About the Author

David Swattridge lives in South Wales. His recent retirement from working as a Commercial Director in Orthopaedics, gave him the opportunity to fulfil a lifetime's ambition to write. He has been married for forty one years, has one daughter and two grandsons.

Dedication

The fallen of World War One, who after a century still remain lost.

Hayley Stroud, an inspiration to everyone she meets.

The Teenage Cancer Trust.

David Swattridge

PALE BATTALIONS

THE DARK LAND

AUSTIN MACAULEY
PUBLISHERS LTD.

A CIP catalogue record for this title is available from the British Library.

ISBN 9781784555009 (Paperback)
ISBN 9781784555023 (Hardback)

www.austinmacauley.com

First Published (2015)
Austin Macauley Publishers Ltd.
25 Canada Square
Canary Wharf
London
E14 5LB

Printed and bound in Great Britain

Acknowledgments

My family, for their belief, and constant encouragement.
Our holidays with Jan and Alan Houldcroft, which provided the inspiration
for this novel.
Poems
Siegfried Sassoon - 'The Death Bed'
Phillip Larkin - 'The Old Fools'
Dylan Thomas - 'Do Not Go Gentle Into That Good Night'
Charles Hamilton Sorley - 'When You See Millions of the Mouthless Dead'
Robert Lawrence Binyon - 'For the Fallen'
Isaac Rosenberg - 'Dead Man's Dump'
Henry Wadsworth Longfellow - 'Evangeline and Other Poems': 'A
Nameless Grave': 'A Psalm for Life'
Wilfred Owen - 'Anthem for Doomed Youth'
John Keats - 'To Sleep'
Songs
The Eagles - 'Long Road out of Eden'
Eliza Gilkensen - 'Calling All Angels'
Peter Gabriel - 'Come Talk to Me': 'Love to be Loved': 'Blood of Eden'
Leonard Cohen - 'The Partisan'; 'Lady Midnight'
Dire Straits - 'Brothers in Arms'
Bob Dylan - 'Blowin' in the Wind'
Novel
The Lost Word - Sir Arthur Conan Doyle

"But death replied: 'I chose him.' So he went,
And there was silence in the summer night;
Silence and safety; and the veils of sleep.
Then, far away, the thudding of the guns."

Siegfried Sassoon – *The Death-Bed*

ONE

'Morbeck – Arnold & Edith
On June 4th 2013 at home.
No flowers. Donations please in lieu, to the CWGC.
We rest in peace. Help those who don't.
'At death, you break up: the bits that were you
Start speeding away from each other for ever
With no one to see. It's only oblivion, true:'

"Jane," Sam called from the conservatory.

"Jane!" No response.

"Jane! Uncle Arnold and Auntie Edith have died."

"Not much to remember a life by!" He thought. *"Just a few lines in the local rag's hatched, matched and dispatched columns."*

"When did they die?" She eventually shouted from the kitchen.

"Last Tuesday. They've asked for donations to the CWGC. Whatever that is."

He re-read the announcement. "Odd wording, 'Help those who don't?'"

"Get round to the house and see what you can do." She shouted from the kitchen. This was followed by silence as the cogs ground away in her brain. "They didn't have any other living family did they?" There was short pause. "They were pretty well off weren't they? That house must be worth quite a bit. What I mean is, it would be a shame to see it go to rack and ruin." Flashing lights illuminated her financial night, as she saw her bank balance moving from deep scarlet to glossy black ebony. "When was the last time you saw them?"

"Jesus!" Sam said quietly to himself. "She just can't help herself. Not a thought for anyone else. All she can see is an unclaimed lottery ticket to pay off her on-line bingo debts." He returned to the conversation with Jane. "It's been at least six months since I've seen them, and then it was usually only twice a month for lunch. I haven't been to their home for at least five years. The last time I saw them was about three weeks ago at their solicitors. They asked me to be their executor, and then we drove down to El Porto's for lunch."

"You're the *executor* for their will! Who benefits?"

"They only made me their executor. It only means I've got to make sure their wishes are carried out after their death. It doesn't mean I know who they've left everything to."

"Call the solicitors now," her voice was still raised but also anxious, "and I'll make you a coffee, dear."

"Dear?" Sam thought. *"The last time she called me Dear, was when I won five hundred on the lottery. My God, she can smell money like a shark smells blood."*

He was sixty in a few months and after thirty years in sales management, he'd decided to take a generous *voluntary* redundancy package he'd been *offered*. It provided him with a comfortable financial blanket, which allowed him to take early retirement at the same time. Unfortunately, within six months his blanket was threadbare. The bulk of the money gone, blown by Jane on on-line gambling.

He lifted Yellow Pages out of the magazine rack. *"Solicitors,"* he thought leafing through it. *"What were they called?"* He ran his finger down the pages. *"Peterson, Grubb and Amos that's them, telephone number 888764."* He picked up the phone and rang them.

He was put through to George Peterson, one of the partners. "Mr Morbeck, I'm glad you called. You were on my list to contact today about the estate of your aunt and uncle."

"I've just read the announcement in today's Argus." Sam replied.

"Shame, great shame. They were such a devoted couple. When can you come around to our offices?"

"Today or tomorrow. Either's fine for me."

"Well I'm free at three o'clock this afternoon. Can you make that?"

"Yes that's fine. I live about ten minutes from the City Centre."

"Excellent. I look forward to seeing you then."

Sam replaced the phone and grimaced. "Shit! I didn't ask him what I've got. She'll be bloody ecstatic. Sod her. If there's any money then it's mine. Jesus, I could walk out and escape to some distant land before she put any legal obstacles in my way."

Chatting with himself was the only intelligent conversation Sam ever got. The conversations had developed over thirty years of their so-called marriage. The standing joke with the few friends he had, was that if he'd murdered her, he'd have been out on parole years ago. A lot richer, single and considerably happier. Chats with his other half, now seemed perfectly natural to Sam, although he'd frequently have to stop himself when walking the dog, as neighbours looked up quizzically at him from their lawns and well-tended flower beds.

His first childhood memory of being aware of anyone talking to themselves, was the old soldier in the faded greatcoat. His father had told him the old man's name was Jimmy, that he was an officer in World War One, he'd suffered terribly, but was harmless. The old soldier, who Sam thought had probably been in his late seventies, would appear at precisely ten o'clock every day at the top of the main street of his village, supported by an ebony walking stick. He'd march up and down the main street, head down, oblivious to everyone, and at twelve o'clock he'd disappear into a side street. At three o'clock the march past was repeated, and at five o'clock the parade finished outside St John's church with an extravagant salute. His clothes were always the same. A heavy wool serge greatcoat, buttoned tightly at the neck with a single tarnished brass button. It strained to break free from the few remaining threads attaching it to the coat; and the remaining brass buttons held the greatcoat together as far as the middle of his chest, which gave the impression of a giant bat with two large flapping brown serge wings. Under the greatcoat was what looked like a thick woollen jacket with brass buttons, and a cracked leather belt with a cross strap across his chest. On his head was a worn green officer's cap with a short peak, chin strap, and a regimental badge resembling a snake climbing up a tree to a crown. His attire was completed by baggy green cord riding breeches, fitted tightly from the knee down, into a pair of brown, once highly polished riding top boots. He would frequently stop, washing his hands in some invisible soap, closely examining them, and never seeming happy with the result, shake his head and continue his march. When he arrived at the railway bridge he'd stop deep in conversation with some invisible long lost comrade in arms. and then curse. "Bastards. They're all bastards. Bloody malingerers. Shoot the buggers. Can't stay here. Shit. Shit. Shit."

School children, including Sam, threw things, whistled and shouted at him, but he never responded to their taunts, raised his head or a hand to them. He simply carried on, head down, as if protecting his face from some bitter winter wind, lost in painful distant memories.

"Cruel what kids do. Sick more like. Poor old bugger. I hope he was never aware of what was going on around him. What did Dad say he was suffering from?" Sam thought. He lay back in the chair and racked his brain for the memory. *"What the hell was it called?"* Finally a drawer flew open. *"Shell Shock? That was it, though that's not what it's called today. What did they call it in Iraq. PTD? PPDS? No PTSD. Post-Traumatic Stress Disorder."* He picked up the iPad, flipped open the folded lid and dived into the wonderful world of Wikipedia.

'*Combat Stress Reaction (CSR), in the past commonly known as Shell Shock or Battle Fatigue, is a range of behaviours resulting from the stress of battle which decrease the combatant's fighting efficiency. The most common symptoms are fatigue, slower reaction times, indecision, and disconnection from one's surroundings…*'

"Disconnection from one's surroundings." Sam said to himself. "Poor sod was disconnected from everything."

"Sam! For God's sake, stop bloody swearing?" Jane snapped as she brought him a mug of instant Cappuccino. "For God's sake will you stop talking to yourself." She hissed at him. "The neighbours already think you're senile."

"Sorry, dear." Sam said. *"Wish I could disconnect from you."* He thought. *"Probably wasn't shell shock the old boy had. Probably PMSD Post Marriage Stress Disorder. How long did you get for manslaughter nowadays? What did they call it? Justified homicide? No, justifiable homicide."* But Wiki would have to wait a few more minutes until she'd finished with him.

"You're coming with me to the GP's. I'm sick of this. It's like living with someone who isn't all ..." There was a short theatrical pause, before with dramatic effect she finished the sentence. "All there." She frowned at him and carried on. "Have you spoken to them yet? The solicitors I mean."

"I've got a meeting with a Mr Peterson at three 'o clock today."

"Well make sure you find out who gets what. If you get nothing, then make sure you ask about how we challenge the will. At their age they must have been a bit senile?"

"I'll make sure I cover everything." He said.

She put the coffee mug on the telephone table next to him. "Don't let that go cold. They're 15p a sachet." She turned and shuffled in her red tweed slippers back to the kitchen, but couldn't resist one last dig at him. "Make sure you get around to the solicitors before three o' clock, and wear that dark blue suit. The one we keep for weddings and funerals." She looked away, but as if to add some *genuine* feeling, said quietly, "I always admired your uncle and aunt. They were such a loving couple." Finally she disappeared into the kitchen, but over her shoulder she had one last personal prod. "And don't ask for any biscuits, or you'll end up on Fat Embarrassing Bodies!"

Sam sighed as her ample rear disappeared out of the room. *"She wasn't always like this."* He thought. *"Mentally or physically. What turns a slim, social, intelligent happy woman into a bitter, twisted, obese, vindictive, sit on my ass all day, pain in the proverbial, close to something resembling a woman?"*

Sam shook his head and returned to Wiki. *"Justifiable Homicide – That which is committed with the intention to kill, or to do a grievous bodily injury, under circumstances which the law holds sufficient to exculpate the person who commits it."*

"God bless Wikipedia" Sam said to himself. Making sure that it wasn't loud enough to be heard in the kitchen. "Any jury would acquit me on that."

He read the announcement again. *"Unusual quote"* he thought, touched the Safari icon and typed in Search, 'At death, you break up: the bits that were you'.

The screen blinked and gave him the answer – 'Phillip Larkin – The Old Fools'. He clicked on the link.

'At death, you break up: the bits that were you
Start speeding away from each other for ever
With no one to see. It's only oblivion, true:
Of choosing gone. Their looks show that they're for it:
Ash hair, toad hands, prune face dried into lines –
How can they ignore it?'

With his sixtieth birthday looming on the horizon, Sam had started taking an interest in his personal appearance. In the private corners of his mind Sam was still in his early twenties, however, the bathroom mirror wouldn't lie, as it starkly reflected his face back to him in all its wrinkled and age-spotted glory, revealing the tragic and unvarnished truth, that he was as Larkin put it, *'Ash hair, toad hands, prune face dried into lines'*.

TWO

Three weeks later Sam met Peterson at Arnold and Edith's home High Wood.

"Good morning Mr Morbeck." The solicitor called to Sam, extending his hand to him as he crossed the street from his car. "Good to see you again, even though the circumstances could be a little happier."

Sam took the limp hand and shook it as firmly as he could without risking breaking bones or dislocating any of Peterson's fingers.

"I'm pretty sure I've done everything you asked." Sam said "All the documents are signed and witnessed. I'm sorry I've not been able to get around to your office since we met, but things at home have been, a little, strained." He opened the battered leather attaché case he was carrying under his arm, and handed Peterson two A4 manila envelopes. "I hope everything's as it should be."

Peterson took the envelope from Sam and turned to the house. "I can check everything once we're inside. My understanding is the funeral is planned for this coming Monday July 1st".

"Yes, everything's organised. It's taken a little longer because of the post-mortems. Arnold and Edith didn't have any known living relatives, so it will only be a small ceremony at the Funeral Home at ten o' clock, and the cremations are at Croesyceiliog Crematorium at twelve. I've arranged to have their ashes interred in their parent's grave at Christchurch Cemetery. There's a small wake at a Country Club close to the crematorium, but I haven't planned for many. Probably just Jane and myself. You'd be very welcome." Sam shrugged and offered his hand again to Peterson. "You really would be very welcome."

Peterson smiled at Sam. "Thank you. I knew your aunt and uncle for a good few years, and I'd like to pay my respects."

For the first time Sam took a good look at High Wood. It was a large detached three storey, red brick Victorian house, with an overgrown privet hedge obscuring the view of the ground floor. With some difficulty, and help from Sam, Peterson pushed open the rusty front gate. It complained loudly as it scraped over the weed infested block paved path, which led up to the front door. The frontage was quite small, either side of the path were lawns, badly in need of cutting, despite the fact that the majority of the grass had been overtaken by a lush covering of moss. In the centre of the lawns, overgrown flower beds were in desperate need of weeding, with unpruned rose bushes overtaking them. Sam scanned the house from the ground floor to the roof, and it looked to be in reasonably good structural shape. The front consisted of two large extended bay fronts reaching up to sharply peaked decorated eaves, and the green front door was protected by a white peeling porch supported by two columns, built into a recess between the bay fronts. The high sash windows looked original, and urgently in need of replacement. Sam scanned them all and his attention was drawn to the windows which all had closed slatted red shutters. The eyes of the house closed in mourning. Fading wisteria, clung to cracked wooden trellises barely clinging to the bricks with a few rusty screws, cascaded like overgrown unplucked eyebrows over the porch, and first and second floor windows.

Peterson turned to Sam and handed him two large bunches of keys. "These are yours now, Mr Morbeck. The key you need is the largest on the bunch. I've put a spot of red nail varnish on it as it's a bit difficult to find among all the others."

Sam took the keys from Peterson and separated the red spot from the others, and estimated there were about twelve keys on each fob.

They reached the front door, and with a little effort, Sam turned the key in the lock. What he anticipated finding inside the house was worrying him. Would this turn out to be a money pit and not the lottery win he wanted? The hundred thousand he'd separately inherited, could be in danger of being sucked up in repairs. As he pushed open the front door, the first thing which confirmed his worst fears was the smell. It was the odour of damp and decay, the perfume of loss and the cologne of death. Chanel RIP. The house felt empty, devoid of anything which had once made it a home. Like Madeline in the 'Fall of the House of Usher', all its emotions had been buried alive in the bricks and mortar of the house. Everything was coated in a thin layer of dust. He walked a short way into the hall, stopped at an Edwardian mahogany hall table close to the front door and blew away the dust covering it. "Do you want to check the paperwork here?" Sam asked Peterson.

"Thank you, yes. It should only take a few minutes to confirm everything's in order."

Peterson opened the manila envelopes and extravagantly brushed the table with a couple of tissues before placing the documents on it. He took a Mont Blanc Meisterstuck from his inside jacket pocket, more for the effect than anything else, started meticulously examining each page, running the tip of his pen down the margins before stopping at each signature, and initialling each of them confirming their authenticity. After about ten minutes he shuffled the papers together, replaced them in the manila envelopes, put them in his briefcase and offered his hand to Sam.

"Everything seems to be in order Mr Morbeck. I'll take the documents back to the office and have a letter drafted to you within a few days confirming the transfer of the property and associated funds and investments to yourself."

"Thanks for all your help. It looks like there's quite a bit of work here to keep me occupied for some time." Sam said.

With both parties satisfied, they shook hands and said their goodbyes.

Sam closed the front door, and with a deep sigh turned to face his inheritance. The hall was about six feet wide, twenty feet long, and the floor wood panelled. At the far end was a wide staircase, to its right a door, and to its left another similar door. On either side of the hall were two doors, one about a third of the way down and the other close to the stairs. All the doors were painted in a depressing olive green with cracked bakelite handles. The walls were decorated with a faded floral green and white patterned wallpaper and the high ceiling was a grubby beige, which must have once been brilliant white. The *decor* was completed by exquisite moulded plaster coving, and two small eight light chandeliers.

What took Sam's breath away, was that since Peterson's departure, everything was now coated by a layer of dust which drifted into the air like clouds of dandelion clocks.

"How in God's name did this happen?" Sam asked no-one in particular. "Where the hell did all this come from?"

"Not a bloody clue." His other half replied.

"But it was … five seconds ago it wasn't here."

"Probably happened when you opened the front door."

"Bullshit."

"No dust." His other half said.

"Ha bloody ha."

"Does it really matter. Decent vacuum cleaner will soon get rid of it. Let's see what we've won."

Sam frowned, but accepted that all this needed was a damn good clean. "At some time they must have been happy here. Why would they let it get like this? I had such good times here."

Sam remembered high teas after school, lunches in the holidays and cold meat suppers after football training, when they would sit around the kitchen table, groaning under the weight of Auntie Edith's irresistible cooking. It was only ever Arnold, Edith and Sam. Sam's parents hadn't spoken to Arnold, Sam's mother's brother, for forty three years. Arnold had committed the cardinal sin of marrying Edith, who was a left-footer, and mackerel-snapper. A devote Irish Roman Catholic from Londonderry. This had been too much for the Morbecks who were high days and holidays not quite committed C of E; God bless her Majesty and all the royal family; re-establish the empire; lapsed racists; how can celibate priests know anything about sex; who the hell does the Pope think he is anyway; it's all Tony Blair and Gordon Brown's fault; bring back the birch, and hanging; know your place and don't get above your station; never a lender or borrower be; nationalise the banks and jail the bankers; ban all medical treatments for the morbidly obese and smokers; triple the price of cigarettes and alcohol, middle of the road British middle class family.

For the last six years, Sam's parents had tolerated each other in sheltered housing, which made Sam's relationship with Arnold and Edith even more difficult to sustain, which resulted in him only seeing them a few times a month, and always out of town in pubs and restaurants. The last time he'd seen them about a month ago, they'd seemed OK, although Arnold did look very tired. He'd put it down to too much DIY, which for someone in his early eighties was somewhat understandable.

"For goodness sake ask me next time." Sam had told them. But it seemed to him there was a lot more they weren't telling him. "Are you sure there's nothing else?"

"Sam we're fine" Edith replied. "We're both getting on a bit. The spirit may be willing, but the body's not quite up to it. Really we're fine. Arnold really needs to catch up with you on a few things, but not here. I know it's been difficult for you to get to the High Wood, but it's important we meet you there. It's more private and there are things we need to show and tell you."

He agreed he'd get around to the house when he could find some time, but he'd never made it. The time demanded of him by his parents, and everything Jane wanted, sucked up any free time he had for himself or his favourite aunt and uncle.

"Why didn't you email me?" He said to the house. "I bought you that iPad and set everything up for you. What did you want to tell me? My God I could do with Psychic Sally right now."

"You should have come around when they asked and told the lovely Jane what she could do." His other half helpfully chipped in.

"That's easy enough for you to say. You don't have to live with her."

"True, but you should have told her to piss off years ago. What exactly does she do to make your life even mildly bearable? For God's sake, at least consider justifiable homicide?"

For once his other half was right. What was it that held their marriage together? Certainly not love. Habit? Fear of the unknown and the thought of the shit which would result from a messy separation? Comfort? Sam loved his house and the creature comforts he'd built up over the years. Stability? At this time of his life the last thing he wanted was change. He'd put up with her for this many years, so a few more until either of them shuffled off this mortal coil would be just about bearable.

All the same, life without Jane. He dwelt on the thought for a few seconds, smiled and with a deep sigh focused back on the house. "I should take a look around. I only ever saw the front room and kitchen when I used to visit."

"Big place isn't it." His other half said.

"Bloody huge. What do you think, start downstairs and work our way up?"

"Yea, sounds like a plan."

Sam looked down the hallway and walked to the first door on the left, the one he knew, the front room, which Edith only ever used for visitors. The door opened surprisingly easily. Sam peered into the room in which he'd spent so many happy hours. Nothing seemed to have changed, although it was a little more tired and covered in the same layer of fine brown dust. He knelt down, rubbed his hand through the dust and examined the brown powder clinging to his palm. He sneezed and the dust billowed into the air like a Saharan sandstorm.

"This isn't dust." Sam thought.

"What is it?"

"Don't know." He rubbed it between his index finger and thumb and gingerly sniffed it.

"What do you think it is?"

Sam frowned and stared at his hands. He smelt them again and then rubbed his hands together to get rid of the dust. "It smells like … like earth or compost."

"It's just dust, from lack of care?"

"No, it's not dust. It's … I don't know what the hell it is."

"But how does this amount of *stuff* get into a house?" His other half asked.

Sam looked around the room. The *dust* was everywhere, coating the furniture, rugs, curtains and light fittings. Sam noticed, that once it had been disturbed, it quickly settled back to the surface it had been coating. He looked behind him, took a sharp breath and frowned. He hadn't left a single visible footprint in the *dust* on the floor.

"How'd you do that, Samuel?" His other half said.

"Don't think I want to know. Come on let's take a look at the rest of the house." He walked out of the room and across the hallway to the first door on the right. It was locked. Sam took a bunch of keys from his coat pocket and decided he'd check again which key fitted which door. The doors on the other side of the hallway were all locked and left for future examination. The small door to the left of the stairwell was locked, but the door to the right, which Sam knew was the kitchen, was open. He turned and looked down the hall, and again, could see no evidence he'd ever been there. "Surely to God that's not normal." He whispered to himself.

The kitchen hadn't changed much since his last meal there. The units, barely visible, under the coating of *dust*, had once been a bright ivory. Most of the white-goods were built in behind them, except for a large walk-in fridge, in the far corner of the room. An oak kitchen table well-worn from countless meals, and six ladder back chairs sat in the middle of the room. Sam pulled out one of the chairs, brushed off the *dust* with a tissue and sat down at the table which had brought him so much good food, company and happiness. With his right index finger he wrote Sam in the dust. Faintly from close behind him he thought he heard a moan, and swung around in the chair but couldn't see anything in the kitchen. "What the hell was that?"

"Nothing." Sam's other half tried to reassure him.

"Nothing my ass. When did nothing moan, and when was the last time you heard a kitchen complain about something?"

"OK. It's the wind. An old house like this must be as draughty as hell." The reassurance continued.

"It was someone moaning, you tit."

The sound of scratching made Sam turn back to the table. Sam had disappeared from the dust, but it was the words which had replaced it which made his stomach twist into a tight knot, and his mouth to turn to sand.

'At Thiepval Where Are You?'

The basic need for flight or fight was comfortably won by flight. Sam flew out of the chair, out of the kitchen and out of the front door, and flight didn't stop until he was on the other side of the street opposite the house.

"What the hell was that?" Sam panted to himself. "How did that writing … who … what did it, and what the hell is At Thiepval?"

"It's probably not a bad idea to go back and find out, you wimp." His other half said.

Sam stared at the house. "Come on get a grip. Did anything try to hurt you?"

"Probably some demon wants to rip off your head off!" His other half helpfully suggested. "Definitely ghosts or poltergeists. You've seen enough of those movies where they don't run for their lives but stay in the house, which is obviously the most dangerous and stupid thing to do. And you're considering stupid and dangerous!"

"We need to take a look."

"As Tonto said to the Lone Ranger. What do you mean *we,* white man?"

Sam ignored his other half.

"So it's going to be stupid man going into dangerous house is it? Why, what's the point? Just sell it and take the money and run. Who gives a shit what, who or where Thiepval is. What we want is the money from the sale, and with that we can put a good few miles between us and the delightful Jane."

"We need to take a look."

"OK fine, take a quick look, but then, sell, sell, sell."

"You're right." Sam begrudgingly replied. "Let's do it!" His feet however hadn't agreed to the plan and remained firmly planted to the pavement.

"Losing your bottle?"

"Piss off. We just need a little pre-planning before we go back into Amityville."

"Pre-planning my ass. Pre-pissing your pants more like."

"Look can you just shut the … just shut up."

"Shit scared, no bottle, wimped out, crapped his pants, pathetic little worm. Missed anything did I?"

Sam ignored the jibes, stared at the house, started to cross the street, and a car barely missed him.

"Asshole!" The driver screamed at him.

"Fuck you, wanker!" Sam shouted after the car.

The scream of brakes, the smell of burning rubber and the cloud of black smoke as the driver slammed on his brakes to further *discuss* the issue with Sam, was enough to get his feet working again. He flew across the road, through the gate and threw himself flat on his stomach behind the hedge before the driver had emerged from his car. He was a thirty-something sales rep, who if he hadn't an appointment in twenty minutes, would have found the asshole that'd stepped out in front of him and *emphasised his displeasure* to him.

"I know you're there, you twat! I'll rip your fucking head off if we bump into each other again." The scream of the wheels told Sam that he could ease some of the tension on his anal sphincter.

"Ooh, Mr Angry has learnt some new words!" His other half chuckled.

"Come on, let's get back in the house."

The front door was wide open. Sam stepped back into the hall and made his way back to the kitchen. The brown dust rose again in small clouds around his legs, but quickly settled back onto the floor, leaving no indication that he'd been there. He pushed hard with his shoulder to open the kitchen door which he'd slammed shut during his dash for freedom, walked across the kitchen, picked up a chair which was wedged under the sink, brought it back to the table and sat down. He'd avoided looking at the table, but now forced himself to look at the dust-covered surface. There was nothing to be seen.

"They were there weren't they? Those words, 'At Thiepval', you saw them didn't you? For God's sake tell me that I'm not losing the few marbles I've still got."

"No they were there." The reply was whispered.

Silence fell like a smoke blanket over the kitchen, smothering the air. What broke the silence stripped away a few more pieces of Sam's will to live. A nerve-shredding sound like nails dragged across a blackboard, shattered the silence with shards of unearthly noise. It was, a cacophony of anguish a symphony of synthesised distress, a distillation of delirium. Sam sat rooted to the chair, unable to speak. Then the stench hit him. It reminded him of rotten meat mixed with the sickly sweet smell of well-rotted manure. Sam's gag reflex projected most of his breakfast muesli, coffee and toast, over the surface of the kitchen table. He sniffed the air, checking that it was fit for human consumption, and gagged again. He turned in the chair and saw a yellowish-brown mist slithering through the kitchen door, which had an odour reminiscent of garlic, horseradish or mustard. The effect was much the same as the first *odour* as the remains of his breakfast and half a litre of bile ricocheted off the table and over most of the chairs. His eyes streamed with tears and his breathing became laboured. His throat burned as he struggled to get air into his lungs, as a comforting feeling of euphoria started to wrap him in a warm blanket. He fell onto the floor and began to wheeze into unconsciousness.

"Sam! Back in the room now! For me, wake up!" His still conscious other half screamed.

Sam shook his head, unsteadily sat up, rubbed away the burning tears from his eyes and coughed to clear his throat of the acrid vapour. He looked around, the mist had disappeared, and breathing was becoming easier.

A loud explosion's concussion knocked Sam onto his back on the kitchen floor. He gingerly sat up, feeling at the growing lump on the back of his head. His ears ringing like the Hunchback of Notre Dame's.

"Now can we please get out of this place?" His other half begged.

"Not yet." Sam peered around the kitchen which looked as if butter wouldn't melt in its mouth. "Not yet. Arnold and Edith wanted to see me here before they died, and there has to be a damn good reason why. The house wants to tell me something, choke me, scare me, or worse? Were Arnold and Edith warning me to stay away from High Wood?"

"I don't really give a toss. Get some professional cleaners in, get it on the market, and sell it for whatever they offer. There is something wrong with this place!"

Sam felt oddly more in control of himself than he had for years. "Arnold would've simply said stay away, and why would he have left me this? They must have known about these things." Sam looked around again at the kitchen, which despite the coating of dust, and the contents of his stomach, seemed in a bizarre way welcoming. "I want to see more of the house." He said.

"You're on your own then!"

"Not possible I'm afraid. Where I go, we go."

"Bastard!"

"Yeh, but you can chose. Upstairs or downstairs?"

"Some bloody choice." There were a few moments of silence. "Upstairs. It couldn't be any worse than down here. Could it?"

Sam walked back into the hall and headed up the carpeted stairs. Their colour and pattern was barely visible under the cloying dust, although the pile still felt deep and lush. It was fitted, up to all the doors of the rooms, whose bottoms had been badly cut to allow them to open over the deep pile. At the top of the stairs the landing split to the right and left. He switched on the lights and looked to the left, where there were three doors on both sides of the corridor. To his right there were three on the right and only two on the left. The final door was directly in front of him.

"Still my choice?" His other half asked.

"Choose away."

"Far end of the landing on the left."

"You sure? Don't want anyone to jump out on us do we?"

"Sod off! That's the one."

Sam walked to the far end of the landing and tried the last door on the left. It was locked.

"You need a key, you tosser. You left the bunch on the kitchen table."

Sam sighed, his signature sound for *'For God's Sake',* begrudgingly turned around and walked back to the top of the staircase, scuffing up the dust on the landing. As he placed his right foot on the first step, he felt a vibration through the floor, making the dust ripple and dance. He held onto the banister with his left hand, as the vibration got stronger. He stood frozen at the top stair as the dust lapped around his ankles like a gentle sea swell. It washed back and fore, up and down the landing, and flowed like a torrent down the stairs.

The opening chords of Deep Purple's Smoke on the Water broke the silence and came close to relaxing an important terminal sphincter in Sam's digestive system.

"Jane. Shit, I haven't checked in for at least four hours. Mission control is in need of an update." He pulled the iPhone out of his jacket pocket and slid the bar to on. "Yes de ..."

"Where the hell are you? At that house? What's it like? What's it worth? Can we sell it? WELL!?"

"I've been looking around the place for hours." He thought it better not to mention the dust for the moment. "It's pretty large and only needs a little spit and polish. It's in pretty good nick all things considered. Garden could do with ..."

"I don't give a shit about the garden. What can we sell?" The words were spat out. "And sell quickly?"

"Christ" Sam thought *"She must have racked up more gambling debts than I know about. How deep in the shit is she?"*

He was suddenly aware that he'd forgotten about the dust which was half way up his calves.

"Are you listening to me?" The words hissed from the phone. "Jesus, why did I ever send *you* to do this? Never send a mouse to do a man's job. Are … you … listening?"

"Yes, sorry, dear. I've just got a few more rooms to look at and then I'll be home." *"Well, to the house"* Sam thought.

"Dinner'll be ready at six. Be there and tell exactly what we can sell. Make a list." There was a thoughtful pause. "The contents as well as the buildings. They must have acquired quite a few things over the years on their travels." There was another long pause. "Have you got the camera?"

"Yes."

"Then make sure you take plenty of pictures. I can look at them on that toy of yours."

"The iPad, dear?"

"Yes the *toy*. Boys and their bloody toys. I'll see you at six."

The phone went dead.

"Yes, dear. So lovely to speak to you. Always such joy." For a few seconds Sam was lost in the delightful thought of getting home and finding her at the foot of the stairs, neck gently twisted to the right, eyes vacantly staring at the ceiling, stone cold and silent. "Such a joy." He was quickly back in the moment and looked down at the dust, which was still rippling on the landing, and the stairs were a raging torrent. He gingerly started moving sideways down the staircase, clinging onto the bannister with both hands.

"OK let's see if we can get to the bottom of the stairs without falling into this."

"No chance." His other half had joined him.

"Oh, back are we?"

"Couldn't leave you on your own could I?"

"Managed it while things weren't too clever, didn't you?"

"She was happy!"

"Don't change the subject."

"She was though, wasn't she? Right pain in the ass. Can't we just get shot of her?"

"She can cook, clean and iron, and she doesn't make any physical demands, thank God. And, well, she smells nice."

"Not much of a Top Ten for marriage is it."

"Look leave it will you. We need to get down these stairs without breaking our neck. So shut the *F* … up and let's get downstairs." He took a few steps and the torrent increased in force. *"One step at a time."* He thought, as he gingerly took a few more steps, struggling to keep his footing.

"Two to go. Almost there now." His other half unconvincingly said.

"Oh will you just shut up."

"Just trying to boost your confidence."

"Well it's not working. So piss off, will you? This stuff, whatever the hell it is, seems to be slowing down."

"Why are you whispering?"

"Whispering?"

"Yes, you know, speaking quietly."

As Sam was about to answer himself, the dust collapsed back into the carpet. He breathed a very short sigh of relief as another violent explosion was quickly followed by a massive concussion, which smashed into Sam throwing him down the last few steps into the wall. The tinnitus the concussion caused, made Sam clamp his hands over his ears. He stretched his neck, and what he saw above him, fully dilated all sphincters. A waterfall of dust was erupting from the ceiling and falling like brown lava, filling the hallway with a choking, pulsating brown plasma. He quickly moved his hands from his ears to his nose and mouth, and clamped his eyes shut as the seething cloud enveloped him. For a few seconds Sam thought his end had come, as inside the cloud there was a strange sense of warmth and well-being.

"If this is dying," Sam thought *"then I don't know what all the fuss is about."*

"Is this is what ashes to ashes, dust to dust means? Is this what happens when we shuffle off this mortal coil?"

"Decided to come back again did you? And its coil not toil."

"OK smart-ass. What play then?"

"Hamlet as it happens. 'To be or not to be' speech."

A second nerve shredding explosion shattered the silence and brought their literary discussion to an abrupt end. If Sam had shuffled off this mortal coil, then he'd no idea what he'd shuffled into. Two more explosions followed in quick succession. There was a brief pause, and then they came one after another in what seemed to be a never ending cacophony from hell. It felt like a tuning fork being repeatedly struck on his head. Ping, ping, ping, creating relentless vibrations. They burrowed into him, deep into his nerves. The sound waves bounced and echoed around Sam at a level and intensity which he was sure would leave him profoundly deaf. The explosions were now constant, and then suddenly they stopped. The silence was golden, as it gently tried to massage away his pounding headache and relieve his screaming tinnitus. The silence seemed to calm the dust storm, pressing it softly back to the floor. Only a thin drifting mist of dust remained, and Sam could now make out details of where he was.

"WHAT CAN YOU SEE?" His other half shouted.

"I THINK I CAN SEE PLANKS?" Sam shouted back.

Another massive explosion shook Sam to the core. He felt like a cage fighter who was taking the mother and father of all beatings.

"PLANKS? YOU SURE?"

"YES PLANKS. WHERE THE BLOODY HELL IS THE HALL?"

Sam's hearing slowly started recovering. "The walls, floor and ceiling are made of rough wooden planks with cross pieces holding them together. There are," Sam squinted into the drifting curtain of dust, "bunks? One, two ..." Sam counted the roughly constructed wooden bunks "... seven, eight. What is this, the seven dwarves bedroom, with a spare for Snow White?" He stood up and cracked his head on the ceiling. His six foot two frame wasn't made for this room. "Bollocks! My bloody head." He rubbed the top of his folliclely challenged pate with his left hand, feeling for blood among the other scabs, scrapes and bruises, all trophies of previous encounters his pate had had with various cupboards, beams and drawers in his house. He put his left hand on the top of his head, gingerly rubbed it and felt cold metal. He lifted his right hand to the top of his head and tapped. Metal! Definitely metal! He ran both hands over the metal dome. At the base was a raised rim under which was a strap. He ran one finger along the strap, along his cheek, under his chin, and along the other cheek to the other side of the metal bowl.

"It's a helmet. For God's sake it's a bloody helmet." Sam said.

"Unless of course you've stepped back into the kitchen and a copper jelly mound with a cloth handle's fallen on your head, and all this is concussion." His other half helpfully suggested.

"It's a bloody helmet, and why am I wearing one? Where the hell are we?" There was a growing level of tension in Sam's voice.

As the dust settled, Sam had a clearer view of where he was. The floor, walls and ceiling were covered in rough wooden planks. In the corner was an entrance covered by a tattered grubby curtain, which flapped back and forth from the concussions of the explosions. Four small chairs and a desk covered in photos and notes, now mostly on the floor, and rough shelving packed with tins completed the basic furniture of the room. Sam looked at the bunks, all empty apart from a thick covering of dust. The room was suddenly silent, it was shattered by three loud blasts on a whistle from outside the curtain. Sam frowned and cautiously moved away from the sound. An odd rustling behind him raised the hairs on the back of his neck. It continued and changed to the sound of cracking knuckles. He couldn't decide if it was better to turn around and take a look, or make a run for the curtain and take a chance on whatever lay on the other side. Curiosity may have killed the cat, but Sam wasn't feeling particularly feline.

"Take a bloody look. The last time anything like this happened was when you were nineteen. You'd dropped a couple of tabs of acid and were being chased down the road by two dinosaurs! Normal sort of thing for a Saturday night in Newport. Sam, all of this is just a chemical imbalance in your brain. Nothing else! Christ, someone who's been locked onto the handle of a bathroom door with stars shooting out of the top of his head, and a few other somewhat bizarre experiences, has got to understand that these things are never real. It's a flashback. Take a look. What's the worst that could happen?"

"Yeah, you're right. It's just some mescaline or acid lodged somewhere in my brain." Sam frowned, not fully convinced by the argument. He turned slowly and focussed on where the noise was coming from. The dust on the bunks was now swirling in clouds above the bedding. Gradually the shapeless clouds began to pulse and the individual dust granules started to coalesce into discernible human forms. Eight human forms sitting on eight rough plank bunks. Eight human forms wearing dome shaped helmets. Eight soldiers. Their forms quickly became clearer and more discernible. They were eight soldiers of the Great War. Eight Tommies. The whistle again blew shrilly. The Tommies jumped down from the bunks, picked up their rifles from a stack leaning against the end of the bunks, and ran through the curtain. Sam pressed himself against the wall of the room, and as the soldiers passed, he gagged at the stench of weeks of ingrained grime, excreta and sweat. One by one they disappeared through the curtain, and silence returned to the room only to be shattered by the loudest explosion so far, closely followed by a massive concussion and a hurricane of dust and rubble which destroyed the curtain. Silence once again returned, and Sam looked around at what remained of the room. The bunks lay in splinters in a large heap at the end of the room looking like a pile of giant's pencil shavings. But what paralysed Sam was the heap of smoking dismembered body parts filling up the entrance to the room. An advanced DIY set for junior doctors studying anatomy. It was a smouldering mound of bleeding flesh which seconds before had been eight men in uniform. Eight imaginary men? Men generated by acid from his youth lodged deep in his neural network? He was suddenly aware of his feet getting warmer. He looked down and saw rivulets of crimson blood soaking into his shoes.

Dum, dum, dum
Dum, dum, da, dum
Dum, dum, dum
Dum, dum

The opening guitar riff of Smoke on the Water broke the silence. Sam ripped the iPhone from his pocket and saw the smiling photo of Jane. He hadn't been so glad to hear from her since she'd called from Tesco telling him she'd tripped and broken her wrist.

"Yes, de ..."

"Any idea what the time is?" Jane spoke slowly and deliberately. Too slowly Sam thought, and far too deliberately.

"Not sure. I've been pretty busy looking around the house. Can't be too late can it?" He looked around. The dug out was gone. He was back in the hall. Had it all been nothing more than a flashback?

Jane's dulcet tones brought him back. "Your dinner's in the dog and your pillow's on the sofa." There was a pause as she seemed to be keeping the worst for last. "It, is a quarter past nine."

He'd been in the house for ten hours! "Look I'm sorry, but there's been a lot to do and I know that you want a quick sale, so I need to know what there is to sell. I've been taking plenty of pictures." *"Please don't ask to see anything."* Sam thought.

"I'll be in bed by the time you get back, so don't disturb me. I'll take a look at the pictures tomorrow." Her tone seemed to soften from granite to slate. "Glad that you've been doing what I asked you to do, but it's pretty simple to phone and let me know where you are."

"I'll be quiet. See you in the morning." He replied with a grimace.

The line went dead.

"The sooner I ..." Sam started to say.

"The sooner you what? You haven't got the cajones to do anything about her. She's had them in the palm of her hand for the last thirty years, and they've shrivelled up." His other half sniggered.

"Oh sod off!" Sam thought to himself.

THREE

It was half past two in the morning, and it had been a less than comfortable night on the sofa. His six feet two frame didn't fit too well on a five foot six sofa bed, and indigestion was eating away at his stomach from the cold remains of last night's curry. He lifted his iTouch from the coffee table, turned it on and smiled as the white Apple logo appeared on the screen. As the icons came to life, he tapped on Music, Artists, The Eagles, Long Road out Of Eden, Album two, slipped the Sennheisser headphones over his ears, closed his eyes and drifted into a world where the lovely Jane couldn't reach him. Don Henley's unmistakable tones oozed like runny honey into his ears. As the lyrics started, they seemed to connect with his *experience* at High Wood.

'Somebody whisperin' the twenty-third psalm
Dusty rifle in his tremblin' hands
Somebody tryin' just to stay alive'

The lyrics struck a note in Sam's head, although it was more like the crashing of a Chinese gong.

"Dusty rifle in his tremblin' hands?" Sam said out loud. "More dust?"

His favourite guitar solo ended, and the song once again took Sam back to Snow White's cottage, the eight soldiers, the weeks of ingrained filth and the overpowering terror he could smell as they scuttled through the torn curtain to God knows what.

'Back home, I was so certain the path was very clear
But now, I have to wonder what are we doin' here?
I'm not countin' on tomorrow and I can't tell wrong from right
But I'd give anythin' to be there in your arms tonight'

Sam became completely absorbed in the song, lost in himself, and the music.

The iPhone on the floor pinged like a submarine sonar. He had a message. Sam paid it little attention, as it was probably some scam offering him thousands he was owed, because of PPI. The sonar wouldn't give up and pinged again. He reached down to the floor, felt around for the iPhone, and eventually found it in one of his shoes. He slid the cursor to on, and a speech bubble glowed at him in the dark.

'25886, 3234, 3439, 1009, 22898, 44567, 7896, 2249'

"What the ..." Sam stared at the screen and slowly read the numbers out loud.

"You've won the lottery." His *better* half was awake.

"The numbers don't quite stack up for the lottery, moron."

There was silence from his *friend*.

The iPhone's sonar pinged again.

'Deighton, Smith, Jones, Hoyles, Bealing, Acklom, Easton, Cross, Lombton.'

Sam swung his feet off the sofa bed and sat up. The speech bubbles glowing at him like alarm signals on a dashboard. He stroked his grey beard and pulled at his earlobe.

"What the hell is this?"

"You'd better reply?"

"Reply" Sam hissed. "Who to, and to what? It's probably a scam. Gets you to reply to some premium rate number and run up a massive phone bill."

The sonar pinged for a third time.

'Sunken Lane, Hawthorn Redoubt, Broadway, White City, Berg Werk, Jacob's Ladder, The Bowery, Carlisle Street'.

"Some mental estate agent?" His other half suggested.

"Bloody insane estate agent." Sam replied.

"Send a reply. What's the worst that could happen? You get a massive phone bill and she'll moan for a few weeks."

"Suppose so, but what the hell do I reply? Nice to hear from you, but who the hell are you and what the hell do you want?" Sam was way beyond tired, and into that alternate state which only the practiced insomniac can appreciate. He was getting more and more frustrated, confused and concerned. He stroked the arrow and pressed the Reply icon. His own empty speech bubble blinked back at him.

'What do you want?'

"I'm really not sure about this." Sam's finger hovered above the Send icon.

"Oh for God's sake just press it. What are you expecting? Pinhead and the other Cenobites to appear in the room, rip off your skin with hooks and chains and drag you down to hell? Hellraiser was only a film you know."

Sam swallowed deeply, held his breath and touched the send icon. Twenty minutes later, the message chain remained stubbornly unchanged.

"I told you it was a scam. Some Latvian is probably hacking into my bank account as we speak! Leave well alone what you don't understand. I should have known better than to listen to you after the shit you've got me into over the years." Sam sighed.

"Great times though weren't they?"

Sam sat in silence staring at the screen. After another ten minutes of nothing he decided a cup of tea and a handful of biscuits could be the solution for his insomnia and frustration. The blue light on the kettle lit up the kitchen with an eerie glow as he emptied the biscuit tin onto a plate. A mixture of biscuits, now all tasting of ginger thanks to a solitary ginger nut hiding at the bottom of the tin, fell onto the plate. Two custard creams, one digestive, three rich tea and the lone ginger nut would make up his feast. The blue light clicked off as the kettle reached boiling point, and Sam poured the steaming filtered water over two tea bags. and let it brew. He liked to taste the tea to the point where the tannin sucked most of the moisture out of his mouth. He took his feast back into the lounge and sat on the edge of the sofa bed. A dunked custard cream soon restored his belief in the small pleasures of life, until the sonar pinged again.

"I told you you should reply." There was the soft sound of laughter.

Sam stood up and a second sonar alarm pinged out, demanding the reply be read. Another speech bubble had been added to the list. Three words glowed back at him in the dark.

'At High Wood.'

"High Wood's Arnold and Edith's home. It's where we've been looking. We need to go back."

"OK, but not now, we'll go straight after breakfast." His other half said.

"Agreed, but there's not much point in trying to sleep. I'll have a look on the iPad and find what I can about these messages." He lifted the iPad and touched the Safari icon. In the search box he typed 'Jacob's Ladder', and Google gave him multiple options.

'Jacob's Ladder – Directed by Adrian Lyne, with Tim Robbins … a haunted Vietnam vet attempts to discover …'

He leaned across the sofa and picked up the writing pad next to the phone. "I'll just keep the main points at the moment." He returned to Google, and reviewed some of the other options.*"*

'A Ladder to Heaven, Patented treadmill, Israel's friendliest musical'.

"Broadway and White City I think I know, so I'll leave them for now." Sam looked at the third message again. "Berg Werk? Sounds Scandinavian."

Google sprang into life again, but everything was in German. There were pictures and videos of the Nurburgring, a restaurant in Berlin and some photographer in Canada. Sam tapped on the berg-werk.com hyperlink. All the photos were of ski equipment shops.

"So what the hell is Hawthorn Redoubt." He typed it into search and waited for the answers. The references quickly appeared and Sam's pulse rate increased. *"This is more like it,"* he thought.

'Hawthorn Ridge Redoubt was a German front-line fortification west of the village of Beaumont Hamel on the Somme. It was the scene of a number of costly …' He tapped the hyperlink for more information. Wikipedia opened up a detailed and expansive reference to Hawthorn Redoubt. The quote finished '… costly attacks by British infantry during the Battle of the Somme in 1916.' Sam read the remainder of the reference article, and noted one particular quote. 'It was also the site of one of the most famous pieces of film footage of World War 1 when the Hawthorn Ridge mine was detonated beneath the redoubt at seven twenty am on July 1st 1916, the first day of the Somme'. "Shit, listen to this." Sam said. "The ground where I stood gave a mighty convulsion. It rocked and swayed, the earth rose high into the air to the height of hundreds of feet, and with a horrible grinding roar the earth settles back on itself, leaving in its place a mountain of smoke"

Sam stared at the messages glowing from the iPhone. "Let's look for High Wood. If it warrants a single message, it must be important."

It was the fourth link which grabbed his attention. 'High Wood is a small forest near Bazentin le Petit in the Somme department of northern France which was the scene of intense fighting for two months …' Sam almost slapped the hyperlink. '... from July 14th to September 15th 1916 during the Battle of the Somme'.

His brain shifted into overdrive, reviewing the information he now had, but it was not much more than a fog. There was too much hurtling around his brain, and bouncing off his skull to make any real sense of what was happening.

"Calm down and let's look at what we know." His other half was trying its best to be a calming influence. "It's pointless getting stressed up about it. We need to sit back and finish the list you started. You've always been good at lists. A bit too OCD at times, but nonetheless, lists have always been a great way for you to organise information. Apart from the texts, what else do we know?"

Sam sat back in the sofa and rubbed his bald head with his right hand. It had to be his right, somehow his left hand didn't have quite the same effect. It was comforting and relaxing.

"Good plan." He picked up the iPad again, hit Notes and started to type. "Where to start?" There was a long pause as Sam thought back over recent events. "I should start with the announcement and work from there." After thirty years in sales management, planning and writing reports still came very naturally to him.

He looked through the magazine rack in the corner of the lounge. "Where are you you little bastard?" The local paper was hiding between Take a Break and Woman. He retrieved it and went back to the sofa.

"OK, deaths, where are you? Bloody hell, someone's selling a mountain bike for fifty quid!" Sam made a note of the telephone number on the writing pad, and leafed through a few more pages before he found the Announcements page.

1. Announcement
   a.   What's the CWGC?
   b.   What does "Help those who can't" mean?
   c.   Who are 'those'?
2.   High Wood
   a.   What the hell is the dust?
   b.   Was everything just a flashback?
   c.   Sell the house now?
   d.   Does the link to the Somme mean anything?
3.   Text 1
   a.   Are they a sequence or a code?
   b.   Are they telephone numbers?
   c.   Are they some sort of reference?
4. Text 2
   a.   Who are they?
5. Text 3
   a.   Are these all places?
   b.   If they're places, then where are they and what's there significance?
   c.   Does the link to World War One mean anything?
Sam read and re-read what he'd written.

"The announcement, what's the CWGC?" It was time to revisit Google.

"OK my friend what do you know?" The links appeared from the ether, and there was one very obvious and common link. The Commonwealth War Graves Commission. He hit the first hyperlink for cwc.org and the text was self-explanatory.

'We commemorate the 1,700,000 men and women of the Commonwealth forces who died in the two world wars'.

It was the two search facilities at the top right of the screen which got Sam's attention.

Find War Dead – Service – Please select & War – Please select'

'Find a Cemetery – Select Cemetery & Country'.

He tapped on 'Find War Dead' and typed in what he felt was the most obscure name, Acklom. Two contacts were found, but further information was requested.

'Name, Rank, Date of Death, Age, Regiment/Service, Service Country, Grave/Memorial reference and Cemetery/Memorial name'.

He had a surname but no initial, a number which could be a service number or some reference to a grave or cemetery, and a place which could be a cemetery? Did any of the information he had match what he'd found on the two Acklom soldiers? One was World War One, with a date of death 21/03/1918 and the other World War Two, with a date of death 23/11/1941.

"Apart from some vague historical interest you might have in this." His other half said. "What's the point? Total, bloody waste of time if you ask me. All that shit today was just your past catching up on you. The house is a total mess. That's all. Get a team of industrial cleaners in and sell it. The texts are some identity fraud. It's what you said, it happens all the time. There was a feature on X-Ray the other night about a woman who'd lost her life's savings to some assholes in Poland. Let's get the funeral out of the way, do our bit, get High Wood on the market and off our hands as quickly as possible."

"Yeah but …" Sam complained without much conviction.

"No buts. Don't stare a gift horse, house, in the mouth!"

Sam sat up and stretched out the muscles which he knew would need more than ibuprofen to get them back into a relatively pain free state. "Much as I hate to say it, you're right. It must be worth at least half a million. Shit what we could do with that!" The thought of a life sans Jane completely outweighed any odd goings-on at the house. He'd somewhat overdone LSD and other hallucinogens in his youth, and he was now reaping a flashback harvest. And It wasn't the first time. There was that recent embarrassing event at Morrison's, which meant he was persona non grata at that particular hypermarket, and the night last month when Jane found him looking for orange frogs in the garden pond.

"Have you been taking your anti-depressants?" His other half asked.

Sam had been taking Prozac for just over a year, primarily to dull the effect of Jane on his already strained mental state. "As far as I know. She feeds me every morning and evening with my happy tabs." Sam said.

"OK so you're still as drugged up as ever. Plan for the rest of this month is, funeral, cremation, wake, intern the ashes and then sell, sell, sell."

At breakfast, Jane was her usual little ray of sunshine. A fourth piece of thickly coated buttered toast and marmalade was rapidly disappearing, flushed down by her third cup of coffee into her overworked and overstretched stomach. Sam was playing with some soggy All Bran which closely resembled something which had just left a cow's third stomach.

"Is … ev … erything … re … ady for tomorrow?" Jane mumbled through a mouthful of half chewed toast.

"I've organised everything with the funeral home, including the wake, and all we have to do is turn up." *"Probably the only ones who'll be there. Shame really,"* Sam thought, staring into the distance where peace, tranquillity and solitude all waved back at him.

"Back with the conscious ,dear." Jane said sarcastically.

"Sorry, just wondering who might be there? I can't imagine there'll be anyone other than us. Sad really, don't you think?"

"What was the house like?"

"That's more like it." Sam thought. *"Get to the money."*

"OK." Sam lied between gritted teeth. "I'm going to arrange for a firm to give it a thorough clean. Once that's done, we can put it on the market. It's a desirable residence as estate agents like to say, so it should sell pretty quickly."

"Good, well done dear." Jane smiled at him.

"She can smell money." Sam thought. *"It's going to be a bloody big shock when she gets my post card from far far away."*

Half an hour later, he was in contact with George at 'Kleen Up – No Messing About'.

"I need it done as soon as possible, but I'm afraid the house is quite a mess." Sam said. "It's been a little neglected."

"No problem Mr Morbeck, just the sort of job we like. A deep clean in a house this size will probably take us three or four days. Do you need the outside, gardens and such like, cleared as well?" George suggested.

"Yes that seems like a good idea. I'm putting the house up for sale, so it needs to be in a great viewing condition."

"Need to take a look first, but on average I reckon that to do a total clear up would take us about a week."

"And the cost?" Sam asked warily.

There was the sound of teeth being expertly sucked. "Obviously I would need to take a good look at the property to give you an accurate cost, but on average ...." There was a long meaningful pause, adding to the effect that a great deal of thought was being given to the calculation. George however was actually scratching an old gnat bite on his arm.

"I really need this done as soon as possible." Sam pressed George for an answer, with the type of comment which had pound signs rattling around George's increasingly grinning face.

"Moron." His other half said. "May as well as tell him to write his own cheque!"

"Bollocks!" Sam said rather too loudly.

"Excuse me, Mr Morbeck?"

"Sorry, George, just spilled coffee over my lap."

"I'd estimate that given the timing, the size and by what you say about the poor condition of the property ..." There was a theatrical pause which only lacked a drum roll. " Around three thousand."

"Told you!" His other half gloated.

Sam's muesli revisited his throat.

"Three, thousand, pounds? I thought it would be nearer five hundred?"

"That *is* only an estimate based on your comments about the condition of the house and your requirements. I can delay the work and get you a full quote," another expertly timed pause, "in the next couple of weeks, but we are very busy at the moment."

"Got you by the short, and now not so curlies hasn't he."

Sam ignored the less than helpful sarcasm.

"No, that sounds fine can you start tomorrow. I need to get the house on the market."

"That's another five hundred on the bill, you tit!"

Sam ignored the abuse.

"I may have to juggle things a little, but that should be OK, Mr Morbeck, I'll get the team on the case first thing in the morning. What's the best way to contact you?"

"On my mobile." Sam replied. *"Shit, I don't want the lovely Jane to know all the details."* "077989444578. I'll drop the keys off at your office this afternoon."

FOUR

Sam didn't do funerals. Never had, never would. He'd written some of his memories of Arnold and Edith for the vicar who was taking the service at the funeral home, and the crematorium. He looked down at the single A4 sheet of hand written notes and frowned. It didn't seem enough, or somehow the right way to celebrate two lives. His notes were brief, but heartfelt, and he'd added a few personal anecdotes about high days and holidays, spent with a couple who had shown him more love than the two strangers who'd raised him. What he was pleased and comforted by, was the poem he'd found. At first he decided to read it himself, but the loss of two dear relatives, was too much for him, and he asked the vicar to include some verses in her eulogy. Thank God for the genius of Dylan Thomas.

'*Do not gentle into that good night,*
Old age should burn and rave at close of day;
Rage, rage against the dying of the light,

Though wise men know at their end that dark is right,
Because their words had forked no lightning they
Do not go gentle into that good night

And you my father, there on that sad height,
Curse, bless me now with your fierce tears, I pray.
Do not go gentle into that good night.
Rage, rage against the dying of the light.'

Jane hadn't made it. Her excuse had been a migraine.

"Hopefully it's a lot more than just a migraine." Sam thought after he'd left her in bed with the covers pulled over her head, and the curtains shut tightly.

He pulled at his collar. She bought everything from M&S, and been a bit too optimistic in the sizes. He was a sixteen not a fifteen collar, a thirty six not a thirty four waist and a thirty six not a thirty four inside leg. Still, he almost looked the part.

Martin Bevan was waiting for him at the door of the funeral home.

"Good morning Sam. A difficult day. How are you? Everything's in place. I've arranged for eight pall bearers to carry the coffins." He nodded to inside the funeral home. "The coffins are in the chapel, and at the end of the service the bearers will carry them to the hearses for the drive to the crematorium." It was a well-practiced welcome, which still sounded genuine despite the hundreds of times Martin Bevan had expressed his condolences to relatives.

Sam forced a smile, shook the hand that was offered to him, and slowly walked into the chapel. Apart from the vicar who was conducting the brief service, he was the only mourner present. The solicitor hadn't made it.

"What a bloody sorry state of affairs!" He thought.

"You're here and I'm here."

"Oh, you made it. Thanks." It was the first time Sam had been genuinely pleased to hear his other half.

"We'll give them a good send off. It's quality not quantity that counts."

"Yeah, you're right. Quality not quantity."

"I'm sorry, Mr Morbeck, what quality?" Elizabeth Roberts, the vicar taking the service, looked deep into Sam's eyes. She was used to grief expressing itself in odd ways, but Sam seemed strangely detached. She was fifty two, five feet tall, slightly overweight, short coloured blond hair, sensible shoes, worn because of painful years standing in cold chapels, churches, crematoria and cemeteries, small beautifully manicured nails and intensely dark brown eyes which revealed an understanding of Sam's deep sadness.

"Mmmm?" Sam looked up into eyes which understood his feelings and offered support. "I'm sorry, I was thinking out loud. I was thinking about ..." He paused searching for something to say. "About ... Mmmm ... Arnold and Edith, that it was about the quality of their life, and not the quantity of years they spent together." Sam swallowed deeply. He seemed to have recovered the situation.

The vicar smiled. "A nice thought indeed. I've read your notes, and made some enquiries of my own about your aunt and uncle, so together with your thoughts and poetry, I'm certain we'll give them the sort of send-off they deserve." She smiled. It was a gentle smile which wasn't forced or practiced, but genuine in its concern for the bereaved. "If you're ready then I believe we should begin."

Sam smiled awkwardly and took a seat in the front row. For the first time he looked at the two coffins lying as they had through life, side by side, now spiritually holding hands.

It was a brief but caring service which Elizabeth carried out to perfection. As the coffins were moved from the chapel to the hearses, Sam for no reason known to him took Elizabeth in his arms and held her tightly to him. It was a physical intimacy, which at that moment all his being screamed out for. He opened his arms and stood back, getting redder by the second. "I'm so ... so sorry ... I've never ... no never done anything like that before." He looked embarrassed and deeply guilty.

"Please don't worry about it. At times like this we all react in different ways." She was genuine in her concern for Sam. "Come with me and let's go to the crematorium together. We can talk in the car." She took his hand and led him like a child behind the coffins to the single black limo. It was a brief, but comforting drive to the crematorium.

"Shit this is a soulless place." Sam thought. *"When I go, I want a hole in the ground in a graveyard in the country, not thirty minutes at gas mark six in a concrete bunker."*

The two coffins were lifted from the hearses onto shining metal trolleys, and wheeled into the chapel. Sam walked slowly behind them, his head bowed staring at the well worn floor tiles. Halfway down the aisle, Sam looked to his right and left. The pews were full. There were people everywhere. He quickly raised his head and looked around the chapel. It was standing room only! The chapel was packed to the rafters with mourners, and everyone whose eye he caught nodded and smiled back in true sympathy at him. Who the hell were all these people?

As at the funeral home, Elizabeth led the service, and after a few hymns, Abide With Me, The Day Thou Gavest and Immortal Invisible, she led a few moments silence and then looked up at the mourners.

Using Sam's notes and her research, Elizabeth gave a heartfelt eulogy and finished with the lines of poetry Sam had selected. After a prayer, she turned to speak to the congregation.

"There is a friend of Arnold and Edith's who would like to say a few words." She paused and referred to her notes. "Isaac Wouters?" She slipped her glasses to the tip of her nose, and scanned the chapel. A small white haired man slowly rose from a row at the back. He took his weight on a silver topped ebony cane and shuffled slowly to the bottom of the steps at the front of the chapel, bowed to the coffins, said a silent prayer and slowly turned around to the packed chapel.

"Friends." He paused as if gathering his thoughts. "We have lost two true angels of mercy. Arnold and Edith were dear friends to everyone here today. I held a special place for them in my heart, and they will be sorely missed. Their passing has left a vacuum we will find difficult to fill." He was struggling to maintain his composure. "High Wood remains one of our strongest beacons, but today, its welcoming light burns dimmer, but we will restore it to all its glory." There were general murmurings of agreement in the congregation. "They showed the way home for so many and we cannot leave those who remain in limbo." He paused and swallowed deeply. "The lost of the Great War drove everything they did, and we continue this work." Isaac was struggling physically and emotionally. "I have chosen some lines from two War Poets, who I know Arnold and Edith loved." He put his free left hand into his inside jacket pocket and pulled out a small sheet of writing paper. "I'd like to read a little of the 'When you see Millions of the Mouthless Dead' by Charles Hamilton Sorley." He paused, composing himself.

"When you see millions of the mouthless dead
Across your dreams in pale battalions go,
Say not soft things as other men have said,
That you'll remember. For you need not so.
Give them not praise. For deaf, how should they know
It is not curses heaped on sac gashed head?
Nor tears. Their blind eyes see not your tears flow.
Nor honour. It is easy to be dead.
Say only this, 'They are dead.' Then add thereto,
'Yet many a better one has died before.'
Then scanning all the o'ercrowded mass, should you

Perceive one face that you loved heretofore,
It is a spook. None wears the face you knew.
Great death has made all his for evermore."

He slowly folded the paper, turned, bowed to the coffins and made his obviously painful way to his seat at the back of the chapel.

Elizabeth rose in the pulpit, giving time for Isaac to return to his seat. "Thank you Isaac." She turned to the coffins, where a special curtain had been constructed to close around them. She bowed her head to give the final words of the funeral ceremony.

"We now commit their bodies to the ground;
Earth to earth, ashes to ashes, dust to dust;
"Does everything have to turn to dust?" Sam thought.
In the sure and certain hope of the resurrection of eternal life ..."

Martin Bevan and another bearer slowly closed the heavy purple velvet curtains around the coffins.

Sam had been asked to choose a piece of music to be played as the mourners left the chapel. He'd selected Nimrod from Elgar's Enigma Variations, which seemed to sit well with the poetry of Charles Hamilton Sorley.

Elizabeth was standing at the door leading out of the chapel offering a hand of comfort to everyone who'd attended the service. Sam hung behind until everyone else had left. He understood why he *didn't do funerals.* Everything was so bloody final, and it was the freezing cold. He was chilled to the bone. It was as if all the natural warmth of humanity had been drained out of the building. The chapel was like a cold storage unit.

'Probably for good practical reasons.' Sam thought.

"Sam." Elizabeth had moved close to him. "Everyone's outside, and the crematorium needs to get ready for the next funeral. They run a very tight ship at these places. Come on let's get some fresh air." Her tone was warm, comforting, almost loving, a sensation he hadn't felt since he couldn't remember when. She offered her hand to him, and as he took it he felt the warmth flow back into his body and soul. He looked up into the dark brown eyes of Elizabeth, which smiled back at him. The moment seemed to last just a little too long.

"Thanks for everything, Elizabeth. The service was wonderful. I honestly don't know what I'd have done without your help and support." Sam realised he was still holding her hand, which she wasn't making any effort to pull away. He let it linger there for a few more seconds and then thought it was probably a good idea to let it go.

She smiled at him. "It was a lovely send off, and it really was no problem at all. It's what I do." She took his hand again. "Arnold and Edith will know what you've done for them. To see so many friends here today must have brought comfort to you. I've rarely seen a chapel so full. It's normal when someone young dies, but for two people who seem to have led such solitary lives, I was very, but happily, surprised. Did you know them well?"

The feeling of warmth was growing. She was a vicar, but my God she was a woman.

"I think you'd better stop what you're thinking!" His other half said.

"Mmmm ... Yeah I know ... but ..."

"Yeah but me no buts. She's a vicar."

"She's also a woman. Something I've a vague recollection of. "

"Look, now's not the time. Once we have the money in the bank then we can think about the great escape. Is she married? I haven't been able to check the left hand."

Sam looked down at the right hand he was holding, and as her left hand reached up to rest on his, his smile was difficult to disguise. There was no ring.

"Sorry, I was just thinking about them." He hoped that his excuse covered his smile. "I knew them so well as a boy, but lost contact with them. They contacted me recently and since then we've met for lunches and dinners. I really don't know much about their recent lives, and I've no idea who all these people are."

"Now's the chance for you to find out. Everyone's milling around outside." Elizabeth let go of his hands, looked outside the chapel, and looked back at Sam. "Time for you to find out? I'd try Isaac first, he seems to be the main spokesperson. Go on Sam, it could be exciting." She moved away to the crowd outside the chapel, shaking hands and offering everyone her deepest sympathies.

Sam left the chill of the chapel for the warmth of the July sun, turned and walked to the area set aside for flowers and wreaths. Despite the request in the announcement, there was one. It was about two feet across, completely made of small red poppies, with a card and an inscription.

'They went with songs to the battle, they were young.
Straight of limb, true of eyes, steady and aglow.
They were staunch to the end against odds uncounted,
They fell with their faces to the foe.
They shall grow not old, as we that are left grow old:
Age shall not weary them, nor the years condemn.
At the going down of the sun and in the morning,
We will remember them.'

Even for Sam the words had a resonance which stirred memories of hearing them before.

"At the service of Remembrance at the Cenotaph." His other and better informed half reminded him.

"I know. Just couldn't bring it to mind, that's all."

A few faces turned to Sam. He was back in audible conversation with himself, and started reading out the words on the inscription to try and cover what he had been saying.

"We will remember them."

"We will never forget them." A frail voice said quietly.

Sam looked down at the white hair of Isaac. He could only see the top of his head, because of Sam's height and that Isaac couldn't raise his head from a bowed position.

"Forget who? I'm sorry to ask, but I sort of know they may be from World War One, but who they actually were I haven't a Scooby, sorry, I haven't a clue. What really puzzles me, Isaac, I hope you don't mind me calling you Isaac?"

Isaac gingerly shook his head. "Of course not."

"What really puzzles me is who you and all these people are? Arnold and Edith always seemed to be a pretty solitary couple, and the house when I went there yesterday wasn't somewhere which would welcome visitors with open arms."

Isaac took Sam's arm. "Let's sit and I'll tell you what I can."

They walked slowly into the garden of remembrance and sat on a bench in memory of Sarah Mallart a young woman who'd died aged twenty six. They sat together, and for the first time Sam could properly see Isaac's face. His skin was the colour of parchment and deeply lined. Age worn, was a term which came to mind. His hair was white, thick and lustrous, his clothes immaculate and his shoes highly polished. But the thing which drew Sam's attention, were his eyes. They seemed huge in proportion to his face, and deep blue. To Sam, they'd seen more than any person should ever see. Seen things which should stay unseen, cried tears for the many, brought comfort and sought understanding and forgiveness. They held Sam's eyes, used them as open channels and gently examined every nook and cranny of his mind. Isaac silently held Sam's attention for what seemed like an age, but what in reality was only a few seconds.

"Where to start?" Isaac eased himself as far as he comfortably could, back on the bench. "How much do you know about World War One?"

"Not much I'm afraid. It started in 1914 and ended in 1918; every year in November there's a ceremony at the Cenotaph; a prince was shot in Serbia; millions died; I did read something on the internet the other day about the Somme, and wasn't there a poster with 'Your country needs you'? Became quite iconic didn't it? I suppose, that's about it really."

Isaac smiled. "Not bad. Most people, particularly the younger generation, have no idea what went on in those four devastating years. Years which took so much potential from a generation." Isaac paused and slowly turned his neck, to look directly at Sam. "You asked who we were. It won't be easy for you to understand what we are and what we do, but I need your help, Sam. Arnold and Edith were sure you could help, but didn't have the time to explain to you what they did without confusing or scaring you."

Sam frowned at Isaac. "Scaring me?"

"I'm sorry, Sam. Possibly not the best choice of words. Arnold and Edith were two of the best we had, and their belief that you could carry on their work, carries a lot of weight with me." For the first time Isaac smiled at Sam. "I need you, Sam." he turned his face away from him. Holding his position had been a painful effort for the old man.

Sam pulled at his ear lobe. It gave him comfort in moments of stress. "Isaac?" He wasn't sure if he should carry on with this conversation. "Isaac, I went to the house for the first time in some time yesterday, and it, how can I say, it was, it's difficult to find the right words?" He was talking to the top of Isaac's head again, but somehow knew he was listening intently to every word he was saying.

"Use whatever words you feel inside. What happened there, Sam?"

"You have to understand I've been experiencing problems with what I think I've been seeing. I took a lot of hallucinogenic drugs when I was younger and I've been experiencing flashbacks. Plus I'm trying to find an antidepressant that works without too many side effects, and you may feel that I'm not the most balanced person to be helping you."

"We are now quite sure that the drugs, LSD and Mescaline, you took in your youth, re-set primal neural connections in the deepest parts of your brain. Recent events have stimulated these connections, and allowed you to sense and experience alternate realities which most never will. Psychics have these connections, and the members of the group and I have them. Without them we wouldn't be able to complete the work we do. Tell me what happened in the house Sam?"

Sam sat back on the bench and stared out at the lines of memorials in the garden of remembrance. They couldn't, but he'd wake up soon. Over the next twenty minutes, he tried as best he could to tell Isaac everything he could remember that he'd experienced at High Wood.

"The *dust* had a life of its own?" Isaac said.

"Yes, it's the only way I can describe it. But it should all be gone by now."

Isaac quickly turned his head to Sam. Much too quickly, as his pained expression showed "It should be gone? What do you mean, gone by now?"

Sam detected a serious concern in Isaac's voice. His eyes burrowed deep into Sam's. "What do you mean, Sam? Gone by now? How can it be gone?"

"I, well, Jane decided to sell the house, so I've arranged for a cleaning firm to give the house a deep clean. It's a very saleable property and we could do with the money." There was a long meaningful silence. "Isaac, there wasn't much else I could do. She's deep in debt and she's dragged me into it to help her clear it. I need to get away from her and the proceeds of the sale will give me freedom."

Isaac seemed to have regained a degree of control. "When are they cleaning the house?"

"Today." Sam replied. "They should be well into it by now."

Isaac's already hunched shoulders sank a little deeper. "You must stop them, Sam. Now!" His voice for the first time was raised. "You must call them now!" His voice became calmer. "Please, Sam, please call them. You must stop this. The damage they will do will be irreparable."

Sam was confused. "What damage, Isaac? They're there to clean and freshen the house, not demolish it." He got up from the bench and knelt on the pebble path in front of him, level with his face. Tears were flowing through the deep facial wrinkles like dried out river beds after a storm.

"Shit, Isaac, sorry, what have I done?"

"Sam, please phone them and see what can be done." Isaac was recovering his composure. "Do you have a tissue?" Sam pulled a crumpled but clean tissue from his jacket pocket and handed it to him. "Thank you, Sam. Now please call them."

Sam rubbed his hands over his bald head and turned to look out at the garden of remembrance. "I don't have their number with me."

Isaac seemed to stop breathing.

"It was just a quick phone call. It was the easiest way to do it." He looked away from Isaac at the garden like a child desperately hoping his father hadn't lost his temper with him.

Isaac crossed his arms over his knees and stared at his feet.

"Isaac, are you OK? Look I'm sorry but I couldn't sell it in the state it was in."

Isaac continued to stare at his feet.

"Please say something." Sam was now pleading.

Isaac's head slowly lifted to a level with Sam's face. He seemed to have visibly aged. His eyes reflected back a sorrow which Sam had never seen. It sliced deeply into him, and for the first time he understood what the house meant to this old man.

"Look I'll drive over there now. You never know, they may not have started yet." Sam was clutching at straws, like a drowning man desperately reaching out for any means of help.

Isaac looked into Sam's eyes, and handed him a small gold embossed business card. "Go now and call me. Let me know what has happened. Then we will meet again. Now please, Sam, go!"

Sam stood up and ran towards the car park.

Elizabeth looked up from the conversation she was having with an elderly woman with jet black hair, and couldn't understand what Sam was doing. Why now? Why here of all places? He was running across the garden of remembrance, just avoiding the small marble headstones and the mourners from earlier funerals.

They turned, angry and confused. "What the hell do you think you're doing?" One young relative shouted after him. "This is a crematorium not an athletics track." He looked after him and despite the place shouted "Prick!"

Sam looked back without slowing and shouted "Sorry! I'm in a desperate hurry."

The young man didn't seem satisfied with this and shouted back "Bloody moron, it's my Gran's funeral today."

"Peter, please not now dear." An older woman took him by the arm and led him away.

"Truly I'm sorry." Sam shouted. He'd only been looking back for a few seconds, but they were a few seconds too many. As he looked around he found himself running directly at the coffin of the next funeral entering the crematorium. The bearer at the front of the coffin shoulder charged him as he was about to crash into it, sending him spinning off into the rose bushes close to the entrance of the chapel. The thorns ripped into his suit jacket, cutting thin red ribbons into his hands and arms. He stood up and stared at the shocked relatives and friends of the deceased. Once again an apology seemed pretty meaningless, so he turned on his heels and continued to run to his car.

Perfectly planned road works; the school run; learner drivers; contraflows; red lights; pedestrians; cones; pigeons; pot holes; pensioners driving underpowered old cars; cyclists who'd written their own rules of the road; ambulances and just about everything possible had thrown itself in his way to slow him down. The latest addition to his problems was a morbidly obese woman in a seriously overstretched bright blue shell suit, who looked like a giant blueberry muffin, oozing over the edge of its paper case. She was chugging along at five miles an hour in the gutter, on a purple, battery powered three wheeled mobility scooter.

"Get off the road and on a diet!" Sam shouted in frustration, immediately regretting it as he did.

The woman looked up from the scooter, peered over the rim of her glasses which had slipped to the bottom of her shiny red bulbous nose, slowly lifted one puffed up hand, smiled at him and daintily raised her middle finger.

"What has he done, Isaac?"

"Hopefully nothing." Isaac was sitting with Guillaume, his younger brother, in a corner of the golf club lounge at the wake, eating a barely adequate lunch. Sam's catering plans hadn't anticipated this number of mourners, and the catering staff were doing their best to accommodate everyone.

"But what if he can't stop them? We'll have to shut down High Wood, won't we?" Guillaume was staring at his plate of a ham sandwich and a small piece of quiche. "How could he do this?"

"He knew nothing of what Arnold and Edith were doing." He looked down at the paper plate and pushed around the few *delicacies* with a crooked arthritic finger. "Let's just wait and see what's happened at the house before we start panicking."

Guillaume stopped prodding what was trying its best to pass as a sausage roll with a plastic fork and looked up at Isaac. "You're right, we need new blood. I don't know how long you and I will be able to continue this work. I just pray that the portal at High Wood is still open. There are so many still to pass through."

Isaac smiled at Guillaume. "They will pass through. None shall remain. The portals will stay open until we have brought them all home."

Sam pulled up outside High Wood and saw a blue and white transit van parked close to the gate. The writing on the side *'Kleen Up – No Messing About'* didn't help his mood. He pushed open the front door wondering what he'd find on the other side, and his worst fears were confirmed as he looked down at a shining highly polished wood floor. Not a grain of dust could be seen anywhere. The hall table, everything, was pristine. Deep clean. He could have no complaints with **Kleen-Up**, they did what it said on their tin. He felt empty, drained of everything, but a voice from the kitchen told him where they were. He walked up the hall over the polished floor which now closely resembled an ice rink, to the kitchen door which was slightly ajar. He gave it a hard push as it jammed on the kitchen floor. Three men were sat around the kitchen table eating packs of sandwiches and crisps.

"George?" Sam said.

The man with his back to Sam turned in his chair. He was in his fifties, shaven headed, wearing overalls which Sam was sure he'd seen them wear on CSI Miami.

"Yes." He smiled at Sam. "Mr Morbeck is it?"

Sam smiled back. "Yes, pleased to meet you." *What's the point of pleasantries"* Sam thought?

"I see you've made a start on the deep clean. Looks very good. Very, very clean."

George looked puzzled. "I'm not sure what you mean. We haven't started on the inside of the house yet. All we've done is some work on the outside of the house. I was planning to call you as I thought we had the wrong address."

Sam looked puzzled. "Wrong address?"

George frowned at Sam. "Yes. Usually when a deep clean's ordered, the house is in a pretty sorry state, but this house is immaculate. I've rarely seen a better maintained house than this one."

Sam sat down next to George. *"What the hell does he mean, immaculate. Where was the dust?"*

The two other men, much younger than George and wearing the same overalls, nodded and smiled at him. It wasn't that often they were given, money for old rope.

"Immaculate? The house didn't need cleaning?"

"No. I could have just sent you the bill, but I want the company to keep its good name. Pete and Steve were all for me sending you the invoice, but that's the younger generation for you." George smiled knowingly at Sam. "No such thing as a free lunch, is there?"

"No and thanks for the honesty, but you're not winding me up are you? The house was clean?"

George's frown deepened. "Spotless. When we arrived it was like a show house. You could have eaten your food off the floor."

"Cup of tea, Sam?" the voice from behind him was a woman's, and very familiar. "Two sugars as usual dear?"

Jane!

"Just making the boys some drinks before they carry on outside. Lovely house isn't it. Should be easy to sell. Isn't it what they call a desirable residence?" She smiled a smile which Sam knew meant *"Got you!"*

"How did you find the house?" He was trying his best not to look surprised or majorly disappointed.

"You left George's telephone number on the writing pad in the kitchen. He was very helpful. He was surprised I didn't have the address! How did the funeral go?" Her smile subtly changed to *"Try as you might, you'll never get one over on me."*

"Good. I mean they had a really nice send off."

"Were there many people there?"

"No, just me the vicar and the people from the funeral home. But it all went well." He was trying to sound as casual as he could, but was certain that the great inquisitor would see through his exaggeration of the truth.

"Good. I'm sorry I couldn't be there, but the migraine was unbearable. I'm sure they'd have understood."

"Bet your sweet life they would if they knew you as well as I do." Sam thought.

"She's got to go." His other half was back.

"She will, and pretty damn soon. I've had enough of this. She's not getting a penny from the sale of this house."

"You've being planning to get rid of her for how long? And she's still here isn't she?"

"Day dreaming Sam? Off with the fairies again?" Sarcasm was a real strength of Jane's.

"Mmmm, yes sorry. Just thinking about how much we could get from the sale." Sam replied with almost a straight face.

He turned back to George. "So when you got here there was no dust anywhere? Nothing?"

"No dust, no grime no dirt, no nothing. As I said, a show house."

Sam felt a vibration from the mobile in his jacket pocket. The glowing screen said *"Number blocked"*. He lifted the phone to his ear.

"Sam, it's Isaac."

"Just a second, please." He tried to look as calm and collected as he could. "Excuse me I need to take this call."

Jane stared at him. "Who is it?"

"No one you know dear. Just someone from the golf club."

Sam turned, walked down the hall and into the front garden.

"Isaac are you still there?"

"I'm still here, Sam. How is the house?" There was concern in his voice.

"It's a little difficult to explain," There was a long pause. "the cleaners are here, but there's no *dust*. The house is in pristine condition."

There was silence on the other end of the line.

"Isaac! Isaac, did you hear what I said? There was no *dust*. It must have been another flashback. I must have imagined everything!"

"Not possible, Sam. I know what the house is capable of. The dust is there. Somewhere in High Wood it's *hiding."*

"My God!" Sam thought. *"He's senile."*

"Hiding? Isaac how does *dust* hide?"

"Sam I know all this sounds strange, but we need to finish the conversation we were having. There are explanations for everything you have seen, and you need to understand them. We need to meet again very soon." There was an urgency in Isaac's voice which was impossible for Sam to miss.

"Sam!" It was Jane, her call was loud, and the message very clear. *"Get your ass back in here now!"*

"Coming." Sam shouted back. "Isaac, I've got to go. I have to be in Cardiff tomorrow, so we could meet at the Millennium Centre in Cardiff Bay. I'll meet you there at 12.30 in the main concourse. We can have some lunch."

"That will be perfect, and I'll wear a red carnation." Isaac said jokingly.

"SAM!" Jane wasn't used to asking twice.

"Isaac I have to go. I'll be there tomorrow. I'll bring my most open mind."

"See you tomorrow, Sam." Isaac sounded a lot less stressed than he had at the crematorium.

"The dust is hiding?"

"Sam can you get back in here and let's decide what George needs to do with the house."

He put the iPhone back in his pocket and headed back to the kitchen. How in God's name was he going to keep her in the dark about anything to do with

High Wood? Until he knew from Isaac what the real story behind the house was, he didn't want it on the market, even though its sale offered the perfect escape plan from her. As he entered the kitchen Jane was sat at the table in deep conversation with George.

"Good of you to join us, dear."

Sam frowned. Did everything she said have to be edged with sarcasm.

"I've been discussing with George the best way forward and we both agree that he should carry on and finish the outside of the house. It will be important to the success of the sale. After that he'll do a complete check on the house, and do any necessary work, but only after he's spoken with me. You're much too busy with other things to bother yourself with this." She stared at Sam and gave him the *'Don't even think about questioning me on this, it's already decided'* look. "I'll speak to some estate agents tomorrow and get the ball rolling. So I'll keep the keys from now on. It will make things a lot smoother if I do."

"Of course, dear, you're much better at these things than I am." After years of practice, he managed to say the words without a hint of sarcasm. She'd already taken the keys from George, but, Sam smiled, she didn't have the second bunch of keys which were locked in the glove compartment of his car.

Jane was back in conversation with George, laughing over some comment she'd obviously made about Sam. She turned her head and dismissed him. "There's nothing for you to stay here for. I'll meet you back at the house. And get the tea on." She turned back to the men at the table.

Sam thought about answering her, but thought better of it and turned to leave the kitchen.

"Tell her to sod off." His other half had had enough.

"That's easy for you to say." Sam had also had enough. *"But she's got to go. Making me look a twat. I could see them smirking."*

"We'd be better off in prison. Let's do something now."

"Leave it to me. I wouldn't give her the pleasure in the afterlife of seeing us in prison. When she goes no one will know. Or care."

Jane shut the door behind George and his team and turned back into the hall. She couldn't stop smiling. The house had to be worth at least a half a million. Goodbye debts; hello Las Vegas; goodbye George; hello tanned, fit, sexually active, young escorts; male or female as it was never too late to experiment; play with the high rollers; get some work done on her face and body, and stick two fingers up to the loan sharks who were making her life a misery.

She'd line up at least six estate agents when she got back to the house and settle on the largest offer. She smiled once more at the house and whispered "God bless you, Arnold and Edith. But it's all mine now."

As she began to turn, she heard, or thought she heard, the click of a door opening behind her. Her mind went into, It's really nothing but the wind and there's absolutely nothing to worry about mode. But the body wasn't listening and had gone into, For God's sake don't turn around and take a look as whatever it is as it's definitely not friendly and I'm sure it'll go away." mode. The deep sigh which followed fused her feet to the hall floor. Flight was desperately trying to win over fight, but both were losing the battle to, This is my bloody ticket out of this shit-hole of a life, and nothing is going to take it away from me, mode. The power of greed was proving a lot stronger than nature's in built survival mechanism. She slowly turned around and looked down the hall. The cellar door was open, and a thick yellow mist was moving slowly in and out of the open door like a gentle Mediterranean swell on a balmy summer's evening.

"Turn around and leave now!" She thought. But the, like the lead in a horror movie who can easily escape the house of the evil dead but decides to stay because he's not sure if the zombies who've taken over the house may have not killed and eaten his girlfriend and the other three friends in the house who he could save in the nick of time from the zombies who he could decapitate with the ancient axe he'd found in the cupboard under the stairs and escape in the van which was still parked in the woods, mode in her brain, was unbelievably winning the argument.

Sam decided to stop at Tesco to grab a coffee. It didn't have the leather seats of Starbucks, but its cappuccino was delicious and about half the price. He picked up a millionaire caramel shortcake, as he needed a sugar-fix before he went back to the house and committed very satisfying justifiable homicide. He settled behind a table set for two, himself and his other self, and started on the millionaire caramel shortcake and cappuccino.

"So, as the three vultures in *The Jungle Book* said, 'What are we going to do now?'" Sam asked his other half.

The old couple sitting at the next table, taking as long as they could over their tea and toasted tea cakes, looked around and stared at Sam.

"I'm sorry I was just trying to remember something for my grandson." It was a faultless well practiced response for those who thought Sam was losing it. "Just thinking out loud. Sorry to disturb your tea."

They looked puzzled at each other, then at Sam, politely smiled and returned to their tea and toasted tea cakes.

"OK so let's think about what to do next. By the way I bloody hate millionaire caramel shortcakes. Next time can we please have a custard slice?" His other half said.

"Yes."

"Yes to both?"

"Yes to both." Sam begrudgingly agreed despite his deep dislike of custard slices. You could never eat them without getting half a ton of custard over your hands, face and shirt.

"If only she'd just disappear. Just vanish into thin air. However much I hate her, I can't think about killing her." Sam was staring at a display, advertising nine toilet rolls for the price of six and trying to look interested in the offer.

"I'll do it. I couldn't give a toss."

"Yeah I know, but unfortunately it's only me who's in contact with the real world. You might be able to do it and get away with it inside my head, but that doesn't exactly solve our problem."

"I know, but at least we could see if it would work or not."

"Yeah, but the basic problem is I couldn't kill anyone." Sam looked away from the toilet roll offer to a free DVD player when you purchased any television."

"Can we at least think it through?" His other half wasn't going to give up easily.

"There's no point. I'm, we're stuck with her, and you never know, with any luck, she may develop some terminal disease."

The opening chords of Smoke on the Water from Sam's iPhone shattered the relative quiet of the restaurant.

The old couple sat at the next table, got up like two first-time marathon runners recovering after collapsing over the finishing line. This sent their table toppling over, scattering their remaining tea, milk, tea cakes, assorted crockery, cutlery, free magazine, birthday card, pen and imperial mints over the floor, and carrier bag containing their meagre amount of shopping.

The mother sitting behind Sam, considered murder, as her baby emitted a scream which could have shattered the windscreens of most of the cars in the car park.

Two other toddlers who were just falling asleep after making their mother's life hell for most of the morning, joined in, and together produced a cacophony of screeching, bawling and howling.

A thin young man in a grey Super Dry hoody slipped on the spilled tea and fell head first into the lap of a none too friendly shaven-headed and tattooed biker.

His emaciated friend carrying two coffees, slipped on the imperial mints and soaked the biker's girlfriend in steaming cappuccino.

The woman at the till turned to look at the commotion and tipped a bowl of soup over her supervisor, who jumped back onto the feet of two nuns.

Who'd actually caused the mayhem seemed uncertain.

The biker had the hoody by the throat; his girlfriend was doing her best to choke the emaciated coffee thrower, Mr Old Couple was mopping Mrs Old Couple with as many paper serviettes as he could lay his hands on, the nuns were clearly not from a silent order or one with a limited vocabulary, just woke up baby was inconsolable, Mummy was shouting at a businessman, who she'd decided was responsible for disturbing her precious little one, because his lap top kept emitting strange alien sounds, as it received his emails, the toddlers were running amok around the cafe followed by frantic Mums, and supervisor was threatening till lady with the sack.

Amongst the confusion in the restaurant Sam quietly strolled out of the store.

"Shit, what else can go wrong today. I've pissing well had enough. Sodding funeral confused the shit out of me. The house, well what the hell can you say about that. The wicked bitch from the west, and her friends the builders. And those bunch of bastards in there! Jesus Christ who have I pissed off?" Sam was sat on the floor talking to a Bob the Builder ride for children. "God in heaven, what did I do in some other life to deserve this?"

"Sam?" The voice came from behind him. "Sam is that you?"

He didn't turn or get up as he recognised the voice. It was Elizabeth. He closed his eyes, screwed up his face, clasped his hands behind his head and like Basil Fawlty began to slowly rock back and fore. He at least had the answer to his question. Today had just got worse. He stopped rocking, unclasped his hands, stood up and turned slowly to face her.

"Elizabeth, thank you for all you did at the funeral." Sam smiled trying to appear unflustered.

"Where on earth were you running to like that? You created, a little, upset at the crematorium. I've never seen anything like it!" Even for Elizabeth her tone was as close to angry as it ever got. "Well, Sam what happened?"

"Think carefully, she's onto you." His other half chuckled.

"Not now please."

"I thought you might need a little help to get out of this."

"Not now! Leave this one to me!"

"Sam are you OK?" Elizabeth was peering into his glazed face. "Sam?" She leaned forward and prodded his shoulder. It had the desired effect.

His eyes refocused on Elizabeth.

But she could see that behind them his brain was desperately looking for an answer. Finally one came.

"I got a text from our next door neighbour. She'd gone around for a coffee with Jane and found her at the bottom of the stairs. She was badly dazed and her shoulder looked like it was dislocated." Sam paused, gathering his thoughts. "She called an ambulance and Jane's in A&E at the Heath."

"So why are you here and not in hospital with her? Donkey" His other half helpfully pointed out.

"Because, she hadn't dislocated or broken anything, there was no evidence of concussion and apart from a few cuts and bruises, she was OK. I've just run her home and put her to bed. I was here to get her something really nice for dinner. What do you think?"

"So so. Just a small point, why don't you have any shopping?"

"Shit! They didn't have what she likes, so I'm on my way home to order a take away. I was sat on the floor because I was pissed off they didn't have fillet steak."

"Liar liar pants on fire."

"Oh piss off and leave me alone."

Sam glazed over.

Elizabeth took him by the shoulders and shook him gently. "Sam are you OK? Come with me. They make a great mug of cappuccino in here, and you look like you need a hot drink, a blueberry muffin and a friendly face to chat to."

"Mmmm?" Sam was back with the living again. "A cappuccino?" Sam's mind was close to meltdown as he remembered Mr and Mrs Old Couple, Mummy and the Baby, the Biker and just about everyone else in the restaurant. He could see her concern was genuine. "Elizabeth, thanks but I really don't feel like coffee at the moment. I'd better get back and see how Jane is. Our neighbour, Louise is sitting with her so I could come down here."

"Would you like me to come with you? I'm very good at providing comfort for the sick."

"No! No!" Sam's response was too quick and too short.

Elizabeth dropped her arms to her side. Surprised and disappointed by his response.

"How to win friends and influence people. A major best seller by Sam Morbeck. Prat!"

"Elizabeth I'm so sorry. I didn't mean to sound so ungrateful. Today's been a little, well, you know." He hoped she wasn't so offended and confused that she wouldn't see him again.

"No, Sam, I should apologise." She'd seen many different responses from people to death and personal crises, and Sam had had his fair share. "Look, if there's anything I can do then please call me." She pulled out an old sales receipt and a well chewed biro from her pocket. "Here are my home and mobile numbers." Her handwriting was copper plate despite the materials. "Please call me at any time." There seemed to be a little more than just an offer of help in her tone and eyes.

"Elizabeth, I'd love to meet again. It's just that things at the moment are, well, I'm sure you understand everything that comes with someone's death. Let alone a couple." He hoped she wouldn't think he was giving her the brush off, could see through the words and into his eyes at his true meaning. "I'll call you in a couple of days when things have settled down a little. If that's OK?"

"Whenever you want to talk I'll be there for you, Sam." She smiled and stroked his cheek with her index finger.

FIVE

Jane held the handle of the cellar door, the viscous yellow mist lapping over her shoes. She pushed at the door trying to close it, but there was too much resistance for her to move it.

"If it won't shut, then how the hell did it open?" She thought.

Her feet disappeared beneath the rippling yellow mist. She struggled to let go of the handle, found she couldn't move her hand, and leant her full weight against the door. As she tried to pull her hand off the handle, there was a soft tearing sound. She tugged her hand away, and the skin of her palm and fingers peeled away leaving a flapping kid glove on the door handle. The house was silent no more. Her scream sliced through the air and bounced off the walls. Jane looked down at her hand which was oozing blood, and dripping into the yellow mist leaving a red trail like a haemorrhaging slug under the door of the cellar. She turned, ran for the front door, and burst out of the house into the afternoon sun.

A balding middle-aged man, dressed for the Tour de France, on what was clearly an expensive racing bike, had propped it against the outside wall, and was running up the path to her.

"Are you OK? Only I heard someone scream?" He was looking at Jane's hand with genuine concern. "Your hand, have you broken it?"

Despite what happened in the house, Jane was again in full control. "No I'm fine thank you. I jammed my finger in a door. Hurt like hell at first, but it's never as bad as it seems." She carried on supporting her damaged hand, and smiled at the wannabe Bradley Wiggins to reassure him she was fine and could be left alone.

"But the scream? It sounded as if someone was being murdered. Are you sure you're OK? Let me take a look at that hand. I'm a GP at a practice quite close to here." He took a step forward and offered to take her hand.

Jane took two steps back. "Really it's nothing. Just needs washing in cold water." She didn't want to explain the actual *nothing*.

The cycling GP stepped closer to Jane. "Please stay calm, shock can have odd effects on patients and your scream would suggest you've done more damage than you think." He reached forward and after a struggle separated her hands so he could examine the damaged right.

Jane's brain shifted into overdrive. *"How do I explain that jamming my finger in a door strips the skin from the palm of my hand? And to a doctor."* She looked at the cyclist as he carefully and closely examined her hand, waiting for the frown, the puzzled look and the questions which would follow, but none came.

With an expression of extreme confusion he gave her her hand back. "I think you must have jammed something other than your hand."

She looked down at the creases and folds of the palm of her right hand. It was a little wrinkled with the recognisable arches, whorls and double simple loops of her fingerprints, but her hand was fine. Jane struggled to conceal her confusion. "I ... Uh ... I ... I must have caught ... I'm really not sure what ... I'll check when I get home ... back indoors. It's somewhere ... rather more intimate." She gave the cyclist a knowing smile and touched her breasts as if to explain her embarrassment.

He smiled at her to indicate he understood, turned to walk back to his bike, and stopped at the gate looking back at her.

"Oh bollocks, he thinks I live here." She thought. *"I'm going to have to go back inside, but I've only got to stay there until he's gone. Should only be a few seconds, and I'll only have to stay just inside the front door."* She waved at the cyclist and walked back into the house.

Sam looked at his grey Swatch, which he wore instead of the Rolex Oyster Perpetual Date Submariner he'd been given by Jane for his fiftieth birthday, from her rare winnings on a trip to Vegas. But since his *retirement* he felt it was a little too ostentatious. When he was working, image was everything in the power game of corporate politics. It was a game you played for all you were worth or if you had any sense, kept well clear of. There were too many casualties of corporate war taking what was euphemistically called *early retirement*, or *seeking a new career opportunity.* They filled the pages of national newspapers and the files of employment agencies, casualties of the dog eat dog battles. He'd played the game for twenty years, eventually lost, and become another faceless casualty of the conflict. The Rolex acted too much as reminder of his battles and scars. Life was now, well up until yesterday, a lot simpler and the Swatch reflected that. He checked the time. It was close to six o' clock. You always lost a sense of time in the bright summer evenings. She'd be livid, but she hadn't phoned, and surely she'd have taken the opportunity to have a go at him. Where was she, and why did he care?

"She's hopefully under the wheels of a bus. Or is life not that kind?" His best friend was back for a chat.

Sam smiled, at his reflection in the glass of the window of the restaurant. He peered through the glass to see a group of arm waving customers shouting at each other. Slowly Mr Old Couple looked up, stopped waving his arms, stared at Sam, recognised him, tugged at the sleeve of Mrs Old Couple who pulled at the sleeve of Mummy and together they angrily pointed at him. Elizabeth thankfully had left, so Sam without fear of further embarrassment sprinted across the car park like a fox with a pack of rabid hounds on his tail. He'd collect his car later when it was dark.

Jane closed the front door behind her, turned to peer through the small glass pane. She could still see the distorted image of the cyclist holding his bike and staring at the house.

"Oh sod off will you." She snarled.

He carried on staring at the house, and then rested his bike against the gate post.

"Oh shit, no. Please don't be the Good Samaritan. Just keep your nose out and piss off." She desperately tried to think of a lie which would get rid of him.

The cyclist started walking up the path.

"Bollocks!" Jane really didn't need this.

As he came within a few yards of the front door his mobile phone rang in his backpack. He slipped it from his shoulder, retrieved the phone and held it to his ear for a few seconds.

"Yes, dear, I know that I'm supposed to be there by now but … I'm sure that she was hurt ..." The conversation became very one-sided, and the result clearly didn't require any more discussion.

"Yes, ten minutes. I'll be there." He looked for a few more seconds at the front door, shook his head, turned and walked back to the gate. He turned for one last look at the house, mounted his bike and sped off to she who must be obeyed.

Jane took a deep breath, sighed, took two small steps backwards into the hall and felt something cold slithering over her feet. Her breathing shortened but she carried on staring directly in front of her at the door. Her brain screamed at her to look down, but no power on earth could make the muscles of her neck respond. Her feet began to feel cold and wet, and the cold gradually moved up her calves. Paralysis slowly progressed up her legs, reached her pelvis, locked her hips, which killed any chance of her responding to the flight response which was screaming at her. The numbing cold had reached her waist, but Jane kept her arms firmly crossed and locked across her chest. But that mad something in her brain wanted to know what the hell was causing the freezing wetness. She unlocked her fingers and inch by inch slid her right hand down the side of her body. She'd no idea what she was going to find, and really didn't want to know, but her primal need to escape needed a little more support information. Her hand finally made contact with the cold, and immediately flew back to the comfort of her chest.

"Once more please. Only this time with conviction." Her subconscious suggested. *"Let's focus and get the hell out of this house!"*

She slid her hand down her side again until her fingers met the source of the cold. She rippled her fingers through what felt like a cold gel.

"You've got to take a look." She thought.

As she looked down, she could see that the entire hall floor had disappeared under a pulsating sea of liquid mud, which spat sticky globs onto the hall walls, like a convict on a dirty protest.

"Move! Now! Anywhere! Get out of the hall! Get to anywhere else in this house or ideally out of the front door! For Christ's sake just move!" Her mind screamed.

She tried to turn back to the front door, but the viscous mud was now inexorably pulling her towards the cellar. She forced her left leg against the strength of the current, and it moved a few inches. With a superhuman effort her other foot followed, and step by step she struggled down the hall until she was within a few feet of the kitchen door. A loud moaning to her left, made her look to where the sound had come from. The cellar door was now wide open, and the liquid mud was gushing through the door and down the cellar steps, like a muddy river crashing over a weir. She tried to make the last few steps to the safety of the kitchen, but the strength of the current dragged her towards the stinking torrent. She leaned forward, desperately struggling against the current of the foul mill race. She'd given up on flight, and flipped to, 'Oh shit I'm going to die. Why does life decide to kick you in the teeth when everything in the garden finally starts to look rosy.'

She started sliding backwards, like Michael Jackson moon walking, her hands clawing at the wall ripping off strips of wallpaper. She desperately struggled to escape the gaping maw of the cellar door, and her hands finally found some purchase against the plaster under the wallpaper. It tore at her nails, but she resisted the pain and pulled herself slowly away from the cellar door. She began to think about possible survival, but as she did, the surface of the torrent rippled and four gelatinous *arms* rose from the surface. They twitched like the tentacles of an octopus, writhed up and wrapped themselves around her waist and arms. She tried to pull away, but the *arms* seemed to be coated in a powerful glue. Her hands lost their grip on the plaster, and she crashed face first into the ooze. She made one last drowning-man-clutching-at-straws effort to escape the inevitable but couldn't overcome the strength of the current and she was dragged through the cellar door. As she flailed for life below the surface of the slime, the cellar door slammed shut, and the hall was once again in pristine condition.

SIX

Sam opened the front door of his house. "Jane?" He called, with as much concern as he thought sounded appropriate. The house was as silent as the proverbial.

"Where the hell is she? She's never out at this time. Food's always on the table at five thirty sharp and in the bin by six thirty precisely." He thought.

"Jane?" He walked into the kitchen. The table was still set from breakfast.

"What the hell! Where's Mrs Perfect?" His other half was back.

Sam stayed silent.

"Sam?"

He stared at the spoons, bowls, the remains of muesli and cornflakes, and two dark green Denby mugs.

"Sam? Cooeee! Back with the living."

He looked up from the table. "What?"

"Where is she?"

"Earlier on, she was at the house. Sucking up to the bloody cleaners, and now the bitch has got her claws into High Wood."

"At the house? She was at High Wood? How the hell did she find it?"

"She phoned the cleaners. I left their telephone number on the pad by the phone."

"Bit clumsy wasn't it?"

Sam frowned, and looked around the kitchen again. Why did he have any concerns about her not being here? He looked at his watch and decided after the day he'd had, an early night was in order.

The deep syrupy tones of Barry White from the radio alarm woke Sam from what had been a surprisingly good night's sleep. Seven a.m. flashed at him, and with a groan he pushed back the duvet and climbed out of bed. The older he got, he found the noises he made when he moved, seemed to be getting louder and more frequent. He rubbed his eyes; scratched his personal equipment; stretched his arms; cleared the sleep from the corner of his eyes; moaned again as he pulled on his dressing gown; hit his toe on the dressing table as he put on his slippers; farted; walked into the door of the bathroom; produced a stream of expletives and sat down on the toilet. When he was younger, his prostate happily allow him to fully empty his bladder, but as the years has passed, it had got a lot grumpier and now demanded more straining and more midnight trips to the loo. Something else which irritated Jane.

"Why can't you stand up and pee like normal men?" She'd snap at him. "You're enough of an old woman as it is, without this."

He flushed the toilet, checking there was no blood; showered; spent too long staring in the magnifying side of the shaving mirror at the state of his skin and pores of his face; cleaned his teeth; sat back on the toilet as his prostate demanded more attention; decided that his nails needed trimming; moisturised his body. and ran from the en suite as a spider the size of a tea plate ran from behind the cabinet under the sink.

"What are we going to do?" He wanted advice from his other half.

"A song and dance. A month's holiday in the Caribbean. Try to stop smiling. Shit, Sam, our dreams have come true. We've won the lottery."

"Shouldn't we call the police? Surely someone will ask where she is. That old bat two doors down is always in and out of the house. She'll start to ask awkward questions."

"What if she does? Who really gives a shit? She was hardly Mother Teresa, was she?" There was a long awkward silence. "OK, if it makes you feel better, call the police and let them know she hasn't come home. They won't do anything for at least twenty four hours, but at least you'll feel better, and the old bat will leave us alone." His other half conceded.

"If they won't do anything for twenty four hours, I'll call them this afternoon after I've met Isaac."

Sam parked the car at twelve fifteen in the Mermaid Quay car park, put enough money in the Pay and Display for four hours, and walked across the busy boardwalk past the Corn Exchange to the Millennium Centre. He looked up at the imposing building clad in multi-coloured Welsh slate, capped with a bronze coloured, and copper oxide treated steel dome. He looked at the lines of the Welsh poet Gwyneth Hughes which were formed by the windows in the upstairs bar areas above the main entrance. 'Creu Gwir fel gwydr o ffwrnais awen.' He'd never really paid any attention to the words before, which thankfully had been also inscribed in English. *'In These Stones Horizons Sing'*. It was opened in 2004, and Sam, without the "I don't want to spend good money on that shit" Jane, had been to see most of the travelling London shows who had taken advantage of the thirty seven thousand square metre stage of the Donald Gordon theatre. He pushed open the doors of the main entrance and walked to the concourse area. He looked around and saw Isaac in the gift shop. He'd picked up a small red dragon wearing a white and green striped T-shirt with a Welsh flag on the chest bearing the legend 'Croeso y Cymru'.

"Something for the grandchildren, Isaac?"

Isaac looked up and smiled. "No it's for me. I have a collection of mementos from my visits to different countries. It's become something of an obsession."

Sam raised his eyebrows and smiled. "Sounds like you have a problem. I'm sure that there must be a help group you could contact." He raised his shoulders and winked at Isaac. "Let's get some lunch. My treat. I called ahead and booked a table at Ffresh. The food is excellent and the menu is mainly Welsh dishes." He took Isaac by the arm and slowly walked across the concourse to the restaurant. They were shown to a quiet table in a corner, which Sam had requested given the nature of the conversation they'd be having.

"Hope this is OK?" Sam looked around the restaurant and then back at Isaac.

"It's fine, Sam."

"Would you like anything to drink?"

"A jug of water with some ice and lemon would be lovely."

Sam ordered water and a diet Coke for himself, the waiter left two menus with them and placed a bowl of olives in the middle of the table. Isaac looked up and down the menu, looked up at Sam, raised his eyebrows, smiled and handed his menu to him.

"I'll leave the choice with you. I'm sure whatever you order will be delicious."

The waiter came back with the drinks and hovered at the table. Sam looked up at the him, pursed his lips as if he was thinking a great deal about his choice.

"What's today's soup?" Sam peered at the waiter's name badge. "John?"

"Leek and potato sir. Really excellent."

Sam looked back at the menu and frowned. "Probably a bit hot today for soup. I'll have two of the prawn and crayfish tail salads to start and two of the rolled shoulder of Welsh lamb."

"Any side orders?"

"Always looking for that extra sale" Sam thought. "Nothing thanks." The look Sam gave the waiter spoke loudly enough to say, *"Thanks very much but now please sod off and leave us alone."*

They sat quietly while the waiter made his way back to the kitchen. Sam took a sip from his diet coke and poured Isaac a glass of iced water. He leaned forward resting his elbows on the table. "Where do you want to start?"

Isaac leaned forward. "As Julie Andrews sang in the Sound of Music, 'Let's start at the very beginning, That's a very fine place to start'." He smiled at Sam as he did his best to sing the words."

Isaac didn't have much of an appetite, but nonetheless enjoyed the meal. They left the restaurant and sat in the shade of an umbrella at an outside table drinking coffee.

"Sam you said when we spoke at the crematorium you'd taken drugs when you were young. Mind altering drugs like LSD, and mescaline?"

Sam nodded.

"Back then, what did you see?" Isaac was peering deep into Sam's face. "Sam, tell me what happened when you took those drugs."

Sam half smiled at Isaac like a schoolboy who's been caught smoking behind the bike sheds. "The best way I could describe it, is that I saw things which I knew logically couldn't be real, but they were staring me in the face, and to me they were absolutely real. Real enough to chase me down the road at midnight and scare the shit, excuse me Isaac, out of me." Sam looked down at his hands remembering the night he dropped two tabs of LSD, and two dinosaurs, the flesh eating variety, crashed out of the bushes on the hill he was sat. They were real. He could hear them, smell them and feel the ground shake as they ran towards him. There was only one thing to do. Run like hell. His friends who'd been with him had no idea what was happening, as Sam screamed, ran up the hill, across a busy road and tried to climb a high metal fence overlooking the M4 motorway. They'd got to him as he reached the top, pulled him back from the brink, and sat on him for twenty minutes as he continued to see the dinosaurs sniffing the ground, searching for him.

"Dinosaurs Sam." Isaac was confirming what Sam had said and not questioning it.

"Yes." Sam raised his eyebrows. "I know it sounds bizarre if you haven't taken LSD, but believe me, what you see, however odd, to you is real."

"I've taken it and know exactly what you mean." Isaac said.

Sam's eyes opened wide.

"Yes there have been other generations who experimented with drugs. Even old timers like me." Isaac smiled knowingly at Sam. "So you've seen things which defy all logic, and yet you've seen them and you know that for you they were as real as the ground you were standing on. Sam, what truly is reality? My reality may be completely different to yours. Psychics understand there are many different realities, and to some this makes them charlatans or frauds. But for them and others, they open a door to alternative realities which most are blocked from. They can also be a link to souls who are trapped in a reality they cannot escape from." Isaac took a sip from his latte and looked around at the open paved area close to the Corn Exchange. It was full of families with children, students, runners, cyclists, food and ice cream stalls, all enjoying the Summer sun.

"Isaac, what's happening to me? What I saw at High Wood was real, and yet yesterday, everything I'd seen and touched was gone. Where was the decay and *dust*? The house was … immaculate." Sam rubbed the back of his neck and twisted it around trying to ease the tension in his muscles.

"You should have been approached years ago, but Edith and Arnold didn't want to disrupt your life. They recognised in you abilities we so desperately need. What I'm about to tell you may seem impossible to comprehend, but you have to believe me that what I tell you is true." Isaac drained the last of his latte. "When anyone dies we mourn for their loss; pay our respects at different ceremonies; celebrate their lives; ensure they have a loving send off; tend their graves where we have a place to visit and talk to them; spread their ashes; keep their ashes in an urn and ultimately have closure. Sam, a great deal of this is not possible if you have no physical remains and don't know how they died or where they lie. We can mourn, but without our loved one's final physical remains, we don't have the comfort of knowing where they finally rest. How can these lost souls rest in peace? What happens to them?"

Isaac drained the last of his latte and smiled at Sam. "Stop me at any time you have a question."

Sam grinned. "If I do that, then we may be here for a very long time."

"Sam I need to talk about the First World War, as it is central to everything we do. OK?"

Sam nodded.

"In World War One, tens of thousands were assigned the description MIA, Missing in Action. They were killed in battle and never found. At Thiepval in

Belgium, there is a memorial bearing the names of about seventy two thousand British and Commonwealth soldiers, who went missing in action during the Battle of the Somme. They were never found and have no known grave. The total for World War One can't be accurately established, but is thought to be hundreds of thousands, who still don't rest in peace. It has been my mission, and our group, to help the missing of the Somme and World War One get home and rest in peace. There are other groups who devote themselves to other conflicts, and between us we cover all major wars." Isaac paused and raised his mug, but the latte was finished. He drained the last of the milky froth and put the mug on the tray they'd carried from the coffee shop.

"Would you like another coffee or something else to drink?" In the brief time he'd known him, Sam had gained respect for Isaac, and in the July heat he was concerned that he could easily become dehydrated. "A mineral water or soft drink?"

"Thank you Sam I'm fine." Isaac looked at the man opposite him. To take on this responsibility at any time was onerous, and for a man of Sam's age it would be tough, but people with his abilities were rare.

"Sam, the Somme wasn't just one battle; it was a series of battles from July to November 1916, and during that period approximately seventy nine thousand British and Commonwealth soldiers were assigned MIA status. The eternal image of the World War One is of soldiers being scythed like fields of wheat by German machine gun fire, and on the first day of the battle twenty thousand British troops were *harvested*. As the battle progressed, thousands more were vaporised by German shells. Others were buried alive, and as the battlefield in November was reduced to a quagmire of liquid mud, soldiers were sucked down into the slime and lost."

Sam had known very little of the World War One, and Isaac's comments brought a chill to the July heat. "What exactly do you do? How do you reassemble a cloud of dust?"

"By entering their reality. A reality which has been unlocked to you by LSD and mescaline."

Sam waved to a waiter and ordered a bottle of mineral water for Isaac and a vodka and tonic for himself. He needed a drink.

Seven hours later Sam was sat at the kitchen table picking at a ham sandwich and sipping decaffeinated coffee. Jane still hadn't come home. It was an odd feeling not to have her whining at him, and there was an eerie emptiness to the house which Sam couldn't get accustomed to. For years getting rid of her had been his greatest wish, and yet now ... They'd been married for thirty two years, and when his friends had asked him what anniversary it was and he'd said jokingly, "Shrapnel".

"It can't have always been bad. Can it?" Sam thought behind closed eyes. *"Surely at some time we were happy?"* He tried to remember a time when they'd laughed, made love, enjoyed each other's company, but struggled to drag a single memory from the vaults.

"Don't start getting maudlin." His other half was having no more of this.

"I know, but, well you know."

"No I bloody well don't know. She's been poison for God knows how many years and now let's celebrate. Let the police know in the morning she's disappeared and then let them worry about her. Bloody good riddance if you ask me."

Sam got up from the table and took a packet of chocolate digestive biscuits from a kitchen cupboard. Every mouthful of the sandwich had stuck in his throat and he needed something sweet. He picked up the mug of coffee from the table, walked into the lounge, picked up his iPod, selected Peter Gabriel, plugged it into the Bose, and put the mug on a coaster on the small side table. "She'll have my guts for garters if I make rings on her beloved wood." Old habits were hard to break.

"That's if we ever see her again." His other half happily replied.

Mercy Street, Sam's favourite Gabriel track started playing. He closed his eyes and tried to make some sense of everything Isaac had told him.

SEVEN

Elizabeth pressed Ctrl/S and sat back in the wooden chair in the vicarage kitchen. The sermon had been easy to write, with inspiration from Sam's selection of poetry at the funeral. She'd never really *got* poetry, but the words of Dylan Thomas perfectly captured everything relevant to old age and death. Like Sam she had an iPad. She'd initially been sceptical of another of the *latest* devices and could see no advantage over her lap top. But now it had become an indispensable part of her life. She searched for the poems of Dylan Thomas and soon found the foundation of the text of her sermon.

There had been a recent spate of deaths in the parish and their effect on the community was an important subject for her to deal with. Particularly as she'd never truly come terms with the recent deaths of her mother and younger sister.

She read most of Thomas's poems over two cups of coffee and found after a few lines, that 'And Death Shall Have No Dominion' perfectly caught the depth of her pain, but it also gave her hope over the finality of the loss of her younger sister Ann, and dearest mother Patricia. She copied and pasted lines into a word document, she'd use for her sermon, and saved the entire poem into her personal folder. She also wrote two lines in her diary.

'*Though they sink through the sea they shall rise again;*
Though lovers be lost love shall not;'

After the death of her mother and sister, Elizabeth felt only a deep unrelenting ache in her heart. There was a vacuum in her which nothing had been able to fill. Her faith had been tested to the limit, to the point where she felt she'd have to give up the priesthood. Funerals were the greatest test for her. How could she reassure grieving relatives that after the pain of death, there was salvation and resurrection, when her own belief was that her loved ones were in the ground and not with God the Father in Heaven. For months her words of comfort to the grieving relatives became nothing more than a script without meaning. She'd searched and searched for anything from the scriptures that would re-establish her faith, but the more she read the more she lost it.

John 14:1-4 hammered another proverbial nail in her metaphorical coffin, *'Let not your hearts be troubled'.* What the hell else could your heart be when you'd lost the ones you loved most in the world?

Corinthians 5:6-8 was the final straw, *'Yes we are of good courage, and we would rather be away from the body and at home with the Lord.'* "Garbage!"

Elizabeth spat at the page. "I want them back in their bodies and at home with me!"

She put down the iPad, took off her glasses and rubbed her eyes.

"I'll print a copy of the sermon tomorrow when I've bought a new set of printer cartridges." She thought.

She got up and carried her final cup of coffee of the day into the lounge, turned on her iTouch and scrolled through the albums until she found her opera play list. She'd come to opera late in life, and now it was an essential part of helping her switch off from the day to day pressures of life. She scrolled down to one of her favourite duets, 'Au fond du temple saint' between Nadir and Zugra from 'Les pecheurs de perles', the 'Pearl Fishers' by George Bizet. She put the iTouch into the Bose and pressed play on the remote control. As the baritone voice of Bryn Terfel and tenor voice of Andrea Bocelli caressed her brow, she lost herself in a warm fuzzy haze.

Meeting Sam had stirred feelings in her which she was sure she'd never experience. She'd returned to the Bible which restored her faith in love, but not yet in death and resurrection.

Corinthians 13:4-8, *'Love is patient, love is kind. It does not envy, it does not boast, it is not proud .... it keeps no records of wrongs .... it always protects, always trusts, always hopes ....'*

The closing bars of the Pearl Fishers brought tears to her eyes, but for the first time in an age, they were tears not caused by grief. She'd call Sam tomorrow, arrange to see him again, and feel him against her. She knew he was married, but sensed he wasn't happy, or was she simply trying to convince herself that adultery was OK? Whatever it was, she wanted him, emotionally, and for the first time since she'd been in University, her body ached for someone physically. Her breath shortened, her chest tightened and there was a glow in parts of her which had been cold and sealed from the outside world for years. She sat back in the comfort of the armchair and let the thoughts of Sam holding her close and the gentle tones of Cavalleria Rusticana – Intermezzo wash over her.

Half an hour later she took the mobile phone from her pocket. Half an hour later for the twentieth time, she tapped on the contacts icon, tapped on Sam, selected SMS and started to type. Calling was just a step too far for her.

"Hope that everything is OK with you. Thought that we could ..."

She tapped the delete key erasing the words.

"How about meeting for coffee at ..."

More deletions.

" .... "

This time she didn't need the delete key, and threw the phone down on the sofa.

"For God's sake how difficult can this be?" She stopped and looked up. "Sorry, Lord, but really how difficult is it to arrange to meet someone?"

She picked the phone up from behind a floral cushion.

"OK I'll call him. What's the worst he can say?" She tapped the contacts key again, tapped on the Sam icon, tapped on the phone number and held her breath. It was ringing. The ring tone stopped and she was transferred to a messaging service.

"Hi, sorry I can't take your call, but please leave a message after the tone and I'll get back to you as soon as I can."

Even hearing his recorded voice was enough to send Elizabeth into a *state*. There was a sharp beep on the line.

"Yes … Hi Sam it's Elizabeth … I was wondering how things were after the funeral and everything … Love to meet up for a coffee and have a chat … Give me a call … Bye … Ummm …" Another sharp tone brought her message to an abrupt end. "Shit! Bloody double shit!" She sheepishly looked up again. "Sorry."

The iPhone in Sam's pocket pinged. He had a voice message, but decided he'd listen to it later, as it was probably only the police following up on his call to arrange a meeting about the missing Jane. He closed his eyes and drifted back to the meeting with Isaac.

"Let's start with the house. High Wood or Bois des Fourcaux as it was originally known in French." Isaac continued. "As well as being the name of Arnold and Edith's home, it was a ferocious battle during the Somme offensive. It was the last of the major woods to fall to the British." He looked up at Sam, silently asking him if he wanted to know more.

Sam leaned forward. "I need to understand what went on, so please tell me what you think I should know, and what part I play in this."

"The attack on High Wood started on the evening of July 14th 1916. Cavalry was involved, the Dragoon guards and the 20th Deccan Horse. Lances against machine guns. What chance did they have? They took about three quarters of the wood but the Germans counterattacked and twenty four hours later retook the wood. It wasn't until September 15th 1916 that the British finally took Bois des Fourcaux. It is believed that around eight thousand soldiers still lie in High Wood, and it's to lost souls like these that we strive to bring resurrection and salvation." Isaac lifted himself in his chair to ease his back.

They sat in silence looking at each other across the table. Seagulls screeched and dived at children eating ice creams as they watched the sailing boats on the bay marina, and overtired toddlers screamed from their pushchairs and prams.

Sam sat back in his chair taking in the sunlit happy scene, and looked back at Isaac and frowned. What was he doing on a day like this discussing lost soldiers of the Somme and how he could bring their spirits back to their loved ones and families?

"Sam, how it works is almost impossible to explain, but let me try. Lost souls travel through time portals connected by channels of energy or ley lines. The first portal was discovered in 1922, by my father at Thiepval, which is now a major memorial dedicated to 'The Missing of the Somme'. It was designed by Sir Edwin Lutyens and built between 1928 and 1932, on the site of the first portal. There are just over seventy two thousand names carved on sixty four stone panels. All of them are missing or unknown, fathers and sons, brothers in arms, sprayed like a giant aerosol into the soil and skies of Belgium and France. The earthly remains of the others were so massively injured, that they were impossible to identify. A jigsaw puzzle of putrid human parts with a missing lid and no picture."

Isaac paused and stretched his neck. "I should tell you something about myself. I am originally from Iepers, in Belgium, and lived in the UK with my family from 1932. My father could see that history was repeating itself in Europe, and decided getting out of Belgium before Germany once again invaded our country, was the safest and best thing to do. My parents, my sister Eveline, my brothers Guillaume and Renaat and I lived with a family on a farm near Woodstock for the duration of the war, until we returned to Belgium in 1948 and set up our new home Beaumont Hamel. You remember it was a key objective of the Somme. It was a village which held an enormously important defensive position for the Germans, and consequently was supported with strengthened positions at Y-ravine, Hawthorn Redoubt, Berg Werk and others.

Sam raised his eyebrows and stared at Isaac. "Hawthorn Redoubt and Berg Werk? Sorry to interrupt you, Isaac, but they were two of the names listed in one of the text messages I got." He felt in his pocket and pulled out his iPhone. "Give me two seconds." Sam scrolled through his messages until he found the mail which had so confused him. "Here it is. It lists Sunken Lane, Hawthorn Redoubt, Broadway, White City, Berg Werk, Jacob's ladder, The Bowery, and Carlisle Street. And the final message said At High Wood." Sam gave the phone to Isaac so that he could read the full message chain. *"Why didn't I mention this at the crematorium?"* He thought.

Isaac stretched, doing his best to take the tightness and pain out of his back and joints. He looked exhausted.

"Isaac?" Sam was concerned about this man who, in the brief time he'd known him had gained his respect. "Isaac, are you OK?"

"Mmmm ..." Isaac scratched the side of his head disturbing his perfectly coiffured locks. "Sam, I'm sorry, this has been a very busy time, and as I said ...," there was a pause as he took a deep breath, "I'm not getting any younger." He rubbed his thighs and squeezed his knees."

"Sam ... " Isaac was carefully reading all the messages. "Sam ... " He carried on reading and absorbing the messages. "These are all places which featured in the Battle of the Somme."

"And the numbers?" Sam jumped in interrupting Isaac.

"They could be regimental service numbers, or grave references, but I'm fairly sure if you researched these you'd find a correlation between the names and the numbers on the messages." Isaac handed the phone back to Sam and smiled. "This confirms you are sensitive to these lost souls. They cry out to you to reopen High Wood. They have found their way to a portal, and from there to High Wood where the door to final rest was slammed in their faces. At High Wood. Sam they couldn't have been any clearer in their cry. They're waiting for you to re-open the last door to their rest and salvation. The dust you saw when you were at High Wood was almost certainly those men. But there will be others at High Wood. A lot of others, who need the final piece of their jigsaw to get back home. Sam you are that piece. They need *you*."

After lunch, Sam took an exhausted Isaac back to his hotel, who insisted that he needed to meet Sam for much longer to explain things fully to him, what he needed him to do, and had suggested he came to Ypres. A trip to Belgium would normally have been completely out of the question, but with Jane out of the way he'd agreed to meet him there the following week. Isaac would organise the flight to Brussels, the train to Ypres, the return trip a week later and his accommodation in Belgium. Sam just had to get there.

He took his iPhone from his pocket and put it on the kitchen table. The message icon flashed at him. He'd forgotten the message he received at lunch.

"Shit, I hope it wasn't the police. It doesn't exactly show me as a caring husband." He picked the phone up and connected to his messages.

"Yes … Hi Sam it's Elizabeth … I was wondering how things were after the funeral and everything … Love to meet up for a coffee and have a chat … Give me a call … Bye … Ummm … Not sure if you've got my number … it's … "

Sam smiled to himself. However garbled the message, it was still great to hear Elizabeth's voice.

"She's up for it!" His other half said.

"Oh piss off will you. It's not like that." Sam was getting a little annoyed with his other half's approach to life, and women in particular.

"Not like what? Not like you'd love to play hunt the sausage with her?"

"For God's sake grow up."

"That's me, the child in you. The teenager who spread your wild oats for you. Didn't have the balls did you? Always left it to me didn't you. Isaac got you sussed straight away. You're an unbalanced loser who could never strike up a conversation with the living. But you always had a great time with your imaginary friends, and now it seems the dead have joined your inner circle of chums."

Sam clenched his fists and stared at the ceiling. Why was this asshole making so many appearances and being so cocky? The antidepressants he was taking had locked him away in the cupboard under Sam's mental stairs, so why was he suddenly out? He looked for his tablets which were always put in the same place by Jane. Tablets! He'd missed last night's and this morning's, and he didn't have a clue where she kept them. They just appeared twice a day and he took them without question. He got up from the table and started rummaging through the kitchen cabinets and drawers. Nothing? Not even a paracetamol. Where the hell did she keep them?

"Who gives a toss where they are. You don't need them. We get on fine without them."

Sam ignored him and walked upstairs to the bathroom cabinet where he knew there was a first aid box. But there was nothing but a few old plasters and the rolled up remains of a tube of TCP ointment.

"Sam look we don't need them. Let's call Elizabeth and do some horizontal jogging."

Sam ignored him. He knew his other half was getting annoyed, as he always started to get cruder. He stood on the landing, frowned and tried to think where she'd keep them. Where did he never go? Anywhere which was *labelled* as Jane's. Where would you keep a lot of tablets? He opened her bedroom door, peered around it and walked in. They'd slept separately for the last ten years, and it was the first time Sam had entered the inner sanctum. It was just what he imagined. Tasteless. Predominantly pink; furry pillows everywhere; soft toys covering the bed; a white 32 inch TV fixed to the wall; mirrored wardrobes; photographs everywhere, but none of Sam; two pink rugs on a beige carpet; a pile of gossip magazines on the bed side cabinet and a full length mirror which reflected back the full glory of the room. Sam opened a few drawers finding mostly lingerie, and as he opened the top drawer of the cabinet next to the bed, he understood how she'd happily avoided sex with him for the last ten years. He lifted two vibrators out of the drawer, stared in amazement at three dildos which made him feel very inadequate, and a selection of *toys* and lubricants.

"She must have been one of Ann Summer's best customer's. And I thought all that buzzing was her shaving her legs." Sam thought.

The mental image of Jane pleasuring herself with what he could see, made him shudder, and feel just a little nauseous. It was like finding your parents having sex on the dining room table. He looked around the bedroom and saw the door in the far corner.

"My God" he thought *"An en suite shower room! I'd forgotten it was there."*

In the cabinet under the sink he found what he was looking for. Pill containers labelled for the days of the week. One blue labelled 'Day' and one red labelled 'Night'. The cabinet was full to bursting with boxes of medication. He took them all out, laid them on the bed, and arranged them into the different drugs. He recognised his three, Simvastin to reduce his cholesterol, Tagamet to control reflux and Fluoxetine, Prozac, his antidepressant. He popped one tablet from each box, looked at the pill containers and saw that up to yesterday there were capsules in the remaining compartments, but the compartments for the night tablets were all still full. He screwed up his nose and stared at the capsules and pill containers on the bed.

"She's not been giving me my Prozac. But I've been taking tablets in the evening? What the hell have I been taking? More importantly what haven't I been taking? Shit, it's no wonder that he's been around so much and that I've been seeing things a lot easier. Why's she doing this?"

"Push you over the edge and have you put away. Sell this house and High Wood and start a new life without you. How about that for a possible scenario?"

"Push me over the edge with your help." Sam snapped.

"No need to be tetchy."

"Tetchy. Me tetchy. What possible reasons could I have to be tetchy. Just leave me alone!" Sam had had enough of just about everything today, and without the Prozac he now understood why he was seeing things and having dark thoughts again.

"Easy way out of all this shit." He thought, looking at the tablets on the bed. *"Plenty of options there."*

"Go on, why don't you do it? What's the point of all this anyway? Some old lunatic has some batty idea about saving some soldiers who've been dead for 100 years! Jesus, and you think you're losing it. Let's take enough of these downstairs, open that bottle of Maker's Mark and sail smoothly down the Styx to Hades."

"Yeah, come on let's do it." Sam agreed.

He emptied one of Jane's small make up bags onto the floor and emptied four strips of Prozac capsules into it. He recognised the name Tamazepam as a sleeping tablet and emptied another four strips in with the Prozac. A combination of these and a few large shots of bourbon should prove effective. He picked up the bag and made his way back to the kitchen to collect the bottle of Maker's Mark, but as he picked up the bottle he saw the message from Elizabeth still flashing on the phone, and re-read it.

"What was that song of Ian Dury's, Reasons to be cheerful? She was a reason to be cheerful, wasn't she? I need a list." Sam thought. *"Reasons to be cheerful. If I can come up with ten then the tablets stay in the bag."*

"Oh for fuck's sake, Sam, get a grip. Reasons to be cheerful? We've got enough reasons to be dead haven't we?"

Sam ignored him and picked up a note pad and biro close to the bread bin. "OK. What have I got?" He started writing.

Reasons to be cheerful

1.   No Jane.
2.   I'm retired. No work.
3.   Money from selling High Wood. Escape.
4.   See the world.
5.   Get a season ticket for the Devils.

"Beginning to struggle? If you come up with ten, then I'm a constipated Chinaman."

Sam ignored him and carried on with the list, although he had to agree that it wasn't exactly easy to come up with ten reasons why he shouldn't shuffle off this mortal coil. Maybe he should have gone for five or six.

6.   Play more golf.
7.   Get HD Sky TV.

"Three to go."

8.   Get an Apple computer.

"Bit materialistic most of these."

Sam refused to take the bait. Only two to go. "Come on Sam, we can do this." 9 ... He leaned back in the chair and stared into space. "Come on how difficult is it to come up with ten things that make me want to keep on breathing?" 9 ... Sam looked at the bourbon and the capsules.

9. Get a new car.

"Still materialistic?"

10. ...

"Not going to make it are you?"

"Oh piss off! Why the hell should I have to decide if I live or die because of some stupid bloody list?" Sam spat the words at the table. "There is only one thing I need at the present to make my life complete."

Sam added one more to the list

10. Elizabeth

EIGHT

"Sister!"

"Sister? Why is anyone calling me sister?" Jane thought. *"Where the hell am I? Am I dead?"* She frowned, struggling to remember what had happened. She'd been at that house when … when what? ... She gently slapped the side of her head. "Remember."

"Excuse me? Remember what? Is there a problem?"

"Sister? Whose sister? I'm definitely either dead, in a coma or drugged up in an asylum." She gently slapped her face again. She should open her eyes.

"Sister Wilmart, Agnes, are you OK? Please, I need your full attention. They've started to arrive and quite soon it's going to be a madhouse in here."

Jane rubbed her eyes and ears. She was hallucinating.

"My God I've caught it from Sam. The bastard must have drugged me. He probably got some acid from a local dealer, and plans to get me sectioned. Bastard's probably been planning something like this for years. Open your eyes and all this will go away. What did Sam always say he'd done on a trip? Fix on something which you absolutely know is real, and everything else must be an hallucination." She opened her eyes and looked down.

"Agnes are you OK? You seem … distracted."

She looked up to her right and saw a hand on her shoulder. This was a hell of an hallucination, as she could feel the warmth of the hand on her shoulder. She looked down at a grey cape with scarlet edging, long white sleeves buttoned tightly at the cuffs, a long white belted pinafore with a red cross in the centre of her chest, a long grey skirt, and a small silver medal pinned to the right edge of the cape. The medal was supported by a mainly red ribbon with two white and navy blue stripes, supporting a silver ring with indecipherable writing and a large capital R in the centre. Even with Jane's sketchy knowledge of history, she could see she was dressed as a nurse, and the uniform rang a faint distant bell. She was sure she'd seen it before in photos at her grandmother's house. Photos of her Great Aunt who'd served in the Queen Alexandra Imperial Military Nursing Service, British Force. The photo had been taken in 1916, during the First World War!

Some force started to take control of Jane/Agnes. She straightened up and looked into the steel blue concerned eyes of Captain James Heyward M.D., F.R.C.S.

"Agnes, are you OK? You had me worried there for a minute. I can't afford to lose my best nurse just before the casualties arrive." He was smiling kindly at her. Not as an officer but as a *friend*.

"I'm fine, James. Just a little nervous. They've served King and Country and we're here to do the best we can for them."

This was an out of body experience. Wasn't it? *"Whose body is this?* "Jane thought. *"Great Aunt Agnes? What did mother and my aunts call her?"* She dredged her memory banks for the name. *"Agnes was definitely her Christian name, but what was her maiden name? Agnes Williams? No it was, Wilson, no, shit what was it?"* She ripped open the dusty cabinets of long forgotten memories, spilling files on the grimy floor, until a file fell open at the right page. 'Agnes Wilmart'. *"Wilmart, yes that was her name. My God she can have only been about nineteen in 1916."*

"Agnes, come, let's go, the first ambulances have arrived and we need to separate the walking wounded from the cases needing urgent attention." He lifted the flap in the tent for her and she followed him across duckboards to a larger tent which served as a receiving area.

The wounded were being unloaded from the ambulances and either being carried in on stretchers, or they were weary stumbling figures in khaki, wrapped in blankets or coats, and bandaged or splinted. All of them caked with blood, dust, salt and sweat, with labels of their injuries attached to their jackets. They came in such numbers that the tent was soon full to bursting. Agnes/Jane moved quickly forward while Captain Heyward whispered suggestions. They soon had stretchers on one side and the standing cases on the other. Leaving the slighter cases to be dressed, Captain Heyward quickly sorted the *bad* ones for resuss, pre-op or evacuation.

Agnes/Jane had dealt with many wounded soldiers, but none with such terrible wounds as these, and it wasn't until six o'clock in the early evening that the receiving area bore some semblance of order. She stretched her shoulders and looked around the charnel tent. It was extraordinary that among all this pain and misery, there was relative silence, and little or no outward expressions of moans, groans or complaints. The badly shocked had passed beyond it, and the others appeared numbed, too tired to complain, or so exhausted that they slept as they stood.

Agnes/Jane, like a ministering angel, floated between the beds, offering a cigarette where it was asked for. Around her were uncomplaining men with shattered heads and ghastly disfigurations of their faces. Shell and bullet wounds of the chest, spitting blood and gasping for breath. Worst of all were those quiet, afraid-to-be-touched men, with an innocent tiny little mark where a bullet had entered their abdomen. Already with a thready pulse, drawn corners of the mouth, an anxious look, and rigid muscles which vividly reflected their terrified understanding of the inevitable outcome they faced.

At the far end of the tent, were the multiple wounded, their bodies riddled with large or small shell fragments, terrible compound fractures and the stumps of torn off limbs. It was like a scene from Dante's Inferno.

She moved around the ward stroking furrowed brows and smiling into staring frightened eyes. She reached the end of the ward lifted the flap of the tent and stepped outside. Even this far from the front the stench of cordite infiltrated her nose. She looked up at the early evening sky and watched the flashes of the guns on the horizon as a barrage of steel and shrapnel rained death and destruction on the German trenches. On the other side of the front, similar scenes to hers were being played out.

"How can man impose such horrors on his fellow man?" She thought.

She looked back at the Clearing Station when a scream from her left made her run to what she knew was 'Resuss'. It was a dreadful place where they sent the shocked, collapsed and dying cases, not yet able to tolerate the stresses of an operation, but who might survive after warming-up under cradles in heated beds or with a blood transfusion. The overworked burial parties would soon arrive.

Captain Heyward stepped out of the mayhem, took her by the arm and led her outside. "OK?"

She looked back at the tent, found it impossible to speak and shook her head.

"Agnes, will you come with me to Poperinghe. It will be riskier than it is here, being that much closer to the front, but you are the best I've got, and the boys at the front need all the expertise we can provide. What do you think? I won't issue an order as I need committed people." He stood close to her. "What do you say old girl. Willing to give it a go for King and Country?"

Jane was becoming a memory, an indistinct face at the back of a group photograph, as Agnes became sharper and more defined. The work done in Resuss, could only have been achieved by Agnes, who'd worked with Captain Heyward, as if she'd done it for years, silently handing him before he asked, scalpels, amputation saws, swabs, needles and sterile catgut as he struggled against the endless tide of the wounded. She turned to face him and smiled. "For King and Country. And for you, James."

"Thanks. It won't be easy. It's already been shelled quite a few times." He looked closely at her and questioningly raised his eyebrows. "No pressure. No one will think any less of you if you say no, and if I was honest, I'd rather you stay here where it's safer, but you're the best at what you do."

Her face, framed in her starched white uniform was smiling, warmly glowing despite the slight chill of the early evening.

"My God" James thought *"No wonder the wounded and dying think they see angels."*

"For King and Country." Agnes pressed her face into his shoulder against the rough material of his uniform. *"If needs be,"* she thought. *"I'll follow you into hell and back."*

NINE

Sam picked up his iPhone, found the note Elizabeth had given him at the crematorium and dialled her number. It was late, but he needed to hear her voice. The call connected and Sam listened to the ring tone. After six or seven rings he was convinced she was either asleep or visiting some suffering parishioner. At ten rings he was about to swipe the 'End Call' red bar, when the line clicked as the connection was completed.

"Hello?"

One word was enough for Sam to know she was *the one*.

"You poor pathetic bastard. The one! Do you think you're in some poxy chicklit novel?" His other half sneered.

Sam ignored his taunt.

"Elizabeth, it's Sam. I'm sorry but I've only just picked up your message. I know it's late but I thought I should call. I hope I didn't disturb you."

There was silence on the line. Oh crap, had he called the right number, or was some middle-age husband now wondering who the hell was calling his wife? Then to his relief she answered.

"Sam it's awfully late. I was just going up to bed when the phone rang."

He felt the heat of a flush of embarrassment.

"I'm sorry. I'll call back in the morning."

"No, please no, it's OK. It's good to hear from you. I was worried when I saw you running from the crematorium. I hope everything is OK?" There was genuine concern in her voice, and not the rehearsed 'You have my deepest sympathy.

He was having another warm flush, but not this time from embarrassment. "Elizabeth thanks. But you're right it is very late. Can we meet tomorrow and I'll let you know everything that's happened over the last few days?"

"And please bring your 'I've suspended belief in reality head' with you." Sam thought.

"Yes I'd love to, Sam. I'm free from around one o'clock. Where do you want to meet?" There was a brief pause. "I'd love to see the house you spoke so much about at the funeral. I could grab some sandwiches from Gregg's and meet you there? I could put the address in my sat nav."

All he wanted was to meet her again, but the last thing he wanted was to meet her at High Wood. But he couldn't, and wouldn't put her off.

"Yes that'd be fine. I'll text you the address and post code and see you there at about one thirty. I'll have a tuna mayo with no onion."

Sam got to High Wood at twelve o'clock, where George and 'Kleen Up – No Messing About' had made a great job of the gardens and lawns. He scratched the back of his head and nervously looked up at the front door. It leered back at him daring him to open it.

"OK let's do this." He whispered to himself. But there was no reply.

His other half wanted nothing to do with this place. Sam waited for the usual sarcasm. "Decided to wimp out have you?"

No answer.

"Bollocks to you then. I don't need any help to find out what secrets this house holds." He looked at the bunch of keys he was holding. He'd asked George to put the keys in sets as he opened each room in the house. Sam had replaced George's paper notes with coloured plastic fobs on the ends of each room key. Red was the front door; blue the cellar; green the first floor bedrooms; yellow the door opposite the top of the stairs; pink the ground floor living rooms; black the back door from the kitchen to the garden; brown the kitchen; white the door to the left of the stairs; the keys with no coloured fobs were for the door at the back of the dining room which opened into the single storey flat roofed extension, and the key with a piece of string tied to it was, well he still had to find the door that matched it. He found the key with a red tag on the bunch, walked up to the front door, sprayed the lock and hinges with WD40 and turned the key. Taking a deep breath he opened the front door and stepped into the hall. It was exactly as he'd left it, immaculate. The rich mahogany floor glowed like warm amber in the sunlight from the front door and the chandelier fired rainbows over the ceiling, walls and floor. The ceiling was a brilliant white and the wallpaper was vibrant, with green orchids on a white silk background. Sam sucked his teeth, frowned and stared around the hall. He must have had the mother and father of all flashbacks when he was first here. The house could have featured in Home and Gardens.

"Explanation?" His other half asked.

Sam didn't answer.

"C'mon, Sam this isn't exactly normal, is it."

Sam just continued to stare at the hall.

"OK, ignore me, but there's something very odd about this house, and I for one say sell it as soon as we can."

"Not yet," Sam finally answered. "Not yet."

"Why?"

"I want to understand what's going on here. I owe that to Isaac, Arnold and Edith."

"Don't owe them a thing. Look after number one. That's all that matters."

"I'm staying. I want to spend some time here at High Wood, so shut up and let's have a good look at the place."

He walked down the hall, spraying the hinges and locks of all the doors with WD40. He walked quickly through the rooms which were all beautifully decorated, and although Sam was no expert, he could see that the contents would have graced any antique shop in Bond Street. The mahogany flooring of the hall extended into all the rooms, each one complemented by rich highly embroidered deep pile rugs. Artwork, each one an original oil painting, hung on every wall lit by small brass wall lights. He walked into the main lounge, where a large marble fireplace dominated the room. Two of the walls were covered in shelves packed with leather bound books, and directly in front of the marble fireplace, a three seater rich red leather Chesterfield sofa took pride of place, with matching wing chairs on either side. There had been no compromise to anything modern in the room. There was no TV, phone, computer, nothing which dragged the room kicking and screaming into the twenty first century. The only nod to modernity was electricity, which powered a sixteen light crystal chandelier on the high ceiling. Sam sat back on the Chesterfield, leaned to one side, took a deep sniff of the leather and relaxed into its welcoming arms. He looked up at the ornate plaster mouldings on the ceiling, at the Chinese blue and white porcelain in the bowed fronted yew cabinets and what looked like Fabergé eggs on wall mounted yew shelves. This place didn't need a cleaner, it needed a team from Sotheby's.

"We've struck gold here. This is the mother lode. Shit, all this must be worth an absolute fortune. We are minted!" His other half was again interested in High Wood.

"Oh, back now you can smell money. You're as bad as she is."

"Oh, come on, you know you don't mean that. Where you would you be without me?"

"Probably in a padded cell, but a lot happier."

"Never mind all that bollocks. What are we going to do with this place? It looks like it could act as a stand in for Downton Abbey."

"I'm meeting Elizabeth here in about an hour and I don't want to hear a peep from you." Sam said between gritted teeth.

"Ooh, hello young lovers. You're not going to let her in on the money are you? Jesus, think of the fit young things around the globe we could be enjoying. Why the hell do you want to replace one bag with another?"

Sam had had enough and decided that ignoring his other half would be the best strategy.

"Doing the silent one on me are you. Well it won't work, you know that don't you? I'll be here when you decide you need me."

He stood up, and walked to the far end of the lounge, where a wood panelled door connected the house to the modern extension.

"Will he help us?" They sat across from each other at an outside table in the hot July sun, sipping cold beers, in Den Klein Stadhuis, in the Grote Markt, the main square of Ypres

Isaac lifted his glass of Rodenbach, and fastidiously wiped the condensation from the sides and bottom of the glass with a couple of paper serviettes. He turned his head and looked up at the Cloth Hall. He'd seen hundreds of times before, but never ceased to be impressed by it. It was originally built in 1304, but lay in ruins after artillery fire devastated Ypres in the Great War. It had been meticulously reconstructed between 1933 and 1967 and now dominated the Grote Markt.

Isaac still had a lot to do before Sam arrived the following week, and was staying at the Hampshire Hotel O just off the Grote Markt. He'd booked Sam a room for the duration of his stay at the Hampshire, which was to say the least a little quirky, but its position located just off the Grote Markt made it ideal for a stay in Ypres. The interior designer of the hotel must have at some time worked as a set designer on Colditz or The Great Escape. The hotel had the feel of a German Stalag in World War Two, however, despite the spartan military theme of the hotel, the small number of staff were extremely friendly, it was inexpensive and the beds clean and comfortable. He drank deeply from his Rodenbach, placed the glass precisely on a beer mat and looked up at his brother sitting across the table from him. "He will do what we need him to do. He is sensitive to the spirits, and his mind is attuned to those frequencies which very few are. He will need a great deal of support, but, yes I believe that he can take over High Wood, and also, I believe, help us at other portals."

Guillaume Wouters put down his glass of Westmalle Dubbel. He'd never been a great lover of Rodenbach. There were only five years between them, but Isaac's time as Chef Charon had taken a massive physical and mental toll on him. It was time for a new Chef Charon, one with psychic abilities, belief, strength of character, sensitivity and boundless energy. Importantly he would have to have no external commitments and no family or emotional ties.

Isaac believed that in Sam, he'd found most of this.

Sam picked a key with no coloured fobs from the bunch, sprayed a small amount of WD40 into the lock and inserted the key, which turned with no resistance. He sprayed some WD40 on the hinges of the door which opened into a small corridor to the extension, at the end of which was more modern door.

"What bloody key does *this* one take?" He scratched his beard, stared at the door, turned around, leaned against the door and quickly got his answer, as it flew open throwing him flat on his back. He lay there for a minute getting his breath back, and then pushed himself back onto his feet. Close to the door were three modern fader switches. He pressed all three, turned them up to maximum, and flooded the room with light. It was about thirty feet long by fifteen feet wide; the ceiling was low with spotlights set regularly every three feet; the walls were painted a matt cream with wall mounted spot lights every six feet; the floor was covered in three by two grey ceramic tiles; at the far end of the room were two windows, covered by metallic venetian blinds; on the left side of the room, a computer was set up with a printer; close to the printer were two substantial filing cabinets; along the entire length of the right hand wall were large maps and charts; in the top right corner of the room a camping table was set up with two collapsible chairs, a kettle, two mugs and some jars containing what must have been coffee and tea and close to the table was a small fridge.

Running down the centre of the room was what Sam could only describe as an enormous 3D ordinance survey map of what had to be France, and was supported by at least ten trestle tables. He walked into the room and stood close to the map. It was definitely of northern France. He noticed a few place names he knew, Boulogne and Calais and some he'd never heard of, Contalmaison,

Pozieres, and La Boiselle. The map was intersected by solid red and blue, dotted red and blue and solid yellow lines, which were labelled with symbols and codes, sealed blue envelopes with numbers and Roman numerals, and others with words and Roman numerals. Fourth XXXX, VIII XXX, 8 XX and XV XXX. The symbols followed the solid blue line along its entire length, and were matched with red sealed envelopes and symbols along the red lines. It was completed by solid blue arrows starting from the solid blue line and crossing the solid red line.

"What the hell is this?" Sam thought. He read more of the place names Mametz Wood, Thiepval.

"Thiepval?" Sam said to no one in particular. "Thiepval was where Isaac said the first portal was found by his father, and a monument, no memorial was built there." He looked again at the map, and behind the first dotted red line two names leapt off the map, High Wood, and Beaumont Hamel. He thought back to his meeting with Isaac. This detailed map had to relate to World War One.

Sam stared at the map, lost in a world of rapidly growing lists of what seemed to be unanswerable questions. He leaned forward on his hands, scanned the map, could see nothing which seemed to be of any further significance, stood up, put his hands on his hips and stretched his lower back. Age came at a price, and it was generally a debilitating and painful one. He turned and scanned the wall in front of him. The computer was a new twenty seven inch iMac. Sam smiled from ear to ear. He'd lusted after this gorgeous creature since he'd first read the review in PC Magazine.

"My God they must have had some spare pennies to be able to afford this beauty. The monitor alone must be worth around seventeen hundred, and every other piece of equipment is Apple. There has to be four thousand pounds' worth of kit here."

"And it's all ours."

"You back?"

"You bet your sweet life. What the hell is this place? One thing's for certain, it's got to be worth many pennies!" His other half started whistling 'We're in the money'.

Sam ignored him and decided that until he understood what was going on here, he'd leave well alone. An odd noise from behind him creased Sam's face into a deep frown.

"Not more trapped mescaline?" He thought, as his brain passed the sound through the 'What the hell is that' filter, and after a few seconds of neural activity he had the answer. Flies, and by the sound of them, probably bluebottles. "Bluebottles? How many of the bloody things are there? It sounds like a swarm." He scratched his neck, rubbed the top of his head and cautiously turned around.

"You're taking something aren't you?" His other half helpfully suggested.

Sam was close to believing his other half, because hovering a few inches above the map, was a seething mass of bloated flies, which Moses would have been happy to use to get away from the Egyptians.

Elizabeth couldn't stop smiling as she input the address and post code into her car's Sat Nav. He wanted to see her. Why else would he have called? She felt the warmth and desire in his hands, had seen it in his eyes, and even her dried up emotions recognised that Sam wanted her. Or was it just that he needed some extra counselling, because his mourning process needed her professional and not emotional support? She sat back in the car seat and stared at the 'Start Route' icon.

"To press or not to press that is the question?" She thought.

The glass half empty part of her was trying to convince her that no one would want her as a woman. Who in their right mind would want an overweight, short vicar with no real life experience. Her hand moved to the ignition key. She'd call and see him another day. He'd understand that things cropped up all the time for a vicar. Elizabeth turned the key, removed it from the ignition and the car fell silent.

Sam stared at the droning swarm. He was no entymologist, but even he knew that these were meat flies, which fed on sugary food, and their larvae fed on decaying meat and faeces. He looked closer at the swarm and saw that it was hovering above Delville Wood. He turned and picked up an A4 file from the table next to the computer desk, stretched forward and waved it into the swarm. It exploded into a million individual flies. A million buzzing individual malevolent insects looking for the attacker of their swarm. They circled for a few seconds in a screaming spiral, stopped, turned and stared at him through countless individual facets of their compound eyes, focusing their combined anger into a single beam of hate at him. Their lapping mouthparts drooled in anticipation of a meal, but Sam was still fresh and not on their menu. Suddenly, as if an order had been screamed by their commander, the synchronised droning started again at a level which hurt Sam's ears. The individual flies morphed into a spinning metallic petanque ball, which began to pulse and change into a spinning funnel like the twisting column of a tornado. The tail of the funnel moved down towards the model until it struck the map at Delville Wood. A cloud of dust exploded from the surface of the map and the vortex burrowed its way into it. Sam stared in disbelief at the swarm, and, too quickly for his back, bent down and crawled under the trestle table to see where the it had gone. But apart from a thick coating of fluff there was nothing.

A loud banging from the front door made him stand up a lot quicker than he'd planned, and crack his head on the trestles. He closed his eyes and kept the expletives inside his head. The banging continued. Sam looked at his watch. It was almost one thirty.

"Shit Elizabeth!"

He ran from the room slamming the door at the back of the lounge. As he reached the front door he tried his best to look calm and collected, took a deep breath and opened the front door. "Eliza …?"

The two police officers standing outside the door looked at Sam and then at each other in that knowing police officer way.

"Good afternoon, sir. We're following up on a report from a cyclist about a distressed woman. Do you know who that might be, sir?" The police officer, a man Sam guessed probably in his late fifties, was accompanied by a pimply youth. The older officer, a sergeant, was holding the ubiquitous note pad and pointlessly licking a pencil.

Sam tried unsuccessfully not to look confused or worried. *They're following up on my missing persons call.* He thought. *But why are they here? And who the hell was this cyclist?*

"He saw a woman at this address, and she was distressed?" Sam said.

"Yes, sir. The cyclist heard," he paused as he read his notes, "he described it as," he paused again for dramatic effect 'a blood curdling scream. I thought that someone was being murdered!' Those were his exact words. Thing is, he only reported it this morning. That's why we've only just come around to look into it. He said that as the woman appeared," again he referred to his notes, "yes here it is. She said that 'She'd caught her hand in a door but she was fine, and then she went back into the house'. He assumed from this that everything was OK, but wasn't really happy about her explanation of the scream. OK if we come in, sir. Bit awkward talking here on the doorstep."

Sam begrudgingly stepped aside and waved his arm inviting them in. "The kitchen is this way. I'll make a cup of coffee while we talk."

The older policeman took off his helmet and nodded to the young constable to do the same. "Tea if that's not too much trouble, sir. Milk and two sugars, and any chance of a few biscuits. Oops, sorry forgot the magic word. Please. I'm always telling the grandchildren. It's been a long time since breakfast and we've had no lunch." He patted his stomach. "Thompson will have the same if that's OK, sir. Thank you." He smiled at Sam.

Elizabeth sat in the car for ten minutes staring at the garage door. She'd rubbed her index finger with her thumb so much that it had become inflamed and sore. Since her childhood she'd kept her lack of self confidence well hidden under a veneer of forced assertiveness. Her confidence had been eroded by years of her comparative underperformance to her elder brother, the blue-eyed boy of the family.

Her father's list seemed endless. "Played for the under twelve's county cricket team; short stories published in The Times; head boy at Worcester College; accepted at Oxford for medicine: rowed in the winning crews in two boat races; a consultancy in Orthopaedics at the Nuffield Orthopaedic centre; four papers published in peer reviewed journals and married with a beautiful wife and three children."

Her father loved rubbing it into every pore at every opportunity, and would really put her down with comments to friends and family within earshot of her.

"Peter, her brother, has been an absolute joy for us. It's helped balance the disappointment of Elizabeth. She's going to be a *vicar*." The word was mouthed, spoken silently as if there was some stigma attached to being a female vicar, as if it was somehow beneath them as a respected family in the local community.

There were never any comments made about her articles published in the Guardian, and being the Junior Ladies Champion at her golf club, a game, her father still believed, was exclusively intended for the male of the species. But she smiled and just carried on. He'd died five years ago, and she'd performed the funeral service and gave a moving eulogy for her father.

She looked at her watch. "Oh for goodness sake, Beth, let's go. If we don't go soon it won't be worth going at all." She pulled at the skin on her elbows and rubbed her knees, put the key back in the ignition, turned the engine on, recalled the address from the Sat Nav and pushed the gear stick into R, having never quite managed the complexities of a manual gear box.

"Lovely cup of tea, sir. Thanks very much, and those custard creams hit just the right spot." Sergeant Lidsay moved his somewhat large frame back and fore in the wooden kitchen chair trying to ease the developing cramp in his buttocks. "Now, sir you say that you inherited this house from your aunt and uncle?" He looked up from his notes at Sam, and paused, clearly waiting for an answer or explanation.

"Yes that's right."

Sergeant Lidsay stared at Sam. His answer obviously not good enough for him.

"Sorry. Yes I inherited the house a few months ago and have only recently started coming here to see what work needs doing. My solicitor can confirm all of this."

"That won't be necessary, sir. Who's been in the house since your inheritance? And may I say that it looks to be a very nice inheritance." There was an intonation in his voice which meant, '*And don't imagine I don't know it's probably worth a small fortune.*'

"Well." Sam paused as if giving the question its due attention. "Not many to be honest, as I've also had to arrange my uncle and aunt's funerals."

There was an understanding nod of sympathy from the police officers.

"The only people who've been here are Mr Peterson, the solicitor handling my aunt's and uncle's will, a firm of cleaners," Sam looked around the kitchen table for George's business card, "yes here it is. They're called 'Kleen Up – No Messing About'." He handed Sergeant Lidsay the business card. "All their contact details are on there."

"Thank you, sir. Anyone else?"

"My wife was here with the cleaners when I was at the funeral. She laid on food and drinks for them. She must have let them out of the house when they'd finished. Then she must have left as well, because she wasn't at home last night, or here at High Wood this morning."

Sergeant Lidsay looked puzzled. "She didn't come home last night?"

"No, but she's done this before. She's got friends who she often stays with if their *sessions* go on very late. They read books and watch movies, usually washed down with a *few* glasses of wine. I did call the police station this morning reporting her missing as she hadn't come home. I thought when I saw you at the door it may have been in response to my call."

Sergeant Lidsay sat upright rubbing the small of his back, and leaned back in the chair, balancing it on its two rear feet. It groaned and complained as he rocked back and forth. He got up, walked around the table opposite Sam and rested his hands on the back of a chair.

"What name is it, sir?"

"Morbeck. Sam Morbeck. My wife's name is Jane."

"I'll just put a call into the station to check that, sir." He walked back into the hall.

"Please no dust. Not now." Sam thought desperately.

The sergeant was back in a few minutes. "Yes, sir, we have a call recorded at ten, regarding a missing person in the name of Jane Morbeck. No news so far I'm afraid. But it's early days. Have you called her mobile? I presume she has one."

"Yes, but there's been no answer all day."

"Bit of a mystery all round this one, Eh Thompson?"

"Yes, Sergeant."

"My God!" thought Sam. *"It speaks!"*

"So it's almost certain that the woman the cyclist spoke to was your wife?"

"Yes, it must have been."

"Can you think of anything which could have made her scream like she did? It was pretty frightening according to Dr Plat."

"Plenty" Sam thought. *"Most of which would have me committed to the nearest asylum. Please don't ask to look around the house."*

"It's a rambling old house, so I suppose a creaking door or some odd sound could make you think there was someone or something else in the house with you."

Sergeant Lidsay stood back from the chair and gestured to the constable to get up.

"Well thanks for your time, sir, and the tea and biscuits. I'll make sure we keep a good look out for her. We tend to find that in most missing person cases they return home within forty eight hours, so I wouldn't be too concerned at the moment. She probably *read* a few too many books." He winked at Sam from beneath his helmet.

They made their way out of the kitchen and down the hall to the front door. As Sam took hold of the door knob there was a loud knock from the outside.

"You never know, it could be the wife, sir."

"Yeah that would just be my luck." Sam thought miserably. He turned the door knob and pulled the heavy front door open.

"Ah it's not the good lady wife, sir, but some parochial comfort. Good morning vicar."

Sam looked into the eyes of Elizabeth and smiled. There was a God!

Elizabeth shook hands with Lidsay, stood to one side, waved goodbye to the police officers as they drove off in their Fiesta, closed the front door behind her and followed Sam into the hall. He walked ahead of her for a few steps and then turned around.

"Sam, is everything OK?" Elizabeth looked into his eyes.

He looked back at her with an expression of relief and affection, quickly closed the short distance between them, and throwing caution to the four windows, took her face gently in his hands and kissed her softly on the lips. "It is now."

Elizabeth smiled at him and pulled him to her. This time the kiss was long and passionate, years of frustration erupting. After what seemed like an age Sam lifted his head back and brushed away a loose hair from her face. Elizabeth buried her face in Sam's neck and the locked floodgates of her suppressed emotions burst.

He held her tightly, and could feel the softness of her breasts against his chest and the rhythm of her breathing. He had no thoughts of taking her upstairs. He hoped that would come with time when she was, in all senses of the word, ready.

"Sam." Elizabeth started to speak but he put his index finger against her lips and whispered. "Shhh."

He took her hand, led her to the kitchen, helped her down onto a kitchen chair, and stood behind her massaging her shoulders. "Something to drink?"

She took his right hand and pulled him round in front of her. "Sit down. Please, Sam, sit down. We should talk." Her mind wanted a lot more than just to talk with him, but Captain Sensible, her own personal Jiminy Cricket, wasn't going away that easily. Sam pulled out a chair and sat down.

"Is this right Sam? I ask couples to promise 'til death do us part', and now I'm doing my best to do exactly the opposite."

Sam understood her reticence and tried to reassure her. "Jane's love for me and mine for her died years ago. Surely 'til death do us part' must also mean 'til an emotional death do us part'? Elizabeth, Jane and I have been existing together. Tolerating each other always seemed to be the lesser of two evils, when compared to a messy acrimonious divorce. It's been habit, nothing more than that." He paused and took her hands in his. "How things have survived until now is nothing short of a miracle. All that was ever needed was a catalyst, something which was stronger than the habit of marriage." He gently squeezed her hands and looked into her eyes. "You're that catalyst."

She leaned close to him. "Any love and emotions I may have had, were sealed in a block of parental concrete, and your," she smiled, "your jack hammer has set me free."

"My God you two make me want to vomit." His other half had heard enough.

"Not now! Please not now!"

"Come on Sam, stop fooling yourself. What would she want with a bald pathetic old git like you? Answer. Nothing."

"I deserve this little bit of joy for the years I've had to put with you and Jane. Now piss off and leave me alone!"

"Getting rid of me isn't going to be that easy." His other half smirked and decided to keep his powder dry until another time.

"Sam are you alright? You looked like, like you were somewhere else."

He rubbed the back of his head and smiled at her. "Sorry. Just remembering what feeling happy was like." He got up from the table. "Can I get you a cup of the proverbial brew that makes everything better? How do you take it?" They both laughed at his unintended double – entendre.

"Thank you George. You've been extremely helpful. Is this the best number to get you on if I need to speak to you again?" Sergeant Lidsay put down his pen next to his note pad, and screwed up his tired eyes. He really needed to start wearing glasses.

"Everything check out with the cleaners, sir?" Constable Thompson put the sergeant's mug of coffee with two sugars, close to the phone.

Lidsay picked up the mug, took a long drink and flicked through the few pages of notes he'd made. "Looks fine. She was at the house when the cleaners were there, made them sandwiches and coffee, Morbeck left before they'd finished and his wife showed them out of the house. I've also checked again with the desk and they did receive a missing person's call this morning from Morbeck. No sign of the wife, though. I've left messages at the addresses Morbeck gave us, but I've not had any replies yet." He took another drink of coffee. "Any biscuits Thompson?"

Constable Thompson took a packet of bourbon creams, the sergeant's favourite, from a tin in the desk drawer and put them on the desk. After dunking and consuming six, Lidsay sat back in the chair and frowned at the computer screen in front of him. There was something which was not quite right about Morbeck. He was becoming an itch he couldn't scratch. Morbeck was too calm for someone whose wife hadn't come home.

"Brightened up when he saw the vicar, though. Didn't think I'd noticed." He thought picking up a paperclip from the desk tidy to clean his ears.

"Sam why were the police here?" Elizabeth was frowning at him.

"Someone reported they'd seen a woman in distress here, and I think it was probably Jane. She was here with the cleaners yesterday." Sam paused and finished his coffee. "She's been missing since yesterday." He desperately tried not to smile. "I reported her missing this morning, so I assumed they were following up on that."

"Did they have any news?" Elizabeth was genuinely concerned.

"No they said that most reported missing persons turn up within forty eight hours, so she should be back today or tomorrow."

"Shouldn't you be at home then?"

"She's a big girl, my mobile phone's on, and she'll call when she gets back, wondering what all the fuss is about."

Elizabeth looked closely at Sam. "Are you really concerned, Sam?"

"Honestly, no. We've been living separately in the same house for at least ten years. I don't want any harm to come to her, but if she's decided to end it, then I'll sleep a lot easier, and smile a lot more." He took her hands across the table. "All I want now is you, and nothing and no one else could make me happier. Let's not talk about Jane. Do you fancy the grand tour?" Sam stood up. "Come on let me show you the house."

"Well at least those parts which will behave themselves." He thought.

She pushed her chair back, walked around the table to Sam, held his hand and smiled up at him, as there was about a foot difference in their heights. They walked hand in hand into the hall. "Where would you like to start?" Sam waved his arm expansively around the hall.

Elizabeth was staring at the cellar door. "What's in there?"

"The cellar. I've not been down there yet. Probably just full of junk."

She carried on staring at the door, let go of Sam's hand, walked a few steps forward and pressed the palm of her right hand against the door. She held it there for only a few seconds and suddenly jumped back. Sam looked at her with concern.

"Elizabeth are you OK?"

"Mmmm? Sam, I uh, there was something, behind the door, pleading to get out. It, they were crying for help, Sam. They sounded so sad, so lost." She sat down on the hall floor tears streaming from her eyes.

TEN

The brothers stood together at the Menin Gate in the warm unseasonal rain. It was eight o' clock in the evening and the last post, being played by the Ypres Fire Brigade. The memorial was a dominant structure in Ypres. It was designed by Sir Reginald Bloomfield, opened in 1927, and combined the architectural images of a classical victory arch and mausoleum. On huge panels inside and outside the memorial were carved the names of fifty four thousand eight hundred and ninety six officers and men who died in the Ypres Salient, during the terrible Third Battle of Ypres. The campaign which ended with the capture in the mud of the infamous village of Passchendaele.

Guillaume shook the rain from his umbrella as they entered the memorial. "Still so many names, Isaac. Still so many. When you see them like this." He paused and looked around at the carved panels. "So many still remain for us to guide home." He walked closer to the panels tracing the names with his finger. "And so many more at Tyne Cot?"

Isaac was stood close behind him, his hand resting on his shoulder. "At Tyne Cot, about another thirty five thousand names recorded as missing and having no graves." He looked around at the panels and like Guillaume suddenly felt like Sisyphus, condemned by the Gods to ceaselessly push a rock to the top of a mountain, where it would fall back of its own weight. The Gods thought there was no more dreadful punishment than futile and hopeless labour.

"We're getting too old for this, Isaac. We need to find a new Chef Charon as soon as possible."

"We've found him, brother, and he will be here in a few days."

Guillaume turned to face Isaac. "Yes he will be here, but will he understand? Will he make the commitment?"

Isaac tried to calm his brother. "I am convinced that Sam Morbeck is the man. He can be the new Chef Charon. His age goes against him, but his abilities greatly outweigh this."

"The others will not agree to this." Guillaume said.

"Yes I know, but nonetheless I believe, Sam has what is needed to carry our cause forward."

"I wish I had your confidence brother. I am anxious that so many may drift for eternity like pollen grains in the summer air."

"Guillaume, we are not alone. Even without a new Chef Charon there are many who will carry on the work after we're gone. No one will stop until we have brought them all home."

ELEVEN

Sam sat beside Elizabeth wiping away her tears, concerned about her reaction. "Elizabeth what happened? What did you sense?"

She turned her head to look at him, wiped away the last of her tears with the back of her hand, and looked up at the door. "Sam we have to help them. I don't know who or what they are, but they've been lost for such a long time. They've been drifting like gossamer on the wind."

He turned her face back towards him. "Elizabeth, I've seen things in this house which I thought were down to a misspent youth, but you've sensed something as well."

Elizabeth looked sideways at Sam and frowned.

"Are the secrets this house holds locked in the bricks and mortar?"

Elizabeth stood up. "I've no experience of anything like this." She shook her head. "Sam, I've no idea what this is."

"Is it something which only a chosen few can sense? Am I losing my mind?"

She turned to him, in control of her emotions. "Sam, you need to tell me everything that's happened."

He looked back at her with an apprehensive look in his eyes.

"Sam, there's nothing to be scared about. Whatever it is, there must be an explanation, logical or otherwise. We can face this together." She gently squeezed his hands.

"I took quite a lot of hallucinogenic drugs in my younger days, and I've tried to convince myself that what I've seen are all flashbacks. However, since meeting Isaac, you remember him from the funeral," Elizabeth nodded. "He told me things which I'm finding difficult to comprehend. Your faith may be able to help you accept them with a lot more ease."

Over the next twenty minutes, Sam told Elizabeth everything which had happened at High Wood and at his home. She sat quietly on the hall floor, asking no questions and making no judgements.

"That's why I was running away from the crematorium. I felt like shit doing it, but I had to get to the house as quickly as possible. Fact is, there was nothing to do when I got there. God only knows where all the dust and disrepair had gone."

"Shakespeare put it well, Sam. 'There are more things in heaven and earth, than are dreamed of in your philosophy'. We've all seen things we don't understand, and sometimes things which we don't want to understand. But nonetheless they exist. Why they exist no one really knows. Probably only the Almighty. Isaac seems to have an understanding of what's happening and the part you play in this, and you're seeing him again next week?"

"Yes. I'm flying to Belgium on Tuesday, and then travelling from Brussels by train to meet him in Ypres. Can you come with me?" He looked pleadingly at Elizabeth.

"No I'm sorry I can't. I've got two weddings, three funerals and two christenings. I've got a pretty busy week."

His shoulders dropped like a child who was expecting a trip to the park, but saw that it had started raining. "No problem. Maybe you can come if I have to go to Belgium again?"

"Yes of course I will. Belgium's a country I've always wanted to visit." She smiled at him. "Next time. It's a promise."

He smiled at her like a child who now has a promise of a visit to the cinema after the rain.

"What are we going to do about the cellar?"

Sam was sat on the floor next to Elizabeth, staring at the door. He reached out and held her hand. They both sat in silence staring at it, when they felt a warm gentle breeze from the gap at the bottom of the cellar door. The breeze was soon followed by a thick yellow mist. They both quickly slid back a few yards away from the door. They held their hands a lot tighter, and tighter still as the Bakelite handle on the door began to rotate and the door slowly began to open.

"We need to take a closer look at that house. There's something not quite right about him or the house, and why's a vicar calling at the house? For all we know Morbeck could have buried his wife's body in the cellar." Sergeant Lidsay was re-reading his notes, finishing off a mug of tea and demolishing a chunky peanut butter Kit-Kat. "Although at this stage, no one's going to give us the time of day to get a search warrant. Other than the cycling doctor, what evidence have we got?" Lidsay shrugged. "So, Thompson, we sit and wait until he makes a mistake." He tapped his red nose with his index finger, suppressed a burp and winked. "Any more tea in the pot?"

"Elizabeth!" Sam shouted. "Elizabeth I need help!" She sat on the floor staring at the door like a rabbit trapped in the headlights. Sam was pressing against the door with his full weight, but his feet began to slide backwards as whatever was behind the door began to win the *push – of – war*. He tried to get some additional purchase, but the highly polished wooden floor offered no resistance. He was beginning to panic. "Elizabeth for fuck's sake get off your ass and help me!"

She looked up at him, shaken by the '*fuck's sake,'* jumped to her feet, threw her weight against the door, and with their combined efforts it slowly began to close. But the yellow mist began to rise up the door, and as it reached their faces they smelt onions and garlic. Sam's eyes started to itch, Jane started sneezing violently and they were both struggling to breathe.

"Push as hard as you can, we've got to shut this and shut it quickly!" Sam's voice was hoarse.

Elizabeth managed to force a smile through streaming eyes, and her nose started to bleed. She pushed as hard as she could, but her feet slipped and began to slide away from the door. Six gelatinous tentacle like arms slowly appeared around the edge of the door, and pushed back against Sam and Elizabeth. Two tentacles suddenly released their grip on the door and snatched hold of Elizabeth's arm. They tugged at her, and pulled her closer and closer to the now gaping opening of the cellar. Sam tried to shout but the choking mist was making it now almost impossible to breathe. Elizabeth stared at him like a salmon caught by a grizzly bear, as the tentacles inexorably dragged her towards the black maw of the cellar. Sam clutched at her free arm, and she moved very slightly towards him.

But to her horror he let go of her arm.

"Sam, please!" She screamed hoarsely, as she started going down for the third time, but he'd felt the pressure on the door easing, and decided to throw both his hands at it and push with everything he had left. The door slowly began to close. One of the tentacles released its grip on Elizabeth, and gripped the door.

"One more effort. Come on we can do this." He managed to croak through what were becoming badly blistered lips.

Elizabeth managed a crooked smile at him. "OK let's send this back to wherever it came from!" She hissed.

They looked deeply into each other's eyes and threw everything they had at the door. Blood began to trickle from Elizabeth's eyes, and Sam's eyes were swollen and closed. The door began to push back against them, but from somewhere deep inside, the instinct to survive spat out one last massive surge of adrenalin and the door slammed shut. Elizabeth turned expecting to see amputated tentacles writhing on the hall floor, but it was empty, unblemished, and shining. There was no mist. Her hand moved to her face, and when she looked at it there was no blood. She looked across at Sam. He was sat on the floor collapsed against the wall. He looked up. His face was unblemished.

TWELVE

Getting the group together in such a short time had been nothing short of a miracle, but Guillaume had achieved it. It was the first time in two years they'd all been together in the same place. Isaac looked around the room he'd booked at the Hostellerie du Chateau des Monthairons, a magnificent mid nineteenth century mansion on the banks of the Meuse, not far from Verdun. The room Guillaume had hired for the meeting had a cool marble floor complemented by an ornate red Turkish carpet, the walls were covered by bookcases groaning under the weight of years of accumulated first editions, orange silk curtains hung from ceiling to floor giving the room a warm comforting glow, a crystal chandelier hung from the ceiling and a small upright piano sat under one of the windows. In the centre of the room was a mid 19th century Louis XVI style oval topped solid mahogany dining table. It was fully extended on six fluted tapering legs ending in brass casters, with six Louis XVI gilt-wood, lyre-back dining chairs and two matching carvers at the ends of the table. There was no modern meeting equipment, and the only nod to a meeting was the coffee and water, set up in two George II sterling silver coffee pots, with additional hot water available in a Meissen yellow-ground hot water jug and the ensemble completed by eight blue onion Meissen cups and saucers.

Isaac cleared his throat. "We should get started. Wir sollten beginnen. Nous devrions obtenir commences."

He took the seat at the head of the table and waited as the others finished their coffees and took their seats. Isaac looked around at the faces he'd known for so many years, Patrice Beaudet, Gilles Vermeulen, George Mainard, Klaus Bauer and Charles Henencourt. There was one empty seat.

"I'm sorry that Ralph Jefferson couldn't make it, but there wasn't sufficient time for him to get here from Miami. However I have spoken at length with him on the phone and he supports my proposal." Isaac examined their faces for any signs of dissension. They were all sat forward in their chairs with their elbows resting on the polished mahogany.

"So to begin." Isaac started his prepared speech. "Why did I ask you to be here today?" Once again he looked at the faces judging their mood. "If you don't mind I'll remain seated. My hips aren't what they used to be. Unfortunately we are all getting old, and to be more accurate, we are all old. I can't speak for all of you, but for me it's all getting to be too much. The physical, mental and spiritual effort which is needed every time I restore is eating away my will and my being." There was a general nodding of heads around the table.

"Für mich ist auch es zuviel immer."

"Please, Klaus, in English." Isaac smiled at the retired General.

"Natürlich. My apologies, Isaac." Klaus nodded to him and sat back in his chair. "For me also it is getting too much. It is with me my knees. One replaced and the other one is nutzlos, useless."

There were nods and groans of agreement around the table. Patrice held up his arthritic hands, Gilles massaged his left shoulder and neck, George adjusted his hearing aids and Charles leaned forward holding his lower back in both hands.

Isaac smiled sympathetically. "It's a miracle that we are all here, ein Wunder,

une merveille. We, and our fathers, have been part of Papaver Rhoeas since the end of the Great War. A war they said would end all wars. A mechanised war of mass slaughter. A war without which the World would have been spared the horrors of civil war, political terrorism and a second total war and genocide in the nineteen forties. A war whose uncertainties created a deeply disturbed Europe, and whose darker side opened the way to Stalingrad and Auschwitz. Our task has been at most times difficult and worst times almost impossible, but we have always remained committed to bringing them back. No one should be Unknown, Inconnu, Unbebekannte. Not at rest, Nicht in Ruhr, Pas au repos. To find those who can follow us has been very difficult, and recently for me almost impossible. How is it with all of you and your fledglings? Klaus?"

"So weit so gut. I have been working with Karsten for over a year now and he is almost, how do you say, Gut zu gehen."

"Good to go Klaus." Guillaume replied.

"Ja, yes good to go. He is ready. He is now living in Fort Vaux in a suburb of Hamburg."

The other members of the group looked at each other for a volunteer.

Patrice Beaudet cleared his throat and took a mint from the dish on the table. "It is also very good en France. Jean Michelle Phoenix, an appropriate surname, is not yet bon d'aller, not good to go, but in a few months he will have taken over from me. He is also living close to one of our beacons, Loos Salient, close to Paris."

"For me things aren't so good." Gilles Vermeulen rubbed his temples and frowned deeply. "No one is interested anymore in the Great War. It is just history taught in our schools like Napoleon, Henry VIII, Julius Caesar, all historical characters who live only on the pages of text books. Ask anyone in Belgium who was Joffre, Ludendorff, or Haig, what happened at Le Minceur – Verdun, Mons, Passchendaele or the Ancre, and how many lives were wasted" Gilles was flushed and clearly angry. "It is just histoire, just names and numbers on a page." He eased himself back in his chair and stared at the plaster cherubs on the ceiling. "Ask them who Mario or Sonic are and they will have no problem. Abrutis!"

The room was silent. Everyone understood Gilles's frustration at the total lack of care or understanding of the Great War by a significant proportion of the twenty first century generation.

"Abrutis. Yes Gilles, morons." Isaac was the first to break the silence. He turned in his chair and gestured to Charles Henencourt. "Charles? Et pour vous?"

"I'm afraid that things are much the same as Gilles. No-one is interested, and to find someone who can commit to the level we need is virtually impossible. I fear that our network of portals and ourselves will all end the same. As dust!"

A deep silence fell over the room. It was as Isaac had feared. No one wanted to share their bad news. Keep it hidden and it will probably go away. They were mostly a group of old ostriches. They sat in silence for a full minute staring at the polished mahogany table before Isaac again broke the hush in the room.

"I have found someone to replace me." Isaac said softly.

There was a perceptible change in the atmosphere in the room.

"Ein Ersatz für sie?"

"Yes even for me. We all have a shelf life and I passed my sell by date a long time ago. Papaver Rhoeas needs a new leader, a new Chef Charon. We all know how rare these individuals are. They are like hens' teeth." He looked at Klaus and the others who looked confused. 'Hennen zähne', 'Dents de poules.' They frowned and looked around the table at each other, and as the lights began to turn on, they smiled and nodded in understanding. "His name is Sam Morbeck. He will be in Iepers next week."

"Sam Morbeck?" Klaus was peering at Isaac over the rims of his gold reading glasses. "Who is this man? Isaac, you can't just call us together and tell us that you've found a replacement for yourself." He angrily shouted." For the Papaver Rhoeas to find a new Chef Charon takes years and also the agreement of all seven members of the Astrea. Sie nehmen viel auf sich selbst." He slapped his hands loudly on the table. "Arschloch!"

Isaac remained calm making eye to eye contact with Klaus. "And now for the group in English as we agreed."

Klaus looked sideways at him. "You take a lot on yourself." There was a deliberate pause as Klaus looked slowly at everyone around the table. "Asshole."

Isaac remained seated, assessing the mood of the group. He turned to Guillaume and raised his eyebrows, as if asking what do we do now. You could have cut the atmosphere with a Japanese sword.

"Thank you, Klaus, for those enlightening comments. I am not suggesting that Sam is the person, but I am saying that with appropriate guidance, he could possibly take over." He paused allowing his conciliatory comments to sink in. "I maybe, and probably am in a lot of people's eyes, how did you say it, an arschloch, but more importantly, we are all very old arschlochs!" The mood of the room perceptibly lifted.

Gilles stood up, stretched and looked at Klaus who seemed a lot more relaxed. "Isaac is right. We are all old, and for me, very tired. The years have taken their toll on all of us. Isaac you say that he will be in Ypres next week?"

"Yes, God willing, he will be in Iepers on Tuesday."

"I suggest we join you at Thiepval on Thursday, and at least meet this man. Does anyone dissent from this?" He looked around at everyone. "Can we all be at Thiepval next Thursday?"

There was a rustling of diaries being opened and pings as smart phones and tablets were turned on.

Isaac turned to Guillaume and quietly asked him to check if they all could make it.

Guillaume opened a small note pad and stood up.

"Gentlemen, can I confirm who can make it."

Klaus looked up from his smart phone. "Bitter, one moment."

Guillaume remained standing. "Certainly Klaus I will start with the others."

"Gilles?"

"I will be there."

"Patrice?"

"Oui, I will be there also."

"George?"

"I will have to rearrange a few things. But it should be OK."

"Charles, how about you?"

"No, I have commitments which are impossible to break, but I am happy with the arrangement."

Guillaume drew his attention back to Klaus. "And yourself Klaus?"

Klaus put down his smart phone and took a sip of water from the glass on the table. He sat back in the chair and massaged his neck, keeping them waiting a few more seconds for the result of his deliberation. "Ja."

Guillaume frowned at him. "Ja, meaning what?"

"Yes, I will be there provided that accommodation is booked and the details are with me no later than this weekend. I will also bring the full profile of Karsten Imlauer with me. We should at least have another candidate to consider."

Patrice raised his left arm.

"Patrice there is no need to raise your arm to be heard. Your thoughts are always valued. Please." Isaac waved his hand across the table.

"Thank you Isaac. It will be good to hear some details about Karsten. You should bring him to Thiepval Klaus." He looked at Klaus who nodded in agreement. "I have a few questions and suggestions." Like most of the others he shifted his weight in his chair, doing his best to relieve the chronic pain of his sciatica. "I would suggest that we meet again on the Friday to come to a final decision. Isaac is right, we cannot delay in finding this replacement. Why not meet somewhere close to Ypres, after we have met this *superman* at Thiepval? Everything can then be decided. We should stay until the Saturday morning." He looked around the room for agreement and found it in their nods and uh huhs. "Excellent. Isaac I will leave all the arrangements to you?"

Isaac nodded in agreement.

"Mr Morbeck should be around for us to have any further discussions we see fit to have with him." Again there were nods and uh huhs. Patrice looked at the empty seat. "What about Ralph? Any decision must be unanimous, and without him any meeting will be meaningless." This time the nods were much deeper and the uh huhs much louder.

Guillaume was still standing. "Gentlemen, given the time difference it is too early to speak to Ralph, but I will email him today and call him this evening to check if he can make the transatlantic trip. Once I have his confirmation I will complete the arrangements and notify everyone by text and email."

George tapped the table with his index finger to gain everyone's attention. "Isaac, what is his link, what is his connection?"

"His Uncle, Jack Morbeck, was recorded MIA at Passchendaele."

"But he hasn't established a spiritual bond yet."

Isaac shook his head. He still had a lot to do before he could convince the members of the Astrea.

THIRTEEN

They sat facing each other across the kitchen table. Still and in silence. Still in the house.

"Elizabeth, I think I know what that was in the cellar." He paused staring at the kitchen door. "When I met Isaac, he tried to explain to me what High Wood is." Over the next ten minutes he told Elizabeth the important details of his meeting with Isaac. Once he'd finished, he sat back in the chair, shrugged his shoulders and pulled a face like a bulldog sucking a wasp. "I know it sounds bizarre, but can someone with your faith and beliefs in heaven believe this?"

Elizabeth leaned forward on her elbows and held her hands to her face as if in prayer. "Sam, I use a lot of literary references and lyrics from songs in my sermons and quite often use them as frameworks to comfort the bereaved. There's a song by Eliza Gilkensen, not exactly as famous as Madonna, called 'Calling all Angels'. She closed her eyes trying to remember the words. "I won't sing, I'm a bit like a crow with laryngitis, but the words I can remember are 'Fallen, like gold leaves in autumn. Fallen, with hardly a sound. Sorrow and sickness is upon us. The darkness is pulling us down. Won't you save us?' She closed her eyes, recalling the words. 'Calling all angels, we're sad and alone. We wandered too far, now it's time to come home. We are fallen lost in the garden …' Oh how does it go?" ' … Liberation is my soul's destiny. My heart wants to fly away home.' She sat back and smiled at Sam. "They want to fly away home, but who are they?"

"I wrote some of their names down somewhere." Sam felt in his pockets and pulled out a crumpled serviette. "Yes here they are, Deighton, Smith, Jones, Hoyles, Acklom, Easton, Cross and Lombton." He pressed the serviette flat on the table. "But even if we know who some of them are, how on earth do we help them? I should just sell this place and never come back. Is High Wood a portal or gateway? Who the hell knows, and how do we know who's trying to fly away home?" Sam rubbed at the palm of his right hand.

"You'll take the skin off that if you rub much harder." Elizabeth smiled at him. "Were they trying to hurt us, Sam?" She played with a fork. "Were they just trying to open the door, to get out. To get home." She paused looking around the kitchen, tapping the table with the fork. "Sam, do you think that something like we experienced happened to Jane?" She raised her eyebrows. "She couldn't have stopped the door from opening on her own, could she?"

He looked up from his now bright red palm, and pressed his middle finger on a spot on his forehead between his eyebrows. A tip he'd never forgotten his secretary had given him about his third eye. If you pressed it, it would relieve any type of headache, and Sam had the mother and father of headaches. Both physically and metaphorically.

"I don't know, and I don't know enough. What do we do?" He dropped his eyes to the table. "Do you honestly think that whatever was out there," he nodded his head to the hall, "could be good? It, they, tried to, well they tried to …"

Elizabeth leaned across the table, smiled and put her hands softly on top of his. They laughed together, breaking the tension of the moment. "We don't know what they were trying to do, but we have to find out. Go to Belgium next week, meet with Isaac, get some answers, and then let's decide what to do next."

Sam didn't move his hands. It felt so good. "OK, Ypres it is then, and hopefully some answers."

Elizabeth nodded to him in agreement.

There was a sudden loud knocking from the hall.

The rhythmic banging echoed around the house, but Sam and Elizabeth had had enough shocks for one day to be phased by it. It stopped, and was followed by a jagged grating noise which Sam recognised as the brass letter flap struggling to open.

"Hello, is anyone there?"

Sam raised his index finger to his lips.

"Hello!" The request this time was much louder and insistent. "Hello, Mr Morbeck are you still here?"

Sam looked up the hall and then back to Elizabeth, if they could, his eyebrows and hairline would have met, if Sam still had a hairline. He whispered to Elizabeth "Lidsay. The sergeant. What the hell does he want?"

Elizabeth smiled back at him and whispered in her best conspiratorial voice. "As long as he doesn't find the bodies in the cellar we should be OK."

Sam raised his eyes to the ceiling.

Elizabeth leaned forward and pulled his head down by his chin. "Lighten up will you. There's nothing in this house we need to worry about." She smiled and opened her eyes as wide as they would go. "Well at least nothing which some policeman close to retirement is going to discover. That's unless of course he's Psychic Sally's brother. Let him in, give him another cup of tea and a plate of biscuits and cakes and he'll leave happy and satisfied. Anyway he may have information on Jane's whereabouts."

He smiled at her. "You really are a little ray of sunshine aren't you." He sighed, turned and shuffled to the front door. There were two more knocks.

"I'm coming!" Two more knocks. "Are you deaf? I'm coming!"

Sam opened the front door, to a beaming Sergeant Lidsay who had his hand raised ready to knock again.

"Ah, Mr Morbeck thanks for answering. I wasn't sure if you were still here or if you'd gone home." He looked over his shoulder into the hall. "Is the lady vicar still here?" He craned his neck to get a better view of the hall, and Sam moved to his right to block his view. Lidsay relaxed his neck and shoulders and smiled.

"What is it you want? Do you have any news on my wife?" Sam was hoping that this was just a quick visit and that Sponge Bob and Patrick wouldn't want to come in the house.

"Would it be OK if we came in? Never like discussing these things on the doorstep." Lidsay took a step forward. Sam turned around and made his way down the hall gesturing that the two policemen should follow him.

"Sergeant Lidsay, this is Elizabeth Roberts." Sam opened his hand and gestured towards Elizabeth.

"It's a pleasure to meet you again, Sergeant Lidsay. Is there something less formal we could call you?" Elizabeth added with a caring smile, being a practiced master at putting people at their ease.

"Please call me Ivor, although I'm mostly known as Jonesy, because I'm always telling people not to panic." He looked at his constable's puzzled expression. "Lance Corporal Jones from Dad's Army?" Thompson looked even more confused. "The old TV sitcom Dad's Army? He was always saying 'don't panic'." Lidsay pulled a face and blew out his cheeks. "Ivor will do fine."

"Please sit down, Ivor, can I get you tea or coffee, and a few biscuits or cakes?" Elizabeth said.

Lidsay patted his stomach and raised his eyebrows. "Probably just a few too many cakes already, but a cup of tea would be lovely. Thompson will have a cold drink." He turned to the young constable who nodded.

Lidsay sat down and gestured for Sam and Elizabeth to join him at the kitchen table. "I'm afraid I've no news on your wife, but she's now an official missing person."

Elizabeth put three mugs on the table and filled a glass from the cold water tap for Thompson. "I'm sorry but we've no ice or lemon."

"Thank you that's fine." Constable Thompson said standing close to the kitchen door.

Elizabeth sat down at the kitchen table and despite Lidsay's protestations, placed a packet of ginger nuts in the middle of the table.

After dunking and devouring six, Lidsay took out his note pad and pencil and leaned forward on the table. "I've spoken to the cleaners." He flicked back through a few pages of his notes. "Ah yes here it is. 'Kleen Up – No Messing About'. Chap's name was George Evans. Very helpful." He seemed to be lost in the moment. "Yes very helpful indeed. He confirmed that your wife was here, that she lay on some lunch for him and his team, and she was still here when they left. The times also match with the report by the cyclist." He looked up from his notes at Sam. "And you stated that she never came home that night?"

"No, she didn't come home. Have you found anything else?" *"He's no Hercule Poirot."* Sam thought.

Sergeant Lidsay closed his note book and sat back in the chair. "No nothing else which has helped us in our enquiries." He unbuttoned the top button of his trousers. "Sorry about this, but I'm certain they're making these smaller nowadays." He pulled at his fingers, clicking them one by one. "So, it seemed to make sense to take a quick look around the house and double check that she hasn't had an accident. Have you checked the house?" He tilted his head to one side.

Over the next hour they checked every room in the house, apart from the locked door at the top of the stairs. Sam explained he hadn't identified the key yet, and Lidsay grudgingly accepted his explanation. The extension did cause some lengthy discussion, but Sam said Arnold had always had a keen interest in World War One, which Lidsay seemed to accept.

"Well thank you Mr Morbeck. She's clearly not here. Although we may need to check that door at the top of the stairs." He pulled his helmet firmly onto his head. "I'd love to take a longer look at that model one day if I could. War games have always been an interest of mine." He looked at Sam like a child in a sweet shop.

"Yes of course. Give me a ring and we can arrange something. I'm sure this won't be the last time we see each other. Hopefully next time you'll have some good news for me." Sam put his hand on Lidsay's arm, making a move to usher him and Thompson towards the front door.

Lidsay recognised the suggestion. "Yes probably time we were back at the station. Thanks for the tea, Mrs, Ms, Vicar."

Elizabeth smiled. "Elizabeth is fine, sergeant."

"Yes thank you, Elizabeth."

He moved to turn away, but stopped, and peered over Sam's shoulder.

"What's in there?"

Sam turned to see what Lidsay was looking at. He was staring at the cellar door.

"The cellar." Sam replied. "I haven't had a chance to take a good look down there yet. Probably just a bloody great mess." He turned around and held Lidsay's arm. "Probably worth having a look when it's been cleaned up?"

Sergeant Lidsay moved his arm away from Sam's. *"Yes I bet you'd like time to clean it up, and whatever's downstairs behind that so conveniently locked door."* He thought.

"I'm here now and we do want to make sure your wife's not had an accident, don't we? Easy to slip down some dark stairs." He moved past Sam to the cellar door. "Is it locked?"

Sam moved next to Lidsay. "No I think the cleaners took a quick look down there." He looked back at Elizabeth, something which was noticed by Lidsay, and with some degree of trepidation gripped the Bakelite handle, turned it and easily pulled the door open. He stepped onto the first stair looking for a light switch, and found a modern switch fixed above the second stair. He flicked it on and a stark white light from a swinging sixty watt light bulb with no shade made him look away for a few seconds. He looked down and saw there were about twelve stairs leading to what looked like a compacted earth floor. He turned around and waved to Lidsay and the others to follow. A gust of damp stale musty air wafted past them.

"Smells like something died down here." Sam joked, but instantly realised that given the time and place it wasn't the best thing to say. At the bottom of the stairs he found a second light switch, and the cellar was lit by nine neon strip lights. He took a few steps into the cellar, closely followed by the others.

Everyone was silent, lost for words. The cellar was huge, and seemed to extend beyond the footprint of the house.

"Quite a cellar Mr Morbeck. You could easily lose something down here. Don't you think so constable?" Lidsay turned and stared at Sam. "She could easily have fallen and got lost in the dark down here. The lights weren't on were they. We'd better take a close look around. Mr Morbeck you come with me. Vicar, sorry Elizabeth, you go with Constable Thompson. We'll go to the far end and meet up with you somewhere in the middle."

Sam counted his steps as they walked to the far end of the cellar. *"It's at least twenty yards long and must extend beyond the walls of the house."* He thought.

The floor was perfectly smooth compacted brown earth. The ceiling had been tiled in what had once been white, but were now dingy grey, foot square mottled polystyrene tiles which Sam could remember seeing in most offices in the seventies. The floor was packed with row upon row of metal shelving, and every inch of every shelf was covered in …. absolutely nothing!

Lidsay ran his fingers along the shelving like a house-proud woman checking if the cleaners had done what he regarded as a *good job.* He looked across at Sam. "Odd don't you think." He was examining his fingers and looking at the empty shelving.

"Odd?" Sam replied.

"Yes very odd." He looked again at his fingers like a child looking at an empty bag of sweets.

"What's odd, sergeant?"

Lidsay looked up at Sam and held up the fingers of his left hand. "All this shelving and nothing on it. Looks like someone was getting rid of … He let the words hang in the air. Do you know what was stored down here?"

"No idea." Sam replied. He was becoming annoyed with this moron's insinuations.

Lidsay gave him a 'I don't believe a word you're saying look'. "Odd that there's not a speck of dust on any of these shelves. Odd wouldn't you say given that it's been shut up for who knows how long." He paused and bent down to the floor and rubbed it with his right hand. "Particularly given that this is an earth floor." He stood up straight holding out the palm of his hand to Sam. It was covered in a fine brown dust. He frowned at Sam and started to walk back to the middle of the room. "Thompson, have you finished yet?"

"Yes, Sergeant. Not that much to see really."

"Oh the innocence of youth." Lidsay thought to himself.

"No there's not that much to see is there." He turned and offered his hand to Sam. "Thank you for your cooperation, Mr Morbeck. Your wife certainly doesn't seem to be in the house. I'll talk to CID when I get back and see how they want to move things forward." He turned away and started up the stairs. "I can see myself out." He called over his shoulder and disappeared out of the cellar door.

Sam sucked in a deep breath, scratched his ears, put both his hands on the top of his head, loudly blew out a breath, glanced at Elizabeth and shrugged his shoulders. "He thinks she's buried under the cellar floor. Bloody suspicious scrote. Before we know it he'll have CSI Cardiff digging up the floor and ripping the house apart looking for her dismembered remains. Jesus what a mess. Why has she gone missing? Probably did it deliberately to cause the maximum negative effect. Such a bitch." Sam sat down on his haunches punching the floor.

Elizabeth moved close to him and gently caressed and kissed the top of his head. "Sam, he said that he was going to hand it over to CID. There's nothing to worry about."

"He's a devious bastard who I wouldn't trust as far as I could throw him. I was on my own with him and believe me he thinks there's been foul play. I'll have to cancel the trip to Ypres."

Elizabeth took his arms and stood him up. "You will cancel nothing. It's vital that you meet with Isaac. You need to know what secrets this house holds, and my God I need to know. I've no explanation for what we experienced, and nothing in my teachings or faith can explain what happened."

They held each other close.

"But what if he, as he will, comes back with flashing lights and JCB's?"

"It's simple. I'll stay here at the house."

Sam pulled away from Elizabeth. "You're joking aren't you?"

She smiled back at him and shrugged her shoulders. "Why would I be joking? I can just as easily cover everything from here as I can from the vicarage, and it will give me the time to properly look around High Wood. Between the two of us we should be able to come up with some meaningful answers."

Sam was lost for words.

"Nothing no say, Sam?"

"Look, we both know there's something in this house which neither of us understands. I can't leave you here on your own. It's too risky." He gazed into her eyes. "I can't lose you. I won't take the risk."

"Sam, you're going to Ypres and I'm going to investigate High Wood. You'll find, as we get to know each other better, that once I decide to do something it's totally pointless arguing with me."

"As we get to know each other better?"

"Yes. Sam neither of us are getting any younger and we can't deprive each other of some love and happiness. Why would we? But we have to discover what we're meant to do with High Wood. I'll go back to the vicarage, pack a bag, and you'd better go home and see if Jane has come back. However bad things have been between you, you need to know what's happened."

He nodded in agreement, realising that any more arguments would be futile.

FOURTEEN

Agnes and Captain Heyward sat in the back of a motor ambulance, holding on as best they could, as it bucked and reared like an unbroken stallion over the rutted roads. They were travelling to Poperinghe in a convoy of twenty motor ambulances which were at the disposal of the Joint War Committee of the Red Cross and Order of St John. The ambulances were all empty of wounded, on their way to collect them from the front line and bring them back to casualty clearing stations. The majority of ambulances had been donated by various organisations and businesses like Breweries; Trade Unions; Charities; Hunts; Worshipful Companies and the Silver Thumb Fund. The ambulance Agnes and Captain Heyward were sharing with three other nurses, was a converted Rolls Royce donated by the Agar – Robartes family of Lanhydrock in Cornwall. The driver was Albert Morris, their chauffeur who'd volunteered and signed up when his beloved Silver Ghost was converted. The majority of the remaining ambulances were Rover Sunbeams, one of which bore the message in large white capitals on the dark green of the body, GIFT OF THE CHILDREN OF NOVIA SCOTIA.

They'd been travelling for about two hours, when they heard the sound of aeroplanes flying above them. The ambulances slowed and then stopped as the troops accompanying them started to open fire on the circling aircraft.

A sergeant from the Green Howard's threw open the heavy sheeting at the back of the ambulance. "Everyone, please, out of the ambulance. There are three German bombers circling the convoy. Quickly please."

James leapt down to the road creating a cloud of dust. He looked up and held out both hands to Agnes and the other nurses to help them down from the tailgate of the ambulance. He looked around assessing the situation and decided that their best option was to get to the remains of a barn about fifty yards back from the road.

"Quickly! Follow me!" He ushered the nurses off the road and across what had once been a busy farmyard into the remains of the barn. "Stay here." He looked back at the convoy. "I'm going to see if I can help." He turned around to look at them. Agnes had never seen him look so serious and concerned. "Do not leave this barn until I return." He turned and ran out of the barn, bent low and sprinted for shelter by the side of the GIFT OF THE CHILDREN OF NOVIA SCOTIA.

A captain of the Green Howard's was issuing orders to a small group of soldiers. "Tell them to aim coordinated fire at the bombers. Deploy the Vickers and keep them at a distance from the convoy where they can't drop any bombs. Good luck." The three corporals and two sergeants ran to different parts of the convoy.

James knelt down beside the Green Howard. "Captain James Heyward. How can I help?"

"Captain Arthur Barker. Glad to have you here." He pointed up at the cloudless sky. "There are two AEG G.IV's circling just outside our range. They're probably just harrying us but I can't take any chances. It's vital we get these ambulances to Poperinghe. The numbers of casualties there have been enormous."

The G.IV's weren't close enough to drop their eight hundred and eighty two pound external ordinance but the twin-engined three-man biplanes were able to strafe the convoy with their Maschinengewehr 08's from the two machine gun positions fore and aft of the pilot's mid-position.

The distinctive pop-pop-pop staccato sound of Vickers machine guns brought a smile to James dust covered face, as the G.IV's turned away and flew north.

Captain Barker stood up and peered around the front of the ambulance. "It looks like they've had their fun for the day. We'll get everyone back on the convoy as quickly as we can. If you'd like to rescue your damsels in distress from the barn, then it shouldn't be too long before we're able to get back on our way." He stood up and started shouting congratulations to the teams manning the Vickers. James stood up to make his way to the barn, but a call from behind spun him around.

"Captain they're turning and coming back." One of the Corporals was pointing to the sky. The G.IV's were completing a 180 degree turn and flying straight at the convoy.

"Open fire at will!" Captain Barker ran to the nearest Vickers team.

James stood, frozen to the spot. The biplanes were making rapid progress towards them, and as he looked up he realised their approach would take them directly over the remains of the farm. He turned and started to run, but the ruts in the road grabbed at his boots and dragged him into the dust. He tried to stand but his ankle gave way under his weight. He looked up again, the G.IV's were almost directly over the convoy. He could clearly make out the honeycomb camouflage on the fuselage of the bomber and the faces of the three crew, peering down at them. The G.IV's weaved from side to side to avoid the Vickers fire, and as they passed over the convoy, James saw them drop their bombs. He rolled onto his back into the ditch at the side of the road, just in time to see the bombers fly over the column. As they flew over, he could see one of the crew in the second plane struggling to release the last bomb, and as it flew over him the release catch opened and the bomb screeched down towards him. He realised that the path of the bomb was taking it away from him, and in relief, blew most of the air out of his lungs in a long deep sigh, until he could see that the path of the bomb was taking it directly at the barn. He tried to stand up, but his ankle gave out under him. He pushed himself up just in time to see the bomb crash through what remained of the roof of the ruined barn. Time stood still as his cry "Agnes!" was lost in the blast of the explosion. The concussion knocked him unconscious.

As he slowly came around, the memory of the explosion and the barn came back to him in all its force. He gingerly sat up rubbing the back of his head, and looking closely at his hands, which were covered in congealing blood. He stretched his eyes wide open and looked straight ahead. The barn was gone, and all that remained was a smoking pile of rubble.

FIFTEEN

Apart from Isaac and Guillaume, everyone else had left. They were waiting for a taxi, sitting in comfortable leather chairs, drinking cloudy white Pastis in what functioned as reception for the Chateau.

"So what do we do next?" Guillaume put down his empty glass and folded his arms across his chest.

"We stick to what we have already planned. I see no reason to change anything. Do you?"

"Well Klaus did seem a little *upset* at what we discussed."

"That's always been his way. He apparently has this wunder kind Karsten, so let's give him a chance and see what he is capable of." Isaac drained his glass and put it down next to Guillaume's. "I see no problem with the others. They have always sought the easy life when it comes to making any decisions about Papaver Rhoeas. Have you had a reply from Ralph?"

Guillaume looked at his smart phone and tapped the mail icon. The message came up at the bottom of the screen, 'You have thirty two new messages'. "I'll see if he's answered." Guillaume looked exasperatedly at the ceiling, and after scrolling through twenty eight of the thirty two new messages Guillaume looked up and spoke to Isaac. "I have to stop all this spam. Ralph replied at ten o' clock local time Miami."

Isaac held out his right hand. "Let me see what he's said." He took the smart phone from Guillaume and read the email from Ralph.

From – rjefferson@gmail.com
To – gmale@gmail.com
12 July 2013 10.02
Subject – Charon
Looks like the Kraut's being his usual self. Cannot make next week. You have my full support on any proposals you have. I could Face Time or Skype if needed.
Best regards
Ralph

Isaac looked up and handed the phone back to Guillaume. "Send this. Thanks for reply. Face Time seems like a good idea. I will mail you the time next week. Thanks for your support. Best regards … " As Guillaume tapped in the response and hit the send icon, a Mercedes E Class pulled up outside the Hostellerie du Chateau des Monthairons. Isaac pushed himself up from the chair. Guillaume's help was ignored. "The taxi is here it's time to go. We have a lot to do before we meet Sam."

The flight to Brussels had been *efficient*. Sam had forgotten how large Brussels airport was, but eventually found the train station below the terminal on Basement Level One. He caught the next train to Brussels Central Station, and from there caught the direct train to Ypres. The journey was comfortable, took about an hour and three quarters, which Sam passed happily finishing 'The Colour of Magic'. He promised himself that he'd read Terry Pratchett, and the book hadn't disappointed him.

He pulled his suitcase off the train and stood on the platform looking for Isaac. A short tanned man in a yellow polo shirt tucked into a pair of khaki chinos, tan loafers and no socks, a dark blue baseball cap with Vasa 1628 on the front and tortoiseshell Oakley's was staring at him from the end of the platform. He was holding a small placard on which Sam could make out his name. He pulled up the sliding handle of the case and walked to the yellow polo man, who started walking towards him.

He slipped the placard under his arm and offered his hand. "Sam Morbeck?"

Sam smiled and offered his hand, which was shaken warmly.

"Isaac is at the hotel waiting for us. His back is not too good at the moment." The accent sounded Dutch. "I'm sorry, I should have introduced myself. I am Guillaume Wouters, Isaac's younger brother. We can walk to the hotel from here it's only about eight hundred metres."

Guillaume took Sam's case and walked alongside him. They chatted about the journey and skirted around the real reason for Sam's visit. It took them twenty minutes to *stroll* to the hotel, stopping in the Grote Markt to admire the Cloth Hall.

"My God, what a beautiful building. Is this the original structure Guillaume?" Sam asked.

Guillaume smiled in appreciation of Sam's comments but also in sadness at its history. "It was one of the largest commercial buildings of the Middle Ages, when it served as the main market and warehouse for Ieper's prosperous cloth industry. The original structure was erected mostly in the thirteenth century, but it lay in ruins after artillery fire devastated Ieper in World War One. It was meticulously reconstructed to its pre-war condition between 1933 and 1967."

Sam turned to Guillaume pointing at the Cloth Hall. "*This* was flattened in the Great War?"

"Ieper was flattened, Sam. The entire city was nothing but rubble. We should make time while you're here, to visit the museum in the Cloth Hall. 'In Flanders Fields' is completely devoted to the story of the Great War in the West Flanders region. It details the effects of the Great War on all those who were directly and indirectly involved. It will give you a much greater understanding of the conflict."

They walked across the Grote Markt, the main square of Ypres and turned right into D'Hundstraat, where The Hotel Hampshire O, was situated only twenty five metres off the main square.

Guillaume looked up at the hotel and Sam's expression. "Yes, I know it doesn't look that impressive, but its position is second to none and the service is excellent." He pushed open the main door into a small reception area.

Sam still looked concerned.

Guillaume smiled at the receptionist and signed himself in. Sam handed over his passport and signed the register. Guillaume picked up his case. "This way, I'll let you decide about the decor."

They squeezed into the small lift with Pat the receptionist, and as Sam would find later, the fountain of all knowledge on anything to do with Ypres, the waitress at breakfast and room maid. It wasn't a big operation.

Pat had moved to Belgium in two thousand to be with her partner Frank who'd served in the Parachute Regiment, and they'd been managing the hotel for the last six years. Their relationship was something like Marge and Homer Simpson and was one of the main reasons people kept coming back to the hotel.

"Been here before, Mr Morbeck? First time in Ieper?" Pat was smiling at Sam and reading a text on her mobile.

"Yes."

"There's plenty for you to see and do. You must see the last post at the Menin Gate." She paused finishing the text. "Shit for brains! What a tosser." She looked up at Sam not in slightest bit embarrassed. "I've seen it too many times to count, but every time it moves me." The lift came to a stop and Pat stepped out into a large airy open area filled with what seemed to be wooden trestle tables and metal chairs. The decor, as Guillaume had indicated, was quirky, and looked like it had been created by a set designer who'd worked on the Great Escape, and had specialised on the POW camp.

Guillaume nudged Sam's elbow and waved his arm around the breakfast room "Interesting decor? The rest of the hotel is themed in the same way."

Sam raised his eyebrows. "And the rooms? Surely not?"

Guillaume's smile grew broader. "If you ever wanted to know what is was like to be a soldier or POW in the Second World War, then this is the place."

"Sam." Isaac was sitting at one of the trestle tables on a chair with a brown worn wooden seat fixed to grey tubular metal legs, which reminded Sam of something he'd sat on in junior school.

He looked around Pat who was obscuring Isaac from his view and smiled. Isaac waved them across to join him. "Sit, please sit. Pat," Isaac waved her over. "I'd like a Hoegaarden, Guillaume will have a Kriek and what would you like, Sam? A beer?"

Sam licked his lips and rubbed them with his index finger. "A beer would hit the spot. Whatever you recommend will be fine."

Isaac looked up at Pat. "I think we'll have a Rodenbach if you have it?"

"One Hoegaarden, one Kriek and a Rodenbach coming up. On your room Isaac?"

"Thank you, Pat, yes that will be fine."

She walked to a large fridge which Sam thought probably functioned as the bar.

"So Sam, welcome to Ieper, we have a lot to discuss." Isaac looked a lot more tired than he had at the funeral.

Pat arrived back at their table with three beers and three tall branded glasses. "I haven't got much at the moment, but would you like anything to eat?" She looked around at the three men, all three shook their heads and started pouring their beers. Pat took the hint that they wanted to be left alone and headed for the lift.

Isaac raised his glass to Sam and Guillaume. "Santé."

Sam drank about half the glass of Rodenbach, ran his finger through the condensation on the side of the glass, smiled and finished the remaining beer. "As they say. I needed that." He smiled at Isaac, and raised his empty glass to him and Guillaume. "Cheers, your very good health."

"Sam I suggest you unpack, take a shower and we'll wait or you here. I've booked a restaurant in the Grote Markt, the Markt 22. They serve Belgian food and it's five minutes walk from here. Please don't rush. We have plenty of time and some of us still have most of our beer left."

Sam stood up and followed the signs to room twenty six. The room followed the same theme as the breakfast area. It was dark, the colour palette mostly shades of brown; the furniture seemed to have been mainly sourced from an Army and Navy store; the bed side table and chairs followed the tubular metal and worn wood theme of the breakfast area and the storage cabinet appeared to be an old ammunition case. It was quirky, but clean. The en suite was modern and a thirty two inch plasma TV was hanging on the wall facing a crisp white duvet on the low bed. However when Sam pulled back the curtains. The position of the hotel made up for everything. He was looking out directly at the Cloth Hall and the Grote Markt.

Fifteen minutes later he was back in the breakfast room refreshed from a hot shower.

Guillaume helped Isaac from the *school chair* and they walked slowly to the lift. Ten minutes later they were seated at the back of the Markt 22 reading the menu. Sam seemed to be having some trouble with it. Isaac smiled at Guillaume, and to Sam's relief offered to order for everyone.

"Another beer, Sam?" Guillaume raised his empty glass to him.

"Thank you that would be great. Could I try what you've been drinking?"

"Of course." Guillaume caught the waiter's eye and ordered a Hoegaarden for Isaac, and two bottles of Kriek.

"What are we having?" Sam asked Isaac. He was now feeling pretty hungry. It had been a long day and he'd only snacked on rubbish.

"We are having Flemish stew, salad and chips. They make an excellent Flemish stew and you know what we Belgians are like with frites and mayonnaise."

Sam looked around the chic restaurant, which was long and narrow, and the decor mainly back and white. There were covered and uncovered tables outside in the square, but despite the warm evening they'd chosen to eat in air conditioned privacy of the back of the restaurant.

Isaac looked around checking they couldn't be overheard, but the majority of the clientele were outside enjoying the balmy July evening. "Sam once again thanks for coming. We have a lot to explain and discuss over the next four days." He sat back as best he could in the straight backed chair. "We, that is myself, Guillaume and a group of other like-minded individuals, are members of an organisation called Papaver Rhoeas." He looked closely at Sam to see if the name rang any unexpected bells. Sam's expression clearly showed that it hadn't.

"Pap ... papave ... row ... rowass?" Sam stumbled over the words.

"Papaver Rhoeas is the Latin name of what is more commonly known as the Corn Poppy, the Corn Rose, or the Field Poppy." He looked again at Sam to detect any signs of recognition. There were none. "Sam, it is best known as the Flanders Poppy. You see millions of them on November the eleventh, Remembrance Day."

Sam's lights turned on.

"World War One, the Great War, brought death and destruction to countless thousands, and many of them were never found. They are the Missing. They wander, locked in an in-between world, drifting on the winds of time. It is our mission to find these Missing, bring them home to the ones they loved and at last to final rest."

Sam was staring in disbelief at Isaac.

"Sam, I know that this seems almost impossible to believe, but we restore them. We reconstruct their shattered and atomised bodies. Bring back what was them, into someone and not something. Someone who at last can find their way to peace, salvation and eternal rest."

Sam was now sitting open mouthed.

"We have abilities which allow us to perform these *miracles*." He took Sam's hands in his swollen arthritic hands and squeezed them as firmly as the deep pain would allow. "Sam you have these abilities. You can perform these miracles."

SIXTEEN

Elizabeth drove quickly to the vicarage, threw a few things into an overnight bag, and decided to collect more after tomorrow's service. She'd written her sermon a few days ago, and just had to *turn up* and *do the business*.

Back at High Wood, she paused in the hall and looked at the cellar door. It was still slightly ajar. She dropped her bags close to the stairs and stood in front of it.

"Just close the door." She thought nervously. *"How difficult can that be? You've been in the cellar and there's nothing there."* Her hand hovered over the Bakelite handle. *"It's not electrified. Just turn the handle."* She grasped it and pulled the door shut. *"You see nothing."*

She picked up her overnight bag, leaving a carrier bag of groceries in the hall and walked upstairs. She'd agreed with Sam she'd sleep in the guest room, which was the second door on the left on the first floor landing. It was like stepping back into a nineteen sixty's furniture showroom. Under the window was a solid teak six drawer dressing table; a large mirror and an upholstered teak stool; two fixed glass topped side tables sat either side of a Danish teak single twin day bed, over which was a yellow, green and brown floral bed spread; set against the opposite wall to the dressing table was a four drawer walnut chest of drawers, on top of which was a black and silver rectangular alarm clock. The effect was completed by brown, blue and white plaid wallpaper, and a deep pile pale green carpet. Elizabeth looked around the room and smiled. It reminded her of happy childhood summer days at her grandmother's in Brighton, and felt like slipping into an old worn but comfortable, if not gaudy, pair of slippers.

"I'll unpack later." She thought, and made her way downstairs to the kitchen to make ham and watercress sandwiches and a cup of tea. Despite being in the house on her own and her recent experience with the cellar, Elizabeth felt genuinely at home. The house had a pleasant ambience, like a comforting travel blanket wrapping itself around you on a cold winter's evening. She sat at the kitchen table, ate her sandwiches and drank her strong milky tea. It was getting towards dusk and Elizabeth decided to switch on a few lights and have a quick walk around the ground floor of the house. Despite the house's friendly ambience, the thought of moving from daylight into darkness, still made her feel a little uncomfortable.

"OK High Wood let's see what you've got shall we."

She walked into the lounge. It was as stunning to her as it had been to Sam. The large marble fireplace; the walls covered in shelves packed with leather bound books; the rich red leather Chesterfield sofa with matching wing chairs on either side; the sixteen light crystal chandelier; the ornate delicate plaster mouldings; the Chinese blue and white porcelain and the Fabergé eggs on the wall mounted yew shelves. Elizabeth would have loved to collapse onto the Chesterfield, but the secrets of the house drew her away to the door at the far end of the lounge.

Sam had given her an outline of what he'd found in the rooms he'd visited, but it didn't prepare her for what she saw in the map room, when she flicked on the light switches. It was pretty much as he'd described, and what took her breath away was the enormous map, which as Sam had said resembled a contoured ordinance survey map. The place names Contalmaison, Pozieres, and La Boiselle he'd mentioned were there, the series of red and blue lines criss-crossing the model, and the symbols and codes. It was an impressive sight. Elizabeth leaned on the edge of the model, scanning everything, trying to take in as much as she could.

"Right let's take a look at the computer and those filing cabinets." The sound of her own voice was comforting in the silence of the house. She turned away from the model and sat down at the computer terminal. Elizabeth rubbed her hands together as it suddenly became very cold in the room. She breathed out and saw the cloudy mist of her breath. *"Odd."* She thought looking at her watch, as it was about six thirty on a warm July evening. She shrugged her shoulders and hit the power button on the iMac. Sam hadn't been able to access any files because they were all password protected, but Elizabeth fancied her chances as silver surfers tended to use pretty obvious passwords.

She clicked the mouse and the request for a password flashed onto the screen. *"OK, what did you use?"* She thought. *"Birthdays, loved ones names, addresses, 1234, anything really which they wouldn't forget."*

She typed 'High Wood', and the message read Access denied; 'Edith26' – Access denied. She sat back in the chair and noticed a curled up yellow post it note stuck to the side of the filing cabinet. She leaned across and peeled it off. In thick black felt pen was written, 'Password – Arnold1234', and beneath it in larger print and underlined was, <u>'DO NOT LOSE THIS!'</u>

"Thank you for the fading memory of old age." Elizabeth said kissing the note.

She typed Arnold1234 into the computer and the shortcut icons to nine folders appeared.

'Monthly Accounts.' "No".

'IFA.' "No".

'HMRC.' "No".

'Gommecourt' "Need to check this one out."

'Serre and Beaumont Hamel' "Another one for checking."

'Thiepval.' "That rings a bell."

'Ovillers and La Boiselle.' "They were on the Map weren't they?"

'Fricourt and Mametz.' "On the Map?"

'Montauban.' "Map's going to take up quite a bit of time."

She picked up a sheet of A4 printing paper, wrote down the password, and the names of the folders she wanted to know more about. She'd work out the complexities of the printer at another time.

Elizabeth sat back in the chair deciding which folder to open first. *"May as well be in the order they came up."* She thought, but as she was about to open the Gommecourt folder the printer at her side came to life. It creaked and groaned as the message 'Preparing to print' appeared in the small glowing window. She frowned and stared at the flashing message. "Did I press print?"

A blank sheet of A4 disappeared into the bowels of the printer, and the sound of printing filled the vacuum in the room. A few seconds later the sheet exited the printer, fluttered into the air, did a gentle spinning somersault with tuck and pike, landed on the floor like a Mayfly at the close of its day long life, and holding to the Laws of Sod, finished print side down. Elizabeth bent down and picked up the A4 sheet, to see what had been printed, and immediately dropped it as if it was coated in acid.

She sat staring at the plain back of the A4 sheet, and after about a minute bent down, picked up the sheet, turned it over and looked again at the image. Staring up at her was a sepia tone picture of a soldier of what she thought to be World War One. She looked back at the computer screen. "Did I open any images? I didn't open any folders, so where did this come from?"

She looked back at the image of the soldier, but there was nothing on it to identify who he was. As she stared at the picture, it slowly began to fade. First at the feet and the remaining image began to disappear like sugar dissolving in a cup of tea. Nothing and no one could have torn her eyes away from the image. Soon all that was left of the soldier was the head which seemed to be desperately trying to hold onto its transient existence. As it began to fade to just the face, it turned and moved from profile into full face. Elizabeth held her breath. The chin began to disappear but before it had gone the lips mouthed something to her which she couldn't understand. She couldn't breathe, and as only the half closed eyes remained visible, they opened wide and made eye to eye contact with her. Finally a narrow shaft of intense blue light discharged from the pupils of the fading image, and the paper was again blank. She sat in the chair for five minutes her eyes transfixed on the blank sheet of paper like the stooge of a stage hypnotist.

"Come on girl. Get a grip. You wanted to know more about High Wood, and it looks like it's trying to tell you."

SEVENTEEN

Agnes's ears were ringing like a treble bob being rung at a wedding , and was sure she knew how Quasimodo must have felt locked in the bell tower of Notre Dame. She crawled out from behind the well and looked back at the smouldering remains of the barn as bright red sparks floated up like Chinese lanterns into the night air.

"Where are the others?" She thought, remembering that she'd left the barn for a call of nature, and quickly understood she was the only one to have survived the bombing. She looked up at the clear starlit sky and realised she must have been knocked unconscious for quite a few hours by the blast. She stumbled over the rubble, around the remains of the barn to the road where the column of field ambulances had been, but apart from a few soldiers brewing tea around a shrouded camp fire, the road was empty. The fire and brewing tea looked inviting, so Agnes wandered across to soldiers.

"My God, miss you're in a bit of a state!" A soldier poking the fading embers stood up and offered her his greatcoat.

Agnes couldn't hear a thing the soldier was saying, as her world was thickly coated in cotton wool. She tapped at her ears with her index finger and mumbled. "The blast. It was the bomb. Have you seen a column of ambulances?"

Understanding her predicament, three of the soldiers got up and sat her down on a bale of hay close to the glowing embers.

"Jack, write it down for her. She's deaf." He turned to Agnes and mimed and mouthed "Like a cup of tea?"

She nodded and smiled, understanding that she could communicate with them, held up two fingers and mimed putting two sugars into a cup.

Soldier two grinned. "Two sugars it is then."

Jack scribbled with the stub of a pencil on the back of an envelope and then moved close to Agnes. He'd drawn a small map with arrows pointing to the left and written 'Column went this way to the front.'

She looked up at him smiled, pointed up the empty road to the left and nodded to Jack.

He looked to where she was pointing, nodded and smiled.

Agnes got up and started to walk down the road in the direction of the front and Jack jumped up and grabbed her by the arm. He shook his head and mouthed "No miss, not at night. Stay here with us until morning."

She understood his concern, but didn't understand most of what he was saying.

One of the soldiers shook his head, frowned and prodded Jack in the back. "Write it down for her."

Agnes read the note, nodded her in understanding and sat down by the fire. It was going to be an uncomfortable long night, but thankfully with the greatcoat and the August weather, a relatively warm and balmy one.

"Miss, miss ..." Agnes could hear sounds as if they were being filtered through a tank of water, but at least she could hear. She'd fallen asleep on the ground covered by the greatcoat and felt like she'd been kicked in the back by a mule. Jack bent down and helped her stand up. Almost straight.

"Thank you." For the first time she took in the face of the soldier. Had they called him Jack? He was probably just about old enough to be serving King and Country. Eighteen or nineteen at the most, and he looked badly in need of a good scrubbing. Dust and what she thought looked like dried blood were on his face and uniform, his boots were caked in dried mud and he was constantly scratching himself from what Agnes knew were the ubiquitous lice which infested so many of the troops.

"I'm afraid this is all we have, but you're welcome to share it with us." He held out a mug of tea and a small slice of bully beef they'd fried over the fire in the remains of a tin. He shrugged and pulled a face at her.

Agnes ate the bully beef and drank the sweet tea as the soldiers rolled cigarettes. Jack turned and offered her a thin cigarette. She shook her head, held her chest and coughed. "Have had this since I got to France." She huskily told him.

They sat together for about twenty minutes until a column of troops from the Sherwood Foresters began marching past. Agnes jumped up and ran towards a sergeant major who was bellowing encouragement to the soldiers.

"Come on you dozy bunch of layabouts. You want to get to the fucking front before the Bosche surrender. Don't you?" He saw Agnes running to him. "Ah sorry miss, didn't see you there."

"I was separated from my ambulance column and need to get to the front. Can you help me get there? I need to get to the clearing station at Poperinghe." She was walking alongside the column.

"Bless you miss, that's where these *soldiers*." He spat out the word as if it tasted of something vile. "Are proudly and bravely headed for death or glory." He turned to the column and shouted. "Death and glory! That's what we're here for aren't we boys."

As one man they shouted back. "Death or Glory. Yes, Sergeant Major."

He threw back his not insubstantial shoulders and chest and bellowed "Good. Let's have a song then shall we. Raise the spirits. How about ..."

A private close to him called out "What about 'Never Mind'?" There was a chorus of approval from the column.

The sergeant major frowned, but after a few seconds smiled. "All right let's have it then."

The song started quietly, but soon spread like a forest fire through the entire column.

"If the sergeant drinks your rum, never mind
And your face may lose its smile, never mind
Though he's just a bloody sot, he's entitled to the lot
If the sergeant drinks your rum, never mind'
'When old jerry shells your trench, never mind
And your face may lose its smile, never mind
Though the sandbags bust and fly you have only once to die."

"There's a wagon at the back of the column, miss. Wait here and jump up on it. It's carrying mostly rations and there's plenty of room. Bit uncomfortable I'm afraid, but better than walking twenty miles to the front." He snapped his heels together, smartly saluted, wished her good luck, and marched off singing with the column.

Jack walked over to Agnes, and tapped her on the shoulder. "Everything in order, miss?"

She turned and smiled at him. "Thank you yes. The sergeant major's offered me a ride to the front on their food wagon." She turned around to see it approaching drawn by two emaciated horses.

"Have you got everything miss?"

"What little I have I'm wearing. My other belongings were either blown up in the barn or are with the ambulance column." The wagon was only a few yards away, Jack jumped into the road and waved it to come to a stop.

"What the bloody hell do you think you're playing at, Private?"

"The nurse needs a lift to the front. Sergeant major says it's OK."

The drover looked down from the wagon and held out a hand to Agnes. "Up you come, miss. Can't have you riding in the back with the weevils can us now."

Agnes gripped his rough hand and pulled herself up alongside him on the wooden bench. He pulled his cap down firmly on his head and tapped the peak with his index finger. "Private Tom Aston, 21st Battalion the Northumberland Fusiliers at your disposal, marm. I've been handed over for the duration to look after these sorry old boys," he said looking fondly at the emaciated horses. "Bless 'em. I used to work on a farm, see. Anyway, better than rotting in a trench eh? Hold on tight now. Don't want you falling off into them ditches do we." He gently flicked the whip over the heads of the horses who pushed what remaining weight and energy they had against the worn leather traces.

She leaned over the side to Jack. "Thank you for all your kindness and help. I don't know your name."

The wagon pulled away following the singing marching column.

Jack looked after the wagon. "JACK" he shouted over the singing of the column "JACK MORBECK."

EIGHTEEN

Sam sat back, sipped the sweet strong coffee and gently rubbed his bursting stomach. A belch would have made it a perfect meal, but manners prevented him from releasing his internal pressure for which he'd suffer later. The meal had been a culinary delight. Isaac had picked at his food, but Guillaume had demolished every course. The restaurant was busy, full of noisy locals and tourists enjoying the cuisine and vibrant atmosphere.

"Isaac," Sam moved his chair closer to him. "This Papaver Rhoeas, Flanders Poppy, this group, why have I never heard of it?"

Isaac turned his head to Sam and smiled. "You've already seen what happens at High Wood. At a portal. If you didn't have your abilities, and you were a normal person, what would you think? We can have no excuses, we created this generation which has moved away from religion, whose values are based on greed, and for whom the World Wars are just pages in a history book. How do you think they would react to what we do? Simply say, why? Who funds this? What does it cost? They would have no understanding of its true value. It would be, as everything else in this world is, broken down to a balance sheet." Isaac leaned on the table. His expression for once showed how truly exhausted he was. Sam put his hand soothingly on his shoulder. Isaac lifted his hand and patted Sam's hand.

"Tomorrow we'd like to take you to places which will show you why we do what we do, and why we need you to help us carry the torch for these drifting spirits. It's late and I'm very tired, so let's agree to meet for breakfast at seven o' clock." He raised his eyebrows to Sam. "We have a lot to do." He took a long deep breath. "One last statistic. Only half of the dead were ever found and identified, a quarter were found and buried as Unknown, and the remaining quarter, a quarter Sam, were never found. We find them Sam and identify the Unknown."

Isaac looked to Guillaume who got up from his chair and helped Isaac to stand. They walked across the Grote Markt to the hotel, and as they exited the lift Isaac took Sam by the arm. "Help us Sam. Help them." He looked deeply, almost beseechingly into Sam's eyes. "I'll see you in the morning. Sleep well."

After breakfast, the three men made their way out of the hotel to Guillaume's car which was parked directly opposite the hotel.

"You sit up front with Guillaume." Isaac said, and with the help of Guillaume he was settled into the crinkled grey leather rear seat of the silver

Mercedes C Class Estate. "It's about ten years old, but it still purrs like a satisfied kitten." Guillaume pulled the seat belt across Isaac and clicked it into place.

Guillaume turned around in his seat and spoke to Isaac. "Thiepval first?"

Isaac nodded in agreement. Guillaume settled back into the driver's seat, fastened his seat belt, smiled at Sam and selected drive.

The journey took about an hour and a half, past road signs whose names rang vague bells in Sam's mind, Arras, Cambrai, many small cemeteries all perfectly maintained, until they finally turned off the D929, the main Albert to Bapaume road, and onto the D73 to Thiepval village. Guillaume parked the car as close to the visitor centre as he could to save Isaac's joints.

The smartly dressed young woman behind the reception desk, immediately recognised them. "Bonjour. C'est si bon de vous revoir."

"Good morning Marie. This is Sam Morbeck, he is with us. Does he need a ticket?"

"Je suis désolé. I am so sorry, Isaac. I am so used to speaking with you en français." She turned and smiled at Sam. "Pardon Sam, if you are with these two gentlemen, then you will not require a ticket to visit the monument. Please enjoy your time here at Thiepval." She handed him a map and a guide. "I wouldn't think that you will need this, but I don't want to upset these two chers amis." She smiled and fluttered her eyelashes at Isaac.

"Vous êtes très méchant." Isaac waggled his index finger at her. "Sam, come we must leave this little minx. We have a lot to do today."

They left the visitor centre, walked slowly down a broad gravel path, across a large semi-circular area and through a large copse of tress. Sam didn't know what to expect, but as they came out of the trees, they entered a broad boulevard of beautifully manicured grass, at the end of which was the memorial.

Isaac and Guillaume kept walking up the boulevard, but Sam stopped dead in his tracks. Guillaume looked back and tapped Isaac on the elbow. He turned, and looked back at Sam, whose expression told Isaac everything he needed to know. The trip was having the desired effect. He now had to make sure that Sam understood the significance of the Thiepval Memorial.

They made their way the few yards back to Sam.

"Impressive isn't it."

Sam stared silently at the memorial.

"Sam, impressive isn't it?"

"Mmmm ... Yes ... sorry ... it's just so ... so ... "

"It's difficult to find words to describe isn't it, Sam."

Guillaume opened a shooting stick and Isaac sat down. It was a perfect summer's day, but here close to the memorial, the air was cool and there was no bird song.

Isaac looked up at the memorial, and even after many years it still stirred emotions in him. He started to talk to Sam, but kept his eyes on the memorial. "It was designed by Sir Edward Luytens and built between 1928 and 1932. There are sixteen piers of Accrington brick, faced with Portland stone. It's forty six metres high, and is the largest war memorial in the world. Its full title is the Thiepval Memorial to the Missing of the Somme. On the stone piers are engraved the names of around seventy two thousand men who died with no known grave in the Somme battles between July 1916 and March 1918." Isaac paused and turned to Sam. "Seventy two thousand, Sam. Come, let's take a closer look."

Guillaume helped Isaac up from the shooting stick, folded it and handed it back to Isaac to use as a walking stick. As they got closer to the memorial, Sam was able to read the inscriptions on the front faces.

On top of the archway was inscribed. 'AUX ARMEES FRANCAISE ET BRITANNIQUE L'EMPIRE BRITANNIQUE RECONNAISANT.'

Just below it was. '1914 1918'

On the upper edge of the left archway was 'THE MISSING' and on the upper edge of the right archway was 'OF THE SOMME'.

They walked in silence up the stone steps to the centre of the memorial, and Sam silently read the inscription.

'Here are recorded the names of officers and men of the British Armies who fell on the Somme battlefields between July 1916 and March 1918 but to whom the fortune of war denied the known and honoured burial given to their comrades in death'.

He looked around at the internal piers faced in Portland stone, engraved with the names of men from the UK and South Africa who had no known grave. He moved close to the piers, and touched the cold stone with his hand, following the carving of some of the names with his right index finger. After a few minutes he stepped back and looked at what must have been twenty poppy wreaths and crosses on the steps of the centre of the memorial.

Isaac was standing with Guillaume alongside Sam. "The inscription says everything for me that this Memorial and we, the Papaver Rhoeas stand for." He put his hand on Sam's shoulder. *Their name liveth for evermore."*

Isaac took Sam's arm for support. "Papaver Rhoeas also works with the CWGC and their teams of archaeologists and forensic pathologists to find and identify the bodies still lying beneath the crops, grass and trees of these Flanders fields. You remember they were mentioned in Arnold and Edith's announcement?"

Sam nodded, remembering the information he'd found on the internet about their work with war graves.

Isaac waved to Guillaume who was looking at the graves on the other side of the memorial. "Let's go back to the car. I'm feeling a little tired. Call everyone and tell them that we will have to rearrange Thursday."

"Klaus will not be happy."

"Is he ever? Tell them that I've contracted influenza. They will understand that for someone of my age how serious that can be."

Sam stopped at the Visitor Centre before leaving and bought a small book 'Poems of the Great War 1914-1918'. As they drove from Thiepval back to Ypres, he browsed through the poem's titles, 'Anthem for Doomed Youth' by Wilfred Owen, 'Enemies' by Siegfried Sassoon, 'Recalling War' by Robert Graves and then one name caught his attention – Isaac Rosenberg.

Sam turned around, Isaac seemed to be sleeping.

"Guillaume?"

Guillaume turned his attention away from the news on the radio. "Yes, Sam?"

"Has Wouters always been your family name?"

"No, it's been Wouters, since just before the Second World War. Jewish names weren't too popular at that time!"

"Was it Rosenberg?"

"Why do you ask, Sam?" Isaac said quietly. His eyes were closed, but his mind was open.

"I was just wondering." Sam replied defensively.

"You must have a reason. Please tell me what it is." Isaac said from behind closed eyes.

"I bought a book of First World War poems at the visitor centre and there's a poet in it whose name is Isaac Rosenberg. It's just that I've not heard the name Isaac very often." Sam seemed embarrassed. "Seems a bit ... stupid really. All there is, is that you have the same first name."

Isaac opened his eyes and smiled.

"Uncle Isaac."

Sam looked over his shoulder at Isaac. "You were related?"

"Yes, uncle generally implies that." Isaac smiled.

Sam blushed and turned around.

"He was a poet at that time. What have they published?"

Sam turned to the contents pages and scanned the list for Isaac's name. "Mmm, 'August 1914', 'Break of Day in the Trenches' and 'Dead Man's Dump', not the cheeriest of titles that one."

"Not a particularly cheery time, Sam. Could you read something for me?" There was a definite note of nostalgia and fond memory in his voice.

"OK, but I'm no great reader." He looked again at the contents page. "OK, pages 12, 24 and 42." He flicked through the small book until he came to August 1914.

"Just read me anything from them, Sam."

"OK." There was a pause as if Sam was preparing himself for a recital, and then there was silence as he scanned the lines of the poems. A silence which turned from seconds into minutes.

"Sam? You were going to read me something from the poems."

Sam sniffed loudly and wiped his nose with a tissue.

"Sam are you OK?"

Sam gathered himself and turned around to Isaac. His eyes were red with tears. "Isaac this is terrible. Just terrible. What in God's name did they go through? How could anyone have lived through this?"

"Please, Sam, read me a few lines." Isaac was pleased with Sam's reaction to the poetry. He knew the poems well but wanted to reinforce the emotions they had released in Sam.

"I'll just read a few lines from 'Dead Man's Dump'."

"The wheels lurched over sprawled dead,
But pained them not, though their bones crunched,
Their shut mouths made no moan,
They lie there huddled, friend and forman,

Man born of man, and born of woman,
And shells go crying over them.'
Sam paused.
"A man's brains splattered on
A stretcher-bearer's face;
His shook shoulders slipped their load,
But when they bent to look again
The drowning soul was sunk too deep"
Sam ran his finger along the poem absorbing the words.

"'Poppies whose roots are in man's veins'. Your Grandfather must have experienced all of these things, or how else could he write such devastating words?"

Isaac had achieved the result he was looking for. Marie made certain that Sam bought the book of poetry, and the verses had done their work.

"Sam read all the poems. They will speak to you better than I, text books, encyclopaedias or TV documentaries can. These are the words of men who lived, suffered and died in the Great War."

During the drive back to the hotel in Ypres Sam read most of the poems, and as they parked the car outside the hotel, he sat blankly staring into the far distance.

NINETEEN

Elizabeth hadn't been frightened by the events in the map room, but she'd been severely shaken. An afterlife was the foundation stone of her faith, and the last few minutes had, in a strange way, strengthened and reinforced her beliefs. She looked back over her shoulder at the now quiet room, and it looked back at her as if butter wouldn't melt in its mouth.

She made her way to the kitchen, unpacked the groceries she'd bought, put the kettle on and made herself a watercress sandwich with plenty of salt. A mug of mushroom cup-a-soup provided the first course, and a Mars bar and a cup of cappuccino packet coffee completed the feast. She found a tray in a cupboard next to the pantry, laid out the food on it, carried it into the lounge, put the tray on the largest of a nest of Yew tables and positioned it close to the Chesterfield. She looked around the room. There was no TV, no radio, no form of entertainment. She got up walked back into the hall, unzipped one of the soft bags she'd brought and lifted out her Bose sound-deck and iPod. There was a relatively modern dual plug point in the far corner of the room, which Elizabeth plugged it into, selected Peter Gabriel, the album Us and touched the play icon. She sat back on the sofa demolishing the watercress sandwich as 'Salisbury Hill' filled the room.

She screwed up the wrapper of the Mars bar and tossed it like an NBA player into the small brass coal bucket next to the fireplace. It hadn't been much, but the meal had the desired effect. She looked at her watch. It was nine thirty. She stretched every ligament, tendon and muscle she could, sighed deeply, closed her eyes and decided that she'd listen to a few more tracks and then head upstairs. 'Come Talk to Me' started playing. She'd listened to this hundreds of times, but as the song came towards the end, the lyrics suddenly had a resonance she hadn't felt before.

'I said please talk to me
Won't you please come talk to me
Just like it used to be
Come on, come talk to me'

The song ended and 'Love to be Loved' started playing. Gabriel's lyrics struck another deep meaningful note.

'And in this moment, I need to be needed'
'With this darkness all around me, I like to be liked
In this emptiness and fear, I want to be wanted

'Cause I love to be loved
I love to be loved'

As 'Blood of Eden' played, Elizabeth felt a discernible drop in the temperature of the room. She opened her eyes and sat up on the Chesterfield. She could see two thin visible streams of breath coming from her nose, like a steam train waiting in the station. She heard the faint sound of footsteps on the wooden floor of the lounge.

"There is nothing to fear in this place." She thought, stood up and turned around. The lounge was in twilight with no lights on anywhere in the house. She looked into the dim light which remained and checked behind the Chesterfield. The door from the map room was wide open.

"I'm sure I closed it when I came out?" She knew the answer but didn't want to reply to herself. She walked around the Chesterfield, looked closely at the elaborate Persian rug and the highly polished wooden floor. Starting from inside the corridor to the map room and ending immediately behind the Chesterfield were the muddy imprints of boots. She knelt down and examined them closely in the rapidly disappearing light. It was difficult to discern how many prints there were, so she tried to count only right boot imprints, and estimated that there had to be about ten pairs.

The music stopped, and Peter Gabriel was replaced by a male chorus. Elizabeth thought that she could hear what sounded like 'Keep the Home Fires Burning', and when she listened closely she could understand the words. Elizabeth ran to the Bose, pulled the iPod out of its station and turned it off, but the singing remained.

'Keep the home fires burning
While your hearts are yearning,
Though the lads are far away,
They dream of home.
There's a silver lining,
Through the dark clouds shining,
Turn the dark cloud inside out,
Till the boys come home.'

Elizabeth quietly spoke into the darkness. "What do you want from me? Who are you? I will help if I can, but please just talk to me!"

TWENTY

During the entire journey, Private Aston regaled Agnes with stories of his farm in Northumberland and his plans for after the War.

"I'm sure he must be able to breathe through his ears." She thought, smiling inwardly.

"We should be there in about twenty minutes, miss. Nice to get my aching ass, apologies for the lewd language, off this seat. Nice to get a real cup of … " He stopped suddenly and looked up at the sky around him. He frowned and moved his hand to a pistol which Agnes hadn't noticed.

"You hear that, George?"

He was talking to a lance corporal who'd fallen to the back in the march.

George was squinting through half closed eyes into the setting sun at a section of the sky directly behind the column.

"Well, Lance Corporal?"

Agnes was aware that the high spirits of the soldiers had suddenly changed, as heads the entire length of the column were turning around and squinting into the setting sun.

"Off the road! Now!" The same command was being bellowed along the entire length of the column.

Private Aston firmly, but calmly took hold of Agnes's wrist. "Best to do what he says, miss. Don't like the sound or look of that." He'd turned around on the seat and pointed in the direction of the setting sun.

Agnes turned, shading her eyes with her hands, and peered in the direction Private Aston was pointing. Set against the orange ball of the setting sun she could just make out the black silhouette of a bi-plane. A silhouette Agnes remembered. It was an AEG G.IV. Slowly its two partners in crime appeared alongside the lead plane.

"Miss, quickly get into the ditch, and as far away from the road as you can."

She jumped down from the wagon and looked up at Private Aston. "Thank you for your kindness. I hope that all your plans work out." She smiled and slid, unladylike, into the eight foot deep ditch.

She heard the drone of the engines and panicked, as memories of the barn came flooding back to her. She started clambering up the loose earth which made up the steep sides of the ditch, but for every step she made up, she slid back two. She was making no progress. The sound of gunfire indicated that the troops had opened fire on the German bi-planes, but they were soon answered by the unrelenting tak – tak – tak of the IMG 08 Spandau machine-guns and the thud – thud – thud of the bullets as they indiscriminately found the road, lorries, wagons, horses and men. Agnes ran down the ditch in the direction of where she thought the forward station was, jumped over the partially buried leg of a soldier, and narrowly avoided the head of another which was protruding from the earth. Then her foot sank deep into something soft. She looked down and saw that her foot was buried half way up her shin in the putrid bowels of what had once been a sergeant. Bile rose into her throat, but she forced it back into her stomach. She pulled her foot out like a navvy pulling his boot from cloying mud, and shook what she could of the maggot infested intestines from her shoe and leg. Her mind was in turmoil, her nervous system in overload, but self-preservation, and the added life force of Jane, gave her the strength to start picking her way through the corpses of men and horses which lined the ditch.

Suddenly she heard a sound which terrified her. It was the same sound which she'd heard just before the barn and the other nurses had disintegrated into a million pieces. The G.IV's had dropped their bombs. She didn't hear the explosions, but was thrown flat against the side of the ditch by the concussions, into the splayed arms of the top half of the remains of a captain. She rolled away desperately trying to climb out of her personal hell, and felt what she thought at first was heavy rain on her back, but they felt more like enormous hail stones, only not hard, but soft. Agnes rubbed her hand across the back of her shoulder and looked at her hand, the *hail stones,* were in reality bloody pieces of soldiers mixed with splinters of wood, earth and rock. Something thudded into the earth close to her right foot. It was the head of Private Aston, 21st Battalion the Northumberland Fusiliers. Agnes's nervous system could take no more. It shut down and she fell into a dead faint close to the smiling face of Private Aston.

TWENTY-ONE

They were having lunch at Market 22, but there was little conversation. Sam's expression hadn't changed much since they'd arrived back in Ypres. It was a complex mixture of disbelief, horror, shame, uncertainty and a deep sadness. The memorial at Thieve and the poetry had had a profound effect on him.

Isaac broke the silence. "Sam we should talk about this morning and our plans for this afternoon."

Sam looked up from his barely touched Veal Cordonbleu, and forced a smile. "I just didn't know. Didn't need to know I suppose." He put his hands together and rubbed the middle of his palm with his thumb. "Why doesn't anyone give a toss?"

"It's no more than history, Sam; some obscure branches on a family tree; frozen moments in time captured in sepia tones; dusty photographs at the bottom of an old sweet tin; a power struggle within an incestuous family; faint echoes of times gone by, and thousands of pages in dull history books. Why would anyone of this generation care, when the soldiers' nearest and dearest are mostly dead." Isaac sighed. He looked a lot more tired than usual. "Those who were identified and buried are cared for by the CWGC and living relatives who've been researching their family history. But those who are still Unknown or Missing, if no-one knows who they are or where they are then who *can* care?"

"But the young should be made to come here and be shown all of this."

"Quite a few do, but they are the exception. It wasn't their war. It wasn't even their century. It is down to us, Sam." Isaac let the words sink in. "Only us. Only we can educate those who are genuinely interested. Only we with the abilities can help the Missing to resurrection."

Sam pushed his frites around the plate with his fork, tried one, found it was cold and pushed the plate away from him. He looked away from the table at the hectic activity in the Grote Markt, where young men and women were getting up from their tables welcoming friends for lunch; businessmen engrossed in their lap tops; teenagers texting with one thumb and chatting at the same time; organised trips playing follow my leader behind a guide with a garish yellow umbrella; women with baskets laden with fresh produce from the open market and groups of old men who'd read the book, seen the film and got more than one t-shirt putting the world to rights.

Guillaume leaned forward and tapped Sam on the shoulder. "Coffee?"

"Mmmm … please. A double espresso."

Guillaume waved to the waitress and ordered two americanos and a double espresso.

Sam gently slapped the table with both hands and sat upright in the chair. "OK, where do we go next?"

From Ypres they followed directions to Poperinge, through Oostlaan, Veurnestraat and finally along the Leeuwerikstraat. After about five hundred yards they passed a cafe on the left, and Guillaume pointed to a sign for a cemetery. As they turned into the junction, Sam could see it was a simple dirt track into woods. After a short drive over a reasonably well maintained track, they came to a bright sunlit clearing, and there was a cemetery. They climbed out of the car and stood at the wrought iron gates. A concrete block on top of the brick gate support read 'DOZINGHEM'. Here in the middle of a dark wood was a beautifully maintained cemetery. Row upon row of white headstones gleamed in the sunlight, and a tall white cross stood proudly at the head of a broad central manicured grass path. Sam walked silently into the cemetery, which was probably a hundred yards long by sixty yards wide. He had no idea how many headstones there were, but estimated that there had to be at least two to three thousand.

Isaac caught up with Sam. "If you're wondering how many are buried here Sam, I should tell you there are three thousand two hundred and forty identified casualties buried here in this small cemetery. And how many unburied were remembered at Thiepval?"

Sam turned to face Isaac. "Around seventy two thousand?"

"Quite right. Imagine filling one of your football stadiums with fans, then kill everyone, and then do that another fifty times and you're still nowhere near how many were lost."

"Isaac, I've seen enough. You've made all the points which you must have wanted to make. Can we please go back to the hotel?"

Isaac took Sam's arm. "There was one specific thing I brought you here to see." They walked solemnly along the rows of graves until Isaac found the row marker he was looking for. "Along here, Sam."

They stopped in front of one of the thousands of white headstones.

"Read the inscription Sam."

He crouched down on the perfectly manicured grass, looked at the face of the gravestone, gasped and fell forward onto his knees. He looked up at Isaac and Guillaume with tears streaming down his cheeks.

24257 PRIVATE
JACK SAMUEL MORBECK
OXFORD & BUCKS LIGHT INF.
14TH AUGUST 1917 AGE 20

"I never knew. Who was he? How did he die?"

"Jack Morbeck was your father Paul's uncle. He is your blood, Sam. He is your connection. These cemeteries were established, for obvious reasons, close to casualty clearing stations. Four were established around a farm called Remi Quaghebeur in Lissenthoek, just south of Poperinghe. It was far enough away from the battlefields of the Ypres Salient to be out of range of the German long-range artillery, and was also next to the railway line which ran between

Poperinghe and Hazebrouck in France. This provided a direct connection to Boulogne where the British base hospitals had been established. He probably died at one of these four casualty clearing stations. I don't know exactly where he was fatally wounded, but given the date and where the grave is located, it's very likely it was at Passchendaele."

Sam stood up feeling the need to salute. "Isaac I don't need to see anymore. For some time now there's been little point to my life and I'm not getting any younger. Although they say that 60 is the new 40." He finally managed to smile, took out his iPhone and asked Guillaume to take a few photos of himself standing next to the grave. Finally he turned away and walked slowly to the entrance to the cemetery. As he closed the gate he turned and whispered. "God bless, Jack. Keep safe. I promise I will do all I can to help the others to a resting place as serene as this." Finally he gave what he thought was as close to a salute as he could manage and left.

In the car Guillaume fixed Isaac's seat belt and smiled. "I think that we have convinced him."

Isaac looked back from Sam and settled back into his seat. "We still have a great deal to do, but I am sure that Papaver Rhoeas will be in sensitive caring hands."

TWENTY-TWO

Despite the after-dinner *entertainment*, Elizabeth had a good night's sleep, but unfortunately found in the morning the boiler hadn't been heating the water, so a *refreshing* all-over cold wash started her day. Breakfast was two cups of strong black coffee with two sugars. She took her coffee into the map room, found the code to the broad band hub, entered it into the settings on her lap top and smart phone, and she was once again in touch with the outside world. She spent the next twenty minutes answering important emails and deleting the spam. Half an hour was spent updating her games, Tribez, Dragon Vale and trying to get through level ninety eight on Candy Crush. Finally, frustrated with exploding chocolate bombs, she closed the lid on the iPad.

"OK." She'd contracted Sam's *let's chat to myself* disorder. "I need to get to the church today and check the arrangements for the services of remembrance," Elizabeth didn't care for the word funeral, "and the other services I've got booked in for this week." She picked up her smart phone and opened her calendar. There'd been a few cancellations, although how anyone could cancel a service of remembrance was a bit beyond her. Weddings she could understand, last minute nerves, he's been sleeping with the bridesmaid, or the groom has come out of the closet. So she was left with a wedding and two christenings on the same day, which gave her a lot more free time.

She packed away the lap top and everything she needed for the day in a battered tan brown satchel, which had served her well since school, took a long look at the house, walked to her car, put the satchel on the back seat and drove to the vicarage, which was close to St Barnabus.

Mrs Mather was already in the church creating her flower arrangements for tomorrow's service, and her husband Bob was cutting the grass in the graveyard.

"Morning, Mrs Mather. They look lovely. Must be a super time of year for you flower arrangers."

Mrs Mather was in her early eighties, always dressed immaculately, hair perfectly coiffured, nails manicured and polished and shoes which you could use as mirrors. Her body had suffered with time, knee and a hip replacements had restored some of her mobility, although Bob had to keep reminding her that swimming and not tennis was probably a better way of keeping fit. However her mind was as sharp as Tamahagane, the layered steel of a Kitana, a samurai's sword.

"It's a marvellous time of year Elizabeth." Mrs Mather said. She'd called her Elizabeth since they'd met, and Elizabeth had never thought of calling Mrs Mather anything other than Mrs Mather. "I haven't seen Gertrude so vigorous for years."

Elizabeth thankfully knew she was talking about her favourite rose Gertrude Jekyll, pronounced Jeekel. Mrs Mather had on countless occasions extolled the virtues of the large, rosette shaped flowers of rich glowing pink and their perfectly balanced old rose scent.

"Shropshire Lad and Captain Christy have both been rampant this year. They've climbed our fence and I only planted them two years ago. Agnes, Cornelia, Felicia, and Francesca have all never looked so beautiful or smelt so sweet."

"More roses I hope." Elizabeth thought. She walked up the aisle to Mrs Mather and sat in a pew close to where she was tying Mother in Law's Tongue to dried Alium flower heads.

"Mrs Mather?"

"Yes, dear?"

"Did you have any relatives who served in World War One?"

She sat back on the pew and turned to face Elizabeth. "Bob's dad signed up when he was seventeen, too young you know, and he survived the whole thing. My dad took the King's Shilling in 1916, just in time to serve on the Somme, but he also must have had the luck of the devil. He was shot on the first day of battle and invalided out. He served out the rest of the war working at Aldershot as an adjutant to the colonel." She stood up peering closely at the flower arrangement and adjusted the length of the pink delphiniums. "Why's that, dear?" She asked without looking up.

"Did you know the Morbecks?"

She stopped cutting the delphiniums, her scissors frozen in mid air, frowned, scratched her head with the handle of the scissors and pulled at her double chin.

"Morbeck … Morbeck? I knew of a Jack Morbeck. They say he was killed at Passchendaele? I'm sure I heard he's buried somewhere in Belgium." She picked her nose, examined her finger and wiped it on the back of the pew. "He had two brothers. Fred survived the War and Bert was too young to serve. Let me think, I'm sure that the younger brother lived, where was it now, big house in, Osprey Close? Yes that was it, the house was called?" She stood up and walked to the open church door. "Bob, where did the Morbecks live?" She shouted across the graveyard.

"What was that, dear?" Mr Mather switched off the lawnmower and cupped his hand around his ear.

"The Morbecks" She paused giving it enough time for it to sink in "Where did they live?"

He sat down on the white marble edge of a grave and scratched his chest. "Morpeth?"

"No Mor … beck."

"Morpeck?"

"Turn it on."

Mr Mather frowned and tapped his ears. "I haven't got them turned on."

"Yes I know, turn them on."

"Turn the lawnmower on?"

Mrs Mather tapped her ears and mimed turning them on.

The penny dropped.

"Do … you … remember … the … MORBECKS?"

"I remember a Jack Morbeck, sad business that, destroyed his mother. Turned the house into a shrine for him, didn't she? Then there were his two brothers, Fred and Bert. Nice chap, Bert, lived with his son and daughter 'til he died in, when was it now, 1972? They lived up in Osprey Avenue."

Mrs Mather shouted at him. "Wasn't it Osprey Close? What was the name of the house?"

"No, it was definitely Osprey Avenue. I remember Phil Roberts, you remember, he was Captain of the Golf Club, died of prostate cancer, he must have lived there for at least twenty years."

Mrs Mather paused for a moment. "Wasn't that Phil Robertson? Captained the tennis club?"

"No, no, Robertson lived in Preston Close. He died in a car crash with his dog. Or was it his cat."

Elizabeth stared at the ground and shook her head. *"Please let me hear the end of this conversation before I die."* She thought.

"Yes of course. His wife was a big woman. Eventually married that butcher from Gloucester."

"Wasn't it Worcester?"

"No, pretty sure his name was Walter."

"It's lovely to hear all this, but what was the name of the house?" Elizabeth smiled at them.

"Ah yes, the house." Mr Mather pulled at his lower lip and blew loudly down his nose. Then a flickering candle cast a little light. "High Way, … no … Holly Wood … no" the candle finally caught flame, High Wood." He smiled as if he'd discovered the meaning of life. "Definitely High Tree … Wood."

TWENTY-THREE

Agnes shook her head, trying to clear the cotton wool from her ears. It was cold and dark, and she'd no idea where she was. She tried to sit up, but a searing pain shot across her right shoulder, and she lay back on the earth. The mists slowly began to clear as she remembered the ditch. The ditch and Private Aston. She remembered stumbling out of the ditch, but after that everything was a blur. She was fairly sure they weren't very far from the front when the column was attacked, but she'd no idea in what direction she'd ran blindly. She put her hands out to try again to push herself up, and bit her lip to hold back a scream, as something pierced both her palms. She brought her hands up close to her face and saw three deep puncture wounds in each palm. She carefully touched the ground around her and felt wire and spikes.

"My God" she thought *"Barbed wire! I must be in No Man's Land!"* Agnes froze. Which way was the British line?

A machine gun opened up and kicked up the earth close to her feet. Agnes lay as quiet and still as her shattered nerves would allow, until the firing stopped. She wasn't sure which direction the machine gun fire had come from and contemplated right or left, forward or back. A sound from what seemed all around her, sent a torrent of chills down her spine. It was a nerve scraping noise like a giant's fingers screeching across an enormous blackboard. She'd no idea what was causing the unearthly sound, but slowly realised that it was coming from the wounded in No Man's Land. Some screaming, some muttering, some weeping with fear, some calling for help, shouting in delirium, and groaning in pain. It was the sound of their distress, synthesised into one unearthly choral wail which broke her heart.

Below, the horror of the cries of the wounded, Agnes could hear whispered voices drifting to her from her right. She lay flat on her stomach and crawled towards them, the barbed wire tearing at her uniform. She could smell cigarette smoke coming from what she could just make out was a trench. *"Thank you Jesus*!" Agnes thought. She started to stand up when she clearly heard the voices.

"Hast du Zigaretten?"
"Nein."
"Keinen Tabak?"

"Nein."

"Dieser Krieg ist eine Nervensäge!"

Agnes threw herself flat against the ground. She'd no idea what they were talking about, but they were definitely not from anywhere south of the Thames. She rolled onto her back staring at the black sky, when a star shell exploded above her, the burning magnesium flare illuminating the scene around her. She lifted her head as far as she thought was safe, and the panorama she was confronted with coated her heart with liquid nitrogen. Stretching from one visible horizon to the other was a clearly discernible network of trenches. Which she now knew, were German. The star shell slowly drifted down on its parachute until it extinguished itself in No Man's Land, leaving the battlefield once again in claustrophobic blackness.

Agnes lay back and stared at the sky, not knowing which way to go. Some hours later as the blue black tones of the sky changed to the orange and reds of dawn, she could see that it was rising on her left. She managed a smile as she realised that if she crawled straight ahead, to the south, she should hit the British line.

Her crawl across No Man's Land was a living nightmare. She'd heard of the casualties left to die and left unburied there, but the numbers she'd fallen into; crawled over; buried her hands into bloated stomachs; found dismembered limbs scattered like shattered tree branches after a storm; breathed in smells which she would never forget or wash from her clothes; slid into bomb craters full of tens of thousands of buzzing flies laying their eggs on the blackened flesh of the dead and picked up pieces of something soft, did their best to extinguish any remaining shreds of humanity she had. Finally just before dawn, she tripped over the half buried lower torso of what once had been someone's husband, son or brother, and laid back and decided to wait for the inevitable.

Suddenly a hand took hold of her by the shoulder. It was the last straw and Agnes fainted, until gentle shaking brought her back into the land of the living.

"Miss." The shaking became more insistent but was still very gentle. Her eyes fluttered open. "Miss?

The voice was quiet but familiar.

"Jack?"

"Yes, miss. Keep as quiet as you can."

"Agnes, please call me Agnes." Despite everything, she was able to manage a smile. It was a smile of unbridled relief and also pleasure at seeing someone British.

"Yes Miss … Agnes." Jack's cheeks flushed with embarrassment. "Follow me. Our trench is only about twenty yards away. I'll get us through the wire. Stay low. Jerry's always on the lookout for an easy kill."

She followed Jack, crawling on her stomach across the last few yards of No Man's Land, until two pairs of welcoming hands helped her down into the trench. Two privates helped her down onto a rough bench built into the side of the trench just above sodden wooden duckboards which lined the bottom. A lance corporal held out a steaming mug of sweet tea which Agnes hugged to her like a new born baby. It slowly began to repair a little of the damage of her night's journey through hell. She looked up and down the trench at the bedraggled band of brothers sitting around.

One of them, unshaven, filthy, his greasy black hair stuck firmly to his head like freshly laid tarmac offered her a bottle of smelling salts. "Might help to clear your head, miss, and it will help with the smell." He pointed up at the top of the parapet. "The older corpses we can't get to are just a bit rank. We do sprinkle Hinchcliffe's, chloride of lime, but it only masks the smell for a short time." He smiled and sidled back into a recess in the trench shored up with timber which served as his accommodation.

In the next *cave* a sergeant, a lance corporal and two privates were jammed in together like sets of siamese twins conjoined at the hip.

Agnes looked up and down the trench. It was cluttered with mess tins; spent cartridge shells; water bottles; canvas bags; split sand bags; cooking utensils; forks; spoons and the general detritus of war. The Tommies looked like a neolithic tribe of troglodytes.

A corporal was unpacking the section's rations which consisted of Quaker Oats; bacon; tinned bully-beef; Maconachie stew; potatoes; bread; butter; jam; cheese; tinned milk; sugar; tea; cocoa and rum. Half a gill per man.

A private was starting to cook on a coke brazier and a scrounged stove.

An orderly, doing his best to support a wounded soldier, appeared around the corner of the trench. Everyone pulled in their feet to make a little more room for him, and as they squeezed past, an officer who was following not far behind them, stopped in front of Agnes.

"Agnes? Sister Wilmart? Is that you?"

She looked straight up into the eyes of James. He grabbed her by the shoulders and lifted her off her feet. "I thought you were dead. The barn … it was … well it wasn't there anymore. How did you … who …" He hugged her close to him and whispered in her ear. "I thought I'd lost you. It was too much to bear."

He turned around to the soldiers in the trench. "Who do I have to thank for saving Sister Wilmart?" There was an embarrassed silence.

"James." Agnes gently pushed him away. "It was Private Morbeck." She thought for a few seconds. "Jack Morbeck." She looked around the grimy faces in the trench looking for Jack, but there was no sign of him.

"He's not here, James. We must find him. Without him I'd be just another name on the casualty list."

"We'll find him, Agnes. Let's get back to the clearing station and have you checked over. You look like you've been to hell and back."

He took her by the arm and led her to a communication trench which led back to a forward clearing station. James gave her a thorough examination, but could find no major physical damage. Amazingly she only had the puncture wounds to her hands, minor abrasions, and cuts and bruises. His concern was more about the mental damage she must have suffered. He didn't have any direct experience of No-Man's Land but had treated enough casualties who'd told him so many lurid tales that he couldn't imagine what she must have been through. A sergeant had told him of the knee of a German soldier partially buried which formed an unnatural stile; the head of another which peered out of the earth looking for his lost torso, and the whole blasted area of No Man's Land was clotted to the very edges with bodies. What he'd seen had looked, as though some celestial undertaker had spaced the corpses evenly for internment and then had been interrupted. To get back to his own trench, he told him, he had to pick his way through a cemetery of the unburied.

James looked at Agnes and held her tightly to him. He was concerned, that he'd seen too many cases of shell shock caused by a lot less than she must have seen.

TWENTY-FOUR

Elizabeth was sat in the church taking in what the Mathers had told her about Jack, Fred and Bert Morbeck.

"They must have been relatives of Sam." She thought. *"I need to go back to High Wood and see if I can find if anyone there is a Morbeck."*

She took her mobile out her handbag, found Sam in her contacts and sent him a text. *'Have more info on your family. Please call. Have made more friends at the house'.* She pressed the send icon and smiled.

Three hours later she was back at the High Wood eating cheese on toast in the kitchen, and despite the earlier fun and games, she didn't feel in any way frightened. The only feeling she had was concern for whoever had tried to communicate with her in the map room and lounge. The questions were how she could meaningfully communicate with them, and how did all this affect her faith and belief in a merciful God.

She strolled into the lounge and sat on the Chesterfield, unsure of what to expect. After half an hour of nothing, she got up and walked back into the hall, looked around wondering what to do next, and remembered there were still some rooms in the house she hadn't investigated. She trotted up the stairs, stopped on the landing and looked at the locked door directly opposite her. It had to be the access to the third storey as she'd checked all the other doors, which led to bedrooms or bathrooms. She'd brought the keys with her and decided that it had to be one of the remaining keys without a coloured tab. The third brass key slid easily into the lock, she turned it and started to open the door when a loud knock from the front door reverberated around the house.

"Sergeant Lidsay, nice to see you again." Elizabeth looked either side of him. "I see that you're on your own this time."

"I was just passing on my way to the station and thought I'd let you have an update on Mrs Morbeck." He looked either side of Elizabeth into the house. "Mr Morbeck not here?"

"No he's in Belgium on business."

"I thought he'd retired?"

"Yes, but this is more of a personal nature."

Lidsay raised his eyebrows. "A missing wife not personal enough?"

Elizabeth's hackles rose. "That's a little uncalled for, don't you think? There's nothing Sam can do here and it's extremely important what he's doing in Belgium." She began to calm down. "It relates to his family history. He met someone at the funeral I conducted, who knew a great deal about what happened to his relatives in World War One." She smiled at Lidsay. "He'll be back in a couple of days. Why don't you call back then and you can update each other."

Lidsay didn't seem satisfied but accepted her offer. "If you speak to Mr Morbeck," He emphasised Mr, implying he disapproved of her use of Sam. "Let him know we have no further information on his wife." He emphasised wife. "However we are continuing our enquiries."

"Thank you, Sergeant Lidsay. I expect I'll speak to Sam this evening. I'll pass on your message and let him know you'll call when he's back." She held out her hand and took a step back into the hall, indicating the *chat* was at an end. Lidsay took the hint, tapped the side of his helmet and walked back down the path. Elizabeth wasn't prone to seeing the worst in people, but she was beginning to develop a real dislike for this particular policeman.

She closed the front door, headed back upstairs, fully opened the unlocked door, flicked the switch on the wall, walked up eight stairs, around a bend and up another six stairs to another locked door.

"Too much to ask the same key opens this." She thought. But fate for once was on her side. The brass key easily turned in the lock and the door smoothly opened.

Elizabeth expected to find a narrow corridor leading to at least another three rooms, but the door opened into a single open space the full length and width of the house. It had been converted into what Elizabeth could only describe as a gallery. Covering all of the available wall space and on both sides of ten twelve feet long panels screwed into the floor, were photographs of what on closer inspection, Elizabeth was sure were soldiers of the Great War. There were row upon row of sepia photographs of expectant young men, smiling at the camera and believing, as all young men do, that they were immortal. But now they were just frozen moments in time, a sepia Bayeux tapestry. All the men were in uniform, soldiers of all ranks and regiments, all walks of life; all classes, all optimistic of their futures, all with plans for after the War, and all in total ignorance of the carnage they were about to face. Fixed to the bottom right hand corner of every photograph was a small white sticker, and on it was written a name, number, division, regiment and place.

What made Elizabeth shudder was that so many of them had no face. She walked closer to one of the panels and looked at the photograph of a faceless Private Arthur Dawes, 221689, 34th Division, 102nd Brigade, 20th Northumberland Fusiliers, Mametz Wood. She walked along the lines of photographs, frowned, and estimated that about twenty five per cent of the soldiers had a face. On these photos, a small white card was stapled to the bottom left, with a simple message '*At peace under an English heaven.*'

She turned to look at the opposite panel and stopped at the photograph of a young man and his new bride. Both with faces. The white sticker read, Captain Edward Upland, 889012, 31st Division, 93rd Brigade, 15th West Yorkshire, Leeds Pals, Gommecourt, and at the bottom left '*At peace under an English heaven.*'

A deep sigh behind Elizabeth, which came from the other side of the panel behind her, span her around. She ran to the end of the panel and looked up and down the photos, but there was nothing obvious which had caused the noise.

"It's an old house. They make more noise than a flatulent pensioner after a curry." She thought, trying to convince herself that she heard noises like it all the time.

She walked up and down scanning the photographs. At each one without a face she felt a deep sadness. As she walked past one she saw what she thought was movement in the photo. She stopped and moved back in front of the photo of Captain Harry South, 76492, 8th Division, 23rd Brigade, 2nd Devonshire, Serre. He had no face, and the photograph seemed to have a 3D-like quality. Elizabeth stared in fascination at what had now become a miniature version of a soldier of the Great War. One which she felt she could pick up. One which was *alive?"*

There was a claustrophobic stillness in the room, and a profound spiritual feeling, which touched the very core of Elizabeth's faith and belief.

Sam was sat in Brussels Airport in a less than comfortable, distinctly un-ergonomically designed plastic seat waiting for his flight to Cardiff. He'd been far too early getting to the airport and still had three hours before his planned departure time. Isaac and Guillaume had dropped him off at the airport after agreeing they would meet next month at High Wood. There were enough rooms at the house for them all to stay until they'd answered all Sam's questions and agreed a way forward for him, High Wood and Papaver Rhoeas.

Airports, Sam had decided over many years painful experience, were sterile, impersonal, high-tech shopping malls for the mass transportation of people, which quite deliberately didn't offer, despite the plethora of shops and goods, stimulation for the mind to make time pass a little quicker. He spent a distinctly non-productive half an hour cruising every duty free shop; sniffing too many fragrances, and smelling as Jane would have put it, like a tart's handbag, sampling too many malt whiskies, skimming woman's magazines, people watching and looking at cameras as if he had half a clue what aperture, CCD, macro, DSLR, purple fringing, which sounded like a euphemism for something slightly pornographic, and resolution, which he thought had something to do with conflict. This was followed by a tuna mayo sandwich and two Danish pastries washed down with two lukewarm cappuccinos with the flotsam and jetsam of mankind in the self-service restaurant. These culinary delights demanded finding a pharmacy for an effective indigestion cure. Sam then made his way to the gate and in another equally uncomfortable plastic chair, read a couple of chapters of 'Portrait of a Killer' by Patricia Cornwell. Still with time to kill, he finally plugged himself into his iPod and listened to a few of his favourite tracks from the album 'I Can't Dance' by Genesis. Eventually, before he had the chance to properly consider painless methods of suicide, relief was brought by the announcement of his flight boarding at Gate 67.

Elizabeth was completely absorbed by the 3D animation developing in front of her. Sepia gradually changed to colour, the soldier and the busy railway station packed with soldiers bidding tearful farewells to their nearest and dearest, was now vibrant in living 3D. Captain Harry South's, 3D facsimile, stood crisply to attention, staring faceless out of the photograph at Elizabeth, stood down to at ease and holding out his hands in supplication. She leaned forward, moved her index fingers close to the photo, and as they neared it a spark of blue light arced between them making a connection. Some form of link had been created between the captain's hands and Elizabeth's index fingers. She jumped back, and the 3D facsimile of Captain South, was stretched and pulled out of the photo. She stared in disbelief at the tiny marionette hanging in front of her, suspended on strings of blue beams of light. Her first reaction was to shake this military Lilliputian off her fingers like a child with a long sticky bogey, but she was too fascinated in discovering what would happen next.

She couldn't take her eyes away from the captain, but the sensation of what felt like coarse sand being blown over her feet forced her to look down. A thin stream of brown coarse grains of *sand* were spiralling around her legs, like a Wisteria climbing the columns of a porch. She tried to move her legs, but the *sand* had substance and like a hungry anaconda constricted tightly around them. The spiral slowly climbed to the top of her legs and continued up her body. As it reached the top of her back, it split into two separate streams which spiralled down her arms, and the blue light bonding her to Captain South, arced like an acetylene flame. The spirals of *sand* coalesced at the ends of Elizabeth's arms, forming a single cloud of rhythmically pulsating grains. Lightning forked through the plasma cloud as the blue light merged with the *sand* storm, and rapidly it enveloped Captain South.

A strong gust of wind blew down the gallery, blowing away all evidence of the *sand* storm, and standing at attention in front of Elizabeth was five feet eight Captain Harry South. His face beamed at her with a smile which for him had been impossible for the last ninety six years. Despite what had happened, Elizabeth felt no fear. She'd no understanding of what had happened, but felt a deep intense satisfaction. He wasn't a handsome man, but he had a face which someone had loved as a son, lover, husband, and father. He was staring at the ceiling of the room, like a child trying to stay awake long enough to meet Santa Claus on Christmas Eve.

Elizabeth looked up to where his eyes were fixed on a small crack of light between the ceiling tiles. It was growing by the second, into a spinning cloud the size of a football of intense white light, but despite its startling brightness, she felt completely comfortable looking at it. She looked away from the light at Captain South, as the *sand* storm returned and spiralled up from the Captain's feet. As it reached his neck he dropped his eyes away from the light and smiled directly at her. The spiral finally began to obscure his head and his face disappeared. But she was sure that he'd mouthed "Thank you".

The *sand* storm collapsed onto the floor and disappeared between the floorboards. Elizabeth looked up to find no evidence that Captain Harry South had ever been in the room. She looked back at the photograph, where everything had returned to sepia, most of the picture was slightly out of focus, but at the centre, standing proudly at attention, smiling broadly at her was Captain South.

TWENTY-FIVE

Klaus had not been happy. Even Isaac's grasp of German didn't extend to the stream of expletives which greeted his phone call.

"Sie sind unzuverlässig Bastarde!" Seemed pretty clear. "Sie können nicht vertraut werden." And. "Sie könnte keinen Fick mit einer Hure organisieren." Seemed colourful in its imagery.

"Klaus I understand your anger, but I can't control my health? You are most welcome to come with Guillaume and me next month to meet Sam. I am sure there is plenty of room at High Wood." Isaac's tone was conciliatory but not grovelling.

"Hohe Holz?"

"Yes High Wood. I'm sure you understand the significance. He now lives there."

"Allein?"

"Yes of course he is alone. He told me that his wife has gone missing, but even if she hadn't the marriage is over."

"Exzellent. Er kann Keine andere verbindungen? Karsten lebt allein und hat keine persönlichen Bindungen."

Isaac was beginning to lose some of his famous patience. "Klaus, I understand your frustration, but can we please communicate in English? And yes as I have said he, like Karsten, has no other ties."

There was a long pause before Klaus replied.

"Ich komme mit Karsten. I will expect you to make all the arrangements. I do not expect things to unexpectedly fall through again Isaac."

"Of course not Klaus, we all work towards the same goal."

"Piss mich nicht über wieder!"

The line went dead. Guillaume came in from the dining room where he'd been listening on another line, and shrugged. "OK?"

"He finished by emphasising to me that he was not a man to piss off. I think that is a reasonable translation." He smiled at Guillaume, "Unfortunately he is very accurate in what he says. He will need to come this time and bring Karsten with him. Make sure that he as all the travel details by next week at the latest. He could still cause us problems."

TWENTY-SIX

The flight to Cardiff had been quick and uneventful. Sam took a taxi from the airport to High Wood, and was stood outside the front door trying to work out how he was going to explain the last few days to Elizabeth.

"It's not going to be easy, is it?" His other half emerged from the shadows. "Do you honestly think she's going to believe your twaddle? She'll be off like a rat up a drainpipe."

"She'll be fine with this. She has a faith which accepts an afterlife as true, so why should this be any different?"

"Oh, by the way, and what about the missus? Remember her, because I'm sure the police haven't forgotten. You never know, with any luck she may be waiting for us in the house."

"Sarcasm was never your strongest point. But you're right, I'd better call that sergeant. What was his name, Lidtropp, Lidman, Lidsay, yes that's it. Obnoxious little shit. I'll call him in the morning."

"Well let's see if the lovely Jane has come home?"

"Piss off!" Sam turned the handle of the front door and entered the hall. "Elizabeth, are you here? I'm back." The house seemed empty, there were no lights on and there was no reply from her. He walked down the hall close to the kitchen door and called up the stairs. "Elizabeth!!" There was still no answer, but Sam could see light on the landing. He dropped his bags, ran up the stairs, and stared at the open door.

"Elizabeth are you here!"

"Sam come up." Elizabeth shouted back.

He breathed an enormous sigh of relief and ran up the stairs to the third storey. The gallery was as big a shock to him as it had been to Elizabeth. He heard a soft sigh from the far end of the gallery, and walked quickly to the sound where he found Elizabeth sitting on the floor between two panels.

She was smiling and staring at the ceiling.

Sam took her by the shoulders and shook her a little too vigorously. "Elizabeth are you OK?"

She looked down from the ceiling into his eyes, appearing to be not at all surprised by his shaking. "Sam."

"Elizabeth why are you up here? What's happened?"

"It's difficult to explain, but it's quite wonderful. High Wood's a doorway to heaven."

He sat down next to her looking deep into her eyes. The last time he'd heard anything like this, was when he was partaking of illicit substances at a friend's house, Pink Floyd were playing Interstellar Overdrive on the stereo, he was lying between the speakers and his brain was up among the stars. "A doorway to heaven? Have you been listening to Led Zeppelin? Have you fallen?"

Elizabeth smiled. "No, not stairway to heaven, a door, portal, gateway, threshold, I don't know what to call this, but believe me Sam its here."

He put his arm around her and gently lifted her to her feet. "Come on let's go downstairs and you can tell me everything."

They started walking slowly down the stairs. Sam went first and helped her down, as he was sure that she'd fallen and was concussed. He made two strong mugs of coffee and sat patiently as Elizabeth told him about what had happened in the gallery. He then made another two mugs of strong coffee and added a good measure of brandy to each.

"You do believe me don't you, Sam?" Elizabeth was leaning across the table holding his hands. "You must believe me. It all happened exactly as I've told you."

"Elizabeth after what I've seen and done in Belgium, I believe you."

She pulled him across the table and kissed him passionately. They held each other tightly and lingered over the moment. There were no apologies when their lips finally parted. Elizabeth dabbed the corners of her mouth with a tissue and smiled at him. "OK you've heard what I've been up to. What happened in Belgium?"

"I'm starving, let's order some food and I'll tell you a tale of mystery and intrigue which Agatha Christie would have been proud of."

She frowned at him. "You'd put your stomach ahead of telling me what happened?" She smiled and pulled a takeaway menu from a drawer in the kitchen table. "Curry OK?"

They sat chatting for the next half an hour catching up on Lidsay's visit, the Mather's revelations and the events in the lounge. The chicken tikka massala, beef madras, nan bread and six popadoms arrived and vanished within minutes.

"I didn't realise I was so hungry." Elizabeth sat back, grinned at Sam, sighed and undid the top button of her jeans. "Now let's have the full undiluted story."

She sat and listened in silence for the next hour as Sam detailed everything he'd learned about Papaver Rhoeas, and what had happened at Ypres, Thiepval and Dozinghem.

She stood up and held her hand out to Sam. "Let's go and sit in the lounge. This is a lot to take in."

They sat close to each other on the Chesterfield, but didn't turn the iPod on. Another visit from the phantom choral society would be just a step too far.

Sam eventually broke the silence. "So Jack's brother Bert lived here with his son Arnold? But why didn't I ever meet him or know anything about him? Who set all this up? The gallery and the map room?" Sam rubbed the top of his head.

Elizabeth pulled him closer to her. "Since I chatted with the Mathers, I thought that we should research your family history. You said Isaac told you that Jack Morbeck was your link, your connection, but Bert and his brother Fred must have a part to play in all of this. I signed up on Ancestry so that we could do some detailed research, and knowing what I did about Jack, Fred and Bert I did some searching around and managed to draw up the beginnings of a Morbeck family tree." She picked up Sam's iPad, touched the Ancestry app., and after logging on entered Morbeck, and brought up the tree she'd started.

"I'll talk you through what I've found so far. Your father Paul Morbeck lived from 1912 to 1977 and had one sibling, his brother Arnold, born in 1925 and who as we know died this year 2013. Their parents were Fred Morbeck who lived from 1899 to 1962 and his wife Emily Court who was born in 1901, and died in 1977. Fred's brothers were listed as Jack Samuel Morbeck born in 1896, and died 1917 in World War One. It was his grave you saw at Dozinghem. The other brother was Bert Morbeck, born 1902, and died in 1972. Fred's parents were Rebecca Millener born in 1876, died 1926 and Adam Cain Morbeck born1875, died in 1915. The 1901 census shows Adam and Rebecca living at 24, Osprey Avenue. It wasn't called High Wood at that time, and in the 1911 census they're still living here." Elizabeth paused for Sam to take it all in.

"Do you have more information on them or the house after 1911?" Sam was sitting forward on the Chesterfield, looking over her shoulder at the graphic of his family tree.

"I can't get any more information on the property, as the most recently available census is 1911, when it was still only 24, Osprey Avenue. I don't know if there's another way to check when it was given the name High Wood. It's something we can possibly check with the council."

Sam pulled at his ear lobe and breathed deeply. "But why High Wood? According to Isaac, Jack was probably killed at Passchendaele."

"I've checked their military records, and it says that Jack died as a result of wounds he suffered at High Wood in 1917, but he died at a casualty clearing station, where is it, it was a long name, two seconds Sam I need to open this file." She navigated through a number of web pages until she found the reference she wanted. "Yes, here it is. Not sure how you pronounce this, Lissenthoek in Belgium."

"Lissenthoek was a casualty clearing station near Dozinghem."

Elizabeth looked up from the iPad at Sam. "Did you notice Adam's dates?"

"To be honest no I didn't."

She opened up the tab where they'd been looking at the family tree and scrolled across to Adam Morbeck.

Sam read the dates and frowned. "1875 to 1915! He died in the Great War, like his son! My God Elizabeth, how did Rebecca cope?"

"She didn't. Mrs Mather told me that Adam and Jack's deaths affected Rebecca so badly that she became a recluse. Apparently the local kids called her the Mad Woman in the Big House. Neighbours never saw her, and whenever anyone called at High Wood, it was one of the brothers Fred or Bert who answered the door."

Sam dropped his shaking head into his hands. "It's no wonder this house is like it is. The despair that must have infected these walls."

Elizabeth sat back against the red velvet cushions on the Chesterfield. "I did find something else when I was researching your relatives." She paused and put her hand on his shoulder.

He sat back and smiled at her. "Something else?"

"Yes I think so." She sat quiet for a few moments looking down at her hands. "What was your wife's maiden name?"

"Why do you want to know?"

"Please, Sam, what was her maiden name?"

"Blanden. She had a brother, Roger."

"Sam, she was my cousin." She let this sink in. "Her mother was my Aunt Joan."

Sam stretched his neck muscles and smirked at Elizabeth. "Sounds like the six degrees of separation to me."

"The six degrees of what?"

"The six degrees of separation is a theory that says everyone and everything is six or fewer steps away, from any other person in the world."

"What about the Morbecks?" Elizabeth said.

"They aren't going anywhere soon, and I need to see what you saw. So come on let's see if we can raise some more spirits."

TWENTY-SEVEN

Agnes spent a week recovering at Remi Quaghebeur, or Corfu Farm as the troops called it, and James kept a close eye on her treatment and recovery. He was happy she was recovering physically, but her mental state would keep him monitoring her closely over the coming weeks.

She was sitting on a bench outside the farmhouse in the early evening sun, when James arrived, looking somewhat embarrassed on a grey mule. He jumped off it and smiled at Agnes. "It was this or a Percheron, and I couldn't get a leg up from anyone."

"You looked very, very military." Agnes covered her mouth with her hands and tried to smother a laugh.

He sat down beside her on the bench, took her hands from her mouth and held them tenderly. They sat for a few minutes in silence, happy to be just with each other in the middle of the madness.

"How are you feeling today? You look radiant."

"I'm ready to come back."

James stared deep into her eyes. "Are you sure? What we do demands that everyone is at their very best."

"James I've had plenty of time to consider this and I've never felt better. Please let me come back."

He sat back, trying his best to look like he was giving her request serious consideration, but finally took her hands and smiled. "We've all missed you, there is so much to do, and we need as many qualified hands as we can get."

"Do *you* want me back, James?"

"Most of me wants to keep you here closeted away from the War, but I have to think of the greater good." He swallowed deeply. "You can start back tomorrow, if that's OK with you?"

By one o' clock the following day Agnes had already assisted in two below the knee amputations; stood with the priest as he read the last rites over four soldiers; kept a sergeant alive by keeping her fingers pressed for ten minutes on a ruptured carotid artery, and removed various shards of shrapnel from the arms and legs of three soldiers.

James had been keeping a particularly close eye on her and after sewing up the stomach of a lance corporal, he walked over to her, tapped her on the shoulder and gestured for her to follow him outside. "How are you coping?"

"Fine. I feel like I'm contributing something again to the cause." She brushed a piece of hair from her face.

"Sure that you're OK? You took a hell of a beating."

Agnes looked up and watched five British Avro 529's fly across the cloudless blue sky, on their way to deliver death and destruction to the German trenches. "Will it ever stop, James? There'll be people like us on the German side who will try to save those who we are about to try and annihilate. Your skills should be used to help the living, not the wounded and dying."

They watched as the Avro's disappeared out of sight.

"Not much we can do other than patch them up as best we can, or try to make their passing as comfortable as we can." James said as the noise of the engines of the Avro's could still be clearly heard. He tilted his head to one side. "Agnes, how many planes did we just see?"

"Five. Why do you ask?"

"It sounds like more than five and one of the engines doesn't sound quite right." He tilted his head again in the direction of the planes.

"James what is it?" Agnes was concerned at his expression.

"Let's get away from the tents." He grabbed her arm and pulled her after him.

"James you're scaring me. What is it?"

He was frowning and looking over his shoulder as he dragged Agnes across the field.

She looked back, stumbled, and a scream which could've shattered crystal glass spewed from her, as she saw the unmistakeable black Eisernes Kreuz, Iron Cross, on the wings and sides of the fuselage of what she didn't know was a Gotha G.V. heavy bomber.

James tripped and pulled her to the earth alongside him. He sat up and looked at the German bomber. "Surely even they wouldn't stoop that low?!" But he remembered the torpedoing of the Britannic hospital ship, and wasn't sure about the bomber's intentions.

They looked together at the bomber, as flashes of red flame spurted from the forward machine gunner. The earth close to the first ward exploded into a thousand individual eruptions of death. As they watched in horror at the plane, they could see it drop four two hundred and twenty pound bombs, followed by a single six hundred and sixty pound bomb. James took Agnes roughly by the arm and pulled her to her feet. "Run for your life my darling!"

James realised the trajectory of the last six hundred and sixty pound bomb, would bring it crashing close to the field they were desperately trying to escape from. As they reached the low hedge at the far end of the field, the world shifted into slow motion, as the concussion from the explosion lifted them up and tossed them like rag dolls over the hedge into a dry drainage ditch. A churning cloud of earth and rocks rumbled over them blotting out the sun and burying them under two feet of debris.

James clawed at the earth, pushing himself up to the *fresh* air, spitting earth from his mouth, unclogging his ears and blinking his eyes wildly to try and relieve the burning in them. He clambered up to the top of the ditch, collapsed onto his back in a field of nettles, shot upright scratching his neck and face as the oxalic acid from the stinging hairs did their best to induce as much pain and irritation as they could. But as he carried on scratching his skin raw, his mind began to clear.

"Agnes!"

He slid back into the ditch and clawed at the earth, like a manic mole, but could find nothing. His heart tried its best to burst out of his chest and tears started streaming down his face as he threw handfuls of earth over his shoulder. A pale hand suddenly appeared close to his feet and James cleared away the earth burying Agnes as quickly and as carefully as he could. He heaved her out of the ditch and laid her on the grass on top of the ditch, but could find no evidence of life.

TWENTY-EIGHT

Sergeant Ivor Wilfred Lidsay sat in his conservatory emptying what remained of a bottle of Kim Crawford Sauvignon Blanc into his glass. His wife had gone to bed hours ago and he was enjoying Inherit the Wind, an old black and white favourite of his starring Spencer Tracy, who he rated as the best actor Hollywood had ever produced. He'd lost count of the times he'd watched it, but the story of two great lawyers arguing the case for and against a science teacher accused of the crime of teaching evolution in a southern US school still held him enthralled.

He had a few more years to go before retirement and just wanted an easy life, but the Morbecks were an irritation that just wouldn't go away. CID had nicely told him to sit behind the station desk and leave crime detection to the professionals, as missing person cases weren't high on their agenda, and anyway in most cases they usually came home. Two murders, a serial rapist and an armed bank robbery were what they were being paid to solve, and not some wife who'd gone walkabout.

"Cheeky bastards" He thought *"I've forgotten more about police work than they'll ever learn."*

He drained the last of the wine and watched as Spencer Tracey drove the final nail of his case into the coffin of Frederick March. He picked up the remote control put the TV on standby, tried to stand up, but the effects of a bottle of his favourite wine and a couple of large whiskies, suggested to him that remaining seated was a better option than falling into the dining room furniture. Disturbing Gloria didn't particularly bother him, but he didn't feel like spending the night being elbowed hard in the ribs because he was snoring like an elephant seal on heat. Four hours later he woke freezing cold and shivering, desperate to have a pee and with a headache which was doing its best to chisel its way out of his skull.

"Never again" He thought *"Well, never again until the next time."*

He stood up unsteadily holding onto the sides of the chairs, and made his erratic way to the kitchen. Turning on the lights was a necessary but stupid idea, and together with the noise of the boiling kettle intensified the relentless pounding in his head. The sweet coffee and seven chocolate digestive biscuits, did little to improve his headache, wellbeing, or mood. He looked up at the kitchen clock. It was four fifteen, he usually got up at six, so it hardly seemed worth making the effort of undressing, cleaning his teeth, trying to get to sleep and then getting up feeling like shit in a couple of hours. He sniffed at his armpits, the odour reminded him of the last time he'd taken his granddaughter to Bristol Zoo, but a liberal spraying with Lynx Africa would neutralise the worst of it. He stumbled into the hall and took a close look at himself in the mirror. It wasn't the prettiest thing he'd ever seen, but then he wasn't trying to win a beauty contest, and stubble was pretty fashionable wasn't it? The greased down hair could be hidden under his helmet for most of the day, and a fresh pair of socks and a pair of Odor Eaters would get rid of the worst of the smell of Stinking Bishop.

He was at the station by five which made the on-duty sergeant happy as he was able to get off earlier than planned. After the handover he chatted with the local drunk in cell five, and made them both a large mug of coffee which resembled sump oil. The caffeine buzz and three Red Bulls carried him through the next three hours on a dark stimulant cloud, and by eleven o' clock he was feeling almost human again. He gingerly walked to the canteen and *forced down* bacon, egg, sausage, fried bread, mushrooms, black pudding, grilled tomato, toast and jam, and a croissant flushed down by three cups of builder's tea.

"Still looking for the missing wife, Ivor?" Detective Sergeant Alan Morris was taking his green tea and wholemeal watercress sandwiches to a free table. "She's probably run off for a dirty weekend with the milkman. You know what they get like at that age. You've got enough experience of one, so you should be able to understand her better than we could." He turned to his partner DC Phil Pretton and smirked.

Ivor stared at the flakes of croissant floating on the last of his builder's tea, but refused to rise to the bait. *"Prick"* He thought *"I'll find her dismembered remains in that house and you'll eat shit pie from my helmet!"* He looked up and *smiled* at DS Morris.

After his shift, despite the levels of blood alcohol, Ivor drove to Osprey Avenue and parked two houses down from High Wood. Two cars were parked outside the house.

"Playing hide the sausage with the vicar, are you?" He thought *"The inheritance and a bit on the side are pretty good reasons for getting rid of anyone's wife."*

After two hours, Ivor's screaming distended bladder and the fact he'd seen no sign of movement in the house, convinced him to call it a day. He glowered at High Wood as he drove uncomfortably past. "Have all the fun you can, because I'm going to crash your party!"

"Have you counted the photos?" Sam had walked up and down the length of the gallery and in and out of all the panels. "I reckon there are at least," he sucked his teeth, "two or three thousand?"

Elizabeth looked around the side of the panel she was examining. "No, I haven't made an accurate count, but I'd agree with you that there must be about two thousand."

Sam waved his hand at Elizabeth to join him. "Is the photo on this panel?"

She looked up and down the rows. "No it was on the one behind us." She turned and pulled Sam with her to the other side of the closest panel. "This is the one." She walked half way down the panel, smiled and pointed at the photo immediately in front of her.

"Meet Captain Harry South, 76492, 8th Division, 23rd Brigade, 2nd Devonshire." She touched the face on the photograph, looked at the white card at the bottom left of the photo and smiled. "Who is at last 'At peace under an English heaven'."

Sam looked more closely at the photos and for the first time noticed that so many didn't have faces. "He didn't have a face?"

"No, he was like these" She pointed out two photos close to where they were standing. "Lance Corporal Albert Cuthwaite, 77651, 29th Division, 87th Brigade, 2nd South Wales Borderers, Gommecourt and Private Geoffrey Bycroft, 99643, 29th Division, 87th Brigade, 1st King's Own Scottish Borderers, Gommecourt, are exactly as Harry was before he passed over." Elizabeth held her hands in front of her almost in prayer. "Sam for the first time I felt I'd found my true calling." She turned to him with an expression which he thought anyone in a state of grace would have. "He thanked me. As he passed through to the other side he thanked me." She looked at her hands and gently rubbed them together. "He'd waited almost a hundred years to be at peace, to be found, to be whole again, and I was his companion on his final journey."

Sam took her hands and looked her directly in the eyes. "Elizabeth I think I know now what we have to do here at High Wood. Isaac gave me some understanding of what he and his group do, and you've already touched these other realities he spoke about." He paused and looked back at the photo of Lance Corporal Cuthwaite. "Have you done any research on him or any of the others with no faces?"

She took a deep breath and turned to the panel. "Not Cuthwaite, but I've looked into the military record of Private Geoffrey Bycroft." She smiled and again and touched the photo. "I found most of what I needed on or through that Ancestry web site." She paused again tilting her head to one side as she studied the Private's uniform and the background of the photo.

Sam was getting impatient. "And?"

"Sorry, and he's recorded as MIA at Gommecourt."

"MIA? You're sure that's what it said?"

"Yes, Sam, MIA. It was very clear that he was lost at Gommecourt."

"Missing at Gommecourt." Sam quietly corrected. "MIA is Missing in Action. Isaac introduced me to MIA and KIA when were at Teepvail, or at least that's what I think it was called. At the top of the memorial it said 'The Missing of the Somme'." He paused and looked around the photos. "Elizabeth, there are about seventy two thousand names on that memorial. All MIA, never found, never at peace, and never properly mourned by their loved ones, who never knew what happened to them or where their mortal remains were. Elizabeth, he has no face because his identity is still lost. His body was either blown to atoms by a shell or bomb, sliced by shards of red hot shrapnel into countless amorphous pieces of flesh and bone, which to this day are still buried in the Belgian soil, floating in the Belgian air, or held at one of the portals." He stopped and stared at Elizabeth. "I have no idea how, but you seem to have the ability to help these lost souls to a final rest." He paused and took Elizabeth softly by her hands. "Isaac seemed to think that the abilities were with me, but it's you. You must have a connection to the Great War that you don't know about?"

Elizabeth squeezed his hands and smiled. "I have a connection. Let's go down to the kitchen, have a coffee and decide what we're going to do next."

Sam watched Elizabeth make the coffee as if they were a normal couple. She picked up the open pack of chocolate digestives, put them with the coffees on an old tray she'd found in a cupboard near the sink, put it in the middle of the kitchen table and sat down next to Sam. He picked up his mug and two biscuits. "You'll be getting me fat." He said with a mouthful of warm soft dunked biscuit.

"You, fat? Bit too late to worry about that." Elizabeth gently squeezed his double chin.

"Cheek."

"No, chins."

"You're definitely getting a bit too cheeky." Sam put down his mug and held Elizabeth's face in his hands. "And I love you for it."

As she leaned forward to kiss him softly on the cheek, Sam turned his head and their lips met. It was like an emotional dam bursting between them, as years of pent up frustration erupted through their fractured barriers. Nothing now would, or could, contain their passion for each other. It should have been a moment of tenderness but all hormonal brakes were off as they staggered into the lounge leaving a trail of clothes behind them. The act of lovemaking was quick, but the explosion of senses at its climax left both of them physically shaking and drained. They lay in each other's arms for what seemed like hours, basking in the warm waves of pleasure washing over them.

Finally Elizabeth sat up. "I'm going to put something on."

Sam held her hand. "Don't be shy or embarrassed."

"I'm just cold, Sam. On the outside that is." She kissed his hand and started collecting her clothes.

Twenty minutes later they were sat at the kitchen table devouring ham sandwiches, salt and vinegar crisps and a couple of Twix bars washed down with a Crabbies.

Sam moved his chair closer to Elizabeth. "I don't know where Jane is, and frankly I don't much care."

"Sam, everyone deserves to be safe."

"You've not met, have you? We've had no emotional link for more years than I care to remember. We've been nothing more than a bad habit, and it's just been easier putting up with each other than facing all the turmoil of a messy divorce."

Elizabeth took his hands and kissed his fingers.

"Sam I don't want to be the cause of any problems."

He frowned at her and then smiled. "You're the only good thing that's happened to me for years." He sat back in the chair and tapped her softly on the end of her nose. "I won't lose you now. Not for anything or anyone. Life's too short and I don't want to be sitting in front of the pearly gates thinking. If only."

Elizabeth put the empty crisp packets and chocolate wrappers into a carrier bag, walked to the sink with the used plates, leaned back against the sink and ran her fingers through her hair.

"Let's go to bed shall we. As you say, life's too short." She tried her best to look sexy under half closed eyes, but couldn't keep it up. "Come on you've had enough time to recover and this time I want to take my time. Sam this is all new to me. I need to learn." She held out her hand to him. "Teach me."

TWENTY-NINE

James sat on the edge of Agnes's bed. He'd stretched all his medical skills to their furthest limits, and had finally brought some faint signs of life back to her. He'd no idea how she'd survived, given her already weakened state, but he was overjoyed she had. One by one he cracked each of his finger joints. He knew it was bad for them, but since he'd been a child he'd found it comforting.

"Captain Heyward."

The voice was indistinct.

"Captain Heyward!"

The voice began to penetrate his emotional fog.

"Captain Heyward, You're needed. There 'as been anover lot of casualties. Bad uns."

The voice was now recognisable as Private Tully. James looked up from Agnes. "Sorry, Tully. What is it?"

"Casualties, sir. Bloody loads ov 'em. Beggin' your parn, sir."

James smiled at Private John Tully, late of the Elephant and Castle. Tully had seen more action than most, and was helping out while his latest wounds healed, before he was sent back to the front to use up his remaining three lives.

"Stand easy, Tully." James tried his best not to smile as discipline was paramount. "How many casualties would you say there are?"

"Bleedin', sorry, again sir, too many if you ask me." He snapped back to attention." There are nine ambulances, sir. They're being sort'd by Captain Smythe for resuss or pre-op. Never seen Lissinook so busy!"

"Lissenthoek Tully."

"Beg parn, sir. Bleedin' langwij. Captain Smythe is waiting for you, sir."

"Thank you, Tully. Go back and tell him I'll be there in a couple of shakes."

Tully crisply saluted with a bandaged hand, turned sharply on his heels and headed back towards the operating theatre.

James stood up and leaned over Agnes. "Won't be long, old girl. We'll soon have you up and at 'em, and back home to Blighty. This war's over for you." He kissed her tenderly on the forehead, brushed away a few stray strands of hair from her eyes, smiled and marched to pre-op.

What greeted him resembled something from the End of Days. The casualties had clearly been exposed to a prolonged shell barrage as the majority of wounds he could see were clearly caused by shrapnel. He walked across the duck boards, soaked in blood, vomit and pieces of flesh to Captain Smythe who was doing his utmost to stem the bleeding from an arm which had been severed just below the shoulder.

"I'm here Charles."

"James, thank God. It's like a slaughter house in here." He looked around the tent and slowly shook his head. "How did we ever get to this over a meaningless assassination in Sarajevo?"

James put his hand on Charles shoulder and gave it a reassuring squeeze. "Who knows, old man? God's probably struggling to understand this carnage. Where do you want me to start?"

Charles scanned the casualties and pointed to a soldier in the far corner of the tent. "Private Morbeck?"

James stared across the tent in disbelief at the young man who was in obvious distress. "Did you say Morbeck, Charles?"

"Yes came in with major wooden splinters in his legs and shoulders. Probable amputations I would think. That's if he survives until the pre-op, let alone the operation."

"What's his first name?"

"Not certain, although I think I heard one of the stretcher bearers say good luck Jack."

"My God you're the one who saved Agnes." James thought.

James did his best to run across the obstacle course which was pre-op, to the soldier who was barely conscious, shocked and clearly in severe pain. He lowered his head close to the chalky glistening skin of Jack's face. His breathing was shallow and laboured, and a menacing pink froth seeped from the corner of his mouth.

"I'm here now, old man. Looks like the Hun's given you more than one Blighty."

The soldier did his best to smile but could only manage a grimace.

"I need to just check your name. Is it Jack Morbeck?"

Jack's eyes fluttered as he desperately struggled to remain conscious, and stay for a few more precious moments in the land of the living. He silently mouthed "Yes, sir".

"OK, Jack, I'm going to get this timber out of you." James made a detailed examination of Jack's wounds, and what he saw didn't fill him with hope. The worst of them was a grave wound to the chest. A large jagged charred splinter had entered his back just below the left scapula, perforating the lung and ribs in front and behind. It had finally lodged below the outside of the left nipple just beneath the skin, and blood was steadily, relentlessly, oozing from the entry wound in his back.

He waved a nurse over. "Get me morphine." He looked to the ceiling. He tried to convince himself that he could work his magic and save Jack, but the evidence of his eyes told him that the best he could do was to make his passing as comfortable as possible.

"What do you want us to do with this one, sir?" A stretcher bearer was standing close to James waiting to process Jack.

He span around glaring at the stretcher bearer, but his discipline and understanding that he was just doing his job, brought a degree of control back to

James. "This *one's* name is Jack Morbeck! You would do well to remember that these *ones*," he waved his arm at the casualties, "that these *ones* have names and families like you, and that it's only through the grace of God and luck that you aren't lying alongside them." He paused regaining his control. "Treat them with respect. Treat them how you would want to be treated. Treat them as their mother would want them treated."

The stretcher bearer reddened and snapped to rigid attention. "Beg pardon, sir! I meant no offence. Only we've got loads of 'em, sorry, loads of casualties needing help, and it's yourselves, sir, who decides who gets treated and who doesn't."

The soldier's stark comment sent a chill down James's spine. Until this moment he'd walked up and down the rows of wounded, performing, as quickly as he sensibly could, spot diagnoses on the severity of their wounds and their chances of surviving any treatment. He'd never fully appreciated that what he was doing, and what he had, was the power of life and death over these desolate men. The power to devastate the lives of their family and friends. The power to eliminate their potential from the population and future generations. He looked down at Jack, did his job, and only in a few seconds made his decision.

"Thank you, you can take him to the holding area."

The nurse arrived back at James's shoulder with a syringe of morphine. He clenched both fists, took the syringe and turned to Jack. He was gone, but the stretcher bearers had only carried him a few feet away. "Wait! Sorry … Halt!"

Both stretcher bearers came to attention.

James moved close to Jack and rolled up the torn sleeve of his blood soaked tunic. The syringe hovered over the vein in Jack's arm. Somehow he'd managed to remain conscious. He grimaced in agony as he slowly lifted his arm and held James's hand, and softly, but very clearly said. "Please."

James smiled into the dimming eyes of Jack, gently inserted the needle into his vein and delivered the morphine into his fading system. "God speed, Jack."

THIRTY

Isaac read the email from Sam a second time. Could it be that the priest he'd met at the funeral held the power he thought Sam had? He'd been certain it was Sam who possessed the sixth or was it seventh sense, but could he have simply misread Sam's energies for Elizabeth's? Or did they, as he now suspected, complement and amplify their individual gifts to a level he'd never seen before? As Sam had requested in the email, they'd both to come to Ypres to meet Isaac and the Papaver Rhoeas. Klaus would again be unhappy, but when Guillaume told him that Sam could not be Chef Charon, his mood would soften.

"Isaac it's time for your medication." Guillaume held a glass of sparkling water in one hand and the first of four daily dosages of the drugs which were keeping his brother alive. The need for a new Chef Charon was genuine, and Isaac prayed that the cancers which were invading his organs would be controlled by the drugs, long enough for him to pass on everything.

"How are you today? You look pale and strained."

Isaac looked up gingerly from the computer and smiled. "I'm fine. Just some niggling backache. Nothing more."

Guillaume knelt on the floor next to Isaac and handed him the pills and water. His eyes glistening with tears. "Isaac, there is no need to keep things from me. We need to go through this together, you must let me know when things are bad."

Isaac swallowed the pills and what remained of the water, and handed the glass back to Guillaume. "Today is not a good day. But we have much to do, and we don't have much time to do it in." He smiled a thin smile at Guillaume, and raised his eyebrows. "I think that I might sleep for a little time. Will you contact everyone and organise a meeting as soon as possible. I could not cope with speaking to Klaus today."

Guillaume knelt on the floor close to Isaac. "Leave it with me. I will arrange everything. What should I tell Sam?"

"Let him know we are arranging a meeting of Papaver Rhoeas, and we will let him have the dates as soon as we have them. Tell him we agree it is important that Elizabeth also comes." Isaac frowned, closed his eyes and seemed to dissolve into the chair.

Guillaume stood up, brushed away some stray white hairs from Isaac's eyes and affectionately kissed his forehead. After an hour of text messages, phone calls, Face Times and emails Guillaume had contacted everyone except Klaus.

August fifth and sixth were the most convenient dates, and it only remained for him to contact Klaus.

"Guten Morgen, Klaus. Ich hoffe, Sie gut sind." *"Surely that should put him in a good mood."* Guillaume thought.

"I am fine thank you." There was a long pause. "Why is Isaac not calling me?"

"He is indisposed and has asked me to call everyone."

"Jeder?"

"Yes he wants to organise an urgent meeting of Papaver Rhoeas, at a date, time and place that is convenient for everyone." Guillaume waited for a few seconds but there was no reply. "I was hoping August fifth and sixth would be OK for you?" There was another long silence.

"Are we now not going to the UK?"

"Circumstances have changed, and Isaac believes more can be achieved if we meet here."

"Umständen? Welchen Umständen?"

Guillaume had learned when Klaus slipped into German it was a good indication that his mood had changed. And not for the better.

"English please, Klaus, my German is not very good."

There was the sound of a deep prolonged sigh at the end of the line.

"What circumstances?" It was spat out as if he was talking to an imbecile.

"Someone else has entered the English equation." He let this sink in for a few seconds.

"Ja, und!"

"Sam has a relationship with a woman which rules him out of any chance of becoming Chef Charon." Guillaume could almost feel the smile growing on Klaus's face. "The issue is that she seems to have greater powers than Sam, and their combined powers we believe are beyond anything we have ever seen before." Guillaume could feel the distant smile disintegrating, and being replaced with a scowl.

"Who is this Frau?" The words were curt and cold.

"She is a priest."

"Ein priester! Of what faith?"

"Protestant, the Church of England."

"At least she's a Christian. God help us if she had been …" The sentence remained unfinished, the conclusion left hanging in the air.

"Klaus, we need to meet them. We urgently need to assess what she, what they are capable of." He thought to himself that with the little time Isaac had left, urgently, was something of an understatement.

"So he will not be considered for the position of Chef Charon?"

"No. As always, the Chef Charon must have no personal commitments. Their complete attention must always be to the Papaver Rhoeas." He knew now that he had Klaus on his side.

"Excellent. Of course we must assess any new talent." His tone was almost conciliatory.

"So can you make the fifth and sixth?"

"Let me check my calendar." There was a clearly staged pause. "Yes I have a space around those two days. Where are we meeting?"

"Iepers. If that suits?"

There was the sound of teeth being sucked. Klaus wouldn't concede that easily. "Iepers?" Another prolonged pause. "Provided that we don't stay at *that* hotel!"

"The O?"

"Yes the O! I would rather sleep on the streets."

"An excellent idea." Guillaume thought to himself. "I have checked the Regina for availability and they can accommodate us."

"The Regina? Give me a few seconds and I'll Google it."

After what seemed an eternity Klaus spoke. "Looks OK." He said begrudgingly." Position seems OK opposite the Cloth Hall. Make sure you also book accommodation for Karsten. Karsten Imlauer. I, M, L, A, U, E, R.*"*

"Thank you, Klaus. I have that." Guillaume scowled at the phone. *"Condescending little shit!"* He angrily thought. "Good to speak to you, Klaus. I'll confirm everything by email. Auf Wiedersehen." He hoped that his true feelings weren't too obvious in his voice.

"Give my best wishes to Isaac. Wir sehen im August."

The line went dead.

Guillaume stared at the receiver in his hand. "I wish I knew the German for fuck off!"

THIRTY-ONE

After five fours in the operating room which resembled a charnel house, James was exhausted. As he stood outside taking in what was loosely called fresh air, he tried not to think about the surgery, or the butchery as it would have been better described. Of the twenty soldiers he'd treated, seven had lost both their legs, three their right leg, two their left leg, three their right arm and the remaining five would be washed and dressed for burial. He crossed his blood soaked arms across his chest and watched a bedraggled rat lapping at a viscous brown pool of something which may have once been water, while another had its head buried in a tin. After everything he'd seen, the rats were just another commonplace part of the scenery of the greatest show on earth. "You should sicken me you know!" James shouted at the rat.

"Sicken you, sir! Apologies, but I couldn't make it to the latrine." The embarrassed corporal had been urinating against the side of an ambulance.

James looked up from the rat realising that even in his exhausted state vermin didn't hold you in conversation. "No, not you, Corporal. Our furry friends over there." James pointed at the now sated rats.

"Can't bear the, pardon me, sir, filthy bastards. Buggers are everywhere. They climb over you when you try to sleep, bite your ass when you're having a crap, beg pardon again, sir. I've seen some of them as big as our tom cat back home. Final straw for me sir was when four of them ate the eyes out of my best mate Ronnie. He was in the Rifle Brigade, got shot trying to get across no man's land, and hung on the barbed wire for a week." He paused, the image playing across his mind. "We couldn't get to him. To any of them. There were hundreds of them hanging on the barbed wire like washing that had been forgotten." He was wringing his hands as he walked off into the darkness. James could hear the corporal sobbing and repeating over and over. "We couldn't get to them."

James sat down on an empty wooden crate and took a letter from his trouser pocket he'd received from his brother Clayton. He scanned it, taking in the good wishes for his safety, but it was the last paragraph which concerned him.

'Goodbye, dear brother, from my grave in the earth. I shall soon become mad in this awful artillery fire. Day and night it goes on without ceasing. Never has it been so bad as this before.

'I've added a few lines which Siegfried wrote on the back of one of those damnable post cards they produce for the Tommies to send back home. Part of

*an idea he's got for a poem. He writes a great deal. Nice chap although his
views are a little eccentric.'*

'Someone was holding water to his mouth.
He swallowed, unresisting; moaned and dropped
Through crimson gloom to darkness; and forgot
The opiate throb and ache that was his wound.
Your dearest brother,
Clayton"

James pressed his thumb to the signature. The War, as his brother had so
poignantly said in the letter, was dismantling him physically and mentally, piece
by fractured piece.

He meticulously folded the letter and put it back in his pocket. Amongst all
this annihilation, there was only one beacon of hope illuminating his life. Agnes.
He could still save her, where he could only dismember or *kill* his other patients.
He pushed himself up from the crate, stretched his stiff aching joints and walked
quickly back to her.

THIRTY-TWO

"Have you had a reply from Isaac?" Elizabeth asked.

They were stood in the map room drinking cold diet Cokes.

"No, but Guillaume has emailed some dates in August. I haven't replied yet as I wasn't sure how your diary was."

Elizabeth looked down and tucked her hair behind her ear. "I'm going to resign from the ministry."

Sam looked up from the map and held her hand. "Are you sure about this?" He was surprised by her decision. What she'd experienced in the gallery had been profound, but he hadn't anticipated Elizabeth would consider such a life changing step.

"To be honest I've been weighing things up for months. My faith has been tested to the point where I find it difficult to offer comfort to those who come to me seeking it. Meeting you was the final proverbial nail in the coffin."

Sam lifted her face up. "Elizabeth, I don't want to be the reason you throw everything in."

"You're not. Just one of many. The incident in the gallery." She smiled. "It sounds like an Agatha Christie novel doesn't it." She kissed Sam on the nose. "What I did for that soldier gave me more satisfaction than anything I've ever done in my life. For once I felt that my life had genuine meaning and purpose." She frowned. "My only concern is the money. I don't have any savings and I don't have any rich relatives in God's waiting room."

Sam pulled her close to him. "Money's not an issue. When Arnold and Edith left me the house, they also left me a hundred thousand." He kissed the top of her head and whispered in her ear, "You can be a kept woman."

The warm glow from the night before was still with them and was still stirring up hormones. They stood back from each other and wickedly smiled.

"Do you think we should?" Elizabeth cheekily asked.

"Do you think I can? Sam feigned exhaustion.

"I'm happy to help you recover."

"Well, if you don't mind, *helping out,* then I think I could just about manage it."

Elizabeth took his hands, laid them on her breasts, and Sam lovingly caressed them. It had been decades since he'd felt this comfortable about something so intimate. "Darling, I'm not exactly pushing up the daisies, but life seems to have been passing me by at times thirty. I don't want to waste another second. I can't afford to waste another second, and if Jane ever turns up I'll get a divorce as quickly as I can. But even without a divorce, we can live together here at High Wood. Jane can have the other house and everything in it. There are no memories held in those bricks and mortar I want to keep. My future, our future lies here. There is so much more still to discover about this house and every mystery it contains, and we can learn and experience them together." Sam paused and dropped to one knee. "Elizabeth, I can't ask you to marry me, but would you do me the honour of living with me?"

She smiled down at him and pulled him up by both hands. "Mr Morbeck, you have a partner. Now let's discover more about the mysteries of the nooks and crannies of our bodies."

"You hussy!"

They kissed passionately.

"You go up and start without me. I'm going to reply to Guillaume that we can make the fifth and sixth."

Elizabeth did her best to smile like Scarlet from Gone with the Wind. "Oh, Mr Morbeck, what kind of girl do you think I am?" She flicked her hair with her hands, turned, swung her hips and pranced out of the room.

Sam smiled at her disappearing back and walked into to the kitchen to let Guillaume know they would both be there for the fifth.

Three hours later they were educated, satisfied, exhausted and showered. The mattress and springs of the bed had been tested to breaking point, and their love and desire for each other amplified to the 'nth degree.

"We really should get out of the house now and again." Sam said.

Elizabeth was boiling four eggs and toasting wholemeal bread. "It's always been a love of mine since my Gran first served them up for tea when I was four. That and Marie biscuits covered in butter."

"Did you ever have sugar sandwiches?" Sam was drooling at the memory.

"Sugar sandwiches? Really? I can't think of anything more revolting."

"Well, what about condensed milk sandwiches?"

"You are seriously having me on, aren't you?"

"No, my Nan used to cut thick slices of white bread, slice cold butter onto them and then pour the thickest condensed milk over them you've ever seen. It would get everywhere. Down your chin, on your jumper, up your sleeves, but it had a taste which would have satisfied the Gods on Olympus if they ever ran out of ambrosia."

She pointed a finger across the table at him. "You're getting very philosophical. How well did you know your Grandparents?"

He took a plate and two egg cups from Elizabeth and started tapping small pieces of shell from one of the eggs. Elizabeth took a knife and sliced the top off the egg. She was a decapitator.

"I really only knew my paternal grandparents." Sam wiped runny yolk from his chin with a tissue. "Fred and Emily, or Bampy and Nanma as I used to call them. My mum's parents died when she was very young and she was brought up mainly by foster parents."

"Fred was Jack's brother?"

"Yes. Did you know your grandparents well?"

Elizabeth played with a piece of toast.

"Didn't really know them that well. They lived in Kent and we lived just outside Exeter in Devon, so we only got together on high days and holidays." Elizabeth stopped and scraped the remaining white of the egg from the shell. "Funny isn't it that until you said what you called them I'd completely forgotten what I called mine." She smiled and finished the remaining egg and toast. "More tea, Sam?"

"Yes please. What did you call them?"

"Mmmm? Oh sorry, Mawnan and Grampty. Don't ask me why, but children just seem to come up with these odd names." Elizabeth looked into Sam's eyes. "They're my link, Sam. I forgot to tell you because we … "

Sam had a knowing and contented expression. "Your link, but how?"

"Mawnan and Grampty were Agnes Wilmart and James Hayward."

THIRTY-THREE

Lidsay had checked with the station and taken two weeks outstanding annual leave. He'd no intention of taking his good lady wife anywhere, but decided it was time to bring that tosser of a detective down a significant number of pegs, and see that twat Morbeck locked away for the rest of his life. Surely that wasn't too much to ask.

He parked in his usual spot two houses down from High Wood and was very pleasantly surprised to see Sam and Elizabeth loading up their car with luggage.

"Off for some sin and sex in the sun? Enjoy it while you can. You'll be picking up the soap in the showers for your boyfriend pretty soon."

He was even happier when he saw through his binoculars that Elizabeth was checking their passports.

"Some overseas sin sun and sex." He looked up and scowled. "Thank you God. I want to see that cheating bitch punished as well, as I'm sure you do."

Sam and Elizabeth drove away for the airport and their flight to Brussels.

Ivor sat waiting in his car for a quarter of an hour making sure they'd gone, and feeling the house was now his, he got out of the car and crossed the avenue to High Wood.

Breaking and entering was a crime, but it was also a skill which was easily acquired from hours and hours of meaningless conversations with burglars in the holding cells. Getting the equipment was a little more difficult, but after a few conversations, he'd made some interesting contacts who were more than happy to help an officer of the law who they might just be able to lean on in the future. Unfortunately for Lidsay, that's exactly what did happen. A little subtle but firm pressure was applied to him, indicating that if he didn't help the local firm, then disclosures would be made to senior officers. He'd have lost too much in pension rights this late in his career, and so what if a few lads got off? They hadn't asked for much. Just a little information on times and routes of patrols, a little *mislaid* evidence and a few extras allowed into some of the lads in custody. In fact they'd been so grateful for his support, they'd started making some anonymous payments into an account in Brighton for him. Nice lads really. Always good to their families and friends.

Entry through the back door was the safest option and had been a relatively easy job for Ivor to open it.

"OK, so where would you bury a body in a house like this?" He felt like the host of 'Through the Keyhole'. Lidsay's stomach decided that he needed a cup of coffee and a few tasty treats before starting any investigations. He was sat at the kitchen table thinking things through and working out a plan of action. "Burial or dismemberment? Dismemberment is messy but a much easier way of disposing of the body. Burial is cleaner, less blood and guts, but time consuming and difficult to conceal a grave for any length of time."

Like Sam, Ivor'd found that after years of marriage to Gloria, the only meaningful conversations he ever had were with himself.

"The most obvious place for either would be the cellar, but there didn't seem to be much evidence of either when we looked around it the other day."

The sound of a key turning in the front door made Ivor spill his coffee over the table and floor. "Shit!"

The front door creaked open and the sound of running footsteps down the hall made Ivor for some incomprehensible reason dive under the kitchen table.

"Sam, hurry or we'll miss the flight!"

From upstairs came the reply. "It's OK I've got it, you weren't to know I'd replaced my passport with a new one. Two seconds and I'll be there."

Ivor breathed an enormous sigh of relief.

"Elizabeth!"

"Yes, Sam."

"There's a packet of mints in the cupboard next to the sink. Can you get them for me?"

Ivor's breathing almost stopped simultaneously with his heart as the sound of footsteps came down the hall and the kitchen door opened.

With one hand on the handle of the door, Elizabeth called back over her shoulder. "In the cupboard next to the sink?"

"Yes they're under the custard creams."

"OK. Anything else you want?"

"No if we need anything else we can get it at the airport."

Elizabeth ran to the cupboard, found the bag of M&S assorted mints, turned around and saw the spilled coffee. The temptation to clean it up was overpowering, but the thought of missing the flight to Brussels won out. She ran for the door and slammed it behind her. The mess would have to wait.

Ivor remained paralysed under the table. He may have had the means and method to be a burglar, but his nervous system was in no way up to this level of stress. The sounds from the hall of two sets of feet and the front door slamming, finally started the process of relaxing most of the paralysed muscles in his body, but he stayed under the table for another five minutes before he felt it was safe to come out.

He picked up the mug, made another cup of coffee, recovered the custard creams from the cupboard Elizabeth had left ajar and demolished half the packet. Finally feeling up to it, he mopped up the spilt coffee, put the biscuits back in the cupboard and his cup in the sink. Not exactly the actions of an accomplished burglar, but he hated mess.

"Right, plan of action. I think a tour of the house would be a sensible start, and suss out how the land lies."

He stood in the hall looking at all the doors and decided he'd start at the top and work his way down to the cellar.

As he reached the top of the stairs, an unlocked door directly in front of him, smiled at him invitingly.

"And what lies behind you?" Lidsay said.

What he saw as he entered the gallery made his chins drop. "My God what the hell is this?" He walked the full length of the Gallery briefly inspecting row upon row of photos of young men in uniform. He walked more slowly back down the Gallery, paying much closer attention to the photos. "Christ, why are so many of them faceless?" He'd been up and down most of the panels when his eye was caught by the photograph of a young officer. He ran his finger along the wording, and read the brief note. 'Lieutenant Robert Hubert Lithrop, 56899, 2nd Division, 47th Brigade, Irish Guards, Passchendaele'.

It reminded him of a photo of his great uncle who'd fought in the Great War. He thought back to Sunday teas with his grandfather Phillip, when they'd spend hours together looking at sepia, and black and white photos of his relatives and listening to stories of heroism, bravery beyond the call of duty, selfless duty to King and Country and of the friendships forged in the heat of battle. But the most heroic of all the stories was that of great uncle Ronald, who'd won the Victoria Cross at the Third Battle of Ypres, Passchendaele.

Ronald's was a story of unbelievable suffering in the liquid mud of Flanders fields, which dragged everything down into to a suffocating slow painful death. Ivor could remember every detail of the story. Ronald and his company were held up by enemy machine-gun fire from concrete emplacements. He organised a party of troops, and rushed one emplacement, captured three machine-guns and twenty prisoners. He then led his company forward under a heavy artillery barrage and machine-gun fire to their objective. Later in the day he organised another successful attack on another machine-gun emplacement, captured three machine-guns and fifteen prisoners. His Victoria Cross took pride of place on the mantelpiece in the front room and Ivor had been allowed the rare privilege of holding it.

He stepped back and leaned against the wall. "What the hell is this place? What in God's name are they up to? How the hell did I miss this when we looked around the house?" He slid down the wall and sat on the floor staring at the panel where Lieutenant Robert Hubert Lithrop's face gazed down at him. He stood up as something drew him back to the photo. He'd not noticed the other note on the bottom of the photograph next to Lieutenant Lipthrop's. *'At peace under an English heaven'.* He walked slowly along the rows of photographs, noting that only the photographs with faces had the words *'At peace under an English heaven'.* Ivor folded his arms across his chest and chewed his bottom lip. "What the hell does all of this mean?"

He slowly walked backwards to the entrance of the gallery, took a last look around and walked down the stairs. As he sat in the kitchen with another cup of coffee and the remaining custard creams, Ivor's mind was in turmoil. None of what he'd seen, could in any way be seen as reasons for murder. Could they? He picked up the empty packet of custard creams, frowned and walked to the fridge. Smiling invitingly at him was a bar of Galaxy Caramel. Cadbury was his favourite, but in times of crisis … he'd force himself.

An hour later he was no closer to unravelling the mystery of the photographs. It was now quite dark in the kitchen, Ivor screwed up his eyes and checked his watch for the time. Eight thirty! Gloria would be pissed.

"No change there then" he thought. He stood up from the table, looked over his shoulder at the house, mouthed *"See you tomorrow"* and left by the back door.

THIRTY-FOUR

James sat with Agnes for three hours and finally slipped into a restless sleep. His dreams didn't give him any respite from the horrors of the clearing station or the War. Images of legless Tommies dragging themselves with smashed bleeding arms through the mud until finally, slowly, they sank beyond sight into the liquid filth; Tommies impaled and bound together on barbed wire weeping in unison in an unholy chorus of suffering; horses with their innards hanging to the ground dragging cannon and being beaten with whips by dismembered arms, and trenches flooded with blood. There was no end or limit to the dreadfulness his mind was able to create.

A loud gasp from Agnes rescued him from the torment of his *rest*. He stood up and leaned across the bed to be closer to her. Her eyes were wide open but they didn't register any real signs of awareness of her surroundings. They were fixed on a point on the roof of the tent. James looked up but could see nothing, and looked back at Agnes whose eyes hadn't blinked or looked away from the spot above her. She was mouthing something which James couldn't understand. He turned his head to one side and put his ear close to her mouth. The words were hushed but distinct.

"I have to go." There was a sharp intake of breath. "I must leave you." Another desperate gasp for air. "I'm the future." A final struggle for breath. "I must follow the light. I have to get home."

James took Agnes by the shoulders and shook her. "Agnes don't go to any light! You belong here with me!" There was desperation and panic twisting his voice. "Agnes!"

The focus of her eyes moved slowly away from the spot above her to James's face, and a warm smile gently caressed her mouth, her eyes softly closed and her breathing stopped.

"No!"

Jane could sense the link between herself and Agnes unravelling, little by little their entangled DNA was disconnecting, unzipping, peeling apart and reassembling its amino acids to recreate the individual beings which were the present Agnes and the future Jane.

Somehow, Jane had sensed Agnes was slipping away, and it was then she began to become fully aware of the absolute need to separate herself from her if either or both of them were to survive. She'd forced one last link with Agnes, to *tell* her as best she could, that without what she was doing, they would both die.

"I have to leave you."

"No, not yet!"

"I don't belong here."

"You are part of me. Don't go!"

"I'm our future. If I stay we don't live on."

"Will we meet again?"

"In spirit yes, but I must go to the light."

"Never forget me. Always remember this."

"You will always be a part of me."

Jane felt the last strands holding them together break, until their union was finally broken. She was aware of floating above Agnes, looking down and seeing James desperately trying to save her. With no sense of fear she peacefully rolled over to stare directly at the intense shaft of radiant white light which seemed to have no beginning or end. It was a shimmering spiralling tunnel radiating bliss. She intrinsically knew what going to the light meant, and it held no fear for her. There was only the impression of a divine consciousness receiving her into an alternate reality. She opened her arms in supplication and effortlessly became one with the luminescence.

James held Agnes tightly against his chest, trying to share his life force with her, and finally, feeling no signs of life, he laid her on the bed and closed her eyes. "Sleep, my darling. You will always be in thoughts, my dreams and my memories. Sleep now. We will meet again, and if this war has its way, then very soon." He dropped to his knees and looked outside the tent to where he knew the stars were, but before he could start his prayer a dazzling pin point of light appeared in the air directly above him. It slowly began to rotate and expand until it was the size of a football. It silently exploded into a million shards of rainbow light, which began wrapping Agnes in a cocoon of pure energy. It moved in a spiral around her for a few seconds, coalesced into a single ball of light, slowly came closer and closer to her until finally it entered her body. At that moment her body flexed into a stiff arch, and floated a few feet above the bed. Her eyes opened glowing with a blue light. Her chest rose and fell as she took intense deep breaths until at last she finally drifted gently back to the bed.

James had no idea what to do. No points of reference, and for the first time in the war he truly felt fear. Agnes gave him the signal what to do. "James, James are you OK?" She was looking up at him with bright shining eyes.

THIRTY-FIVE

The flight to Brussels had been quick, smooth and uneventful, and a driver was waiting for them in arrivals. "Mr Morbeck?"

"Yes."

"I am to take you to Ieper. Monsieur Guillaume has arranged this for you. Please come this way."

They followed the young driver who was dressed in a black suit, crisply laundered white shirt, black tie and highly polished shoes. All that was lacking to complete the image was a peaked cap, which Sam saw lying on the front seat of the Mercedes. He took their luggage from them, expertly stored it in the boot, opened the back door for Elizabeth and settled her into the rear seat.

Elizabeth sat back into the deep leather of the seat and smirked like a young child on Christmas morning. "This is … I feel like royalty. Didn't you have to get the train the last time you came?"

"Yes," Sam said with a forced frown. "But with you with me your ladyship," He paused for effect, "only the red carpet is good enough."

Elizabeth prodded him in the ribs and kissed him on the cheek.

The journey to Ypres was smooth and relaxing. They stopped for a natural break and a coffee, and the journey of around eighty miles took only just over an hour and a quarter. Elizabeth had been full of questions about the cemeteries she could see from the road and place names which had started to mean a little more to her. Questions which the driver, Jean Philippe, was more than happy and able to answer.

They arrived at the Hotel Regina at around five o' clock. Jean Philippe handled the luggage, ensuring that the concierge understood the importance of the guests.

Sam thanked Jean Philippe and gave him a twenty Euro tip.

"This is very generous."

"Please take it, you've been extremely efficient and very friendly. I'll let Guillaume know what excellent service you've provided." Sam shook him by the hand. Jean Philippe nodded, jumped into the driver's seat, waved and moved off into the rush hour traffic.

Elizabeth hadn't moved from the pavement and was staring at the Cloth Hall. "Sam, it's magnificent. And it was completely destroyed in the War?"

He followed her gaze across the square, and despite the fact that he'd seen it before, the building was still an architectural triumph. "Completely flattened. I'll have to take you inside, they have the most amazing World War One museum." He looked up and down its hundred and twenty five metre length and couldn't help but be impressed by its majesty. "But that's for another day. Right now we should find Isaac and Guillaume."

Elizabeth looked a little anxious.

"There's nothing and no one to be nervous of, my love. They are the kindest, gentlest people I've ever met. You'll love them, and they're going to love you." He squeezed her hand. "Come on let's check in."

Guillaume was waiting in reception for them, drinking an ice cold glass of Kriek. He waved as he saw Sam, spilling some of his lager over his jeans. "Sam it's so good to see you again. And this … this must be Elizabeth." He offered his hand to her and nodded. "How should I address you, Elizabeth? I am not familiar with the Church of England."

She instantly liked Guillaume, who had such a friendly manner and excellent manners. Such a rare thing in the modern world.

"It's lovely to meet you, Guillaume, and please, it's Elizabeth or Beth, I respond to both."

Guillaume had already checked them in, and being unsure about their relationship, he'd booked two singles. Sam smiled and whispered to Elizabeth that she should leave her door on the latch.

"Isaac is taking a rest at the moment so I'd suggest we have a beer in the Grote Markt. Unless you'd like to freshen up after your journey."

Sam looked at Elizabeth and smiled. "Guillaume, a cold beer right now would be, as we say, exactly what the doctor ordered."

Guillaume laughed to himself. "I must remember this …. Tout ce que le médecin a ordonné. Yes excellent."

They walked to the corner of the Grote Markt close to the City Hall and sat at a table outside 't Klein Stadhuis, Little City Hall, as the August evening was warm and pleasant.

"You must try their beer. They brew it themselves."

Although she wasn't a regular beer drinker, Elizabeth joined Sam and Guillaume in a cold glass of Klein Stadhuis.

"This is really good. It makes a change from my usual glass of Sauvignon Blanc. Can you buy this in England?" Elizabeth asked.

"I'm afraid not. It is local to Ieper and this restaurant, but I can arrange to have some shipped over to you if you'd like?"

Elizabeth glanced at Sam who was vigorously nodding in agreement. She looked back at Guillaume. "I think that's a yes."

Sam hadn't realised how thirsty he was as he drained the glass in a couple of gulps. "Another?" He raised his glass to Elizabeth who shook her head. Guillaume smiled and waved over the waiter to take their order. He took hold of his sleeve and turned to Sam and Elizabeth. "Shall we eat while we're here? Isaac probably won't join us until tomorrow and I imagine you don't want to eat too late?"

Sam and Elizabeth looked at each other and nodded to Guillaume. "Thanks, that sounds like a good idea. It's been a long day and I don't really want to be too late getting to bed tonight." Sam smirked at Elizabeth.

"If we could have some menus please, two more Klein Stadhuis." Guillaume looked at Elizabeth, "And a glass of your best Sauvignon Blanc."

After a simple dinner of mussels, veal cutlet, fries and ice cream, they strolled across the busy Market Square to the Hotel Regina.

Elizabeth got their keys and handed Sam's to him. "I'm going up I'm dog tired." She kissed Guillaume on both cheeks. "Thanks for a wonderful evening. See you in the morning." She turned and gently kissed Sam on the lips. "See you in the morning." They would keep up the pretence for as long as was required.

Sam turned to Guillaume. "Time for a night cap?"

"Just a very quick one, Sam. We have a lot to do tomorrow."

They found a table in the corner of the hotel bar and ordered a glass of Boulard, Grand Solage Pays d'Auge, Calvados for Guillaume and a glass of Cognac Leyrat, VSOP for Sam.

"How ill is Isaac?" Sam asked.

Guillaume sipped his calvados. "Not good." He stared at the table. "Not good at all. He has asked me not to tell anyone about his illness, but you're different Sam, and I think you should know. But Isaac must never know that you are aware of his condition." He finished the calvados and waved the empty glass at the barman. "I think I need another. How about you, Sam?"

Sam knew his limits which he was very close to exceeding. "I'm fine Guillaume. Thanks."

They sat in silence until the calvados arrived, which Guillaume drank in a couple of gulps. He shuddered slightly, pulled his chair conspiratorially closer to the table, looked around the bar and stared directly into Sam's eyes. "He has prostate cancer." He paused for a few seconds. "But it has spread."

"How widely?"

"The cancer is an aggressive form. We originally thought he had an enlarged prostate, BPH, Benign Prostatic Hyperplasia, but it was quickly and correctly diagnosed as Prostate Adenocarcinoma." Guillaume swallowed hard. "It's pretty widespread now. The cocktail of drugs I give him are just palliative. At present they control most of the pain, but he tires very easily. He has written a living will, and when the drugs become ineffective he has arranged to go to Veritas in Switzerland." Guillaume looked down at the table. "I don't agree with him, but I will respect his wishes and be with him at the end."

A bottomless silence settled over the table.

Sam stood up, walked around the table, stared out of the window, sat down next to Guillaume and held him by the shoulders . His body quivered as the emotional dam of months of stress finally burst.

Sam lifted him from his chair. "Come on, let's get you to bed."

The next morning Sam met Elizabeth in reception for breakfast, and as they entered the restaurant Sam began to grin.

"What is it? What's tickled your fancy?" Elizabeth said.

He pointed to a table in the corner where Guillaume and an old man immaculately dressed in a blue suit, white shirt and navy sweater were sat together looking at an iPad. The old man looked up as best he could, recognised Sam and waved him over.

"Isaac, so good to see you again." Sam sat down beside him, held out his hand to Elizabeth for her to sit next to him. "Isaac, this is Elizabeth."

Isaac looked up at her from his hunched position. "My dear it is so good to meet you at last. Sam has told me so much about you, and if half of it is true then you will soon be canonised."

Sam ordered coffee and pain au chocolat, and Elizabeth tea and pain au raisin. He pulled his chair closer to Isaac. "Are you feeling better? Guillaume told me that you were feeling a little tired?"

Isaac smiled at him and slowly nodded his head. "Yes a little weary. I'm afraid it's a price we pay as we get older. However after a good night's rest I am refreshed and ready for what should prove to be an interesting day." He finished his coffee as Sam and Elizabeth's breakfasts arrived. The waiter without asking topped up his coffee. "Sam I need to explain what is planned for today and what I would like to achieve. We will be meeting the other members of Papaver Rhoeas." He left this hang in the air for a few seconds.

Sam looked concerned. "All the members?"

"Yes. Some important decisions need to be taken, and taken very quickly. Everyone is arriving today for a meeting tomorrow, but I wanted us to have time to prepare before we meet them. I want to, how do you English put it, ah yes, have all my geese in a row."

"Ducks, Isaac."

"Yes ducks in row, whatever the relevance of that is. Lets go up to the meeting room we've booked and I can explain my plan.

The meeting room was well appointed and set up for twelve people. Sam looked at Elizabeth, shrugged his shoulders and they all sat close to each other at one end of the table.

"Sam, when we met a few weeks ago I explained what we, the Papaver Rhoeas, do. Have you outlined this to Elizabeth?"

"As best I can. But I hope the next few days will give her a much better understanding."

"Excellent. Elizabeth, we are not misogynists, but so far, no woman has ever entered the Papaver Rhoeas. I have no rational explanation why, but it seems obvious from what Sam has told me, that you have the abilities which would provide Papaver Rhoeas with an outstanding member."

She looked down at the table and blushed.

Guillaume turned on the projector linked to his laptop, turned down the lights in the room.

Isaac took a sip of water and took two codeine capsules. "First slide, please, Guillaume." The screen burst into life as an image of the Great War filled the screen. This was followed by ten other harrowing images from the war to end all wars. "These are some of the reasons Papaver Rhoeas was formed."

A picture of the Thiepval Memorial came on the screen. "This memorial is a flagship for why we are still needed today. It is our mission, Elizabeth, to find the missing, bring them back to their loved ones and to their salvation and resurrection. I hope that as a priest you can understand this."

Isaac paused and took a sip of water.

"The fundamental laws of physics tells us that matter cannot be created or destroyed. It can only change its form. When the Missing were blown to pieces, they weren't destroyed. They changed their form, into a pure life force. The existence of these life forces can only be detected by a very select few. They are sometimes called sensitives, psychics, or mediums. You," he pointed to Elizabeth and Sam, "are sensitive to the life forces of these missing souls, who drift on the breezes of time like threads of gossamer. However you and a very few others, have additional abilities to find and guide them to their home. You've seen the faces on the photographs in High Wood?"

"Yes, and those with no faces."

"They are the ones who are after almost a century still missing, manquant, fehlende, пропавших без вести. In a thousand tongues they remain gone, but never, never forgotten." He sat back in the chair and sighed.

Guillaume bent close to him, and whispered in his ear.

"No, no I'm fine. Now let's get on." He took a laser pointer from the desk tidy in front of him. "Guillaume, the members please." A sepia photo appeared on the screen of a colonel of the French Army in World War One. "This is Patrice Beaudet's father, Colonel Maurice Alfonse Beaudet. One of the most decorated heroes of France. Sadly he was killed at Amiens, but his body was never found." The next picture appeared. "His son, Patrice Beaudet, one of the founder members of Papaver Rhoeas. His father was and still is Patrice's primary reason for playing a vital part in establishing our group." He gingerly turned to Sam and Elizabeth. "Patrice is an ally. He will support anything I propose."

The next image appeared. "Giles Vermeulen, Belgian, another ally. A good and true friend. His father was lost in the mud at Passchendaele."

Pictures of the other members of Papaver Rhoeas quickly followed with a brief pencil history by Isaac. Each one was identified as an ally, undecided or anti. Isaac finished with Klaus Bauer. Isaac stare at the screen for a few seconds and then continued. "Klaus Bauer. Klaus was a decorated General in the Oberbefehlshaber Netherlands."

Guillaume turned off the projector and turned up the lights.

Sam looked puzzled. "Very little on Klaus?"

Isaac and Guillaume exchanged glances. "I'll let you meet and you can make your mind up about Klaus." Isaac left it at that.

Sam looked at Elizabeth and shrugged. "Isaac thanks for explaining who we'll be meeting, but why are they allies, undecided or antis? Surely you all have one and the same purpose?"

"Sam I'm not getting any younger and it is vital we find a new Chef Charon, a leader of the group. These members of Papaver Rhoeas will vote for who will become my replacement. But it has to be someone who has the necessary abilities and can commit all their time and energies to our cause." He paused. "I saw this in you, Sam."

There was silence around the table.

"In me? You saw me as your new leader?" Sam began laughing. "Isaac, you really can't be serious can you? I know nothing about the group and even less about how to bring back these lost souls. I came here believing that you wanted me to take over from Arnold and Edith, and I've no problem with this. But Chiron?"

"Charon, Sam."

"You say potato I say potato. Isaac I came here because I have seen abilities in Elizabeth which make mine look like cheap conjuring tricks. I thought you should assess what Elizabeth can do for your *Poppies*. But whatever it is, we will be doing it together Isaac. I couldn't possibly commit all my time to this. Elizabeth and I have finally found each other. I believe this made her acutely aware of her skills and amplified them. It isn't me that has the real powers, Isaac, it's Elizabeth."

Silence fell on the room. Isaac stared at the table playing with a pencil. The silence remained unbroken for what seemed like an age. Isaac broke the uncomfortable vacuum. "Then we have a problem."

Sam sat forward. "Isaac, we always used to say in business that there were no such things as problems. They were only opportunities."

"An opportunity for a problem. I said that I *saw* it in you to be leader."

"Isaac, I understand that you are upset, but … saw?"

"Yes Sam, *saw*. As soon as I became aware of your relationship with Elizabeth, I called this meeting so that we could agree on a new Chef Charon. Not you Sam."

Sam sat back in his chair, almost disappointed in Isaac's comments. "But you did think I could have been Chef Charon?"

"Yes, Sam. I did think you could."

Sam smiled. "Elizabeth and I will take over High Wood, and will continue the work of Arnold and Edith. You have our absolute commitment on this, and the answer to your new Chef Charon is in this room."

"Elizabeth!"

"No, no, I've explained that we intend to work together at High Wood. Since we met at the funeral, virtually all of my communications have been with Guillaume, and my understanding of your cause has come from emails, Face Times, Skypes and phone calls with Guillaume. Isaac you were the catalyst, the spark which ignited the fire, but it is Guillaume who manages everything around Papaver Rhoeas. It is Guillaume who understands the fine details of running this organisation. Your brother, Isaac, your new Chef Charon, has been with you for the last fifty eight years. Let's meet Papaver Rhoeas, and help you convince them that Guillaume should be the new Chef Charon."

Isaac remained silent for several minutes. "Guillaume are you party to this? Is this some plot you've been hatching up with, Sam?"

Guillaume stood up and left the room.

Sam stared in disbelief at Isaac. "You're the world to your brother. Without him where would you be today? In some soulless hospital ward, a hospice or … Switzerland."

"You know? He told you despite everything I asked?"

"Yes because he is desperate and he cares, and because if he loses you he loses part of his soul. He's in pieces, but he carries on because you need him, not just as a carer, not just as a member of Papaver Rhoeas, but as your only brother. Your blood." Sam stood up and took Elizabeth by the hand. "Come on, we need to find Guillaume and check he's OK. This ..." He waved his hand towards Isaac. "Doesn't seem that he needs anyone, and certainly not us or his brother!"

THIRTY-SIX

Jane's memory of her separation from Agnes was still raw. She'd developed a strong physical and spiritual, bond with her. They'd become one body with two souls, with the will power, strength, and life force of two. Two souls which had been slowly merging into one, until … It had felt like an elastic band stretched to its limit until it finally snapped. There'd been genuine pain, both physical and mental, but now Jane was once again a single entity. Once again her unique self.

She had no sensation of time or space, but felt the stirrings of memories of drifting on a balmy sea, being lifted from gently lapping waves, wrapped in a fleecy blanket, joyful memories of nights spent playing cards with a gentle old man, dogs named Furgle and Arnie, a car accident, a funeral, a new home, misery, abuse, hatred of men, a violent death, a verdict of not guilty, a love found, a wedding day, a love lost, a wasted life of bitterness, a house, Agnes, the light, and Sam. What *had* she done to Sam. She knew it was too late to rebuild anything between them, too much damage had been done. Was it too late to ask for forgiveness and understanding, and to free him from her suffocating presence? Jane had no idea how she'd ever do this, given she was now certain she must be dead. But where and what she was, were still mysteries. Surely this had to be, what did they call it, Purgatory? She was in a holding pattern between heaven and hell, and she had a sneaking suspicion which final destination she was heading for.

She'd no sensation of time passing. Floating in a void. Somewhere in that world in between awake and asleep. Numb. No awareness of anything. Gradually a dim light growing brighter and brighter. A light very different from *The Light*. It was flickering, red and yellow, with a warmth which was both welcoming and threatening. She felt herself sinking deep into a warm pool, and finally into yielding, silky, quilted softness. Into *sheets*? She could smell lavender and sense warmth. She could move her arms and legs, and then all her body. The Eagle had landed. But where and when?

"Is this Heaven?" She thought. She spread out her arms and patted where she'd landed. It had a comforting familiarity. A sense of home? *"If I can move, then do all my senses work?"* The thought teased her. *"Go on open your eyes. What's there to fear? Nothing if you think you're in Heaven, but everything, if this is some scam of the Devil."*

"Trust me." The thought teased.

"Trust you! Look what my life was like, thanks to me trusting you!"

"Unfair, Jane. Unfair."

"Unfair my ass! Trust your instincts they said? I'd rather trust politicians or journalists."

"Open your eyes. Go on. You'll be pleasantly surprised. Really you will."

She chewed this over and despite grave misgivings, slowly opened her eyes. At first everything was unclear, lost in a swirling mist. Fleeting shadows almost in focus but then quickly gone. She rubbed her eyes, stretched her neck and again opened her eyes. This time the mist began to clear, and what she saw in sharp focus took her breath away. She was in the master bedroom at High Wood. The fire in the hearth was lit and the logs crackling and sending out a warm welcome to her.

"Told you, didn't I?" Instinct one, Jane nil.

"Mmmm ... Could be."

She pushed herself up on her elbows and looked around the room. She hadn't spent much time at High Wood, but she'd taken a whistle stop tour of the house while the cleaners were eating their lunch, and decided that this room would be hers. She swung her legs off the bed onto the carpeted floor and slid off the bed. She wasn't in any way unsteady on her legs. She walked to the door and opened it onto the landing. "Anyone here?" She called into the dark emptiness of the house. The house was silent. She felt along the wall to where she remembered seeing the light switches, flicked them all on and lit up the landing and stairs. It was definitely High Wood. "My God. I'm back! And in one piece." She walked to the top of the stairs and started to make her way down to the hall. Halfway down she heard a sound like nails being dragged down a blackboard. It was the scraping of the bottom of the back door on the kitchen floor.

THIRTY-SEVEN

"Captain Heyward."

James looked up from Agnes at a gangly youth in the uniform of the Irish Guards and insignia of a 2nd Lieutenant standing ram rod straight at attention.

"Stand at ease, Lieutenant."

The change from standing to attention, to at ease, was almost imperceptible. "2nd Lieutenant Ronald Lidsay, Irish Guards. Sir."

"Please call me James."

2nd Lieutenant Lidsay looked puzzled.

"I'll call you Ronald and you call me James." He smiled. "Give it a try."

Ronald stared at James and rubbed his thighs.

"Go on, Ronald. For me."

"Yes, sir. I'll try as requested."

"Excellent. Now what is you want, Ronald?"

"GHQ asks if you could help out the Canadians at Vimy, sir. They have suffered serious casualties and are finding it difficult, almost impossible, to cope with the number of casualties. There is a Clearing Station at Agnez – les – Duisans, close to Arras, where the most help is required. I have transport waiting to take us."

"Transport! You want me to leave now?"

"As soon as possible, sir."

"But I have patients here who still need my help."

"GHQ was clear and very insistent, sir. You have an exceptional reputation in battlefield medicine, and it is felt we should assist our allies to the best of our abilities."

James understood this was a well-rehearsed speech, and that he shouldn't shoot the messenger. Orders were orders. He looked down at Agnes. She seemed to be OK and he'd ask Simon to keep an eye on her for him. "I'll be there in fifteen minutes. Wait for me in the transport. I know where they're usually parked."

2nd Lieutenant Lidsay snapped back to attention, smartly if not over elaborately saluted, turned on his heels as best he could on the boards, and marched out of the tent.

Agnes was smiling angelically up at him. "You have to go. They need you. I'm fine, and I'll be on a boat back home soon." She took his hands and kissed each of his fingertips. "These are too precious to just care for me." She raised his right hand to her face and wiped away a tear. "I will miss you, James, but God willing, you'll come through this and we'll be together again. We haven't survived all this not to spend the rest of our lives together." She smiled. "I know that ladies don't, but if you hadn't already guessed, this is a proposal."

He sat on the bed and lifted her hands to his face to stem the two rivers of tears which were streaming down it. "I will. And I'll come back for you."

"I know. Now go. I think that poor 2nd Lieutenant may be close to having a heart attack."

They looked deep into each other's eyes and started to laugh. Agnes prised her fingers from James and pushed him to his feet. "Go, I'll be fine."

What greeted James at Agnez-les-Duisans was worse than anything he'd yet experienced or could have possibly imagined. He was greeted by Colonel Robert Gough who took him on a quick tour.

"Glad you're here, Captain Heyward. I hope that 2nd Lieutenant Lidsay was …. let's say …." He smiled knowingly at James. "Reasonably communicative? Doesn't have the greatest abilities in the area of personal relationships, but on the battlefield he undergoes a miraculous transformation. Heart of a lion, and the men would march into hell and back for him. Hates the duties he has and wants to get back to the front."

James raised his eyebrows and smiled at Colonel Gough. "He was full of good manners and very helpful. Got me here in one piece, and I hope he gets another chance at the front."

"He will." Colonel Gough rubbed the stubble on his chin and frowned. "Unfortunately, I've seen his orders, and they're putting him in charge of a troop of tunnellers. I just pray that he's not claustrophobic." He paused, shook his head and smiled at James. "General Byng was very specific he wanted you. You must be very good? Things here have, let's say, been difficult. Do you know Vimy?"

"No sir, not really. I was aware of a planned offensive, but things are kept very close to GHQ's chest."

"Overall, the battle was a great success, the Germans were driven out and we now control Vimy Ridge. However, we are still dealing with its aftermath, and it's this I'm sure you can help us with. The injuries are what you will have already seen, but it's the numbers we're struggling with. There have been around eleven thousand casualties and four thousand killed." Colonel Gough put his hands on his hips and stretched his overworked painful back.

"I will do everything and anything I can to help, sir."

"Thank you James. I'll pair you up with Captain Le Chartrois. Jacques as he prefers to be called. He's from Quebec and speaks fluent French, although he will tell you what *he* speaks is pure undiluted French, unlike the bastard tongue which the locals in France speak. He's a good man and good at his trade. Now let's get you settled into a billet. I imagine that you haven't eaten much today?"

"No, sir. Just a few bits and pieces."

"Well, you'll be pleased to know our cook worked at one of the finest restaurants in Vancouver, and is a genius with Bully Beef." He laughed, put his arm around James's shoulder and walked out into the cold night air.

James's thoughts were still with Agnes. He wouldn't relax until he knew she was safely back in England.

THIRTY-EIGHT

Klaus was the first to come to the conference room. "Guten morgen, Guillaume. Wo ist Isaac?"

"He will be down in a few minutes. Good morning, Klaus."

"Good morning. Is Isaac still unwell?"

"He is OK. He has good days and bad days. Today is a good day."

"That is good news."

The door opened and Isaac, supported by Patrice entered the room. "Guten morgen, Klaus. Wie geht's dir?"

"I am well, Isaac. How are you?"

Isaac sat down in the chair next to Guillaume, on the opposite side of the table to Klaus. Patrice stood close to the door finishing his coffee and croissant.

"As they say in America, let's cut the crap and talk turkey." Isaac said.

"We should wait for the others." Klaus said.

"Of course. If you are in agreement, I propose that only the members of Papaver Rhoeas meet first, and when we have concluded our business we meet with Karsten, Sam and Elizabeth."

Klaus nodded in agreement.

"Good. Guillaume, will you chase up the others and tell Karsten, Sam and Elizabeth we will let them know when we have finished our formal business."

Guillaume stood up and left the room as Gilles, George, Ralph and Charles came into the conference room.

Isaac waved them to take a seat.

The group looked around at each other, nodding in greeting as they came to each member of the group. Isaac tapped his water glass with his pen and the sound brought everyone's attention and eyes to him.

"Friends, firstly thanks for coming at short notice." He slowly turned to his right. "And particular thanks to you Ralph. Boston to Brussels is no short journey."

Ralph nodded in thanks and silently waved his comments away.

"OK, to business. We have a number of things to determine over the next few days. Firstly, whether or not we invite Sam, Elizabeth and Karsten into Papaver Rhoeas, to replace Arnold and Edith in the UK and Helmut in Germany. Secondly, we must appoint a new Chef Charon." He paused sipping from his iced mineral water. "It is I'm sure no secret to everyone that I am terminally ill."

The bomb shell landed and had its desired effect.

A gasp followed by a deep sympathetic sigh ran around the room.

Gilles Vermeulen was genuinely shocked. "How long have you … have you known?"

"About six months."

"And how long have you … got?" The last words were lost in a tearful mumble.

"About the same. Six months, if I let it run its course, but I may take things into my own hands if life becomes particularly unbearable. This is why I have called us together, as I have no idea when bearable discomfort becomes unbearable pain."

George Mainard raised his hand. "What's the protocol for this? You are the first and only Chef Charon. What determines your replacement?"

"Thank you, George. I'll come back to that if I can and deal with new members first. Accepting new members is straight forward. We all to have see and accept they have the genuine abilities we seek and are prepared to accept the strictures and demands of a life in Papaver Rhoeas."

There were sounds of agreement from everyone.

"How do you propose we test them?" Klaus asked.

"I propose, with everyone's agreement, that tomorrow we go to Vimy and Langemarck."

Klaus tapped his pen on the table. "Langemarck I understand as a test for Karsten, however Sam and Elizabeth are not Canadian? They have no connection to Vimy or Canada, so we should test them at Tyne Cot. It would be much more suitable." Klaus looked around at the others, seeking and getting their agreement.

Guillaume came back into the room. "I have seen them and suggested they spend a few hours across the square at In Flanders Field museum in the Cloth Hall. I've asked them to be back for lunch."

Isaac smiled at his brother and tapped the seat next to him. "Excellent, thank you, Guillaume. My thoughts on the choice of memorials is that the next generation of Papaver Rhoeas need to have abilities beyond ours, and I believe they have these. I know so far as Sam and Elizabeth is concerned about their local skills, and Klaus has given me every assurance that Karsten has similar exceptional skills. Is that no so, Klaus?"

"Ja."

"So I believe that Karsten will make Canadian contact at Vimy and Sam and Elizabeth will make German contact at Langemarck. We will then have members who are not land-locked and can help others."

Hushed individual conversations broke out around the table discussing Isaac's proposal, which only lasted for a few minutes when it appeared clear that Ralph would be their spokesperson.

"There is some thought that we may be expecting too much of these people. We still need the help in each country, and there is a concern this could dilute that. However, our curiosity outweighs these concerns and we agree that Vimy and Langemarck should be used."

Isaac rubbed his hands together and nodded. "Excellent. I agree with your summary and suggest that any final decision isn't taken until we've all had sufficient time to assess their potential."

Ralph looked around the room at nothing but nodding heads. "We are in agreement."

An uncomfortable silence fell over the room.

Klaus broke it. "Firstly I believe we owe Isaac our eternal gratitude for his decades of leadership and commitment to our cause."

There was applause around the room.

"I would also like to propose we offer similar thanks to Guillaume. We complain every time he calls, but without his tireless work the group would have withered and died on the vine years ago."

The applause was as warm and genuine as it had been for Isaac. Guillaume bowed to the group.

"Gentlemen. We have an important decision to make. What do we want in our next Chef Charon? Most of it sits opposite me, embodied in Isaac."

Hands rhythmically tapped on the table.

"We are all Europeans. Apart from our north atlantic member." Klaus nodded to Ralph. "Members of the same united club, which has succeeded where the League of Nations singularly failed, and we all have connections to the Great War which singles us out as combatants. I believe that as a nation, Germany has established itself as the leading economy in Europe and has finally washed away the poison of Adolph Hitler. I also believe that I am the person best placed to name the next Chef Charon." Klaus looked around at nothing but shaking heads. "I also believe that you misunderstand my words. I am best placed to name Chef Charon as I have been with this group from the beginning, and I have also been trying to establish links with similar groups in Russia, who we should never forget suffered almost eight million casualties." He paused to let this sobering thought be digested. "Isaac often complains of my English. It is not my natürliche Sprache, so if you will permit me I will speak in German, and I'm sure that Isaac or Guillaume will translate for me. Then hopefully my words and meaning will be better understood."

Isaac moved in his chair. "I'm sure that I speak for everyone, Klaus, when I say we will translate. It is never easy to translate one's true feelings into another's language."

Klaus stood up. "Liebe Freunde. Ich schulde dir so viel zu Isaac. Und weil Zeit kostbar ist, werde ich kurz."

"Dear friends. I owe Isaac so much. And as time is at a … premium … I will be brief."

"Es ist nur eine offensichtliche Wahl, haben wir als Chef Charon."

"There is only one obvious choice we have for Chef Charon."

Klaus looked around the room at everyone, daring them to contradict him. "Dieser Mann. That man, is Guillaume Wouters."

Isaac started to translate but was brought up short by Klaus's conclusion.

There was stunned silence in the room.

"Does anyone disagree?" Klaus was still standing, arms crossed, daring anyone to speak against him.

"As I believe it is said at marriages, Jetzt sprechen oder für immer schweigen."

"Speak now or forever hold your peace." Isaac slowly translated through tears and a beaming smile.

There was silent accord in the room until spontaneous applause burst out led by Patrice.

Two hours later, Sam and Elizabeth hugged Guillaume and warmly shook his hand. Karsten patted him on the shoulder.

"Isaac saw the light then?" Sam asked.

Guillaume smiled and put his hands on Sam and Elizabeth's shoulders. "It was Klaus."

Sam and Elizabeth frowned at each other and then at Guillaume. "Klaus, surely not? I thought he wanted to be the new Chef Charon. That he saw it as his natural inalienable right." Elizabeth said.

Guillaume smiled again. "Even a leopard it would seem can change its spots." He squeezed their shoulders and grinned. "Even one of Germanic birth."

"But how? Why?" They said in unison.

"Isaac has the title, but it has been me with the unswerving support of Klaus who has kept Papaver Rhoeas functioning." Guillaume sat down on a sofa just outside the meeting room in an open area where lunch and coffee were about to be served. He patted the sofa beside him, gesturing them to join him. "We are a group of old men. Yes, committed to our cause, but nonetheless old, old and tired. We need fresh young blood to rejuvenate the organisation."

Sam looked himself up and down.

"OK Sam, maybe not quite so young, but I'm sure still very fresh." He smiled. "My role is now and has been for some time primarily logistical. I keep the wheels oiled and turning. Klaus may seem brusque, you know, a bit German, but he still possesses the greatest abilities, desire and energy of the group. Probably stronger than they were thirty years ago. The others are, well, without being rude, are getting, how do you British put it … a bit past it? But they are as dedicated today to Papaver Rhoeas, as they were at the beginning. Don't ever underestimate them." He stood up. "Come, let's get something to eat before the others smell lunch. Their energy may be less than it was, but their appetites and waist lines, are still pretty impressive."

THIRTY-NINE

Not long after breakfast Lidsay was back at High Wood. The back door must have swollen with the overnight rain as it jammed on the kitchen floor. He pushed against it and eventually it succumbed to his bulk. Despite having eaten three pieces of thickly buttered toast, a bowl of porridge, two croissants all washed down with two large mugs of sweet tea, he found that he just about had enough room for three cold sausages, crouching behind a gently quivering piece of overripe Brie at the back of the chiller cabinet in the fridge. He stood up from the kitchen table, walked into the lounge and sank into the Chesterfield staring at the door to the map room. He'd slept very little in the night as he tried to think of what the hell was going on at High Wood. Even in his fevered imagination he had to begin to concede that perhaps the twat's wife wasn't …. well …. dead. Despite this, his inner man prayed there was someone rotting away in the house. He'd never get another chance like this to piss on that cocky little bastard of a detective's chips, and if some innocent bystanders ended up as collateral damage, then so what. But where to look? He knew he couldn't rip up carpets and flooring. Well not yet anyway. So what would CSI Miami do?

Jane listened to the sounds coming from the kitchen. If it was a burglar, then he was making himself at home. She was still trying to come to terms with whatever the hell had happened to her. Had Sam spiked her food or cranberry juice? Unlikely. Her mind drifted back to the hall and the … what the hell had it been? Preservation of her sanity had blocked out most of the events of her last day at High Wood, but blurry glimpses, fleeting shadows and spectres of past events were labouring to prise open the padlocked doors of the cabinets of her memory. Everything after that last day at High Wood sat in her mind like pieces of a jigsaw with no box or picture. Agnes and James, the pain and suffering, the wounded mutilated and dying boys, Jack Morbeck, the singing of the Sherwood Foresters; '*If you get stuck on the wire, never mind And your face may lose its smile, never mind Though you're stuck there all the day, they count you dead and stop your pay If you get stuck on the wire, never mind*'. and Private Aston's head. The spectres prised the door open another inch.

Lidsay walked into the lounge, sat on the Chesterfield, undid the top button of his jeans and satisfyingly scratched his nether regions. "Why the hell doesn't she buy me trousers with zips?"

It was one of his pet hates, and Gloria knew it. Too many buttons, too tight and too short. She would always smile when she bought anything for his, *best kept covered*, leg department, as she knew Ivor would spend most of the day pulling up his unbuttoned trousers and then pulling them down again as they sat so fashionably two inches above his ankles, so delightfully showing off the Simpsons socks she'd bought at the same time.

"Bitch." He thought. *"I'm sure she does it deliberately to make me look a div at the station."* The creaking sound of footsteps on the stairs swiftly focused his mind back on the job. "Anyone there?"

"You fucking moron!" He silently screamed at himself. *"Anyone there? My God, what if it's Mr and Mrs Crippen, missed their flight, come home early and slept here last night? Good morning, sir, vicar. We had a report of a possible break in and as I was passing on my way to the station, I called in to check on things. Looks like the back door's been forced, but apart from them apparently having fed themselves, there doesn't seem to be any evidence of theft or vandalism. I'd believe that at a stretch."*

He remained seated, grabbed some paper from the coffee table, acted as if he was making notes, and looked at the open door.

Jane reached the bottom of the stairs and peered into the kitchen. The table was a mess of crumbs and spilt tea or coffee. Her natural instincts shouted at her to clean this up, but her greater overdeveloped nosey nature won. The hall was empty, but she sensed there was someone in what she remembered was the lounge, which was quickly confirmed by "Anyone there?" She looked around for anything which would serve as a blunt instrument, but could see nothing sufficiently threatening. She glowered at the open door to the lounge, girded up any loins she may still have possessed, and strode, almost confidently into the lounge.

Lidsay hadn't taken his eyes off the door. A sheen of sweat glistening on his bald head. "I am a policeman."

"Jesus, that's about as bad as 'anyone there'." He complained to himself. He stood up as he felt that this put him in a much stronger position, but a sudden panic loosened his bowels.

"You're not in uniform!" The panic increased. *"Think! Think for God's sake think!"* The muscles of his various sphincters prepared themselves for mass evacuation. *"I'm in plain clothes helping out CID while they've got two detectives on long term sick."* The muscles settled back into a slightly more relaxed state. *"Shit that's not too bad, and almost believable."*

Jane stood in the doorway of the lounge staring at Lidsay. Why was he looking past her at the door? Why did he look like he hadn't long climbed out of bed? She frowned, gazed at him, and walked up close to his face and blew at him.

Lidsay jumped back as a cold breeze chilled his face. *"Bloody draughty these old houses. Must have been the wind in the cracks moving things. 'Cause as sure as hell there's no one here."*

"He can't see me!" Jane lifted her hand to Lidsay's face, and it passed easily through it, like a glider through a cloud. She walked around him and prodded his back with her ring finger. It disappeared into him as if she was kneading soft dough. She was fascinated by what was happening, like a child who's been shown a magic trick by her Grandfather and is still full of wonder.

She stared down at her hands and gripped Lidsay's arm. It felt like soft marshmallow. She walked round to his front and could detect absolutely no reaction in is his face. She walked through Lidsay and sat on the Chesterfield, patted the cushions and found they reacted to her touch. The cushions which were flat and creased were now pumped up. She patted the arm of the Chesterfield and felt the cold of the leather.

Lidsay shuddered. "Shit, someone just walked over my grave."

Jane smiled. *"Don't know how close you are."* She thought.

He turned around, moved two of the cushions to one side, and sat next to Jane on the Chesterfield.

She leaned forward and playfully squeezed his knee. No reaction. She sat back and drummed her fingers on the arm of the sofa.

Lidsay's head flicked towards the sound.

"So you can't see or feel me, but you can hear me." The thought excited and also intrigued her. *"OK. So I can't interact directly with you,"* she stared at Lidsay's startled face *"but I can interact with things which you can see, feel and hear."* She looked down at the Chesterfield and drummed out a simple rhythm on the seat.

Lidsay's expression and blood froze.

"Getting a bit concerned are we? And by the way, what the hell are you doing in High Wood? Breaking and entering? Tut tut, everyone at the station won't be at all pleased will they?"

Lidsay stared at the leather seat as the surface moved in and out in time with the tapping.

Despite everything, Jane was beginning to enjoy herself. She got up from the Chesterfield, walked across the room to the book cabinet, took a copy of Pride and Prejudice, carried it back to the sofa, sat down, opened the book and started to read.

What Lidsay saw, was a book rise from a shelf, float across the room, settle down next to him, open itself and the pages start to turn. Everything screamed at him to run, but fear held a vice like grip on his muscles.

Jane dropped the open book onto the floor and gave Lidsay's knee another squeeze. The noise of the book regaining its attraction to gravity, released the padlocks from Lidsay's muscles and joints. He leapt up, ran across the room, tripped over the rug, crashed into the door, splitting his lip, staggered down the hall, fell into the hall table, wrenched at the locked front door, span around as he heard the sound of doors opening in the hall, scuttled back down the hall into the kitchen, looked back and fell over some low steps, produced a stream of expletives any experienced sailor would have been proud of, crashed through the open back door into the garden, fell into a tangle of brambles, improved his vocabulary of expletives, got up, looked back, fell over next door's cat and finally with tears in his eyes ran around the house to the relative safety of his car.

Jane sat down at the kitchen table convulsing with laughter as she heard Lidsay's car scream into life and speed off down the avenue. She sat at the table for a few minutes pushing the crockery around. The laughter subsiding as she came to the realisation that despite the fun she'd had with Lidsay, she couldn't be seen or felt by people.

The ginger cat from next door, still shaking itself from its meeting with Lidsay, ran into the kitchen and jumped onto the table. Jane put out her hand to smooth its long downy coat, and it passed straight through it. She rested her elbows on the table and pushed a plate to one side which spooked the cat. She watched it skid across the floor and out of the door. For the first time since she'd *returned* to High Wood, tears welled up in her eyes.

"So ... not just people. I can't ..." Tears spilled down her cheeks like early morning rain. *" ... I ..."* Sobs worked together with the tears to disrupt her thoughts. She took a couple of deep breaths and swallowed hard. *"OK Jane let's compose ourself and think calmly about what's happened."*

She walked back into the lounge, crumpled into one of the wing chairs and started to recall the last few days, weeks, or had they been months? Time seemed to have lost all meaning. She closed her eyes, held her face in her hands and pressed x30 on her mental rewind. When she reached Sam and the cleaners leaving the house she hit pause. She wanted to, needed to know what had happened, recall ... the ... She hit x6 and watched the replay.

The open cellar door, the yellow mist, the skin peeling from her hand, her scream, the cyclist, the numbing wet cold, the pulsating liquid mud, the surge of the river of mud, the open cellar door and the claustrophobic darkness.

"Isn't there supposed to be a light? Not dark?" She screamed in her head.

"Is this all there is after death?" She used the word for the first time. *"Christ, I'm dead? Is this Purgatory? Am I in God's waiting room?"* She felt more numb than sad. Strangely almost at peace, Jane looked up at the ceiling. "So what happens next?" There was no reply. "Just another part of Your great mystery?" Still no answer. She picked up a dusty empty wine glass and threw it against the wall.

"Feel any better now?" There was a brief pause.

"Yes."

"Well I can at least talk to myself." She thought gloomily.

Jane had left her replay on x6. An image materialised. Shaky, black and white, but it was easily identifiable.

"Agnes?"

FORTY

James collapsed like a well-loved rag doll onto his bunk. It had been fourteen hours since he'd slept, and he was utterly drained. He'd used up the last reserves of his adrenalin hours ago, and what was loosely called will power was all that had kept him on his feet.

"Du vin, James?"

Even James feeble French understood the offer. "Merci. Je, voudre, beaucoup. Sorry about the French, Jacques."

Captain Le Chartrois put the tumbler in James hand. "A bientôt."

James smiled. "Cheers." He raised the glass to Jacques and drained it of the excellent red wine. He stared in disbelief at the empty glass and held it up to be refilled. "Where did you find this? It's … C'est merveilleux!"

"Très bien, James. I'll have you fluent before this War is over. The wine is a 1920 Chateau Haut – Brion, Pessac – Leognan." He drained his glass and refilled both of them. "Chateau Haut-Brion was conceived and laid down at the beginning of 1533 by Jean de Pontac, which makes it the oldest wine estate in Bordeaux. Please don't ask how I came by this, petit trésor."

James simply nodded and took a little more time savouring the rare wine.

"You are exhausted. I will leave you to rest." He took his empty glass, without any resistance, pushed him down onto the bunk and walked outside.

James's sleep was deep and untroubled. Then his dreams began. Contented dreams of Agnes; a new home; a blissful marriage; four children, two girls, Emma and Poppy, two boys, Peter and Alan; balmy summer days; mists and carpets of rust coloured leaves; brilliant white hoar frosts; Christmas and peace on earth to all men. Dreams which transformed into nightmares of Agnes's burial; Jack Morbeck, an ungainly ambling corpse, dead eyes staring into the abyss of eternity, hundreds of needles stabbed deep into the bleached parchment like skin of his naked arms; horrendous scenes of human carnage; charnel houses saturated with blood, liquefied flesh and decomposing corpses hanging like putrefied washing on a rusted barbed wire line. The explosion close to his tent shook him from his bunk onto the floor, dragged him back to consciousness and the realisation that he'd moved from one nightmare into another.

"Captain Heyward!" Unknown arms helped him from the floor.

"Jacques?"

"No sir it's 2nd Lieutenant Lidsay." He fell flat on the ground dragging James down with him as an enormous concussion blew the remains of the tent away from around them.

"What the hell's going on, Lidsay?" James was shouting at the top of his voice. The concussion of the shells had deafened him.

"Sorry, sir, I can't hear a thing you're saying." He bellowed back, tapping his ears, shaking his head and raising his hands to where the tent should have been.

Any meaningful communication was going to be impossible, so James simply pointed in the direction of where the flap of the tent had been and ran for his life. They stumbled and ran through a hail of earth, canvas, metal, wood, blood and dismembered body parts. In the mayhem and confusion they became separated. James turned, looking for Lidsay and stumbled into a trench.

Deafness had been replaced by a piercing ringing in his ears, which was more debilitating than the deafness and considerably more painful. He stayed bent low as he got up from the muddy duck boards covering the bottom of the trench, and climbed down into the opening of a dug out. He looked around again for Lidsay, but couldn't see him anywhere.

Four soldiers emerged around the corner of the trench. "Can't stay here, sir. The Huns have started a major counterattack. We need to go." A shell landed close to the trench, and the dug out, and the four soldiers were blown apart. James was blown down the steps of the dug out, and only saved by the combined mass of the soldiers' dismembered bodies, which smothered him in a protective shell from the physical effects of the blast. But not the mental devastation it cleaved deep into his psyche.

FORTY-ONE

They travelled to Vimy in two Audi Q7's driven by Guillaume and Gilles. After about an hour they passed through the village of Thelus. Sam touched Elizabeth's arm and pointed at a road sign indicating they should turn left at the next junction to Foret Domaniale, Memorial Canadien and Canadian National Vimy Memorial.

"Canadian memorial?" Sam whispered to Elizabeth. "What the hell have we got to do with Canada? All our links are to Britain."

"They must know what they're doing." Elizabeth said.

Sam looked around the Q7. "Remember what Guillaume said." He paused and looked around again to check that no one was listening to them. "They're past it."

"Sam!" Elizabeth had forgotten to whisper.

Four surprised heads turned to look at them.

"Sorry everyone, Sam had fallen asleep on my shoulder."

After a few frowns, they looked back at the road ahead.

"Sorry, Sam, but that was uncalled for. I've never met such a group." She looked up. "They're, it's hard to find a suitable word. They're … glorious."

"Sorry, that was a little wide of the mark. But why are we at a Canadian memorial?"

Elizabeth took his hand and kissed it. "Whatever they've planned must have some sense and meaning. Let's just wait and see. It can't be too far now."

Within ten minutes they were turning into the car park of the memorial. Everyone gingerly clambered out of the Q7's, stretched and turned towards the memorial. Sam and Elizabeth were already transfixed on it.

Klaus put his hands on their shoulders. "Beeindruckende, Ja." They turned to face Klaus.

"Es tut mir leid, I am sorry. I find it is so much easier to slip into my mother tongue." He moved between them and pointed at the memorial. "It is impressive."

They turned and looked back in awe at the two towering white limestone pylons.

Sam was the first to speak. "Is this just dedicated to the Canadians who died at Vimy?"

"No. There are about eleven thousand names carved into the pylons, and the memorial stands as a tribute to all Canadians who served their country in battle and particularly those who gave their lives."

"How many?"

Klaus scratched his chin. "I believe there were about sixty six thousand Canadians who lost their lives during the war."

Elizabeth turned around. "Can we get closer?"

"Of course. Once the others have, stretched their joints a little."

Elizabeth and Sam walked ahead with Klaus and Karsten, and stopped about fifty yards from the memorial. The white limestone blocks of the hundred and fifty feet twin pylons silhouetted against the deep blue of the sky, were like sentinels silently guarding a now *peaceful* world.

"It's wonderful isn't it." Klaus had interlinked his arms with Sam and Elizabeth. "How much do you know about it?"

Sam shook his head. "Nothing."

Klaus pulled them close to him. "It took eleven years to complete and was dedicated in 1936 by Edward VIII. The dedication took place only three years before the madness started all over again." Klaus raised his eyebrows and shrugged. "It's made from six thousand tonnes of Yugoslavian, sorry Croatian, limestone." He briefly paused before carrying on. "The pylons, or as I prefer to call them the towers, represent Canada and France. It's about two hundred and fifty feet across at the base. You can't see them all from here, but there are twenty sculptured figures gracing the monument. The two you can see at the base of the steps, are mourners, a man and a woman. The most famous figure is carved from a single thirty tonne block of limestone and represents a brooding Canada watching over the graves of her dead. She is best known as the Weeping Woman. We will be able to see her at the front of the memorial."

The others by now had caught up with them, and were slowly walking to the memorial.

Klaus tugged at Sam and Elizabeth's arms. "Come or the pack will get there before us." He looked at them and smirked.

They walked around to the front of the monument and stood below the Weeping Woman, a cloaked and hooded figure facing eastwards towards the new day.

Isaac was sitting on the wall close to her feet.

Klaus looked up, his whole face beaming. "Ich liebe sie einfach. Sie ist großartig."

Isaac smiled at them. "He likes her."

Sam could understand his feelings. He'd never appreciated art in any of its forms, but this … it stirred emotions deep within him. It seemed as if an emotional tuning fork had been struck on his heart. He turned around to look for Elizabeth.

She was standing close to one of the pylons, her hands and face pressed close to the stone. Her entire body seemed to be trembling, and as Sam ran up the steps to her she shuddered and collapsed.

Klaus, Patrice and Ralph had seen what had happened and were quickly by Sam's side, who'd put her into what he thought was the recovery position.

Ralph knelt down and carefully adjusted the position of her arms and head. "Has she done this before, Sam?" He asked in a calm but obviously concerned manner.

Sam was transfixed on the prostate figure of Elizabeth.

"Sam! I need to know if she has ever had an episode like this before."

"Ummm … no … Not since I've known her, but that's only a few months at the most." He looked up at the group who were now surrounding them in a protective human shield.

Ralph checked her pulse and breathing and seemed satisfied that she wasn't in any immediate danger. "Karsten, check if anyone has any blankets or ideally some sort of wheelchair or stretcher."

"Should we move her?" Sam asked in a panic.

"Not wishing to use a hackneyed old phrase, but, trust me I'm a doctor." Ralph took his hand and gave it a reassuring squeeze.

"Everything points to her having had an epileptic fit, probably a grand mal. They're always very disturbing to see, but if we keep her comfortable then she'll soon recover."

"What was she doing when she collapsed?" Isaac asked.

Sam stood up, stretching his hips and knees. "She was leaning against this wall." He turned and pointed at the white wall, covered in the names of those Canadians who had fallen at Vimy. He walked closer to it and could clearly see the outline of Elizabeth's hands on the white limestone. They were either side the word Lieutenants and directly above the name J.W.Lester. Sam ran his finger through the carved letters, and stared at the name.

"Why you?" He thought.

"Sam, she's coming around." Ralph was supporting her head in his arms.

Elizabeth looked up hazily at the sea of faces above her and blushed. "What happened?" She was clearly still dazed and confused.

Sam sat on the ground next to her. "You gave us all a nasty scare." He said between deep swallows. "How do you feel? Has this happened before? Do you need any medication? When …"

"Sam, let her rest." Ralph had come to Elizabeth's rescue.

She sat up and rubbed the back of her neck. "Please help me up. I feel a lot better now."

With the support of what felt like most of the group, Elizabeth was helped back to her feet. She brushed herself down and straightened her hair.

"Come on, let's get you away from this." Sam was beginning to calm down, just a little. He wrapped his arm around her and turned to make their way up the steps and back to the car.

Elizabeth glanced to her right and her expression iced over. "Lester." The single word was murmured and barely audible.

"Elizabeth what is it?" Sam's relief was changing to concern.

"Lester, Letourneau, Lewis, Lane, Legros, Lickiss, Lindsay, Livingstone, Lloyd, Lodge, Lyons, Lindell, Logan … "

Klaus was listening closely to Elizabeth.

"Sam look at the wall. Look at the names."

Sam turned to face the wall.

Elizabeth continued. "Lancaster, Lanning, Latham, Laurie, Lawrie, Ledingham ..."

Klaus moved closer to the wall and pointed to each of the names Elizabeth was listing.

"Leishman, Lemon, LeRouge, Lewis, Little, Livingstone, Long, Long, Lowe, Luff ..."

Sam stood between Elizabeth and the wall, blocking her view, but the seemingly endless list of names continued.

"Lycett, Lydiard, Lynch, Lancy, Lark, Latimer, Latter, Lawlor ..."

"Klaus we've to get her out of this place. I don't know what's happening to her but it scares me. Please help me."

Klaus and the others in the group were transfixed by what they were seeing and hearing. They'd wanted proof of the abilities these newcomers possessed, but nothing had prepared them for this.

Sam moved around them, shaking them by the shoulders. "Patrice, please, Gilles, Isaac for God's sake, George, Charles." He stood back and screamed at them for help.

The litany continued. "Lawlor, Lawson, Leeming, Leger, Lemax, Lennox, Lewis, Linnen, Little, Lockett ..."

Klaus finally stopped tracing the names on the wall and came to help him. They took Elizabeth by the arms and helped her up the steps. The other visitors to the memorial watched as Klaus and Sam carried her back to the car.

"Lusier, Lyall, Lingford, Longley, Lydiatt, Lawson, Lindsay, Lund, Labelle, Laberge ..."

Sam had become desperate as he watched the woman he loved disintegrate into what could only be some form of psychosis. He only had one solution to restore anyone in this state to something resembling normality. He slapped her face.

"Sam, for God's sake you could make her catatonic." Ralph shouted.

"Sam?"

"Elizabeth."

She was softly rubbing her glowing cheek and smiling at him. "Did you slap me? Truthfully." She raised her eyebrows and tilted her head to one side.

He nodded like a child caught eating a bar of chocolate just before dinner.

"I presume you must have some good reason for *abusing* me. Is this what I can expect from a relationship with you?" She'd taken his hand and was examining his palm.

Sam lifted his hand to her face and gently tried to smooth away the raw red stain on her cheek. "I am so sorry but you were scaring me. All those names!"

Elizabeth took a few steps back from Sam. "Sam, how could I scare you? The last ... I'm not sure how long it's been ... is just a blank." She turned and looked at the memorial, and a strange expression started gathering on her face. Sam grabbed hold of her shoulders and turned her to face him.

She blinked and looked directly into Sam's eyes.

It was a look he'd never seen on any human face. A look he never wanted to see again. A look which seemed to concentrate all the anguish and suffering of humanity into one pair of staring eyes. He looked back at the memorial and suddenly felt what Elizabeth had connected with. The memorial, like a sponge, seemed to have soaked up the memories of all those lost souls whose names were carved into its limestone. Their tortured memories transmitted from the landscape, retrieved from the polluted soil and the blood stained earth, and collected by the limestone of the memorial. The raw emotion generated in the War to end all Wars by torture; indescribable agony; aching loneliness; burning hate; fathomless despair; unbearable torment; unending ordeal; slaughter and death, could not be neutralised by any of the countless of acts of heroism, sense of brotherhood, comradeship and the eternal love of those loved ones left at home.

Sam leaned back against the Q7 and studied the memorial. A realisation suddenly came to him of what it was that Elizabeth and he were tuned into. For him the memorial was some sort of twentieth century monolith.

Vimy was only one of a chain running across Europe transmitting distress signals from the lost souls of the Great War.

Klaus stood close to him understanding his expression. "Damit Sie verstehen?"

Sam turned back to Klaus. "I don't speak German."

"You now understand." He frowned. "It was not meant to be like this. Elizabeth will, I'm certain be fine. She has great strength."

"You should have warned us. Given us some inkling of what we could expect." Sam's fists were clenched.

The others arrived at the cars.

"How is she?" Guillaume asked anxiously.

"Not good thanks to you and your Papaver Rhoeas cronies!" Sam was livid. "You used us for your own ends. Why not tell us about this place. How long have you all known about this … this *Transmitter*?"

"Sam I understand your anger."

"You have no idea."

"Believe me I do. Please, come let's sit in the car. Elizabeth needs to rest and I need to give you an explanation. I promise that no one expected such a reaction from Elizabeth. In all the time of Papaver Rhoeas no one has ever responded in such a way." He paused as Klaus helped Elizabeth into the Q7. "She seems to have, I find it difficult to find the right word, seems to have, immeasurable, unlimited … Sam she has abilities which I've never seen. And I have seen and experienced many." He took his arm. "Now come, Elizabeth needs you."

"We should head back to the hotel." Sam was leaning across the back seat.

"Yes of course we will, Sam. We need to check Elizabeth over." Klaus pressed the button on the door and his passenger window silently opened.

"Guillaume!"

In the other Q7 Guillaume looked across at Klaus and opened his window. "What is it?"

"We're going back to Ypres. To the hotel."

"OK."

Klaus frowned a little but then smiled. "Gilles, let's get back to Ypres."

"We're going nowhere. I want to stay here. I need to understand what just happened." Elizabeth was sitting up at the back of the Q7, and her expression suggested she wasn't prepared to discuss it.

Klaus turned in his seat and spoke to her. "We need to get you away from this place. You can rest at the hotel. There is too much energy here and I don't want to expose you to any more risk."

"Klaus, I need to understand what just happened to me and going back to Ypres isn't going to do that." She pointed at the memorial. "I made a connection with that and I need to know why and how." She was clearly in no mood for discussion.

Klaus called across to Guillaume, who was watching them. "Elizabeth wants to stay. So, Chef Charon, what shall we do?"

Guillaume smiled and rubbed his temple. "Elizabeth, we can't stay here. At present, the power of Vimy is too much for you."

She frowned and started to speak, but Sam held his finger to her lips.

"Please let me finish." He pushed himself up in the car seat. "In time I'm certain you will be able to cope with the memorial, but not today. I suggest that we drive, only a few minutes, to the Memorial Park and the Interpretive Centre and give you, Sam and Karsten a little more understanding of what Vimy and the other memorials are."

Elizabeth grudgingly nodded.

Klaus tapped Gilles on the shoulder. "We are going to the Memorial Park."

Five minutes later they pulled into the car park at the Memorial Park. Guillaume retrieved a cool box and vacuum flask from the rear of the Q7 and distributed coffee and sandwiches to everyone. "There are toilets here if you need them." He said. "And given everyone's age and prostate condition, I'm sure you'll want to use the facilities."

Klaus raised his eyebrows and smiled.

Sam and Elizabeth gratefully accepted the coffee and quickly ate the BLT's the hotel had provided. Sam brushed the crumbs from his lap and put his and Elizabeth's styrofoam cups in a black bin liner.

Klaus was already outside. He turned, waved at Sam, Elizabeth and Karsten to join him. "Isaac is a little tired, so Guillaume and I will show you around and give you some more background information." He waved his arms around at the woods. "Follow me please." They walked a few yards through trees into an open gravel area, and from there they could see the preserved trenches.

"My God."

"Mein Gott."

"Shit."

"Yes, impressive isn't it." Klaus grinned at Guillaume.

"But how have they preserved the sandbags?" Sam searched through his pockets for his iPhone. He'd forgotten his camera but the new 5's camera was brilliant.

"During the construction of the Vimy memorial, they had to wait for the limestone, so the Major in charge of the project, I believe his name was Simpson, had the trenches rebuilt with sandbags filled with concrete. It helped prevent any natural damage due to the weather and undergrowth. What you see is a short section of the Allied and German front lines, with a few metres of No Man's Land between them."

They walked up the trenches to the Allied front line.

"If you climb up here you can see the German front Line." Klaus said.

Elizabeth was helped up by Sam, and quickly turned to Klaus with an astonished expression. "They were that close to each other! They can only be fifty yards apart at the most." She looked back and stared in disbelief at the narrow piece of land between the two front lines. "They could have spoken to each other!"

"They often did." Klaus said.

Elizabeth stepped down from the lip of the trench. "Sam, Karsten, you must see this."

Sam stood on a platform close to the concrete filled bags and stared in amazement at the space in which you could have played tennis.

"There are also tunnels here which are even more fascinating, but you have to book a guide and we don't have the time."

Klaus walked out of the trench and stood at the highest point of the Allied front line. The others followed him to the vantage point.

"From here you get a much clearer perspective of how they literally were on top of each other, and you can see how badly pitted the ground is from shell fire." He paused. "You must remember that the Western Front was pretty much like this for almost five hundred miles. He let this sobering thought hang in the air. "Anyone need the toilet?"

They were all grateful to be brought back to reality.

It was a strange thing that however much Sam didn't want to go to the toilet, as soon as *the toilet* was mentioned, his bladder demanded evacuation.

"Klaus when are you going to explain what happened at Vimy?" Elizabeth had taken his arm and was quite insistent.

"Not here. It's not that conducive."

"Then where the hell is conducive?" Elizabeth's mood and patience were strained.

"Elizabeth, I understand your frustration."

"Do you, do you really?"

"Yes, of course."

Elizabeth shot him a look which was abundantly clear in its message.

"My concern is for you, Elizabeth. I have never seen anyone so affected as you were at the memorial. I felt that a short break would be sensible. We still have a lot to see and do today, and if you are feeling OK." He took her by the shoulders. "Really OK."

She nodded.

"Then we should get some lunch at a restaurant I know close by. The Auberge De La Coulotte has excellent food, and after lunch, we will, I promise, answer all your questions. Does that sound OK?"

She nodded.

It was only a few miles to Souchez and the Auberge De La Coulotte. The atmosphere was welcoming and the staff attentive. After an excellent lunch of local cuisine washed down with several carafes of wine, Klaus, Guillaume, Isaac and Ralph ordered coffee in the lounge. They pulled enough well-worn chairs together, sipped their sweet coffees and began to explain how it all worked.

FORTY-TWO

Jane wandered around the house, touching, tasting and smelling everything. She sat at the kitchen table with a cup of coffee and an open packet of digestive biscuits. She'd decided to experiment a little, to understand what she could and couldn't do. Did she still need to eat and drink? Could she still eat and drink? She stirred the coffee and pushed the biscuits around the plate.

"Come on." She thought nervously. *"What's the worst that can happen? You are ... well you are aren't you, ..."* The word was difficult to use and admit its finality. "Either dead or passed over to somewhere or something I don't as yet understand." The words were whispered.

"Pick up the drink and eat the biscuits."

"But I don't feel hungry or thirsty, so what's the point."

"The point is, we need to find out everything we can about what the hell has happened to us."

There was a loud knock from the front door.

"Shall we have a little fun?"

"Let's."

She got up from the kitchen table and walked down the hall to the front door. There were two more loud insistent knocks, so she took a deep breath and slowly opened it.

George had been a driver for UPS for ten years and was used to people not being at home to collect their deliveries. He'd tried to deliver a parcel to Beech Tree, the house next door to High Wood, but the occupiers were out. He looked down at the electronic device which required him to get a signature confirming he'd delivered the package, heard the door opening and looked up ... at nothing. He took a step into the hall and looked around the back of the door.

"Anyone here?" He frowned, scratched his head, looked over his shoulder and peered back into the house. *"They must have left the door unlocked, and a draught's blown it open."* He thought.

Jane walked past or more accurately through, George and picked up the parcel.

He took a few steps into the hall. "Hello! Anyone here! I've got a parcel for next door!" It was the last package on the van and he didn't want to take anything back to the depot and risk losing a bonus. *"They never check the signatures anyway. Sign it yourself."* He thought.

He looked at the device and signed J. Morrison with his left hand. It looked fine, and anyone could have been at the house, couldn't they? He turned around to pick up the parcel. It was gone. He walked out of the front door, onto the drive and looked around the front of the house. "What the hell?"

Jane had walked back through him, lifting the parcel over his head as George was forging the signature. Smiling to herself she carefully placed the parcel halfway down the hall.

After finding nothing outside, George walked back into the hall. The parcel sat smirking at him. He stared at it in disbelief, looked over his shoulder again, grimaced, rubbed his temple with his index finger, sucked his teeth and sniffed loudly.

"Probably kids pissing about." He thought. *"Little bastards"*

"I know you're there you little buggers. You'd better stay hiding." But despite his comments, George couldn't help but smile. It was the sort of thing he'd have done when he was young. What happened next however was outside his normal sphere of experience.

Jane bent down, picked up the parcel, walked down the hall into the kitchen, put the parcel on the kitchen table and ran back into the hall to enjoy the show.

George was lying prostrate on the hall floor.

"Oh shit!" She ran to him and tried to give him cardiac massage, but her hands passed straight through his chest onto the hall floor. Reassuringly his chest was still rising and falling. *"*

Please, just have fainted!" She desperately thought.

She ran to the kitchen, filled a tumbler with cold water and ran back to the hall spilling water onto the hall floor. She stood over George and poured the water over his face. To her relief he gasped, sucked in two lungfuls of air, opened his eyes, sat up, looked down the hall, suddenly remembered the floating parcel, vomited and ran for the door.

Jane watched him disappear at a rate of knots out of the house and sighed.

"Not much fun, was it?"

"No."

"Bit immature wasn't it?"

"Yes."

"Need to have a real think about where and what the hell we are and what we're going to do. Don't we?"

"Yes."

FORTY-THREE

The counterattack had been repulsed with significant casualties, but Vimy Ridge remained in the hands of the Canadians. James, despite Colonel Gough and Captain Le Chartrois' entreaties, resumed his duties.

"Really colonel, I'm fine. Not a scratch on me, unlike those poor blighters whose dismembered carcasses saved my life. Where's 2nd Lieutenant Lidsay? We were separated in the mayhem."

"Lidsay's fine. He almost got what he wanted. He's been promoted to lieutenant, and is back at the front in charge of a platoon. Unfortunately, it's with a troop of moles. Tunnellers." He smiled. "Like any good soldier he took it in very good spirit." He frowned at James. "You, however, were found covered in the remains of God knows how many soldiers."

"There were four of them." James said quietly.

"A sad loss. Something like that may not have marked you physically, but I've seen enough men who've buried major mental wounds until it's too late to do anything for them. Take some leave, find Agnes, go to the coast, and get away from the front for a few weeks. You need to get over this."

"I need to do all I can for these men." He looked around pre-op at the shattered bodies. "There but for the grace of God and their comrades remains, would have gone I. I owe them a deep personal debt, which I aim to repay in full."

Colonel Gough put his hands on James shoulders, realising that ordering him to take leave, would probably do more harm than letting him stay. "One week and then we discuss how you are. That's all I'm prepared to agree to."

James started to speak, but Colonel Gough raised his index finger to his lips.

"This is not for discussion. One week, and we will talk again." He turned on his heels and marched out of pre-op.

James tried to speak again, but Jacques put his hand over his mouth.

"Accept the compromise. Personally I agree with Colonel Gough. You need time to recover. Not only from the dug out, but everything else which you've told me happened to you and Agnes. It must have affected you."

James sat down on a stool, dropped his head into his hands and wept.

Jacques wrapped his arm around his shoulders.

"Find Agnes and take some time together. In this war none of us knows what tomorrow holds, so if there is a chance, however small, of some love and happiness, grasp it with both hands."

James looked up, wiped away his tears leaving muddy streaks across his face, and nodded.

FORTY-FOUR

Lidsay drove as far as the nearest pub, and ordered a large vodka and Coke. At least Gloria wouldn't smell anything on his breath. He stared at the glass, wondering if alcohol had contributed to what he'd *seen* at the house. The vodka and Coke disappeared in two gulps.

"Bollocks! If it was the booze, then I'll be buggered if I'm going to give up one of the few pleasures I still have. Sofas that drum out a rhythm, books that float and turn their own pages, cold winds in your face and doors that open and close by themselves! What the hell is going on in that house? And where have they buried the body?

"Did I just say that out loud?" He thought.

The salesman, and his client at the next table, looked him up and down as if he'd spat in their beers. "Bit early to get in that state." The salesman said just loud enough for Lidsay to hear.

He looked them both up and down, opened a packet of pork scratchings, tossed two into his mouth, belched, and gently lifted one cheek and farted.

The salesman thought about making something of it, but the deal he was negotiating, wouldn't be helped by him scrapping with some drunk. He leaned across the table, whispered something to his client who nodded, and they both stood up, and moved to a couple of stools at the bar. There was a short conversation with the barman, and a lot of finger pointing. Even a novice in lip reading could make out "I'm sorry".

Lidsay looked away, and carried on eating his scratchings. He heard footsteps, but maintained his gaze at the table.

There was a polite cough, which he ignored, followed by a more insistent clearing of the throat.

"OK, time to apologise." He thought.

"Excuse me, sir, but you're not a regular here, are you? I like to keep a quiet house, and don't like my customers being upset, and annoyed, by, well it is a little early in the day, isn't it, sir." His tone could have etched his name into bullet-proof glass.

"I'm not drunk! This is the first drink I've had today."

"I've no reason to disbelieve you, sir. However, why don't you finish it and find another pub to fantasise in."

"I've every right to drink here." Lidsay was getting arssy.

The barman bent low so his mouth was only a few inches from Lidsay's ear. "If your ass isn't out of this pub in thirty seconds, then I and my other two colleagues, will assist you in your departure from this establishment." There was a short pause. "Now fuck off!" He stood up straight, pulled Lidsay's chair out from under him and pulled him up by his collar.

Lidsay's first thought was *"I can take him"* until he saw his two *colleagues* standing behind the bar. Either of them could have easily acted as a stunt double for the Incredible Hulk. Lidsay tried to shake the barman off his collar, but his vice like grip wasn't released, until he was rather brusquely helped to a seat on the pavement. He could hear laughter coming from inside the bar.

A group of women indulging their devotion to shopping, gingerly stepped around him, looked him up and down as if he was something that they'd just trodden in, loudly tutted and sailed off to the nearest store.

Embarrassment was not something Lidsay ever suffered from, but the glowing of his cheeks suggested to him that it might be sensible to make his way home. Gloria would be out for at least another three hours, so he'd have time to review the events at High Wood, and decide what his next actions would be. As soon as he got home, he made himself a strong cup of Builder's Tea, took a pack of Kit Kats from the fridge, walked into the lounge, and looked around at the scene of disorder.

"What the hell do you do all day, you lazy bitch." He shouted at the house. He pushed three magazines from his favourite recliner onto the floor, breathed a deep sigh and sat down. *Her* cat came in from the hall, and wrapped itself around his legs. He pushed it away, but it span around, and nestled its head into his calf.

"Piss off, you mangy bastard. I've had enough flea bites off you this year to last me a lifetime. Although your *mummy's* certain it's next door's equally mangy dog."

Lidsay picked up Waffles. *"What sort of bloody name is that for an animal"* he thought, and launched her up the stairs. "And bloody stay up there!" He was no animal lover. He looked around the room for any other possible disturbances and sat down again in his recliner.

"OK, Ivor, what do we do next?"

"It's impossible to report any of this at the station. That cocky bastard already thinks I'm an imbecile, and who'd believe me anyway?"

"So what do we do next?"

He pulled at the lever on the side of the chair and the footrest sprang forward. Another couple of pulls and pushes, and the chair was virtually a fully reclined bed.

"If that place is haunted, then maybe his wife's just ran off and refused to go back?"

"Have you checked his home?"

"Well High Wood is his home. Isn't it?"

"No."

"Where does he live then?"

"Need to find out, don't we."

This epiphany restored Lidsay's belief in Sam's murderous guilt.

"That's why I didn't find anything at High Wood."

"Lights coming on now are they?"

"The bastard did her in at home, and that's where she still is. He focuses all his efforts, and everyone else's attention on High Wood, while he's bumped her off and disposed of her at home!"

"So next action is?"

"Find his address from pretty much any database at the station I choose, and pay it a visit."

"And?"

"And. What?"

"And what about floating books?"

"Bollocks to floating books!"

"There's something in that house which despite everything, seems to keep dragging him and his tart back for more."

There was a long pause as Lidsay's cogs slowly turned.

"Shit!"

"Another revelation?"

"If they've seen what I have, and surely to God they must have, then it can only be something of real value that the old couple hid in the house. Given the time they spent there, Darby and Joan must have squirrelled it away somewhere they haven't found yet."

"Bingo! Give that man a cigar!"

"Whatever's in there, must be worth a fortune, otherwise why hasn't he put the house up for sale? There was one pretty much the same at the other end of the avenue I saw in the estate agents window, asking for offers in the region of six hundred and fifty thousand. So whatever's in there, has got to be worth more than that, hasn't it?"

"Oh yes."

"Oh yes indeed."

FORTY-FIVE

The journey from Agnez-les-Duisans, to the clearing station at Poperinghe, was uneventful but uncomfortable. James wasn't too concerned about the discomfort, as all his thoughts were on seeing Agnes again.

His welcome at the clearing station was warm and heartfelt. Private Tully beamed at him through a thick layer of blood streaked mud covering his face. "Good to see you again, sir. If you don't mind me saying, it 'aint been the same since you left."

"Excellent to see you, Tully. I've missed your laconic humour."

"La ... kon ... Sorry I never was much of a singer, sir?"

James smiled to himself. "Wouldn't say that, Tully. I've heard your rendition of 'Hanging on the old Barbed Wire'."

Tully smiled sheepishly. "I 'ave been known, now and again, sir, to tickle my tonsils so to speak."

James smiled. "Do you know where Sister Wilmart is, Tully?"

"Yes, sir she's 'elping out in recovery. They wouldn't let 'er into Resuss. She wasn't very 'appy about it I can tell you, sir. Strong willed lady that one, sir. No offence meant."

"None taken, Tully. I'll make my way down there and surprise her."

"And a very pleasant surprise I'm sure it'll be, sir."

James patted Tully on the shoulder and made his way to recovery.

Agnes had been tending the post op wounds of ten soldiers, and offering as much human kindness as she could, given the brief time she could spend with each of them. Five of them would be back at the front within a few weeks, two would be in wheelchairs for the rest of their lives, two were so badly disfigured, that simply getting them back into society would be a major task, and then there was Private Seldon who was slowly drowning in his own blood. In an odd way Agnes was happy that Seldon wouldn't recover from his wounds as he'd been literally ripped apart by shrapnel. James, she thought, wouldn't have put him through this and would have *helped him on his way*. She was sat with him, wiping his forehead with a damp cloth, his cough was getting worse and the red foam in his mouth had become a constant irritant.

He gazed up at her through dimming eyes. "Not ... long ... now ... miss." He sounded as if he was gargling as he struggled to speak.

"Until we get you home? No not long."

He grimaced at her in ever increasing pain and discomfort. "No ... Not."

Agnes had seen the gleam of life drain from a lot of suffering eyes and Private Aston's were thankfully beginning to fade. "Just rest now."

His body was racked and shaken with a juddering cough and fresh crimson blood began seeping from his nose and the corners of his mouth. He was desperately struggling to hang onto life, but the fight was almost over. His chest arched upwards, his head flew back, and Agnes and the bed were drenched in a deluge of blood which exploded from his throat. The struggle for life was over.

James saw her at the far end of Recovery. She was sitting with a soldier and seemed to be mopping her face with her apron. As he got closer, the full extent of what had happened became clear to him.

"My darling." He took her in his arms, soaking himself in Private Seldon's blood.

Agnes looked up at him, her faced streaked red and her hair matted with blood. "James!"

There were no more words. They weren't necessary.

Orderlies arrived to *take care* of Private Seldon.

James lifted her to her feet, and helped her out of Recovery into the fresh air. He sat down next to her on a bench made from crates, and softly wiped away the blood from her face. "Better get you washed up." He tried to smile, but nothing would come.

Agnes stood up and looked down at him. "Give me a few minutes. I'll wash and put some fresh clothes on."

He could see from her face, that she was still in shock, but now wasn't the time for platitudes. What she needed couldn't be provided here. He had to get her away from this nightmare before she was destroyed by it.

She was back in about fifteen minutes, looking clean, fresh, and deeply upset. She sat next to James and rested her head on his shoulder. "How can there be a God. How can He be merciful, when we see what we see every day? What sin had that poor young man done which demanded that his death should be one of so much suffering? He hadn't lived life long enough to have done so much evil." She started to weep inconsolably.

James let the violent emotions drain themselves from her.

Eventually she sat up, took his face in her hands and kissed him tenderly. "What next?"

He stroked her cheek with his finger and did his best to wipe away her tears. "Next, my love, is that we get as far away from this misery, and torment as we can." He lifted her up, and sat her on his lap. "I've been told to take three weeks' leave."

Agnes frowned at him. "Are you OK? What's happened?"

"Nothing really, just an accumulation of little things I suppose. I just need a break. Away from," he waved his arm at the clearing station. "All of this."

"And after three weeks?" She was close to tears again.

"Sssh. Let's not think about that now. Who knows what will happen in three weeks. We don't know about the next three minutes most of the time." He took hold of her hands. "And you, my darling. For you the war is over."

"Not if you have to come back. So long as you're here, my war can never be over." She stood up furiously shaking her head.

"It's not open for discussion. I have the papers which release you from active service. You are going home." James said.

She folded her arms belligerently, and scowled at him.

"Agnes, you can't argue against orders. When this is all over we'll never take an order again. We might hand out a few to our children."

Finally she smiled. "Children? And how many do you plan to have?"

"Oh." He stroked his chin. "Probably, six or seven."

"And is this after we're married or will all of them be born out of wedlock?"

James dropped to one knee.

Agnes gaped at him.

"Agnes Wilmart."

She half closed her eyes and grinned at him.

"Please, this is serious."

She took a deep breath and held down her rapidly developing smile.

"Thank you." James said in false seriousness. "Agnes Wilmart, I have loved you from the first time we met. I can't lose you or this love. These are difficult times, and we need to make the most of any rare joyful moments we're given." He took her hand. "Agnes will you make me the happiest man in France and be my wife?"

"Captain James Heyward, there is nothing in this world, or the next, that I would be happier to do."

They fell into each other's arms.

FORTY-SIX

Klaus, Guillaume, Isaac, Ralph and Gilles, had taken their coffees out onto the veranda, and were sat in the warm afternoon sun with Sam, Elizabeth, and Karsten.

Isaac leaned forward, nodded at Klaus, Guillaume and Ralph, who nodded back. "Firstly, on behalf of us all, our apologies for what happened at Vimy and Langemarck." He smiled at each of them. "We have never seen such reactions to these places, and it confirms that you will be important members of Papaver Rhoeas." He paused and drank some of his coffee. "So where to start? You know why we exist?" He looked around at each of them and Sam, Elizabeth, and Karsten all nodded.

"Excellent." He stretched his shoulders and sighed. "I will keep this as brief as I can." He gestured to Guillaume for some tablets.

"Are you OK, Isaac?" Elizabeth asked.

He smiled, took the tablets from Guillaume, and washed them down with the last of his coffee. "You deserve facts. Just facts. So, firstly … I am dying. To be frank, I don't know how long I may have left."

Elizabeth's face drained of any colour, Karsten tried to speak, but Isaac raised his hand. "We have decided as a group that Guillaume will assume the position of Chef Charon and handle the day to day management of Papaver Rhoeas. Klaus will lead our programmes in Europe and work closely with Guillaume as Co-Chef Charon." He smiled at Klaus. "Ralph will lead the US and Canadian operations, Gilles will develop our links with Russia, and offer assistance to the Rest of the World. We want Elizabeth and yourself, to lead the UK and Karsten to lead Germany, Austria and eastern Europe." He paused and asked Guillaume to organise some drinks.

"Let's start with Vimy. Why did Elizabeth react as she did? When it was built, Vimy was always meant to be seen by the general public as a place of remembrance and commemoration, but this was secondary. During the Great War, as you now understand, unimaginable horrors took place in these fields. The war generated vast amounts of discharged life energy of the men who died, and this drained into the earth. The founder members of Papaver Rhoeas discovered they were sensitive to these energies."

Two bottles of mineral water and a jug of coffee were brought to the table. Guillaume thanked the waiter, signed the receipt, everyone refilled their cups and glasses and Isaac continued.

"They discovered that in the fields were highly concentrated, interconnected areas of life energy, or Foci. Do you understand what Ley Lines are?"

Sam, Elizabeth and Karsten looked at each other, frowned and shook their heads.

"Ley lines, are places of alignment of geographical, and more importantly, historical interest. The concept originated with Alfred Watkins in 1921. He noticed on a field visit, that he saw, as he put it, 'like a chain of fairy lights' a series of straight alignments of various ancient features, like standing stones and hill forts. He also noted that many of the footpaths in the area seemed to connect from one hilltop to another in a straight line." Isaac stopped and looked at each of the newcomers checking that they understood what he was saying.

There was no dissension.

"The founder members also recognised that these ley lines acted as channels for the life energies, connecting the Foci. Foci were first detected at Thiepval, Tyne Cot and Vimy, and it was here that memorials were constructed. The architects were members of Papaver Rhoeas and incorporated design elements which stored amplified and transmitted the life energies through further ley lines to their home countries, where they were received by buildings and homes which sat on ley lines and acted as receivers."

Everyone smiled.

"Vimy bears a striking resemblance in its structure to a radio transmitter, and the curved Wall of Remembrance at Tyne Cot viewed from above looks like a radio dish." Isaac sat back in the chair, closed his eyes, rolled his neck and grimaced.

Klaus leaned forward, resting his elbows on the table. "Would you like me to continue Isaac?"

Isaac nodded slowly.

"When the verloren, the lost were killed, they didn't pass over. How could they? What was there to pass over? Their mortal remains had been blown to the four winds by shells; sliced into a thousand pieces by red hot shrapnel; drowned beneath liquified mud; reduced to smouldering ash by flame throwers; evaporated by mines or simply rotted and disintegrated, in No Man's Land. There was nothing to pass over. All that remained was their life energies. These memorials exert a pull on these drifting disparate fragments of human essence, draw them from the 'ley lines', filter and concentrate them in the Foci and re-assemble them into their unique human forms. To use the current terminology, their human genome. This is then stored in the memorial like energy in a battery to be transmitted to the buildings and homes in countries around world." Klaus paused and pointed at Sam, Elizabeth and Karsten. "Those buildings and homes where you my friends and all those like you, live and help them to their final rest."

Klaus stood up, drained the remains of his tepid coffee, shuddered and refilled his cup from the flask. "Is everything so far reasonably clear and understood?"

"I think I'm beginning to understand." Sam said with a deep frown.

"I'm starting to get the picture." Elizabeth seemed the most relaxed she had been for some time.

"Ich bin immer noch ein wenig verwirrt."

"Karsten, das verspreche ich, dass alles deutlich wird."

Karsten smiled and nodded.

Klaus turned to Isaac and the others. "So far OK?"

No one disagreed.

Isaac glanced at Klaus. "A good time to pause I think. Let's take a twenty minute comfort break."

FORTY-SEVEN

Jane found the only real change to her existence, life didn't seem to be the right word, was her inability to physically interact with any person or animate thing. She'd experimented with cats, dogs and a number of passer-byes. All with the same result. Not a hint or a glimmer of recognition of her being there, except when she picked up recycling bins and carried them to the other side of the road. She'd quickly decided that she'd enough proof and she didn't want to draw any more attention to herself.

Everything else remained the same. She ate anything she liked; drank everything, hot, cold or alcoholic; read magazines and books; watched TV and movies; listened to the radio; showered and bathed; cooked; pottered in the garden; slept soundly every night, although she had no memory of any dreams. She'd came to realise that she didn't develop hunger, thirst, a cross legged, tap dancing, bladder bursting need for a pee or tiredness. This was in itself good news, because she'd no idea where everything *went* that she consumed, or how she would have restocked the fridge and food cupboards. But even so, she enjoyed these physical acts and sensory experiences, which were reminders of a life once lived.

She was standing in front of the pretty much Mother Hubbard bare cupboards and fridge which didn't improve her mood.

"I wonder if he's sold the house." She thought. *"I haven't seen hide nor hair of Sam for, shit, I can't remember, and don't really seem to care."*

She picked up the last Kit Kat from the fridge and wandered into the map room. She'd been in there quite a few times, but until now she'd not really paid any attention to anything.

"If I can't get a response from anybody, then I won't be able to communicate with anyone face to face or with a phone." She held her face in her right hand and squeezed her cheek. *"Mmmm? However."*

She walked over to the computer, sat down, pulled the chair forward and hit the power button. Arnold's convenient password reminder gave her quick access to the computer, she moved the cursor over the email icon and clicked the left mouse key.

"User Name and Password required."

"OK. Password must be the same as the one I just used." She picked up the Post-it note and typed, Arnold1234.

"Now your user name." Jane drummed her fingers on the desk.

"User name is pretty much always your email address. So, given that this has opened in BT Yahoo, your email must be, a.morbeck@btinternet.com. The screen disappeared and was replaced by a BT Yahoo home screen. Jane moved the cursor to the email icon, paused and then hit the left mouse key.

"OK. New message." A blank page appeared on the screen and she hit the Contacts icon.

"You must be in here somewhere."

She scrolled through the names until she found Sam and pressed enter. The cursor blinked over the empty page. "So what are you going to say? Sorry I haven't been in touch, dear, but I've been back to the Great War; joined with the soul of my long dead Aunt Agnes; been through hell and back; astrally projected from Agnes and the Great War back to this house; frightened the shit out of an obnoxious policeman and discovered that I'm probably a ghost." She smiled to herself. "Pretty accurate, but maybe just a little too much information for now."

She shuffled the chair forward and started to type.

Sam and Elizabeth were walking in silence in the gardens of the restaurant, sipping something a little stronger than coffee. They sat down on a cast iron bench close to a bed of delphiniums.

"Want to go home?" Sam scratched his ankle where he'd been bitten by one of the local insect population.

"You'll make that septic if you keep on scratching it." Elizabeth chided.

"Thank you, Mum. So, want to go home and forget all of this?"

Elizabeth finished the last of the Sauvignon Blanc and stared at the empty glass. "I've spent twenty five years in the ministry and in all that time I've never experienced anything as spiritual as I did at High Wood." She kept staring at the glass. "I've never felt as gratified as I did when that soldier passed over. Passed over because of me." She carefully placed the glass on the gravel by the bench. "If I'm able to do that only once more then I'll feel my life has been worthwhile." She took his glass and drank the remains of Sam's Merlot.

"So that's a yes?"

"Mais oui, monsieur."

"Bon."

Jane handed Sam the empty glass, stood up and did the closest thing she could to a tap dance. She stopped and looked at Sam who was frowning. She sat sheepishly next to him and tenderly took his hand. "And what about you, Sam?"

He took his hand away from hers, crossed his arms, closed his eyes and deeply sighed.

"Sam?" Elizabeth was nervous. "Sam, what is it?" She held her breath.

"I feel the same as you."

Elizabeth noisily breathed out.

"But?"

She held her breath again.

"At my age do I need this? Do I need this responsibility? Isn't anything we do just a drop in the ocean?" He uncrossed his arms and turned to face her. "You don't need me to do this. You have the gift. Not me."

Tears were welling up in her eyes.

"The only part I have to play, is that I had a relative who died in World War One, who had a relative who had a house which I now own. It's hardly a spiritual link is it?"

Elizabeth sat closer to him. "OK so what about all the things which happened at the house? And please don't say they were all flashbacks. I believe the reason we work so well together is that you can enter their reality and their time. You bring them to me." She held his face close to hers. "You have a connection with these poor lost souls. Whatever it is doesn't matter a toss, but what's important, is that you have it and they need that connection to bring them at last, back home."

Sam kissed her nose.

"Listen, if we draw an analogy to what Klaus just told us, then you're sensitive to their transmissions and can somehow enter portals which they can use to find me at High Wood, and I help them to pass over." Elizabeth said.

Sam was clearly not entirely happy. "So what happened at Vimy, if it's me that's the sensitive one to their *transmissions*?"

Elizabeth had been thinking about the events at Vimy and thought she understood what had happened. "How did Klaus describe it, that these memorials attracted, focused, amplified and transmitted these forces. These memorials are warehouses packed to the rafters with lost souls desperately struggling for a way to pass over. If, as I believe, I am their conduit to the other side, then at Vimy, they were fighting for my attention." She kissed him again. "Sam. It's more proof that what I believe is true."

He sat back on the bench, mulling things over in his mind.

After what seemed to Elizabeth like an eternity, he turned again to face her.

"OK. We'll do it."

"Is that it?"

"Is there anything more?"

She smiled, stood up and did another less than impressive impression of Ginger Rogers.

Sam took his iPhone out of his jacket pocket, swiped it to on and checked his messages. Nothing. He stroked the email icon. Twenty six unread messages. He started at the oldest and worked his way up the screen. They were mostly spam until he came to the most recent email, and the subject struck him dumb.

Subject – For latest news on Jane – Read on.

FORTY-EIGHT

Agnes and James spent two blissful weeks at a London hotel. When they weren't making love, they took in several shows, did all the sights and visited relatives of James in Wimbledon.

They were stood outside Westminster Abbey, contemplating where to have lunch.

"Why not try the Ritz?"

"At their prices."

"To hell with it, I'll be going back in a few days and it is, as they say, only money."

Agnes turned away from James, took a handkerchief from her pocket and dabbed at her eyes.

"My darling I'm so sorry. I wasn't thinking."

"It's … it's." Agnes struggled to speak.

James took her in his arms and did his best to comfort her. "This time it will be fine. I've been appointed head of surgery at a base hospital in Boulogne. My days at the front are over."

"Really? No more Vimys or action?"

"None. They want me to use my skills to ..." He paused and looked at the slow moving surface of the Thames.

"James?"

"Sorry, I'll be creating programmes to ..."

"James what is it?"

"I'll just be sending them back as cannon fodder. More grist to the mill and more carrion for the rats and crows."

"But you'll be away from the front. You'll be safe."

He carried on studying the ripples in the river's ever changing surface.

"James, I can't lose you. I won't lose you."

They leaned together against the Cathedral railings holding hands.

Agnes broke the silence. "James, promise me you won't go back to the front. I know it's a lot to ask of a soldier, but when this war ends, as it will, we can rebuild a normal life. Without you I've no future."

Her expression told him she was sick to her stomach with fear that she could still lose him.

He raised his left hand and placed his right hand over his heart. "Agnes Wilmart I solemnly promise that I will not expose myself to danger, stay well away from the front line, avoid the enemy at all costs, always change my underwear and," he lowered his hands and took gently took hers, "promise with all my heart that I will come back to you."

Two days later they said their goodbyes in their hotel room. It was hard enough coping with her own private anguish, and she couldn't face a railway station, as it somehow concentrated the emotions of the milling crowds into one great ball of grief which sucked the life from everyone.

They'd agreed she should take up a nursing post in England, and Agnes had made enquiries and been accepted at Newton Abbott's Seale Hayne in Devon. She'd read about a cure for shell shock which had been developed there by Arthur Hurst, an Army Major. She'd seen so many cases in France where it was seen as a sign of emotional weakness or cowardice, and in the some terrible cases, shot for cowardice. She was aware of the current harsh treatments of solitary confinement, disciplinary treatment, electric shock treatment, shaming, physical re-education and emotional deprivation. But what Hurst was doing in Newton Abbott, seemed to offer hope and understanding, leading to a possible cure.

Three days later, she arrived at Exeter station at around five o' clock and was collected in an ambulance driven by a young hospital porter in his early twenties.

"I'll pop your bags in the back here, miss. No other passengers today."

Agnes left her two suitcases on the road and climbed into the passenger seat.

"Been over in France, miss?"

"Yes."

"What was it like?"

"You've not been?"

"No, miss." He looked embarrassed and stared straight ahead at the road wishing he hadn't raised the subject.

"Why's that?" Agnes sounded interested rather than inquisitorial.

"I'm a Quaker, miss. We're pacifists. I had to go up before a board of enquiry and they were satisfied my beliefs were genuine, so I was excused duty. I've done everything I can to support our boys. I started here about three months ago, and before that I was working at the docks in Bristol. I haven't been shirking, miss. I would have loved to have gone, but God demands that we do not make war."

Agnes smiled at him. "What's your name?"

He blushed. "Sorry, miss. Franklin, miss. Franklin Quincy."

"Well Franklin, I'm Agnes Wilmart, and France was hell."

"Hell, miss?"

"Hell Franklin. I've seen things which no one should be expected to see. You may think you've missed the *show*, but believe me this has been a *show* I would want no one to see."

Silence fell as Franklin decided Agnes didn't want to refresh any memories buried deep in her psyche. They drove the rest of the way to the hospital in silence. He parked the ambulance at the entrance gate to Seale Hayne, took Agnes's luggage from the back of the ambulance, helped her down from the cab and nodded his head for her to follow him.

They entered through a short tunnel at the base of an imposing tower into a large quadrangle. The buildings which made up the four sides were two storeys high, made from red brick with vivid green ivy clinging to the mortar. A tall man dressed in a plain black suit, white shirt and blue tie stood at the bottom of the steps of the entrance. He was clean shaven with piercing blue eyes, swept back greased black hair and a smile which played at the corners of his mouth. He stepped forward and offered his hand to Agnes.

"Welcome to Seale Hayne Sister Wilmart. I am extremely pleased we were able to bring your knowledge and expertise here to Seale Hayne." He was quietly spoken, with an underlying positive tone.

"Thank you, but who am I speaking to?"

"I am so sorry. Arthur Hurst, I run this establishment." He shook his head in embarrassment.

"Major Hurst. You're the main reason I wanted to come to Seale Hayne. To observe and learn your techniques for shell shock."

He seemed even more embarrassed and kicked at the gravel on the quadrangle. "Please call me Arthur. I try to keep things here as informal as possible." He stepped forward and picked up her cases. Franklin tried to take them from him.

"That's fine, Franklin, I'll show Sister Wilmart to her quarters."

Their feet clattered on the wooden floors of the hallways as they passed wards and closed rooms with frosted glass windows.

"I'll give you the full tour tomorrow. Dinner will be at around eight thirty in the main dining room." He stopped and opened double doors into a large wood panelled room with high windows, where a long highly polished mahogany table was set up for dinner.

Arthur turned and waved his arms around the room. "It's not too far from your room and as you can see you'll be able to meet just about everyone."

Her room was small but cosy, well appointed, and importantly her own. She took out the few photographs she had, placed them carefully on the bedside cabinet, picked up the photo of James, and kissed it affectionately.

"Well it seems very nice here, my love. I'm having dinner with most of the staff in about an hour. I'll write every week and have these little conversations with you every day. I pray you keep your promise to me and that the Archangel Michael wraps you in his arms." She kissed the picture again and lay down on the bed with it held tightly to her breast.

FORTY-NINE

Despite everything which had happened at High Wood, Lidsay's avarice and belief that there was buried treasure somewhere in the house, easily overcame his innate spineless fear. He finally talked himself into it, with the thought that if whatever it was at the house wanted to harm him, then why did it just want to read a book to him? Probably just a bit lonely. Thoughts of any dismembered wife had long since disappeared and been replaced with a 'Get out of Jail Free' card which he planned to use, as soon as he'd decided which part of the world would suit him best. He parked in his usual spot about two hundred yards from High Wood, walked past the house a couple of times to check if anyone was at home, and finally walked down the path to the front door. He decided that he'd at least make it look like he was trying to speak to someone in the house before breaking in again through the kitchen door, and knocked loudly, rang the bell, stood back, looked at the house, shook his head and walked down the side of the house.

Jane sat up in bed. She never seemed to feel the need to sleep, but just lying there and reading Patricia Cornwell was still a very pleasurable experience. She slid out of bed, and looked down at herself. She hadn't at any time thought about what she was wearing. She walked to the dressing table, bent down, and looked at herself in the mirror. What she saw made her stumble back and sit on the floor. She looked about thirty. And despite having spent the night in them, her clothes were immaculate. "How … " She touched her face. "This is … " She ran her fingers through her now long blonde hair, and frowned at her reflection. "How? … If I'm dead, then how am I … " She stroked her cheeks and gently touched the corners of her eyes. *"Death becomes her."* She thought and started to smile. "I was quite a nice bit of stuff. Shame no one can see me." She looked again at her clothes. *"Handy that."* She thought. *"At least there's no washing and ironing in the after life."* She stood up and sat on the edge of the bed. "Why can't anyone see my clothes?" She pictured in her mind Claude Raines in the Invisible Man, walking around in a suit, with his face covered by bandages. They could see his clothes, so why couldn't they see hers?

"He was still alive." Her conscience suggested.

"Could be." Jane replied. "So everything that's directly in contact with me becomes part of me?"

"Seems a reasonable conclusion."

She hopped off the bed, patted herself down and padded a short way down the landing in bare feet. The knocking and ringing had stopped, and Jane contemplated going back to bed to finish 'The Bone Bed'. She leaned back against the wall considering what to do, and it gave under her weight. She turned and looked at the depression she'd made in the wallpaper, and tapped around it with her knuckle. It was hollow. She stood back and looked up and down the landing. Her bedroom door was on her right, the middle door was a bathroom and the next door another bedroom. The far door opposite the stairs, she hadn't investigated. She looked up and down the doors on the left. There was a door on the far left, one in the middle and the depression she was standing in front of, directly opposite her bedroom, where a door should be.

Jane looked up and down the wall. Surely there had to be a blocked up door behind this? And behind any door has to be a room.

"Bit of common-sense please, Jane."

"Mmmm?"

"Do we really want to find out what's in this room."

"Mmmm?"

"Someone believes, and has taken the time and effort, to make sure that this door stays hidden."

"Mmmm?"

"So what do we achieve by opening it?"

"Could be there isn't anything in there to be afraid of. They may have wanted to stop anyone getting in. Thought of that?"

"Mmmm?"

"There are so many peculiar things in this house, the odds are that it's probably something they wanted to keep locked away like some mad relative."

Jane ignored her conscience. "So how are we going to get past this?" She pointed at the wall.

"Probably something in that shed in the garden?" Her conscience had conceded defeat.

Jane made her way quickly down the stairs, through the kitchen and into the garden.

Lidsay reached the kitchen door and found it wide open. Despite this meaning he had quick and easy access to the house, it disturbed him. Had some other opportunistic burglar decided there had to be something in the house worth nicking. He walked softly into the kitchen and listened closely for any noises. Nothing, the house was as quiet as a mute mouse.

"Where to start?" He thought. *"Where would you keep anything of value? Not downstairs. Too accessible. Upstairs? I've not really taken a good look at the bedrooms."*

He ambled into the hall, walked up the stairs, and decided to start at the door furthest away from the stairs. Halfway down the landing, he stopped and mentally counted the doors on each side.

"Odd." He thought. *"Why no door on the far right."*

As he reached the far end of the landing he had his answer.

"Bloody thing's boarded up. What are you devious bastards hiding?" He thought. *"What have you got squirrelled away in there?"* He kicked the wall and almost broke his toe.

"Shit, ass and bollocks!" He hopped around the landing, stopped, swore a little more and stared at the obstacle in his way.

"Wouldn't need much to break through that." He thought. *"But no bloody tools!"*

He turned, walked down the stairs, out of the kitchen, quietly around the side of the house and out to his car. Home wasn't too far, and his tool box waited for him there. As he pulled away from the kerb, an unseen yellow tool box floated down the garden, into the kitchen, up the stairs, across the landing and crashed to the floor as it slipped from Jane's hands.

FIFTY

Elizabeth looked at Sam. "What is it?"

He turned the iPhone to face her.

She took it from him and visibly paled.

Subject – For latest news on Jane – Read on.

"What does it say?"

Sam carried on staring at the ground shaking his head.

"Do you want me to read it?" Elizabeth asked.

The ground continued to hold his attention.

"Sam?"

He slowly nodded his head.

She opened the email and started to read it out loud.

"Sam and friend."

She paused looking at the words and wondering what tone they'd been written in.

Sam finally looked up from the ground at Elizabeth. "Problem?"

"No it's nothing." She carried on reading.

"You may, or more likely not, have been wondering where I was. Where to start? I suppose the first thing is to say that I'm pretty sure I'm dead."

Elizabeth dropped the phone.

Sam knelt on the floor, picked it up and carried on reading the message.

"Sorry to drop it on you like this but to be honest I'm not really sure what I am. All I can really say is that it's complicated. But I can tell you where I am. High Wood. Some knob of a policeman was around here. Although I'm not sure if he'll ever be back. Sam, we've both known that whatever we once had ended a long time ago, and in my present state it's most definitely over. Please come to High Wood so that I can try to understand what the hell's going on. When you get here come to the room with the map, stand next to the computer and I'll let you know more. Please bring your friend with you. At least one of us deserves a little happiness. Sam, please come. Jane, Remember Desperado."

Elizabeth was staring at Sam's expression. "What do you think?"

He shook his head and carried on staring at the message.

"Sam!" Elizabeth prodded him in the ribs.

"Mmmm?"

"The email, what does it mean? Is somebody just trying wind us up?"

"It's from her."

"You're sure?"

"Certain. Only Jane would know about Desperado." He produced the deepest sigh Elizabeth had ever heard.

"Desperado?"

"In the early days we had some odd conversations, and one of them was what music we wanted at our funerals". He smiled remembering what had been good times. Times which had quickly soured like week old milk, and the resulting yoghurt, their relationship, had left nothing but a sour taste in the mouth. "I decided while everyone was milling around making small talk I'd have Song for Guy, you know, Elton John, and as my casket was being wheeled out of the chapel of rest, the Intermezzo from Cavalleria Rusticana."

Elizabeth frowned.

"It was used as the theme for 'Raging Bull'."

She nodded.

"As everyone was leaving the chapel at the crematorium, the grand finale would be 'Always look on the bright side of life'. You know, Monty Python, 'Life of Brian'."

Elizabeth smiled and nodded. "Very memorable. And Jane?"

"Yes, sorry, Nessum Dorma, Nimrod and", he stopped and noisily sucked his teeth, "'Desperado' by the Eagles". He stared at the iPhone. "No one else could possibly know that. No one! We need to get back and find out what the hell's going on".

Elizabeth turned his face to hers. "Sam, if it's Jane then we have a lot to think about, and we need to finish things here before we jet off to Cardiff. We owe that to Isaac and the others. Don't we?"

Sam released another stomach wrenching sigh, but then smiled. "You're right. If it is her, then she does at least acknowledge that our so called marriage is over".

Elizabeth looked deep into his eyes. "Sam you knew her for a long time and if you have any feelings of loss, then it's OK".

He held her face, tilting it up for him to kiss. "Any feelings I had for Jane disappeared I can't remember when. If I have any feelings left for her then they're only contempt and disappointment for the wasted years".

She tried to speak, but he put his index finger gently on her lips.

"I understand your faith tells you to forgive, and I'm happy to forgive Jane for most things, but how can I forgive her for a lost life". He pressed a little firmer on her lips. "However, for you, I forgive her everything". He took his hand away and raised it above his shoulder. "I swear by whatever you hold sacred".

Elizabeth smiled at him. "Let's go back to the others, take the time we need to finish up things here and take our scheduled flight tomorrow".

They stood up and walked arm in arm to the restaurant.

FIFTY-ONE

Time passed quickly at Seale Hayne. Agnes closely observed Arthur's treatment sessions learning his techniques for shell shock. The soldiers exhibited so many different symptoms that Agnes had difficulty understanding how Arthur could have developed one central treatment for hysteria, anxiety, paralysis, limping, muscle contractions, blindness, deafness, nightmares, insomnia, heart palpitations, depression, dizziness, disorientation and loss of appetite. The anger she felt developed for the ignorance of the British high command, the officer class and a high proportion of the British public, who saw shell shock as a sign of emotional weakness or cowardice. She'd heard from Arthur of those who had been charged with desertion, cowardice and insubordination. The many stories of those who on their return home were treated as deserters and made to feel nothing but shame, appalled her.

Arthur's pioneering methods were humane and sympathetic unlike the accepted techniques. The main work was occupational therapy, labouring in the Devon landscape and stimulating creative techniques. The soldiers produced a magazine with a gossip column called 'Ward Whispers', and Arthur had reconstructed the battlefields of Flanders on Dartmoor to help the men relive their experiences. Above all, the men were treated with dignity and humanity.

Agnes was sat with Arthur in his office where he'd set up a projector. He had the foresight to film his techniques so that others would have the proof they demanded.

"Unfortunately the press have dubbed me the *Miracle Worker*." He was carefully feeding film into the projector. "But what I want to show you does rather support that epithet." He finished setting up the film, drew the curtains and started the projector.

The film ran for about ten minutes and showed the treatment of Private Percy Meek who'd been driven almost mad during a massive bombardment on the Western Front. The images of Private Meek, who'd regressed into a baby-like state and was sat in a wheelchair, distressed her.

Arthur squeezed her shoulder. "It's OK, Agnes. Percy has that effect on everyone."

She watched as Private Meek gradually recovered , and finally could be seen walking and laughing with Arthur in the grounds of Seale Hayne. "As you can see, he recovered the majority of his faculties." Arthur opened the curtains.

"Miracle's a good word." Agnes said.

Three months later Agnes was drinking coffee with Arthur in his office.

"I've got a new case which I'm sure you could take the lead on." He smiled. "What do you think? There's no pressure to do this. You're doing a marvellous job for me and I don't in any way want to compromise that, but you have something which sets you above the others, and these poor souls should benefit from that. So are you ready for a challenge?"

Agnes stood up, took a step back, and frowned at Arthur.

"Is that a yes?"

She drew a deep breath and spoke almost in a whisper. "Are you sure?"

"Agnes I knew almost immediately when we met what you would be capable of."

She drew another deep breath and looked across at him. "Yes I'd like to do it?"

"Grand. Go down to ward three, meet me back here at about three o' clock and let me know what you've learned about this man."

Agnes stood up and turned to leave, but as she reached the door she turned. "Can you tell me anything about him?"

"He was found buried in a collapsed dugout. They think he'd probably been in there for about three days." Arthur stood up and walked from behind the desk. "Agnes he was buried with what they estimated to be the remains of eight other soldiers who'd been killed when the trench took a direct hit from a German shell. He was catatonic."

Agnes's face showed the shock and sadness she was feeling.

"Don't worry, he's not dangerous. Far from it. Just visit him and let me know what you think. No more than that."

She stood in silence for a few seconds and then with some trepidation, made her way to ward three. She spoke to the sister in charge who told her that the captain was in a private side room, and that she shouldn't be shocked at anything she saw. She entered the small room, where the bed was perfectly made, the creaseless sheets crisply tucked under the mattress and the pillow showing no impression of a human head. In fact the room seemed to be unoccupied.

She walked out of the room into the corridor and called to the sister. "There's no one in here?"

The sister said only three words. "Under the bed."

Agnes pointed down and the sister nodded. She nervously walked back into the room, and looked closely again at the bed. There was no sign or evidence of life, so she dropped to her knees, crawled to the side of the bed, bent down close to the floor and peered at the dark space under it. It was difficult to see anything in the dim light, but after a short time she could just make out the shape of a man's back huddled against the wall. Her neck and back were aching so she sat back on her haunches and stretched her legs.

In times of stress Agnes had the habit of singing to herself. She quietly started to hum 'Keep the Home Fires Burning', got up from the floor and sat on the bedside chair. 'Keep the Home Fires Burning' was followed by 'Pack Up Your Troubles', 'It's a Long Way to Tipperary' and 'Never Mind'. The last song bringing back sad memories of France. After half an hour she decided she'd have to go back to Arthur and admit that she failed to achieve anything. She stared at the bed and started to talk. "Who are you? What in God's name did you suffer in that pitch black tomb with those other," she couldn't find the right word, "… men. Someone somewhere's missing you." She felt an unquenchable sadness spread over her.

There was a brief muffled sound from under the bed. "I miss someone."

Agnes felt goosebumps race all over her body.

"I can tell you about the soldier I miss if you like."

There was a sound of springs moving.

"His name is James, and we plan to get married after this nightmare is over. Do you have a sweetheart? "

A pale hand appeared from under the bed.

Agnes caught her breath. Was this what Arthur meant he thought she was capable of?

"What's her name? Mine's Agnes, what's yours?"

The hand became a forearm.

"My love is a Captain. He's a surgeon. What do you do?"

A shoulder emerged.

"You're in a wonderful place."

The shoulder slowly disappeared back under the bed.

"Don't talk about Seale Hayne." She thought.

"I want to start a big family with James, and create a new generation and start replacing the one we're losing. Do you have a large family?"

The shoulder reappeared, and Agnes could see that the unknown soldier was wearing a grubby blood stained vest.

She swallowed hard. "I haven't seen James for about four or five months now, although it feels a lot longer. I haven't had a letter for about six weeks." Her thoughts drifted away to France. She sighed and looked back at the bottom of the bed. The back of a head was now visible. A head with only wispy strands of hair, covered in the angry red scabs of healing abrasions.

She swallowed hard.

Two hands were now clawing at the floor pulling itself inch by inch from under the bed. When the upper torso was clear of the bed the body began to slowly rotate, and as the face gradually became visible, Agnes's face screwed up into an expression of horror, and she collapsed onto the floor in a dead faint.

The face was Captain James Heyward's.

FIFTY-TWO

It took Lidsay half an hour to find the tools he needed in what he liked to call his *Gloria Hole* in what at one time had been the garage. Gloria took little interest in what he was doing, offered him a cup of coffee and shouted at his back as he left that she would be at the Bingo whenever he got back.

Twenty minutes later he was back at the High Wood, unsure what the neighbours would think about a stranger walking around the house with a set of tools. But, *"Sod it."* He thought.

Jane tore the wallpaper from the blocked door, and the wood which she could now see, was only hardboard and was simple to rip off. She stood back and looked at what was still to be done. Two bolts were screwed into the door and locked it into the frame. The topmost bolt was rusted and wouldn't budge. She rifled through the tool box and found a tin of WD40, and after a few squirts of the miracle oil, the bolt slid back with enough resistance to show that it wasn't going to give up without a fight. She sprayed the remaining bolt and left it for a minute to let the WD40 work its magic. As she slid the second bolt back, the door seemed to sigh in relief. She held onto the handle, turned it, pushed it and pulled it, but it wouldn't move.

"Keys! Shit where did I leave them?" She thought for a few seconds. "Hall table? No. Shit what did I do with them?" She slapped the door, and a light came on. "Map room."

As she was turning, she looked back at the door and noticed that screwed into the bottom was a cat flap. "Inside the house?" She stared at it, frowned, and made her way downstairs to the map room.

Lidsay was happy to see the kitchen door still open, as the weight of the tools was burning his shoulder. He dropped them noisily in a heap on the kitchen floor, scratching the tiles.

"I'll take another look at that door and see what I need before I cart this lot upstairs." He thought.

Half way along the landing he thought his eyes were playing tricks on him. In the middle of the landing was a pile of torn wallpaper and ripped sheets of what looked like hardboard. He stared at the pile and scratched his stomach. "How the …?" Had the loving couple come back and decided it was time to collect the loot from the room? "Don't be a knob." He chuckled to himself. "Their car wasn't parked outside." He kicked at the hardboard. "Still … gift horses and mouths." He gripped the handle and pushed. Nothing. Pulled.

Nothing. The stream of expletives he produced would have embarrassed the most experienced builder or football fan.

"Bastards have already come, gone and locked the door! Shit! Shit!" He punched the wall grazing his knuckles, and then threw his not insubstantial bulk against the door. He bounced back and screamed as he aggravated an old shoulder injury. The boot was next to try its luck. This time a repaired achilles tendon came close to rupturing. He hopped, limped and rocked back and for in agony like a demented Irish dancer, and fell on his back in the opposite bedroom. His mood and nervous state were not improved when a bunch of keys floated down the landing, stopped opposite the door, turned over a few times until a key was selected, inserted into the lock and the door opened. The keys floated into the darkness of the room and the door closed.

Lidsay's overriding demand for getting the hell out of it, was just about overcome by greed and an insatiable curiosity, which his mind reminded him, had killed the cat.

"Bollocks. Let's take a look." He thought.

The room was in pitch blackness. Jane tried the light switch close to the door, but nothing happened.

"Back downstairs then. I'm sure there's a torch in the kitchen."

Lidsay's hand was hovering over the door handle when it turned and the door began to open. This time greed comfortably lost, and he ran back into the bedroom on the other side of the landing. He put his ear to the door, but could hear nothing. He dropped to one knee and squinted through the keyhole. He was directly opposite the *other* bedroom and could see the door now wide open, but no sign of anyone or anything else. Greed began to win again.

Jane was frowning and staring at the pile of tools on the kitchen floor. "These aren't mine. I took them upstairs didn't I?" She sat down on the edge of the table and scratched her head. "They were in the tool box." She smiled for a moment, and then scowled as she wondered who'd dumped them here. "They're not mine and they weren't there before I went back to the shed."

The scream from upstairs instantly gave her a clue as to who's tools they were.

She ran for the stairs and in a few seconds was standing outside the open door. She peered into the darkness but could only make out barely discernible outlines, which the torch quickly turned into shape shifting shadows. She walked in and shone the torch slowly around the room. The decor, furniture and fittings were at best spartan, bare floorboards were partially covered by two worn patterned rugs, a faded blue armchair sat under the window, a single bed with no headboard was tight against the far wall, the sheets were stained and grubby, the flat pillow could have offered no comfort or support, a small table and wooden chair, had been fixed to the floor in the centre of the room, the window was covered by a blackout blind, a doorway had been built between the bedroom and the central bathroom, there were no drawers or cabinets and Jane realised that there were no mirrors or pictures. She opened the door into the bathroom, and the condition of it was very similar to the bedroom. A chipped sink which had no plug or taps, a cracked soap dish with a sliver of what at one time must have been a bar of soap, a badly stained toilet with a wooden seat she wouldn't have risked sitting on, the door to the landing had been nailed to the frame, there were no towels, flannels, sponges or mirrors and the bath had a deep black scum line. This was no luxury apartment. And who'd screamed?

FIFTY-THREE

Through a torrent of tears, Agnes stared at the bearded face which she knew so well. Despite his dreadful appearance, it was definitely James, but his eyes were lifeless, hollow and vacant. She wanted to take him in her arms, but something told her any sudden movements would send him scurrying back into his sanctuary under the bed.

The door to the room opened. Arthur stood on the threshold, wide-eyed, staring at the bed. "Are you OK, Agnes?" He was visibly shocked. He'd hoped that she would have an effect on this patient, but never to this degree. "Agnes, Agnes look at me." He whispered.

She turned her head towards Arthur, but her eyes remained fixed on James. "I … I … know him." She sobbed. "I … love … him"

James' eyes followed the direction of Agnes's head, and as he saw Arthur he rapidly retreated back under the bed, like a tortoise into its shell.

Arthur took Agnes's arms and helped her to stand. "Come with me. There is nothing we can do now for some hours."

She stared at the dark space under the bed and wondered what had caused this. She leaned on Arthur and walked slowly with him to his office.

"Please drink this." It was a small glass of brandy. "Now take these." She swallowed the tablets not knowing what they were, but trusting Arthur's clinical judgement that she needed them. "And now drink this slowly."

He handed her a cup of hot sweet tea.

They sat quietly for five minutes while Agnes sipped the tea recovering from the shock of seeing James.

"Agnes, do you think you can talk now?"

She looked up and nodded.

"OK. So please take as much time as you want, and tell me all you can about this man."

Over the next hour she told Arthur everything they'd experienced together in France, the horrors of the casualty clearing stations, the bombing and destruction of the barn, the shelling, being buried, No Man's Land, the rats, Seldon, Jack Morbeck, the indescribable slaughter, the second bombing, the list went on and on.

Arthur made notes of everything she told him, filling in the mostly blank sheet of Captain James Heyward. "Agnes I understand how difficult this is for you, but the more we understand about Captain Heyward, the easier it becomes to penetrate his private reality and bring him back to ours." He paused and put down his notebook. "Would you like any more tea?"

"Thank you yes."

Arthur looked into the tea pot and called to his secretary for a refill. "And a few biscuits if you can find any." He smiled at Mary, who'd been with him for ten years. "Thank you. Agnes, I need to be completely open and honest with you. I did know his name and had learnt about the relationship he had with you."

Anger flashed across her face. "How dare you take advantage of me!"

"Agnes, I won't try to justify ..."

"How dare you. How dare you use me like that!" She was incandescent.

Arthur sat silently for five minutes while she fumed at him, but eventually she seemed to run out of steam, sat down, crossed her arms and glowered at him.

"Agnes, I am so very sorry, but I never had a case as bad as James and I needed you to see him without any preconceptions of his condition, or who he was. Your deep personal connection would have coloured the way you reacted." He pulled his chair around the desk closer to her, and she started to stand up. "Please let me speak." He opened his arms to her and she sat back in the chair. "For the first time today he came from under the bed of his own volition. He came out for you. The bond you have is strong. Stronger than any I have ever seen. Strong enough, I believe, to bring him out of this catatonic state. What concerns me more is how you've survived as much trauma as you have without any apparent mental scars?"

She uncrossed her arms and smiled at Arthur. "I had help from a friend."

What Arthur couldn't possibly know, was that Agnes had survived the horrors of France, because, she'd possessed the combined strength of two women's will power and life force. Herself and Jane.

"She's gone and I'm on my own now." Agnes smiled at Arthur who understood she didn't want to discuss this any further. "I have scars," she continued. "and they're buried very deep. One day they may burrow their way to the surface, and then I'll need help, but now James is my concern. Do you know what happened to him after I left him in France?"

"They will burrow their way out." He thought. *"But I'll be there for you when they do."*

"Let me fill in the gaps," Arthur said, "about what happened to him. He was in Boulogne for about two months at a base hospital, and was due to come back to England, but was asked, as a personal favour to General Craig, to make one last trip to Ypres to try and save his son who'd been badly wounded."

"For his son?"

"Yes, James was a close personal friend of General Craig and had been to school with his son Edward."

"But he should have been coming home!" She said between angry sobs.

"Agnes I understand your frustration and anger, but you knew James better than anyone."

She nodded.

Arthur looked caringly at her. "He would have gone willingly. Do you want me to go on?"

She nodded slowly.

"On his way to Ypres, he stopped to treat a Tommy who'd broken his ankle after dropping a tin of petrol on his foot. After strapping it up as best he could, the other soldiers in his troop asked James to join them in their dugout for a brew. He was pretty close to Ypres so he didn't feel he could turn down their offer."

Agnes put her hands to her face.

Arthur paused.

"Carry on."

"As they were drinking their tea the Germans started a counter attack. James was well behind the front line, but the shelling was aimed to hit the support lines behind the front. That's really all I know other than our troops held their positions and pushed the Germans back, but it was some hours after the fighting had stopped that a sergeant noticed there was a crater where his dug out had been. It took them eight hours to dig him out, but he'd been buried for almost three days. What remained of the others was covering the floor, walls and ceiling of the collapsed dug out. They collected what they could of them and buried them in a mass grave. James was catatonic. When they lifted him out of the dugout he had a blanket over his head, and when he arrived here, an orderly took it from him. He dived under the bed, and has been there ever since. He eats, drinks and, well does everything under the bed."

Arthur could see Agnes was finding this very difficult to listen to. "Let's take a break and meet again tomorrow morning to agree what we do next for James."

Agnes nodded.

Arthur hugged her and kissed her forehead.

She walked slowly back to her room, fell onto the bed, and eventually fell into a deep disturbed sleep.

FIFTY-FOUR

Elizabeth was worried about Sam. Since they'd rejoined the others, he seemed distant and disconnected from them. "Sam." She touched his arm.

"Mmmm?"

"We're going to Langemarck. Klaus wants to see how Karsten reacts to the concentration of German dead at the cemetery."

"Mmmm?"

She held his arms and gently shook him. "Sam. What's the matter with you? Come on, we're going to Langemarck."

"Sorry, yes, Langemarck." He stood up and walked to the Q7.

Elizabeth watched him walk away and shook her head.

On the drive to Langemarck, Sam sat in silence focussed on something distant and remote.

As they neared Langemarck, Karsten became increasingly agitated.

They stepped out of the Q7's and stood in silence close to the cemetery.

The cemetery was a sombre scene, but unlike the British and French cemeteries, there were no visible headstones or crosses. All that could be seen were what looked like concrete slabs set into the grass, and at the far end of the cemetery the statues of four mourning figures.

Sam was the first to speak. "Where are the headstones?"

Klaus stopped close to him. "There are no headstones because after the War the Belgians were, let's say less than willing to give up land to the German enemy. So it became necessary to erect shared graves." He paused and swallowed deeply. "What today we call mass graves." He waved his arms towards the cemetery and frowned. "They take up less space." He sighed and pushed his hands deep into his pockets.

"Mass graves?" Elizabeth's expression was one of shock.

Klaus stretched his shoulders. "Elizabeth you have to remember that at the end of the First World War we Germans were persona non grata in Belgium. We were justifiably hated for what we had done to their country and their citizens. A lot of atrocities were carried out during the War and most of their towns and villages were reduced to rubble. The German Army and nation were regarded as, Kinder des Teufels, Children of the Devil. Any thought after four years of war of surrendering *any* land to Germany for *any* purpose, was understandably an anathema to them."

Klaus led the group into Langemarck, but Isaac remained in the Q7 with a few of the older members who by now were very tired.

They stopped in front of an oak panel which listed the names of the German soldiers buried at Langemarck.

Elizabeth stood close to it examining the long lists. She turned her head to Klaus. "How many are buried here?"

Klaus had been pointing out certain names on the panel to Karsten. "Entschuldigen sie mich Karsten."

"Natürlich."

Klaus took Elizabeth gently by the arm and led her into the cemetery, followed closely by Sam. He pointed at a large concrete slab set into the grass. "In this 'Comrades Grave' are buried about twenty five thousand German soldiers." He pointed at a set of brass plates. "Their names and regimental insignia are carved into those panels."

Elizabeth stared at him in disbelief. "In this single grave are twenty five thousand men?"

"Twenty four thousand, nine hundred and seventeen to be precise." Klaus said quietly.

Elizabeth shook her head and stared at the concrete slab. "So many in such a small space."

Sam was scanning the cemetery, to where small crosses were dotted around. "What are those?"

"They don't signify burials. They are just symbols."

They walked silently around the cemetery examining the small flat stones set into the grass.

"These are?" Elizabeth asked.

"These stones mark the graves of German soldiers. In each are eight." Klaus was looking over his shoulder for Karsten. "Have either of you seen Karsten?"

Sam turned to Klaus and pointed to an original blockhouse along the north wall of the cemetery. "I'm pretty sure I saw him go in there."

They ran across to the blockhouse, the sound of their feet echoing loudly in the empty space. At first they could see nothing as their eyes adjusted to the dim light. Elizabeth was the first to spot Karsten. He was crouched in a far corner like an airline passenger locked in a brace position. They tried to move him, but he was paralysed, petrified into stone.

"How do we move him?" Klaus said desperately to Sam and Elizabeth. "Bitte helfen sie mein sohn."

Sam raised his hands to the ceiling. "I don't understand."

"Es tut mir leid, I am sorry." He was almost in tears. "Please help my son!"

Sam exchanged a quick glance with Elizabeth "He looks like you did at Vimy. How are you?"

"Fine, but you're right, Karsten looks ..."

"... Looks like you did?" Sam finished her sentence.

"Don't know how I looked, but he looks a lot like I was feeling." She said.

Klaus was hugging his son. "Verzeih mir. Ich habe Sie zu weit geschoben." Tears were streaming down his face.

Sam bent down close to Klaus and Karsten. "Klaus, we need to get him medical help."

Klaus continued rocking back and forth. "Mein Sohn was hab ich dir getan?"

Elizabeth firmly but tenderly lifted Klaus up and looked into his eyes. "Klaus, Klaus."

He looked at her desperately through clouded eyes, reddened by tears.

"We have to get Karsten out of here and to medical help." She looked at him and nodded.

Klaus took several deep breaths and tried to smile at Elizabeth. He took out a tissue, wiped his eyes and noisily blew his nose. "Ja, you are right. I must control myself and think only of Karsten."

They looked down on the collapsed body of Klaus's son. Elizabeth and Sam took hold of him under each arm while Klaus lifted his feet. The others in the group rushed across to see what they could do to help. Those in the Q7's could see the activity and as *quickly* as they could, made their way to the cemetery gates.

By the time they reached the cemetery gates, Karsten had regained consciousness. He was staring at the sky and constantly rubbing his fingers across his palms. Klaus sat down next to him and gently touched his shoulder. "Karsten?" He touched his shoulder again. "Karsten?"

His son turned his face to his father and frowned. "Es ist kein Platz. Sie sind zusammen wie die Sardinen in der Dose verpackt. Sie hatten keine Ruhe. Seit hundert Jahren hatten sie keine Ruhe!"

Sam stared in confusion at Elizabeth. "What did he say?"

"I've no idea."

Guillaume who was standing close by touched them on the back. "He said that they have no room. No space." He paused, the meaning of the words striking him like a sledgehammer. "That they … that they are like sardines in a can. That they haven't been able to rest for a hundred years."

FIFTY-FIVE

Jane stepped back into the bedroom and closed the bathroom door, behind which was a cowering Lidsay.

He'd been stood next to the table when a torch floated into the room. His memory of his last visit and floating books sent him flying in terror behind the bathroom door, where he was still curled in a twitching ball of fear. In his innermost thoughts he started to pray.

"Dear Lord, I have not led a blameless life, but I'd like to live it a bit longer before entering your Kingdom, if that's what you've decided for me. I swear I will start working for charities, I'll go to church. Whichever is your personal favourite. I'd rather it wasn't the Mormons as I don't really have much disposable income left over at the end of the month. If there's anything you have a preference for then please send me a sign. Only nothing too frightening. Just an email with some ideas would be great."

He'd watched as the torch floated into the bathroom, illuminated the bath, toilet and sink and after a few breathless seconds, floated out of the room. He was glad there was a toilet close by, but wasn't too sure about whether any bodily matter would be flushed away by the stained decaying plumbing, and the prospect of exposing his nether parts to the cracked heavily discoloured toilet seat helped him recover control of his bowels.

Jane took one more brief look around the room and decided, that tomorrow, she'd open the blinds and the shutters, and examine the room in daylight. She left the bedroom door open, and decided to go down to the lounge and listen to the news on Radio 4.

Lidsay watched as the light disappeared from the room leaving him in total darkness, feeling like a victim in a Freddie Kruger nightmare. He cautiously stood up, listened one more time, and stepped back into the bedroom, which now was partially illuminated by the light from the open door. What he could just make out sitting at the camping table vented all bowel contents.

A woman dressed in a luminous white medical gown with ties at the back, exposing a bony spine, was scratching at the table with her nails which were breaking off and bleeding. Her greasy white hair was matted to her head and her bare feet caked in dirt.

Lidsay stood motionless, paralysed to the spot. She was sat with her back to him and he prayed to all possible deities that she wouldn't turn around and see him.

The lady in white stopped scratching the table, and started drumming a repetitive rhythm on the table with her bleeding fingers. Lidsay tried desperately not to gag from the stench of the contents of his bowels which were coating most of the tail of his shirt, jacket, trousers, underwear, shoes and socks.

The drumming stopped and the woman's head slowly with a grinding sound turned on its axis until her face was staring directly at Lidsay.

"She can't see me." He despairingly thought.

"Jack, is that you?" The voice was hollow, like someone talking into an empty bucket.

"Don't answer. For fucks sake do not open your mouth. She can't see you!"

"Jack, I've been waiting for you. They told me you were dead, buried somewhere in Belgium." As she stood up the joints in what once had been her body cracked like jumping jacks. "Have you seen your father?" Her question was full of despair. It was a desperate cry for help. "He didn't come home. They couldn't find him."

Lidsay had a few options. Faint, vomit, scream, have a chat, die or run like hell out of the door. There was only one feasible option. He tore out of the room leaving a trail of excrement behind him, virtually fell down the stairs, slithered across the kitchen floor, crashed into the kitchen table, got up and tripped over the neighbour's cat which attached itself to his leg with its claws, screamed and fell headfirst into the walk in fridge, limped out of the back door, stepped on a slug and fell face first into a rose bed. He stood up carefully removing thorns from his arms and legs and hobbled to his car.

Jane heard the commotion as the cat howled and Lidsay screamed, but by the time she reached the kitchen all that remained of whatever it was, was a swinging kitchen door, the kitchen table on its side, a smear of blood on the fridge door, a pile of broken flower pots, flattened roses and an appalling smell from what was most probably a blocked drain. She closed the kitchen door, locked it, poured half a bottle of bleach down the sink, took a lemon yoghurt from the fridge and went back to the lounge to listen to Eddie Mair and the Prime minister debating who was responsible for the crisis in the prolonged rail workers strike.

FIFTY-SIX

Agnes was still fuming. How could Arthur have abused her trust and regard for him so badly. To take advantage of her like that. To expose her to the shock of seeing James like he was. Over the months she'd seen many shocking cases of shell shock, but nothing like James was suffering from.

"I shouldn't have left you my love?" She thought hopelessly.

There was a soft knock at her door.

"Agnes."

It was Arthur. "Agnes, please listen to me. I need to explain to you."

There was an icy silence.

"Agnes I know that it was unforgivable what I did."

The permafrost got deeper.

"I believed, and obviously I won't know for some time, but I truly believed, and still do, that his reaction to you might be the trigger which started him on the long road to recovery."

The winds whistled across the steppes.

"I understand your anger so I'll leave you in peace. But please, I implore you, work with me, and we can get the man you know and love back from the abyss. Sleep well and I'll see how you are in the morning."

As Arthur turned away, the door opened few inches and he could see Agnes's tear filled eyes.

"You believe that you can cure him?"

Arthur smiled. "Cure isn't a word I like to use with this condition. But yes, I believe we can help James confront his personal demons, send them back to hell, and give you back the man you love."

The door fully opened. "Arthur I'm sorry please come in."

He hugged her and kissed the top of her head. He wasn't jealous of James but he could understand how that disturbed man had fallen so deeply in love with this extraordinary woman. A love which he was convinced would be the trigger to his recovery.

Later the following morning, Agnes was back in James's room, silently waiting for him.

James lay in the cloying dark, aware of nothing but the constant concussion of the shells obliterating men and machines.

"We stay here."

"Mmmm"

"We stay here."

"Mmmm"

"We stay here."

The circular conversation continued in his brain as it had for the last two months. His brain locked in an impenetrable self defence shield, made of six inch tempered steel. There'd only been one disturbance. A sound, a resonance of things past, a chink in the armour, a glimmer of light in the bleak murky blackness. It was fleeting, a passing moment of recognition, a whisper which momentarily evoked the likeness of a face. A faded silhouette.

"We stay here."

"Mmmm"

"We stay here."

"Mmmm? What if?"

"We stay here!"

"Captain Heyward." A different crack in the cocoon. "Captain Heyward."

"We stay here. Do not answer. Don't give us away."

"Captain it's Jack Morbeck."

Deep in James's brain a minute but discernible crack began to repair itself.

"We stay here!"

"Mmmm? What if?"

"Dear God. We stay here!!"

"Captain, the boys and me wanted to help. Seeing the bother you're in. Only way is to dig you out. Can't do it yourself. Can you?"

"We stay here!!"

"Mmmm? He wants to help."

"Dear God. How many times. We stay here!!"

"Captain, we're going to start digging. It's going to take a little time as you're buried pretty deep and we don't want to start another collapse. Just hold on in there and we'll have you out as quick as we can."

"Mmmm? He wants to help."

"We stay here!!"

"But they've started."

"Captain Heyward," it was a different voice, "she did all she could for me, but I was too damaged. Tell her that Joe Aston sent his thanks for her care in his last moments. Listen to her, Captain, *your* damage can be repaired, but you must listen to her."

"We stay here."

"Mmmm? What if?"

"Dear God Almighty. We stay here!!"

Above him James could hear the faint sounds of scraping. Of hands painstakingly removing soil.

"We stay here."

"But it's."

"Dear God Almighty. We stay here!!"

"James."

"That voice."

"James."

"That voice ... it ..."

"James."

"It ... It ... Ag ..."

The door to James room opened and an orderly walked in backwards carrying a lunch tray of brown Windsor soup and steamed fish. Agnes looked at the congealing mass on the plate and shook her head at him.

"Thank you, I'll get him something else in a few minutes." She said gratefully.

The orderly sneered and nodded. *"Too bloody good for the likes of you is it?"*

He span on his heels, and caught the edge of the tray on the doorframe, sending it crashing to the floor.

A massive explosion and concussion smashed into James haven.

"We stay here!!!!"

FIFTY-SEVEN

Sam and Elizabeth decided to take in the local atmosphere and walk around Ypres's streets, shops, bars and restaurants, before packing for their flight home.

Karsten seemed to have fully recovered, and Klaus had taken him back to the hotel. His son's reaction to Langemarck, had disturbed him and he was undecided what to do next. The survival of Papaver Rhoeas was vital, but not at the cost of his son.

The group had agreed to meet again at five o' clock and determine what should happen next.

Sam bought a Dead Man's Penny in a small shop close to the Menin Gate. They were tokens of gratitude given by the British Government to the fallen service men and women's next of kin. It was the name on the Dead Man's Penny which caught his attention – Adam Cain Morbeck.

Elizabeth was drawn to Pip, Squeak and Wilfred, the 1914 Star, British War Medal and Victory Medal. She'd no idea why she bought them, but somehow knew that she had to have them, despite knowing nothing about Ronald Hubert Lidsay 2nd Lieutenant Irish Guards.

They were sat in a cafe in the Gross Markt drinking cold beer and eating crisps. They'd swapped purchases and were closely examining them.

"This was Adam's. Remember what I told you about him and your family tree?" Elizabeth said.

Sam looked up from Squeak. "I get a bit confused with second removed this." He smiled at Elizabeth. "But I do remember he was Bert, Jack and Fred's father, which would make him my … great grandfather?"

"Remember his wife's name? She lived at High Wood with the two sons."

"Rebecca Milliner? Shit I don't know where that came from."

Elizabeth beamed at him. "Yes Rebecca Milliner. She was your …"

"Great grandmother."

Sam put Squeak on the table and took the Dead Man's Penny from Elizabeth. "So she lost her husband in 1915 and her son in 1917! My God, what was it the local kids called her?"

Elizabeth breathed deeply, sighed and said quietly. "The Mad Woman."

Sam drained the remaining beer in his glass and ordered two more. "Is there anything else you know about her?"

Elizabeth drained the last few drops of her beer and took a fresh glass from the waiter. "From the brief research I've been able to do, particularly in the local press, it seems that Rebecca was the backbone of the family. The death of her husband in 1915, didn't seem to have had any visible effects on her. She still had two teenage sons. Bert would have been thirteen and Fred fifteen, and add to that the worry of nineteen year old Jack who was in the trenches in France, then her mind would have filed away her loss into a dark corner of her mind."

"Why was Adam in France?"

"Not completely sure. His age was damn close to the maximum age for service, but there were such massive losses that they were taking anyone who could hold a rifle. He may also have had a trade which the army was desperate for."

"Even so, to leave your wife to fend for herself with two teenage boys wasn't exactly, thoughtful."

"Sam they were different times. Service to your King and Country was seen as a duty. Women were still handing out white feathers."

He played with the condensation on the side of his glass. "Why did they call her mad?"

"It said in the local papers that she could be seen at an upstairs window for days on end, staring down the avenue, waiting for Adam and Jack to come home. Apparently this went on for about six months, and then she simply disappeared."

"What from sight? Out of the window?"

"No, she literally disappeared. Anyone who went to the house was only ever met by Bert or Fred, and when they were asked where she was, they would always say she'd gone to visit her younger sister Maud, who'd also lost her husband in the War."

"Didn't anyone check?"

"Sam every last man was being sent to France, so no one was in the slightest bit interested in some batty old woman who'd gone to see her sister for comfort."

"So no one ever checked if she'd gone?"

"Her sister lived in Exeter, and no one as far as I could discover ever checked if she was there." She picked up the glass and drained it until only threads of froth were left. "And I couldn't find any record of a death or burial."

Sam looked up from the menu. "What! No record of a death, or burial? Bit bloody odd, isn't it? Is that all we know about her?"

"After she was reported going to her sister's in Exeter, she became of little interest to the local press." Elizabeth looked at her watch. "We should get back. I still have to finish packing and we need to find out what they've decided to do."

Sam tapped his glass on the table. "Yeah, I suppose you're right. Still when we get back, I'd like to find out what happened to her."

They walked to the bar, settled the bill and walked across the Gross Markt to the hotel.

Karsten had recovered fully and was sitting in the lounge, drinking coffee with Klaus and Guillaume.

Elizabeth bent down to him and kissed his cheek. "How are you feeling?"

"I am good thank you. I feel much better now." Karsten said.

Sam pulled over two chairs, ordered beers for everyone and sat down with them. "It's been an eventful few days."

"They have been, somewhat, ein wenig seltsam, a little strange. Perhaps just a little too strange." Karsten replied.

Klaus loosened his tie and unbuttoned the neck of his shirt.

Sam leaned forward. "Where do we go from here?"

"We go back to our homes and carry on the work. There are still countless thousands of lost souls seeking salvation. They remain our first and last priorities." Klaus said.

Guillaume seemed distant.

"We won't meet again before we fly home tomorrow?" Elizabeth was concerned about loose ends. "Surely we need to finalise a number of things?"

Klaus placed his hand on Guillaume's. "We will meet again quite soon, but for now it is time to go home." Klaus picked up his glass of beer, examined it in detail, raised it to the ceiling and indicated to everyone to pick up their glasses. "Sam, Elizabeth, a few hours ago," he drank from his glass and raised it once again, "we lost a true friend, ein außergewöhnlicher Mann, der große Geist, Mitgefühl Ad Menschlichkeit, of exceptional spirit, compassion and humanity." His mind seemed to drift away to a far off place. "Isaac … passed away on the journey back to Ypres. It was peaceful and Guillaume and I were with him at the end."

Elizabeth sank into the chair and dropped her glass which shattered on the tiled floor. Her face collapsed into a trembling, tear-soaked mask.

Sam jumped up from his chair and held her tightly against him. He could feel hot rivulets coursing down his face, his chest tightening, breathing becoming difficult and a growing void in his abdomen. He knew that Isaac was terminally ill, but Sam didn't handle loss well. And the two words he hated more than any had started rebounding inside his skull. *"If only."*

A profound silence fell over the group.

Elizabeth gently pushed Sam away and sat forward. "I would like to officiate at the funeral. Would that be OK?" She looked at Guillaume.

He looked startled, and looked at Klaus who nodded. "Elizabeth I am sure Isaac would have approved. The problem," he spoke caringly "is that we are Jewish and we have different rituals to yours."

Elizabeth nodded in understanding. "Then perhaps you would allow me to say a few words at the ceremony?"

"Of course, of course. That would be wonderful."

Sam sat back in his chair and wiped away his tears. "Guillaume," he paused, looking for the right words, but couldn't find them.

"Sam, words aren't necessary. I understand and appreciate your thoughts. Isaac has been suffering, suffering terribly, for months. We had a date and time booked at Veritas in Switzerland to end his personal torment." He was staring at nothing in particular. "Next Thursday. It was something which I'd agreed to, but something about which I had enormous trepidation. The end of life is something we all know is inevitable, but to specify a place, time and method was too much like an *execution* for me. God forgive me that I don't believe I could have been there at the end for him. But now, now I was there for him." The emotional dam finally burst.

Klaus stood up. "I think I should get Guillaume up to his room." He bent down and tenderly helped Guillaume get up. He held him from one side while Karsten supported the other. As they stopped at the lift Klaus turned and spoke to Sam and Elizabeth. "Please wait for me. I'll be a few minutes."

They sat back into the chairs and glanced at each other.

"I've seen bereavement many times Sam, but I have never felt it as deeply as I do now." Her tears had dried up and her eyes looked red and sore.

"Does this change everything?" Sam asked.

Elizabeth pulled her chair closer to him. "Isaac knew he was dying. All this was planned well in advance to ensure that his work was carried on. The change, is that our commitment to this must be even stronger than before. We must never let these souls carry on drifting aimlessly in the ether. It was his, and now it must become our life's work."

Half an hour later Klaus emerged from the lift looking drained. Sam quickly got up, mimed a drink to Klaus who nodded and indicated he'd like a large one.

Klaus quickly drank half of the malt whisky, sighed deeply and forced a smile. "Guillaume is resting. Ralph has given him something to help him sleep." He finished the remaining malt and waved his empty glass at the barman for another. "We need to speak. I know it may seem inappropriate at this time to be discussing these matters, but we all return home tomorrow, and we know the last thing Isaac would have wanted was Papaver Rhoeas to lose its focus." He took the glass from the waiter and signed the bill for the group. "We will all meet again very soon under very difficult circumstances at Isaac's funeral. I will keep in touch with all the details and Guillaume will, I know, want to organise everything. But then will not be a time to try to think calmly and clearly." He leaned forward and took them both by the hand. "You both understand what is needed of you?" He looked deeply into their eyes. They both nodded. "Good. Carry on the work you have started, and, I hope now, you better understand us and our mission."

They nodded in agreement.

"Soon, after the funeral, when we have started the healing process we will meet again and talk more of the future. But for now let's raise a glass to," Klaus's tears ducts had recovered, "to, I can't find the words in English. To Isaac. Gott segne dich, mein liebster freund."

FIFTY-EIGHT

PM had finished and was followed by the shipping forecast.

"Is anyone really interested in what the weather is like in North Utsire, Fitzroy, Malin and Dogger, although I suppose I can see there would be some interested parties in Dogger ... ing?" She thought, chuckling to herself at her attempt at a pun. She lay back on the Chesterfield, hugged a cushion and stared at the ceiling.

"What the hell was that room for?"

"No idea." Her conscience replied.

"Yes but was it to keep something or someone in, or something or someone out?"

"No idea."

"Not much bloody use are you. At least have a guess."

"Well, given what was in the room, then someone was, well, *living* in there."

Jane sat upright. It still seemed strange to her that as far as she was concerned she still existed, but didn't live. Her body still seemed to function normally, with the obvious exception of not being seen or heard by any living thing, and that she didn't need to eat, drink, sleep or excrete to keep going.

"I'm bored. Bored fartless."

"So what do you want to do?"

"Tell you what, let's see how far we can get away from this place. At least we'll get a change of view."

She walked up to the front door. and slowly pushed it open. She knew that she could walk through it, but wanted to try to keep things as *normal* as she could. She reached the gate, looked up and down the avenue and decided that for today, she'd go no further. She turned around, frowned deeply at the house and flashed two fingers at it. What was staring back at her from High Wood got her attention.

The shutters of all the windows were thrown open and in the furthest room on the right, the boarded up bedroom, staring vacantly past her, was a woman, probably in her forties, in what once must have been a crisply laundered white nightgown, but which had long since become tattered, faded and a grubby shade of grey. Her attention seemed to be fixed on the avenue, her unblinking eyes straining to see over the horizon. An expression of pain and deep despair etched into her face. A modern Penelope, unravelling Laertes shroud, still waiting for her Odysseus to return home from the war.

What she saw at every other window made her question her sanity. If you still possessed such a thing in death. Every other window, upstairs and downstairs, was crammed with soldiers, whose faces seemed to be *blurred*, their features erased, all jostling for a place at the front. A hand would appear and drag one away to be replaced by another. They were like waves crashing against the window panes as new soldiers replaced those fighting to stay at the front. She stared in disbelief at the ever changing tableaux. There didn't seem to be any threat or danger, but only an anguished cry for help. She felt no fear, and the only emotions she felt were pity and a deep profound sadness. She took a couple of steps towards the house and the bedlam at the windows slightly subsided. She took a few steps away from the house and the mayhem reached a new intensity. The closer the calmer, and the further away the greater the turmoil. It was like turning a volume switch up and down. She took one more look at the soldiers, walked quickly up to the front door and strode into the hall. As she closed the door, a sense of calm seemed to descend over the house. It was as if it had simply relaxed.

She walked into the kitchen. For Jane it held the most potent feeling of normality in this abnormal house. Despite having no feelings of thirst or hunger, she made a large mug of coffee and decided to finish the last of the now almost stale chocolate digestives. Once they were gone, then Mother Hubbard's cupboard would be bare, until Sam came back to replenish the shelves.

"Where do we start?"

"Not sure really. None of it frightens me, although it doesn't exactly inspire a sense of well being."

She dunked and finished the last biscuit.

"So, where do we start?"

"Not much point in putting it off is there?"

"Suppose not."

She drank the last of the coffee which was stone cold, and shuddered.

"Bloody hate that."

She stared at the mug and turned it upside down on the table, a small liquid brown rivulet growing from its rim.

"What about the heads? You couldn't see their faces."

"Putting it off are we?"

"Well, what about them? What the hell is this house? Some waiting room for the faceless departed before it's finally decided if they go up or down? If it is, then I think this one's slipped the Almighty's mind as there seems to be a little overcrowding."

"They were all in uniform."

"Do you think they're connected to those photographs."

She paused, pushed back the chair and stared at the ceiling looking for Divine intervention, some epiphany, some help.

"OK, this is what we're going to do."

"In charge now are we?"

"Someone's got to be. The only threat seems to be from the woman at the window. The shutters are open now so finding something in that room with some personal details will be a lot easier."

"My thoughts precisely."

She stood up from the table, made her way up the stairs, along the landing and into the bedroom. Sunlight illuminated the room reflecting off millions of fine dust particles drifting in the air, but there was no sign of the woman. There was no breeze or any sort of air movement in the room, but the dust seemed to be moving in unison like macrophages attacking foreign cells. As she walked towards the bed the dust wrapped itself around her, forming a tight thin layer over her entire body, leaving only her face uncovered.

"Bit odd don't you think?"

"I'm probably full of static."

Jane walked to the bed and opened the top drawer of what must have been the dressing table. There were a number of books neatly laid out across the base of the drawer. The covers, which once must have been vibrant primary colours, were badly faded and worn at the edges, where strands of white threads hung like unkempt fringes. One by one, she picked them up and noted their title and authors.

The Lost World – Arthur Conan Doyle
Robin Hood – Henry Gilbert
The Night Land – William Hope Hodgson
Death in Venice – Thomas Mann
Tarzan of the Apes – Edgar Rice Burroughs
Evangeline and Other Poems – Henry Wadsworth Longfellow

"Anything?"

"No not really. There are no dedications, no notes, no names. Nothing."

She put down The Lost World, picked up Evangeline and Other Poems, carefully opened the book and searched the pages for anything which might throw some light onto this mysterious page. As she turned the pages, she noticed that certain lines of poetry had been underlined in what was probably pencil.

"Found something?"

"Not sure. Someone has underlined some of this poem."

"Mean anything?"

"I'm no literary critic. The last book I read was Fifty Shades of Grey." She looked back at the page and began reading out the highlighted text.

"SPEAK! Speak! Thou fearful guest!
Who, with thy hollow breast
Still in rude armour drest,
Comest to daunt me!"

She looked up from the page and frowned.

"Wrapt not in Eastern balms,
But with thy fleshless palms,
Stretched, if asking alms,
Why dost thou haunt me?"

She started to read again, but heard an unnatural low whimper from the bathroom. It gradually increased in volume until it reached a crescendo, reverberated off the walls and ended in a chorus of screams. Longfellow dropped to the floor, and Jane stared in the direction of the bathroom.

"What the … was that?"

"Just the wind in the pipes?"

"Wind my ass."

"Wind *from* your ass more like."

Jane bent down and picked up the book. Her coat of many particles quivered like leaves in an autumn wind and then gripped her like a vice. She stepped back and sat on the bed still holding the book.

"It's extraordinary isn't it?" The voice was unknown and distant.

Jane's head snapped to her right.

"Quite, quite extraordinary isn't it. 'Picked his bones in whispers. As he rose and fell. He passed the stages of his age and youth'."

A young Rebecca Milliner was sat next to her on the bed.

Jane stared at her feeling no fear, only a strange but wonderful bond to this woman. Instinctively she held out her hand to Rebecca, and every nerve fibre in her body fired as Rebecca took her hand and squeezed it.

"You can see me and touch me!" Jane cried.

"Of course. Why wouldn't I?" Rebecca said.

"Because no one else can."

Rebecca looked confused. "Why?"

Jane was puzzled by Rebecca's reaction.

"Because we, well, I am I believe, we are ..." she was concerned about using the word, but there was no other, "… dead."

"Oh I know I'm dead, I've had the company of faceless soldiers since I can't remember when. They've all tried to help me find them. But I'm still here." Rebecca squeezed Jane's hand.

Jane frowned and touched Rebecca's face. "I'm Jane." She said. "Jane Morbeck. I couldn't explain to you how I ended up here." She smiled.

Rebecca's expression moved between confusion and happiness. "Morbeck?"

"Yes my husband's name is Sam Morbeck. Apparently his family's lived here for some time."

"Since the beginning of 1899."

"Since when?"

"I moved into the house with Adam in 1899. We needed a large house as we planned to have at least six children. We were lucky, and Jack, Fred and Bert soon filled the empty spaces of the house. Adam was a miner." She seemed to drift into her own personal land of memories.

Jane tapped Rebecca's hand and she glided back to the present.

"Yes Adam was a miner. Worked down the pit."

"I still don't know your name." Jane said softly.

"Rebecca. Sorry, forgetting my manners. Rebecca Morbeck." She grinned at Jane whose expression had frozen.

"I believe that I must be your husband's great grandmother?"

Jane's face remained frozen.

"Purgatory's odd isn't it? We sit here waiting for, after all this time I still don't know what, release to somewhere or something." Rebecca looked directly at Jane. "Do you believe in Heaven or Hell?"

"Sam's great grandmother! But you're only fortyish?"

"Fifty."

"When did you die?"

"1926."

Jane stared at Rebecca in disbelief. "You haven't aged."

"Can't explain it, but time seems to have stopped here. What's the year?"

"When I first came here it was 2013. It may still be 2013, but I couldn't be sure. Let's go downstairs, have a cup of tea and see if we can," there was a long silence as they stared at each other. "… Oh shit, I don't know, but let's at least sit somewhere more comfortable." Jane suggested.

Ten minutes later she'd made two mugs of tea from the last of the tea bags, sugar and milk, and walked into the lounge where Rebecca was stood looking out of the window.

"Tea?"

Rebecca turned, her forehead deeply furrowed. "I don't eat or drink. Don't feel the need to."

"But wouldn't it be nice to just taste some hot sweet tea?"

"You eat and drink?"

"Mostly when I'm bored, and it sort of reminds me of days gone by." She offered the mug to Rebecca. "Go on. Live, well, haunt a little dangerously."

They laughed and Rebecca took the mug. "It's hot."

Jane raised her eyebrows and drank her tea.

Rebecca tentatively raised the mug to her lips, sipped a tiny amount of tea, smiled and then swallowed about half the mug. "That is so good."

"Isn't it."

"But I don't understand how we can? And what happens to the tea?"

"I have no idea. This is all new to me. But what I'm pretty sure about is that we seem to be able to interact with anything inanimate, not living." She walked across to the bookcase and took a large leather bound volume from the shelves, carried it across the room and deposited it on the coffee table. "Anything inanimate, but I'm certain that we can't physically interact in any way or be seen or heard by anything animate. You know, people or animals."

"Some have seen me at the window." Rebecca said. "I think if you want them to see or hear you they can."

They sat down on the Chesterfield cradling their mugs of tea.

"Why are you still here after all these years?" Jane asked.

"According to the Bible, you can only enter Heaven if you are in a state of grace. So you and I can't have achieved that. The Church says that this place, purgatory, is where we gain that state of grace." She smiled. "I must be a lost cause if I still haven't achieved it after all this time."

"You're a wicked woman Rebecca Morbeck."

They laughed and finished their tea.

Rebecca relaxed back into the comfort of the Chesterfield's cushions. "You know I never come down here. I'd forgotten how lovely it was. I've always stayed in that room or sat in one of the other bedrooms. Until they locked me in."

For the first time Jane could detect an air of sadness. "Why?"

"I was becoming, it's difficult to explain, but I was becoming hard to control. Violent, physical, destructive, dangerous and impossible to live with. I've never held any malice against the boys for what they did. Life was difficult enough, and I was making things very hard for them."

Jane decided she'd let sleeping dogs lie. "Why do you really think you're still here?"

Rebecca sighed. "I think that we stay here if we have unfinished business."

Jane turned her head towards Rebecca. "What have you got that's unfinished?" *"And for that matter, what have I got that's unfinished?"* She thought.

"I'm waiting for Adam and Jack." Tears welled up in her eyes.

Jane let her speak when she felt ready.

"In 1915 I lost my husband Adam. He was forty. They sent me a telegram. Just a few words typed on some strips of paper which ended my world. Your husband is missing in action presumed dead. Two years later I got another telegram. Your son has been killed in action. Twenty one. That's all he was. They sent me his things. I locked them away in one of the rooms on the third floor. They told me where he was buried, but I never got a chance to visit his grave." For the first time in almost a hundred years tears were streaming down Rebecca's cheeks.

Jane leaned over and pulled her close. She could feel the sobs rocking her body. They sat huddled together for quite a while until Rebecca recovered herself enough to start talking again.

"They never found him you know. Nothing, not even a hair. Just nothing. Blown to the four winds. My husband, my only true love just didn't exist any more. How can that be? How does someone just not be there anymore? Their record on this earth erased. How can you mourn? How do you ..." Tears were freely flowing again.

"Rebecca, it's OK, I don't need you to tell me any more if it's so deeply painful for you."

Rebecca sniffed and tried to smile. "I never grieved. I couldn't. I need to do this. I locked myself away inside my head. I locked everything away that I'd been sent of Adam and Jack. My other sons had to cope with the loss of their brother, father and then mother. I shut myself away in the room upstairs. Inside my room and my head was my comfort blanket. I tried to forget everything. With no memories, how could I feel pain? But there are things which cannot and should not be forgotten."

Jane sat quietly and let Rebecca drain the sorrow of a hundred years.

"I have no memory of my death. But what I know with all the certainty I have, is that I have to find Adam before I, we, can move on from here to whatever lies over the next horizon."

"Why don't we get their things from upstairs? That may help you find him." Jane suggested.

Rebecca thought for a few seconds and then nodded in agreement. They walked together to the landing, and up the stairs into the gallery. They stood together staring at the rows of photographs.

Rebecca wandered up and down the panels. "None of this was here. It was three rooms." She pointed at the panels. "None of it. I put their things in a box under the floorboards." She looked around trying to get her bearings. Finally she pointed to a far corner of the room. "Over there. It was over there. I'm sure."

They ran across the gallery to the back-most corner of the room. Rebecca looked around and pointed to the floor. "Here. They're here."

They looked down at the vinyl covering on the floor and frowned.

"It'll just have to come up." Jane said.

"But how?"

"Luckily, there are a few tools just outside your room."

Ten minutes later, they'd ripped up most of the vinyl in the corner exposing the boards, and examined them for any evidence of them being disturbed.

"Can you see anything?" Jane asked.

"No. But I'm sure I put them here." She closed her eyes, trying to remember the moment and then suddenly opened them. "I made marks on the floorboards." She closed her eyes again. "It was their initials, ASM and JSM." She dropped to her knees and started to closely examine the floorboards.

Jane ran her fingers over the surface of the floorboards and felt indentations in the wood. "Rebecca! Here, there's something in the wood."

Rebecca crawled across to Jane and peered at the faded impressions.

Jane stood up, took a screwdriver from the tool box and began tracing the shapes of the marks. "A, can't really make out the next one. This looks like an N ?" She carried on scraping the dust and grime from the marks. "Must be an … I? Next one is definitely an S. She carefully picked at the last mark. And this is another N."

Jane sat up and stretched her shoulders. She didn't feel any aches or pains, it just seemed the natural thing to do. "So we've got A something N and ISN. Has to be here. Near enough to ASM and JSM for me." She jammed the business end of the screwdriver into the gap between the floorboards and tried to lever one up, but time and rusty nails resisted her efforts. "No problem. Give me a couple of seconds. I left a crowbar outside your room."

Left on her own, Rebecca tenderly traced with her index finger the initials she had carved into the floorboards in 1917. "I'll soon have you back my darlings. I'll find you."

FIFTY-NINE

Agnes and Arthur had finished breakfast and were discussing James. It had been three weeks since she'd first *discovered* him under the bed and little seemed to have progressed.

"I don't seem to be having any affect at all on him." Agnes said.

"It seems a trite thing to say, but these things do take time. James is a complex case and you have the best insight into his time in France, and what could have precipitated this major psychosis."

Agnes picked up her tea cup examined the pattern of tea leaves in the bottom, and wished she could interpret their hidden meaning to see what the future held for her and James. "His entire time in France was horrendous. The things he saw would have been enough to turn the mind of any sane man." She put the tea cup down and pushed it away in frustration. "How any of the medical teams remain in control of their reason amazes me."

Arthur walked across to the service hatch, brought back a pot of coffee and two mugs, poured two strong black cups, added two sugars to each, nodded at her to follow him and carried them back to his office.

They sat in two easy chairs drinking their coffees.

"Agnes I understand your frustration, but believe me, what you've been doing has had a positive effect on James. It doesn't seem that way at present, but I know from painful experience that what these men need more than anything else are time, patience and love. All of these James gets from you."

"But I just sit and talk and never see or hear him." It was clearly beginning to take its toll on her.

Arthur recognised her torn emotions. "Would you like me to have someone else talk to him for a few weeks and you could take a well earned break?"

Agnes sat stiffly up in the chair "No! Absolutely not! If he hears someone else's voice then God knows what that will do to him." She looked deep into Arthur's eyes. "I will bring him out of this."

Arthur smiled, he was delighted with her response. "My dear, he will remain in your care for as long as you want."

She looked down at the worn carpet and blushed. "Sorry for my reaction, but he means so much to me."

"I know my dear, and it's that which gives him his best chance of recovery. Finish your coffee and let's see how he is today."

Arthur had arranged for a comfortable chair to be put in James' room, and Agnes had been deeply grateful for the comfort it gave her during the long hours with James. The chair was always kept close to the window near the top end of the bed, but when they entered the room, it had been moved close to the bottom end of the bed.

"You've changed the position of your chair Agnes." Arthur said.

She frowned and looked around the room. "No. I always keep it in the same place. I don't do anything which might disturb the feeling of constancy. Did you arrange this Arthur?"

"No." He turned and walked out into the corridor. A few minutes later he came back. "No one has moved anything in the room. I've spoken with Sister Mada and she's given strict instructions that the only persons allowed in the room other than her, are you and me."

They looked at the chair, glanced at each other, looked back at the space beneath the bed, looked at each other again, looked again at the space beneath the bed and finally hugged each other. "It must have been James?" She whispered.

Arthur beamed and nodded his head. "Who else?" He spoke softly. He pointed at himself and then the door indicating he'd leave Agnes alone with James. He raised his thumb to her, and she smiled and nodded.

Her first thought was to move the chair back to the window as the view helped pass the long hours, but decided that if James had moved the chair, he'd have a good reason. She opened the cupboard against the wall which acted as storage for the few remaining earthly possessions of the patient, and took out his kit bag. She opened the top and quietly looked through its contents. Among the expected soldiers' paraphernalia was a small pile of books tied together with string. She carefully undid the knots holding the parcel together and looked at each of the volumes. The Lost World, Robin Hood, The Night Land, Death in Venice, Tarzan of the Apes and Evangeline and Other Poems. She decided that a good rip-roaring adventure would provide the sort of escapism James needed, so she opened *The Lost World* and started to read.

"Chapter One – There are heroisms all around us: Mr. Hungerton, her father, really was the most tactless person upon earth – a fluffy, feathery, untidy cockatoo of a man, perfectly good natured, but absolutely centred upon his own silly self."

She carried on reading for about a quarter of an hour.

"Chapter Two – He is a perfectly impossible person: My friend's fear or hope was not destined to be realised. When I called on Wednesday there was a letter with the West Kensington postmark upon it, and my name scrawled in a handwriting which looked like a barbed wire railing."

She stopped and picked up a glass of water.

"Odd sort Mr Hungerton?" The voice came like a gentle summer zephyr from under the bed.

Agnes spilt most of the glass of water over herself.

"I thought when I read it first he sounded a bit *unusual*."

Agnes didn't know what to say or how to react.

"Please carry on."

Agnes sat in catatonic silence.

"Oh please don't stop. You read so well and your voice reminds me of someone."

"A chink of light." She thought. "The contents were as follows:- Sir – I have received your note, in which you claim to endorse my views ..." Agnes didn't want to stop reading but her throat was on fire. "... although I am not aware that they are dependent upon endorsement from you or anyone else."

Twenty minutes later her throat was only producing a hoarse croak. "I'm going to have to stop now. I have a desperately sore throat, but if you'd like I could come back tomorrow and carry on with The Lost World."

A sigh came from beneath the bed which drove daggers into Agnes's heart.

"That would be lovely. I look forward to it. I hope you didn't mind me moving the chair. I couldn't see you with the light behind you."

Agnes frantically wanted to dive under the bed and take James in her arms. How could he talk like this but still remain paralysed under the bed? "I'll be back early tomorrow." She stood up, replaced the book on the bedside cabinet and laid her hand on top of the sheets.

"Take care, my love," she whispered.

"Stay with me," James' words were spoken as softly as a baby's kiss.

Agnes ran from the room, slid down the corridor wall and disintegrated into wailing inconsolable tears.

Arthur appeared around the corner of the corridor, swept Agnes up in his arms, and carried her to his office.

She sat for ten minutes utterly inconsolable. Eventually she looked up at Arthur. "He spoke to me."

Arthur stared at her in disbelief. "Spoke to you?"

"Only a few words, but it sounded like James used to sound."

"What did he say?"

"He said a few things about the book and asked me to ... st ... stay." She couldn't contain the emotions.

He waited for her to find herself again and poured them two cups of Earl Grey, his particular favourite brew. "Agnes, the books must have some special meaning for him. There are so many in the library. Why these?"

"I found them in his kit bag. It's probably why *The Lost World* got such a reaction. He must have read them when he was in France."

"Yes very likely." Arthur picked up *Tarzan of the Apes*, drumming his fingers on the cover. "What were the other books?"

She rubbed her forehead. In some strange way it helped her think. "*The Night Land, Robin Hood, Death in Venice* and *Evangeline and Other Poems*."

"Ah, Longfellow, I approve."

"Arthur, what does this mean? Is this real progress? Will he ever recover?"

"Time is James's main ally, and your time is the most precious to him. You may not sense that every day, but your presence is the key factor in his recovery. This demands tireless patience. Patience which will be stretched to its very limit and beyond. But the result, the pot of gold at the end of this particular rainbow, is beyond value."

She nodded in agreement and smiled. "I should get back to him."

"Of course, my dear. I hope the book," he tapped the sleeve cover, "soon has you both swinging through the trees like Tarzan and Jane."

She kissed him on the cheek, took the book from him and made her way back to James's room. When she got there her chair had been moved back to its original position. She dropped the book and covered her mouth with her hands.

All her attention had been on the chair, but her shock became astonishment when she'd looked at the bed. In the centre was a large lump covered totally in blankets and sheets. It was without question a hunched body. Agnes was paralysed. Should she leave and call Arthur? Start reading Tarzan? Pull back the sheets? Dance with joy? Scream thank you to the heavens?

"Be calm Agnes." She thought frantically. *"This is another step."* She fought the absolute desire to scream in joy. *"What would Arthur say?"* Her mind was in turmoil. *"Be calm Agnes. Please be calm."*

The door behind her opened. "I thought that I might sit in on the readings if that's ..." Arthur stood in the open doorway his eyes wide and his mouth gaping at the mound on the bed. He took Agnes's hand, pulled her into the corridor and swung her around. "I think you're making progress!"

SIXTY

The flight to Cardiff was spent mostly in silence. Their thoughts drifting between events at Thiepval, Vimy, Langemarck, Ypres, Papaver Rhoeas and the death of Isaac.

Sam was sitting as comfortably as was physically possible in the narrow cramped space of the aisle seat. He turned his head to Elizabeth who was sat equally uncomfortably in the opposite aisle, frowned, shrugged his shoulders looked at his watch and smiled. "Comfy?"

"Like a home from home. Only it belongs to a six stone midget."

They laughed at each other and sat back as a stewardess offered them refreshments from the trolley.

"Two coffees for myself and," Sam pointed at Elizabeth, "milk and sugar, bacon sandwich, chicken sandwich and two Kit Kats, please."

After completing the gastronomic delights of the airline, Sam stood up and gestured to Elizabeth to follow him to the rear of the cabin.

"Shame we couldn't get seats together."

Elizabeth smiled, did a little dance and disappeared into a vacant toilet.

Sam had become accustomed to her regular need for the facilities.

"What do we do when we get back?" He asked Elizabeth as she finished wiping her hands with her own wet wipes.

"What Klaus and Guillaume said. Carry on. We've still so much to learn and so many to help."

"Yes I know, but after Isaac's death, I wasn't sure what to do."

"Sam if there was only one thing to remember from this trip, it's that there are thousands of lost souls who desperately need our help." She paused and squeezed his hands. "What do we do about your wife?"

He pulled a face and chewed his bottom lip. "First of all we find out if that email was just a wind up." He frowned. "Secondly, if it is genuine, then we find her at High Wood, and I'm a widower. Oh and thirdly I marry you."

Elizabeth grinned at him. "Got it all sorted?"

Sam blew on his nails and polished them on his sweater. "Yes."

"Being a little presumptuous aren't we?"

"Mmmm?"

"All this is assuming I give up the clergy, you find your apparently dead wife, and I shack up with you in some odd house."

"But I thought that we were, you know, a couple?"

"A couple of what, Sam?"

"A couple who loved each other and wanted to be with each other?"

Elizabeth's expression relaxed. "Of course I love you and want to be with you, but we need to be realistic about things. If Jane isn't dead then we can expect war. Despite the lack of anything between you, she will be hurt and vindictive."

Sam kissed her softly and pushed some loose hairs behind her ear. "As soon as we get back I'll take legal advice and find out exactly how things stand. I know a good solicitor in Cardiff. He's a friend of someone I knew at work."

Elizabeth kissed him on the cheek and gently moved him to one side. "I really do need to use the loo again."

Back in their seats it was difficult to carry on a meaningful conversation across the aisle, so they agreed to get back into their books and decide on a plan of action when they got back to High Wood.

SIXTY-ONE

The crowbar made light work of lifting the four floorboards they needed to lift to access Rebecca's keepsakes. They were knelt on the floor examining what they'd found in the space beneath them.

"They sent me these." Rebecca was holding two Dead Man's Pennies against her tear-stained cheeks. "We all got these." She bent forward and lifted out two tattered buff envelopes. "Got these telegrams. Couple of words which destroyed my life." She held them against her face and then looked back into the space beneath the floorboards. In the bent cardboard box were some faded wedding photos, a tweed cap, a miner's lamp, a photo of the family at the seaside, a woollen scarf, a pair of brown children's shoes, calendars for 1915 and 1917 with days crossed out, two army caps, regimental badges, and a copy of the Bible. "This is all I have of them. Not much is it. Two lives in a box. But it'll do for now until we're together again."

For the first time in years, Jane could see the love two people could hold for each other. A love which could transcend everything the world could throw at it. An indivisible bond that sailed across the rough oceans of time. It was a love she'd never seen in anyone who'd been close to her. Her parents had a mutual hatred of each other which culminated in a messy divorce. This left Jane spending weekdays with her mother and every weekend with her father, which soon became every other weekend and finally only high days and holidays. In her young mind he'd deserted her, and the love she'd given him had been tossed into the bin like an old sock. Her mother quickly found a new love of her life who could do no wrong, and had abused the attractive teenager. Something her mother knew about, but was prepared to *tolerate* to keep her new partner happy. The only thing Jane could see which came from love was heartache and physical pain.

Finally, in Rebecca she'd seen real freely given love. Love which she'd resisted, feigned with Sam, used as a means to an end, given her power over men, but ultimately corroded her spirit and soul, and led to a wasted life. For the first time in years tears started to course down her cheeks.

"Jane?" Rebecca leaned across the hole in the floor to the kneeling Jane and touched her knee.

Jane looked up and tried unsuccessfully to wipe away her tears. "I've been thinking. Something I should have done a long time ago." She sat back on her haunches and sighed. "Anyway, spilt milk and all that. There's something about this house which …" she looked around at the panels, "What are all these pictures?" A glimmer of an idea glinted at the back of her mind. "Have you ever taken a close look at them?"

"I told you, I stayed in my room. This wasn't here when we lived here. I'd remember. I didn't know this place existed."

Jane grinned. "Then don't you think we should take a look?"

A glimmer started to illuminate Rebecca's mind. "To see if there's … do you think there could be … a … a photo of Adam?"

Jane stood up and helped Rebecca get up. "Let's take a good look at all of them. We've plenty of time."

They started walking up and down the panels, looking closely at each photo.

"Why haven't a lot of them got faces?" Jane was frowning. "It must be something to do with these Post-it notes."

"Post whats?"

"Sorry. Post-its. They're these small coloured notes." She pointed at them and read them out to Rebecca. "You see, this photo which has a face, has 'At peace under an English heaven' written at the bottom, but this one without a face doesn't."

Jane was reading the notes at the bottom of the picture. They looked at each other and a second glimmer sparked between them. "These are all at rest but Adam isn't. So we need to find Adam's photo. It must be among all these others." Jane paused and held Rebecca's hands. "When we find him," she squeezed her hands a little tighter, "… if he's like these," she nodded to the photos they were looking at, "… then he won't have a face."

Rebecca swallowed and nodded. "But we're going to give him his face back aren't we."

Jane smiled, and kissed her on the cheek.

SIXTY-TWO

They were standing close to the bed staring in disbelief at the motionless mound of blankets and sheets.

Arthur gestured to Agnes to follow him out of the room. "I'm lost to know what to say." He scratched his head and rubbed his neck. "I've never seen this type of recovery. What's very clear is the bond between Captain Heyward and yourself finally reconnected. What do you think was the key?"

Agnes frowned and shook her head. "I'm not entirely sure." She stared at the floor tiles looking for some spark of inspiration. She thought back over the time she'd spent with James. "It has to do with the readings."

"Agnes," Arthur gently moved her away from him, "you must continue with the readings. You have to continue to strengthen the connection between you." He walked back into the room and returned with the books from James's kit bag. "You were about to start reading Tarzan?"

Agnes nodded. "Yes, it seemed that given the effect of *The Lost World*, something in a similar vein like Tarzan might work its magic."

Arthur was examining the six books. "I think you should try this one." He lifted up *Evangeline and Other Poems*. "I think Longfellow could stimulate thoughts which James has buried, and needs to confront." He opened the book and ran his finger down the contents. "Try this one, 'A Nameless Grave'. " He handed her the book with his index finger on the title of the poem.

Agnes read it and looked up in shock. "Are you sure this is the sort of thing he should be hearing? Isn't this what he's been desperate to escape from? My God, I'll send him screaming under the bed." She threw the book back at Arthur.

He stooped and retrieved it from the floor. "Agnes, this is difficult. More difficult than I can imagine, but please understand these fractured spirits must confront their demons and send *them* back under the bed." He offered the book to her but she turned away. "Agnes if you ever want the James you loved back in your arms, escaped from his Hell into your Heaven, then you must do this." His arm was still extended holding out the book. "Please, Agnes. Not for me, but for James and all the others who will benefit from this." He touched her on the shoulder with the book. "Please, for me?"

She turned slowly. "If he becomes worse and I lose him, I will make you pay, Arthur." Her voice was not full of menace, simply cold. Permafrost cold. She took the book, silently turned and walked back into James's room. She stared at the page for at least fifteen minutes until she finally gathered up everything she had to read some lines from the poem.

"A soldier of the Union mustered out'
Is the inscription on an unknown grave
At Newport News, beside the salt sea wave,
Nameless and dateless; sentinel or scout
Shot down in skirmish or disastrous rout"
The silent mound on the bed seemed to softly tremble.
"Of battle, when the loud artillery drave
Its iron wedges through the ranks of brave
And doomed battalions, storming the redoubt.
Thou unknown hero sleeping by the sea
In thy forgotten grave! With secret shame"

A soft trembling of the sheets, gradually increased in intensity until it became a disjointed juddering. Agnes looked up hearing the noise of the quaking sheets, but bit her lip and carried on to the end of the poem.

"I feel my pulses beat, my forehead burn,
When I remember thou hast given for me
All that thou hadst, thy life, thy very name,
I can give thee nothing in return."

The sheets and blankets rose and fell like the gentle swell of a summer sea, until they slowly tumbled onto the floor. On the centre of the bed was what once been Captain James Heyward. An officer renowned for retaining a remarkably smart, if not pristine appearance was now been reduced to nothing more than the bare supporting framework of the man he'd once been. She couldn't be certain it was James. Until he spoke.

"You have given me everything and more."

It was a brief sentence. A few words. Words which Agnes would remember and cherish forever. She sat frozen to her chair, totally unsure about what to do next. Her instincts screamed get up and hug him, but the converted believer in Arthur's methods whispered, *"Speak to Arthur."*

Arthur opened the door a few inches and peered into the room. Agnes caught his eye and nodded at him to come into the room. "What do I do?" She whispered to him.

He looked at the bed, stepped back, shrugged his shoulders at her and mouthed. "Go with your instincts."

Despite everything which was screaming at her to race to him, the *Arthur* in her took control and helped her slowly stand up and move quietly to the bed, smile, sigh more deeply than she thought possible, sit softly on the edge of the bed, offer her left hand to James, smile; wait for him to react to her, suppress the almost uncontrollable need to cry, until James looked down at her hand, up at her face and finally wrapped his cold fingers around her hand. Not until that moment did she throw her other arm around him and pull him so close to her that they became one.

SIXTY-THREE

Sam unlocked the front door, pushed it open with his knee and stood back to let Elizabeth into the hall.

She turned her head to him. "Cup of tea?"

He put the cases down, pushed the front door shut with his bottom and picked Elizabeth up in his arms. "I can think of nothing nicer. Well actually that's a lie. I can think of a lot of things which would be considerably nicer and probably just as hot and wet."

Elizabeth fluttered her eyelashes at him. "Why, Samuel Morbeck, I do declare, I am a vicar you know."

He kissed her neck, and in a very poor impression of Rhett Butler whispered in her ear, "Frankly, Miss Elizabeth, I don't give a damn."

She bowed her head in mock embarrassment and prodded him in the ribs. "Sam, let's leave the luggage for now, we can unpack tomorrow. I'm starving let's go out and have a curry. There's no way on this earth I want to cook."

He needed little persuading, turned and quickly left the house. Elizabeth smiled and followed him outside. "Sam, Sam, where are you going?"

"I'm going back to Charleston, back where I belong. Although I think that first I must go to the Four Mughals for a Chicken Passanda. Will you accompany me sugar?"

"Great balls of fire, don't me call me sugar."

"How fickle is a woman."

Elizabeth stopped, her feet set astride. "Right, Rhett, I've had enough of *Gone With the Wind*. After all," she stared into the far distance and flicked her hair, "...tomorrow is another day."

Sam smiled, bowed deeply, kissed her hand and softly took her chin in his right hand. "You should be kissed often, and by someone who knows."

"Fiddle-dee-dee! Now can we have a bloody curry!"

Upstairs in the gallery, Rebecca and Jane fell silent and crooked their heads to the sounds they could hear downstairs.

Jane was the first to speak. "It's Sam. After all these years, I'd know his voice anywhere. Rebecca he can help us. I'm not sure how yet, but he's been preoccupied with this house since he inherited it." She stood up and opened her hands at the photos. "There's got to be a reason for all this, the maps and the stuff downstairs." She stopped and listened again to the voices. "He's not on his own." She frowned.

"Jane are you OK?" Rebecca stood up, staring at her.

"Mmmm, yes I'm fine." Her smile returned. "It must be that vicar. Stupid isn't it. I've had no feelings for Sam for as long as I can remember, we've been sleeping separately for at least ten years, but there's still something in me which really objects to the fact he's found someone else. He's mine. My property I suppose. I don't want him, but I don't want anyone else to have anything which is mine." She was frowning again.

"Jane let him go. To be honest, you don't have much of an option, as you're dead. Eternity's a long time to spend being angry. Let him know he's free. Didn't you say that you could e-mail him?"

Her smile had returned. "Yes you're right. Not much point in being mean-spirited. Good idea on the e-mail. Let's go down to the map room and decide what it is we need to say to him and his trollop."

They picked up the Dead Man's Pennies, joined hands, made their way downstairs to the map room and turned on the computer.

"OK, so what do we need to say?" Jane opened a new blank email, entered Sam's email address and sat with her fingers over the keys.

"You should probably tell him that you're only here in spirit?"

"Yes, he probably thinks my first email was a wind up." She scratched the back of her neck. "Right, one, explain about me, two, explain about you, three, tell him the problem we have, four, what can he do to help us?" Jane turned to look at Rebecca who was gazing at the computer screen.

"You can send messages with *this*?"

"Yes. Just with the press of a button."

"Does it call someone to take the message to Sam?"

Jane smiled. "No. This machine sends messages through the air, and Sam has a machine which collects the messages which he reads."

Rebecca's eyes had grown even wider. "Like telegraphs down wires?"

"Yes just like telegraphs. Only quicker."

Rebecca seemed to accept this and Jane could see no reason to complicate things any further, and she started to type.

Subject – Jane

Sam I thought I'd write again to make sure you understood my email wasn't a wind up.

There's no easy way to put this. I'm dead. Just a spirit. How I died is still a bit of mystery to me. I get flashes of memories but these are still cloudy and vague. What I do remember are two names. Agnes Wilmart and James Heyward, but I don't know who they are or maybe were. God knows how I'm able to write this, but for some reason, I seem to be stuck in Purgatory, which for me is High Wood. I know this is difficult to take in, but I promise you, this is not a wind up.

I'm not alone. There's someone else here in the house with me. Rebecca has been stuck here since 1926. Her surname is Morbeck. She must be a relative.

She lost her son and husband in the First World War. Her husband was never found. She believes she's stuck here because she hasn't been able to see Adam rest in peace. We've seen the photos, and found him. He hasn't got a face. Can you help us find him for Rebecca?

Sam, we were never good together. I'm gone, so you're free. I wish we could have been happier together but the dice didn't roll for us. If you've found happiness then grab it with both hands. Life is shorter than you think.

See you soon.

Jane

Sam and Elizabeth had demolished three popadoms and mixed chutneys when his iPhone pinged that an email had arrived. The restaurant had free Wi-Fi and he was expecting an email from Klaus, but his face froze as he read the mail.

Elizabeth was concerned with his expression and the time it was taking him to read and re-read the mail. "Sam. What is it?"

He looked up from the iPhone. His expression was a mixture of surprise, confusion, disbelief, disappointment, anger and the hint of a smile. "She's definitely dead."

"Dead?" Jane said. "Who?"

"Jane." The word was spoken blankly.

Elizabeth was happy she was sitting down. She couldn't remember being lost for words but she recovered. "Who sent the email?"

"Jane?"

"Jane Morbeck? Jane your wife? Jane your dead wife?"

Sam was staring again in disbelief at the email. "It must be a hoax. A hoax in pretty bad taste." He looked up and scowled. "But how could she know about Rebecca Morbeck? Remember, you told me about her, her husband and her sons. What does she mean, 'When you get back to High Wood I'll prove it to you'."

The waiter delivered their curries.

"I've lost my appetite." Elizabeth was staring at the nan, rice, chicken passanda and beef madras sat on the warming plates.

Sam sat back and put his hands on top of his head. "Me, too. We'll still have to pay for it."

Elizabeth pursed her lips. "Ask them to put it in trays for us and we'll take it back to the house. You never know we may feel like it later on."

Twenty minutes later, carrier bag in hand they opened the front door and walked into High Wood.

"What should we expect?" Sam walked into the kitchen and put the curries on the table.

Elizabeth leaned on the table. "Sam, I've absolutely no idea. After I've dust to dusted anyone, then only God truly knows what happens next. Where do we start?"

"She mentioned the photos in the email, so I suppose the gallery is as good a place as any."

They held each other's hands more firmly than they had before and made their way upstairs. Sam walked in front of Elizabeth up the narrow stairs into the gallery, with a degree of trepidation.

"What do we do now?" Sam asked.

"Let's see if we can find that photo Jane mentioned in her email." She looked around at the panels and countless photos. "What was the name again, Sam?"

"Adam Morbeck." He rubbed the back of his neck. "My great grandfather."

"OK, so where do we start?" She pulled at her ear lobe and sighed.

"Let's split up. I'll start at the far end and you start here. If you find anything, just shout."

They nodded at each other and Sam made his way to the furthest panel.

An hour later they hadn't found Adam.

"Do you want a coffee?" Elizabeth shouted.

"Good idea. I could do with a break."

Jane was sat in front of the computer with Rebecca, when they heard voices in the kitchen. She stood up and smiled at Rebecca. "Let's get in touch with them shall we?"

Elizabeth and Sam were sat at the kitchen table drinking coffee. Decaffeinated, which Sam particularly disliked, but it was all that was left in the cupboard.

Jane and Rebecca entered the kitchen and sat in the chairs opposite Sam and Elizabeth. Rebecca looked apprehensive.

"Can you hear me, Sam?" Jane said, checking if she could be heard. There was no response.

"They can only hear and see us, when *we* want them to." Rebecca reminded her.

Jane stood up and walked around the table brushing past Elizabeth, who stood bolt upright sending her chair flying across the kitchen.

"Elizabeth!" Sam jumped up from his chair and grabbed her arms. "Elizabeth. What is it?"

"I … I felt something? Something brushed past me. It was like a cool breeze."

Sam frowned, looked around the kitchen and picked up Elizabeth's chair.

Jane stood close to Sam, and blew in his ear, and his hand flew up to his head

He looked around the kitchen, frowned, but then smiled.

"Sam? What's happening?"

"I think this is Jane letting us know she's here."

"Could have been a draught?"

Sam smirked at her, sat down at the table and took a deep breath. "Jane is that you?"

Rebecca moved close to Jane. "Shall we let them see us?"

Jane smiled wickedly and shook her head. "Not just yet."

Elizabeth sat down and pulled her chair closer to Sam. Despite her faith and beliefs, she wasn't prepared for this. They held hands and squeezed hard when a cupboard door opened and a bag of flour floated out of it, across the room and settled on the table. The top of the bag opened, the contents spilled like an avalanche onto the table top, and it slowly spread out into a thin layer covering the top of the table.

"Sam, what's going on?" Elizabeth whispered hoarsely.

"She's getting in touch," Sam said trying to sound calm, but the tremor in his voice gave away his true feelings.

Jane stood at the table and started writing with her index finger in the flour. "It's Jane. Sorry if I scared you."

Sam and Elizabeth stared wide eyed at the words as they appeared letter by letter. He leaned forward, brushed out the words and started to write with his finger.

"Are ..." Sam turned to Elizabeth. "I don't know what to say."

She smiled and started to write. "Is Rebecca with you?"

The words disappeared as they were brushed away.

"Yes."

"Can you hear us?

"Yes."

"We can't hear or see you."

"I know."

"But you can move things."

"Yes, but only inanimate things."

Sam touched Elizabeth on the shoulder. "This is going to take all night." He stood up and looked at the other side of the table at Jane and Rebecca. "I'm going to get paper and pens."

He ran into the lounge, took a reporter's pad and two biros from the top drawer in the sideboard, ran back into the kitchen, grabbed a towel, brushed the flour off the table, and put the pad and pen in front of where he believed Jane was.

"I'll speak and you write. Is that OK?"

"Yes."

"It's too complicated for us to understand how you're here, so for now, how can we help?"

The biro hovered over the pad and started to write. "Rebecca lost her husband Adam in 1915. His body was never found. I think this house is important. Is it?"

"I'm pretty sure it is. I've been to Belgium and met a group who bring back the lost souls of soldiers killed in World War One."

"Can they help Rebecca?"

Sam turned to Elizabeth who nodded. "I think so."

Jane turned to Rebecca who'd no idea what was happening, but understood the writing on the pad. "Sam thinks they can help."

"Even after all these years?" Rebecca seemed a little sceptical.

Jane shrugged her shoulders. "Who knows, but shall we give it a try?"

Rebecca nodded.

Jane wrote her reply. "What do we do?"

"Show us where Adam's photo is. We couldn't find it."

Rebecca blushed, put her hand into her pocket and pulled out the crumpled photo of a faceless Adam. "I'm sorry Jane but I couldn't leave him there so soon after finding him."

Jane stroked her cheek and wrote her reply. "We'll meet you in the gallery."

SIXTY-FOUR

A month later, James looked like the man she loved. His weight had just about recovered, the pallor of his face had been warmed and tanned by the early autumn sun, the beard was gone, his hair had begun to recover, he was wearing his uniform, he was eating and sleeping relatively normally and had suffered only two brief relapses.

Agnes and James had continued their readings, and he'd become enthralled with the poetry of Longfellow. Thankfully for Agnes he'd lost interest in the 'Unknown Grave' and could recite most of 'A Psalm of Life', which seemed to reflect his recovery and renewed appetite for life. They were sat under an oak tree and he was reciting it to her.

"Life is but an empty dream!
For the soul is dead that slumbers,
And things are not what they seem.
Life is real! Life is earnest!
And the grave is not its goal;
Dust thou art, to dust returneth,
Was not spoken of the soul."

Agnes loved these precious times with James. To see and hear the man she thought she'd lost, restored her spirit.

James looked back to the sky and carried on.

"Not enjoyment, and not sorrow,
Is our destined end or way;
But to act, that each to-morrow
Find us farther than today."

He sat down on the bench close to Agnes. "How long is it since we were in France?"

This was a subject Agnes knew would come up, and she'd prepared herself for this moment. "Probably about four or five months." She held his hands, and despite the autumn sun they were icy cold. "Are you OK, my love? Your hands are so cold."

"Cold hands, warm heart." He tucked his hands under his thighs. "Do you think I've recovered?"

Agnes shrugged her shoulders. The question was one she didn't want to answer.

He looked her in the eyes. "The doctors seem to think I've made a remarkable recovery. Do you?"

She shrugged her shoulders again. "James, I'm not a doctor."

"Yes, but being as close as you have been to me over the period of my recovery, you must have established your own view?"

"You've come so far, that it would be easy to say you've recovered. If your recovery is complete, I couldn't say. I'm just so happy that I have you back." She leaned forward and kissed him tenderly on the lips. "Can you remember much of when you were … not with us?"

"Under the bed? We have to be open about it."

"Yes, of course."

"So you think I'm pretty much back to myself?"

Agnes was concerned that James was almost demanding she confirmed his full recovery. "James I've said all I can." She stood up. "Come on let's get back inside. The afternoon's getting chilly." She turned and started walking towards the gate house.

"They want me to go back you know."

Agnes froze in mid stride. Every internal organ was pitched into a maelstrom, her blood congealed in her veins, fuses in her brain were blowing, she was struggling to breathe, she felt she knew what it must be like to have *bought one* in the stomach, but somehow she managed to turn to face him.

"I've been thinking it over." He said calmly.

She turned, her face flushed with anger and fear. "What's there to think over?" Her arms were flailing like a demented windmill. "My God, how many lives do you think you've got?" Tears started tracing rivulets down her cheeks. "You've given enough! We've given enough!" She turned away from him. "This should be our time. We deserve it. What else can they possibly want from you?" She turned and pummelled his chest with her fists. "You owe me this. This is our time! They've had their slice of our lives. Their pound of our flesh."

James took hold of her hands and kissed them. "My darling." Agnes tore her hands away from him. James reached out and fought to hold her close to him, and her struggle against him gradually began to subside.

"I'll come with you." She sobbed into his shoulder.

Arthur had seen them from the house and was running across the lawn to them. "Is everything alright?" *"What an idiotic question!"* He thought.

Agnes moved away from James and wiped her eyes and nose in her sleeve.

Arthur moved closer to James.

"OK, old man?"

James looked up and smiled at Arthur.

"What's happened?"

"They want him to go back!" Agnes jumped in.

Arthur looked surprised. "Go back? Who asked you to go back James?"

"Field Marshal Haig. He came to my quarters a few days ago and told me my skills were desperately needed at the front."

"Field Marshal Haig came *here*?"

"Yes. He was incognito, in disguise. You wouldn't have seen him." James tapped the side of his nose and looked cautiously around the garden.

Any hope Agnes had that James had recovered, collapsed like a child's burst balloon.

"James, we wouldn't want anyone to know about this would we." Arthur scanned the grounds. "Let's go back inside where it's a lot more secure." He took their arms and led them towards the house.

Thirty minutes later, James was back in his room, Agnes and Arthur sat with him. His entire demeanour had changed. He was drumming his fingers on the wooden arms of the chair, tapping his left foot and gently rocking back and forth. His eyes were clear and open, but focused on some obscure distant point. He hadn't spoken for fifteen minutes, when the finger drumming and foot tapping suddenly stopped.

"Did Haig say anything to you Arthur?" James whispered.

Arthur nodded and smiled conspiratorially at him. "He did call in to see me, and told me his visit was very hush hush, so I kept it to myself."

Agnes turned and frowned quizzically at him.

James leaned forward in his chair. "What did he say?"

"He believes that the work we're doing here is fundamentally important to the overall victory. Getting soldiers back to front is a vital component of his plan, and this is the only place which is returning good numbers of shell shocked troops to the front line."

Agnes's frown grew even deeper, but Arthur continued.

"He believes, in fact he is convinced, that if you work with me here, your contribution to the British victory would be significant. More so than patching up the wounded in the casualty clearing stations and hospitals. His view, is that if the British public see *these* soldiers returning to the front, then it will show them that there is no condition which will keep a British Tommy from fighting the Bosche."

James was staring intently at Arthur absorbing every word like a child listening to a story from his grandparents. "But he told me he wanted me to go back. He was very clear about it."

"You misunderstood him, James. His meaning was for you to get back as many to the front as possible. He made this very clear to me. In fact, he told me it was a direct order."

James carefully studied Arthur's face, eventually stood up and offered him his hand. "When do we start?"

Agnes smiled. She now understood. She leaned across and squeezed his arm. "Thank you."

SIXTY-FIVE

Lidsay was bored. He'd begrudgingly taken up the superintendent's *offer* of an early retirement on full pension, after it had been made abundantly clear to him that if he didn't, he'd be facing disciplinary charges. There'd been no party, no leaving presents just a smirk from that bastard of a detective.

His daily routine was set in immovable stone. He got up late, expecting his breakfast to be on the kitchen table, watched BBC news for an hour, showered when the need demanded it, wore ill-fitting jeans and a sweatshirt bearing the faded legend 'Rock the Kasbah', drove to Tesco, bought The Sun, had two coffees and a doughnut in the restaurant, drove home, watched the Discovery channel for an hour, expected sandwiches and coffee to be ready by one o' clock, watched anything which was on Sky Sports until two thirty, dozed and slept for an hour, read the paper until four, watched the quizzes on TV until six, expected dinner to be on the dining room table at six fifteen, slowly drank two large glasses of whisky, watched UK Gold for a few hours and went to bed at nine thirty.

Gloria's life *had* changed, but for the worse. When Ivor was working, life was just about bearable, but now she was beginning to understand how you could be driven to murder. She'd thought of quite a few innovative ways to kill him and then effectively dispose of his body. It occupied most of her quieter moments.

"Isn't there anything you'd like to do?" Gloria asked despairingly, praying that she could get him out of the house.

Lidsay mumbled something through a mouthful of toast.

"For God's sake, Ivor, at least have the decency to speak with an empty mouth."

He washed down the toast with the last of his coffee and waved the empty cup at her.

After picking his teeth and belching, he turned slowly to face her. "I've plenty to keep me occupied." He stared at her, waved the mug again and turned the kitchen TV on to BBC News.

Gloria took the mug, mimed beating him over the head with it, silently screamed, and thought of more imaginative ways of death for her so called husband.

Later that morning he was drinking his second cup of coffee in Tesco, when a face passed by the window which blew the dust off memory files in his mind.

It was Morbeck. Samuel Morbeck, murderer of this parish and owner of the means to get him away from Gloria and God's waiting room.

It was just a fleeting glimpse of his nemesis, but it was enough to bring back thoughts of escape. He couldn't give a shit about Morbeck, his bit on the side, or that snot nosed dip at the station, but whatever was hidden at High Wood still called to him.

"Is it worth the hassle?" He thought. *"Life may be boring but there's not much risk involved and Gloria's a non-demanding sort."* He picked at the remains of his doughnut and stirred the dregs of his coffee. *"What's the point of dropping myself in it, ending up in the cells and letting that knob at the station take the piss".* He got up, strolled over to the magazines, flicked through the pages of 'Gardeners World' and found an article on pruning clematis which occupied him for five minutes. *"Still, a quick recce wouldn't cause any problems, and my uniform is still in the downstairs closet"*

"All right, Sarge'?" It was snot-nosed Detective Dip from the station.

Lidsay looked up from the article not even trying to force a smile. This was the last thing he wanted. "OK."

"How's the life of leisure?"

"OK."

"The wife's well?"

"OK."

"Been on any courses on conversation?"

"No."

The sarcasm was lost on Lidsay.

"Nice to have seen you, Sarge. I'll pass on your best wishes to the boys at the station."

"Mmmm ..." Lidsay had his nose back in the magazine.

Snot-nosed Detective Dip turned and walked away. "Miserable old scrote." He said, just loud enough for Lidsay to hear him.

Lidsay ignored the comment, replaced the magazine on the rack and left the store.

Back home, he prised open the door to the closet under the stairs, and among the four discarded umbrellas, ironing board, two buckets, Dyson, shoe polish and dusters, toilet rolls, hula hoop, thing to pull down blinds in the conservatory, wild bird seed, wellington boots, bleach, sundry cleaning products, light bulbs, torch and batteries was his uniform packed flat in a vacuum storage bag.

Two hours later he was sat outside High Wood in his uniform. Half an hour later he was still sat in the car. His personal Jiminy Cricket was sat on his shoulder doing a reasonably effective job. of keeping him out of mischief. He eventually brushed him onto the back seat and got out of the car. High Wood smirked at him.

"You won't beat me this time you poxy shit." He spat at the house, pushed open the gate, walked down the path and knocked loudly on the front door. A few seconds later the door opened and Sam's familiar features frowned back at him.

"Good day, sir."

"Sergeant Morbeck." Sam couldn't disguise his displeasure "What an unexpected pleasure. Come in." He turned and gestured for Lidsay to follow him down the hall. Half way, Sam unnecessarily shouted, "It's Sergeant Lidsay."

Jane and Rebecca stayed seated at the table, Elizabeth grabbed hold of a dust pan and brush and started ineffectively trying to clear up the flour. As Sam and Lidsay entered the kitchen there was a soft white haze in the air.

"Sorry about the mess, we were going to make some cakes and spilt a bag of flour." Sam lied convincingly.

Elizabeth put down the dust pan and brush and took Lidsay by the arm. "Let's go into the lounge. It's a lot more comfortable and a lot less floury."

Sam and Elizabeth sat on the Chesterfield and Lidsay sat to their right in an armchair. After a few minutes of small talk, Lidsay brought the conversation round to the topic of Jane's disappearance. "Have you heard anything from your wife?" He emphasised the word wife and stared at Elizabeth.

"No," Sam replied "we've been in Belgium. Do you have any news?"

"Afraid not, sir. She seems to have vanished into thin air."

"Oh, I thought seeing you here meant you might have some news for me." Sam said pointedly.

"No, no, I was just passing and thought I'd check on how you were." Lidsay lied. "There've been quite a few burglaries in the area and I wondered how up to date your security was. Very happy to take a quick look around for you. All part of our service to the community." He leaned forward in the seat trying to look as genuinely concerned as he could.

Sam looked at Elizabeth. The last thing he wanted was this devious sod looking around the house, but he didn't want to do anything to arouse his suspicions. "That's very thoughtful of you. There are a lot of sentimental things in the house, and I'd be devastated if they were stolen. I'll walk around with you and make notes."

Lidsay sat back and tried not to scowl. "Always best if I do the initial check on my own. I'll make notes of the relevant things which will need sorting out and we can go through them together after." His tone was one of '*I know what I'm doing so please don't interfere*'.

"If you're sure?"

"Normal procedure. Not a problem. I'll start upstairs if that's OK?"

Sam nodded as Lidsay stood up and left the room.

They walked back into the kitchen to see the note pad flying off the table and the disembodied pen scribbling a note.

"That asshole was sniffing around here while you were away. He must have broken into the house as everything was locked. Don't know what happened when he was here, but all I heard from him were screams as he ran out of the house." The top sheet was torn off and handed in mid air to Sam.

Rebecca took the pad and wrote. "I think it may have been my fault." She smiled. "He saw me up in my room, and I'm never at my best there."

Jane put her arm around her shoulders, kissed her on the cheek, took the pad back and added her own note. "I may have taken a book from the cabinet and put it on the Chesterfield next to him and perhaps blown in his ear."

Elizabeth leaned across to read it and laughed. "I know how he felt, but if he had such a scare last time he was here, then why's he come back?"

They stood up and walked back into the lounge.

"Not a clue. Unless ..." Sam stood up. "Unless ... surely he doesn't think that ... no ... Even he couldn't be that suspicious ... could he?"

"Could he what?"

"Think that I've killed Jane and hidden her remains in the house?"

Jane looked at Rebecca, laughed and dramatically threw herself onto the Chesterfield. "He done away with me, cut me up in bits and hid me under the floorboards."

Elizabeth felt the Chesterfield shake, looked at the dent in the seat next to her and smiled at the invisible Jane. "Sam you should follow him around."

"What's the point, there's nothing for him to find, and certainly no dismembered corpse in the attic."

"Yes, I agree, but there's plenty in the gallery which could be awkward to explain?"

"He'll find nothing. He's too inept."

Lidsay was beginning to think this hadn't been such a good idea. What the hell did he honestly expect to find in this rambling house which he hadn't before, and what was he going to report to them on their security? He also didn't want to bump into the Woman in White again. After ten minutes of pacing up and down the landing he decided he'd tell them he'd need a lot longer, and another officer from the station. So he'd call them in the near future and make an appointment.

Sam, Elizabeth and their two *lodgers* were still in the lounge when there was another loud knock at the front door. Elizabeth got up. "My turn."

"If it's the Mormons then tell them I've converted to Buddhism." Sam said.

Elizabeth opened the front door to a tall smartly dressed young man.

"Hello, madam, I'm Detective Constable Rogers. Is Mr Morbeck at home?"

Elizabeth waved him into the hall. "Yes he's in the lounge. I didn't realise that the police were so attentive."

DC Rogers frowned at her. "I'm sorry, I don't understand."

"You're the second in the last twenty minutes. Just like London buses."

DC Rogers appeared confused, but his bewilderment was answered as ex – sergeant Ivor Lidsay recently *retired*, stepped down from the last stair into the hall, face to face with snot-nosed Detective Dip, whose confusion rapidly changed to what could only be described as a wicked grin.

"Sergeant Lidsay. Fancy meeting you here. I'm sure we can discuss things down at the station with Inspector Morton. I'm really looking forward to seeing why you're here." He turned to Sam who was stood in the lounge doorway. "I just popped around to update you on your wife."

Jane smiled.

"No news I'm afraid, but as I said before, these things do tend to resolve themselves. Please keep in touch and hopefully we'll be able to discover what's happened." He smiled, shook Sam and Elizabeth's hands and turned to Lidsay. "I'll give you a lift back to the station, Sergeant."

Lidsay was rooted to the spot, tried to regain his composure, but could only manage to hoarsely whisper, "Oh bollocks!"

SIXTY-SIX

"How are things?" Klaus was on the phone to Guillaume. It had been a week since Isaac's death, and he was concerned about him. Isaac and Guillaume had been inseparable, and the bond between them obvious to even the most insensitive person. He had real concerns that Guillaume was putting on a little too much of a brave face. He'd been too chirpy, too normal, too settled and just too Guillaume.

"They've still not released Isaac's body. So I haven't got a date for the funeral. They still haven't determined a cause of death, but I'm hoping things will get resolved quite soon."

"I'm planning to come down on Wednesday."

"You must stay with me."

"That's very kind Guillaume."

Klaus inwardly smiled. He could now spend some time with Guillaume and properly assess how he was doing. He had concerns for the running of Papaver Rhoeas which had to outweigh his personal feelings for Guillaume. "I will let Sam and Elizabeth know what's happening. I've been in touch with the others but I've been avoiding calling them. They got so close to Isaac in such a short time." There was a long silence. "Guillaume, are you OK?"

"Mmmm … Sorry Klaus … just thinking about Isaac … I miss him you know."

"I know. We all do." Klaus's concern was palpable. "I'll come earlier. I'll be there tomorrow. I should be with you by lunchtime. You shouldn't be alone."

"Odd isn't it."

"Odd?"

"Yes. Odd how we all believe we're immortal. But in the blink of an eye, beyond our shelf life, passed our expiry date, we become just footprints in the sand, autumn leaves blown away, a snowman in the sun, shifting shadows, frozen moments held in silver frames, remembered faces and events, a smell, a sound, a feeling, a taste, nothing more than a memory, one more branch on a family tree." Guillaume said.

"It's a road we all travel. A road on which we think we can find alternative routes, but whatever we do, the destination never changes. You think you can cope with anything. That life has prepared you for just about everything it can throw at you, but the only real certainty life can offer us is death." Klaus thought carefully about his next words. "The lost souls we help have no anchor, no direction. Isaac knew this. We all do. It's what drives us. It's what drove Isaac, and it's what drives you."

"You're right. Isaac's spirit is still with me and I know where his physical … where his … where he lies."

"Tomorrow we will talk. Talk of Isaac and remember good times. I will contact Sam and let him know what's happening. Put plenty of bottles of that Belgian beer in the fridge and we will toast old friends and fond memories."

"Sounds like a good idea." Guillaume's voice had lifted.

"Yes a damn fine idea. I'll call you tomorrow when I'm close. Take care."

"I look forward to seeing you and thank you so much for calling."

The phone went dead. Klaus replaced the handset and sat back in the chair. He was a little happier with the Guillaume he had said goodbye to than the grieving brother he'd called. He lifted the lid of his laptop, reopened email, found Sam in contacts and started a new mail.

Subject – Isaac

I hope that you and Elizabeth are well. I don't have a date yet for Isaac's funeral. I'm going to see Guillaume tomorrow. He hasn't been too good since Isaac's death. Sorry that we've not been in touch. Things have been a little hectic. As soon as I have a date for the funeral I will let you know. Any questions please contact me. We will meet soon.

My very best regards

Klaus

He opened the bottom drawer in his desk, took out his favourite malt whisky and poured himself a large shot. It was a little early, but he needed some enhancement to his mood.

SIXTY-SEVEN

Agnes and Arthur were sat in his office having afternoon tea. The rays of the late afternoon sun transformed the dust in the air into dancing jewels. She finished the last piece of her scone and wiped away the clotted cream and strawberry jam from the corner of her mouth with a napkin. Arthur sat back in his chair wiping away the cream from his moustache with the knuckle of his index finger. They looked at each other and smiled. It had been six weeks since James had *received* instructions from Field Marshal Haig and his overall physical health had dramatically improved. His mental condition however was still fragile. The delusion that Haig had made a personal trip to see him was still a reality to James. This left Arthur with a problem, in that on the surface James was an incredibly quick learner, and, under supervision, had become a valuable member of his team. His work with the patients, so far as Arthur could determine, was helping his mental recovery, but James' refusal to accept the visit from Haig was only imaginary, remained a serious concern to him.

"How do we convince him that Haig was never here?" Agnes asked.

Arthur blew his nose, as he was suffering from a bad cold, and frowned. "I've been wondering if we should. It's Haig's visit and orders which transformed him, and if we persist in trying to dissuade him of it, then I'm worried he may rapidly regress." He wiped his red eyes. "I think for the present, we should let sleeping Haigs lie." He got up and walked to the window. "We have a somewhat larger problem."

Agnes suddenly had that empty feeling in her stomach, and an uncomfortable feeling of foreboding.

Arthur continued looking out of the window at the low sun. "I have regular visits from senior brass to determine how many of our patients are fit to return to duty."

Agnes was finding it difficult to breathe.

"The most recent visit was the day before yesterday." He paused and breathed deeply. "Colonel Pritchard." He folded his arms across his chest. "He saw James working with Private Longue, and later, Pritchard had a long chat with him."

Agnes could feel her eyes welling up with tears.

"Pritchard came to my office with a list of names he wanted released for duty. Unfortunately there is little I can do to argue against his decisions. They are so short of troops at the front, that provided you can stand upright and hold a rifle, you should be fighting for King and Country and killing Bosche." He turned, vainly trying to smile at Agnes. "He was most impressed with James and wanted to know why Captain Heyward wasn't at the front helping the wounded."

Agnes sat silently staring at Arthur in disbelief.

"He's left the relevant papers to have James returned to France for active duty at a casualty clearing station or hospital as yet to be determined."

The words struck deep into Agnes like red hot shards of shrapnel. She'd lost him again. "But surely you explained about Haig to him?" She said in desperation.

"I did, but he's old school. shell shock to him and others like him is merely a coward's way of avoiding war. A sham, an easy way to feign illness, something true men, brave men don't suffer from, a feeble excuse created by pacifist conchy medics like me to save lives and let Germany win the war. He assured me in very clear terms that if he had his way, everyone in this establishment would be on the next transport to France. His conversation with James, convinced him that he was ready to go back to the front and help the cause, and that he'd been forced to work with me. After that, Colonel Pritchard assured James he'd be on the earliest possible ship to France."

"Is there nothing we can do?"

"Absolutely nothing. James will be leaving on Saturday. All the papers have been received."

"But he's not well. The first exposure to anything … anything ..." Her words were lost in tears.

"Agnes, what can I say? The technology of war has moved on, the means we have invented to slaughter each other becomes ever more efficient, but the understanding of its effects on men's minds, is, and will remain a mystery to the generals. All they require is numbers. Bodies to offer up for sacrifice to the great god Mars. They work with the statistics of conflict. Kill more of them than they can kill of us, and we will ultimately triumph." He sat down, utterly deflated. Was the creation of a body factory all that he'd achieved? All he would be remembered for? What was the point of restoring men to health so they could be fed into the meat mincer that was the Western Front? How many had he sent to brutal deaths? How many were among the missing? How many had been sucked down into the depths of the quagmire of Flanders? He closed his eyes and started to weep.

Agnes stood up, knelt in front of him and hugged him tightly to her. Sobs racked his body, his tears soaked Agnes's shoulder. She gently pushed him away from her. "Arthur! Arthur look at me!"

His head remained paralysed, locked to his chest. She put her fingers under his chin and slowly brought his face up to hers. His eyelids partially opened revealing reddened eyes. "I'm going back with him. They need nurses, and we worked together well as a team. I'll keep a close eye on him. I know your techniques, and if I believe his condition is worsening then I'll … I'll shoot him in the foot." She paused in thought. "You don't suppose I could accidentally shoot him now and get away with it?"

Something resembling a smile flickered across Arthur's mouth. "You will stay here. This war won't last forever and your work will carry on long after this is forgotten."

She held his arms, perhaps a little too firmly. "I will bring him back, we will come to see you and work together again. In a time of peace."

"Agnes you must not go back. You won't have enough strength for both of you. You know better than anyone the daily hell you'll be facing."

"We'll live together or die together. Life without James is not worth contemplating." She stood up and walked to the window. The orange ball of the sun was doing its best to cling to the horizon. "Will you call Colonel Pritchard or whoever it is we need to organise my papers?"

Arthur nodded.

"Thank you. I'll go around and tell James the news."

SIXTY-EIGHT

Jane still wasn't comfortable with Sam being with Elizabeth, and told Rebecca that she didn't want Sam and Elizabeth to see or hear them. However, they agreed that they needed something for them to know where they were, and decided on two hats from a wardrobe.

What Sam and Elizabeth saw as they entered the gallery were a peacock feathered duck egg blue, and a black lace creation floating in mid air.

"Jane is that you?" Sam asked?

The duck egg blue hat nodded.

"So Rebecca, you must be black lace. Good thinking. At least now we can see where you are."

Black lace nodded in agreement, and walked to the most central panel in the gallery and stopped halfway down. Sam, Elizabeth and duck egg blue followed. Rebecca unfolded Adam's photo from her hand and replaced it on the panel. Sam had brought the note pad and pens with him, and offered them to what he now knew was Rebecca.

She took the pen from his hand and pointed at a photo. Sam read the note – 'Private A. C. Morbeck, Royal Engineers, Brigade Mining Section, and 28th Division'.

He spoke to the black lace hat. "Was Adam a tunneller?"

Jane picked up the note pad. "Rebecca do you know what he means?"

Rebecca smiled softly "Yes. He was a miner most of his life, and late in 1914 a call went out for experienced miners and clay kickers, men who'd worked on the London Underground. That's why despite his age, Adam was recruited into the Royal Engineers. A year older and he wouldn't have gone."

Jane wrote a simple. "Yes."

The note pad conversation continued back and forth.

"Do you know where he was sent?"

"*We think it was France.*"

"Town?"

"*Don't know.*"

"Any idea of where he served or may have stayed?"

There was a longer pause than usual.

"*The only thing Rebecca can remember, was Hill 60?*"

Sam looked up from the note pad. "I need to go down to the map room and do some research on the internet." He turned and walked to the stairs. "I should only be a few minutes."

Rebecca and Jane sat on the floor, and what Elizabeth saw were two hats sinking lower and hovering about three feet above the floor. She sat down next to them. Jane picked the note pad. Elizabeth looked down as words began to appear.

"I'm glad that Sam has found happiness with someone."

A new note pad conversation had started.

"He's happy, but I'm not sure how I should feel. Having a conversation with his dead wife is a little … strange."

"I understand, but you can at least still feel."

Elizabeth smiled at the joke and turned in astonishment She could hear Jane. "I can hear you!"

"Well that should make things a little easier." Jane replied.

"But I still can't see you."

As Elizabeth spoke, she could see the hazy outline of two women start to appear next to her.

"I felt that now we could let ourselves be seen by those who we want to see us. Up until now, I just didn't want to be seen by you. It's odd, even when you've fallen out of love with someone to see them with someone else is … hard to bear."

"I didn't ever intend for this to happen." Elizabeth said.

"And I certainly didn't intend for this to happen to me either."

Elizabeth smiled. "I'll be good for him."

"I wasn't, and he really is better off without me."

"There must have been some good times?"

"Very few. It was a marriage of convenience. Mostly my convenience."

"Why do you think you haven't passed over?"

"Not a clue, but I think Rebecca's stuck here because of Adam."

"Can I ask Rebecca something?"

"Yes."

"Can you tell me a little more about Adam." Elizabeth said.

Rebecca smiled, remembering fond memories. "He was a wonderful husband and father. Hated life down the pit. Everyone liked and respected him. He'd help out anyone who needed it. He suffered terrible with his chest. From the mines, all the dust, but despite that he loved singing in the local choir."

Elizabeth thought she might have found a way to help find Adam. "Did he have any favourite hymns or songs?"

"I'm not sure of the titles, but I'll do my best." Rebecca hummed the songs she could remember he loved to sing.

"That's great. I'm sure that one was 'Rock of Ages'."

There was a slightly longer pause as she hummed another tune. "I think I've heard the Welsh sing this. Is it Bread of Heaven?"

"Excellent. Actually it's called 'Guide Me O Thou Great Jehovah'."

"Right up your street this." Jane chipped in.

"A street I know very well. Keep them coming."

Rebecca hummed again.

"Got that one I think. 'Praise him, Praise him'." Elizabeth said. "I think that that should do."

"Thank God for that. Sorry vicar." Jane said.

Elizabeth laughed. "Bless you my child."

"I'm afraid it's a bit too late for that."

Elizabeth easily slipped back into her vestments. "It's never too late for a blessing and forgiveness in God's house."

"I wish I could believe that."

"Believe it, Jane, and your journey will be a lot easier."

Sam reappeared in the doorway. "I know they say it's a small world, but Hill 60 is about three miles southeast of Ypres. We were almost there Elizabeth." He walked into the gallery, stumbled and leaned against the wall, as he saw three women sitting chatting to each other as if it was the most natural thing in the world to do. "I can see you!" Sam said. "But how?"

"Because they want us to see them." Elizabeth said.

"But how?" Sam persisted.

"Sam, as one famous President of America once said, "Read my lips", Because … they … wanted … us … to … see … them."

Sam looked at Jane. "What happened to you?"

"It really doesn't matter. It can wait until another time." Jane answered. "We've been having a nice chat." She smiled at Elizabeth. "About things, and you."

Sam stared at her in silence.

"Lost for words. Never seen that before, Sam."

"I'm not sure what's more scary. Speaking to fresh air, or seeing … what are you?"

"Spirit, ghost, phantom, anything you like to call me, Sam. But we're just plain old Jane and Rebecca."

He sat on the floor next to the three women and shrugged his shoulders at Elizabeth.

"Everything's fine, Sam. What have you discovered?" Elizabeth asked.

"Sorry, but this is a little … I'm not sure what." He turned to look at Rebecca. "Lovely to see you Rebecca. You're sure it was Hill 60 and not any other number? There were a lot of hills in the Great War."

"Yes I'm certain it was 60."

"Do you know the date he was … lost?"

"May 3rd 1915."

"Hill 60 must be where Adam was lost." He pulled some crumpled sheets of A4 out of his pocket and flattened them out on the floor. "The Battle for Hill 60 was fought from," he ran his finger along his notes, "April 17 to May 7 1915. The French had built a mine gallery under the hill and it was extended," he tapped the notes, "it was extended by experienced miners from Northumberland and *Wales*." Sam smiled broadly at Rebecca. "This has to be where Adam was killed." He regretted using the word as he said it, and looked down at his notes. "Initially there weren't many casualties, but the fighting became very heavy. Germany used poisoned gas shells in early May, when they recovered Hill 60."

Sam turned to his second page of notes. "Massive mines were eventually completed and were fired with seventeen other mines in June 1917 at the Battle of Messine." He checked his notes "A hundred and twenty three thousand pounds of high explosive." He folded up the notes and pushed them back into his pocket. "Anyone or anything anywhere near that explosion would have been vaporised."

They sat in silence for a long time.

"So how does this help?" Jane asked.

"If Adam was at Hill 60, then he was close to Ypres. This should mean that his spirit should be close to or at Thiepval, Vimy or the Menin Gate. I don't expect you to understand, but these structures attract and *store* lost spirits. I still don't understand how, but believe me Jane, they do. If Adam's spirit is at one of these places, then Elizabeth has a good chance of helping him become Adam again and passing over."

"Have you been taking that stuff again?" Jane said under raised eyebrows.

Sam laughed. "I thought the same as you. But it's true."

"OK, let's say we believe you. What do we do next? We must help Rebecca, Sam. She's been waiting for Adam for almost a hundred years."

"Once he's here at High Wood, Elizabeth can help him. High Wood is full of souls, but I don't believe Adam is one of them. Elizabeth would have felt his presence, and if he was killed near Ypres then one of the memorials will have attracted his spirit to it." He moved closer to Rebecca and whispered to her. "I will find him for you. I know people in Belgium who'll be able to help us. If anyone can help, then Guillaume and Klaus will."

Rebecca took hold of Sam's hand. "I have waited almost a hundred years, and if I have to, I'll wait another hundred. Time's passed slowly for me, but I don't feel that I've changed. If you find my Adam, will he still be my Adam? Will he remember me? Have I waited for nothing?"

"Let's go downstairs," Sam said, "and agree what we're going to do next." He turned to Rebecca. "Can you bring Adam's photo down to the map room."

Half an hour later Sam had scanned the photo, saved a copy to file and printed six copies. "I think I should go to Ypres, and you," Sam gestured to the others sitting around the kitchen table, "should stay here and be ready if Adam comes through."

"Sam we're going with you. Elizabeth can stay here, but if anyone can find Adam then it must be Rebecca." Jane said.

Sam was frowning, but Elizabeth was nodding in agreement.

"You think this is a good idea?" He said.

"Jane's right, Sam. Rebecca is the closest to Adam and she'll need Jane's support."

"Fine, so let's say they come with me. How the hell are they going to travel? Can they travel? They don't have a separate channel and border control for the dearly departed!"

"No one can see us who we don't want to see us, so who's going to notice anything out of order? Unless of course they're psychic."

"But can you move outside the confines of this house? I thought *this* was your Purgatory, and not some undefined geographical area."

"I can, but we'll need to see what Rebecca can do." Jane turned to Rebecca. "Have you ever left the house?"

"Not since …"

"Have you ever tried to leave the house?"

"No."

"So you may be able to."

"I don't know, I think I should stay here at High Wood. Don't make me go outside. I may miss Adam." Rebecca sounded distraught.

Jane put her arm around her and pulled her close. "You won't miss Adam. We're going to find him in Ypres." She squeezed her tightly. "After all these years I'd want to try anything to bring him home." She gently moved her away from her. "Wouldn't you?"

Rebecca managed a smile and nodded. "Let's see what I can do."

"We're going outside. Wait for us here." Jane said.

Elizabeth gripped Sam's arm. "They need to do this Sam. Having them with you has got to help." She paused and thought to herself. *"At least I hope so."*

Jane stood outside the open front door and Rebecca cowered in the shadows of the hall. She'd been trying to coax her outside for five minutes. She walked back inside and held her hand. "What have you got to lose? Trust me. Come to the door and stand on the step. If you feel OK then try a step outside? Close your eyes and trust me, I'm a doctor."

Rebecca frowned.

"Sorry." Jane said. "It's a very old joke. Now close your eyes."

Rebecca took a firm grip of Jane's hands and took a few tentative steps.

"That's my girl." Jane said encouragingly. "Just a few more."

Rebecca's grip became vice like, but encouraged by Jane, she took more steps.

"There, I'd say that's far enough for a first attempt. Take a look."

Her eyelids were clamped shut.

"You've made it this far. You may as well see what you've done?"

Rebecca allowed tiny slits of light enter her eyes.

"Just a little more?"

The slits slowly grew until Rebecca found herself staring wide eyed at the garden.

Jane's grip grew firmer as Rebecca tried to run back to the house.

"I've got to see what they're doing." Sam ran to the front door. "I can't see anything. They must be still in the house." He shouted back to Elizabeth who was standing in the kitchen door.

"Probably in the back garden? A little more private for what they're doing." Elizabeth smiled as Sam pushed past her, apologised, ran through the kitchen and out of the back door. Elizabeth followed and stood alongside him. Tears started flowing freely at what they saw.

Jane and Rebecca were skipping around the lawn. She looked at Sam who was quietly trying to wipe away his tears. "So can they go?" She asked rhetorically.

He looked at her, wiped away some of her tears, cupped her chin in his hand and smiled. "How could I say no. But I'm still not entirely sure how they," Sam pointed at the *girls* dancing around the lawn, "will be able to travel by air."

SIXTY-NINE

Lidsay wasn't having a good week. Made to look a knob at Morbeck's, made to look an even greater knob at the station, his pension threatened with termination, possible legal action for impersonating a police officer, banned from two of his favourite pubs, thrown out of Tesco for upsetting customers, ripped off a nail on a tin of soup, trod in cat's shit on his lawn and carried it into the house, sprayed weedkiller on his favourite rose, and to top it all off, he'd been diagnosed with type two diabetes. Someone had to suffer for all of this and it was Gloria who bore the burden, and the bruises. Long sleeves and scarves covered most of his handiwork, but no one really believed her walking into a door as a reason for the black eye. The final vindictive straw which broke her personal camel's back was Ivor pouring half a bottle of domestic bleach into her aquarium.

He walked down to the corner shop to buy a paper and a bottle of milk, insulted the shopkeeper by discussing his ethnic origins and right to be in Britain, called a pensioner a drain on society, told a teenager he was sponging off the state, knocked over a bucket of cut flowers, hurled abuse at two cyclists, threatened a pimply youth selling the *Big Issue* and returned home empty handed.

His week was perfectly rounded off when he found a suitcase outside his front door with a yellow post it note stuck to it bearing the succinct message.

"Had enough. Sod off."

He spent the next half an hour disturbing the neighbours as he tried to batter down the front and back doors. Gloria turned the volume up on the radio and sang along to Michael Buble. The full extent of his vocabulary of expletives, surprised even the most liberal of his neighbours, but common sense made them resist the need to correct some of his more colourful imagery and language, and simply enjoy the entertainment from behind the safety of their curtains.

Twenty minutes later a police car pulled up outside the house, and two officers well known to him made their way to where he was now sitting on the front step.

"Everything alright, Sarge?"

Lidsay looked up. "What the fuck do you think?"

"No need for that Ivor. We're just responding to calls from several people in this area about a domestic disturbance."

Lidsay turned his head to the house. "Happy now, bitch!"

"Not going to ask again, Ivor. Tone it down. Don't want another visit to the station do we." He was finding it hard not to smirk.

Lidsay looked up. "Something tickling your fancy, George?"

"Can we go inside and discuss this?"

Lidsay pointed over his shoulder at the house. "Don't know. You'd better ask the Wicked Bitch of the West. I'm locked out."

George knocked on the front door and called through the letterbox to Gloria. "Can we come in and discuss this Gloria?"

"You can, but that bastard can piss off!"

George turned around and spoke to Ivor. "Seem to have a bit of a problem, Ivor. You appear to be persona non grata, so why don't you find somewhere to stay for tonight and we'll all come back tomorrow when things have calmed down."

Lidsay stared aggressively at George. "You as well? Work with someone for twenty years and you think you know them. Any ideas where I might stay tonight?"

"Always a place in the cells for you, Ivor." George had had enough of this.

Lidsay finally gave it up as a lost cause, picked up the case and stormed off down the street.

SEVENTY

Seale Hayne seemed like a lifetime away to Agnes. They'd been back at Agnez-les-Duisans for two months, and when Agnes looked at the highly skilled surgeon with the bed side manner of St Michael, stitching together a macabre patchwork of flayed skin and pieces of flesh, replacing internal organs in gaping bodily cavities, precisely removing foreign, in all senses of the word, objects from every conceivable part of the body, amputating hands and arms which had held lovers close and fought suitors away; amputating legs which had graced football pitches and cricket squares, removing eyes which had stared in wonderment at the birth of their sons and daughters, and those who eventually surrendered to the demands of a greater power as major blood vessels ruptured and drenched James in what had once brought life to the dismembered young man lying in front of him. She had to struggle to remember the days and weeks she'd spent trying to coax him from his shell under the sanctuary of his bed, and desperately trying to recall the broken man from his personal hell. Their time at Seale Hayne was now a rapidly fading memory of good times and bad.

James stretched his spine as far as was possible without dislocating any vertebrae and sighed deeply. All days were hard, but today …

Agnes looked across the operating room at him and was concerned at his expression. She waved at him to meet her outside.

He looked up, smiled, nodded and mouthed, "Just be a few minutes."

She paused briefly and watched him as he walked across the blood soaked boards to a soldier who he'd simply had to stitch up, as there was no chance of any surgical repair to his massive internal wounds. Agnes had never got used to these pointless deaths, so she turned and walked outside into the chill November air.

"Cigarette?" James didn't smoke, but always carried a battered packet of Players Navy Cut and a box of Aeroplane matches for *moments of stress*. The young infantryman nodded painfully, James lit a coffin nail and placed it between the soldier's cracked lips. He drew in an enormous breath, hacked violently but satisfyingly and blew out the smoke.

James looked closely at the ashen, swollen, badly bruised face and searched through his memory files. This shell of a man, this facsimile of a human being, this echo of a life rang bells, which suddenly chimed in unison. "Tully, Private Tully?"

"Reporting for duty, sir."

"What in God's name happened to you?"

"German shrapnel, sir. Couldn't just sit around here and watch my mates …" he grimaced in agonies which morphine could no longer control, "… go to the … slaughter … sir." His face crumpled into a mask of suffering. "Had … to … do my … bit."

James had no idea how long Tully could last, but decided that he wouldn't leave him until he'd passed to a place where he prayed that suffering didn't exist.

"Passchendaele was it?" James asked.

Tully struggled to take a breath, coughed up a bright red froth which soaked into the cigarette paper making it look like a tiny stick of peppermint rock. He bit into the cigarette and hoarsely whispered. "Poelcapelle." He spat the cigarette onto the floor. "Their shells were exploding … in the mud and showering us … with filth." He gasped for air. "They were … shredding our dead lads' rotten flesh."

Blood, too slowly for James, was filling Tully's lungs and drowning him.

"At least … I … didn't drown … in the filth … of one of those … shell holes …" He coughed and scarlet blood ran from the corner of his mouth.

James stood up and held Tully's hands. He knew that relief was close at hand. "Take it easy, Tully. We'll all soon be out of this hell."

His words were faint and gargled through the blood spewing from his throat. "Let … the wife know … going to … think … tell her … I …" His final words were washed away, lost in a scarlet torrent.

James felt Tully's death grip through his hands. In a final desperate moment of release, the left hand limply fell away, and James had to prise open the fingers on his right, as it clung to a few last moments of contact with the living. James leaned forward, cleaned away the blood from Tully's face with a swab and tenderly closed his eyes.

A familiar voice offered some comfort. "There was nothing you could do. It would have been better for him if the shrapnel had been a few inches higher. At least death would have been instantaneous."

James turned around and collapsed into the arms of Captain Jacques Le Chartrois.

Half an hour later Jacques was stood with Agnes in their quarters, he'd examined James and was sat by his bunk looking closely at him. "The shell shock was that bad?" Jacques had no idea that James had been hospitalised and was shocked at the story Agnes had told him.

"Worse than I've said." Agnes had used up all her tears.

"But why did they send him back?"

"Because there are few men with James skills to quickly repair broken men so they can be fed back into this ravenous war machine. If that means he …" she looked away from James "… if he suffers, then so be it. It's a small price worth paying, and what's one more shattered life among the tens of thousands of others."

Jacques moved closer to Agnes and held her tightly. "We must get him out of this."

"Yes. But how? They won't send him back until he breaks down again."

"He'd get back with a Blighty." Jacques smiled at Agnes.

"We need to shoot him." Agnes said quietly.

Jacques quickly but gently, put his hand on Agnes's mouth and mouthed "Shhh."

"We need to get him shot?"

"But something that's not dangerous. Only something which means that he will be shipped back to England." Jacques whispered.

"But how? The chances of James being anywhere near any action are tiny."

"Accidents happen all the time." He said with a wink. "We just have to make sure that it isn't seen as a deliberate act of cowardice."

Agnes frowned at Jacques. "So he could be shot at dawn?"

He laughed. "Very unlikely."

"But possible. Yes?"

Jacques sighed. "Yes anything is possible, but extremely unlikely." He looked around the empty room as if every ear in the Army was listening to them. "Once he has recovered we will arrange to go to Ypres. On the way, surely it would be possible that a stray German bullet could hit James in the foot? Entirely plausible," he paused and looked around the tent, "wouldn't you say?"

Agnes cautiously smiled, but still felt very uncomfortable about Jacque's plan, but what was the alternative? Wait for James to disappear again into his own personal hell. Only this time never to emerge?

"He'll never agree to it." Agnes knew James too well.

"He'll never know about it." Jacques replied, smiling.

"He'll never forgive us."

"He'll have nothing to forgive, Agnes. A stray German bullet. What could we possibly have to do with that?"

Agnes walked aimlessly around the tent, occasionally looking at the sleeping figure of James.

"A man of his principles would never countenance this." She thought. *"If he did ever discover the truth he'd never forgive me, I'd lose him. But if he stays here I'll lose him anyway. He can't cope with this any longer. I need to get him back to Seale Hayne and Arthur."*

She turned to Jacques. "What do we have to do?"

SEVENTY-ONE

Klaus had decided to stay with Guillaume until the funeral. He was reading Sam's latest email, when the phone rang.

"Bauer." He always answered the phone in the same abrupt way.

"Klaus, it's Ralph. How's Guillaume?"

"About as well as could be expected. We have a date for Isaac's funeral."

There was a short silence.

"That is ... good news. When is it?"

"Next Tuesday. A memorial service at a Synagogue at one o' clock followed by burial in their family plot."

"Have you told any of the others?"

"No. We're emailing everyone today."

"How are you holding up?" Ralph was concerned.

There was a longer silence.

"Not well."

Another silence.

"I am so sorry I can't be there, but my wife's starting chemo and I have to be here for her."

"Your priorities lie with her. Guillaume knows that you would be here if you could." Klaus said.

"Give him my heartfelt best wishes, and say a prayer for Isaac for me." Ralph was finding it difficult to speak.

"We'll call you when it's all over." Klaus said.

"I'd welcome that, Klaus. It will be good to talk. Take care. This has taken its toll on you as well."

"There are, six days to the funeral. There will be plenty of time to recover then, but for now I must be strong for Guillaume. Auf Wiedersehen."

"Goodbye. Take care."

Guillaume came into the room with two coffees. "Who was it?"

"Ralph. He sends his best wishes. He won't be able to attend the funeral. His wife is ill." He paused. "Very ill."

Guillaume left it at that.

"I've had an email from Sam. I'll reply to it and let him know the details of the funeral." Klaus said.

"How are they?" Guillaume was genuinely interested in Sam and Elizabeth. He'd developed a true friendship in the short time he'd known them.

"OK."

"Only OK?"

"Well it's a little difficult to explain."

"Klaus please try."

"He has, I'm really not sure of the words. Er hat gefunden, entdeckt, Gespenster, Geister am hohen Holz."

"Ghosts, spirits! What spirits?" Guillaume's voice gave away his shock.

"Der geist ... the ghosts of his wife Jane, and of a missing soldier's wife Rebecca Morbeck."

"They are in High Wood?"

"Yes. High Wood was Rebecca Morbeck's home and High Wood is the last place his wife Jane can remember being at before she died." Klaus remained utterly factual in his answers.

"Who was Rebecca's husband?"

"Adam Morbeck. He was Sam's great grandfather. Do you remember, we found his great uncle Jack Morbeck's grave at Dozinghem."

"Yes, but there is also Sam's wife!"

"Ja, Sam's Frau."

"She is dead?"

"Ja Guillaume, ghosts are usually like that."

"He is certain of this."

"It is beyond doubt. Elizabeth has confirmed everything."

Silence.

"This is unexpected news. The fact that he and Elizabeth have made direct contact with these spirits, confirms they possess the powers Isaac believed they had. He would have been very happy." Guillaume said.

"You should also be aware that Sam wants our help. He is coming to Ypres with his two new *friends*."

"The spirits! His wife and Rebecca?"

"Yes they all plan to travel. Sam believes that Rebecca will be able to contact Adam if he is trapped in Belgium or France."

"Can they travel? This is unprecedented."

"Sam believes they can, so having no previous experience of such things, I must bow to his knowledge."

"And when will they be here?"

"Friday." Klaus said.

"Do you want me to pick them up?" Guillaume asked.

"Nein Danke, mein Freund. Just get me one of those beers I like."

"La Chouffe?"

"Nein, no, it sounds like roman ... romanblack?"

Guillaume laughed for the first time in weeks. "Rodenbach?"

"Ja, ja Rodenbach? Es is sehr guht. It is good to hear you laugh." Klaus sensitively replied.

"It seems a very long time since I smiled."

"Time is a great healer Guillaume. Today it feels that nothing will ever repair your broken heart, and nothing ever will completely. Only having Isaac here could do that. But time does heal. Time and friends."

They smiled at each other and walked arm in arm into the kitchen to the beer.

SEVENTY-TWO

Sam was sitting in departures at Cardiff airport checking the status of his, their, flight to Brussels on KL1058. It was still on time and boarding would be through Gate 1. Sam looked across the departure hall to where Jane was showing the bewildered Rebecca around the duty free shopping area.

"And these are for listening to music?" Rebecca asked in amazement.

Jane smiled. "Yes you can keep a thousand songs on this."

"But it's so small. Where do you keep them?"

This was territory Jane didn't want to, or couldn't enter. "I haven't got a clue. All I can say is that it works." She picked up a demo model and carefully put the headphones over a suspicious Rebecca's ears. *"Nothing too loud."* Jane thought.

Rebecca's hands instinctively went up to her ears, but Jane caught them before they could rip the strange things from them.

"It's fine. Honestly." Jane said reassuringly. "Just listen." She searched through the track list and selected 'Cavatina' from the 'Deer Hunter'. As the soft lilting Spanish guitar of John Williams started to play, Rebecca smiled and started crying. Jane tried to take the headphones off, but Rebecca stopped her and smiled.

"It's wonderful." She said through tears.

Sam got up and walked quickly across to the duty free shops. He couldn't believe no one else had noticed the headphones floating in mid air. As he reached them, he saw Jane take them from Rebecca's ears and drop them onto the counter.

Rebecca was startled. "Jane that was wonderful."

"Yes but also strange." She smiled at Rebecca and looked around the shop. "You don't often see headphones floating in mid air."

Only one other person had noticed. An eight year old boy was desperately, but without much success, trying to tell his parents about it. "But they *were* floating. Honestly!"

"Calm down Peter. You're getting over excited. We'll soon be on holiday, and Mickey Mouse is getting everything ready for us in Paris."

"Why won't you believe me?" He was getting exasperated with his dismissive parents.

"Peter, headphones do not float." His father picked up the nearest pair of headphones and dropped them onto the floor. "You see, they don't float."

"But they do get damaged!" The electronics sales person was standing close to Dad as he picked up the headphones.

"They're not damaged. Look." Dad pushed the headphones under her nose.

She took a step back and took them from Dad as if they needed decontaminating, examined them closely and held them out to Dad pointing at what appeared to him to be nothing. "They're cracked. I can't sell these now. You have to be very careful with electronic goods. Health and safety."

Dad stared at the headphones in disbelief and looked around at the small crowd which had gathered to enjoy this early morning entertainment. "What bloody crack." He offered them back to the sales person who crossed her arms.

"I think I'd better get the store manager, sir."

Dad's wife poked him in the ribs. "Alan! Pay for them and let's get away from here!"

Dad gritted his teeth. "Look there's no need for that. How much are they?"

"£69.99."

"How much! I didn't want to bloody well buy the shop!"

"Alan!!" The single word and tone was sufficient to tell Dad that if he didn't want a week of misery, he'd shut up and pay.

"£69.99? That's fine." He handed her his boarding card and master card, entered his pin, waited for the receipt, took his goods and was escorted by his embarrassed and angry wife to a coffee shop.

"Poor little tyke." Rebecca said. "Hope he doesn't get into any trouble because of us."

"He'll be fine." Jane replied. "Not so sure about his father though."

Sam was unsure how to start any sort of conversation with Jane and Rebecca, without making the assembled mass of travellers think he'd escaped from some home for the mentally unstable. "Having fun?" He whispered.

An orange-faced woman selling a new fragrance from Chanel turned and sarcastically whispered back. "No not really. I've been here since five o'clock this morning, but thanks for asking."

Sam smiled and walked a few steps away. He looked at Jane and Rebecca, who were both in hysterics.

"Really, Sam, chatting up women at this time of day." Jane said, desperately trying to keep a straight face.

"I'm not chatting … " Sam stared at Jane and Rebecca," … It … I … was just …"

"Oh really, I didn't realise I was chatting with you!" Orange face was getting annoyed with Sam.

"No not you." Sam turned to Orange face. "Her." He said pointing at the display of perfumes.

"Who?" Orange face's complexion was now bordering on scarlet.

"Her." Sam looked to where he was pointing, and swallowed deeply.

"Oh *her*. I didn't realise that *she* was here."

"Sam I'd back away now. There are a couple of security guards who seem to be taking an interest in you." Jane said to him.

"Oh, piss off!" Sam bit his tongue a little too late.

"Charming!" An older woman with a blue rinse; dressed in a beige suit with trousers that were just too short, sitting too high above shoes which were too pink, hissed at him as she picked up a bottle of Flower Bomb. She turned to her overweight and heavily tanned friend, wearing a poorly fitting black wig, jeans two sizes too small, a long black loose blouse which just about managed to cover her bulging posterior, luminous green Nike trainers, and in a voice which was loud enough to ensure that everyone would know who and what she was talking about, spat out. "You'd think someone of his age would know better. How they can drink so much at this time of the morning is beyond me, Lesley. Probably on benefits and an alcoholic!"

"Do you actually want to buy anything, sir, or would you like to get a coffee and sober up! I can always ask security to give you a helping hand?" Orange face had had enough of travellers who couldn't resist alcohol at eight o' clock in the morning.

Sam did his best to be apologetic, "I'm really sorry," and come up with some plausible excuse for his odd behaviour, "I'm going to a funeral and I'm extremely upset. A very dear friend you see." He offered his hand to Orange face who looked at it as if it belonged to an infected tramp. She turned on her heels and started selling her wares to a young man whose girlfriend clearly needed the most expensive perfume she had to offer.

He was about to say something, but became aware of the number of eyes fixed disapprovingly on him he walked across the hall to a news stand, bought a copy of The Times, some mints, and ambled across to a coffee shop avoiding the glances of most of the passengers who'd heard the *discussion* in the duty free shop.

"Medium latte and a croissant please." Sam asked as he handed over a ten pound note.

"Obviously trying to sober up, Lesley. Probably impossible for the likes of him." Blue Rinse was two behind him in the queue. "Family's probably all the same. They usually are."

Sam folded his arms and bit his lip as hard as he could without causing any permanent damage. He picked up his coffee and croissant from the end of the counter and found a table in a far corner of the coffee shop. Blue Rinse looked after him, pointed and made some derogatory comment to the waitress and Black Wig. He found a table for three in a corner of the coffee shop and Jane and Rebecca joined him.

"OK if I sit here?" An elderly traveller asked Sam.

"Uh, sorry no they're taken." Sam replied.

The old man looked closely at the two apparently empty seats. "By whom may I ask." He said courteously.

"Oh sorry, they're in the toilet. But they should be back in a few minutes."

The coffee shop was packed with travellers. The old man looked around at the full tables and raised his eyebrows at Sam. "Would it be OK if I just sat down until they came back? Only my hip is playing me up."

Blue Rinse overheard the conversation and was glowering at Sam.

Jane stood up and whispered in Sam's ear. "Let him sit down."

Sam gestured to him to sit down.

"Thank you. I understand how difficult it is to keep a seat when it's this busy." He gingerly sat down and sipped at his latte. "Travelling far?"

"No not really. Just to Brussels and then Ypres." Sam replied.

The old man smiled. "Ypres? My father was wounded very close to Ypres in World War One. His brother, Philip, was sadly killed." He sipped his americano. "Never found his body. So sad." He dunked a digestive biscuit, and got it to his mouth just before it collapsed into his mug. "Damnedest thing though, his other brother, Albert, he was the eldest, survived the war and married a bloody German." He drank a little more americano. "Can you believe that! Kill the buggers for four years and then bloody well marry one." He chuckled to himself, completely unaware of his very politically incorrect feelings. "Family disowned him of course. Never spoke to him again. I tried to keep in touch, but he moved to Germany with his wife and set up home in Dresden. He was killed in the firestorm after the bombing raid in March 1945. Poetic justice if you ask me. Survive the war to end all wars with Germany, and then get killed by the British." He chuckled again to himself, picked up his mug and drained the last of his americano. "Are you going to pay your respects to anyone?"

"My Uncle is buried at Dozinghem. He was killed at Passchendaele." Sam answered.

The gentleman frowned and shook his head. "God awful place Passchendaele." He slowly pushed his chair back and stood up. "Just called my flight. Hope you have a good visit. Nice to speak to you."

Sam stood up and offered his hand. "Nice to meet you as well … Mr?"

"Sorry how very rude of me. Arthur Tully, and yourself?"

"Morbeck, Sam Morbeck. Enjoy your holiday. Where are you going?"

"Las Vegas. Go every year. Wouldn't miss it. Gamble a little, win some, lose some, see some shows, revisit the Grand Canyon and wander up and down the Strip." He smiled to himself. "Heaven on Earth." He turned, waved and started walking slowly to Gate 5.

"KLM flight to Brussels is now available for boarding from Gate 1."

Sam stood up, grabbed his hand luggage and said. "Just follow me and find somewhere on the plane where you're not in the way." He immediately regretted not whispering.

Blue Rinse turned in her chair, narrowed her eyes and looked up at Sam. "I pray to God I'm not on the same flight as *you* and that our paths never cross again. If I ever see you again it will probably be on some crime programme!" She turned to Black Wig and shook her head.

After a thankfully incident-free flight, Sam exited the arrivals lounge and spotted Klaus and Karsten leaning against the metal barrier. Klaus opened his arms and hugged Sam.

"So good to see you again my friend." He turned to Karsten. "Grab the trolley and bags will you." Karsten smiled at Sam and shrugged.

They made their way to the car park and loaded Sam's bags into the boot of the Mercedes.

Klaus looked all around Sam. "Did your friends come with you?"

Sam nodded.

Klaus and Karsten frowned and smiled. "Where are they now?" Klaus said.

Sam looked over his right shoulder, "Jane is here," and then his left and nodded, "and Rebecca's here."

Klaus sharply clicked the heels of his shoes together, nodded and smiled. "Willkommen Sie in Brüssel sehr geehrte Damen. Excuse me please. Welcome to Brussels, dear ladies."

Karsten was staring into the empty space around Sam. "Vater, kannst du sie sehen?"

"Ich kann sie nur spüren. Excuse me Sam, I was telling Karsten that I could only sense them. I have felt the presence of so many spirits over the years that I know immediately when *friends* are with us. Welcome again, ladies. Will they travel in the back with you, Sam?"

"Yes, and thanks for your understanding." He smiled and slid onto the middle of the three back seats. Jane shuffled through Sam and sat on his left while Rebecca sat on his right.

"This is very nice." Jane said to Sam.

"Klaus has always been very generous in his hospitality." Sam replied.

Klaus turned around in his seat. "Did you say something, Sam?"

"I was just telling Jane how generous you were."

Klaus looked across the back seats of the car and smiled at Sam. "I must have a conversation with them when we get to the hotel."

For the first time since he'd *found* Jane and Rebecca, Sam didn't feel *strange*. He should have realised that Klaus's past experiences with so many lost souls had made him ultra-sensitive to any residual spirit energies.

Rebecca was still in a trance.

"You OK?" Jane asked her.

"It's all just a little …"

"I understand." She leaned across the seats through Sam and squeezed Rebecca's arm. "It would be like me finding myself stranded in 1914 London."

Klaus looked back over his shoulder. "It would be impossible to comprehend. I can't imagine what it would be like, Rebecca, to find myself in a time completely alien to me." Klaus smiled at Sam. "I think that you both look very beautiful."

Jane and Rebecca turned and looked at each other at precisely the same moment. Their jaws on their chests. "You … c'can … h'hear … and see us?" Jane stuttered. "But we didn't *let* you. Did we? How can you?"

Klaus pulled down the sun visor and smiled in the illuminated mirror at them. "I have spoken with so many spirits over the years, my dears. Is it good to know that you are not alone, Sam?"

Sam nodded and smiled.

"He's German." Rebecca whispered to Jane.

"It's OK, we haven't been at war with them for almost seventy years." Jane whispered back smiling. "The war to end all wars didn't. A second World War followed the carnage of the first after only twenty one years. Unfortunately we don't learn our lessons very quickly. Millions more needed to be slaughtered before we almost began to understand the sheer idiocy of it all. Even now we still massacre each other. Ethnically cleanse has become more politically acceptable than holocaust."

Twenty five minutes later they were checking in to their hotel.

"I have booked a separate room for the ladies." Klaus whispered to Sam. "I thought that it would be more … *suitable*. The hotel believes that these guests will be late arrivals, and I've told them they will collect their keys from myself. I'd suggest that we all have a quick shower and meet in the bar in about half an hour? I have a restaurant booked for nine. I'm sure ladies," he spoke quietly at the space between Sam and Karsten, "I'm sure you will be able to occupy yourselves?" Jane nodded at Klaus who smiled. "Excellent."

Dinner was adequate. Not the best or worst Sam had eaten, but at least it filled a hole. They were sat in the lounge of the hotel drinking night caps, and Jane and Rebecca were sat on a rug in front of them.

"What do you want to do tomorrow, Sam?" Klaus lifted his empty glass to the waiter and gestured that he wanted a refill.

"I was hoping that you'd have some ideas?"

Klaus smiled as the waiter returned with his whisky. He drained the glass, sat back in the red leather chair, steepled his fingers and pressed his lips with his index fingers. "After your email I looked into Adam's service in the war, and the possible part Hill 60 played in his death."

Rebecca's head turned to Klaus.

"There is a cemetery close to where Hill 60 was located, and I think that's where we should start." He turned in his chair to look at Rebecca. "Rebecca, your connection with Adam should help us find any traces of him. That's all we need, and once we have found this trace, we can …" Klaus paused, as he noticed that a couple sat at the bar had taken a keen interest in the conversation he was having with the rug. The barman was leaning forward on the bar and seemed to be indicating to them that he'd served Klaus with four or five whiskies. Klaus glared at them, shook his head and looked back at Rebecca and smiled. "As I was saying, once we have a trace of where Adam was … is, then Sam can make contact and direct him to Thiepval. From there he will soon be back at High Wood and Elizabeth."

"Will I see him?" Rebecca was leaning forward and staring intently at Klaus.

"Honestly. I don't know. I have had no experience of another spirit waiting for a lost soul."

Rebecca's face collapsed.

"But." Klaus leaned forward in his chair. "My belief is that because of the strength of your ties to Adam, he will not move on until you have been reunited."

She held hands with Jane and smiled. "We will see each other again. Won't we?"

"I have no doubts." Jane squeezed her hand and smiled.

The following morning an Audi Q7 collected them from the hotel. Klaus knew the driver from previous visits, who wasn't in the least bit surprised at odd conversations that took place on the short drive to Hill 60 south-east of Ypres. The driver pulled into the car park, everyone disembarked and took a close look at the contemporary photos and back ground information placed by the Westhoek Tourist Board. At the front of the site was a memorial to the 1st Australian Tunnelling Company.

Sam looked at it closely. "There are bullet holes in it!"

"Not from World War One, Sam, this area was fought over again in World War Two. We never seem to learn." Klaus explained.

Sam was still staring at the memorial. "These tunnellers were Australian."

"Yes they were the main strength of the mine which was excavated here." Klaus replied.

"But I thought this was where Adam probably died?"

"There were British soldiers supporting the Australians with their expertise, and with Adam's knowledge of mining, he would have been a prime candidate for that type of role."

Sam walked on a few paces, looking around the memorial site. "The ground's still badly scarred and cratered. What must it have looked like when you stripped away the grass, trees and all signs of civilisation? I've seen photographs, but until you see this with your own eyes ..."

"The ground was preserved not only to leave the scars visible for future generations, but also as a mark of respect for those who died here." Klaus paused for a few moments. "The site is essentially a mass grave." He looked back at Sam and Karsten. "You will both need to be careful here. There are many life forces concentrated in this place."

Karsten was looking to his right. "These depressions in the ground were caused by what?"

"The mines." Guillaume had joined them. "These smaller craters are from 1915 and 1916." He started to walk further into the site and waved to the others to follow him. He stopped at a much deeper single crater. "This was one of the nineteen mines blown at the start of the Battle of Messines. In 1916, the British started a mining offensive against the German-held Witjschate salient. The conditions for mining were particularly difficult, but despite this the sappers dug tunnels eighty to a hundred feet down into the blue clay."

Karsten looked over at Klaus who seemed distracted, and was looking around the edge of the crater.

"Can you believe that Karsten?" Guillaume was staring into the crater and hadn't noticed Klaus racing around the edge. "A hundred feet down, and they excavated around six thousand yards yards, of galleries, deep under the German front lines." Guillaume looked up to see Sam chasing after Klaus around the rim of the crater.

Klaus reached Jane and Rebecca who were standing transfixed close to the rim of the crater. "Rebecca, I should have asked you to stay in the Q7. This is too much to expose you to so early."

Rebecca kept staring into the crater.

Jane looked up and smiled. "It's OK Klaus, Rebecca's fine." She turned back to her and gently put her arm around her shoulder. "It's the first time since Adam left for the war that she's felt close to him."

Rebecca looked down into the crater. "He's here. This is the place."

"Klaus!" Jane shouted.

Klaus turned and gasped. Sam was stood on the edge of the crater which was beginning to crumble. Klaus rushed to him, but as he reached out to grab hold of him he toppled like a rag doll into the crater.

On the other side of the crater, Guillaume watched in disbelief as Sam rolled and tumbled down the crater until he came to a crashing stop in a bramble bush at the bottom and disappeared from view. He jumped into the crater and slid down the side, avoiding the tearing brambles and stinging nettles like an Olympic slalom skier. When he reached the bottom he ran to the bramble bush Sam had crashed into, but couldn't find him in the tangled mass of thorns.

"Sam!" Guillaume shouted in panic.

No response.

"Sam!" Guillaume grabbed a stick beating at the brambles.

"Guillaume, can you see him?" Klaus was stumbling down the slope desperately trying to get to Guillaume. "Is he there?"

Guillaume pushed the brambles aside with the stick, and peered into what remained of the bush. He looked up to Klaus and slowly shook his head.

SEVENTY-THREE

Alone in High Wood, Elizabeth didn't feel uneasy or afraid, just lonely. Without Sam there, she'd begun to appreciate how quickly he'd become a vital cog in her life. For years she'd led a single life, but now understood that a life led alone was incomplete. Not just in the eye of the Lord, but also there was little satisfaction in not being able to share the good things in life with someone close. It was too late for the joy of children, which was a nagging sadness, but one which she would bear. The physical side of their relationship, even though it was still very early days, was something which had added a level of satisfaction she'd never experienced before. More satisfying than those warm moments as a teenager, she'd didn't really understand, trotting around Mrs Abbott's paddock on her favourite grey mare Charlotte. This was more direct, more intimate, more fun and less bruising. She smiled. The satisfaction was as much in the anticipation as it was in experiencing his ejaculation and her orgasm, orgasms. She smiled again. Ejaculation and orgasm were words which had never featured in her vocabulary and still sat a little uncomfortably with her.

She sat bolt upright in bed, as the sound of the kitchen door scraping against the tiled floor, woke her from a deep satisfying sleep.

Lidsay hadn't had many worse weeks in his life. Kicked out by Gloria, made to look a twat again, at the station, threatened with losing his pension, cautioned by the Assistant Chief Inspector, staying at a cheap B&B, eating a diet which consisted mostly of pie and chips, and his car had failed its MOT. So what was there to lose, at least in prison he'd get a bed, three square meals and no bills to pay. He was still convinced there was something in High Wood. Something they wanted to keep secret, and something which offered him a way out of this shit hole of a so called life. He grimaced as the kitchen door complained as it dragged across the kitchen floor. He was sure there was no one in the house, as there were no cars to be seen anywhere, Elizabeth had taken a taxi from the vicarage, and no lights shone a warning in the house. But he still had real concerns there could be someone in High Wood as he'd not been monitoring the house, and this visit had been on impulse.

Elizabeth swung her feet out of bed onto the carpet, feeling in the darkness with her feet for her slippers. She stood up and shivered, as much from fear as the icy cold of the bedroom. She was still unaccustomed to the layout of the room and bit her lip as she kicked the leg of the dressing table with her little toe. Her hand finally found the light switch but resisted turning it on. The benefits of illumination she decided were outweighed by the risks of alerting whoever it was that she was there.

Lidsay froze in the darkness. Cold and fear were a toxic combination. He decided to leave the door open and flicked on his torch. The stark narrow beam of light didn't ease his fear as it created sinister shape shifting shadows.

"Shit! I'm too old for this." He thought as he shambled into the hall.

"If that ... whatever it was ... is still up there ... then ... I'm ... Oh bollocks ... come on let's get the gold. What's the worst that can happen?" He stopped thinking as he started imagining the worst things that could happen. He made it up four stairs when he heard an odd sound from the landing.

"It's nothing."

"Bollocks, is it nothing!"

"Look it's nothing."

"Piss off!"

"So what the fuck is it?"

"I have no intention of finding out!"

Lidsay was finding it hard convincing himself that this was all worthwhile. The hollow tapping sounds from the landing didn't make going up the stairs a lot easier.

"So what the fuck was that?"

"Old houses move all the time. It's the wood. It warps."

"You're pissing warped if you think I'm going up there to say hello to ..."

The sound of the top stair creaking as it gave under the weight of ...

Lidsay wasn't going to wait to find out what. He span around, fell down the few stairs he climbed, stumbled into a small table, smashed a vase, dropped the torch and ran into the darkness of the house.

Elizabeth's foot hovered over the second step at the top of the stairs, but the sound of crashing furniture and shattering china made any further progress impossible. Her breathing was fast and shallow, her skin clammy, her hands clenched into frozen fists, her eyes wanting to close but refusing and staring into the darkness. Something shapeless shot into the blackness, whimpering as it ran. Elizabeth frowned. Not many spectres whimpered. Did they? Animals whimpered.

"Some stray cat smelling food, has pushed open the back door and panicked." She thought. She crept down the stairs and tripped over the overturned table, cutting her hand on a shard of broken china. She pulled a tissue from a pocket in her pyjama trousers and held it tightly against the cut to stem the bleeding. "Puss! Puss! Here puss!" She called into the inky blackness.

Lidsay's nervous system was close to meltdown. *"It's her."* He thought. *"She's looking for her bloody cat."* He stumbled backwards across what he didn't know was the lounge and into the map room.

Elizabeth heard the noise and called out to the cat again. "Puss! Here puss!"

Lidsay fell against a light switch on the wall of the map room, and the glare of the strip lighting temporarily blinded him.

Elizabeth saw the light from the map room, and the thought of a cat turning on the lights, somewhat evaporated her hope that whatever was in the house was of feline origin. She edged back out of the lounge and crept into the kitchen. She needed something to provide her with a little more physical protection, and a meat tenderiser gave her a better feeling of security.

Lidsay felt frantically for the switch and turned the lights off.

"Please find your cat!" He desperately thought as he closed his eyes and gracefully slid down the wall onto the floor. *"God, if you want to take someone before their planned departure date and give someone else a bit more time down here, then take me now. Because if there's any point to all of this, then I'm afraid its lost on me."*

A shuffling sound to his right made him clamp his eyes shut even tighter.

"Take me now! Please take me now!"

The shuffling began to move further into the room.

Lidsay rolled to his left and felt for the opening of the door, crawled into the lounge, out into the hall, and whispered what he thought was close to a Hail Mary. In the cloying darkness he lost all sense of direction. To his left he could see a thin strip of dim light.

"Has to be the front door." He thought. *"It's the light from the street lamps."* He crawled to the strip of light and like a blind man reading braille felt over the surface of the door until he found the handle.

"Sweet Jesus thank you." He stood up, quietly opened the door, stepped inside and fell down the stairs of the cellar.

"Lidsay." Someone or something hissed his name from the darkness.

"Oh shit, she knows my name." He thought.

"Lieutenant Lidsay." The hissing continued. "Where are you?"

"Lieutenant?" It was a clearly a man's voice. Lidsay put his hands to the ground to push himself up, ready to run back up the stairs to whatever lay in wait for him, but what he felt under his palms disturbed him. It felt chalky and granular. *"Calm down. The floor down here was soil, wasn't it."* He felt a little reassured as he remembered his last look around the cellar.

Elizabeth gingerly walked out of the kitchen, weapon in hand and flicked on the light switch in the hall. Out of the corner of her eye she noticed the cellar door was open. She grabbed the handle and slammed it shut.

Lidsay looked around for the steps, but they were gone, replaced by the white chalk walls of a tunnel. The grime streaked face which emerged from the pitch black of the tunnel almost finished him.

"He's here, Sarge'." The words were whispered over his shoulder. "But he looks in a bad way." The face moved closer to Lidsay illuminated by a flickering candle. "It's OK, sir, we'll have the lights working again in no time." The face looked deeply into Lidsay's eyes. "I think he's gone, sir. Lost it. Dark can do that to a man."

A second grime-streaked face appeared in the candle light and stared closely at Lidsay. "Doesn't look good does 'e. We'd better get 'im out of 'ere as quick as we can." He turned and hissed into the darkness, "Smiff, if you don't get these 'effin lights back on in the next two minutes I'm going to shove this candle up your arse!" He turned around and spoke to grime face. "Get 'im back up the tunnel and into the open. If 'e really *goes* down 'ere then Gawd only knows what will 'appen." He turned and walked away into the darkness threatening Smiff with untold physical misery.

Lidsay sat paralysed against the tunnel wall. Grime face reached out to him but he just stared at the hand as if it was leprous.

"Come on now, sir. Let's get you out of here shall we?"

Lidsay couldn't have answered even if he'd wanted to, as terror had paralysed his vocal cords.

Grime Face moved closer to Lidsay and firmly took hold of his arms. "OK, sir, just let me show you the way. It'll be a lot better when we get you out of here."

Like a submissive child, Lidsay let Grime Face guide him down the claustrophobic tunnel. Light bulbs, hanging on wires along the ceiling of the tunnel like long forgotten Christmas decorations, suddenly exploded with a blinding light which rebounded off the stark white chalk of the tunnel. Grime face instinctively let go of Lidsay and covered his eyes. Lidsay didn't react as quickly, and screamed as the blinding light seared into his eyes. Burning tears streamed down his cheeks. It was a level of pain he'd never felt before, and prayed he'd never feel again. The light had scorched the retinas in his eyes.

Grime Face carefully opened his eyes to small slits, squinted and saw the trouble Lidsay was in. He tore a strip of cloth from his sweat stained vest and told Lidsay to close his eyes. "Let me wrap this over your eyes, sir. It'll help." It took Grime Face two hours of immense physical effort to get Lidsay through the slippery waterlogged tunnels and up a steep shaft to the surface.

An officer and a medical orderly were standing close by drinking tea. They looked across, ran to Grime Face, and helped carry Lidsay out of the tunnel entrance and into a nearby ambulance.

"You're lucky we were passing so close to you." The officer said. "How long has he been like this?"

"Not sure, sir, but the lights were out in the tunnel for at least twenty minutes. I've seen men go, well, go a little barmy in only a few minutes in that blackness. We had candles, but when we found him he didn't have any with him. When the lights came back on, halfway down the tunnel, well" he nodded at Lidsay on the stretcher, "his eyes, well he had them open, sir."

"Has he said anything at all?"

"Not a word, sir."

Lidsay's mind and body were operating on auto pilot.

"And his name and company?"

"Lieutenant Ronald Lidsay, Irish Guards, sir. Been with us clay kickers for about a month. Nice chap. Seemed to be getting on OK with everyone."

"Lidsay?" James immediately recognised the junior officer who'd saved his life. "Thank you private. We'll take it from here."

"He'll be OK won't he, sir?"

"We'll have him as right as rain in no time and back down that rabbit warren with you and the other troglodytes."

"Troglo … what, sir?"

"Never mind, Private. With you brave men."

"Thank you, sir. I'd better get back. There's still a lot to do before the big day." He tapped the side of his nose, winked, crisply saluted and walked back to the well concealed tunnel entrance.

"What's your name, Private?" The officer called after him.

"Morbeck, sir, Adam Morbeck."

"Thank you, Adam, I'll do all I can for him."

Captain Heyward turned back to the stretcher. "Well, old man. What are we going to do with you?"

SEVENTY-FOUR

Elizabeth stood in the hall, meat tenderiser in hand. The house seemed to have regained its calm and whatever had caused the disruption, was gone. Despite the hour, she didn't feel the need for sleep, wandered back into the kitchen, made a cup of milky coffee, and took it and a handful of biscuits into the lounge. She put the cup and biscuits on the small table in front of the Chesterfield, turned on the iPod and Bose, selected Leonard Cohen and sat back. Cohen's songs suited her mood. Friends had always called it music to kill yourself by, but since Elizabeth had first heard 'Bird on the Wire', she'd fallen in love with his songs and poetry. His gravel voice and the lyrics of the Partisan made their gentle progress around the room.

'There were three of us this morning
I'm the only one this evening
but I must go on ...
Oh the wind the wind is blowing,
through the graves the wind is blowing ...

Elizabeth slowly became aware that she wasn't the only one listening to Leonard. She didn't feel afraid or threatened but simply aware that there were others in the room with her. A few more songs played and she could sense they didn't seem to mean so much to the *others,* until Lady Midnight started playing.

'I asked her to hold me, I said "Lady unfold me,"
but she scorned me, and she told me
I was dead and I could never return.'

There was an audible sigh, which seemed to suck all the warmth from the room. A choral sigh of immeasurable sadness and loss. A requiem for despair. Elizabeth stood up and looked around the room which was softly lit by the light from the hall. The margins of the room were in shadow and were packed with clearly discernible swaying human shapes. She still felt no sense of danger. Only an all encompassing sorrow.

"What is it you want?" She asked as she turned full circle in the middle of the room. "How can I help? I am only here to help?" She held out her arms in supplication. "Are you lost souls from the Great War?" The sigh was replaced by a hollow moan, unintelligible whispers and the sound of shuffling feet. "I can help you. I have helped one of you, and he is free. He has returned home, and I can do this for you."

The whispering grew in intensity, and Elizabeth could sense a growing nervousness in the room. An insecurity. A feeling of abandonment. There was no anger, no aggression, only an overpowering sense of a lack of trust. A murmur behind her made her turn around and look into the hall. It was dark, but visible in the darkness were groups of swaying figures. She walked into the hall and looked up the stairs, which was packed with an undulating mass of bodies. As she watched in fascination, more and more figures appeared out of the walls. The house was alive, saturated with souls.

"Let me help." She said calmly. "Come with me to the gallery. Show me who you are and I will show you the way home. I cannot comprehend how you must feel after waiting for so many years to return home and rest, but I know I can help you complete the last stage of your journey."

Elizabeth started to climb the stairs, and the figures, parted like the Red Sea. As she passed through them she became more and more relaxed. In tune with them, but when she climbed into the gallery, she found herself alone. She looked back down the stairs of the gallery, at a seething mass. She waved to them to come up, but none accepted her offer.

"I'll pick a photo and see if I can get that soldier to come to me." She thought.

Elizabeth switched on the lights in the gallery, walked into the second row of panels, and randomly stopped at the photo of a faceless Tommy standing to attention. The notes at the bottom told her that it was Corporal Albert Thomas, 22409, 31st Division, 94th Brigade, 13/York & Lancaster (Barnsley Pals 2nd). The photograph was taken in a studio, long before Albert was exposed to the full horrors of the trenches. She reached out, touched the photo and felt a jolt of static. An image briefly flashed through her mind of Albert sunk up to his knees in a quagmire, screaming for help. Elizabeth gasped as she stood back from the photo, because hovering to her right, a few inches above the floor, was what looked like a sculptor's unfinished clay model of a man. She was transfixed by it, as some invisible expert hand started to sculpt the surface. The gouged clay, close to the floor, began to take on the shape of square-toed standard issue B5 boots. The sculpting continued into puttees, wound like a mummy from ankle to knee, breeches; tunic, deep pockets, brass buttons, belt, hands, shoulder straps, insignia and turned down collar. There was a pause as the invisible sculptor prepared for the most difficult part of his creation. The face. Elizabeth moved closer to the Tommy as the neck and an Adam's apple appeared. Then gradually the smooth features of the young face of corporal Albert Thomas became clear, topped off by a peaked cap. She reached out and touched the cold clay and could feel her hand getting warmer. The smooth clay began to morph into Albert's well dubbined tan boots, long wool serge strips and cotton tapes of his puttees, tight fitting khaki service dress trousers, loose fitting tunic, peaked cap with a stiffened peak and rim, and the cap badge of the Barnsley Pals.

Corporal Albert Thomas snapped to attention and crisply saluted. "Reporting for duty, Mam."

Elizabeth still felt no fear. "Albert."

"Yes, Mam. Corporal Albert Thomas 22409."

"Do you know where you are Albert?" Elizabeth asked.

Albert frowned. "Not exactly, Mam. Seem to have been … don't really know how to say it, Mam."

"It's OK, Albert. I'll try to explain." Elizabeth had no real idea how she was going to explain this.

He was looking at the photos. "Who are these men?"

"Soldiers who fought in the Great War."

"Why are they here?"

"So I can help them."

"Help them do what?"

Elizabeth tried to change the direction of the conversation. "Albert, what's the last thing you remember?"

The furrows in Albert's brow grew deeper as he struggled to prise open the long closed and rusted filing cabinets of his memory. "It was raining. It was always raining." Shaky black and white images stuttered across Albert's mind. "The roads were rivers. In any hollow the mud was as deep as a man's thighs, and off the roads the ground was one vast bog, our dugouts crumbled in and our communication trenches collapsed."

Elizabeth stood silently as Albert's memories recovered.

"We had to repair the parapets blown up in the day in the communication trenches." He clenched his fists, desperately trying to recall that night. "We had to stoop in the pitch blackness, heads bent forward, fronting the rain with our tin hats. Captain Blacker was doing his best to keep our spirits up." The images were becoming sharper. "Most of the trench had crumbled into the slime of the bog, and walking was almost impossible. You just put one foot into the mud in front of the other and then lugged out your back foot. It took it out of you." He was staring somewhere back into the far dusty recesses of the distant past. "Filling a sandbag could take ten minutes. The clay stuck to your shovel so you had to shove it in the sandbag with your hands. The weather got so bad that we couldn't do a thing. Captain Blacker tried to rally our spirits, but the electric lights failed and we pretty much gave up. We were sat soaked to the skin. Exhausted, shivering and coughing." The memories were becoming tangible as Albert shuddered.

He stood motionless, looking again like a clay statue, struggling to remember the final events of that night.

"What happened then?"

He swallowed deeply and stared directly at Elizabeth. "The shelling started again. We shouldn't have been there. George was the first." He looked around the gallery, forcing doors open in his mind. "He shouldn't have stood up. We was told never stand up in a trench. But he stood up." He massaged his temples with his hands. "His brains were all over Arthur and me. Top of his head was just … just not there anymore." Files began to fly open in Albert's mind as the memory of that night became clearer and clearer. "Ed was next, or was it Tom? No it was Ed. He … he … well he just lost it. Climbed over the top of the trench and marched off into no man's land." He paused again as the files replayed their terrible images. "Didn't get very far. You could hear the machine gun, a sort of muffled scream, and then a muffled splash. Must have fallen into a flooded shell crater. Shot to pieces or drowned." Albert was now just staring at the floor.

"Captain Blacker wasn't up to it. Young chap. When the corporal and the sergeant bought it, he, well he just followed Ed and crawled out of the trench. Stood on the parapet. Sniper must have got him. Single shot to the chest. Dropped like a stone. A body is full of a lot of blood you know." He looked up and stared at Elizabeth. "You sort of forget that when you've seen so much …" This was beginning to become a nightmare for Albert.

"Albert it's OK you don't need to go on." Elizabeth said caringly.

Albert's posture stiffened. "No, Mam, we need to remember our fallen comrades." He paused again as more stark images projected inside his head. "The rest of us, well we didn't have much of an idea what to do next, but the German's made up our minds for us." Albert's mind wouldn't give up the last piece of the jig saw. Elizabeth could see his face contorting as he struggled to open the last file.

"What happened, Albert? What did the Germans do?" Elizabeth asked.

"It was shells. More bloody shells. Shells and a curtain of mud and filth. Not sure how many, but about three shells exploded close to the trench. There was this silence and then this … it was like a huge wave in a storm at sea. An avalanche of slime, blood, guts, barbed wire and mud flew over us. Flew over us and then like a breaker on the shore in a winter storm, it crashed down on top of us." Albert's final memory had opened. "It buried us. All of us. I couldn't move. Couldn't see. Couldn't breathe. Tom had hold of my hand. I felt him squeezing it until it went limp. I was panicking. I was trying to hold my breath and not swallow the mud, but my head was exploding." The final piece of the jigsaw fell into place. "I couldn't hold it any longer … I sucked in the mud. It filled my lungs. Your life doesn't flash in front of your eyes you know. There's too much pain and panic. The pain in my chest and head was …" The jigsaw was complete. The memory recalled. Reality and truth revealed.

Elizabeth held out her hands to Albert.

"I died?" He whispered, and took Elizabeth's hands.

"Yes."

He let go of Elizabeth's hands and looked down at himself. "Then what's this?"

"I believe that what you are now, is the energy which remained when you died. Your body, the physical you, was never found, but your energy survived the years. You never found final rest and peace, but you were attracted to something which brought you here. I can help you find peace."

"Will I see my family again?"

"Not in this life, but in the next. In the next we will all be together again, but you have to pass over to be with them. You've been locked in this space because you were never laid to rest by your loved ones. I am here because I can guide you and your lost comrades to the next life. Guide you to where you can again be reunited with your loved ones. Take my hands and we can finish the journey you started so many years ago. Let's end the torment and send you home." Elizabeth offered her hands to Albert.

His expression began to subtly change from fear to hope. He held his hands close to Elizabeth's and smiled. "Take me home."

"I will."

Elizabeth felt a warmth begin to flow from the tips of her fingers into Albert. A yellow aura began to form around their hands and slowly move up their arms. It moved across their bodies, caressing them as it flowed, and in a few minutes Elizabeth and Albert were surrounded by pulsating yellow auras out of which red sparks erupted and flew like exploding sun spots. The auras began to change from yellow to orange, then green, then blue, then brilliant white until they finally began to slowly fade. Their hands fell to their sides and Elizabeth stood back a few paces, smiling at Albert who smiled back at her. His boots were the first to change as they lost their hard worked shine and became the dull brown of clay. The coarse texture of Albert's puttees were next, as they became smooth and brown. The metamorphosis slowly moved up Albert's body, as the texture of the coarse wool serge of his uniform once again became clay. Albert's smile remained unmoved as the change moved ever upwards, until his face began to solidify into clay. Finally his peaked cap was transformed into clay, and the metamorphosis was complete. Elizabeth's eyes were welling with tears which she'd held back as best she could, but now the dam burst as she looked at the soldier standing in front of her. His smile was frozen, but still beaming from his face.

Without thinking, Elizabeth started to recite.

"They are not dead
Who leave us this great heritage of remembering joy.
They still live in our hearts
In the happiness we knew, in the dreams we shared.
They still breathe
In the lingering fragrance, windblown, from their favourite flowers.
They still smile in the moonlight silver,
And laugh in the sunlight's sparkling gold.
They still speak in the echoes of the words we've heard them say again and again
They still move,
In the rhythm of waving grasses, in the dance of the tossing branches.
And laugh in the sunlight's sparking gold.
They are not dead;
Their memory is warm in our hearts, comfort in our sorrow.
They are apart from us, but part of us.
For love is eternal,
And those we love shall be with us throughout eternity."

As she recited the final lines of the poem, the clay of the soldier began to dry and crack, until it resembled an Egyptian artefact discovered after centuries in a lost tomb. Elizabeth reached out, and Albert collapsed into brown dust covering her feet, and filling the gallery around her in a swirling cloud. Quietly like an eddy in a slow moving stream, the dust began to rotate around her legs, gradually moved away from her and began to form what looked like a storm cloud in an early evening sky. At its centre was a brilliant white spinning globe, about the size of a tennis ball, around which orbited countless tiny pinpoints of light. Elizabeth watched them in fascination. It looked like images she'd seen of galaxies taken from distant satellites. She could feel an intense but bearable heat generated by the cloud, which seemed to wash away and ease all her aches and pains. She felt totally at peace. The speed of the pinpoints of light suddenly increased, until they became just a blur, and then accelerated into the spinning centre of the globe of light, which began to pulsate. Elizabeth still felt completely safe despite the surface which resembled a boiling lava lake. Finally it began to rise to the ceiling and in an instant was gone.

Without thought, Elizabeth bowed her head and recited from memory,

"For as much as it has pleased Almighty God to take out of this world the soul of Albert Thomas, we therefore commit his body to the ground, earth to earth, ashes to ashes, dust to dust, looking for that blessed hope when the Lord Himself shall descend from heaven with a shout, with the voice of the archangel, and with the trump of God, and the dead in Christ shall rise first. Then we which are alive and remain shall be caught up together with them in the clouds to meet the Lord in the air, and so shall we ever be with the Lord, wherefore comfort ye one another with these words."

In her mind she clearly heard *"I am home. Thank you."*

Elizabeth smiled to herself and thought. *"Rest in peace, Albert. Be with those you love now and through eternity."*

SEVENTY-FIVE

Sam sat hunched in a foetal position, cold and wet. His mind had decided that blocking any visual input would be a good protective mechanism to adopt, but despite this, in a far away nook of his neural crannies, a little something was niggling away that it would be a much better idea to take a look where he was, and it was beginning to win.

He cautiously opened his eyes, and immediately wished the little something in his brain had kept its mouth shut. He was sat in about six inches of freezing filthy brown water in what he soon realised was a tunnel. It was eerily silent and dimly lit by flickering candles fixed to the wall. It was about seven feet tall, six feet wide, and the walls, ceiling and floor were all braced with strong timbers and planks. He pushed himself up out of the freezing water and looked as far as he could see up and down the tunnel. A shuffling noise behind him made him flick his head around, and what appeared out of the darkness of the tunnel stimulated his bowels.

"It has to be a British soldier. It's got two legs and most of what looks like a uniform." Sam thought.

But it was the skull cap, face piece, two tubes like those on a vacuum cleaner attached to a large canvas back pack and the plumbing on its side which tested Sam's sphincters. A large mud encrusted hand came up to its face and pulled down the face piece. "Jack?" It whispered.

Sam was now fully spooked. This had to be a flashback. How else did this think it knew him?

"Jack is that you? What the hell are you doing here? I heard you were up near Passchendaele. Sorry about all this." It gestured at the equipment. "It's meant to protect us from the gas, but I'd rather rely on my canary to be honest. Bloody thing stinks, and it's murder just trying to breathe." He laughed, walked up to Sam and hugged him tightly.

"Come on, son. Lost your tongue have you? What're you doing down here, boy" He stood back frowning at Sam. "Christ you haven't deserted have you!"

"No, of course not." Sam didn't know where the reply came from, but was glad it had.

"So, Jack, why are you here? To see your old dad?"

"You're my father?" Sam thought. *"You think I'm your son?"* Sam's cogs turned at the speed of light. *"If you think I'm Jack, and I'm your son ... then you*

must think I'm ... Jack Samuel Morbeck?" The thought was too bizarre to consider, but the last few weeks had shown Sam that anything was possible.

"You're Adam Morbeck?" Sam said.

Adam stared back at him in false anger. "Now then, son, I know its been a while, but you can't have forgotten me that quickly?" He grabbed him by the shoulders and kissed him on the cheek leaving behind a muddy streak. "My God it's good to see you. I was on my way up top for a breather. Come on it'll be a lot more comfortable talking up there." He turned, looked at Sam, smiled and gestured for him to follow.

Sam followed Adam to the end of the tunnel, up the ladders and steps of the vertical shaft to the entrance and exit of the mine. The weather was mild for October. Adam looked up into the late afternoon sun and walked across to a converted lorry which provided basic food and drink. They collected milky hot weak tea and chocolate and sat on duckboards to enjoy their *feast*.

"So, how did you manage to find me?" Adam asked.

"Brain in gear before mouth." Sam thought. *"Take a minute."*

"Jack?"

"Sorry, but it was more by luck than judgement. I was on my way back to Ypres and got talking to some troops."

"Good non-committal start." Sam thought.

"Once I told them my name, they said they knew a tunneller called Morbeck at Hill 60. I had a word with my Captain and he gave me two days to look for you. Morbeck's not that common a name, so once I got close to Hill 60, finding you was easy."

"Might have just got away with it." Sam thought.

Adam scratched his nose and smiled at Sam. "No there's not many of us. Quality not quantity eh, son?"

Sam sipped his tea and thought about what he knew of Adam's death. *"What did Rebecca say?"*

"She didn't say very much."

"Oh, back are we. Been away a long time?"

"I've been doing some research." His other half returned from the shadows.

"And?"

"And, I know where Adam is recorded to have been when he went missing."

"Is that it?"

"Don't get tetchy, at least one of us has been busy and not just swanning around Belgium and France."

"So what's the discovery?"

"And, the last place Adam was seen alive, drum roll, was here in the mine under Hill 60. Buried in a grave he'd dug himself. The irony of it."

"Oh do piss off."

"Charming, after all I've done for you." His other half was as annoying as usual.

Sam reined in his neck. *"OK. Thanks for that. Shame is that I already knew. Why the hell do you think that I'm here."*

"Just trying to help. At least we know where he went missing, so X marks the spot, doesn't it?"

Adam was staring at Sam. "Cat got your tongue, son? Thought you'd be rattling away like you normally do."

"Sorry, Dad, this war's been horrendous. You want it to be over, be back with the ones you love, and now I've got half of that, it's a bit overwhelming."

"Big words for you, Jack." Adam chided. "Swallowed a dictionary since you signed up?"

"Bloody officers. You know what they're like. Talking with plums in their mouths. All public school boys."

"Look, boy, I've got to get back with the others, what did he call us, troglidives. Well it was something like that. Nice chap that Captain Heyward. Hope that lieutenant Lidsay is OK. He seemed to be in good hands." Adam said.

Sam sat bolt upright. "Lidsay, Dad?"

"Yes, Lidsay, Irish Guards. I found him in the tunnel." Adam shook his head and frowned. "He didn't look too good to me."

Sam left it at that. Trying to draw some loose connection to a pain in the ass policeman from a hundred years in the future probably wouldn't achieve very much. He was however considering options about Adam, but his other half was still hanging around.

"Not a good idea."

"What's not?" Sam queried.

"What you're cooking up isn't a good idea."

"Don't see why."

"Ever heard of the butterfly effect? Keeping Adam out of that mine and avoiding his death, will not guarantee Rebecca's future will be a bed of roses."

"I wasn't considering that."

"Bollocks you weren't. That man sitting there is your great grandfather. Are you seriously telling me if you save his life and he goes on to live a long and fruitful life, it will have no effect on you or anyone else in the Morbeck line?"

Adam stood up ready to return to his subterranean world.

Sam jumped up beside him and took his arm. "I'll walk back with you."

"That'd be nice, son."

"Dad, do you have to work underground? Must be something else you're good at it. Can't be healthy for a man of your age to be down there."

"Man of my age. Cheeky sod. From what I've seen of what goes on up here, I reckon it's a damn site safer down there." Adam waved his arms towards the pock marked ground.

"Is there much still to do?" Sam asked.

"Not too much. Sorry, boy, but secrets is secrets." Adam knowingly tapped the side of his nose.

Sam took a firm hold of Adam's arm. "Please don't go back down that hole. I beg you."

"Now then, now then. We've all got our bit to do and mine's down there." Adam nodded to the concealed entrance to the mine shaft. "This will be over soon. That's what the top brass tell us, and we'll be back with your Mam before you know it." He smiled at Sam, prised his hand from his arm, tussled his hair and disappeared into the bowels of the earth.

Sam watched him go knowing that Adam would never see Mam again.

"At least," he thought, *"not in this world, but I'll make damn sure that you meet again in the next."*

"If we manage to get out of this particular period of history." His other half reminded him. *"And not the way your ex good lady wife did."* He emphasised.

Klaus stood at the bottom of the crater staring in disbelief into the bramble bush. "You're certain this is where he finished?"

"No question. This is the exact spot." Guillaume replied.

Klaus looked up to the crater's edge. Karsten was sat on the ground rocking back and forth with his head in his hands.

"So many German dead." Klaus thought. *"How many were evaporated when the mine exploded under their feet? Karsten's head will be spinning out of control."* He scanned the rim of the crater. Jane and Rebecca were holding each other close and peering down at Klaus. He gestured at them to come down. He needed them. Jane to find Sam and Rebecca to find Adam.

"Hold my hand tightly," Jane said to Rebecca, "and we'll be fine. Something's wrong and they need our help. Not sure how we can, but the answer is down there at the bottom of this crater."

Rebecca nodded in agreement and, not quite like two mountain goats, they gingerly started climbing down the slope. It took longer than Jane had thought as they slipped and slithered down the steep incline of the crater, but after a few minutes, they were stood by Klaus.

"Thank you. Both of you. I'm not exactly sure what we do next. Something like this has never happened before. We are always trying to help the dead move on, not get the living back from the past."

Jane's face betrayed that she didn't believe they could do what Klaus wanted.

"You're unsure about this?" Klaus asked Jane.

"Very unsure. When I went back, I came back like this." Jane replied looking herself up and down.

Klaus rubbed his cheeks firmly with the palms of his hands.

"I can still help find Adam can't I?" Rebecca asked.

Klaus smiled. "Of course. But again, I don't know how. We have never sought the help of the departed's loved ones spirits."

Rebecca grinned. "The dead."

"Yes, my dear. The dead."

"What if I just walk around and see what happens?" Rebecca asked.

"I'll do the same." Jane agreed, "Can't do any harm, can it."

Klaus shook his head. "No. I can't see why it would."

Jane and Rebecca started walking in opposite directions around the bottom of the crater.

Guillaume was stood by Klaus's side. "Will it help?"

"Who knows. I'm not sure if even Isaac would have an answer." Klaus said softly.

Guillaume was looking up at Karsten who was still rocking back and forth. "We should get to him?"

Klaus followed Guillaume's eyes to Karsten. "I have taken him to places he wasn't ready for. Even I am struggling to maintain control. The energies here are enormous. So many dead concentrated in such a small space."

Guillaume held Klaus firmly by the shoulders. "This is not easy for all of us, but we need your strength. Karsten needs your strength."

"You're right, Guillaume. The last few months have been difficult for all of us. Particularly you." He smiled and squeezed his arms. "I will fetch him. We need to conclude this."

Sam decided to follow Adam into the mine, and see what happened.

"This is not a good idea." His other half was angry.

Sam ignored him.

"Are you listening? You can't meddle with the past. It has consequences."

Sam walked through the entrance and saw Adam disappear into the mine. He stayed far enough behind not to be noticed, but still had no idea what he planned to do or how the other tunnellers would react to him.

"Sam, it's not too late. Please!"

"Give it a rest will you."

"Isaac wouldn't approve. You know that, don't you?"

"Isaac ... Isaac isn't with us. He's ..."

"I know it's hard, Sam, but if he was here, he'd tell you to get the hell out of here before you do something you, and God knows who else will seriously regret. That's if we still exist after you've done whatever it is your planning."

"I just want to keep an eye on him. That's not interfering. Is it?"

"No I suppose not."

Adam didn't look back and Sam followed him for twenty minutes into the galleries of the mine.

"You'll never find your way out of here." His other half said.

Sam just kept tracking Adam further and further into the dim light and the smothering silence.

"As quiet as the grave." He thought. *"And hopefully not Adam's."*

As Adam took a right at a T-junction a massive explosion and concussion in the tunnel knocked Sam flat on his back, which was immediately followed by the sound wave and heat of the explosion. After a few seconds of deafness and confusion, he stumbled to his feet and ran around the corner of the T-junction. The tunnel had totally collapsed into a smouldering mound of earth, wood and chalk. Sam peered through the dust and smoke, and could just see an arm sticking out about a foot above the freezing water. He ran and started scrabbling at the earth, until he could see a shoulder and part of a neck. He pulled the arm as hard as he could, instinctively dropping it as the earth smeared face of Adam emerged into the twilight of the tunnel.

"Adam!" Sam screamed. "Too late, too bloody late!"

"It's for the best, Sam." His other half said.

"Not for him it's not." Sam spat back at him.

"Easy, tiger. You can't change the past. You can only affect the present."

Sam knelt down in the freezing water close to Adam and tried to wipe away some of the earth from his face and out of his nostrils.

"I'm not dead yet, son." Adam opened his eyes and smiled at Sam.

"You're …" Sam sat back in the freezing water.

"Not dead?"

"But you're buried."

"Bloody Germans. We picked up the sound of their workings a few days ago, and now they've blown this bloody camouflet. So this part of the tunnel's buggered. But there's a lot more tunnel ready to blow under them, and we won't just bury them. Won't be nothing to bury when all that amotal goes up under their boots."

"What about the others on the other side of the collapse?" Sam asked.

"They'll be fine. Plenty of other ways out of here."

"Right, then let's get you out from under this rubbish." Sam said.

"Not much point Sam." Adam replied.

Sam's hands froze in mid-air.

"What there is of me that's stuck under here, isn't going to be of much use to anyone. I can't feel anything below my waist, and I'm not going to be a bloody hopeless cripple sat in a corner by the fire." A rasping cough shook Adam and a small crimson trickle of blood flowed from the corner of his mouth. "Just make sure that your mother knows I died fighting for King and Country." Another shuddering cough turned the trickle to a steady flow. "Stay with me, son."

Sam was in pieces. This man wasn't his father, but the feelings that were ripping him to pieces could only be for a close loved one. The past was beginning to mould Sam to stay with it until Jack's death in 1917.

"Sam!" His other, and for now, better half was concerned. *"Sam, this is what was meant to be. Sam, he isn't your father. We had to find him for Rebecca, and we've done that."*

The stoney frozen expression on Sam's tear-streaked face scared his other half.

"Sam what we have to worry about is how we get out of here and back to the crater. To our present. Not his. We … Do … Not … Belong … Here!"

Sam looked down at himself. His clothes had started to change into a dirty khaki uniform, and strangely, it didn't in any way frighten him. It seemed quite natural. He felt like a plain caterpillar transformed into an exquisite butterfly, albeit a grubby dirty khaki variety.

"Sam!!" If Sam wasn't worried then his other half was panicking.

The dirty khaki transformation had moved up as far as Sam's waist, and if his other half could have shaken himself, Sam's teeth would have been rattling.

Like constricting pythons, grimy Puttees started wrapping themselves around his legs.

Rebecca and Jane were walking around the crater in ever decreasing circles, and as they came close to passing each other for the fourth time, they stopped dead in their tracks, fell to their knees and put their hands on the ground.

Klaus had found it difficult to bring Karsten down into the bowels of the crater, and was acutely aware that his son's abilities were turned up to full volume. Even Klaus was finding it hard to keep focused as the concentrated mass of human energy did its best to drown them. Guillaume scrambled up to meet him and helped them down the last few yards to the bottom of the crater.

"Is he OK?" Guillaume asked as they sat Karsten down on the damp grass.

Klaus shook his head. "I don't know. This is getting to be too much even for me." He gently massaged his temples.

"Klaus. What do we do?" Guillaume asked.

Klaus looked down at Karsten and shook his head.

"You don't know?"

Klaus avoided Guillaume's concerned face and shook his head again.

Guillaume looked up in desperation. Things were slowly coming apart at the seams. He looked across at Rebecca and Jane and frowned. They were lying flat on the grass, and their arms seemed to be burrowing into the ground. He grabbed Klaus by the arm and pulled him towards him. "What are they doing?"

"Sie sehen, wie sie? You see them?"

"I have for some time."

"Aber ... but ... you ..."

"Klaus I see them, but I do not know what they are doing. Do you?"

Klaus looked across at the two women, whose arms had now completely disappeared into the soil of the crater. His head snapped around. "Guillaume, keep a close watch on Karsten!" He ran across to Rebecca and Jane as their shoulders began to sink into the ground. He stumbled and fell heavily over a boulder, splitting open his eyebrow. As he knelt up, he saw the two women gracefully disappear into the ground like dolphins beneath the waves.

Sam ignored Adam's comment and slipped his hands under his armpits, but couldn't move him.

"Told you." Adam hoarsely whispered. "There's timbers and all sorts under here. Give it up, son. Just keep my head above the water and be here for me."

Sam's other self stood back and looked Sam up and down. The transformation from Sam to Jack was almost complete, as the past, present and future merged into a single reality.

Sam sat down in the freezing water and cradled Adam's head. His skin felt cold and clammy and his breathing was almost imperceptible. The life force was draining from this man who had spliced himself into Sam's life. He'd never been with anyone at the moment of death and a strange fascination began to take him over as he watched this man move from one reality to another.

Adam weakly coughed and mouthed the words. "Stay with me."

"I'm not going anywhere."

"Never was a truer word said." Chipped in his other half. *"We are now well and truly stuck here for good."* Other than a peaked cap, the transformation was complete.

Sam was oblivious to everything except making sure that Adam's last moments were as peaceful as the surroundings would allow.

"Adam!?"

"Sam!?"

Rebecca and Jane appeared like fragile, drifting morning mist close behind Sam and Adam. They stood transfixed, shocked, staring at the tragic scene confronting them.

Sam's head span around.

Rebecca's eyes fixed on Sam and then moved slowly to the ashen face of her husband, Adam. "My two boys. My two sweet boys. How did it come to this?"

Jane frowned and looked around at Rebecca. *"My two boys?"* She thought.

Rebecca span around and grabbed Jane's arms. "We've found both of them. All the years of misery and waiting were worth it." She turned and through her tears smiled to where she saw her husband and *son*. "My family is back together."

Jane softly smiled at Rebecca. *"My two boys?"*

Klaus stared at the empty space where the two women had been and pointlessly patted the grass. Blood seeped into the corner of his eye from the cut on his eyebrow and he dabbed at it with a tissue.

"Mein Gott. Wo sie sind?" He sobbed.

Karsten had recovered his senses and was looking across at Klaus. "What's happened?" he asked Guillaume.

For once Guillaume was lost for words. "The … Sam … they disappeared … Rebecca … Jane …"

Karsten gripped him by the shoulders. "Slowly now. Where is everyone?"

"Isaac, where are you now when I so need you?" Guillaume desperately thought. "This is not easy." He started.

"That's fine just take your time."

"We are in a crater where Hill 60 was in the War. It was blown up by an Allied mine and hundreds were obliterated. Mostly German. They were literally dashed to the four winds. It is their spirits, their concentrated life energies which have overwhelmed you. There are so many in such a small area." Guillaume paused and nodded at Karsten to see that he understood.

Karsten released his grip on Guillaume and nodded.

"Rebecca and Jane have … they just … just sank into the ground." Guillaume looked across at Klaus who was sitting back on his haunches staring at the ground and shaking his head. "We should go to Klaus. We can finish this later."

Karsten followed his gaze and nodded.

"Was zu tun ist? Was zu tun ist?" Klaus kept repeating. "Was zu tun ist?" He rocked back and forth and slowly shaking his head from side to side. "Ich habe so was noch nie gesehen. Wo sind sie?"

SEVENTY-SIX

Elizabeth had never felt so balanced and in control. All her years as a priest had never given her such a sense of fulfillment.

She remembered the evenings spent with her father looking at the stars. Names she could never forget, Andromeda, Cassiopeia, Aquarius, Perseus, Pleiades and her favourite Aldebaran. She believed then that the points of distant light were Gods, Angels and the Spirits of departed souls.

"Are you up there with Aldebaran, Albert?"

She felt a warm glow as she recalled his spirit leaving this world, looked back at the gallery, and thought of the size of the task she faced. She thought again about the stars and wondered if there was enough space in the vast galaxies to take all these tortured lost spirits.

She made her way down to the map room, sat in front of the computer and opened a blank word document. She needed a plan. A method of handling the seemingly endless numbers of spirits locked in the house. She started typing.

1. How many souls are there? – Count the pictures with no faces. Write down their names and input them into the computer.
2. How to record and monitor them? – Have to be on a spreadsheet. That's all I know how to use.
3. How do I prioritise them? – Date they were recorded as missing?
4. How long will it take? – Need answer to 1.
5. Have I got enough time? – See 4.
6. Do I need help? – See 5.
7. Do they all want to go? – ???

Elizabeth sat back and stared at the brief document. *"Not much of a plan."* She thought and pressed Cmd/S and saved the document as 'Aldebaran'.

Writing down the names was laborious and time consuming. Elizabeth sat on the floor and looked at the three pages of names she'd written down. It had taken her two hours and her wrist was bitterly complaining. She needed a quicker and easier method.

"The smartphone." The idea shone brightly. *"Take a picture of each of them and save them on the computer."* She smiled and stretched her aching wrist. *"Genius!"*

The loud knocks on the front door made her spill her glass of water.

She opened the front door and smiled at the woman standing in the rain. She was short and obviously overweight, a polka dot umbrella with two broken supports, flapped ineffectually in the strong wind, a knitted blue woollen hat was pulled down firmly over her ears, revealing a few strands of grey greasy unwashed hair, her blotchy complexion was unconcealed by little or no make-up, a tartan scarf tied tightly around her neck, flapped stiffly behind her, making her look like a bedraggled Scottish Biggles, a cracked olive green Barbour jacket, straining at its buttons, just revealed the merest hint of a grey sweater and baggy maroon jogging bottoms hanging just above barely white, slightly too large Nike trainers, completed the ensemble.

She spoke in a hushed whisper. "Sorry to call at this hour."

Elizabeth could barely understand what she was saying. "I'm sorry?" She replied.

"Sorry!" She shouted. "I'm Gloria Lidsay. We've never met, but I think my husband may have been here?"

Elizabeth took a few steps back and gestured for Gloria to come in out of the rain. She flapped her umbrella until Elizabeth thought it would finally fall apart, laid it in the porch and walked into the hall.

"Please follow me. It's a lot more comfortable in the kitchen."

Gloria peeled off her woollen hat, revealing greasy unwashed grey hair which lay like a perished swimming cap, tight against her scalp, and followed Elizabeth into the kitchen.

Elizabeth made two mugs of coffee and sat opposite Gloria at the table.

"Lidsay you say." Elizabeth stared at the ceiling. "Can't say that I've heard the name before."

"He was a sergeant at the local station."

Elizabeth's eyes opened wide. "Sergeant Lidsay! Yes of course. He came here about three or four times. Sam's wife, sorry Mrs Morbeck went missing a few weeks ago and he was looking into it. Is that who you're looking for?"

"Yes. Ivor and I had a bit of a, *misunderstanding*, and I've not heard from him in days. It's not that I'm worried or anything, but it's so unlike him. We've had misunderstandings in the past you see, but he's never not got back in touch with me." She sipped at her coffee. "Very nice. I use Kenco. What's this?"

"Douwe Egberts I think." Elizabeth replied.

"Very nice. Must get some the next time I'm in Asda." She drank some more coffee, mmm'd, put the mug back on the table and ran her finger around the rim of the mug. "Yes, very nice."

Elizabeth frowned. "Sergeant Lidsay is your husband?"

Gloria looked up from the coffee. "Sorry, yes. We've been married ..." she looked up to the right at nothing in particular trying to remember how long they'd suffered together. "Probably about, thirty years. Time flies so quickly, doesn't it?"

Elizabeth nodded and smiled. "And he's missing?"

"Yes, missing. I sort of threw him out, and I'm worried about him. Can't really cope on his own. Funny isn't it that however much you grow to despise each other, you miss them when they're not there." Gloria was gazing into the distance again and smiling inanely.

"Gloria, it's OK if I call you Gloria?"

She nodded.

"When did you last see him?"

Gloria frowned and began staring into the distance again. "Last Thursday, or was it Friday, no it was Thursday, at about ten o' clock that night. I'd packed a case for him and left it outside the house."

"And you haven't seen or heard from him since."

"Not a dicky bird."

"Have you spoken with anyone else?"

"Went up to the station, but they didn't know anything. Didn't really seem to give a shit." The expletive surprised Elizabeth. "He wasn't liked you know." Gloria picked up her mug and finished her coffee. "Very nice. He wasn't really liked by anyone. I never met his parents, or anyone from his family." She looked into the empty mug. "Do … you … egg … bat? Could you write it down for me. Very nice. Must get some."

Elizabeth scribbled Douwe Egberts on a napkin and pushed it across the table to Gloria.

"Thank you." She crumpled up the napkin and pushed it into a pocket in the Barbour, and sat back in the chair. "Lovely house this. I've always wanted somewhere with a bit more room. What would something like this cost?"

Elizabeth was getting a little frustrated with Mrs Lidsay and could begin to understand how the sergeant might have become a little *annoyed*.

"I really don't have a clue." Elizabeth looked very obviously at her watch, but Gloria didn't take the hint. "If I remember anything I'll call you. Do you have a number I can ring?"

"Mmmm. Yes." She took one of the napkins, nodded at Elizabeth's pen, and wrote two numbers. "That's my home number." She said tapping the number with Elizabeth's pen. "And that's my mobile." She repeated the tapping.

Elizabeth picked up the napkin and stood up.

Gloria finally took the hint. "Well I'd better be going. Thank you for the coffee. Very nice. If you remember anything, please call me?"

"Yes of course. I hope you find him." *"But for his sake, not too soon."* She thought.

Elizabeth opened the front door and stood back to let her *guest* leave. As Gloria opened the broken umbrella, a gust of wind blew it inside out. She tutted, folded it under her arm, waved over her shoulder and walked down the drive. Elizabeth closed the front door and couldn't help but laugh.

"What has happened to you, Sergeant?" She thought. *"You were very interested in High Wood. Weren't you."*

SEVENTY-SEVEN

Agnes re-read the letter from Arthur for the fifth time and smiled. It had a desperate tone, he'd been inundated with cases of severe shell shock, was struggling to cope, and he needed their help and experience. If she could only convince James that returning to Seale Hayne and working closely with Arthur would be as fulfilling as the work he was now doing. She knew it wouldn't be easy, as he was totally immersed in new and better techniques of treating the wounded. The *physically* wounded.

She didn't know if it was a result of his own shell shock, that he'd become, not intolerant, but unsympathetic to the many tortured cases of *mental* wounds he'd seen. He'd carefully packed up his own nightmares, sealed them in lead lined boxes, bound them with chains and stored them as far away as he could in the deepest recesses of his mind.

Sadly for Agnes, he'd adopted the, come on old man, stiff upper lip, don't want the others to see you like this do you, what would your family think, for King and country, can't let the side down can you, never see the Bosche behave like this, come on now, shake yourself, get a grip old chap, what about your pals in the trenches, is that soldier with no legs making a fuss, one last push and victory will be ours, is this how Tommy Atkins would behave, tried and tested Army techniques of treatment designed to constantly replenish the industrial mincing machine at the front.

She neatly folded the letter, put it back in the envelope and tucked it in her apron pocket. This wasn't a Bull at the Gate time. He'd need gentle but firm persuasion. She knew where he'd be, and made her way to recovery.

James was where she'd expected to find him, checking the dressings of a sergeant who'd been badly tangled in barbed wire, which had sliced multiple ragged cuts into most of his legs and arms. He'd spent close to two hours stitching him back together. The scarring would be significant, but mainly hidden by clothing, provided that no major infection took hold.

"How are you feeling sergeant?" James asked.

"Like a carved roast joint on a Sunday, sir. Give me a couple of pills and I'll be right as rain."

James smiled. The soldier's attitude reconfirmed his view that the so-called shell shock cases he was seeing were just slackers and cowards. This brave suffering sergeant was an example to all of them. "I'll have to see if I can find you a bit of crackling then." He said winking at the him.

The sergeant blew out his cheeks and grinned. "That would be nice, sir. A real treat."

Agnes tapped James on the elbow.

"This is Sister Wilmart, sergeant." He gently nudged the sergeant's arm. "Closest thing this place has to crackling."

Agnes heard the comment and blushed. "Captain Heyward. Really." She said in mock embarrassment.

James gently squeezed the sergeant's shoulder. "I'll be back to see you later on. Get some sleep."

Agnes smiled at the sergeant who grinned back through a haze of pain and drugs. She linked arms with James. "Come on, let's get some fresh air. I've had a letter from Arthur."

They sat outside in the early evening together.

"What's this letter then." James asked.

"Oh, Arthur was just asking after us. Wondered how we were getting on here at the Front." Agnes answered in a matter of fact tone.

"That's all?"

Agnes, looked at the ground and spoke quietly. "He wanted to know if we'd like to go back to Seale Hayne and start working with him."

James smiled. "Yes that would be marvellous. We'll need something to fill the gap after all this ends. Can't think of anything better than working with Arthur. Lovely chap. Not so sure about his thinking and methods, but I'm sure that over time we could develop a good working relationship. We'll need somewhere for these damaged men to convalesce after the war. They'll need a lot of support to fit back into society, and Seale Hayne would be a wonderful place for them to rehabilitate. It's the perfect environment, far removed from the Hell they've been living in."

"After everything he did for you, you don't have belief in his work on shell shock?"

"Agnes, our minds are fundamentally driven by primal instincts. Self-preservation is one of our strongest drives, and if the mind can find a way of ensuring this, then surely it will. Most of our troops have strong enough will power and pride in their King and Country to resist and suppress this urge, so we must stimulate their true patriotic instincts, and remove these unpatriotic self-centred desires for self-preservation."

"James," Agnes was taken back by his comments, "were *your* primal instincts too strong?"

"I was weak. Nothing more, nothing less."

"You were ill, James. Very ill."

"It was personal weakness. I let myself, my family and my country down. It was something I was eventually able to recognise in myself, and put right, and Arthur may have had a small part to play in this,.

"Living under your bed for weeks was just through personal weakness?"

"Yes. It was a method of recovery. I needed isolation, and once I'd identified in myself what needed to be done, then restoring my true patriotic instinct was just a matter of time. In times like this we have to forget self and do all we can to work for our country and comrades. Our lives are secondary to defeating the evil that is Germany."

Agnes stared at James in disbelief. She knew that a full recovery would take time, but his refusal to accept that Seale Hayne and Arthur were integral to his recovery, were difficult for her to accept. He'd most definitely recovered all his medical skills, but she was now seriously concerned that his underlying mental state was deteriorating. "So you'll be happy to go back to Seale Hayne?"

"Absolutely. Once, and only once, this damn war is over. These soldiers," he turned and pointed back to the tents where the wounded and dying lay, "are needed at the front, and my skills will get them back quicker than anyone else I know."

"That could be months, even years!"

"Yes. But the sooner these men are back killing Bosche, then the sooner this war will be over."

SEVENTY-EIGHT

Karsten was finally beginning to feel in control. The energies which were still bombarding him had become manageable. A filter in his sub-conscious was preventing the mental overload which up until then had paralysed his mind. He'd never seen Klaus not in control and the image of his father sobbing was disturbing and upsetting for him. He dropped to his knees and for the first time in his life, cradled his father.

"Give them a focus, Karsten. They will need something to guide them back."

Karsten knew the voice, but didn't understand why he could hear it inside his head.

"Put your hands on the ground, and concentrate your thoughts through them."

Karsten's mind was desperately trying to find a reason why he believed he could hear Isaac's voice.

"Karsten, it is your time. Guide them back. I will be with you."

Karsten looked over his shoulder around the crater. "Isaac?" he whispered.

"I am with you, Karsten. I always have been. Guillaume will care for Klaus. You must focus on the others."

"I'm not ready."

"You have always been ready, and now is your time."

Karsten gently let go of his father and gestured to Guillaume to take his place. "I'm ready." He walked a few yards away, dropped to his knees and stared at the ground. A patch of grass close to his knees began to glow a dull rusty orange. He made his hands into fists and dug his nails into his palms. He had no idea what would happen next, but was prepared to accept whatever it was.

"Put your palms on the grass and think only of Sam. Only one of them needs a point of return to follow. the others will come with him."

Karsten leaned forward and cautiously placed his hands on the glowing patch of grass, and a gentle kick of what felt like static electricity tingled through them.

"Just hold that. That is all you need to do for now."

Karsten stared at the glow and trusted in Isaac.

"Rebecca," Jane asked "who do you see?"

Rebecca frowned at the odd question. "Adam and Jack of course. I should know my own husband and son."

"You think that Sam is your son."

"Sam is my son." Rebecca was becoming exasperated. "Jack *Samuel* Morbeck"

"He looks like Sam … Jack?"

"Of course!"

Jane was confused and worried. She'd come here to save Sam, her *husband*, not Jack/Sam her, whatever distant relation he was.

Sam stared at Jane. Something deep in his psyche was *itching*, and it was becoming an itch he was desperate to scratch. A flea bite which no amount of antihistamine would ease.

"Come on, Sam!" His other half screamed. *"You know who she is! She's here to get us back! You need to remember who you are."*

"Who is she?"

"For God's sake, she's … she was, your wife. It's Jane!"

"Jane?"

"Jesus! Yes! Jane!"

"And I'm …"

"Sam Morbeck her ex-*husband*. Not *Jack* Morbeck, Rebecca's son and soon to be demised soldier of the Crown. *He* is somewhere near Passchendaele."

Sam's attention came back to Adam as he felt his breathing change. It was shallower and more laboured. His eyes had rolled back into his head leaving only the whites visible.

Rebecca sensed the change and ran to Adam's side. "I'll look after him now son. He should be with me at this time."

Sam tenderly passed Adam to Rebecca, stood up and walked to Jane.

"Jane … it is … you?"

"Yes, Sam, it's me."

"What happened to you?"

"I died."

"You … but how are you here?"

"I haven't got a clue, but I am definitely dearly departed."

"But … you … you disappeared. Didn't you? Vanished into thin air. We even had the police looking for you. We didn't have a clue where you'd gone."

"I still don't have a clue, and I was there."

"How are you here?"

"I could ask the same question, Sam."

Sam shrugged. "Good point. It's just a little *strange* to be chatting with your dead wife!"

"Are *you* dead, Sam?"

Sam hadn't considered this option. "I … I …"

"You don't know?"

"No. I don't think I am. I think I'm supposed to be helping him." Sam pointed to where Adam was slipping away in Rebecca's arms.

"How?"

"It's complicated."

"Try me."

Sam took a deep breath, as *Sam* made a full recovery. "Adam is one of the Missing. He died in the Great War and his mortal remains were never found. His, essence, spirit, soul, what made Adam, was scattered to the four winds. He's never rested, and drifted for a hundred years on the winds of time. The trips to Belgium were to try and understand all of this. There is a group called Papaver Rhoeas. They, we, help Adam and those like him to finally find a final resting place, back with those who miss and love them."

"That wasn't so hard was it?" She'd dragged him back from the precipice.

"No, not so bad."

"Sam, I can't say I understand any of this, but if it means that Rebecca finally has closure, then it has to be a good thing. Does it really matter if we understand any of this?"

He shook his head.

She smiled at him in a way he'd not felt for … ever. There seemed to be genuine caring in her eyes. "What do we do?"

He shook his head.

"You don't know?"

He shook his head. "I'm still learning."

She smiled at him. "Never too old to learn, Sam."

"No, but it may be too late."

He felt a warmth on the back of his neck and looked up at the ceiling of the tunnel, where a small but distinct circle of orange light was pulsing and slowly growing in size.

A stifled cry from Rebecca made them both look in her direction. It was obvious from her demeanour that Adam had died. Her head was buried in what of his chest was free from the collapsed tunnel.

Scattered fragments in Sam's mind, like the pieces of an unfinished jigsaw, began to come together and form a clear sharp image. He walked close to Rebecca and spoke softly to her. "Rebecca, this is what we knew had already passed. Nothing has changed. But we can change the future, and you can have Adam back. He is closer to you now than he has been for a hundred years, and we need to help him make that final step to be with you through eternity."

She nodded and forced a smile.

"Jane, come here." Sam said. "Rebecca, keep holding Adam's hand as firmly and as lovingly as you ever have."

"You think that you know what you're doing?" His other half asked.

"I'm going on instinct and a voice which keeps whispering to me."

"Like that reassures me."

"It'll have to."

Sam took hold of one of Jane's hands and one of Rebecca's. "Jane take hold of Adam's other hand." Sam followed the whispered instructions. "Now we have a circle." He knelt with Jane in the icy water close to Rebecca and Adam. The glow above them was now a brilliant crimson. "Look to the light. Everyone look to the light."

They all stared through half closed eyes at the spinning crimson vortex and felt a growing sensation of weightlessness. They began to spin, slowly at first, but then closer and closer to the rotation of the vortex. As they rose and span around they were forced to release each other's hands. Silver and gold threads like silk from a spider's spinneret exuded from Adam's palms and began to wrap themselves around Sam. As they span quicker and rose higher Rebecca, Jane and Adam merged with the circle of crimson light. The threads multiplied and began to form a cocoon around Sam, as the others disappeared from his view into the vortex.

Karsten struggled to keep his hands on the grass as the temperature increased. He could feel a pressure on them which wanted to force them into the air. Everything he was doing, like Sam, was on instinct and in line with the instructions he was receiving, as only he knew, from Isaac. The surface of the ground beneath his hands began to rise like an ancient burial mound. The mound began to collapse in its centre and earth started to erupt from it. Karsten was thrown onto his back by the force of the eruption. He stared at the centre of what now resembled a small volcano, where what appeared to be a huge silken cocoon was appearing above its rim.

Klaus looked up at Guillaume who was transfixed on the cocoon. He stood up and followed his frozen gaze, and what he saw shocked even him.

SEVENTY-NINE

Elizabeth slept well as she always had at High Wood. She turned over and looked at the alarm clock. "Bloody hell, it's ten to nine!" She pressed the 'On' switch and snuggled back under the warm duvet as Radio 2 serenaded her into the day.

"Bugger it," she thought, *"another half an hour's not going to bring the stock market to its knees."*

The knock on the front door ended any thoughts of a few more precious minutes under the covers. She hit her toe as she fumbled around for her slippers, produced expletives which she didn't know she was capable of, pulled the dressing gown from the back of the bedroom door, tied it too firmly around her waist, pinched her skin, produced a variant on the earlier expletives, slipped halfway down the stairs, and jarred her back which further expanded her vocabulary.

"This had better be worth it." She thought angrily as she pulled back the front door. It wasn't.

Gloria was back, and so far as Elizabeth could see she'd slept in the clothes she was wearing the day before, and probably, by the greasy appearance of her skin, hadn't washed.

"Yes, Gloria." Elizabeth's welcome wasn't warm.

"Sorry to be a pain so early." She said as she looked Elizabeth up an down, "Didn't get you up did I?"

"Pots and kettles." Elizabeth thought. "No problem at all." She lied effectively, regaining her self-control. "Please come in, it's a little draughty on the doorstep."

They walked to the kitchen and Elizabeth made mugs of *very nice* coffee.

"OK?" Elizabeth asked.

"Very nice."

"Thank you." Elizabeth replied desperately trying to hide the sarcasm in her voice. "What was it that brought you back so soon?"

Gloria smiled, exposing unbrushed, unflossed off-white teeth. "I found this in Ivor's wardrobe. It was in one of his shoes. I was cleaning last night." She handed a dog-eared note pad to Elizabeth. "It's mostly notes about, well they seem to be about, watching this house and you and Mr Morbeck. He's not very pleasant about you. But the main reason I brought it over, was that he seemed to think there was something of value worth having in the house, or that someone, his wife had been murdered. He must have been in the house, because he describes rooms and things … odd things." She paused, pulled a pained expression and raised her eyebrows.

"Murdered!" Elizabeth shouted. "If that's the case then why didn't we get any visits from any detectives not some dimwit of a sergeant?" She was angry and suspicious of this woman. Were the noises she'd heard the other day Lidsay?

"I'm only telling you what he wrote." Gloria said defensively. "If you look at the page where I've put a tissue in, you'll see what I mean."

Elizabeth threw her an angry stare. She opened the note book at the tissue and removed it like an infected swab with the tips of two fingers. The writing was like a child using a crayon, but the words were clear.

'Got into the house through the kitchen. Nobody home. He's probably with his tart. Whatever they're hiding I reckon is upstairs or in the cellar. If anyone else reads this then I swear that I saw this and I'm not mental. There's a locked room at the end of the first landing. Someone'd forced it open. They've got a mad woman chained up in there. But she can't be real. She was doing things which I've only seen in horror films like the Exorcist. I swear she was possessed or some sort of ghost. There was things happening which I can't write about as I don't know the words. I'm never going back upstairs in that house.'

Elizabeth looked up from the note pad, frowned and squinted at Gloria. "You're sure he wrote this when he was sober?"

"He used to drink a bit, but never enough to make him see things." Gloria answered defensively.

"Drugs?" Elizabeth had had enough of this scruffy woman.

"There is no locked room or mad woman upstairs." Elizabeth lied effectively. She'd tidied things up around Rebecca's room and locked the door "I've been sleeping up there for a few weeks and I think I'd have noticed something like that." She continued, praying that Gloria wouldn't want to check upstairs.

Gloria raised her eyebrows. "Finish reading what he wrote."

Elizabeth narrowed her eyes at Gloria and carried on reading.

'Went back to the house. They were both there. Said that I was going to check on their security. That twat of a detective came to the house at the same time. Up before the beak tomorrow. See what happens. Hopefully won't lose my pension. Must go back to the house. It or her body must be in the cellar. They're always twitchy when I mention it.'

"And you believe this, this fantasy? This admission of criminal activity?" Elizabeth said very directly to Gloria.

"Why shouldn't I?" Gloria's unwashed hackles were up. "Why's a vicar shacked up with a man who's wife's missing?"

Elizabeth cheeks flushed but she managed to control her anger. "We aren't as you so eloquently put it, shacked up. I am staying here in my own room, paying my way, helping Sam through what has been a very difficult time for him. He recently lost two people who he was very close to. Your husband, *I thought*, was helping to find his missing wife, but he seems to have become some sort of burglar. These notes seem to suggest he had other motives, and he was taking drugs!" Her anger begun to seep to the surface.

"Well I want to look in the cellar and upstairs!" Gloria hissed. She was standing, leaning forward on the kitchen table and being as threatening as she could manage.

"Well you can …" Elizabeth bit her lip. "You can of course take a look. But only when Sam gets back from Belgium. It's his house and he should say who can and can't wander around it."

"That's not good enough. Ivor's not been home for days and he knew something about this house. I think he's still here!"

Elizabeth couldn't suppress the nervous laugh which had been slowly developing in her stomach.

"You think this is funny?" Gloria leaned further forward on the table.

"Yes I do."

Gloria blew her cheeks out loudly and slapped her hands on the table, slipping and cracking her chin on it.

Elizabeth did her best not to let her laugh turn into hysterics.

Gloria sat back down on the kitchen chair, trying to maintain her composure and cradling her chin.

"Are you OK?" Elizabeth asked in as concerned a manner as she could muster.

"I'm vine." Gloria replied through a cracked tooth, bleeding gums and split lip.

"Do you want something for that?" Elizabeth asked pointing at her mouth.

"Yes, shumfing cold would 'elp."

Elizabeth got up silently shaking with laughter, got a pack of frozen peas from the freezer, wrapped it in a tea towel and gave it to Gloria.

"Fank you."

They sat in silence for five minutes as Gloria held the cold against her mouth. Finally she broke the silence. "I still want to she the sheller."

Elizabeth managed to keep a straight face and stood up. "Please, follow me."

Gloria followed her into the hall and down the steps into the cellar. "Big ishn't it." She said looking around at the large space. "You could hide anyfing down here."

"It is, as you can see, just full of empty shelving."

"It is now. But what was it like before Ifor got interested?"

"I really don't like your insinuation." Elizabeth said.

"True though, isn't it. How do I know what dis was like a few weeks ago. You could 'ave 'ad any amount of work done down 'ere. New floor." She waved her arms around.

"Look, unless you propose to dig up the floor with a JCB, then I suggest you leave. If you want to come back with a search warrant then please do, because there is nothing to find here." Elizabeth's patience was at last broken.

"Where's that mad woman? Where's she locked up?"

Elizabeth was about to take her arm and escort her from the premises when a loud knock from the front door shattered the air. "Wait here, I need to see who that is." She ran up the cellar steps, down the hall pulled open the front door and in a none too welcoming tone said. "Yes. What is it?"

"Ma'am have you ever considered how Jesus could help you in your life?"

"Frankly yes I have." And she slammed the door shut in the young American evangelist's face.

Muffled behind the door she heard. "Bless you."

"Bollocks!" She thought and started to open the door, but the thought of ejecting Gloria from the house was a much more attractive option. She turned and headed back to the cellar. The scream which came from it sent shivers down her back. She ran to the cellar door and jumped down two steps a time into the cellar. What she saw, tested even her faith. Gloria was sat on the floor of the cellar with her back as firmly as she could get it against the first row of shelving. Her eyes were wide open and fixed on a spot at the end of the row. Elizabeth followed her gaze. Floating in the centre of the row was a spinning vortex of crimson light about two feet across, making no sound.

"Gloria." Elizabeth called to her, but there was no response from the paralysed woman. 'Gloria!" There was still no hint of a response. Elizabeth gripped onto the shelving, and shuffled to Gloria. "Gloria!!!" The eyes blinked as a few neurons recognised the external stimulus.

"Mmmm?"

"Gloria, take my hand."

"Mmmm?"

Elizabeth slid down to the floor and grabbed Gloria's left hand. Her head snapped to the right and her terrified eyes began to understand that help was at hand.

"Gloria, come with me. It's OK. Just follow me up the steps. We'll be out of here in no time at all."

Despite recognising Elizabeth, Gloria's motor functions had not recovered and she sat in a heap on the floor. Her muscles turned to jelly.

"Gloria, please, I can't do this on my own!"

The heap collapsed further in on itself.

Elizabeth glanced at the vortex which had stopped rotating and was edging slowly towards them.

"Gloria! Gloria come with me now!"

The quivering mound remained paralysed against the shelving.

The crimson vortex moved closer.

Elizabeth desperately tugged at Gloria's arms, trying to drag her to the steps and possible safety. She could feel heat from the vortex pulsing at her elbow.

Gloria was an immobile, paralysed, trembling living corpse.

Elizabeth felt a jolt in her shoulder as the vortex brushed close to her.

Gloria slipped into unconsciousness and Elizabeth decided that self-preservation overrode everything else She took one last look as Gloria was enveloped by the vortex, and ran for the steps.

EIGHTY

Lidsay lay motionless in the bed. His eyesight was slowly recovering, but his mental state was at best, disturbed. Which of the realities he'd experienced was true. The sergeant or the lieutenant? Both were completely plausible, but which was reality and which was generated by his own psychoses.

"So how are we doing?" The doctor who'd brought him from the tunnel was standing over him with an attractive young nurse.

Words wouldn't, or couldn't come.

"It's OK, don't worry, these things take time. Main thing is that your sight seems to have recovered. OK if I take a look?"

Lidsay nodded his approval.

James examined his eyes and checked his other vital signs. "Yes. Everything's looking very good. We'll have you up and back at the front in no time."

"Back at the what?" Lidsay thought. He tried to speak, but the words still wouldn't come.

James put a caring hand on his shoulder and smiled. "Don't say anything. I know how important getting back to your comrades is. Give it a few days and you'll be chasing Sister Wilmart around the beds." He patted him on the arm, and turned left to tend to another soldier with an amputated leg.

Agnes stayed at his bedside. "I understand what's happened to you." She said quietly. "I know that this will not be OK in a few days. Believe me when I say that I will make sure you don't go back to the front." She smiled at Lidsay. "Not in your condition." She gently squeezed his hand and followed James to the next patient.

Lidsay lay quietly in the bed staring at the canvas ceiling of the tent. Which reality should he choose? This was becoming difficult as any reality before this present one was rapidly becoming a vague memory. He'd been a sergeant, had he been promoted? Who was Gloria? Hazy images of arguments flashed through his mind, but he could find nothing good or anything of joy in these recollections. Nothing to make him choose it as his reality of choice, but then what was there in this one which offered more?

"What is this?" He thought. *"Must be a Hospital? Am I at war? That officer said that I could go back to the front? What front?"* He looked around at the uniforms of the nurses, orderlies and doctors. *"It's no recent war."* He carried on thinking. *"My God, it's World War One!"*

"Nurse!" He shouted.

Agnes turned back to Lidsay. "Yes, lieutenant?"

"Everything is hazy. I find it hard to remember things. Where am I?"

"That's completely understandable." Agnes said reassuringly.

"I'm not really sure about who I am or what I'm doing here. Wherever here is."

"You're in a casualty clearing station in France. You were found in one of the mines. You're a lieutenant in the Irish Guards and your name is Ronald Hubert Lidsay." Agnes smiled. "Does that help?"

Lidsay's brain was in turmoil, but he kept his expression as calm as he could. "What year is this?"

Agnes, frowned. She'd never seen a patient so completely lose his understanding of time. "It's 1915 lieutenant."

Lidsay sat up in the bed and looked around the tent at the assembled group of dismembered shattered parts of a mutilated, tormented lost generation. A generation of which he wasn't a member.

"How am I here?" He thought surprisingly calmly. *"1915? How?"*

"You should rest lieutenant."

"I feel OK," Lidsay replied.

"Nonetheless, as they say, the doctor knows best. So please lay back."

Lidsay complied.

"Thank you. Now let's check you over." Agnes checked his vital signs again, but could only guess at his mental state. "You seem to be recovering well. How do you feel in yourself?"

"A little hazy on things."

"Hazy in what way?"

"I have no idea how I got here."

"Do you know who you are?"

"I thought I did, but I didn't think I was Ronald Hubert Lidsay. The last time I looked at my passport it said Ivor Wilfred Lidsay and it was 2013."

Agnes stood back from the bed in shock, this man's psychoses were worse than anything she'd ever seen at Seale Hayne. He was, she couldn't find the words, like no-one she'd ever met. Like someone from another world. from another time and place?

"You're sure this is 1915?"

"It was until a few moments ago."

"Am I in a coma? That would explain most things."

"I'm going to bring the doctor to have another look at you." Agnes had never seen such a bad case. "I'll be back in a few minutes. Get some rest."

Five minutes later, Agnes was back with James. She'd outlined Lidsay's comments and mental state and that she thought that there was a lot more to this soldier than just being trapped down a mine.

"So what's this about not knowing who we are?"

Lidsay sat up. His memory flashing intermittently like a TV receiving a corrupted signal. He stared at Agnes and James, while the left hemisphere of his brain desperately tried to unscramble the external stimuli it was receiving.

Synapses fired and did their best to decode what they *could* see into what they knew they *should* be seeing.

"Lieutenant? What do you see?" James sat on the bed close to Lidsay.

Lidsay's eyes were wide open, pin hole pupils fixed on James. His mind in turmoil. *"What's that smell? It's like putrid or decomposing flesh, it's like a few suicides I worked on. Who are these mangled men? Why don't they complain? I've been locked up in some bloody asylum? They've got me on drugs? Where the hell am I? Are those explosions? Is all of this just inside my head? Why do my hands look so young?"* His brain was fast approaching overload and needed to shut down all unnecessary functions and circuits. All incoming data needed urgent cross referencing against every known memory bank. Lidsay's frazzled brain flicked its power switch to standby mode. He was paralysed in a sitting position, his eyes glazed and unresponsive. The line between Ivor and Ronald becoming fuzzier

Agnes sat on the edge of the bed and tried to lay Lidsay flat, but his body was locked. Muscles and joints set in stone. "James, what do we do? He's all the classic symptoms of shell shock, but I've never seen anyone as bad as this before."

He slowly shook his head. "Don't know. Probably for the best if he doesn't regain full consciousness."

"James!"

James stared at Lidsay and examined him again. He stood back and stroked his chin. "Agnes, you think that this is shell shock."

She nodded.

James shook his head. "He exhibits all the classical signs of poisoning. He's been exposed to something. This isn't shell shock." James looked up with an expression like Newton hit by the apple. "This soldier's been exposed to some toxin." His eyes opened even wider. "It's a gas. It has to be. God only knows what the Germans are using against our troops. You've seen the effects of mustard gas. They've developed a chemical which directly affects the brain and incapacitates the soldier." He marched up and down the ward clapping his hands together. "It makes them incapable of fighting! Imagine the effect on an army exposed to it. Germany could simply march into whatever country they wanted, without a bullet or shell ever being fired." He frowned deeply. "They'd have world domination in a few months."

"But we've seen nothing like this before." Agnes said.

James smiled. "Haven't we?"

"What on earth do you mean?"

"How often have we seen soldiers who've lost all control of their senses? Soldiers who can't control their muscles? Who can't sleep? Who twitch uncontrollably?" James paused and raised his eyebrows. "Who don't want to fight? Ring any bells?"

Agnes stared incredulously at him. "You're not suggesting that this supposed unknown gas or chemical is the cause of …."

"… shell shock!" James finished her sentence. "It makes perfect sense, and if I can discover what this gas or chemical is, then we can develop an antidote and simply treat affected men. We would have them back at the front after a simple injection or tablet." He smiled to himself, thinking of the gratitude of High Command for his genius.

"James, it's a mental disorder. You surely can't believe that shell shock is the result of some unknown German secret weapon?"

He shrugged.

Agnes shook her head and tried again to get Lidsay to lay flat on the bed, but he was still paralysed. "James help me to get him comfortable."

They slid their arms under his, lifted him to the head of the bed and propped him up against a stack of pillows.

"Agnes we have other men who have a greater need of our skills. We can come back and check on him later. I need to think how to determine what this poison is."

She nodded, shrugged, took one last look at Lidsay, but what she saw made her grab James's arm and pull him around. "Look at his eyes!"

Lidsay was staring as far to the right as was possible without his eyes popping out of his head, and the pupils had grown to the size of dinner plates.

Agnes followed his gaze. He was staring wildly at the entry to the tent, where a nurse was stood, silhouetted by the evening sun. Agnes shaded her eyes to try to see her face but couldn't recognise her. She tapped James on the shoulder and pointed to the nurse. "Who's that?"

James stared at the silhouette of the nurse and shook his head.

The unknown nurse took a few steps into the tent and her features became clear.

Agnes raised her eyebrows and shook her head at James. "Do you know her?"

"No. We have so many new replacements lately that it's difficult to keep up with everyone. I'll find out who she is." He waved across the tent at the nurse who smiled and pointed at herself. James nodded and gestured for her to come across to them.

She was in her late twenties, about five feet tall, startling blue eyes, blond hair, small feet and hands, a wonderfully engaging smile and the only distinguishing mark was a small scar above her right eye. She smartly saluted and smiled at them.

"Captain James Heyward and Sister Agnes Wilmart. And you are?"

"My apologies, sir, I only arrived this morning and I've been finding my bearings. I'm the replacement for Nurse Ackroyd. My name is Gloria Perron."

Lidsay gasped. Perron rang peels of bells in his mind. It was … It was … Shit what was it … Did I have a wife? … Was this her? … What was her maiden name? … Was this Gloria?

EIGHTY-ONE

The cocoon toppled over the edge of the mini Vesuvius and rolled close to Karsten's feet. He pushed himself up onto his knees and stared at the it. The surface was rippling and rhythmically pulsating. It seemed to be made of pristine brilliant white silk threads, which weren't contaminated in any way with soil or any form of debris. His first thought was to rip open the surface of the cocoon, but Isaac's voice suggested otherwise.

"Open it too early and you will kill the butterfly."

"Butterfly?"

"The new life. It will soon open. You must have patience."

Karsten stood up, crossed his arms and watched the metamorphosis happening at his feet.

"Karsten, are you OK?" His father was concerned about his son.

"I'm fine. I have a guide."

Klaus turned to Guillaume shrugged his shoulders and frowned.

"Leave him. He seems to know what he's doing." Guillaume said.

"But a guide?" Klaus replied.

"I sense that Isaac may be with us." Guillaume said smiling at Klaus.

"Isaac? You feel your brother's presence with us?"

"Yes. Given what we know and do, I see no reason to believe we will not move to another place. Isaac has not yet gone, and is with Karsten." For the first time since Isaac's death, Guillaume felt at peace with himself. He touched Klaus's shoulder and smiled the smile of someone who'd found the answer to life the universe and everything. "He will speak to us. This I know."

Klaus accepted what his friend was saying and watched as Karsten concentrated on the cocoon.

"He is fine my friend. Trust your son. He has come of age."

"I … I … Isaac?" Klaus stuttered.

"I don't have long to stay with you. Time is precious."

"But I have so much to ask."

Guillaume stared at Klaus as he spoke to the sky.

"There will be time for answers when we meet again."

"When?"

"Thank God this is something none of us know. Make everything of the time you have. Have no regrets. Leave no stone unturned. Guide as many back as you can."

"Isaac, there was so much I didn't …"

"I know, my friend."

"Isaac?" Guillaume understood who Klaus was speaking with. "Brother. Speak to me. Please." But there was silence in Guillaume's mind. "Why them and not me?" He dropped to his knees and uncontrollably wept.

The cocoon suddenly became still.

"Guillaume something is happening." Klaus had dropped to his knees close to him and was doing his best to comfort him. "Look. The cocoon. Something is happening."

What appeared to be an arm was protruding from one side of what now looked like a giant inflated condom. At its bottom the shape of a foot distorted the surface. The three men crawled back. Another arm pushed the opposite side out, quickly followed by another foot at the bottom. It was when the deflated condom sat up that all three men turned and ran up the side of the crater. They stopped a few yards away as curiosity won over self-preservation. The condom was sat up and two hands appeared to be, like a chick in an egg, trying to tear the membrane to escape from it, but the membrane was particularly resilient. It stretched but resisted all efforts to break it.

"Should we help?" Karsten asked.

"How?" Klaus replied.

"Help break that membrane."

Guillaume and Klaus looked amazed at each other.

"Der Junge ist sauer!" Klaus said.

"Ja. Wie die Engländer sagen ist er mit der Feen."

"Yes." Klaus laughed, "Off with the fairies. But perhaps we should see what is inside?"

Guillaume grudgingly nodded in agreement.

"Karsten. Wir müssen es aufzubrechen." Klaus said.

"Sie sind sicher?"

"I am sure."

Karsten looked around the ground close to them and picked up the broken branch of a bush. He moved closer to the cocoon and prodded at the membrane with the stick. Like a balloon, it simply bent inwards and then back to its original position.

"You'll have to push a lot harder." Klaus said.

Guillaume was looking around for something more suitable, and saw something rusty in a bramble bush close by. As he pulled at it he could see it was a section of barbed wire still attached to its metal spike. He pulled it clear of the brambles and carried it across to Karsten. "Try this?"

Karsten turned and smiled. "That should do it. This stick is … nutzlos."

Carefully avoiding the rusted barbs, Karsten dragged the wire across the middle of the membrane, which stretched and resisted, but after a short time tore and ripped open. A cloudy white fluid gushed out of the tear and the cocoon began to deflate until it hung like a wet plastic sheet over what was clearly the body of a man.

The three men stared at each other, speechless.

A hand appeared from the tear, quickly followed by another. They gripped the slimy membrane and began to pull it back from the unseen man. As it peeled back over his head, Klaus, Guillaume and Karsten like a barber shop choir gasped in unison.

Although the face was covered in a glutinous liquid and the hair was matted tightly to the head, they could clearly see who it was.

"Mein Gott! Sam!!"

Karsten ran forward and tried to pull Sam out of the cocoon, but it was like trying to extract a wet bar of soap from a dish of olive oil. The others ran to help him, and between them eventually managed to drag Sam from the slime.

Klaus quickly put Sam in the recovery position and did his best to clear his airways and eyes of the opaque mucus. "Give me your sweater." He shouted to Karsten. "I can wipe this stinkenden Scheiße off him."

Karsten pulled off his red sweater and threw it to Klaus who started wiping off as much of the filth as he could from Sam's face and neck.

Sam's chest heaved as his lungs convulsed, desperately trying to spew out the filth which was choking him.

Klaus massaged his back. "It's OK Sam we're here."

More and more cloying mucus erupted from Sam's throat as his lungs began to win the battle, and after a few minutes of throat scraping retching, he rolled onto his back and did his best to smile at Klaus.

"Take it easy, mein freund." Klaus whispered.

Sam tried to sit up, and with Karsten's help and support, sat with his head resting on his flexed knees.

"Take it easy, Sam." Guillaume said. "Everything's going to be fine."

Sam straightened up and looked around him. "The others …" he croaked "the others … where" He violently coughed as the last of the mucus flew from his lungs, "where … are they? They were with me. We found … him … Adam … we found him. Where is he? Where … are … they?"

Klaus, Karsten and Guillaume stared at each other and shook their heads. "There *is* no-one else, Sam."

"But they were there!" Sam insisted. "The four of us were …" Sam spat out hopefully the last of Klaus's stinkenden Scheiße. "Have you got any water?" He asked.

Klaus looked at Karsten and gestured for him to run to the car and fetch what they had. "Karsten will fetch some for you." Klaus said. "Sam, tell us what happened."

He told them what he could remember of what happened in the tunnel. Adam trapped under the collapsed ceiling, Rebecca being with Adam at the end, the light in the ceiling of the tunnel, the silk threads, the others disappearing into the light and the guiding voice.

Karsten down-hill skied the side of the crater with the water.

Sam drained the bottle and then slowly looked at each of them. "There was a voice. A voice in my head. It was telling me what to do. It was … it sounded like …"

"Isaac?" Guillaume softly said.

They all looked at each other.

"Yes, it was Isaac."

"He spoke to me as well." Karsten said quietly. "I am certain it was Isaac. He didn't say his name, but I know it was him."

Klaus sat back on his haunches. "He came to me." The tears began to flow. "He told me to make everything of the time I have. To have no regrets. To leave no stone unturned, and to guide as many back as I can."

EIGHTY-TWO

Elizabeth stood with her back pressed against the wall of the cellar, her breathing shallow and laboured. She turned her head and peered back at the shelving. The spinning vortex was motionless, hovering just above the floor, but Gloria was nowhere to be seen. Elizabeth swallowed hard and slid gently down the wall to the floor.

"This cellar has to be the centre of activity." She thought. *"It's acting like a receiver. and a transmitter. That's what's happened to Gloria and Jane. Maybe this is where that sergeant disappeared?"* She thought back to Ypres and how they'd described how the memorials worked with the local receivers in each country. *"They must arrive here, wander the house looking to be found by ... me. I'm the final stage of their journey. Through me they find final salvation and rest."* This for Elizabeth was an epiphany. Through all the years of her work in the ministry she'd never felt closer to God than she did at High Wood. "Lord thank you for guiding me here."

A disturbing thought struck her. *"If it's a receiver? Then can anything come in?* What else was floating out there in the ether and wasn't as *friendly* as the lost souls of her soldiers?

She stood up and walked into the cellar away from the vortex, deciding to double check if there was any sign of Gloria, but after a few minutes it was obvious she wasn't anywhere to be found.

A sound like a child's balloon bursting span her around. The vortex was gone, replaced by a swirling opaque cloud which curled and eddied over the shelving and into the all corners of the cellar. It wrapped itself around Elizabeth's legs and climbed up her body like a hungry reticulated python. She looked around the cellar which was now completely buried up to the level of her waist in a swirling dense fog. She moved towards the steps, her legs pushing through the mist, and as she approached the steps, the fog seemed to shudder and ripple like the surface of an ultrasonic cleaner. In the centre of the room it started spinning like a whirling dervish into a violent whirlpool, and as it span faster and faster the fog from around the cellar was sucked into the eye of the whirlpool.

Elizabeth felt no pull into the whirlpool, stood on the last step of the cellar and watched as the fog rapidly disappeared like cloudy soapy water down a bath's plug hole. As the last of the fog disappeared and the cellar cleared, she could see three figures huddled together where the centre of the whirlpool had been, and as they stood up, she gasped and fell back against the wall of the cellar.

Jane, Rebecca and Adam slowly stood up and looked around.

Elizabeth stood frozen to the spot. In the few weeks she'd been at High Wood, she'd seen things which would normally have sent her screaming for the hills. But this was … it was just … just.

Jane was the first to see her and ran across to her. "You look like you've seen a ghost."

Elizabeth did her best to smile. "You're pretty close to the mark."

"Sorry to arrive unannounced like this. But you know that time tunnels are like London buses, you don't see any for ages and then three come along at once."

This time Elizabeth genuinely smiled.

"Sorry, Liz. It just sort of happened, and we had no control over it. Where's Sam? He was with us." Jane looked around the cellar and up the steps. "Where is he?"

"I only saw the three of you *appear*." Elizabeth replied.

"But he was with us. When we found Adam he was with us. He was with us when a crimson glow appeared." She looked around again as if Sam had found the perfect spot for hide and seek. "But he's not here?"

"I haven't seen him Jane." Elizabeth was beginning to panic. "So where is he?" Jane's expression offered her no reassurance that Sam was safe.

"Liz I've never done this before. It's as strange to me as it is to you. I can't even begin to try and explain what's just happened. But I'm sure Sam is OK." She took a few steps back and pointed to Rebecca and Adam. "You should meet the happy couple."

If Elizabeth was confused, then Adam's mind was rapidly dismantling itself, as the thought *"No previous experience!"* bounced around his skull. "Becky, how can this be? When … what … where is this?" He massaged the nape of his neck and shook his head. "I'm unconscious, and I'm imagining this." He reached out and held Rebecca. "But I can feel you against me. I know it's you. But you can't feel dreams. Can you?"

Rebecca was desperately worried this was all too much for him. She was struggling herself to understand everything which had recently happened. "My darling, I can't explain any of this." She pointed at Elizabeth and Jane. "Who they are. Except that without them, I'd have never found you and still be locked in that room upstairs." The tears were freely flowing. "I have you back. I have you back forever."

"But …" Adam's face was creased with lines.

Rebecca put her finger to his lips. "Don't try to understand, and just accept what is. I've been waiting so, so long for you." And for the first time in almost a hundred years, they kissed and reignited the fire.

"But, Sam …" Elizabeth was in panic mode.

Jane gestured to the reunited couple. "Come and meet Adam. Wherever Sam is, I know in my bones he's safe. He'll come back to you."

They both jumped in shock as the phone in Elizabeth's pocket pinged. Elizabeth scrambled to get it out of her trouser pocket and read the message. Panic mode remained as she recognised Guillaume's number, but it soon disappeared when she read the text message. She turned the phone to Jane so that she could read the message.

'I'm OK. Don't know how. Are Jane Rebecca and Adam with you? – LOL – Sam'

Despite the sentiment, Jane smiled. She had no feelings left for Sam, but was happy that he'd found someone like Elizabeth.

Elizabeth had never been adept at texting, but her reply took only a few seconds to write. *'They're all here. What do I do? Come home. – Luv U'*

Ping

'Sorry. Not until after Isaac's funeral. Should be home in a couple of days.'

Ping

'What do I do with them?'

Ping

'Don't know. Should you help them move on?'

Ping

'All of them?'

Ping

There was an obvious delay before the next text came through.

'Yes All of them.'

Ping

'I'd rather wait until you get back.'

Ping

Another delay.

'OK. Probably a better idea. Take care I'll call after the funeral.'

Ping

'Give Guillaume my love Take care.'

Sam read the final text. "Guillaume, Elizabeth sends her love."

Guillaume smiled and nodded in gratitude.

Klaus stood up and wrapped his jacket around Sam. "We had better get back. There are still things to do before the ..." He swallowed hard. "... the funeral."

Karsten helped Sam to his feet and the four men slowly made their way up the side of the crater. It took quite some time as they took it in turns to support Sam as he stumbled through the bracken and long grass. When they reached the car, Sam turned to Klaus and said through a smile. "Your jacket's ruined."

EIGHTY-THREE

Lidsay, *Ivor* Lidsay, was inexorably changing into Ronald. The appearance of Gloria as a replacement for another nurse, now seemed perfectly normal to him. Something was niggling at the back of his brain, but like any itch, with enough scratching, it would eventually go away, and Mrs Gloria Lidsay and the future would soon fade into grey.

"This is Lieutenant Lidsay, Nurse Perron, he's been with us for a few days now." Agnes looked closely at Lidsay, his expression had changed. The distant look in his eyes had been replaced by a strange clarity, and he was smiling. She looked back at Nurse Perron who was smiling at him. "You seem to have a magic touch, Nurse Perron."

She blushed not taking her eyes away from Lidsay. "What's he being treated for?"

James moved quickly forward not wanting Agnes to mention his *discovery*. "Poor chap was trapped down one of the mines in total blackness. Panicked and his eyes were then badly affected by lights in the tunnel." He looked at Lidsay and back at Gloria. "Agnes is right, you do have a magic touch. This is the best we've seen him look since he was admitted."

Gloria smiled. "Thank you , Captain. I seem to feel a close affinity with the lieutenant."

"Ronald, please." Lidsay was sat up in the bed.

"Nurse Perron, I'm going to leave you with Lieutenant Lidsay for a few minutes as you seem to be having such a very positive effect on him. Wait here and Sister Wilmart will be back to take you to matron who will assign you your duties." James took a nearby stool, placed it close to the bed, tapped it and gestured to Gloria to sit down. "We'll leave you to it."

As they walked away James turned to Agnes. "You see, what better proof do you need, that just below the surface of this cancer shell shock, is the true man. Lidsay will be back at the front in days." He frowned, looked back at Lidsay and smiled. "He's probably developed his own antidote to the poison. I need to analyse his blood. " He frowned again and stared at Lidsay and Nurse Perron. "We should keep them together. She seems to have a positive effect on him." He turned and walked away, very happy with himself.

Agnes frowned, and bit her tongue. If James thought there was some miracle cure associated with an antidote to the *'poison'*, then perhaps she could convince him to report this in person, to Arthur at Seale Hayne. "It certainly looks to have real promise. I've never seen such a rapid recovery."

"Yes, discovering what poison the Bosche are using, could be the answer everyone's been looking for, for this so-called illness." James stopped, clearly lost in thought.

"We really should see Arthur about this, James. With the facilities at Seale Hayne, you could develop potential antidotes. You could even inoculate against the poison." Agnes suggested.

"I hope that that wasn't a little too enthusiastic." She thought.

"You're right, but I can't leave here without my leadership."

"No, of course not, but we could at least start the wheels turning. Once GHQ know about the speed you could get men back to the front, and critically, prevent them getting this so-called disease, then I'm certain they'd want to get you and Arthur together as soon as possible."

"But do I need Arthur? Surely I just need to develop an antidote? I could do that anywhere."

"You need a chemist to find an antidote and, you can't do any research here, so we need to go back to Seale Hayne."

James massaged the back of his neck, frowned, sighed, chewed his thumb, sighed again, shook his head, stared into the far distance, turned and looked back at Gloria and Lidsay, smiled at Agnes, shook his head again, closed his eyes, blew out his cheeks, massaged the bridge of his nose, opened his eyes and looked around the beds at the damaged humanity he'd repaired, pulled at his earlobe, sighed once more and walked out of the tent.

Agnes shook her head as he disappeared outside. *"Pushed him a bit too strongly."* She thought. *"Softly, softly, as they say. Not crash bang wallop."*

James ran back into the tent and grabbed Agnes by the shoulders. "You're right. I need to see Arthur, but he could come to me, and that would kill two birds with one stone. I can keep treating these," he waved his arms around the tent, "desperate souls, Arthur could bring a chemist, and we could work together to get a truer understanding of what we are seeing in Lieutenant Lidsay." He squeezed her, kissed her on the cheek and laughed out loud. "It's the perfect solution to everything."

"Oh God no." Agnes thought. She ran back to her quarters and wrote the quickest letter of her life.

'Dear Arthur,

You will have received, or will soon receive a letter from James. Please do not comply with his request for you to come to France. I am desperately worried about him. He is functioning better than ever as a surgeon, but his mental state seems extremely unstable. I need to get him back to you at Seale Hayne. Please, please make up anything which you think will convince him to come to Seale Hayne to meet with you there.

Sincerely

Agnes'

She read it, re-read it, sealed and addressed the envelope and dropped it into the post box.

"Writing home, old girl?" James was standing just a few feet behind her.

"Yes just catching up on the local gossip." She was frantically worried that he'd seen the address.

"Gossip from Seale Hayne? You should have told me you were writing to the girls. I could have put your letter in with mine." He kissed her cheek. "I've written to Arthur like I said." He rubbed the palms of his hands together. "Any luck, he should be, God willing, with us in a few weeks." He frowned. "Only problem is my star patient Lidsay, is making a marvellous recovery and I should have him back in the trenches in a few days! I can't keep him here. The entire point of this is to get these men fighting fight fit as quickly as possible, and pushing the Bosche back where they belong."

Agnes saw a chink of light. "But you need him and his blood. Why don't we take him back to Seale Hayne, while he's still with us? It would only take a couple of weeks at the most, and I'm sure GHQ would approve given the extra troops it would generate for them."

James sucked in his cheeks and pulled at his fingers, loudly cracking them. "But we couldn't just turn up at Seale Hayne."

"Why not?" Agnes could sense the chink getting larger.

"Well for one thing ..." James screwed up his face. "For one thing, Arthur could be far too busy to spend any time with me." This seemed to partially placate James's wavering concerns.

"Is there any way to contact him quicker than the mail?" Agnes continued to prise the gap open.

"I suppose that Bob could send a telegram for me."

"Bob?"

"Captain Robert Dabin. Works at GHQ. Owes me a couple of favours." Light was beginning to flood in.

Agnes realised it would only take a small nudge to completely open the flood gates. "Let's get hold of him." She suggested.

"Could phone him I suppose. Provided that the damn lines haven't been destroyed by the shelling." James was almost there. "Come on then let's go up to see Corporal Stewart. He can tell us if his precious communication lines are open."

Corporal Able Stewart, owed his life to James, after he'd sewn the torn shreds of his stomach back together. He still suffered badly from severe indigestion every time he ate, but he was alive and had been given this cushy number in communications. "No problem at all, sir. Give me a couple of secs and I'll get GHQ on the line for you." He expertly manipulated the telephone board and, good to his word, he soon had GHQ on the line.

"Tell them that I need to speak to Captain Dabin." James said quietly.

"Captain Dabin. Yes, sir."

It took a couple of minutes to find the captain, and as his voice could be heard at the end of the line, Corporal Stewart smiled and handed the handset to James.

"James, you old bugger. Haven't spoken to you for ages. How are you old boy? How can I help?" The crisp cut old Etonian tones of Robert Dabin crackled down the fragile telephone line. "I wouldn't chat for too long. These bloody lines are always going down."

"Good to hear you again, old man. Give my regards to Audrey when you next write to her." Pleasantries out of the way, James explained what he needed.

"No problem. Just shout out what you want to say. Keep it brief and to the point. I'll shorten it if I need to." He paused. "OK, I've got paper and a pencil, off you go."

Ten minutes later Captain Dabin was watching as Private Absolom tapped the message.

'FROM – Capt J Heyward TO Maj. A Hurst Seale Hayne, Devon – URGENT Have SS patient and have cause of SS must see you STOP ASAP'.

"Thanks private. Bit shorter than he dictated, but needs must. I think I've got the gist of the message."

Two days later a reply was delivered to James.

'FROM – Maj. A Hurst TO – Capt J Heyward Come as soon as you can'.

He took the telegram to Agnes, who managed to maintain her self composure as she read the short message. "You can go then."

"*We* can go. GHQ have already OK'd everything. Transport will be available when we request it." For the first time in weeks, James seemed to be genuinely smiling.

EIGHTY-FOUR

Guillaume contacted the airline and pushed Sam's flight back by two days. He wanted him to stay for a few more days, but Sam was insistent that given what had happened at High Wood he needed to get back as soon as possible.

They arrived late at Guillaume's home in Uccle. He smiled sadly as they approached Bloemenwerf, where he and Isaac had moved after Beaumont Hamel. Built in 1895, the house and its interior were designed by Henry van de Velde a Belgian painter, architect and interior designer. It had been inspired by the Arts and Crafts movement and specifically William Morris's Red House. Velde had incorporated the same patterns of embellishments and flowing linear shapes. Guillaume had always loved the house and was sad to be away from it. The door below the large central porch, seemed, as it always had, to be smiling and welcoming him home. He looked up at the three Dutch gables and the shutters in the four windows set in the white walls of the front of the house, all closed since Isaac's death.

Klaus climbed out of the car and stretched his back. It had been a long drive and his sciatica was sending a deep aching pain down his leg into the sole of his right foot. He looked around at the familiar front and gardens of Bloemenwerf and remembered cold beers and open sandwiches on the lawn. He knew that although Isaac was gone, his spirit would always live on here.

The others climbed out of the car and made their way up the steps to the front door.

"You have a beautiful home." Sam said. "You must have been … you are … very … happy here." He felt embarrassed at his struggle to find the right words.

Guillaume reassured him with a gentle smile. "It's OK, Sam. Times like these are difficult for all of us and words are difficult to find." He opened the front door and gestured for him and the others to follow him into the house.

After settling into their rooms, they all met in the dining room and sat around the table drinking cold Leuven beers.

"Is everything arranged for tomorrow?" Klaus asked.

"Yes. Roger, a close friend, and his brother Stefan, have been attending to all the details for me. Roger has also been my Shomer. My watchman. In our tradition the deceased should not be left alone or unattended, and the Shomer, will stay with Isaac from his death until the funeral and burial. I should have arranged everything for my brother, but …" Guillaume's resolve finally gave way and he sat back in his chair sobbing.

"He would understand Guillaume. He was, is, a good man. A saint among men." Klaus put his arm around Guillaume's shoulders. "He is still with us. Those of us who were at the crater know this." He looked around the room and smiled. "Are you here now my old friend? Give us a sign."

Guillaume walked to the sofa and stopped. He looked around at the others and smiled. "He has sent me a sign. "He bent down and picked something up from the rug. As he turned to face his friends, he opened his hand, and sitting on his palm was a perfect white feather. "He is with us."

They all raised their glasses and offered a deep heartfelt toast to Isaac.

Guillaume dabbed at his eyes with a tissue. "Is anyone hungry?" He asked.

"Not me." Klaus replied. "This," he raised his glass, "is all I need." He looked at Sam and Karsten who nodded and raised their glasses. "I think what we all need is a good night's sleep. We will need it for tomorrow."

Everyone agreed, drained their glasses, got up, turned the lights off in the dining room, climbed the stairs, said goodnight to each other on the landing and settled into their rooms for what for all of them would be a restless night's sleep.

The following morning after a breakfast of mainly coffee, they dressed for the funeral. Guillaume was sitting in the lounge with Stefan while Roger, who was Shomer, was with Isaac.

"Is everything in place, my friend?" Klaus asked.

Guillaume slowly nodded, his face expressionless. This wasn't going to be an easy day for him. He stood up and embraced Klaus, Karsten and Sam, and as he did he pinned a black ribbon to the right side of their jackets.

"This is K'riah, it is tradition. It represents the rending, tearing, of our clothes, and is symbolic of the tearing of our hearts. You must wear it for seven days." He thinly smiled. "And it does save on having to buy new clothes." He winked at Klaus.

Klaus was relieved that Guillaume had still retained a glimmer of humour.

They were met at the synagogue by their Rabbi. "A sad time Guillaume."

Guillaume nodded but said nothing. His throat was constricted and nothing would come from it except sounds of desperate sadness.

Isaac's plain coffin was at the head of the Synagogue.

"There are no flowers," Sam whispered to Karsten.

"It is their custom." Karsten replied. "They are considered … I believe the word is frivolous."

The synagogue was packed with mourners and Guillaume spent as much time with them as he could, accepting their condolences.

After about fifteen minutes of recitations, psalms and scripture readings, Klaus walked forward to deliver the eulogy. He acquiesced to Guillaume's request, to remember Isaac. He had no notes. Everything he needed to say would come from the heart. He turned to face the congregation, bowed to Guillaume and swallowed hard.

"I am proud to say that Isaac was my friend, and that his brother remains my closest friend." He took a deep breath. "His work for his fellow man was done without need for thanks and in the true spirit of humanity. He lived a full life. A rewarding life. We enjoyed many Kriek and Leffe together." He patted his paunch and smiled. "Probably a few too many." There were nods and muted smiles amongst the mourners. "The lost of the Great War was his passion. A time in our history which has crawled into the dimly lit corners of the minds of today's young. To them it is just pages in a book, documentaries on TV, endless lists of the names of young men of a lost generation, sacrificed among Flanders' poppies and fading memories treasured and remembered every November 11th. Isaac always said their suffering must never be forgotten and we will continue to ensure that it isn't. So many years together ..." Klaus took a tissue from his trouser pocket and dabbed at his eyes. "Forgive me." As one, the mourners put a metaphorical arm around his shoulders. "This is not easy for me so I will keep it brief." He dabbed his eyes again and screwed them up to hold back the torrent which was welling up behind them. "The poets of World War One put into words what we can only imagine, and I know it meant a great deal to Isaac. I've chosen some lines by Wilfred Owen, which I believe sum up why Isaac did what he did, and why we continue his work." Klaus pulled a small sheet of paper from his pocket.

"What passing-bells for those who die as cattle?
Only the monstrous anger of the guns.
Only the stuttering rifles rapid rattle.
Can patter out their hasty orisons.
No mockeries for them: no prayers nor bells,
Nor any voice of mourning save the choirs, -
The shrill, demented choirs of wailing shells;
And bugles calling for them from their sad shires.

What candles may be held to speed them all?
Not in the hands of boys, but in their eyes
Shall shine the holy glimmers of goodbyes.
The pallor of girls' brows shall be their pall;
Their flowers the tenderness of patient minds,
and each slow dusk a drawing-down of blinds."

He walked to the coffin, tenderly laid his hands on the plain wood, bowed his head and said a few silent words.

"Goodbye old friend. Come back and see us again. You are missed."

He stood upright and turned to the mourners, his cheeks awash with tears as the dam burst. "I'm ... sorry ... he was my ... friend is not enough. He was ... my ... I can find no word." He blew his nose and pushed the tissue into his jacket pocket. He'd learnt some words of Hebrew and closed his eyes to recall the words. "בשלום נוח. שלי ידיד לך מברך אלוהים." There was a murmur of approval and nodded heads from the mourners as they wrapped their arms around him again. He sat down between Guillaume and Sam, who put their arms warmly around his shoulders.

Guillaume leaned close to him. "Thank you. Isaac would be very happy."

"It was all I could manage. It wasn't enough." Klaus sobbed.

Sam squeezed Klaus's shoulder. "It was perfect."

Klaus nodded, but Sam could sense that Klaus was suffering.

The Rabbi graciously thanked Klaus, and a few minutes later they were following the coffin into the graveyard.

Guillaume stopped and spoke quietly to Karsten, Sam and Klaus. "It will seem strange to you, but at the graveside we will take part in the burial. It is Chesed Shel Emet. It is the final unselfish act of love which Isaac's family and friends carry out for him. Watch me closely and I will guide you."

Sam, Klaus and Karsten looked at each other and then solemnly nodded in understanding to him.

The burial was difficult but strangely comforting. The four friends stood at the graveside and silently said their last goodbyes to Isaac, and when the time came when they had to tear themselves away from the grave, they each dropped a keep sake, a Flander's poppy, onto Isaac's coffin.

They turned to walk away from the grave, and saw a double line of mourners stretching away to the synagogue.

"It is a Shura." Guillaume said. "It is tradition for us only to receive words of consolation and comfort after the burial. They are given through the Shura. Words from the heart go directly to the heart." He smiled and whispered. "Follow me."

As they walked through the Shura, the feeling of love and sympathy was overwhelming. An elderly woman reached out and touched Sam's sleeve. "May you be comforted among all the mourners of Zion and Jerusalem."

Much later that evening when all the mourners had left, Klaus, Guillaume, Sam and Karsten sat together around the kitchen table.

Guillaume was the first to speak. "I will not be able to leave the house for the next seven days. This is required by Shiva." He turned to Sam. "I cannot travel, but I will be here for anything you need. Things at High Wood will not be easy. Despite Rebecca being reunited with Adam, the dead, after they have been locked for such a long time in Purgatory, can develop an unquenchable desire to stay with the living". He paused and took a sip of water. "They may not be happy to leave, to move on. When they are lost and alone it is much easier. They want to be reunited, but if they are already reunited, then why would they want to go from a place they know and love, to who knows what. Finally being with the one they love after so many years, restores memories of a life lived and a time gone by. They will cling onto this like a limpet to a ship's hull, chain themselves to them and demand to stay." He took another sip of water. "You will need to be careful Sam. The desire to stay can transform the friendliest spirit."

"Transform into what?" Sam was frightened by Guillaume's comments.

Guillaume looked directly into Sam's eyes. "I have seen this only once." He glanced at Klaus. "Klaus I know has seen it quite a few times."

Klaus frowned and nodded.

"Guillaume, transform into what?" Sam was now seriously worried. Elizabeth was in High Wood, on her own with three spirits, and she had no knowledge of what Guillaume had just told him. He took his phone from his pocket, frantically scrolled through his contacts and touched Elizabeth's mobile number. He looked back at Guillaume, still waiting for an answer. The call connected and Elizabeth's phone rang, and rang, and rang. He looked back to Guillaume, his expression frozen in panic. "Guillaume!"

"I know that we should have told you before, but Isaac wanted to wait until you were fully committed to Papaver Rhoeas. Then he died …" He looked down at the table. "I'm sorry, Sam."

Sam turned and looked at Klaus. "Tell me. Tell me now. She's not answering. What's happening?"

Klaus leaned forward, sighed loudly and rested his elbows on the table. "Sam." He ran his fingers through his hair. "There are rare occasions when the spirit of a soldier becomes so lost in Purgatory, that this in-between world becomes home. Sam, you and I can never truly comprehend what they suffered, so after the horrors of battle and the agonies of death, they find themselves …" Klaus stroked his chin. "Have you seen those isolation tanks where you float in a salt solution in total darkness?"

Sam nodded. He hoped that Klaus would soon get to the point as he was terrified about what might be happening to Elizabeth.

"They find themselves in a place where pain and suffering don't exist. They suffered so much in the trenches, when they find themselves suspended in this, other world, a tranquil Eden, there are a few, only a very few, who won't leave. They resist being helped to move on. Their memories fade until they evaporate, and all that remains for them is the present. All they know is Purgatory, and if they are forced to leave, then they don't react well. This is the same for those who are reunited with their loved ones who have also not moved on." He paused and raised his eyebrows. "Like Rebecca and Adam."

Sam had visibly paled, and looked like he was about to faint.

"Karsten, get Sam some brandy." Klaus shouted.

The brandy was downed in two. "Klaus. I understand, … well I think that I sort of understand. But what do they change into? Please tell me."

"They become, untote, undead. This does not have the right meaning." Klaus spoke to Karsten. "Wie sagst du vampir?"

Karsten's eyes opened wide. "Ein vampir?!"

"Ja, ein vampir."

Karsten didn't understand why Klaus was asking this but replied quietly. "Es its das gleiche, es ist vampir." He pronounced vampire in English. A little too loudly as Sam slammed his hands on the table.

"Vampire! Did you say vampire?" Sam's fuse had burnt out and his bomb exploded. "Are you seriously telling me that she's at High Wood with Dracula and the Bride of Dracula?"

Klaus held Sam's hands. "It is possible, but highly unlikely."

"What sort of pissing answer is that. Is she or isn't she? And why would they suddenly develop a taste for blood?"

"Not blood Sam. On the few times …"

"How many is a few?" Sam angrily asked.

"It's difficult to put a number on it."

"Then try!"

"Maybe ten."

Sam seemed relieved by the answer. "That's nothing isn't it? If that's all you've seen since this organisation started operating then that's hardly any at all."

"Ten a year, Sam."

Sam's relief was short lived. "So what do you mean by vampire?"

Guillaume sat forward to take some of the pressure off Klaus. Karsten was also intently listening, as all this was new to him.

"Sam," Guillaume started, "even after all these years, we still don't properly understand this phenomenon. Having seen the results of what they do, then we believe they are desperate for any means to stop them moving on. It is our belief that they think if they take the life force from a living being, then they will remain here."

Sam was shaking his head. "This is like some cheap horror film. You're all deluded. Things like this are only thought up in the minds of people like Stephen King. You're talking bollocks."

"I wish we were, Sam. But I have seen this at first hand, and I have lost dear friends. This is a dangerous and unpredictable quest we have set out upon, and we are dealing with altered states and forces no one claims to even partially understand." Guillaume stood up and stretched. "Sam, you are right that our first priority must be Elizabeth." He drank the remainder of his glass of water. "I cannot leave the house, Shura demands this of me. I would not be paying my brother the respect he deserves." He put down the glass and matched Sam's glare. "You must call Elizabeth. Only by speaking to her will we know what has happened." He nodded at Sam's phone. "Try again. She may have been out?"

Sam redialled the number and waited as the phone rang and rang. "You've got to get me on an earlier flight! Drive me to the airport. Take me NOW!"

"Sam it's late."

"I don't give a flying fuck what the time is. Get me to the airport. I must get on the earliest flight. God only knows what's happening at High Wood." He pulled his hands away from Klaus and glared at him and Guillaume. "If she's … she's … I'll never forgive you! You'll wish that we'd never met!"

"We were wrong not to have told him. Klaus you must go with him. He will not know how to deal with what he may find there. Use our plane. You can be in the UK by lunchtime."

"Isaac?" Klaus exclaimed.

EIGHTY-FIVE

Organising documentation and travel, had been a lot simpler than Agnes had anticipated. Captain Dabin proved invaluable as he oiled the wheels, and a week later she was driving down the familiar road to Seale Hayne.

James had spent most of the journey in close conversation with Lieutenant Lidsay and Nurse Perron who Lidsay had insisted must travel with them, as her appearance *may* have played a part in Lidsay's recovery.

"It's beautiful isn't it. A world away from the guns and death." Gloria was staring out of the window at the sweeping grounds of Seale Hayne.

"We had some marvellous times here. The work can be distressing, but the results Arthur, sorry General Hurst, has achieved with his patients is nothing short of miraculous." Agnes replied.

"And all of this is to treat shell shock?" Gloria asked in a tone which Agnes took exception to.

"You don't believe that shell shock is a genuine condition?"

"Do you?" Gloria grinned.

"Then why are you here?"

"Chance to get away from all that damn suffering I suppose."

"All that damn suffering?"

"Don't tell me you didn't get sick of the smell and the noise. Why can't they just die quietly? It's not as if they'd ever recover to what they were before the war? I mean, when your number's up, then shuffle off this mortal coil with a bit of decorum and thought for others."

Agnes was struggling to believe what she was hearing wasn't the deluded ramblings of a lunatic.

"I mean," Gloria continued, digging the hole deeper and deeper, "most of them could barely read and write. It always seemed to me it was the officers who suffered the most. Having to write those terrible letters to wives and mothers. Lying about how Tommy had fought bravely and died protecting his comrades. Not much fun that, is it?"

James and Lidsay were still deep in conversation, and thankfully, Agnes realised, hadn't heard a word of their discussion.

"James will need to know. We can't allow her to stay here for what's just a holiday!" She thought.

Thankfully for Agnes they arrived at the main entrance of Seale Hayne and Arthur was standing at the bottom of the steps waiting to welcome them.

Private Owen moved from behind Arthur and opened the rear door of their car. "Lovely to see you again, miss. Pardon, Sister." He said through a broad smile. "And of course you as well, sir." He said to James.

"So good to see you again, Owen. How have things been since we've been away at the front?" Agnes asked.

"Considerably better now that you're both back with us, miss." Owen's sentiment was genuine. He'd a secret crush on Agnes which was showing through his bright crimson cheeks. "Warm isn't it, miss?" He continued trying to cover his embarrassment.

"Very unseasonal, Owen." Agnes answered.

"James, welcome back. Your telegram was very exciting and a little mysterious." Arthur stepped forward and warmly shook his hand.

"Good to see you, Major." He stepped to one side and theatrically waved his arm at Lidsay. "And this is Lieutenant Roger Lidsay." He waved across Gloria to meet Arthur. "And Nurse Gloria Perron."

"So very pleased to meet you both. I look forward to talking with you, but for now please follow me. I've organised some sandwiches and tea. I imagine that you need both after your journey."

Everyone nodded in agreement.

Arthur turned and quietly spoke to Private Owen. "Organise the luggage will you, Owen."

Owen crisply saluted. "They'll be in their quarters before you've finished your first cup of tea, sir."

Arthur patted him on the shoulder. "Good man." He had a lot of time for this quiet but efficient soldier.

After they'd eaten their fill of sandwiches and drained an urn of tea, Arthur proposed that Agnes, Gloria and Lieutenant Lidsay, made themselves at home in their new quarters, and as if by magic, Private Owen appeared and took them to their rooms.

"I wanted to have a private word with you, James," Arthur said quietly, leading him to a couple of well-worn but very comfortable green leather armchairs.

"Of course, Major," James replied as he relaxed back into the chair.

"Arthur. Please, James, call me Arthur. If in public you feel that major is more appropriate, that's fine. But in private, please call me Arthur."

James nodded and smiled.

"Excellent. Now tell me about this German poison and Lidsay."

"Yes. In all my time in this damnable war I have never seen such a dramatic recovery. And suddenly it came to me. Poison gas. The Bosche are using gas more and more. Lidsay was exhibiting many classic shell shock symptoms, but his recovery was sudden and dramatic. My thoughts were he'd been exposed to a massive dose of this new poison, but had developed his own antidote to the poison. My belief is this was the reason for his apparently miraculous recovery. The effect the nurse had, may well have had some *influence* over him as well, but developing an antidote is the key. That's why I thought coming to see you was the best thing to do." James conspiratorially leaned forward in his chair.

"To be honest I was for sending him back to trenches, but he may have something in his blood we need."

Arthur stared at James and frowned. "Back to the trenches?"

"Yes, that's why I wanted to see you. I believe that if we work together and use your contacts and knowledge, we could determine how this poison works, and develop an antidote. We could then disprove this whole fallacy of shell shock and have these men, these malingerers, back where they're needed, at the front." James sat back in the chair beaming and obviously very pleased with himself.

Arthur was speechless.

Owen had returned and was stood at attention in the doorway. "Everyone settled into their quarters, sir."

"Thank you, Owen. Perhaps you could show the captain to his quarters." Arthur needed to be alone to take in what James had said. He stood up and shook him by the hand. "I'll see you at dinner. Usually meet at about eight for a few drinks."

"Splendid. I could do with freshening up." James saluted and followed Owen.

"I can see what Agnes was worried about in her letter." He thought. *"He's bordering on the psychotic."*

EIGHTY-SIX

Adam looked down at his feet, scratched his head, looked up and stared wide eyed at Rebecca. "I was in France? In a war?"

This wasn't going to be easy. "Yes, that's right, you were in France, fighting in the war. Do you remember what you were doing?"

"Doing?" The head scratching started again. "What was I doing?" He looked at Jane and scowled. "Who's she? Bloody house is full of women."

"She helped me. Please, Adam, think. What were you doing in France?"

He didn't lose the scowl, but looked away from Jane. "I … I was digging. Yes, I was digging. It was like being back down the mine. Bloody wet, and freezing cold. Rats everywhere. So quiet. Quiet as a mouse. Feet rotting." His eyes glazed over as memories began to take shape in his mind. "I was on my own. I was coming back from …. I saw *Jack*. Rebecca, I saw Jack. What did he ask me? What was it?" He pulled at his nose and ear lobe. "Don't go back down the mine. That was it. Don't go back. But I had to. Couldn't let the others down, could I?"

"Of course not, my pet." Rebecca said quietly.

"Didn't get back to them." Memories were taking on greater clarity. "Explosion. Tunnel collapsed. Buried." Fear grew in his eyes. "Couldn't breathe. Couldn't feel my legs. Pain. So much pain."

Rebecca started to cry as he remembered his personal hell.

Adam was back in the mine. "Just wanted to die." He looked up at Rebecca. "Wanted to see you and the boys. But the pain, so much pain. I couldn't bear it. Lungs on fire. My arm … arm was … snapped. Could only see out of one eye. Could only taste blood." He stopped, the memory too cruel and vivid to have to relive again. Then his expression softened. "Jack came back for me. Becky, he came for me. He was with me." Adam's expression changed again into frantic despair, as the complete memory played itself out in his mind. "I died!" He patted his body. "How am I here? Arm not broken. How am I like this? How are we together?"

Rebecca reached out and held his hands. "We are spirits, my darling. Ghosts." There was no easy way to say it.

Adam jumped back, dropping her hands.

"There is nothing to be afraid of. I promise." She crossed her heart.

He stood silently staring into the far distance.

"Adam?" Rebecca was terrified that she'd pushed him too far too early. "Come with me." She offered him her hand which he stared at for a few seconds, but eventually took tenderly. "Let me show you some things which will help."

They walked hand in hand past Jane and Elizabeth, up the cellar steps and into the kitchen. Rebecca took him to the calendar pinned to the larder door, and pointed at the year. 2014. Adam peered at the sheet of days, weeks and months trying to take in what his eyes refused to believe they were seeing.

"The year is 2014?" He whispered.

"Yes."

"But …"

"The house has changed, hasn't it. Look, this is the house we lived in, but it isn't the home we built. I've been trapped here waiting for you to come home to me. Trapped for almost a hundred years. We swore 'til death us do part, but I wasn't going to have it end, so I waited, and waited, and waited. They called me the Mad Woman. Thought that I didn't know, but …"

Adam tried to speak, but she shook her head at him.

"I've been walking the corridors and rooms of this house praying that one day I'd see you again." She beamed at him. "And here you are. I don't care how you got here, only that we're together."

Adam smiled at her. "I've missed you."

She smiled back at him. For the first time sensing that he'd begun to understand.

He stood back, frowning. "What happens next?"

Rebecca still smiled at him. "We move on. We move on into the light. Move on to what lies next for us."

He still frowned. "And what's that? What does lie next for us?"

"I don't know what you mean." She was frightened by his response.

"Where do we go when we leave here?" He was becoming agitated.

"I don't know. It must be to Heaven."

"Or Hell?"

"We led good lives. Why would you say Hell?"

"What about what I did in the war? Was that right? Whose side was God on."

"Ours of course."

"How do you know that?"

'I don't, but God wouldn't … side with Germany."

Adam stared at the calendar, deep in thought. "Do we have to move on?"

"Pardon?"

"Do we have to move on? You say you've been here for a hundred years, so why shouldn't we stay here for another hundred?"

Rebecca shook her head. "I don't know."

"Exactly. We don't know. So why risk losing each other again if we move on? We've no idea what's next for us, so let's stay here?"

Rebecca had no answer. Why move on? Adam was right. They could lose each other again. Couldn't they? She nodded to him.

Elizabeth and Jane followed Rebecca and Adam to the kitchen, and were surprised and happy to find them smiling at each other, and more importantly, at them.

"Everything OK?" Elizabeth asked cautiously.

"I'm sorry, Elizabeth, all this is …" She smiled at Adam, "It's a little, too much for us to take in." She took Adam's hand and moved closer to Elizabeth. "You haven't been introduced. This is my husband, Adam."

Elizabeth tottered and held onto the table to keep herself upright. "Your husband? Adam Morbeck?"

"Yes."

Elizabeth looked at Jane. "You found him?"

"Yes. Well, actually Sam found him, and then we found Sam."

"But if Sam was with you, then where is he?"

Jane shook her head.

Worst case scenarios ran through Elizabeth's head. *"He's stuck in 1915 and can't get back. He's been killed. He's lost somewhere in the ether. I'll never see him again."* Her mind was in turmoil.

"Elizabeth are you OK?" Jane was concerned.

"Mmmm … yes fine. Just worried about Sam." She couldn't disguise her anxiety.

"He'll be fine. Believe me I've known Sam for quite a few years, and despite all his failings, he's a survivor. Believe me, like the proverbial bad penny, he'll turn up."

Elizabeth put her hands in her pockets and felt her mobile. She took it out and realised she hadn't turned it on. She fumbled to press the on switch, watched the screen come to life and saw she had six missed messages. She opened them and started to read Sam's frantic chain. Her expression told Jane that Sam had *turned up.*

"From Sam?" She asked rhetorically.

Her expression was better than any spoken answer.

"Told you. What does he say?"

"The first few are just where are you, then there are a few where the hell are you," She laughed between the tears, "then finally he says they're on their way here to High Wood."

"On *their* way here? Who are *they*?" Jane asked.

"Klaus, Karsten and Sam."

"The three musketeers, riding to the rescue." Jane laughed. "Want to hold each other's hands?"

Rebecca's reply wiped the smile from her face. "We've decided to stay."

"To stay!" Jane gasped. "But the whole point of this was to allow you and Adam to move on together."

"Yes, but we talked things over, and we've no idea what's on the other side of this. We know this, this place. High Wood was our home, and we want to stay here with what we know rather than risk losing each other again."

"But you can't stay." Jane continued.

"Why?" Rebecca asked testily.

"Well, because, … Elizabeth, talk to them." Jane turned to Elizabeth and raised her arms.

Elizabeth looked at the couple separated by many decades and now reunited. *"Why would you want to risk it all again."* She thought. *"Would I chance it?"* She smiled at them. *"Why couldn't they stay?"* She frowned, struggling to find a reason why they couldn't stay at High Wood.

"Elizabeth?"

"I was just thinking." She replied.

"About what."

"About why they had to go. What harm is there if they stay?"

"Well … it would … it would …"

"You see. It's impossible to come up with a plausible reason why they should move on into uncertainty."

"But what about the rest of their family?" Jane smiled, as though she'd found a chink in their argument.

Elizabeth looked at Adam and Rebecca. "She's right. What about your boys? What about your family?"

Adam nodded at Rebecca to answer. "At some time in the future we will move on, and please God, see them again. It's in the natural way of things. We know that, but for now, and until then, we want to be together. We know it can't be anything like it was before. We're just shadows of what we used to be, but what makes us, us, hasn't changed. Now, we're together, and that's all that matters. I know now that we don't have to stay here. That we can move on to somewhere else, so if you don't want us here, then we'll leave, but this was our home and we want to stay here at High Wood." They smiled at each other, turned together with expressions like lost puppies.

EIGHTY-SEVEN

The Cessna 182T was arranged by Guillaume, and getting an early morning slot, through his personal contacts, had been pretty straightforward. Klaus had flown the Cessna many times, and would pilot the flight to Cardiff.

"You need to be at the airport by seven." Guillaume told the others as he came back from the study. "Pack very light. The plane is only a four seater."

Klaus nodded his approval and thanks. He turned to Sam. "Any reply from Elizabeth?"

Sam shook his head. "Nothing."

"She will be fine, Sam. There will be no problems. When we get there tomorrow she will be, how do you say, trigon die Kaffeekanne."

Karsten laughed. "Putting on the kettle. Not wearing the coffee pot."

"Gut, werden also Sie die Kaffeekanne stellen, auf. Bitte."

Karsten smiled and clicked his heels. "Coffee is on it's way."

Sam looked to Guillaume who shrugged. "A German joke."

After coffee, the four men wished each other good night.

Back in his room, Sam set his alarm for four o' clock, picked up his iPhone and tried unsuccessfully to get hold of Elizabeth, before trying to get a few hours sleep.

The flight to Cardiff had been smooth and passed quickly. Klaus had piloted the Cessna expertly through UK air space and was taxiing to his space at Cardiff airport.

"OK everyone, it's just a short walk to the terminal and then we can get a taxi to High Wood." Klaus said.

Karsten was sat at the back of the plane. He wasn't a good flier and travelling in a flying SUV, as he saw it, hadn't filled him with a great deal of confidence, despite his father being the pilot.

"Doors are ready for us to deplane." Klaus spoke over his shoulder. "Be careful. There are only a few steps, but still be careful when disembarking."

Everyone nodded and carefully got out of the plane.

A VW Sharan was the best available taxi on the rank. They all piled in, Sam gave the driver the address and emphasised, with the promise of a decent tip, it was vital that they got to High Wood quickly.

"I just believe you need to move on." Elizabeth was unsure about Rebecca and Adam's desire to stay.

"Why?" Adam's question was short and direct.

"Well, because it's the natural way of things."

"Is it natural for Rebecca to be stranded here for decades?"

"No, but there is a reason."

"What?"

"Rebecca had unfinished business. You were lost, and as the hymn says, but now I'm found. She can now move on, move forward."

"Why?"

Elizabeth sighed.

"Am I boring you?" Adam asked angrily.

"No, no, of course not. This is so difficult for all of us. Even my faith and beliefs are stretched to their limits. This isn't exactly covered in Christian teachings."

"So if this is too difficult to understand, and none of us really knows what's going on, then why are *you* so sure we've got to move on?" Adam was visibly getting angrier.

Elizabeth looked at Jane for some moral support, but she was shaking her head and mouthing "He's right, isn't he?"

"Well!" Adam had moved closer to Elizabeth. His breath was hot and smelt of decay.

"Adam, please, we're not against you. we just want to help." Jane said.

"Odd way of showing it." He glared at her and then menacingly stared at Elizabeth.

"Adam …" Rebecca tugged at his sleeve. He tore it away.

"*You* want us gone. That's what *you* want. Isn't it!"

Elizabeth wouldn't look away from his gaze, even though it terrified her. She looked closely at his eyes at the dramatic change in the colour of his irises, which were now a deep red, and his dilated pupils looked like he'd been snorting cocaine.

"Adam, I want what is best for you and Rebecca. Nothing else." Her voice was quivering.

"Liar. Lying bitch." His voice had dropped to a deep bass.

"Adam, please, I don't deserve this. What's happening to you?" She looked frantically at Jane and Rebecca, silently pleading for help.

"*You* seem to be the only one who wants us gone." He leered at her. "So if *you're* gone, then *we* stay."

The taxi pulled up outside High Wood. Sam almost fell out and started to run for the house.

Karsten quickly followed, while Klaus paid the driver.

Sam burst in through the unlocked front door, ran down the hall, stumbled and crashed into the hall table. "Bollocks, my bloody knee." He shouted.

Karsten, close behind him, couldn't stop and fell headlong over Sam's body, slid along the hall floor and crashed headfirst into the cellar door.

Klaus quietly pushed open the front door which had swung back on its hinges, and smiled at the scene of mayhem and destruction.

"The energy of the young," he said through tears of laughter, which abruptly stopped as they all heard the scream from the kitchen.

Adam put the tip of his right index finger on Elizabeth's forehead and closed his eyes. She felt a tingling in her lips and then something close to an electric shock. It was this which had caused her to scream.

"Adam, stop now!" Jane grasped his shoulders and tried to pull him away from Elizabeth.

"Adam!" Rebecca tried and failed to get between him and Elizabeth, who felt what she could only describe as a magnetic pull on her heart. Some force was trying to rip it from her chest. Her throat was constricting and her breathing becoming laboured.

They were completely unprepared for the scene which greeted them. Sam stared in disbelief, Karsten gasped, and Klaus uttered some German expletives.

Sam moved closer to Elizabeth, who was surrounded by a flickering blue aura, which rippled from her feet to the top of her head, in a constant rhythmic flow like a gentle swell on a summer sea. It then span into a vortex, which formed a spinning crystal clear azure ribbon which disappeared into the centre of Adam's forehead. Although Adam had form, as did Rebecca and Jane, he lacked what Sam could only call substance, which was changing as the energy from the ribbon flowed into him. There were perceptible changes to his head, which appeared denser and more solid. Sam looked from Adam to Elizabeth and put his hands to his face as he saw that Elizabeth's head exactly matched Adam's, only in that where his was gaining substance, she was losing it and becoming translucent like the bell of a jelly fish.

Karsten moved alongside Sam. "We need to break this ... this ... Scheisse ... Diese Magie ... Dieses Übel!" He dived at Adam's waist trying to knock him off his feet, but flew straight through him and crashed into the kitchen table, knocking the breath out of himself.

"No substance." Sam thought. He looked again at Adam's head, its solidity had extended down to his neck. The wheels in his brain span like a runaway roulette wheel. He flew across the kitchen and reached out for Adam's neck. His hands met resistance, and his fingers closed like a tripped mantrap.

Adam's eyes snapped open, as he stumbled back and toppled over. The evil, dieses Übel, diese Magie, the magic with Elizabeth was splintered, but not completely broken.

Sam sat back holding onto Adam's neck. Karsten regained his composure, joined Sam and grabbed Adam's shoulders which now had substance. Together they dragged him across the kitchen floor. As they pulled him further away from Elizabeth, the spinning azure ribbon grew thinner and thinner, until it was just a single strand. The substance of his head, neck and shoulders started to fade, until, as they reached the door of the kitchen their hands closed on nothing but fresh air. They looked at each other and immediately looked up to see Adam moving back towards Elizabeth, the azure strand now growing thicker the closer he got to her.

Klaus had been watching in disbelief as things developed, and understood when Adam started back across the kitchen floor, what he had to do. He ran forward, wrapped his arms around Elizabeth's waist and dragged her across the kitchen to the back door. "Help me!" He shouted to Sam and Karsten. "We need to get her out of this place!"

Sam and Karsten, ran as quickly as they could to Elizabeth, put their arms under her armpits as Klaus supported her feet. Together they struggled step by step carrying Elizabeth out into the garden. As they reached the lawn, they broke into a cold sweat as they saw Adam coming out of the kitchen door, floating about a foot off the ground his eyes a pulsing crimson.

EIGHTY-EIGHT

The following day after breakfast, Agnes was sat opposite Arthur in his office drinking coffee. She'd asked to meet him privately to discuss James.

"When did he start having these bizarre ideas about shell shock?" Arthur sat back in his chair and sipped his steaming coffee.

Agnes shook her head. "I honestly don't know how long he's been constructing this theory about a secret German poison gas, but it was definitely brought to a head by the recovery of Lieutenant Lidsay."

"It was that dramatic?"

"Like Lazarus rising from the dead. I've never seen anything like it. One moment Lidsay was completely out of it, then he was awake, alert and talking to us." Agnes replied.

"And it was this, *miracle*, which turned on the lights in James' head."

"Without doubt. His response was as dramatic as the lieutenant's."

Arthur blew on his coffee and sipped more of Owen's excellent brew. "Where are all of them?"

"James is resting in his quarters and the lieutenant and the nurse are walking in the gardens." She stood up and looked out of the window. "They're sitting under that oak tree." She pointed out of the window at the grounds of the house.

"I just can't help feeling we've met before." Roger said to Gloria.

Gloria dropped her eyes to look at the grass. "I had the same feeling when I walked onto the ward that first time."

"You did?"

"Yes. It was like, like, what do they say, dayla voo?"

Roger smiled at the top of her head. "Deja vu. You've the feeling you've done something before."

She looked up, blushing. "Yes, that's it. Only it was more like a feeling you'd felt before."

Lidsay was now 95% Roger, but 5% Ivor was still hanging on in the deepest dankest caverns of his mind, and the 5% was doing its hardest to be heard.

"I was married to her? That's what you can feel. Although, it was admittedly not much of marriage. Time; money; frustration; booze; work; no kids; not enough we time; her bloody mother; my bloody father; that cow next door; New Zealand Sauvignon Blanc; those poxy holidays in Turkey, and nothing physical for years. We never really had a chance. Shame really because at the beginning we were good together. Remember those cheap holidays in

Spain; the dogs; the cats; that first flat, what a shit hole that was; living with your parents and that first car. It would have been quicker and warmer to have walked everywhere. And then I joined the police. Beginning of the end that was. Downhill from there. Shame we couldn't have another try. Wipe away the past and start again."

The 95% took control again. "I know what you mean, but I can't believe we've never met before. I would have remembered you."

"Smooth, very smooth." 5% thought to itself.

"I made a pledge to myself at the start of the war that I wouldn't get involved with anyone, as there was such a high risk of … separation."

Gloria nodded. "I did the same. So many have been killed that I'm sure we were right." She paused. "Don't you?"

"Absolutely. There are already too many widows and brokenhearted lovers. We shouldn't risk adding to them."

"Smoother than a baby's bottom." 5% smiled to itself.

"Yes. Too many shattered lives." She squeezed his hands.

Roger smiled lovingly at her. "If we weren't in this damn war, would you have considered …"

"Not too smooth now. Don't push too hard." 5% was strangely beginning to want 95% to win the argument.

"Consider what, Lieutenant?" Gloria was blushing.

"Well … perhaps we could have …"

She leaned forward and kissed him softly on the lips. But quickly sat upright and took her hands away from his. "I'm sorry."

He smiled, took her face in his hands and kissed her. Not softly, but with a passion that took their breath away. This time there were no apologies.

"We should live for the …" Gloria gasped.

He put his finger to her lips. "Don't say the moment. This should be forever. This has to be forever."

"I was going to say the rest of our lives together."

"Maybe this was meant to be?" 5% thought. *"Is this my second chance? But what happens to me? Is this the end of me?"* The thoughts were becoming whispers, soft murmurs on the winds of time. 5% was slowly getting smaller and smaller. Four to three to two to one. Until all that was left of Ivor was a soft whisper in the shadows. *"Is this the end of me …?"*

Agnes and Arthur smiled at each other. A moment of love in a time of hate.

"He'll be back in trenches in the blink of an eye if James sees them." Arthur said. "He's not aware of their feelings for each other?"

"No. It's a surprise to me." Agnes replied.

"We should keep this from him. I'm sick of being just another factory for producing fodder for German guns." He sat down and sighed deeply. "What's the point of everything I do, Agnes? As soon as they recover to anything close to health, the brass send someone in to assess them and send them back." He rested his head in his hands. "Such a damnable waste of a life."

"But what about those who don't recover?"

"Broken men with splintered minds. Men who will never fully recover to live a normal life with their friends and families. Human jigsaw puzzles with too many pieces missing to complete the picture of their mind. And there will still be those who will always see them as just cowards and malingerers. Nothing will change *their* bigoted minds. So these shattered souls will vegetate here and just survive. Is that a life worth living? What is the point of all of this? Why don't I just help them just slip away." He sat upright in the chair and stared hopelessly at the ceiling.

Agnes was terrified by Arthur's sudden loss of belief in himself and his treatment of these broken men.

A few hours later Arthur and James were sat together reviewing the notes they'd prepared on Lidsay and Gloria.

"I can't find anything unusual about either of them." Arthur said looking up from his notes. "Nothing that sets them apart from any other lieutenant or nurse in the British Army."

"I have to agree." James replied." But something dramatic happened when they met. One minute he was catatonic, and the next he was as lucid as you or me. What we haven't done." James continued, shaking his head. "Is take blood samples from them. How else can we find an antidote to this damn poison? Who do you know who can analyse it?"

"There's a professor of biochemistry at Exeter University who owes me a couple of favours." Arthur said.

"Excellent. This is the key. Once we have it we can develop something to neutralise it, and inoculate the men against it." James was lost in a world of his own. "We should also see how they react with each other. There's something unique about their relationship. Perhaps *she* has the antidote in *her* system."

"What I've seen of them together," Arthur thought, *"is the last thing I want you to see."*

"We should organise this for this afternoon." James stood up and walked over to the window. "I can see them walking in the gardens. Leave it with me, and I'll organise things for two o'clock. Straight after lunch."

Agnes came around the corner of the corridor and saw James's back disappearing into the garden. "Where's he off to in such a hurry." She asked Arthur.

"Take a look." Arthur said glumly pointing out of the window.

Agnes peered out of the window. At first she didn't notice anything, and then saw James trotting across the lawn shouting and waving at the trees. She swallowed hard as Roger and Gloria emerged onto the lawn. James quickly reached them, put his arms around their shoulders and animatedly started explaining what he wanted to do that afternoon. There were clearly nods of agreement all round, James shook their hands and walked briskly off into the grounds.

"Ah, not good," Agnes said as she turned from the window. "How do we prevent this?"

"Bit late don't you think?" Arthur replied gloomily.

"Arthur?" Agnes pulled a chair next to him and sat down. "I don't understand what's happened to you since we arrived back here with them." She

364

waved her hand over her shoulder at the window. "What is it about them that disturbs you?"

Arthur looked away from her avoiding eye to eye to contact. "They represent the possible end of everything I've worked for. I have no doubt that there is no German poison, or anything miraculous about these two young people. But if James makes his *miracle* as public as he says he will, then with or without evidence, the top brass will be sending buses to Seale Hayne to collect everyone to ship back to France. They've been secretly praying that someone would state publicly that the men here are nothing but shammers. Cowards of the first order, who've let down their comrades and country." He slapped his hands on his knees. "What happened in France was purely coincidental. The lieutenant would have recovered if Nurse Perron had been a hundred miles away. There's no secret poison gas, and she's nothing to do with his recovery. I've seen this before. An apparent spontaneous return to normal." He looked back to Agnes. "But it never lasts." He stood up and walked to the window.

"So why have you supported James in this?" Agnes asked.

"To prevent him from crashing back into the nether world he occupied when he was here. Agnes he's balancing on a very thin high wire. If he falls, he will never get back up again. He'll be lost forever in a place whose thick forests you and I will never penetrate." He shook his head and massaged his temples, another headache rapidly developing. "This is my quandary. Protect my patients, myself and my reputation, or protect James's sanity. The self or my doctor's oath. One will have to lose."

Agnes got up and crouched in front of him. "Arthur, my love for James is …" Her eyes welled up with tears. "… it's … I've never felt about one person as I feel about him. And I would do anything I could to protect him." She took a deep breath. "But what you do here is beyond measure. The men you treat are fractured souls. I still don't fully understand how the treatment is so successful, but having been through the nightmare of trench warfare and it's results, then I understand why the mind simply can't cope with the horrors it's exposed to. Horrors of a magnitude of which they have no previous experience. How could they. These men were working in offices, farms and factories, where you don't see your mates suddenly explode into bloody pieces of flesh, their pals in the pub aren't disembowelled in front of them, family decapitated or shredded by red hot shrapnel, rats eating people, bodies allowed to rot, to get home from work they don't have to walk across cess pits on bridges made of human corpses, or listen to their family screaming from no man's land as they slowly die from their wounds. There is a reality in France from which the majority of the British population have been protected. This alternative reality is sold to us as our patriotic duty to serve King and country, and if we choose not to take the King's shilling, or even worse, run away, then God help us. White feathers and abuse from the suffragettes and their friends, or ridicule as cowards and wasters who deserve to be locked up or shot. Arthur, until your treatment of these men received grudging approval, these broken minds were, and in the main still are, treated as pariahs. This work cannot be stopped." She wiped away the tears from her eyes.

Arthur stood up and lifted her from her crouched position. "A fine speech, my dear. And one which should be heard more widely. Unfortunately, you would be branded as a reactionary, or revolutionary traitor, and locked up in some dank prison cell." He lifted her chin and tried his best to smile at her. "You realise what you're saying?"

She slowly nodded.

"If I push him over the edge then he will probably never come back to you."

Once again she nodded her understanding.

"I pray I may be able to save him, but I am not confident of it."

Agnes looked directly into Arthur's eyes. "For the greater good."

"I'm not a religious man, but for years I've found great solace in Buddhism. The Buddha says 'For the good of the many, for the happiness of the many, out of compassion for the world'. This I believe is what I strive to do."

They hugged each other tightly.

"You're sure about this, Agnes?"

"With all, well almost all of my heart." She smiled wanly.

"Then we'd better catch up with James as he seems to have things well under control."

EIGHTY-NINE

"Think Sam! Think!" His mind was operating at close to overload. *"Shit, now come on, concentrate. Not easy, but necessary."* He stared at the scene developing in front of him. *"I can't grab hold of him. Oh Jesus what do I do?"*

A whisper at the back of his mind became a murmur, which became almost audible, until he finally could clearly hear the voice.

"Think back to the mine Sam. What did he say to you?"

"Isaac?"

"Yes, Isaac."

"But … you're …"

"I know, Sam, but not now. The mine, what did Adam say to you?"

Sam dragged his mind back to the mine when he first found Adam.

"Come on, Sam. What did he say?"

Sam was beginning to lose it. Panic was crushing logical thought,

"Sam!!"

"Oh shit yes. Sorry."

Adam was almost on top of them.

"Oh God no. He … Adam … said … he said …" The lights came back on. "He called me, son! He thought I was Jack!"

"You'd listen to your son wouldn't you?"

"Adam. Listen to me." Sam said as calmly as he could.

"The mine Sam. Remember the mine."

Sam smiled as best he could as Isaac gave him a mental nudge.

Adam was now within a foot of Sam. The crimson irises of his eyes glowed like hot coals. Sam could feel the air around him chilling. His breath was like mist on a winter's morning.

"The mine Sam! What did you say!?"

"Dad it's me. It's Jack!" Sam shouted.

Adam stopped.

"Dad it's me, Jack. We were together in the mine. Mam's in the house. She's waiting for us."

Adam's eyes focused on Sam's face.

"Jack?"

Jane and Rebecca stared at each other in disbelief at what they were seeing.

"What's happened to him?" Rebecca turned to Jane, panic in her voice.

Jane shook her head. "This is all new to me as well." She said. "It seemed to start when he insisted he wanted to stay."

"Yes but not like this."

"Quick, we need to go outside and see what's happening."

They ran out of the kitchen into the garden. Adam was standing, not hovering, in front of Sam, who they could see through Adam's translucent body. Rebecca started to move towards Adam, but Jane stopped her. "Just wait a few seconds. Sam may have this under control."

Sam held Adam's gaze which was becoming softer.

"Jack, is that you?" Adam was calmer but suspicious.

"Yes, Dad."

"How are you here?"

"Does it matter, Dad? You're here and Mam's here." He pointed over Adams's shoulder to where Rebecca was standing.

Adam slowly turned and stared at the two women. "Who's she?"

"Mam, of course."

"No, the other one. Who's she?" Adam's mood was darkening again.

"She's a friend of Mam's?"

"Never met her!"

Sam tried desperately to remain calm. "They met, after you went to the war. Jane moved from Bristol. She's a good friend."

Adam still scowled. "Bristol, don't know anyone from Bristol."

"Just think about, Mam, Dad. She'll tell you about Jane."

Jane whispered to Rebecca. "Go to him and reassure him. Bring him back."

Rebecca walked towards Adam. Despite her love for him, she was scared of whatever it was her husband had become. "Adam, where have you been? We've been looking for you. I was so worried. But here you are safe and sound." She smiled at him and opened her arms.

Something in Adam's head, like a leech, wouldn't let go. It whispered to him. *"It's a trick. He's not your son. And who's she?"*

"Adam, my darling, it's me Rebecca." She was now standing close to him.

He examined her face in minute detail, reached out and brushed wisps of hair away from her face. His frown relaxed, the furrows less deep.

"Rebecca?" He leaned his head to one side and he looked deep into her eyes.

"Yes, my darling, it's me."

"Jack's here." Adam turned his head and nodded at Sam.

"I know. It's so wonderful we're together again."

"Yes wonderful." The leech in Adam's head was still screaming at him. *"This is all a lie!"*

Adam started to become a little calmer. His belief that Sam was his son, Jack, was almost complete, but the leech kept niggling.

"So why aren't you at the front." Adam asked Sam.

"Had special permission to come to see you." Sam wondered how long he'd have to keep up this charade.

"Where have they got you posted?"

"You know I can't tell you that, Dad." Sam wagged his finger at Adam who smiled knowingly.

"All I can say is I'll be in Belgium." He winked.

"Understood." Adam winked back.

Sam stood up and walked back towards the house. "How long do I have to keep this up?" He asked Klaus quietly.

Klaus shook his head.

"You don't know?"

He shook his head again.

"Going somewhere, son?" Adam asked.

"Just stretching my legs, Dad. Bit stiff. I need to get a drink of water."

Adam nodded and started talking to Rebecca.

Sam walked into the kitchen, leaned on the sink, and poured himself a glass of water.

"How did I get here?" He thought.

"Because it was meant to be, Sam." The reply echoed around his head.

Sam stood bolt upright and quickly scanned the room.

"Over here, Sam."

Sam looked around the kitchen, and in the far corner he could discern the silhouette of a very familiar shape which began to raise its head. Sam held his breath.

"Hello, Sam." Isaac stretched his shoulders and stood ram rod straight. "One of the benefits of death." He smiled. "Surprised to see me?" He walked across the kitchen, closer to Sam. It was Isaac, but a younger version, and the most striking difference was his posture. The bent figure he knew, was now standing tall straight and the skin of his face was smooth and glowing. "Say something Sam." Isaac, the younger, was still smiling.

"Shit!" Was the only word Sam could mumble.

"Very eloquent my friend. But we need to discuss things," Isaac replied. "I've had experience of this. Of souls finding a kindred spirit and demanding to stay."

Sam nodded, lost for words of more than one syllable.

"I'll carry on until you've recovered the power of speech." Isaac continued. "I've only experienced this once in my life. I found the wandering soul of a soldier from Leuven, but at precisely the same moment, the spirit of his brother who was killed in the same battle came through." Isaac shrugged. "The best laid plans of mice and men. They met and wouldn't leave. The older brother Marvin was the main problem. Peter was less of an issue." He gestured towards the chairs around the table. "Shall we sit. It will be a little more comfortable than this."

Sam felt like sticking pins in his eyes to make sure he was either still alive or in the middle of the biggest flashback he'd ever experienced. They sat at opposite ends of the kitchen table.

"You *can* smile, Sam." Isaac said mischievously.

Sam did his best to change his expression, and eventually forced the muscles of his face to construct a smile.

"There, that wasn't difficult was it?"

"No." Sam managed a word.

"Progress." Isaac laughed.

"How are you here?" Sam was beginning to recover the power of speech.

"No stopping you now."

"It is you isn't it?"

"Sam, not too many weeks ago if someone had told you you'd be sitting talking to a ghost, then you'd have laughed. But here you are."

Sam managed half a smile.

"More progress." Isaac leaned forward and offered his hand to Sam.

Sam looked at it as if it was leprous.

"You can touch me Sam. I won't break."

Sam leaned to meet Isaac and took his hand. "It's not cold!"

"Wooh. Wooh!" Isaac waved his hands and arms like Casper the Ghost.

"Very funny." Sam finally said, smiling. "But why are you still here?"

Isaac shrugged. "Unfinished business."

"What unfinished business?"

"You, Sam. You and Elizabeth."

"Unfinished. How?"

"You need to ask? You're not ready, Sam. Not even close. The others will help, but it was me that brought you to us, and so it falls to me to make sure you're ready. This is a difficult path you have chosen to take, Sam. It is good in some ways that Adam has appeared now. It is a steep learning curve, and after Adam it will seem much easier."

"What do I do about him?"

"You let him stay."

Sam looked at Isaac in amazement. "I let him stay?"

"You let *them* stay."

"But he's dangerous. Why would I take such a risk?"

"Experience, Sam. The two men in Leuven, were causing me real problems, and I tried and tried to move them on, but all that happened was that someone ended up in a coma, and truly there was no need. Sam what is the issue with them staying? Why can't they stay together in the house?"

"But they're, he's dangerous. Isn't he?"

"Yes he is, Sam."

"So we should move him on?"

Isaac slowly shook his head. "When we tried to do the same with Marvin and Peter, my other brother Renaat ..."

"You had another brother?"

"I *have* another brother, and he's still in a coma. The night we decided to move the brothers on, was after weeks of trying. We did everything we could to get them to move on. We went back to the house and got everything ready to force them to leave."

"What did you have to do?"

"It's not worth telling you Sam, as what we did that night will never happen again. It was a mistake which will be never be repeated. Let them stay. Trust me when I say this. It's my fault that my brother is on a life support machine, and

Guillaume has never forgiven me for that night." Isaac sat back in the chair and sighed.

Sam stood up. "Isaac, wait here." He ran out of the kitchen door and waved at Klaus to come in.

"Sam, what is it?" Klaus asked.

"Isaac."

"Isaac?"

"Isaac's in the kitchen."

Klaus stared at Sam in amazement.

"He's here to help us with Adam. He hasn't moved on yet. He says he has unfinished business. He said it was me, but I'm pretty sure that it's unfinished business with Guillaume."

Klaus frowned. "With Guillaume?"

Sam slowly nodded. "Renaat."

"He told you about him?" Klaus frowned. "Isaac is here?"

Sam slowly nodded over his shoulder and pointed to the kitchen.

Klaus walked slowly into the kitchen and looked across at the familiar, but younger face of Isaac.

"Klaus."

Klaus sat down close to Isaac. "You spoke to us at Messines."

Isaac nodded.

"How long will you be here?"

Isaac shook his head. "As long as it takes."

"To be forgiven by Guillaume?"

Isaac looked down at the carpet and nodded.

Klaus's heart reached out to Isaac. "I'm, sure he has nothing to forgive. We all knew the risks, and Renaat was as aware of the dangers as we all were. Why did you believe he held you responsible?"

Isaac looked up into Klaus's eyes. "I don't know. As the eldest brother, I held myself responsible. I suppose I assumed he would do the same."

Klaus shook his head. "Never for a moment."

Isaac smiled and held Klaus's hand.

"I c'can f'feel you!" Klaus stuttered.

"Because I want it so." Isaac smiled at Klaus. "You must tell Guillaume for me. My time is short and we must deal with the matter of Adam."

"I will speak to Guillaume as soon as I can." Klaus promised. "Isaac we failed at Leuven. What is different here?"

"They are different. Adam and Rebecca lived and loved here at High Wood, so why not let them stay? What harm is there in there being another two spirits with all the others who are already here."

"You want them to stay?"

"Ja. Why risk anyone like we risked Renaat? Let them stay. Eventually they will move on. Everyone does."

"Will you move on?" Klaus asked softly.

Isaac nodded. "Once I have completed things here. Then I will go."

"Do you know where Isaac? Is there nothing to fear?"

"Nothing but the sad farewells we make. But there are also happy reunions with those we loved. They are waiting for us, beyond these realms of Purgatory." Isaac's expression was one of perfect peace. "I am sad to go, Klaus, but I know that I will meet you and Guillaume again, and this gives me the strength I need for the journey."

Klaus dabbed at his eyes with a tissue.

"Sadness is fine Klaus and mourning is natural, but our memories live on. Take joy from remembrance of times past. Let Adam and Rebecca stay and things will take their natural course. Give Guillaume my love, Sam, and Elizabeth my hopes for the future. Karsten good luck and you Klaus, a friend's undying love to carry you through the hard times ahead." Isaac stood and walked to the door of the kitchen. "Look after Renaat with Guillaume for me."

"Isaac, stay." Klaus's request was heartfelt. "Please, please stay."

Isaac started to become translucent; to emit a soft blue glow, to float a few inches above the ground, to slowly rotate emitting a soft, almost indiscernible comforting hum. What had been Isaac, gradually began to lose its mortal form and change into a column of pure energy, which, like an upside down whirlpool entered the ceiling and slowly disappeared, until only the remnants of a blue glow could be seen on the ceiling.

Klaus stared at the circle of blue light and wept. "Stay, please stay."

NINETY

They caught up with James as he was coming back into Seale Hayne closely followed by Roger and Gloria.

"Ah, good you found them." Arthur said cheerily.

"They were sitting under the oak." James replied with a smile.

"Let's go to my office and start." Arthur suggested.

James nodded in agreement and the group followed Arthur to his office. They settled into chairs and Arthur started speaking.

"Gloria. We want to speak to you together to try and understand what happened in France. How you, lieutenant, suddenly overcame what to James seemed appalling shell shock." He looked at James who frowned. "Agnes will take notes, and I think it will make things much more relaxed if we use first names." He looked again at James who was now smiling and nodding. "Good." He turned his chair to face Gloria who was sat on the same side of the table. "Gloria, what did you think when you saw Roger for the first time."

"That it wasn't the first time."

Arthur frowned. "*Not*, the first time?"

"Yes. It was odd. I didn't feel I knew him, but that I *would* know him. Know him in the future? I'm sorry. I know it sounds odd, but I can't find any better way to describe it."

Arthur looked at James and Agnes and raised his eyebrows. "Please carry on."

"As I said, I had a feeling that this man would be a part of my future and he needed my help." She paused, thinking about the events of that day. "I felt a link, no a bond with this man. I'd no idea why, and I've never had a feeling like it before, but I could feel his pain, and I knew I could help him."

Arthur swung around in his chair and spoke to Roger. "What did you feel when you saw Gloria?"

Roger was staring intently at Gloria. "I'm sorry, Arthur, you were saying?"

"What did you feel when you saw Gloria?"

Speaking to Arthur, Roger kept his eyes firmly on Gloria, who was smiling at him. "Until I saw her, I wasn't really aware of anything. Everything seemed to be happening around me. I felt like I was watching it all from outside myself. Like I wasn't me anymore." He paused. "It's so hard to put this in words."

Arthur smiled. He'd taken control of the meeting. "That's perfectly OK. Your words are the best to describe how you felt. Please carry on."

"You know when you do or say something and think that you've done or said it before?"

"Yes. Deja vu."

"Yes. Well this felt like I was seeing someone who I was yet to meet, but someone who would mean everything to me. I suppose like love at first sight?"

"Do you think that's what it was?" James spoke for the first time.

Roger scratched his head for a few seconds. "No. It was profoundly more than that. I absolutely knew that this woman would be my life partner." He looked at Gloria and smiled.

"How do you think you came to be in the hospital?" James was now leaning forward, and looking very intent.

Roger frowned. "I'm not sure." He scratched his head again and for a couple of minutes stared at the floor. A small guttering candle began to flicker at the back of his mind. "I was in the dark? I'm sure it was dark. But really dark. No light at all." He looked up from the table and stared at Agnes. "Then there was light." He smiled. "Not in the biblical sense. It was light like I never want to see again. Like the sun had been trapped in a glass bottle." He stopped again and closed his eyes. " I couldn't see." His eyes snapped open. "I couldn't see. I was blind."

"Do you think you imagined you were blind?" James was becoming slightly agitated. "Did you think it was all in your head?"

"No I couldn't see."

"Or was it that you didn't want to see?" James was pushing him.

"No, no, I couldn't see. I was blind."

"But blind men don't recover their sight, do they? And you can see. Can't you?"

Tears were beginning to well up in Roger's eyes. "I'm not lying. I'm not a coward. I was blind."

"And now you can see. Something of a miracle don't you think?"

"No! Not a bloody miracle!" Roger shouted.

"Then what?" James pushed.

"I'm not a bloody doctor! How the hell should I know?"

Arthur had heard enough. "James, let Roger tell us about the time in the hospital."

"But I want to know more about …"

"Please! James! Let Roger tell us, in his words. Not what you want to hear." He tried to hide his anger, but was finding it very difficult.

James frowned and sat back in his chair, like a sulking child who's been told that it's time for bed while he's watching his favourite programme.

"Roger, please carry on." Arthur said.

Roger, dabbed at his eyes with a handkerchief and flashed an angry look at James. "OK." He breathed deeply and carried on. "I felt like I was in a dream, when you desperately want to wake up, but you can't. You know, when you're being chased and can't get away? You're sure it's a dream, but something niggles away at you that it isn't. I became more and more convinced it wasn't a dream and I could wake up and get away from whatever it was that was trying to get me."

Agnes was smiling and nodding in agreement. "I know exactly what you mean." She said supportively.

"It's just so hard to put it into words."

"You're doing fine." Agnes said.

Roger smiled and carried on. "Like I said, I felt I was in a dream, but not? And it wasn't until I sensed and then saw Gloria, I knew for sure that it was a dream and I could wake up." Roger beamed. "That was it. It was a dream and you woke me from it." He looked across at Gloria and smiled at her.

Arthur held his hand up to James who was preparing to attack again. "Roger, your mind was protecting you from the trauma around you, and recognised that you were physically damaged and decided to shut itself down to the outside world which had caused the damage. It felt that inside it's own protective cocoon, your body would be better able to heal itself."

"Rubbish." James almost whispered.

Arthur ignored him, but Agnes threw him a look which could have cut through steel.

"The question is still, why did Gloria have this affect on you?"

Gloria sat silently listening to everything, but now leaned forward and spoke. "I believe that we live only one life, but it takes different paths, at and during different lives and times."

They all looked at her in surprise.

"We have life partners who we meet over and over again during each of our new lives. For us it always seems that it's the first time, but it's just a remembrance of times past. What Roger and I felt that day was a vision of our future, and the continuance of a relationship which has not yet, but will, blossom in this life."

They looked at each other again in disbelief. Hearing this level of philosophy from this young woman.

Gloria smiled at them. "You're thinking where did all that come from." She slowly shook her head. "How can a simple nurse possibly be able to postulate such things." She smiled again at their expressions. "I studied philosophy and religion at Oxford before the war." Their jaws dropped metaphorically. "I got a first with honours." She let this bombshell settle for a few seconds and then dropped another. "I have a PhD. You should really call me doctor not nurse." She said wickedly.

"My apologies, my dear. I didn't know." Arthur said quietly.

"You didn't ask."

"No, no you're right. Books and covers I'm afraid."

Later they joined each other for dinner and were sat drinking what was doing its best to be coffee.

"Sorry about the hot brown liquid." Arthur apologised with a smile.

"It's OK." Gloria subtly exaggerated.

"Please, I know that it tastes as much as it resembles tepid dishwater."

Gloria smiled and drained her cup.

"You feel ready to go back to the front, Roger?" James had been waiting impatiently for this opportunity.

Arthur and Agnes scowled at him. But he ignored their displeasure.

"I hadn't really thought about it. Of course I want to, but I want to be at my best." He paused, his cheeks flushing. "Still not feeling quite there yet."

"But you look in A1 shape," James persisted.

"Appearances can be misleading," Gloria said testily.

"Misleading for who?" James was being particularly aggressive.

Gloria didn't answer, got up and walked to the window.

"Are you misleading anyone, Roger?"

Roger looked at the floor.

"Roger?" James persisted.

Roger locked his fingers together and began to slowly rock back and forth.

"Silence, Lieutenant? Silence isn't always golden you know. When do you think you will be back at the front?"

Roger kept his eyes firmly fixed on the floor. "Soon, very soon."

"The war will be over soon. You surely don't want to miss the action do you? Your comrades are dying as we speak. Britain needs every able-bodied man in the trenches. Don't you feel the slightest twinge of guilt?"

"James, enough!!" Arthur's final straw had been broken. "Leave the man alone."

"They are all malingering." James replied. "Physical wounds can be seen and treated. Don't you think it's a little convenient the injuries they claim to suffer from can't be seen? How many KIA's were down to mental wounds?" He stared directly at Arthur, looking for a fight.

Arthur was incandescent, but refused to let James have the pleasure of seeing that he'd angered him. "Tell me James." He said calmly. "Why were you under that bed for months? What physical wounds made you take refuge in the dark space beneath a bed? Could you show them to me?"

The wind was briefly taken out of James sails.

"I was … I was in … in shock." He stuttered.

"From a mental wound?"

"No, it was just the manifestation of a physical wound. My mind was perfectly clear the whole time."

"Which presumably was why you were totally mute for the whole time?"

James began to gradually implode.

Arthur kept pushing. He'd never pushed anyone back into a mental illness, but James had clearly never recovered from the original psychosis.

"Arthur, please don't do this." Agnes hissed.

"If I don't do this you'll lose him forever. In this deluded state he is untreatable. He is very close to a major mental breakdown and I need him to recognise his disorder."

James was rubbing the arms of his chair with closed fists and staring into the far distance. "It was a physical wound." He murmured. "I can only treat physical damage, where you can see it and repair it. If the damage is beyond repair then death follows as surely as night follows day. How can you repair what you can't see. It's not possible. Shell shock is nothing more than mumbo jumbo. Black magic. A conchy's way of getting out of serving his King and Country, and laying down his life for his fellow man. They have to be eradicated."

Agnes stared at him in disbelief at what she was hearing. She turned and looked at Arthur in despair. He gestured at her to follow him out into the corridor.

Arthur frowned and shook his head. "His mental state has deteriorated much faster than I thought possible." He walked up and down the corridor shaking his head. "I should have done something as soon as I saw him."

Agnes's eyes filled with tears. "Can you save him?"

Arthur avoided her gaze. "I'm not sure, I'm really not sure. He is close to falling into a bottomless pit."

"What do we do? How do we save him?" Agnes pleaded.

"He will need to stay here at Seale Hayne for treatment." He looked at Agnes and shrugged. "But do you think he would stay voluntarily."

She shook her head.

"Then we have to convince him or make him."

"We will have to make him." Agnes conceded. "He'll never admit he's ill, and certainly not mentally ill." She walked close to Arthur and lowered her voice. "What do we have to do? I'll do anything you say, if it means I will get James back."

Arthur took her hand. "I only have one option, which I do not like to use, but it will achieve what we want."

Agnes looked very concerned at his comments. "You're frightening me, Arthur."

"What I'm proposing, is that I section him under the Mental Deficiency Act. In that way I will have full control of his treatment, and only I can revoke the sectioning." He paused and leaned forward in his chair. "I will need to sedate him, Agnes. I would rather have control of his consciousness, and not let his mind take control again. If it does, then I'm afraid he'll spend the rest of his life in an asylum."

Agnes burst into tears.

Arthur gently took hold of her hands. "You must understand how ill he is my dear, and what will happen if we cannot treat his condition. You will need to be strong for him and more importantly for yourself. The coming weeks and months will be hard, very hard. But if we don't take this course of action, then I am certain we will lose him forever."

Agnes wiped away her tears and tried her best to smile at him. "Tell me what I have to do."

Arthur smiled. "Come, we have to save Roger from another mauling from James."

NINETY-ONE

Sam looked at the ceiling of the kitchen and gasped as he watched the blue whirlpool of light, slowly make its way across the ceiling and disappear.

"He was here with me. We talked. He believed that Guillaume blamed him for Renaat." Klaus looked up, anguish written deeply into his face. "He's gone Sam." Finally he completely broke down.

"I'm so happy you could see him. I thought I was … well … imagining it all." He sat down next to Klaus, unsure what to do to comfort him. "Klaus?"

"It's OK, Sam, just you being here is all I need. Words aren't necessary."

They sat in silence for a few minutes.

"What happened?" Sam asked.

"We spoke about many things, and now there is no misunderstanding about their brother Renaat. He was always kept as a family secret which no-one spoke about. But Guillaume and I will visit Renaat more regularly at the home." He steepled his fingers and smiled. "We also spoke of Adam. Or rather of Adam and Rebecca."

"And?"

"Isaac says we should let them stay."

Sam said nothing.

"Isaac said to me why not let them stay? His brother, Renaat, is in a coma because we tried to force two spirits to move on." He paused and sighed. "He has been in a coma …"

Sam raised his hand. "I know about Renaat. Isaac told me. Remember I mentioned it to you?"

Klaus stared at Sam and shook his head.

"It doesn't matter. What we need to do now is decide what we do next. Do we simply walk into the garden and tell Adam and Rebecca they can stay, and everything in the garden will be rosy? Is it that easy?" Sam walked to the window, scratching his head.

Klaus followed him and touched his shoulder. "I think it is Sam. There are no magic spells, just a welcome to stay here at High Wood with you and Elizabeth. I think it's that simple."

Sam stared out of the window at the garden and suddenly frowned. "What do we do about Jane?"

"Presumably, we ask her if she wants to stay as well?" Klaus replied.

"But she's my wife!"

"You're *ex*-wife, Sam. Jane is a spirit, and you are a widower."

"It would make life very awkward for Elizabeth. Living, well being in the same house as my late wife, who'd still be walking the corridors and rooms. I mean when we go to bed, she'll … well … well she'll be able to …"

"Be able to what, Sam? Besides Jane may want to move on. To still be here, she must have unfinished business. Do you know what it is?"

Sam turned around to face Klaus. "Yes."

"And what is it?"

"Me."

"You?"

"Yes. She believes that in life she … wasn't … well she wasn't the best wife she could have been, and she wants to see me happy."

"But that's wonderful. Surely that's exactly what you want for Elizabeth and yourself?"

Sam sucked in his cheeks and sighed. "I don't trust her."

Klaus frowned. "In life, Sam, but not in the after-life, and especially not in Purgatory there is too much at risk to put any, how do you say it, black marks in your book. She is being genuine, Sam. She has no choice. If she stays she will not interfere in your relationship. I know this. Believe me, Sam, I know this."

In Bloemenwerf, Guillaume was stood by the window looking out at the rear garden, when a familiar figure appeared on the lawn. *"Isaac!"* His brain screamed. He ran out of the back door and down to the lawn.

"Guillaume, my dearest brother." Isaac said softly.

For the first time in his life, Guillaume was lost for words.

Isaac was stood on the well mown lawn. He was almost transparent, and surrounded by a pale blue shimmering aura.

"Cat got your tongue?" Isaac chided. "I just wanted to say goodbye. I didn't get a chance when … it … happened. So auf wiedersehen my brother, or should I say, as I know we will, au revoir."

"Isaac, there is so much I need to say."

"There is little time. I have told Sam what he must do and said goodbye to Klaus." Isaac smiled. "I spoke with him about Renaat."

Guillaume swallowed hard. "Renaat. We haven't spoken about him for some time."

"And we should have. He is our brother. I have always held myself responsible, but Klaus helped me …"

"He told you that I didn't hold you responsible?" Guillaume said.

Isaac nodded.

"We were all responsible, brother. We all knew what we were doing. What risks there were."

"And yet we locked it away, like we did Renaat." Isaac shook his head. "Time should never be wasted, brother. It is fleeting like an early morning mist. Make the most of the time you have left. Enjoy every moment. Do not mourn for me, I go to a better place, where we will meet again."

"Can you stay a little longer?" Guillaume begged.

Isaac shook his head. "It is time." He began to gently fade into an azure mist which floated up into an ancient Oak tree and dissipated among its branches.

"We part as brothers should." Guillaume finally smiled and sat on the low garden wall. Bloemenwerf would never be the same, but Guillaume could spend his remaining years in the comforting knowledge that his brother would be waiting for him.

Sam and Klaus looked at each other and nodded. "They can stay."

"Mein Gott! Das ist wahnsinn!! Die ravings eines toten." Karsten angrily replied and then bowed his head. "I am sorry father. My comments were … unangemessene."

Klaus's anger quickly subsided. "They weren't inappropriate, they were … taktlos."

"Ja, taktlos."

Elizabeth's shout from the garden brought their discussion to a rapid end. They flew out of the kitchen, to find Elizabeth pinned to the lawn by Adam.

"Let her go!" Sam screamed.

Without thinking Klaus dived at Adam, passing straight through him and crashing into the shed, dislocating the index finger of his right hand. "Scheisse!" He shouted.

Faint yellow streams of mist had started to flow from the corners of Elizabeth's mouth into Adam's eyes.

Sam jumped forward, grabbed Elizabeth's shoulders and dragged her away from Adam, who despite everything, had completely changed into a *vampir*. He lifted Elizabeth in his arms and blindly ran into the kitchen, through the lounge and into the map room. He sat her in the computer chair and gently stroked her face. "Elizabeth?" He kissed her cheek. "Elizabeth?"

She stirred and flapped her arms at Sam. "Leave me. Leave me alone."

NINETY-TWO

At breakfast the following morning, Agnes arrived late. Arthur, Roger and Gloria were finishing their porridge, but there was no sign of James. She walked up to Arthur and wished everyone good morning. "Any sign of James?" She asked.

There was a general looking around at each other, shrugging of shoulders and shaking of heads.

She looked at Arthur and frowned. "I'm going to look for him."

Arthur tried to smile, but failed miserably. "Let me know when you find him." He gestured for her to come closer to him. "We will need to start things today. I received a telegram from GHQ late last night, ordering James back to the front in two days time." He shook his head.

Agnes gasped in disbelief. "He can't. They can't. He's … he's …"

"Not ready yet?" Arthur completed her sentence.

Agnes shook her head. "I'm going."

Arthur nodded and squeezed her arm. "Be careful. He's very close to the edge."

Agnes ran out of the dining room for James's quarters. A few doctors and nurses wished her good morning, but her mind was elsewhere.

"Charming!"

"And you!"

"Ignorance of the young."

"Who does she think she is?"

"Excuse me!"

Echoed off the corridor walls, as she dashed past them.

As she ran past the wards, she glimpsed the patients she'd helped Arthur treat, and as she came to Kipling Ward, she stopped dead in her tracks. Standing in the doorway, rocking back and forth was Sergeant Major Frank Mansden. She'd grown close to Frank over the weeks of his treatment. His tremors, nightmares, violent outbursts, abuse and periods of catatonic shock had all significantly improved. And now, here he was, standing half way out of his ward, dishevelled and partly undressed. As she got closer to him she could hear him quietly, and constantly repeating over and over again, "No head, no arms, no legs."

A nurse pushed past her, pulled Frank into the ward and slammed the door.

Agnes tried to open it, but the key audibly clicked in the lock. She stood back staring at the frosted glass. Were Arthur's techniques only short term? She chided herself about her doubts, reluctantly turned away from Frank's ward, ran down the corridor and up the stairs to the first floor where James' quarters were. He was sat at the end of the bed in full uniform, mumbling something which Agnes couldn't understand. As she got closer to him her heart froze. He was holding a Webley Mark IV 38/200 service revolver in his left hand, and spinning the cartridge cylinder with his right. Her first thought was to make a grab at the revolver, but the possible outcomes terrified her. She walked closer to him, but he was totally oblivious to her. As she got nearer to him she began to understand what he was saying.

"Both legs partly torn away at the knee, one arm broken, other wounds, still conscious. Morphia or chloroform. To sleep, to dream." Still unaware of Agnes, he looked down at the Webley and smiled. "You know what to do for these poor souls." He looked up through Agnes. His eyes focused on some distant point. "Then … then you … you see them shaking and swearing, unable to walk, unable to talk, unable to sleep, fouling themselves, hiding in corners, frothing at the mouth, finding God, finding the Devil and creating their own Demons …" He looked down again at the Webley. "Malingerers and cowards, bringing shame and dishonour on their families and friends." He span the cylinder and smiled. "Only one treatment for them. Treat them as I would any other poor soul who couldn't survive to live a normal life." His smile changed to something closer to a leer. "Let them sleep." He lifted the Webley to his ear. "You can make them sleep?"

Agnes panicked.

James held the Webley lovingly against his cheek. "Are you sure?"

A small voice in his head answered. *"They will sleep when I kiss them goodnight."*

Agnes's panic grew, but she was paralysed with terror of what she believed James was considering.

He kissed the Webley and stood up.

Agnes desperately tried to shout or move, but her brain was in Possum mode, which was reinforced when James started quoting poetry.

"O soft embalmer of the still midnight,
Shutting, with careful fingers and benign,
Our gloom-pleas'd eyes, embower'd from the light,"

Agnes stared through fixed eyes at James as he completed the poem.

"Save me from curious Conscience, that still lords
Its strength for darkness, burrowing like a mole;
Turn the key deftly in the oiled wards,
And seal the hushed casket of my soul."

"O soft embalmer of the still midnight?" Thought Agnes. *"Shutting … gloom-pleas'd eyes … Turn the key deftly in the oiled wards?"*

James stood up and walked past her as if she didn't exist. He reached the bedside cabinet, unlocked the top drawer, kissed the Webley, placed it tenderly in the drawer, locked it and replaced the key in his trouser pocket. He looked around the room, still completely unaware of Agnes, checked his appearance in the mirror and left.

"What do you mean to do?" Agnes thought. With James gone, her paralysis disappeared. She sat on the bed and came to a conclusion she didn't want to reach. She shook her head, *"He's a doctor. He wouldn't. He took an oath."* She continued to try to dismiss the answer she'd reached.

An hour later, after she'd freshened up, Agnes was sat in Arthur's office drinking tea in an awkward silence.

Eventually Arthur broke the silence. "Agnes, what is it?"

She looked up from her cup and shook her head.

"Please, tell me what it is." He leaned across his desk. "Agnes. Tell me."

She placed the cup on the highly polished desk top, not worrying about any rings which might be made on the mahogany, swallowed hard and started to speak. "I think James plans to shoot the patients."

Arthur sat bolt upright in the chair, his face frozen in an expression of utter disbelief. "You ... b believe, that James ... p plans to kill ... to k kill ... my patients?" He fell back into the chair almost knocking it over. "Why? What ... what makes ... you ... you th think this?"

Agnes sat back in the chair and looked directly into Arthur's eyes. "He has a pistol. A Webley. He keeps it locked in his bedside cabinet."

Arthur frowned, but looked a little relieved. "But he's a serving officer. They all have Webleys."

"He was quoting poetry."

Arthur began to smile. "War tends to bring out the poet in all of us."

Agnes shot out of her chair and shouted. "He was quoting something about shutting their eyes, their ... gloom ... gloom-pleased eyes, keys in oiled wards." She struggled to remember the words. "Something about," she screwed up her eyes, "about a soft embalmer?"

Arthur sat down and held his head in his hands.

"Arthur?" Agnes said. "Arthur, what is it?"

"He's quoting Keats. It's a poem called 'To Sleep'." He lifted his head and stared at Agnes. "What else happened? Did he say anything else?" He stood up and walked around the desk. He took hold, a little too firmly, of Agnes' arms. "Think, Agnes. For God's sake think."

Agnes pulled away from him. "You're hurting me!"

Arthur shook his head. "I'm so sorry, but what you've said frightens me." He walked back around the desk and sat down. He gestured her to sit down. "When I studied medicine at university, I also developed a keen interest in the romantic poets of the 19th Century. Shelley, Blake, Byron, Wordsworth," he paused, "and particularly John Keats." He pulled open his desk drawer and pulled out a dog eared, well-thumbed book. He lifted it up and showed it Agnes. "Keats. I studied his works. I dissected them for their meanings."

Agnes shrugged.

"I understand the true meaning of 'To Sleep'."

Agnes shrugged again.

"The meaning of the poem is a metaphor. It really means to die."

Agnes held out her hands and shrugged again.

"Keats wants *'The Sleep'*. He wants to fall asleep. He wants to die because of his suffering. Because of his illness, he knows that his end is coming soon and he doesn't want to suffer. He sees death as a liberation." Arthur raised his eyebrows, checking that Agnes understood.

She frowned and nodded.

"James has treated men with horrific wounds, and rather than see them suffer, he gave many of them a peaceful end with morphia?"

Agnes nodded. She'd seen so many shattered bodies, so many of what once had been men, dying in unbearable agony, who'd been helped out of their torment by his caring and skills. She remembered Private Polton. His abdomen split open and his bowels, steaming and bloody, sitting on his lap. He was staring down at them, touching them like a child prodding a dead hedgehog he'd found on the road. James had assessed Polton, and immediately decided he was untreatable. He'd told her Polton would never survive the journey to the Clearing Station, and that he'd help him out of his suffering. Agnes frowned. She remembered the last thing James had said to the private before he injected the morphia. For some unknown reason they had burnt themselves into her mind. She quietly repeated them to Arthur.

"O soothest Sleep! if it so please thee, close, in the midst of this thine hymn, my willing eyes."

Arthur looked up to the ceiling. "We both heard what he said to me yesterday." He massaged his eyes.

Agnes shook her head.

"About men suffering from shell shock being malingerers and cowards? You remember now."

She nodded.

"You look at what he said, the poem he quoted today and what you saw in his room, then you can only come to one conclusion."

Agnes looked down at her feet.

"He plans to save my patients from, as he sees it, their feigned suffering, by helping them to sleep. To die, Agnes. The same relief as he would give to the wounded in France. The questions are, when does he plan to do it, and how do we get the Webley away from him?"

She scratched the side of her head. "He must be going to do it at night. The poem talks of darkness, and at night there's only a skeleton staff. It must be tonight or tomorrow night, before he has to go back. Getting the Webley will be a problem."

"We can only do this ourselves." Arthur whispered to Agnes as they stood a few feet away from James' quarters. "He doesn't know about the recall yet, but will have to be told tomorrow. If, and I pray that it is if, he plans to do what we fear, then it will be at the latest, tomorrow night." He massaged his temples and frowned. "James is well respected by the senior brass, we had better be right about this."

They both laughed nervously.

Arthur pulled a bottle of chloroform and a wad of cotton wool from the pocket of his white coat. "Once he's asleep, I'll use this," he looked at the bottle of chloroform, "and then take him to my car in that wheelchair." He pointed to the corner of the corridor.

Agnes frowned. "You've decided not to section him?"

"After a lot thought, I've decided that keeping him sedated, which I'd have to, for such a long time, would be dangerous to his health. Senior staff know he's here and there are a lot of them who agree with his current thoughts on shell shock. They would come here looking for him." He looked closely at Agnes. "I have thought at length about this. Keeping him here against his will is not a good idea. We need, in the short term to keep him away from the front and any immediate danger."

"Are you sure about this Arthur. I'm terrified about sending him back to the front in his condition."

"I have contacts who will be able to help. We can make sure he stays at a base hospital, a good distance back from the front. But actually physically stopping him going anywhere near the front will be a difficult."

"I'm not entirely happy about this Arthur. However, I understand your reasons." Agnes smiled to herself. She had an idea which she'd thought of in France, which would definitely stop James going anywhere.

"As the chloroform wears off I'll sedate him, and tomorrow morning we'll drive to Exeter and put him on the first available London train. If anyone asks, then he had one last binge before returning to France. I'll put his orders in his pocket, and we can spill a little whisky on his clothes. Waking up either on his way to, or in Paddington with orders, feeling the way he will and smelling of whisky will hopefully convince him that a good night was had by all. I've written a note to put in his pocket, and I'll need one from you to make it all seem real." He pulled a notepad and pencil from his pocket and held it out to her.

She took them and put them in her apron pocket.

Noises from James' room made them run to the corner of the corridor. They stood with their backs pressed against the wall as they heard the door open. Arthur pressed his finger to his lips and Agnes nodded her understanding of the need for silence. They heard footsteps in the corridor which grew louder and closer to them, but they stopped and grew quieter as James turned and walked the other way.

"We need to follow him." Arthur whispered.

Agnes looked puzzled. "Why? He'll come back and we can do what we need to then. It's going to look a little suspicious if we overpower him in the corridors, and we'd still have to get him back to his room. Let's just wait here. He's probably gone to the loo."

Arthur frowned. "What if he's decided to shoot everyone tonight?"

"It's too early. There's too many staff around." Agnes said.

Arthur relaxed. "I'll go back to my office and get something for us to drink."

Agnes leaned back against the wall. "Good idea. Even when he gets back, we still have to wait for him to go to sleep."

Arthur walked off into the half light of the corridor towards his office.

Agnes looked after him until he was out of sight. *"Time to get his revolver?"* She thought. *"What have I got to lose. Even if he comes back and finds me in his room, he can't possibly find anything wrong in that. If I'm going to stop him going back to France, I need that revolver. A Blighty is all he needs."* She peered around the corner of the corridor, ran to James' room and quietly closed the door behind her.

Making love had been spontaneous for Roger and Gloria. They barely knew each other, but the bond between them had developed over many lifetimes. They lay back on the bed comfortable and relaxed in their nakedness.

Roger lifted himself up on one elbow and looked up and down the length of Gloria's naked body. He felt no lust in what he was doing, but only a feeling that he knew this woman. Knew every inch of her intimately. Not because of their last hour of passionate love making, but something else, something deep within his psyche was telling him that he'd known this woman before, and would know her again.

The rush of endorphins through Roger's endocrine system had revived and boosted Ivor to nearer 10%, and it was through Ivor's eyes that Roger was seeing this woman's body, a personal recollection of a future event.

Gloria looked up at him and smiled. "You look like the cat that got the cream."

Roger grinned. "The double cream." He said with a mock leer.

"Lieutenant Lidsay, really." Gloria feigned embarrassment.

He got up from the bed and started dressing. "I'd better get back to my own bed, before anyone misses me."

"Do you have to go?" Gloria pleaded like a blushing teenage girl.

Roger smiled through half closed eyes at her. "It's difficult enough as it is getting these trousers on, without your help."

Gloria pulled the sheets up over her and giggled at Roger's problem. "I could find a use for that." She said from beneath the sheets.

"Nurse Perron I'm sorely tempted to discipline your insubordination, but I haven't got the energy."

10% Ivor, like a peeping tom, had been watching everything, through Roger's eyes, and what he'd seen had stimulated the recovery of another 5%.

"Was it ever like this?" He thought. *"There must have been times when we ... when we were ... were lovers. Times when our marriage meant something?"* 15% was growing in strength. *"What the hell went wrong?"* He struggled to recall memories of future events, but the strength of Roger's present day memories were still damping them.

"You're very quiet?" Gloria said as she emerged from beneath the sheets.

"Mmmm?"

She looked closely at Roger. He seemed distracted, somewhere else, not here with her. "Penny for them."

"Mmmm?"

"Penny for your thoughts." She said. "Roger, what is it? What's wrong?"

"Nothing." He replied unconvincingly.

"Regretting what we did?" She sounded hurt.

"No. No. Of course not."

"Then what is it?"

He shook his head as if he was trying to clear it. "There's something … something inside my head." He frowned deeply. "It aches."

Gloria climbed out of bed and massaged his neck. "Probably just a headache?"

"Yes. Probably just a headache." He smiled unconvincingly at her. "Too much pleasure. It's been such a long time. I thought that my head was going to burst."

Gloria smiled, but wasn't convinced by what he said. "Get some aspirin from the pharmacy, and get a good night's sleep. I can finish bursting your …" She smiled wickedly at him. "Go on. Get some tablets and sleep."

Roger tenderly held her face and kissed her gently on the lips. "I think I may have fallen in love with you, Nurse Perron." He finished buttoning his trousers and walked to the door. "But you'll probably still turn into a sour old cow." He said quietly as he left the room.

She fell back onto the bed and pulled the sheets around her, suddenly aware of her nakedness and vulnerability. Had she misheard what he'd said?

NINETY-THREE

Elizabeth eventually regained control of herself.

"Sam." She threw her arms around his neck. "Sam, what's happening? This isn't how it's supposed to be."

He slowly shook his head and screwed up his face in disbelief. "I know what's happened and what we need to do." He paused and swallowed hard. "Isaac came to me."

Elizabeth dropped her arms from around his neck and jumped back. "Isaac? Our Isaac?"

"Yes. Our Isaac. He had unfinished business and had to see us to complete it."

"What unfinished business?"

"Something to do with Guillaume and another brother." His eyes filled with tears. "It was hard when he died, but to see him again and then to lose him again so soon is tough to handle."

Elizabeth stroked his cheek and dabbed away the tears with a tissue. "It at least reassures us there is somewhere after all this and we are going home to God."

Sam took her tissue and blew his nose. "Still tough."

She nodded her head. "So what do we do?"

"We let them stay."

Elizabeth frowned. "Stay? But stay where?"

"Here."

Her frown deepened. "But how? I mean ... it's ... well it will be ..."

"Difficult to find any reasons why they shouldn't. Isn't it. I've been thinking about it since Isaac said this was what we should do. And I'm stumped."

"What about the others?"

"Klaus and Karsten agree. I'd better get back to the kitchen and see what's happening." He held Elizabeth's hands and stared deeply into her eyes. "You. Stay here. No arguments. Stay here."

Sam entered the kitchen with a degree of trepidation, unsure of what he would find, and what he would do.

Klaus and Karsten were stood at the open back door, Jane was pressed up against the sink and Rebecca was still sat at the kitchen table with her head in her hands. Adam was no longer floating but simply standing in the centre of the kitchen with his back to Sam. From the direction of his head, he seemed to be watching Klaus and Karsten, so Sam stayed where he was and silently waved to Klaus, who simply smiled, not wanting to draw any attention to Sam.

Jane moved away from the sink and took a few steps towards Rebecca.

"Leave her!" The voice was deep and threatening.

"But she's frightened, Adam. She's …"

"Leave her!" This time Adam's head turned towards Jane.

"But, Adam …" Her sentence was cut short when threads which looked like the hanging tendrils of a Portuguese man of war, spat out of Adam's mouth and wrapped themselves around Jane's face, blinding and smothering her.

Sam panicked, but Klaus shook his head and waved at him to stay where he was.

Adam saw Klaus's movement and span around to face Sam. He seemed swollen, more defined, more living than dead, and his face was like a demon's from 'The Triumph of Death' by Breugel. Sam was no art critic, but he knew what he liked and since his teenage years he'd found Breughel's imagery both compelling and horrific, adjectives which summed up Adam's face very well.

Adam slowly turned his head from side to side like a demented owl, his eyes never leaving Sam's.

Sam's eyes were burning, but he wouldn't blink and lose this battle of wills.

Adam seemed to be retching. Slowly at first, but then a violent spasm shook his chest and throat.

Sam had seen this happen earlier, when Jane had tried to intervene. He frantically looked around him for the closest thing he could use as a shield. He dropped to his knees and ripped the closest cabinet door off its hinges. As he looked up, the tendrils were rushing towards him. They hit the door like wet chamois leather slapping against a window. Sam breathed a little easier, but soon regained his tight chest as the tendrils began to ooze over the edges of the door and coil themselves around his wrists. He desperately tried to drop the door, but the tendrils were covered in octopus like suckers.

As the writhing coils reached Sam's elbows, Klaus and Karsten decided that it was time to act. To do exactly what, they had no clue, but to simply stand and watch wasn't an option.

Sam was hyperventilating, his blood pressure rapidly rising as the blood in his arms was squeezed into the rest of his circulatory system. Like a party balloon, his arteries and veins would only take a certain pressure before bursting.

Elizabeth managed to stay where she'd been told for about a minute, but what she saw as she reached the kitchen door made her blood pressure drop like a stone, and she fell into a dead faint.

Sam heard something fall behind him, but couldn't turn his head to see what it was, as the tendrils were keeping him *occupied*.

Klaus and Karsten stopped a few feet behind Adam and stared at each other, with completely no idea what to do.

"How do we stop this?" Karsten whispered.

Klaus looked at him and raised his eyebrows as far as he could. "What if we … Im namen der Gotter wie solte ich wissen?

"Es tut mir leid."

Klaus quickly scanned the kitchen work tops. "Get the knife!" Klaus whispered, but Karsten couldn't see it and shrugged. Klaus stabbed his finger towards the sink where a knife block stood. "Das messer!!"

Karsten nodded, ran to the sink and took the carving knife from the block. He frowned at Klaus. "But we can't stab or kill him. Can we?"

Klaus shook his head. "Cut the threads."

Karsten smiled in understanding. "Now?"

"No. I'll grab hold of Sam and pull him away. When the threads are stretched and taught, you cut them. After that …" He shook his head.

Klaus ran around Adam and took a firm grip on Sam's leather belt. He looked up at Karsten, nodded and pulled with all his strength. Karsten ran around Adam and started hacking at the tendrils, but the blade of the knife just bounced off them.

The tendrils were squeezing Sam's throat and he was getting dizzy.

"I suppose this is where I meet Isaac again. Earlier than I'd planned. But that's life I suppose." He thought as he began to slip into unconsciousness. Almost at the point of no return, Sam started to hear singing. Singing in a wonderfully calming soprano voice. *"Angels."* Sam thought. *"Not long now."*

Karsten, Klaus and Jane all turned their heads to the kitchen table. They looked at each other in disbelief at the angelic voice, like liquid honey, which was trilling from Rebecca's throat.

She'd walked a few paces and was stood close to Adam's left shoulder. She was singing gently to him.

'I'm a young girl, and have just come over.

Over from the country where they do things big,

And amongst the boys I've got a lover,

And since I've got a lover, why I don't care a fig.

The boy I love is up in the gallery,

The boy I love is looking now at me,

There he is, can't you see, waving his handkerchief,

As merry as a robin that sings on a tree.'

Adam's head rocked to one side, as if trying to hear the singing better.

Klaus kept pulling for all he was worth and Karsten was now pulling at the tendrils with his hands, which were becoming entangled and achieving nothing.

'The boy that I love, they call him a cobbler,

But he's not a cobbler, allow me to state.

For Johnny is a tradesman and he works in the Boro'

Where they sole and heel them, whilst you wait.

The boy I love is up in the gallery.

The boy I love is looking now at me,

There he is, can't you see, waving his handkerchief

As merry as a robin that sings in a tree.'

Klaus sensed he was beginning to win the battle. The tension on the tendrils was weakening. Jane ran to Rebecca's side, and as best she could, joined in the singing. Sam slipped into unconsciousness and collapsed to the floor taking Klaus with him. Karsten rocked back as the tension on the tendrils suddenly relaxed. He smiled briefly, but was terrified when the slack in the tendrils meant that they were able to coil around his arms and shoulders much quicker than before.

'Now if I were a Duchess and had a lot of money,
I'd give it to the boy that's going to marry me.
But I haven't got a penny, so we'll live on love and kisses,
And be just as happy as the birds on the tree.
The boy I love is up in the gallery,
The boy I love is looking now at me,
There he is, can't you see, waving his handkerchief,
As merry as a robin that sings on a tree.'

As the final lines were sung, Adam turned and looked questioningly at Rebecca.

"It's me, my love. Remember our song. Sing it with me. Just the chorus. That's the bit that you like the best. Sing with me, Adam. Like we used to at the music hall on a Saturday night. Sing with me."

Rebecca started the chorus.

"The boy I love is …"

She smiled at Adam and nodded for him to join in.

"Come on, my darling. You know the words." She spoke the next line slowly. 'The boy I love is looking now at me.' Remember, you'd always look at me when you sang that?" Adam's expression began to soften. Jane stepped back from this deeply personal and intimate moment between a husband and wife. Between two lovers who's passion for each other hadn't diminished in almost a hundred years of separation.

Klaus was desperately tearing at the tendrils around Sam's throat. Jane had joined him and was doing her best to help. Suddenly they both stopped and looked up. The singing voice had changed from soprano to baritone.

"There he is, can't you see, waving his handkerchief, as merry as a robin that sings on a tree."

Rebecca threw herself forward and hugged her husband. She felt Adam kiss her neck and whisper "I love you."

The tendrils began to dissolve, and Klaus found himself pulling away a mass of mucus slime from Sam's neck and head.

Karsten was shaking his hands like a demented conductor, throwing the slime all around the walls, work tops and floor of the kitchen.

Klaus pushed two fingers into Sam's mouth and did his best to clear the slime from his throat and airways.

"Is he alive?" Jane asked.

Klaus shrugged and turned Sam over into a recovery position. Sam didn't move.

"He's dead isn't he?" Jane shouted.

"Klaus do something. For God's sake do something!" Elizabeth screamed.

Sam slowly became aware of the blurred image of the lounge. He tried to sit up but felt hands holding him down.

"Stay there, Sam." It was Klaus' voice.

"Klaus?" Sam whispered hoarsely.

"It's me, Sam. You need to rest."

"Elizabeth?"

"She's fine Sam. *You* need to rest." He said firmly.

Sam's vision began to clear. He was lying on the Chesterfield. Standing around him were Klaus, Karsten and Elizabeth. He tried to push himself up on his elbows, but they wouldn't support him.

"Sam, listen to Klaus. Rest." It was Elizabeth.

Sam smiled and blew her a kiss.

"Drink this Sam." Elizabeth lifted his head and put a cup of hot sweet tea to his lips. "Slowly, its hot."

He drank the tea and his head felt a little clearer. "I want to sit up." He croaked to Elizabeth. "Please, I need to sit up. I'll be fine."

Elizabeth nodded, Klaus and Karsten put their hands under his arms and gently lifted him up against the back of the Chesterfield.

Sam smiled and rubbed his neck. "Where are the others?"

"They're together in the kitchen, Sam. Do you remember anything?" Karsten asked.

Sam shook his head. "I've a vague recollection of," he stopped and smiled, "of a giant jelly fish?"

Klaus laughed. "Quite close, my friend. Quite close."

"What did happen? Are they OK?" Sam asked.

Klaus sat down next to him. "It is as you say, a long story. A very long story, and we have plenty of time to tell you about it. But for now, please rest."

Sam frowned and stared into Klaus's eyes. "I saw Isaac."

Klaus nodded and looked up at Karsten. "We saw him as well, Sam. He came to help."

Sam lifted his hand for Elizabeth to hold.

She took it and gently squeezed it. "We were worried about you."

"I love you." He mouthed to her, his throat burning like acid.

She squeezed his hand a little firmer, touched her lips with two fingers and blew him a kiss.

"I want to see Adam." Sam whispered.

The others looked at each other and nodded. Karsten left the lounge and returned with the three spirits, who all came close to the Chesterfield and smiled at Sam.

"Thought that we'd lost you." Jane said.

"Glad to see you looking better." Rebecca added.

Adam knelt down close to Sam. "I am so sorry. I understand now what was happening, what I was doing. And ..." he looked up, "Klaus?"

Klaus nodded.

"Klaus told us we could stay. Stay here at High Wood."

Sam looked up at Klaus and smiled.

"Isaac said this was what should be done." Klaus said.

Sam smiled and nodded, beginning to remember a little of what had happened. He said softly. "He came to see me, to see us." He frowned and looked at Klaus. "He wanted to ... to ... talk with you."

Klaus's eyes filled with tears, remembering Isaac's words. "We talked. Nothing was left unfinished. He … he has passed over." He dabbed at his eyes with a tissue. "We will meet again. I now know this for certain."

Adam stood up, spoke quietly to Rebecca and Jane, and after a short time turned and spoke to the others. "We understand what should be happening, where we *should* be, but this is all still …" he looked around the room, "odd, difficult, almost impossible for us to understand." He looked at Sam. "You must see that? You were there with me in that tunnel."

Sam nodded.

"And now we're here in the same time and place? How can that be? I'm a simple man, and this is …" He shrugged his shoulders and rubbed his head. "How can I do this?" He rubbed his head again. "I can feel myself. But I'm dead." He looked despairingly at Klaus. "What am I?" He waved at Jane and Rebecca. "What are we? Do any of you know?"

Sam patted the Chesterfield for Adam to sit down beside him, understanding the utter confusion in his mind. A few months ago, Sam would have asked the same questions, and even now after all that had happened, every day still confused, frightened and amazed him. "I'll try to explain who we are, what we're doing and why we're here." He looked up at Klaus and Karsten. "And these two fine gentleman will fill in all the gaps." He took a glass of water from Elizabeth and drank deeply to ease his throat.

"Sam if it is difficult for you to speak, then I can take over." Klaus offered in a concerned voice.

Sam shook his head and smiled. "I am as new to this as Adam, Rebecca and Jane, and they've been through a lot more than I have. I'll see how far my throat will let me go, and you may have to finish for me."

Klaus nodded and sat down in one of the armchairs.

Slowly, and for most of the time hoarsely, Sam outlined as best he could, what had happened to him over recent weeks.

Adam and Rebecca listened intently, and Jane kept shaking her head as she began to understand what had happened at High Wood.

Sam let Klaus explain to them about Papaver Rhoeas, which seemed to strike a chord with Adam.

"So you help us, the ones that went missing, to … to find our loved ones again?" Adam said.

"Yes we do." Klaus replied. "But you are an exception. Most of the souls we help home, have no loved ones who are still with us. They have already passed over, and we help them meet again on the other side."

Adam nodded. "But why is Rebecca still here?" He looked up and smiled at her.

Klaus smiled at the reunited couple. "Because she couldn't move on. When a soul has unfinished business, or they are so strongly bound to either a place or a person, they will not move on until they are reunited or choose to go. Rebecca was held here because of her great loss and sadness, and her love for this house. She was waiting for you. She couldn't, wouldn't move on until she found you. The worst part for her was not knowing what had happened to you. She knew about your son, and although this broke her heart, she knew what had happened to him and where he was buried."

Adam's eyes flew wide open. "My son? Which … who…?"

Rebecca quickly sat down next to him, "Jack died of his wounds at High Wood in 1917." She let this sink in. "You'd already been reported missing in 1915, so you weren't … you didn't know. We are all dead, my darling. Our boys are waiting for us. All that we love is on the other side."

Adam stood up and walked out of the room.

Rebecca looked after him. "He will need a few minutes on his own. You are all intelligent men. Adam is a simple man. All this, is beyond him. But he will understand it. It will take a little time, but he will understand this."

Jane had silently, and patiently listened to everything. "How did I die?" She softly asked. "Why am I still here? I understand Adam and Rebecca, but I still don't understand what happened to me."

Klaus gestured to Sam that he would answer Jane. "It is difficult to explain, but I will try."

Jane smiled and nodded.

"High Wood is like … like an airport, a terminus, where passengers fly in and passengers fly out. It is one of many airports around Europe. High Wood allows souls to fly in and souls to fly out, but there are no traffic controllers. Souls can arrive at any time, and we never know when. But they need someone to help them move on. So I suppose we are like passport control." Klaus knew that he was stretching the analogy to breaking point, but Jane seemed to be understanding most of what he was trying to explain. "OK so far?"

Jane frowned, but smiled and nodded.

"Good. It isn't easy. Shall I continue?"

"Please." Jane answered.

"Souls can fly out to pass over to the other side, but souls can also fly out from here to anywhere in the past. High Wood is a connection to the past, present and the future. It is a connection which no-one can control. It opens and closes as it chooses. You were at a door when it opened to the past. I have no idea what happened when you were there, but at some point the door opened again and you *travelled* back to High Wood."

Jane sat on the Chesterfield close to Sam. "I think I know what opens the door." She said. "A link to the past is what drags you back. A personal link. It must be the strength of the bond which pulls you back. Agnes called me. Agnes Wilmart, she married an army surgeon and became Agnes Heyward. She was my great aunt. A nurse in the Great War, my mother told me about." Jane frowned deeply. "I … I think that I became her. We sort of merged."

Elizabeth walked slowly in front of Jane. "Agnes Heyward was my grandmother. She was a nurse in the War. My grandfather was James Heyward. He was a captain in the RAMC. He was a surgeon."

NINETY-FOUR

Agnes scanned the room, and in the bright moonlight from the window saw James' trousers hanging over the back of a chair. She put her hand into the pockets and felt for the key which she'd seen him put there. Nothing. She lifted the trousers off the chair, held them upside down and shook them. There was a light metallic tinkle on the floor and Agnes's hopes lifted, only to be dashed when she saw James's fountain pen glinting in the moonlight.

"Where are you?" She whispered to herself. "Where have you put it?"

She rifled through the drawers of the desk which functioned as a dressing table, checked all his other trousers and anything hanging in the wardrobe which had a pocket, emptied his wash bag, pulled his suitcase from the top of the wardrobe, checked inside it and finally dropped to her hands and knees to look under the bed. As her head disappeared beneath the bed, her heart stopped as the door to James's quarters opened.

"How can there be no coffee at this time of night?" She heard him complain. "Hate cocoa, but needs must."

She heard him blow a couple of times, cooling the hot cocoa, and swear as he'd clearly not cooled it enough. She lay silently squeezed between the bed and the wall, struggling to keep her breathing quiet, as the rusty springs bitterly complained under James weight. He puffed, swore, and something landed on her stomach.

"Bloody biscuits." She heard him say. "Where have you gone my little beauty?" She heard the springs complain as James rolled over on the bed.

"Down here are you?" His hand appeared over the side of the bed, fumbling for the lost biscuit.

Agnes's breathing became shallow and rapid, her skin clammy, her mouth dry, her senses at fever pitch.

James's hand reached lower down the side of the bed searching for the floor and his biscuit.

Agnes gripped the frame of the bed and started pulling herself into the small space under the bed, scraping her knees and hands on the rough metal of the frame. The biscuit fell from her stomach onto the dusty floor, and she felt James' hand brush her hip as it finally found the biscuit.

"Ah there you are my little beauty. I thought I'd lost you."

For one moment Agnes thought James was talking to her, but it was his desire for the shortcake biscuit now covered in fluff. She heard him complain again about the room not being cleaned, but this was quickly followed by the sound of satisfied munching. There was relative silence for a few minutes as James consumed his late night snack, and then she heard him unlocking what she thought must be the bed side cabinet.

"There you are. Have you been lonely? Sorry to have left you for so long, but I'll soon have you shutting their gloom-pleas'd eyes."

Agnes heard the distinctive sound of metal being lifted from the drawer.

"Bit early yet though. Let them sleep a little longer, and then we'll release them all from their suffering at two o' clock. I'll set the alarm and then you and I have work to do."

She heard the revolver being replaced in the drawer, and the scraping of the warped wood as it was closed, but she didn't hear any key turning, locking it.

The springs complained again as James settled down for a few hours sleep before his *mission*.

She lay in the dark and dust under the bed until she thought James had enough time to fall asleep. As she started to pull herself from under the bed, her movement disturbed the dust which rose like a mini tornado making her nose itch uncontrollably. The tickling and itching was unbearable, and the response to sneeze was almost impossible to control. She pushed herself from under the bed and slid against the wall until she was clear of it, stood up, and prayed that James was still asleep. His eyes were shut but moving. Agnes tiptoed to the cabinet and tried to pull the drawer open. Like the bed springs it complained bitterly as the ill fitting drawer scraped over the wood of the cabinet. She stopped as James muttered something in his sleep, looked at the bed side cabinet and saw the alarm clock.

"If he doesn't wake up, then he can't do anything." She thought.

She lifted the alarm clock and moved the third hand to ten o' clock. *"You can miss breakfast as well."* Her mind decided. *"But I still need the revolver, and my hands are pretty small."* She thought, comparing the size of the gap to her hand. *"I think I could pull it through that gap."* She slid her hand easily into the drawer, and found the barrel of the Webley. Gripping it with her thumb and two fingers, she slowly pulled it until she could feel the cylinder and then the hand piece. She started to lift it and got the barrel clear of the drawer when cramp struck her fingers and the Webley fell back with a crash into the drawer. Agnes held her breath. James stirred, but stayed with his dreams of the Sussex Downs.

Her hand and fingers were small enough to get in and out of the drawer, but she didn't have enough strength in them to lift the heavy revolver out. She looked around the moonlit room for a solution, and after a few seconds, saw it hanging on the handle of the wardrobe. She softly walked across to the wardrobe, and picked up the metal coat hanger.

"I can use the hook to fish it out by the trigger." She thought.

She bent the hanger into the rough shape of a handle, lowered the hook into the drawer, and after a few unsuccessful attempts, hooked the ring of metal around the trigger.

"Easy now. We don't want this one to slip off the hook. Easy, easy."

The Webley appeared over the edge of the drawer, swinging gently on the hook. She pulled it out a little further, the swinging got faster and the Webley looked like it would win again. She made one last hard pull with the hanger, lifted the revolver clear of the drawer, and as she did, the Webley slipped effortlessly off the hook and fell back towards the drawer. Agnes's other hand shot out like an English slip fielder and grabbed the handle as it fell into the drawer. It rattled loudly against it, but James was enjoying himself far too much on the Downs to be woken. Agnes lifted the Webley out of the drawer and like a new born baby, held it tightly to her chest. As she stepped out into the corridor and closed the door, a hand on her shoulder, released a scream which had been welling up in her for the last half an hour.

"Agnes it's me." Arthur hissed.

James sat bolt upright, the Downs left in the realms of sleep, swung his legs out of bed, cracking his knee on the open cabinet drawer. "Shit! Shit! Shit!" He wailed as he hopped around the room, slipped and fell headlong into the wardrobe, splitting his eyebrow and breaking his wrist.

Agnes and Arthur, heard the commotion, looked briefly at each other, ran into James' room and flicked on the light. The scene was one which wouldn't have been out of place in the saloon of a western movie. James was lying in a crumpled heap, his back against the wardrobe door, his left hand trying to stem the flow of blood from a gash on his eyebrow, his right arm hanging by his side and an angry red mark on his right knee, showing through a tear in his pyjama trousers.

"My God James, what's happened." Agnes asked running to him in her best, but forced, caring nurse manner and tone.

"I … I heard a … I think it must have been a scream?" He moaned softly and tried to stand up, but his right leg collapsed under him. He screamed in agony as the medial collateral ligament of his right knee ruptured.

An orderly ran into the room. "Can I help, sir?"

"Give me a hand to get him onto the bed."

They lifted him together and put him as gently as they could onto the bed.

Arthur did his best to assess what damage James had done to himself. It had been some time since he'd had to deal with physical trauma like this, but between himself, Agnes and the orderly he was happy that they'd at least made James comfortable.

"Bloody drawer was open." James mumbled. "I'm sure I shut it."

"Don't worry about that now." Agnes reassured him. "Let's get you fixed."

"It was bloody closed you know." He pushed himself up on one arm and moaned in pain. "I put the …"

"Put what, James?" Agnes asked.

"Oh, I put … a … book I was reading in there before I went to sleep."

Agnes looked in the drawer. "It's not here now. You're sure you put it in the drawer? Because there's a book over here on your suitcase." Agnes walked over and picked it up. "Is this it?" She held it close to James.

He nodded. "I must have been mistaken."

"A blow on the head can easily disorient you, old man." Arthur held James wrist and took his pulse. "Just rest for now. As soon as Dobbs gets back we'll get you stitched up. Tomorrow I'll get a doctor I know over from Exeter to check you over and see what needs doing."

James nodded in mock understanding. Telling them about the Webley wouldn't have been a good idea. *"Where is it?"* He thought. *"I know it was there. So who's got it?"* He looked back at Arthur and then Agnes, and the shape of the bulge in her apron pocket gave him the answer.

His expression told Agnes he knew where the revolver was.

"Anything we can do?" Roger and Gloria were taking a post-coital stroll, heard voices and stopped to see if they could help.

"What have you been up to?" Roger asked.

"Nothing that you two have, by the expressions on your faces." Agnes answered.

"Are you OK old chap?" Roger asked.

"Yes. Just bloody clumsy. Fell over the cabinet and into the wardrobe. Nothing heroic I'm afraid. You two get back to your quarters. You look like you need a rest." James waved them away with his good arm. "And your own separate quarters."

They blushed. "If you're sure?"

James waved them away again, and they disappeared down the corridor, arm in arm. "Young love. They may as well make the most of it."

"They're …" Arthur exclaimed.

"Yes they're …" James replied.

"But …"

"But what? At times like this they need to grab every moment of pleasure they can. They'll be back at the front in a few days."

Agnes screwed up her face and peered at James. "What do you mean, back at the front in a few days?"

"I telegrammed HQ to let them know that Roger was A1. They seemed very pleased. I picked up my orders to return at the same time." He let these words hang in the air, but Agnes and Arthur didn't respond as he'd hoped.

Agnes was lost for words.

"But he's not ready to go back, and you'll be here for some time yet." Arthur snarled.

Despite his cuts, bruises, ruptured knee and broken wrist, James was clearly in full control of his senses. "I may be stuck here while I heal, but Roger's as ready as he'll ever be. Troops need to see that their officers are ready to lead them into battle."

"James, he's not ready. He's still very unstable." Arthur, despite understanding that James was still in the deepest chasm shell shock could take him, was losing his temper.

"When did you last see action?" James pointedly asked Arthur.

Arthur's cheeks flushed like ripe tomatoes. "I've been … well this treatment … well it … it takes time to …"

"Not recently then?' James level of sarcasm was becoming uncomfortable for Agnes.

"No."

"Spent any time just at or close to the front?"

"No!"

"Well I would suggest that given my direct experience of the effects of war, I probably have a better understanding of what drives men to desert their comrades."

Arthur was speechless.

"My view, which has been reconfirmed since being here again, is that these men are all, how can I put it not too harshly, traitors to their King, country, comrades and family." He laid back in the bed, beaming. "They will burn in hell if they are not corrected." He closed his eyes and smiled to himself. "If their attitude cannot be appropriately and correctly realigned with the vast majority of our brave troops, then they should be removed from society, and not mollycoddled in some warm bed, by doctors and nurses who should know better." He opened his eyes and scanned Agnes and Arthur for their reactions, which were plain for anyone to see. "I now need to rest. A few aspirin would be OK and I'll see your friend in the morning Arthur." He closed his eyes and lay back on the bed. "Goodnight. Thank you for your care. Oh, and Agnes, could you put my Webley back in the drawer." He dismissively waved them away.

Arthur started to speak, but Agnes touched her lips and gestured to the door.

"Don't forget the Webley, will you dear." James said as a parting comment.

NINETY-FIVE

"Why didn't I survive the journey back?" Jane asked Klaus. They were stood in the gallery looking at the photos.

"Some survive the journey, and some can't. Sam can. We've evidence of this with yourself, Rebecca and Adam. This is still new to me, but I believe that the bond you formed with the past was stronger than any bond you had with the present. It was possibly the strength of the bond with which kept your physical side in the past, and released your spirit to move on."

Jane stroked the photo of a pilot and sighed. "You're probably right. I wasn't a good wife you know. Quite a bitch really. I made his life a misery. He seems happy with Elizabeth don't you think?"

Klaus nodded. "They seem very much in love."

"We were like that. But only for a brief time." She walked over to the window. "I miss all this you know."

"Miss?"

"All of that." She pointed out of the window to the street where mothers in their cars were rushing to collect their offspring from school. "Never had any. Could have. But we just never got around to it. Sam had his work and I had … well I got used to being idle. The thought of having screaming kids around the house demanding my time was too much to bear. What a bloody waste of a life." She turned away from the window, unable to keep looking at the living. "I need to put it right."

"Is this your unfinished business Jane?" Klaus asked quietly.

She looked up at him and tried but failed to smile. "I think so. Maybe I'll get another chance in another life?" She tilted her head at Klaus, seeking an answer.

He shook his head. "We devote our lives to helping these lost souls." He tenderly touched the photos. "But until I make the final journey …" He shook his head again. "Who knows. All I can say is that the more I see, the more I am convinced that this shell is only one of many we inhabit over countless lifetimes. Buddhists call it reincarnation. I believe that what we see, is a variation on their theme, but I have no doubts that they are very close to the ultimate truth."

Sam appeared in the doorway. "You two solving the problems of the world?"

"Should you be up here?" Klaus replied.

"Probably not, but sitting around isn't going to get anything done." He walked to where they were standing. "Young weren't they?"

"I was saying the exact same thing." Klaus replied.

"What were you talking about?" Sam asked as he looked at the fresh face of the airman.

"Oh, just putting the world to rights."

"Nothing too major then." Sam joked.

"No nothing too major." Klaus winked at Jane and smiled.

"So they're going to stay?"

Klaus looked puzzled. "They?"

"Adam and Rebecca."

"Ah yes. They will stay here at High Wood."

"I'd like to stay as well." Jane said quietly.

Sam and Klaus's heads snapped around.

"You want to stay as well." Sam said rather too sharply.

"Bother you does it?" Jane sniped back.

"Yes it bloody well does."

"Tough. If it's good enough for them, then it's good enough for me."

Sam turned away and muttered some unintelligible expletives.

"Was it always like this with you two?" Klaus said softly.

Sam turned around and nodded. Jane ran her fingers through her hair and laughed. "Pretty much." She said. "Only a lot more unpleasant." She smiled at Sam. "Wouldn't you agree, dear?"

Sam tried not to, but couldn't help but smile. "Like two cats in a sack."

"Well my feline friends. We need to address the location of Jane as well as the other two spirits." Klaus said.

Sam nodded in agreement. "It would just make things a little uncomfortable for Elizabeth and me. It would be bad enough living under the same roof as your ex-wife, but with your wife's ghost?" He laughed out loud. "Why would you want to stay?"

Jane looked at the two men. "I believe that I can help you."

Klaus and Sam looked quizzically at each other. "Go on." Klaus said.

"Your organisation searches for lost souls, spirits, ghosts like me."

They nodded.

"There are ghosts in this house aren't there?"

Sam nodded.

"And you find it difficult to, well, to speak to them. To let them know why they're here and how you can help them?"

Sam sighed and nodded.

"So, who better to communicate with them and overcome their fears, than me." She opened her arms offering her services to Sam and Klaus. "They've already briefly spoken with me. They don't know where they are, aren't even sure who they are, what's happened to them, what's going to happen to them and … Sam, they can't comprehend that they're dead. Even I find all this just a bit odd. These men's minds, like their bodies were, torn apart, sliced and shattered."

"She makes a lot of sense," Klaus said to Sam.

"Unfortunately yes," Sam replied.

"If you stay, where will you stay?" Sam asked Jane.

Jane frowned and tipped her head to one side. "I don't understand?"

"Where will you live … I mean stay. I mean …"

"Sam I am not in the slightest bit interested in you and Elizabeth. If you're afraid I'll come floating into your room while your, well you know what I mean, you're, being friendly with each other, then don't. We were finished a long time ago, and believe me when I say, that I am truly happy for you both."

"You see what I mean, though?"

Jane nodded.

"Let's go back downstairs and see how all this is going to work." Klaus suggested.

Sam and Jane smiled at each other, and nodded at Klaus.

For anyone visiting the house for the first time, the scene in the kitchen would have seemed a little chaotic. Sam, Elizabeth, Klaus and Karsten were sat around the kitchen table, apparently talking intently to the fresh air between them, and the floating mugs of coffee would probably have been a step too far.

For those sat around the table, Adam was stood between Klaus and Karsten, Rebecca was stood between Sam and Elizabeth and Jane was making coffee for those who would be able to enjoy it.

Jane placed the mugs on the table and Klaus nodded in thanks. "Two sugars?" She said.

"Perfect." Klaus replied smiling at her.

Sam tapped the table with a tea spoon. "Working together."

Jane pulled a stool from close to the oven and sat down. "We," she pointed to Adam and Rebecca. "are on the same plane, or whatever you want to call it, as all the other souls who are stuck here in High Wood. We can become your eyes, ears and voices with these souls. Give us names and we can find out if they are here or if they need to be found and brought here. From what I understand, Sam is able to travel back and fore into the past and find these lost souls and guide them to High Wood. This is what happened with Adam, isn't it?"

Sam nodded, although even to him what Jane said sounded bizarre.

"You're right." Klaus said as he walked back to the table, pulling a chair behind him. "You must understand that this is as new to us as it is to you. We have never had spirits stay and offer their help." He sat down. "They've always come and gone. They've never stayed. We've always made sure they pass over."

Jane smiled. "So we're all learning something new?"

Everyone nodded, and murmured their agreement.

"So let's learn together. Adam and Rebecca are from the same time as the lost souls you help. They must be able to communicate better than anyone with these spirits who are at best confused, and at worst terrified of the unknown. Surely reassurance from Adam and Rebecca, can only help?"

Klaus looked to Karsten. "You've been very quiet."

"I am as new to this as Sam and Elizabeth. We are all trying to understand, to believe what we see with our own eyes. Things which anyone else outside this circle would say were at best demonic."

Klaus frowned and shook his head. "Far from demonic my son."

"To us no, but to an outsider it would seem like … I cannot find the word in English. Vater, hexerei." Karsten said.

"Witchcraft." Klaus translated.

"Yes witchcraft. But we know that it is God's work, not the Devil's, and for me, I say that we accept all the help we can. I, we need it. Where is the danger in this?"

"What happens if we say no." Elizabeth asked.

"We'll just haunt the house. Make your lives a misery. Moaning and screaming all night. Chains rattling, beds shaking, demons rising from the pit, blood running down the walls, mass murder, all the crockery smashed and a really nasty smell in the loo." She looked around the table at everyone and burst out laughing. "Your faces." She carried on chuckling to herself. "It's what won't happen if you say no that is more important."

Sam was amazed at where all this had come from. This wasn't the woman he'd been married to, but as he thought back, he remembered the woman he'd known before they got married, and he understood why at the start they'd loved each other, and why bitterness, spite, on-line bingo and separate lives had eroded their marriage.

"Shame." He thought.

Klaus leaned forward and rested his elbows on the table. "As Mr Dylan once sang," and in a very bad Bob Dylan impersonation he sang, "the times they are a changin. We must embrace change. It is the only true constant. Isaac is no longer with us, and I couldn't believe he would ever go. We all try to feign to others, that we graciously accept our mortality and that death holds no fear for us." He smiled. "This of course is horse shit."

"Bull shit." Sam corrected quietly.

"I'm sorry Sam. Yes, bull shit. It terrifies all of us. Do we honestly know where the missing go when we send them on? I have no idea. I have my beliefs, but we could be sending them into, who knows what. Until we make the journey ourselves, we will never know for certain what lies ahead of us, and by then it will be too late. I pray every day that they've gone to a better place. That they are once again with the ones they loved and lost. That Isaac is with his parents, and that he will be waiting for me when I die." He drained the last of his coffee. "Seeing and speaking with Isaac, and being here with Jane, Adam and Rebecca, has strengthened my belief that the spirit does live on, and we go to a better place." He turned and looked directly at Jane. "Work with us. There will come a time I'm sure when you will want to move on."

Jane shook her head.

"You will. If only to meet those who have gone before."

She shrugged and slowly nodded.

"But until that time, we must change and work together." He raised his empty coffee mug in a mock toast. "To us all here now, and to those who we will meet again."

Everyone raised their mugs, clinked them against each other and said, "Cheers. Prost."

NINETY-SIX

Agnes stared at James and shrugged. "Your Webley?"

"Yes. The Webley you have in your apron pocket." He said quietly.

Agnes shrugged again.

James became agitated, but kept smiling, and pointed at her apron. "That bulge! What is it?"

"This?" Jane replied tapping her apron. "A stethoscope."

James shuffled around on the bed, but couldn't stand because of his injured knee. "Show me!"

"You've seen a stethoscope before."

"I'd *like* to see *yours*!"

Jane smiled at him. "I have to go."

"Jane! Show it to me *now*!"

Arthur linked arms with her and led her out of the room. "Let him let off some steam. He's not going anywhere with that wrist and knee."

"Come back here. That's an order!" Steam was coming out of his ears.

As they walked down the corridor, they could hear him hurling abuse after them.

"We'll leave him until Robert gets here to look at his wrist and knee." Arthur said. "At least he won't be *helping* any patients tonight."

Agnes smiled. "Shouldn't we give him some painkillers?"

"The level of pain he has will keep his mind occupied."

"But shouldn't we at least give him something?"

"Robert won't be long. He was going to leave once he put the phone down." Arthur looked at his watch. "He'll be here in about twenty minutes. James will be fine until then. But to be certain, I've asked George to keep an eye on him." He stared at Agnes' apron. "Is it his Webley?"

Agnes nodded.

"Better give it to me to lock away."

She pulled it out of her apron pocket and thought of the death something as small as the Webley could cause, and the level of slaughter the assembled weaponry of each army was reeking on each other. Arthur took it from her and locked it in his desk. He dropped the key in his pocket and patted his leg. "It will be safe in there."

Roger turned to Gloria as they walked back to their quarters. "What do you think happened?"

Gloria shook her head. "Seemed a bit odd to me. Falling over like that. Does he drink?"

Roger shrugged. "No idea, but I couldn't smell anything could you?"

Gloria shook her head. "Do you think they know?"

"About us?" He replied.

"Yes, about us."

"Sounds like it."

"So what do we do?"

"More of the same I hope?" Roger smirked.

"Roger! You know what I mean."

"Well, we can save on their laundry and heating."

Gloria looked puzzled.

"Living in one room?"

She blushed. "We can't do that. We're still on active service. The Army wouldn't allow it. Would they?"

Roger raised his hands to the ceiling, and shrugged. "Coming back to my place?" He said raising his eyebrows as high as they would go.

"You're incorrigible."

"Just insatiable." He laughed and linked arms with her. "Come on, it's late and I need my sleep."

He walked her to her quarters and kissed her tenderly goodnight. "I really do need my sleep."

As he pulled the sheets up to his neck, Roger smiled at the memory of Gloria's naked body pressed against his, and the pleasures they'd willingly given to each other.

"Stop it!" He thought. *"Can't do anything about it now."* He looked down at the bulge in the sheets. *"Start thinking about bell ringing or stamp collecting."*

The surge of Roger's hormones started to fuel Ivor's recovery. Roger's preoccupation with the delights of Gloria, diverted his mind from keeping Ivor sealed away deep in his psyche. 10% grew to 15% and quickly to 20%. Roger's thoughts of stamp collecting weren't working as he was lost in the pleasures of self-satisfaction. 20% imperceptibly became 25% and Ivor started to regain self-awareness.

"What the hell is this?" Ivor's recovering consciousness thought. *"How can I just be thoughts? Where's my body?"* He became aware of another entity. A soul intimately intertwined with his, which seemed to have control of his physical self. As Ivor struggled with this new reality, Roger carried on blissfully pleasuring himself, lost in a deep physical sensation, with no sense of the growing presence of Ivor.

"What are you doing?" Ivor asked itself. *"I've died and gone to hell."* He thought. *"I'm stuck in some other bastard's body while he wanks off over my wife. How do you turn this off? Think about something else. Those bastards at High Wood. Sam and Elizabeth. The killer and the vicar. Devious bastards. Give me one more chance to bring them down. Cocky sods."*

The strength of Ivor's hatred of Sam and Elizabeth, accelerated his rate of recovery. 25% soon became 35%, which in no time soared to 49%. Almost the tipping point. Ivor suddenly became tangibly aware of a sensation like a zip slowly unfastening. The bond that was holding him to Roger was breaking down like replicating strands of DNA.

Roger suddenly stopped pleasuring himself as he felt a surge of heat run from his head to his chest. His hands flew to his chest as he thought his rib cage was about to split apart. He pressed his hands hard against his ribs, desperately trying to stop his chest exploding. The heat briefly moved to his abdomen and then tore down his legs.

"I'm dying" He thought. *"What a way to go! A heart attack induced by a ... The post mortem results will make interesting reading. Hope they'll be able to close the coffin lid."*

As the separation process finished, Ivor lost all sense of where he was, but not of who he was. He'd transformed into energy. The essence of Ivor Lidsay, concentrated into it's purest form. A life force plasma.

Roger's body became rigid.

"This is it." He thought. *"Didn't expect it to end this way. Thought that the Hun would play a part in my shuffling off."*

His eyes peered down at his stomach, where a blue glow had become visible beneath the cotton sheet. He felt no pain. No sensation of any kind. He felt cocooned in soft velvet. His mind seemed to be separating from his body.

"I'm dying and it's not as bad as I thought it would be. Quite pleasant really. Like sinking into a warm bath."

Ivor felt like he was floating in a balloon.

Roger watched the blue glow rise from his body and hover above it. *"My soul?"* He thought. *"My God it's beautiful."*

Ivor's balloon was suddenly hit by bullets from a German biplane, but he felt no panic or fear. He looked up as the balloon collapsed into a flapping tube.

Roger's body relaxed. His mind recovering the lost space Ivor's spirit had taken up. He was beginning to feel alive. He shook his head as his senses recovered. He saw the blue orb with new eyes and sat bolt upright in the bed. "What in the name of all that's holy is that?" He shouted at the darkness.

In the next room, Gloria had found it difficult to go to sleep, as her imagination had been as colourful as Roger's. The shout from the next room made her leap out of bed, and despite her partially dressed state, she ran next door to him. As she ran into the room and flicked on the light switch, she could see Roger staring and pointing at the ceiling. She followed his finger and looked up.

"It's gone!" He shouted. "It's gone! My soul's left me!

Ivor's balloon plummeted towards the ground.

Gloria ran to the bed and took Roger in her arms. "It's OK, my darling. You're having a nightmare. Nothing else, just a nightmare." She murmured reassuringly.

He looked from the ceiling to her. "Just a nightmare?" He whispered. "Nothing more than that?"

Gloria smiled at him. "Just a nightmare." She said softly and kissed him on the forehead.

Ivor's balloon smashed into the ground.

Agnes spent a sleepless night, her mind trying to make sense of what had happened to James. She talked with Arthur into the early hours. When Arthur's colleague arrived at two o' clock, she left them to treat James and made her way to her quarters.

At eight o' clock, a bleary eyed Arthur knocked on her door. "He's sleeping."

Agnes put her hands to her face and sighed.

"Robert has dressed his cuts, and fixed his wrist and knee with plaster of Paris. He thinks that the damage to his knee is quite severe."

Agnes tried unsuccessfully to suppress a smile.

"He's injected him with a heavy sedative, and he'll sleep for quite some time. When he wakes we need to decide what to do next. Robert will come back tomorrow to check on him, and has agreed to write a medical report for me which I'll send to his battalion headquarters. I will contact them today to let them know what has happened." He smiled at Agnes. "He won't be going back to France for the foreseeable future."

She rushed to him and threw her arms around his neck. "Arthur …" Her words were lost in a flood of tears. After a few minutes she calmed down. "What are we going to do?"

"Finish the treatment we started for his shell shock. It's still at the root of his problems. If we are to break this cycle then we have to complete what we started."

She nodded her understanding and agreement. "When do we start?"

"Immediately."

She looked puzzled. "How? He's sedated?"

"A perfect condition for me to use auto suggestion. While his mind is under the control of the drugs, it is pliant and open to suggestion. This has worked well in the past and I believe it will work well with James." He looked Agnes up and down. "Get dressed and meet me in the dining room. We'll have some breakfast and then start work with James."

She pulled a sheet around herself, blushed and waved Arthur out of her quarters with a smile.

Roger and Gloria were already in the dining room when Agnes arrived. Roger pointed to his plate of kippers and mouthed the words "Very good. How are you?"

She nodded and smiled. "See you after."

Arthur stood up and pulled back a chair for her. "Some tea?"

"Coffee please. Very black, very sweet and very strong. I need it." Agnes replied. "And just a little toast please."

"Jam?"

"Marmalade please."

Roger and Gloria finished their breakfasts and joined Agnes at her table.

"How's James?" Roger asked.

"Not great. Arthur's friend came in the early hours of the morning and patched him up. He's sleeping now, but he won't be right for some time." Agnes said.

"Bloody shame." Roger continued.

"How so?" Agnes asked.

"We were planning to go back to France together. We've had our orders to return to France."

"James told us he should have been going as well." Agnes said.

"Yes, I saw his telegram when I picked mine up and transport has been arranged to pick us up tomorrow." He turned and smiled at Gloria. "Looking forward to it aren't we, old girl."

Gloria managed a wan smile, and raised her eyebrows to Agnes.

"Can't wait myself. Big push must be due soon. Oops, sorry, loose talk and all that. I didn't take offence at what he said you know. Heat of battle and all that. People say a lot they don't truly mean when they're under stress. I do hope we'll be able to get together soon and chew the fat."

Agnes smiled. *"Bravado just for us?"* She thought.

Arthur arrived back at the table with her coffee and toast, wished Roger and Gloria a very good morning, and said to Agnes that they should finish their conversation in his office when she'd finished breakfast.

She smiled in agreement and drank most of the bitter coffee in one gulp.

"We should have a drink tonight. You know to say au revoir. Hate goodbyes. So final don't you think?" Roger said.

Agnes nodded.

"So we'll see you in the mess at about eight o' clock."

"Look forward to it." Agnes mumbled through a mouthful of toast and marmalade.

Roger and Gloria stood up. "Plenty to pack. See you later then." They waved and left the dining room.

An hour or so later Agnes was sat at the end of James' bed, listening intently to Arthur as he read softly to the sedated sleeping James from the notes he'd written.

"You have helped so many men, James. It's this you will remember. Remember the men who lived. The men you saved. The men you put back together. Remember your love for Agnes. Remember the men with shell shock. Remember your shell shock and the time you spent at Seale Hayne. Remember Arthur and how you worked together. When you wake you will remember all these things and feel rested. You will want to stay at Seale Hayne. You will have no desire to go back to the front."

He repeated the words four times, and then sat upright in the chair, stretching his neck and back. "We'll do this every two hours until he wakes."

"This will work?" Agnes asked.

"I believe it will. These are still early days in completing my work, but the results I have seen so far, give me encouragement that we will get back the man we knew. Or at least one who understands his condition and accepts that treatment is necessary."

"If you don't mind me saying, there's an awful lot of hope and maybe in what you said."

Arthur smiled and shrugged his shoulders. "Hope always springs eternal my dear." He stood up and gestured at the door. "We'll come back," he checked his watch "at eleven fifteen. I'd suggest you try and get some sleep."

As they left the room, Agnes touched Arthur's arm. "Did you know Roger and Gloria were going back to France, and that James knew about his recall?"

"No to question one, although it doesn't surprise me they would want them back at the front. It saddens me, but it's no real shock. So far as James is concerned, his manner and extreme agitation, makes sense if he was anticipating a quick return to France. He would want to complete his work before going back, so last night would have been his penultimate and most realistic chance of doing it."

"Is there nothing we can do for Roger and Gloria?" Agnes asked with pleading eyes.

"Afraid not. They're both in rude health, and want to go."

"Roger might, but I'm not too sure about Gloria."

"They'll be fine. It will probably be all over before they get off the ship."

He walked down the corridor, whistling, 'It's a long way to Tipperary'.

About an hour later, Agnes went back to James's quarters to find Arthur administering an injection to him. "Does he need that?" She asked.

Arthur stood up and turned to face her. "He does. If Roger and Gloria are leaving tomorrow, I don't want him getting a hint that they're going back to France." He wiped a drop of blood away from the injection site. "It's just a repeat of what Robert gave him last night."

Agnes frowned and looked concerned. "You're certain about this?"

Arthur smiled and nodded. "Yes, my dear. As certain as I've ever been about anything." He sat down close to James, took out his notes and began repeating them to him.

NINETY-SEVEN

They sat around the kitchen table discussing how they could best work together until it began to get dark.

"I think it's time we stopped and had something to eat." Sam suggested.

There were general sounds and nods of agreement around the table.

"I think I would like one of your famous curries." Klaus said patting his empty, paunch.

"I think there's a menu in that drawer." Sam pointed to the unit close to the oven. "Yes that's it Karsten. Bring it over here and I'll phone an order through."

An hour later, the table was littered with mostly empty foil containers, and the kitchen smelt like a restaurant in Bangalore.

Klaus belched loudly, blushed and immediately apologised. "That was a wonderful Dhansak, but I think the second nan was a little too much for me." He sat back and massaged his now very full stomach.

Jane joined them as Indian food had been a great passion of hers, and the smells alone were driving her mad. Adam and Rebecca stared at the food and shook their heads, as they'd never seen Indian food before.

"Let's clear up in the morning." Sam suggested.

No-one objected, and they all moved into the lounge.

"You're here for another day?" Sam said to Klaus.

"Yes, and then we've got an early afternoon flight, so we'll need to be at the airport by about eleven thirty. Will you take us, Sam?"

He nodded. "Of course. So we have tonight and tomorrow to agree how we're all going to make this work."

There was general agreement in the room.

Elizabeth stood up. "I've only helped a few of these lost souls, and those I haven't are hiding in the shadows, terrified to show themselves. The few I've helped had faith and a belief they were going to a better place, but these others, the majority, died in traumatic circumstances and are still utterly confused and frightened." She looked around the room into the shadowy corners. "They're here now. I've seen and heard them. I can show them to you if you like?"

There were a few moments silence, before Klaus spoke. "You should show us." Everyone in the room nodded nervously.

Elizabeth walked over to the Bose and iPod, flicked the switch on the wall and scrolled through artists until she found what she was looking for.

"They seem to like music." She pressed play and the distinctive guitar of Mark Knopfler and Dire Straits broke the silence.

'These mist covered mountains
Are home now for me
But my home is the lowlands
And always will be
Some day you'll return me
Your valleys and your farms
And you'll no longer burn
To be brothers in arms'

There was a nervous silence which no-one wanted to break, but Sam whispered to Elizabeth. "Will this work?"

"Give them a few moments. They've never had an audience before."

Sam smiled and crossed his fingers.

Knopfler started singing the haunting lyrics again.

'Through these fields of destruction
Baptisms of fire
I've witnessed all your suffering
As the battle raged higher'

There was a soft murmur from the shadows. Karsten and Klaus peered over their shoulders into the dim corners of the room. Adam and Rebecca began to smile. Jane felt fear, but one which was more of the unknown than of a danger to herself. Elizabeth smiled and held her finger to her lips for quiet.

'And though they did hurt me so bad
In the fear and alarm
You did not desert me
My brothers in arms'

Almost imperceptibly, barely discernible shapes began to emerge from the shadows. Klaus gasped, Karsten swallowed hard, and Sam stared in disbelief. Elizabeth smiled as the lost souls moved into the light. Adam and Rebecca moved forward to greet them, and Jane started to weep.

From each corner and side of the room, faceless Tommies were shuffling into the light.

Adam suddenly stopped dead in his tracks and stared at Rebecca. "Is that?"

She nodded, tears streaming down her cheeks.

"Jack!?"

'Now the suns gone to hell
And the moon's riding high
Let me bid you farewell
Every man has to die'

One of the Tommies lifted his head and stared across the room at Adam and Rebecca. "Mam? Dad?"

Adam and Rebecca ran to him, and the three hugged each other. Their first contact in almost a century.

"But how are you here? And you have a face." Adam said. "Sam saw your grave at …" He looked across at Sam.

"Dozinghem." Sam answered. "It was Dozinghem, Adam, and it was clearly marked with Jack's name and details. He was killed in 1917."

Jack shook his head. "We all have faces. Can't you see them?"

Adam and Rebecca looked around at the soldiers, and could see that all of them had faces.

Adam turned to Sam. "You can't see their faces?"

Sam shook his head. "None of us can."

Klaus walked closer to Sam. "They exist in the same reality as the spirits of the soldiers. If they can see their faces then identification will be so much easier. A good reason for them to stay?"

Sam smiled and nodded.

Adam turned back to Jack. "Who's buried at Dozy … ham?"

Jack rubbed the back of his neck. "Ralph Peters is buried there."

"How?" Adam asked.

"He needed some leave and I didn't want to use mine, so we sort of swapped identities. He was killed when he was me. *I've* got a vague memory of our sergeant shouting mortars, and then … nothing, until I woke up in a casualty clearing station." He closed his eyes trying to recall his last moments spent in an earlier reality. "A doctor … he … he helped me. He stopped all the pain, then there was … there was nothing, and then I was here. Where is this? Most of us think we're in hell. Being punished for the killing. Are we, Dad? Are you in hell with us?"

Adam held him close and kissed the side of his head. "No son, you're not in hell. You're home."

Mark Knopfler sang the last of the lyrics. Words which drew all the Tommies into the light of the room

'But it's written in the starlight
And every line in your palm
We're fools to make war
On our brothers in arms'

NINETY-EIGHT

The transport, was as expected, on time to collect Roger and Gloria. Arthur said his goodbyes at breakfast, and left to keep a close watch on James.

Agnes was trying unsuccessfully to hold back her tears, and had already soaked one handkerchief. "I'll miss you both." She sobbed. "Take care. For God's sake take care."

"We'll be fine." Roger said with a standard issue stiff upper lip. "It'll all be over before we even get to the front. The Hun's on the run." He smiled at his unintentional lapse into poetry. "I could be a Sassoon." He smiled at Agnes. "Take care of yourself.

Gloria was having less success in controlling her emotions. "I don't want to go. He's afraid, but won't show it." She whispered in Agnes's ear as they hugged each other. "I want to stay with you."

Agnes held her close and tight. Her opinion of Gloria had changed, for the better, since her first comments about shell shock. "Don't go."

"I have no choice. Orders. Damn orders." She stood back and wiped away her tears, putting on her standard issue brave face. "You take care of yourself and James." She blew a kiss and climbed into the transport behind Roger. They leaned out of the windows and waved goodbye as the transport pulled away down the drive.

"Take care!" Agnes shouted after them.

Arthur was sat with James, who was beginning to become awake and alert. "How are you feeling?" He asked.

James rubbed his eyes, carefully touched his knee, looked down at his wrist and around his quarters. "Bit of a night."

"You could say that."

"To be honest, it's a bit of a blur. What happened?" He raised his hand and winced.

"A simple accident. You tripped and fell. Nothing more."

James shook his head. "Walking around in the dark I suppose?"

Arthur nodded. "Looks like that's what happened. A few things had been knocked over and you were in a heap against the wardrobe."

James smiled in embarrassment.

"How are you feeling? I mean apart from the pain from your wrist and knee."

James seemed to think for a few seconds before answering. "Pretty good, to be honest. It feels like, like a weight's been lifted off my shoulders." He smiled. "Haven't really felt this good for some time. How long will I have these on?" He nodded down to the plaster on his wrist and knee.

Arthur shook his head. "Not my area of expertise I'm afraid." He smiled at James. "What would you the doctor tell you the patient?"

James chuckled. "Be a little more careful?" He looked across at the door, and smiled as Agnes came into the room. "Just discussing my injuries." He explained. "I'd say that it's going to be at least a month before I could use the hand normally again, but the knee I have no experience of what I've damaged. When's your friend coming back?"

"He'll be back today to take a look at you. Probably just after lunch." Arthur smiled reassuringly at Agnes. "Talking of food. Shall I organise some breakfast for you?"

James nodded. "Full English please. If that's possible?"

"I'm certain that Ruth can pull something together that's quite close to that." Arthur stood up and left the room. "I'll leave you two alone."

Agnes sat on the edge of the bed. "You look well, all things considered."

James nodded. "Never felt better, apart from." He lifted his hand and nodded at his knee. "I feel like I've slept for a month."

"You must have needed it."

"You're probably right. Things have been a little fraught over the last few months." He held Agnes's hand. "How are you? You look tired."

She shrugged her shoulders. "I'm fine. You know me."

"Yes I do." He said. "And you don't look well. You're overdoing it, aren't you."

"Possibly, but they need my help."

"They?"

"The patients here at Seale Hayne." She smiled at him. "And now you!"

"Sorry. Bit clumsy I'm afraid." He lowered his eyes in mock shame. "Are Roger or Gloria coming to see me?"

Agnes had been fearing this conversation more than most. "They left early this morning before you woke. They didn't want to disturb you, but they sent their best wishes."

"Left?" James frowned. "Left for where?"

"Should I lie?" Agnes thought. *"Probably best not to."* She swallowed deeply. "They were recalled to France." *"Honesty is the best policy."* She tried to convince herself.

James frown deepened. "Recalled to France?"

"Is there an echo in here?" Agnes tried but failed to inject a little humour.

"Echo?" His frown couldn't get any deeper. "Why wasn't I told about this?"

Agnes stood up and looked down at him in the bed. "Roger said that you knew about it, and you haven't exactly been with us for a few days, so it would have been understandable if you'd forgotten."

"Oh." He almost seemed satisfied with her answer. "Lucky buggers."

Agnes bit her tongue. There was nothing in her vocabulary which could describe what Roger and Gloria were about to do as lucky.

"Shame. I'd have liked to have said goodbye to them. Good egg, Roger. Gloria was a bit, well a bit emotional, but she knew her stuff. Damn good nurse. Troops will love her." He lay back on the bed. "Lucky buggers."

Two months later, Gloria was stationed at a casualty clearing station close to Poperinge. It wasn't the safest of postings, but she felt somehow closer to Roger here, than she would at a base hospital. She was carrying out the part of her job she hated. Washing, preparing and dressing a soldier who'd succumbed to his wounds. As she checked his personal effects, she found a letter which hadn't been posted. The creased, muddy envelope was unsealed, and her first reaction was to pass it onto the officers who'd make sure it got to his nearest and dearest. But the top of the letter was visible and Gloria carefully pulled it out, unfolded it and started to read the soldier's last words.

"Dearest Mol, Hope all is well and the children are being good. I miss them so much. Kiss them good night for me. Has Emma's cold cleared up? Tell Dad and Mam that I'm doing OK. I love you my darling and miss being with you, Emma and Alfie. I don't know if you'll get this. They censor most of our mail. But I wanted you to know the truth. I know you'll make sure everyone knows about what we're suffering over here. God willing I will survive this hell."

The letter finished with a post script.

"We stagger around in the mud, slipping and sliding, tugging our boots out of it every time we take a fresh step. Jerry's shells shower us with filth, they disturb the riddled and broken corpses, and re-shred their putrid flesh into scraps. A lot of the lads have gone missing. If you get hit, the chances are that you'll slip into some yawning shell-hole full of greyly opaque water concealing unmentionable things and drown there.

For pity's sake. Tell them about us."

Gloria sat on the bed and wept, folded the letter, put it carefully back in the envelope and in her apron pocket. She stood up and looked down at the unshaven white face cut down in the first flush of life.

"I will make sure she gets this." She thought. *"And everyone will know how you've suffered. Now rest in peace."*

Roger, to his great personal embarrassment, had been awarded the Victoria Cross, which he'd asked his commanding officer to keep private. He'd asked to be sent straight back to the front, had been promoted to lieutenant and posted to the 8th Battalion, 7th Somerset Light Infantry, where he'd taken command of a troop of thirty soldiers. He was sat in his dugout with his 2nd lieutenant having a mug of very early morning tea, before going over the top, to retake Polygon Wood. The weather was favourably dry and outside a mist was rising which would provide them with unexpected cover from the German guns.

"Polygon Wood and we follow the barrage, sir?" 2nd Lieutenant Peter Le Fevre nervously said. He knew of Roger's gallantry and his VC.

"Yes, Peter. Mind you, there's not much of a wood left. Shelling's taken care of most of that. There'll be a five layer creeping bombardment, and we must follow this with the precise timing we've discussed." Roger tipped his head forward, checking his 2nd lieutenant's understanding of their orders. "First time, Peter?" Roger asked casually.

"Umm, yes, sir." He stood to attention. Attempting to show his commitment and bravery. "Looking forward to giving Jerry some steel like you did, sir. When will you get the VC?"

Roger smiled. "It's only a piece of metal. Everyone who was there deserves one." He patted Peter's shoulder, and quickly changed the subject. "When did you get to France, Peter?"

"About three weeks ago, sir."

"So you've not seen any action as yet?"

"No, sir, but I'm as ready as I'll ever be."

"You know the survival rate of officers, don't you, Peter?"

"Yes, sir."

"Doesn't worry you at all?"

"No sir. Just as much chance of being run over by a bus, sir."

Roger smiled. What this officer lacked in experience, he made up for in bravado, and if that motivated his men, then damn good for him. "Where are you from, Peter?"

"Bristol, sir."

"Like it there?"

"Born and bred. All my family's there. New wife and baby." He smiled with pride. "Young boy. Charlie."

"Good. Well we'd better make sure you see them again."

"Yes, sir." The 2nd lieutenant was still at attention.

"At ease, Peter. What's the time now?"

"Five twenty, sir."

"OK." Roger drained the remainder of his tea and stood up. A private handed him his helmet and revolver. "Thank you, Smith. See you later for tea and cake?"

"Absolutely, sir. Victoria sponge is in the oven as we speak."

"Good man. Save me a large slice. I'll bring back some German sausages."

Private Smith smiled at his lieutenant's euphemism.

Roger checked he had everything, and for a final time synchronised his watch with 2nd lieutenant Le Fevre. "Good luck." He shook him firmly by the hand. "Follow orders and do nothing too heroic."

They walked up the wooden steps from the dug out, along the duck boards smiling and encouraging the assembled troops. "Morning everyone. Ready to dish it out?"

There was a general murmuring of expletives and nodding of heads. Despite Roger's best efforts, everyone knew of his bravery and would have marched into hell and back for him.

"Excellent." Roger looked at his watch. "Five minutes, everyone. Get to the ladders. My whistle and we go over together."

Outside, Roger was the perfect example of the British officer, but inside his stomach was in a turmoil, his mouth was as dry as sand, his hands were bathed in sweat and he'd developed a twitch in his right eye. All of which were fairly standard reactions to going over the top. So far despite everything, he'd beaten the odds, and was still confident that he'd see Gloria again. What concerned him was the burning sensation at the base of his back which was moving slowly up his spine like red hot coals. He rubbed his back and checked his watch. "Two minutes." He climbed halfway up the short ladder, revolver in his right hand and whistle in his left. He watched the second hand inexorably start a one minute countdown. The searing heat in his back had reached his neck, it felt as if his spine, vertebra by vertebra, was fusing. "Thirty seconds!"

"At least the mist will give us some element of cover. God be with us." He thought. And at precisely five thirty a.m., Roger put the whistle between his lips and blew as hard as he could.

There was a shrill chorus of whistles as the trenches vomited their human targets into no man's land. Roger reached the top of the ladder and with revolver in hand marched slowly into the mist. As he took his first steps, his body momentarily went rigid, and his vision blurred. It lasted for less than a second, and he put it down to the heat of moment, but the real cause of his reaction, was a little more complicated.

Lidsay, the 49% Ivor, who'd split from Roger, hadn't made it home to High Wood. The attraction back to Roger, had been too strong for the channel of energy flowing to High Wood. Ivor felt dizzy and confused, and had no idea where he was. The fact that his spirit was co-existing in the body of a lieutenant in World War 1, would have blown most of his neural network, so his brain was doing its best to keep him in ignorance to protect itself. The problem it had was that Ivor was receiving the same external stimuli as Roger was. Ivor's self, worked as hard as it could to shut these out, but their intensity proved too much. Ivor began to see, hear and smell what Roger was directly experiencing. The safest option his neural network had was to simply shut down.

NINETY-NINE

Sam, Klaus, Karsten and Elizabeth were stood in the middle of the lounge, surrounded by translucent shapes, all standing to attention.

"What do we do?" Sam whispered to anyone who was listening.

There was silence.

"Any ideas?" Sam said a little louder.

"Where are the others?" Elizabeth asked.

"I thought they were here." Karsten replied.

"They're in the kitchen." Klaus said.

"Jane!" Sam shouted. The assembled mass moved a few paces back.

Jane, Adam and Rebecca tried to run into the lounge, but the stairs, landing, hall and lounge door were packed solidly with soldiers standing shoulder to shoulder.

"I didn't realise there were so many." Rebecca said. "What do we do?"

"No previous experience." Jane replied.

"Now then. Give us a bit of room! Stand aside!" Adam barked.

There was an immediate and coordinated response as a channel opened between the men. "Follow me." Adam said quietly. "Not sure how long they'll believe I'm NCO material."

A narrow but clear path led them into the lounge and up to the four statues.

"Problem?" Jane chuckled.

"Answer?" Sam replied.

"Not a clue," Jane said.

"Marvellous," Sam replied.

"You?" Jane asked.

"Soiled." Sam eventually replied smiling.

"Unfortunate." Jane chuckled again.

"Very amusing, but what on earth do we do?" Klaus said.

"I'd suggest we all go back to the kitchen and decide what to do next," Sam said.

Everyone nodded and squeezed their way down the narrow corridor between the troops.

"Does anyone have any previous experience of this?" Sam asked as they stood around the kitchen table.

Klaus nodded. "The closest I have seen to this was in Verdun. We were helping a couple with six German soldiers who'd been buried in what became the foundations of a house. When the couple were having work done in the cellar, they disturbed them."

"And what did you do?" Sam did his best to hide his frustration.

"We showed them the way."

"But how?" Sam asked.

"We didn't have any spirit help," he looked across at Adam, Jane and Rebecca, "so a local medium communicated with them for us. She told them they needed to move on to meet their loved ones. They seemed to listen and ..."

"And?" Sam wasn't hiding his frustration.

Klaus frowned. "At first they did nothing, but when Heidrich opened the portal in the house, they could see the way."

"There was a portal in the house?" Elizabeth said.

"We were very fortunate. Without it we would have had to move them to Thiepval." Klaus answered.

"Move." Elizabeth said.

"Yes, my dear. Move. There are circumstances where souls are too far from a ley line or transmitter, and we need to contain them and remove them from their place of rest. At these times we use a container and then transport them to one of the main transmitters. From there they will find there final place of departure." Klaus explained.

"Do you have any with you?" Sam asked optimistically.

Klaus shook his head. "They are designed for, let's say, smaller numbers."

"How small?" Sam asked.

"Two, three at the most." He answered.

Sam sat down at the table, resting his head on his hands. "And you have the most experience of these things." He said sarcastically.

"We've never had the support of anyone from the other side, and we've never had a house like this one. Your Aunt and Uncle's death left these souls here, with no-one here to guide them on their way. That's why they are all so confused." Klaus waved his arm towards the hall. "Firstly they suffered the trauma of a violent death, then instead of moving on to the other side, they find themselves in limbo, floating somewhere between here and there, and with no sense of being. Eventually they arrive here, then more and more arrive and so they sit around kicking their heels, frustrated, bored, becoming angry as no-one tells them what is happening, *until* ... Let's hope we never find out what happens if they reach *until*. They're travellers, who find themselves locked in limbo and with no information on when they will leave." He paused to let things sink in. "They listened to Adam, and they will not, or possibly cannot hear us, but they can hear him. And they may listen to Rebecca and Jane, although being women, who knows with these men of their time."

"What should we do?" Sam persisted.

"Their path home lies through Elizabeth." Klaus answered.

"But she can't possibly manage all of them."

"Not quickly, no, but Adam, Jane and Rebecca can give them information on when they can expect to be leaving, and identify them for Elizabeth. If it was us Sam, then isn't the most frustrating part of being stuck in an airport waiting for a delayed flight, simply the not knowing. Expectation management, Sam. It is a tried and tested technique. It works. It will work here. I know it."

"For certain?" Sam asked.

"Nothing in life, other than death is certain, but what *is* certain is that we have to do something, or we may start to find out what *is* after until." Klaus placed the palms of his hands firmly on the table, ending the discussion. He turned to Elizabeth. "How long does the process take?"

Elizabeth shrugged. "So far I've helped only one soul. Only one Klaus, and now we have, how many, probably hundreds." She shook her head.

"How long Elizabeth. How long did it take?" Klaus asked gently but firmly.

She looked up at him. "Probably about five minutes, but I was exhausted after it."

"So if we said that with rest between each, could you manage one an hour?" Klaus asked.

"Probably. But at the start I'd have to play it by ear."

"Of course, my dear. But let's assume, not a good word I know, but let's assume you could manage one an hour. So let's say on average you might be able to help, how many shall we say, six to eight a day?"

Elizabeth looked pleadingly at Sam.

"Don't you think we're expecting too much this early?" Sam strongly suggested.

"We don't have the luxury of being able to have a long learning curve. This is new to all of us, and we will all stay until we are happy Elizabeth, and everyone else involved can cope." He waved his arm again in the direction of the hall. "Let's at least try one and see how we go from there?" Klaus tilted his head to one side and smiled.

Elizabeth nodded. "Just the one. It's getting very late."

Klaus reassured her. "You are right Elizabeth, it is late, so we should not start until the morning."

"That's fine." Elizabeth said.

"Adam can you talk to the soldiers and try to explain what is happening. Is that OK?" Klaus said.

He nodded his head. "I'll try."

HUNDRED

James mental state was much improved, and Arthur was pleased with the progress he'd made, but this was threatened by the fracture to his wrist. The break had been more severe than at first thought, and important nerves had been damaged in his right hand. James had very little feeling in any of his fingers, and for a surgeon this was almost certainly career ending.

"Heard anything from Roger?" James asked Arthur as he entered his quarters. After two months James's knee wasn't fully healed, but with support from elastic bandages, he could walk with the a stick. But James, more than anything, wanted news on his wrist.

Arthur smiled and held out an envelope to him. "One for you, and one for me. We'll have to compare notes.

James clumsily opened the envelope, and swore under his breath, carefully unfolded the two sheets of paper, and sat on the bed to read Roger's latest epistle.

'My dear chap, Greetings from the front and best wishes to Agnes.

I have written separately to Arthur. How's the knee and wrist? Coming on well I hope. I am now Lieutenant Lidsay VC. I'll be a Major before you yet.'

James jaw literally dropped to the floor. "He's won a VC!"

Arthur dropped his letter and stared at James. "A VC?"

"Just drops it in the letter like he's won a raffle."

"How did he win it?"

"No idea. He just says," James looked back at the letter, "I am now Lieutenant Lidsay VC."

Arthur sat speechless, praying this news wouldn't undo all the progress he'd achieved with James. "What else does he say?"

"Mmmm?"

"Anything else of interest in the letter?"

"Mmmm?" James carried on silently reading the letter.

The cuisine still doesn't compare to Seale Hayne. Still enjoying Maconochie's out of my Dixie lid. Managed to get my hands on a few tins of Van Camps Pork and Beans, Fray Bentos bully beef and a tin of plum and apple jam which makes the standard issue biscuits almost palatable.

Our last ration carriers were all killed by mortar fire. The water and food was scattered about the mud and shell-holes. Water is so much more precious now than victuals. It's everywhere 'but not a drop to drink.' The full petrol cans are cruel burdens to shoulder over a mile or so of the battle-field, and the water still tastes like petrol.

Real treat yesterday, Private Bird, our platoon scavenger, got his hands on some bacon. For anything from an hour to two hours the most vicious noise to be heard in the trench was the sizzling of bacon. Of course this couldn't last. Some machine gunner, cheerful from his meal, broke the spell with the 'pop-pop-pop-pop' call on his Vickers, which didn't fail to evoke the slower 'pop-pop' from some heavy machine-gun in the German lines.

Looks like we'll be seeing action again quite soon. Obviously can't say anything, but it will be good to be having another crack at the Bosche. The men are all up for it.

Some men further up the line have been stuck in mud up to their waists. Where we are it varies from ankle to waist deep and it is almost impossible to keep rifles clean. Therefore, rifle inspection seems almost pointless, it is monotonous and unsatisfactory, as a few hours later the rifles are rusty and muddy again, and need another inspection.

Spent yesterday showing our new snipers how to search the trench systematically from left to right, noting the exact position of anything that looked like a loop-hole, or steel plate, and especially the thickness of the wire, what kind, and whether it was grey and new, or rusty-red and old; whether there were any gaps in it, and where they were.

The last twenty four hours have really been a blank. The usual rounds at night, visiting sentries, the usual slipping and stumbling over abandoned trenches and mud-holes in the dark, the usual stand to arms at daybreak, and then to sleep. Which is where I am bound next.

I'll write again as soon as I can.

Best wishes to everyone

Roger

James neatly folded the paper, put it back in the envelope and placed it in his bedside cabinet. "When am I getting out of here, Arthur? Much as I enjoy your company, I want to get back to France before the whole damn show's over." James said.

"Roger is due just after lunch, so I'd suggest we sit down with him and see what additional physiotherapy you need to help your knee, wrist and those fingers. Any more sensation in them?" Arthur asked.

James shook his head. "I'm finished as a surgeon." He held up his hands. "These are the tools of my trade. Without them I couldn't even consider sewing up the seam on a dress."

"If, and I emphasise if, they don't sufficiently recover, there are a multitude of other specialities in medicine other than surgery." He let the idea sit with James for a few seconds. "You know I'm always looking for more expert help here at Seale Hayne."

"Surgery is my, life Arthur."

"Isn't the preservation of life as important?"

"Of course, but this has always been my path, my raison d'être."

Arthur moved away from the subject. "How are you sleeping?"

"Like a baby. Eight hours a night."

"Nightmares?"

James shook his head.

"Thoughts on shell shock?"

"Difficult to treat. Your work here at Seale Hayne leads world thinking."

"You've no doubts that the physical symptoms are produced by the mental trauma the patients have suffered?"

James shook his head and smiled. "I know where you're going with this, Arthur. Those days are past. I remember the bed. I remember how I was. I understand what happened to me and that I could relapse if I was exposed to the same stimuli again." He smiled as Agnes entered his quarters. "Come to check on me as well?"

"Good morning, James." Agnes said.

He smiled. "Good morning, Agnes."

"Better?" She replied.

They laughed at each other.

"It's so good to see you happy," Agnes said with a crooked smile.

Arthur stood up. "I'll leave you young lovers to yourselves. I'll come back when Roger arrives." He turned to leave, but stopped and spoke to James over his shoulder. "You should think seriously about alternatives. Nerve damage, as I'm sure you know, is extremely difficult to repair. Think about what I said?"

James slowly, very slowly, nodded.

Agnes looked after Arthur and frowned. "What are you thinking about?"

James sucked his teeth. "Giving up surgery."

"What!"

He lifted his injured hand and stared at it. "The nerves don't seem to be healing." He paused, clearly very emotional. "How many one-handed surgeons have you met?"

Agnes sat on the chair next to him. "You have a gift which doesn't have to be expressed through surgery, there are so many other branches and specialities in medicine. So many new discoveries still to be made."

"I know, but surgery is my passion." He rubbed his affected fingers. "Arthur wants me to work with him here at Seale Hayne."

"That's wonderful." Agnes thought carefully before going on. "You want to help get soldiers back to the front?"

"Of course."

"Treating soldiers here will support the effort at the front. This isn't a surgical repair, but it's a repair, isn't it?"

James looked her in the eye and forced a smile. "I suppose so."

"Thank God!" Agnes thought. *"Progress."*

"But ..."

Agnes pressed her index finger against his lips.

"But me no buts, James."

"Thank you, Mrs Centlivre." James laughed.

"It's good to hear you laughing." She said. "I haven't heard you laugh for months." She kissed him tenderly on the lips, hiding her concern that James was still burying the trauma and stresses of France.

Roger led his platoon into the swirling mist as part of the second wave, encouraging them to keep alert and be prepared for the fight to come. A breeze started to disperse the mist and reveal the landscape in front of them. The German line followed points of eminence, always providing them with a commanding view of No Man's Land. Immediately in front, and spreading from left to right as far as the eye could see, was stark evidence that the first wave of the attack had been brutally repulsed. Hundreds of dead, many of them strung out like wreckage washed up to a high-water mark. As many had died on the wire as in open ground, and they hung in grotesque postures like fish caught in a net. Some looked as if they were praying. They'd died on their knees and the wire had stopped them falling. A 2nd lieutenant, Roger knew, was hanging on the wire, and troops were trying to lift him off, but it was clear that the Germans had two or three fixed rifles firing at his body every few seconds, riddling it with bullets, certain they would kill anyone who tried to rescue him. He swallowed hard. He'd seen so many die that he was becoming oblivious to the horror and pain, but the sight of his friend twitching on the wire as bullet after bullet hit him, and the brave men falling alongside him, had a greater impact than he'd imagined. Concentrated machine gun fire commanding every inch of the wire, had done its terrible work.

"They must have been reinforcing the wire for months. You can barely see daylight through it." Roger thought desperately.

Ivor's senses had recovered, and were straining to look away from the carnage, but the images were almost hypnotic, compelling in their horror. How was this possible? How could men do this to their fellow men? He'd been taken as a schoolboy to an abattoir, but the scene in front of him, made that look like an average scene from a Bruce Willis film. The stuttering images he'd seen in so many documentaries on the Great War, were here in glorious colour and 3D, with the added special effects of smell and taste.

"No CGI here." He thought. *"I have to get away from this. From him. This idiot's going to be shot or blown to pieces, and me along with him. But for God's sake how? What the hell is happening to me? My God, police work and Gloria were like heaven compared to this. If there is a God then please get me out of him, and here! I will change. I must be dead. I knew that I'd end up down below. Shit this really is hell. Is that what wars are? Hell spewed out onto the surface of the earth, and the Devil playing Risk with real armies?*

The second and this time final separation began, as Ivor's stress levels strained to their limit the bonds holding Roger and him together. The molecular velcro strips bonding them together were tearing apart. Ivor felt as if someone was ripping an enormous plaster from his body, and then he lost the nearest thing he had to consciousness.

Roger shuddered as Ivor began to separate from him for the final time. His head was suddenly becoming clearer, his sight and hearing sharper. His thought processes were focused again on the battle and his men. He reviewed the situation he was confronted by, and it was obvious to him, that in the equal way the dead seemed to be spread out, there were no gaps in the wire.

There was an eerie silence, before the next barrage, as the platoon stared in disbelief and terror at the horrific scene. The creeping barrage started again, but the salvoes exploded too far in front of them.

"Pick up the pace men, we need to be closer to the barrage." Roger shouted.

They increased their pace and got closer to the ear shattering explosions, which were throwing storm clouds of earth, and body parts of the unburied dead, raining down on them. The wire seemed to be simply rising into the air, and then gracefully falling back into an even greater tangled mess.

"Jesus!" A corporal shouted, as the ragged rotting remains of the torso of what had once been a Grenadier Guardsman knocked him onto his back. He clawed at it, but only succeeded in tearing the torso into more stinking pieces. He started to scream as more and more rotten flesh and guts covered him.

Roger kept the troops as close to the creeping barrage as he dared. A shell exploded overhead and showered them with shrapnel. A shard of red hot metal, the size of a tea plate, tore through his elbow amputating his lower arm and cauterising it at the same moment. He felt no pain, and it was only when he tried to raise his arm, that he saw the smoking stump where the lower half of his arm used to be. Blood loss and shock dropped him to the ground like a stone. He heard the slow repetitive 'pop-pop-pop-pop' of German machine-guns, and as he looked around through the smoke, his expression froze as he saw his platoon being cut to ribbons by the monsoon of German bullets. Bloody pieces of the platoon, were falling around him like joints of beef in a Butcher's window. The ground, already soaked, was awash with crimson blood. He fell back into the mud, his arm still numb, but his emotions agonising. An arm landed close to his head. He stared at it, and recognised on the back of the hand, the unmistakable tattoo of a dragon. The hand still clamped in a death grip, on the butt of his pistol. The barrel blown away. Roger knew his 2nd lieutenant's pride in his heritage and country of birth, Wales. He closed his eyes and lay back. Death would soon come and release him from this horror. Surely even hell itself couldn't be as bad as this. He'd soon be walking the Downs again with his Border Collies, Arnie and Furgle, stopping at the Crown for a pint of Solomon's best, sitting under the oak tree in his garden reading Shelley, dead-heading the roses, watching the bats in the early evening swooping and soaring around the garden, sleeping in a bed with clean crisp linen, listening to the silence, smelling the fresh air, drinking a cool glass of water which wasn't tainted with petrol and above all else, not living in a slaughter-house.

The massive trauma fractured any of the tenuous remaining links between Roger and Ivor. Ivor's spirit coalesced into a pure ball of energy, which flew high above the battlefield. A signal in search of a beacon. It hovered, sending out pulses, which were finally detected by a ley-line to Thiepval, and from there to High Wood. It burrowed into the death soaked earth of the battlefield, until it found the ley-line, and streamed into it like a leaf caught in a flooded storm drain. At Thiepval it was connected to a High Wood ley line, and the portal out.

HUNDRED-ONE

The next morning at about ten, Sam walked into the gallery with a flask of coffee, digestive biscuits and a bar of chocolate. Elizabeth, as she'd asked, had been on her own for about an hour, and Sam was relieved at what he saw. She was sat in a green canvas camping chair, making notes on a journalist's writing pad. She looked up and smiled as Sam walked towards her.

"How are you?" Sam asked.

"Surprisingly relaxed." Elizabeth replied. She stood up and took the flask from him. "Coffee?"

He nodded.

"Perfect. Just what the doctor ordered." She screwed off the plastic lid and unscrewed the stopper. Steam and the satisfying aroma of fresh coffee caressed her nose and cheeks. "I'll have some of that chocolate please."

Sam snapped a strip off the bar, handed it to Elizabeth, and smiled as she dipped it into the hot coffee. It was one her great pleasures in life. "Anyone passed over yet?" He said.

Between mouthfuls of melting chocolate and sips of steaming coffee, she told Sam that one soul, Lieutenant Alfred Doyle, had happily moved on. "He was smiling, Sam." She recalled. "He looked so … so … oh happy's not the word … so at peace. It was as if a great weight had been lifted from him." She smiled, finished the chocolate and started on the digestive biscuits. "It takes it out of you."

Sam chuckled.

"It does!" She laughed.

"So, what happens next?"

"I wait I suppose. Wait for the next, then the next and …" She sat down again thinking about the size of the task in front of her.

Sam walked close to her and put his arm around her. "We don't have to do this you know. Say the word and we'll get a flight to somewhere sunny on the other side of the world."

She shook her head. "Sounds wonderful, but if you'd seen his face, Sam, felt his relief and seen through his eyes the thoughts of seeing those he loved again, then there is only one thing I can do." She kissed his hand. "You see that don't you?"

Sam smiled. "Of course, but for now, I'll stay with you." He raised his eyebrows. "If that's OK?"

Elizabeth didn't answer.

"Elizabeth?"

"I don't know if that's a good idea, Sam. This is such an intimate thing, that I wonder if anyone else is present, they may not come to me."

Sam moved away and looked into her eyes. "I'll only do what you think is right."

"Let me help another and then we can talk again."

Sam put the flask, biscuits and the few remaining pieces of chocolate on the floor beside her, bent down and kissed her on both cheeks. "Be careful. Call if you need me. I'll just be below on the landing."

"I'll be fine. They don't want to hurt me. I think that after all they've seen and done so many years ago, that all they want is peace." She stood up from the chair, hugged Sam and kissed him. "Now go."

He nodded, walked to the stairs and made his way down to the landing.

Adam stepped into the cramped hall at the back of the crowded ranks of soldiers.

"Just tell them what's happening." Rebecca whispered.

"It isn't that easy." He replied. "I need to understand what's happening myself before I can tell them."

"Tell them what you know. Start there."

Adam smiled. "I'll try."

Rebecca turned to Jane. "Do you think he'll be OK?"

Jane shrugged. "I think if anyone of us had been told that this is what we'd be doing, then we've had had them committed. But, here we are." She scratched the side of her head. "I think he'll be fine." She said unconvincingly.

They held hands as if their lives depended upon it.

"Everyone!" Adam said. "Please!" They all stood facing the lounge, a low murmuring just barely audible. "Everyone, please!" He turned around to Rebecca. "This is hopeless."

She took his hand and smiled. "They're soldiers, Adam. Speak to them like Tommies."

He nodded and turned to face them. "'Tent-ion!"

The hall echoed, as the mass of troops snapped to attention and span on their heels to face Adam.

"Stand easy." He ordered. "Can everyone hear me?"

There was a general nodding of heads.

"I'll speak to those of you in the hall first, is that understood." The nodding was repeated. "Good." He turned his head and grinned at Rebecca and Jane. "I'm Staff Sergeant Adam Morbeck, and this won't be easy for you to understand. Please listen and then I'll try to answer any questions. These ladies are also here to try to answer your questions."

Klaus and Karsten appeared behind him in the lounge doorway.

"These gentlemen are also here to help you. There is nothing and no-one to fear in this place. Everyone is here to help you."

Heads turned and whispered to each other. Someone shouted from the back. "Thank you, Staff Sergeant, first piece of information we've had. I'm Captain Chris Forster, Grenadier Guards." He walked close to Adam. "What the bally hell is going on? I've no idea how long we've been here, why we're here or how we got here. Mixed regiments, mixed ranks, won't do, Staff Sergeant. Not good for morale. Men need to know their place, don't you know. Glad you're here. Get some action at last. Anything I can do? Uniform's not quite right?"

Adam saluted. " Waiting for a replacement, sir. The other was torn to shreds on the wire." Adam paused believing that he'd given the captain a plausible excuse for his uniform." Nothing you can do at the moment, sir, but I'm sure your presence will be of great help to the men's morale."

"Thank you, Staff Sergeant." he turned and stood at ease close to Adam. "I'll stay here. Gives everything a bit more authority."

Adam nodded. "Yes, sir. Thank you, sir."

"Now everyone." The captain bellowed. "Listen to the staff sergeant. Listen well." He turned his head to Adam. "All yours, Staff Sergeant."

"Thank you, sir." Adam snapped his heels together.

Klaus spoke quietly to Karsten. "The British. How did they ever win two World Wars?" He smiled.

"Stand on a chair." Captain Forster suggested. "Easier for them to see you."

Adam nodded and turned to Rebecca. "Could you get me a chair?"

She walked back to the kitchen, grabbed a chair and took it to Adam.

Feeling very uncomfortable, he stood on the chair and looked down on the sea of faces looking expectantly up at him. "This is not going to be easy to say." He began. "Please listen to everything I have to say." He cleared his throat. "We are in a place where we are waiting to move on to another place."

"Bit non-specific, Staff Sergeant." Captain Forster said.

"Has to be, sir. Need to know."

Captain Forster tapped the side of his nose. "Understood."

"We ... we ..." Adam swallowed hard. "We ..."

"Spit it out, Staff Sergeant."

"We are all dead." He let the words hang in the air. "We were all killed in action, but our bodies were never found." Heads were turning and shaking. "I understand that this is difficult."

"Bloody right it is." A private shouted from the back.

"We can't leave this to him." Klaus said to Karsten. "It's completely unfair." Klaus stepped forward. "I'll take over."

"Is that a good idea?" Karsten asked. "A German telling them what's happened?"

Klaus smiled and shook his head. "Probably not. Jane, tell Adam that I'm Belgian. An ally. And I will explain what has happened."

The soldiers were getting raucous.

"If I'm dead, then how am I standing here?"

"He's right."

"Load of bloody rubbish if you ask me."

"This is a POW camp."

"Where's the senior officer?"

"Who put you in charge?"

Elizabeth tapped an ever increasingly nervous Adam on the shoulder. "Klaus will speak to them. Tell them he's a Belgian officer, General Wouters. You will need to tell Klaus what they say and do."

Adam looked back and frowned. "General Wouters."

Elizabeth nodded. "Tell them he's in civvies."

Adam turned to the noisy crowd and Captain Forster raised his hand and ordered silence. Adam smiled in thanks and explained to the hushed ranks what was going to happen.

"General Wouters?" Captain Forster queried. "Never heard of the man."

Klaus turned to Jane. "Explain to the captain that I can see him but he needs to let me hear him."

Jane quickly spoke to Captain Forster who nodded in understanding.

"I'm a recent appointment." Klaus said to what he still saw as a faceless captain. "I'm sure that I can explain to the men what is happening."

Captain Forster moved to one side. "Can you hear me now?"

Klaus nodded.

"I'd use the chair," Captain Forster suggested.

Klaus nodded, and changed places with Adam.

There was a lot of murmuring from the troops.

"Silence!" Captain Forster ordered. "I will not tolerate such insubordination. This is General Wouters. He is a Belgian and will explain things to you." He turned to Klaus. "General."

"Thank you Captain." Klaus turned to what he couldn't see was a sea of scowling faces. "Why you are here, is difficult for anyone to understand." He held up a copy of the Times. "To make your understanding a little easier, I am going to give this to your captain, and I will let him read the date on it."

Captain Forster smiled and took the newspaper from Klaus. His smile immediately disappeared as he read the date. He looked up at Klaus, his eyes wide with shock. "How can this be?"

There were whisperings among the soldiers as the Captain's reaction was passed from one soldier to the next.

"It is correct." Klaus calmly replied to the Captain. "Let's go into the kitchen, and I'll try to explain. It will probably be better then if *you* speak to your men."

Captain Forster looked *shell shocked*.

Klaus spoke to the troops. "We will just be a few minutes. Your captain has some questions for me. We will not be long." He turned to Adam and Sam before leaving. "Keep an eye on them. If things begin to turn ugly, call us."

They nodded and turned to face the now ever increasingly agitated mass.

Klaus and Captain Forster sat around the table.

"You saw the date?" Klaus asked, not being able to gauge any of the captain's reactions.

"Yes, but, but surely this must, it must be … it's a misprint. Isn't it?" The captain almost whispered.

"It is no misprint. That is today's date. The year is 2014."

"No, not possible. How … I mean …"

"Look around the room. Does this look like any kitchen you ever lived or ate in?"

The Captain looked around, frowned, shook his head and sighed.

Klaus spoke to Karsten who was stood in the doorway. "Turn on the TV."

Karsten walked across the kitchen and using the remote control turned on the TV. HD colour images of a Spanish football match appeared on the screen.

Captain Forster's jaw literally hit the floor. "How, they are, moving, real … do they live … colour … how …"

"Captain, for you, all this is all a level of shock which I cannot even try to understand."

Captain Forster's eyes were wide open, unblinking, fixed on the screen.

"Captain." Klaus tapped the table.

The captain looked away and managed to close his gaping mouth.

"The truth is this." Klaus took a deep breath. "The War was won by Britain and her allies in 1918, and it is now 2014. It's nearly a hundred years later, is it likely that you and your men wouldn't have aged?"

Captain Forster shook his head.

"You have no recollection of the War?"

"Yes, a great deal, but it all stops abruptly. For me everything stopped at … it must have been, or was it, no it was Cambrai. But after that … I seem to have … here."

"When your memories ended at Cambrai," Klaus paused, he needed to be sensitive about the next things he said, "when they stopped, everything stopped. What is your last memory?"

Captain Forster looked up at the ceiling. "I was leading an attack on a German defensive position." He paused, searching his mind for anything. "Sergeant Philips was next to me … we heard the pop-pop-pop of their machine-guns … they cut him off at the knees. Lieutenant Marple … he … Oh my God … he was hit in the chest. Went down like a sack of potatoes. They were falling around me … falling like … like freshly cut saplings. A few of us … we … we reached their trench. I shot two of them. Corporal Mann … he … he shouted something. What was it?" His eyes suddenly closed as the memory opened up for him. "He shouted grenade." He put his head in his hands. "He just exploded into a thousand bloody pieces, and then there was heat, heat and searing pain … and then nothing." He looked up at Klaus. "I died. I died, didn't I? We all did, didn't we?"

Klaus nodded. "Yes Captain you were killed in action, but you were never found. You are still recorded as Missing in Action."

Captain Forster nodded, and stared at the floor. "Bit of a shock really. Thought that we were just in some … not really sure what."

"You are still what made Captain Forster you. All that has gone is your physical body, but your spirit, your essence, is what has survived the years. It is this that needs to move on, and reunite with those you loved who have already passed over."

Captain Forster raised his eyes and looked directly at Klaus. "The troopers are all dead?"

Klaus nodded.

"But why are we here? What is this place?"

"Because you've never, this is not easy, because you were never laid to rest, your soul cannot find peace. It is stuck here, caught in an in-between world called Purgatory, and you need to find final rest. You need to meet up again with those you loved. They were never able to find peace, not truly knowing where you were or what had happened to you. We are a group who can give you that peace. We can help you move on to join them. Some call it Heaven, others have different names, but it is the place where all souls meet again in final peace. We are here to help you make that last journey. High Wood, this house is, is a gateway to that final resting place. There are people here who can open that door for you. For you and your men."

Captain Forster looked like a rabbit caught in the headlights.

"Please take a moment. This is, well it's almost too much to expect anyone to comprehend."

Captain Forster nodded. "Let me speak to the men. I'll do it in small groups. I may need your help. Probably will, so please don't go anywhere."

Klaus raised his eyebrows. "You are certain about this?"

Captain Forster nodded. "You have an odd Belgian accent, general."

"Mea culpa, Captain. My name is Klaus Bauer. I was a general in the war which came not long after yours, and I am German."

"So even our enemies are part of this?"

Klaus smiled. "Enemies no more, Captain. We lost both the wars, and we lost millions of men, many of whom, like you, are still caught in limbo. We help everyone who was killed and is still missing."

"Is there somewhere I could speak to small groups of men?"

Klaus nodded. "We'll get out of here and let your men in in groups of five?"

Captain Forster nodded. "That should be fine. We'll have to play this by a very large ear."

Klaus and the others left a shocked Captain Forster sitting at the kitchen table, while they organised the troops.

Ten minutes later, after some uncomfortable conversations, they managed to get the agreement of the men, that three small groups would speak with the captain, and they would then decide amongst themselves if any others would meet him. This seemed a reasonable compromise to Klaus, and the first five soldiers were decided by drawing straws.

Klaus and the others stood nervously outside the closed door of the kitchen. Five minutes passed, then ten, then fifteen, and when twenty minutes had passed, their nervousness and apprehension got close to panic. After almost half an hour, the door slowly opened. Klaus heard the indistinct sound of conversation, and then the soldiers reappeared. Their lack of faces meant they had no idea how things had gone.

Captain Forster followed them out of the room.

Klaus looked him directly at him. "How did it go?"

He rubbed his forehead with the edge of his thumb, and an unseen smile began to lift the corners of his mouth. "They don't understand everything, and like me, probably never will, but they accept what has happened, and what needs to happen to reunite them with their loved ones and families."

Klaus turned to Sam, and Karsten and shook their hands. "If I could I would shake your hand, Captain. this is wonderful news. What about the others?"

"We will continue as we discussed, and then the first five men I spoke with, will start speaking with their comrades as well." He beckoned them into the kitchen. "How do we decide who will, will, *pass over* first?"

"In the order they are spoken to?" Sam suggested.

"Not by rank then?"

"Well, that is a possibility." Sam looked at Klaus for help.

"I think it best if we leave that decision to you, Captain. You understand the men so much better than us." Klaus said.

Captain Forster nodded. "Thank you. I will discuss it later with the other junior officers, but for now let's talk to everyone."

Sam's head flew around as he heard a crash in the cellar. "I'll check and see what that was," He said to the others.

"I'll come with you," Karsten said. "I don't know why, but I feel that something isn't quite right."

"I'll be fine," Sam reassured him. "Something's just fallen over down there, and needs picking up."

"I don't know Sam," Karsten replied, frowning at him.

"If I need help I'll shout. OK?"

"OK."

"Good. I'll be back in a few minutes." He turned, walked into the hall, down the cellar steps, and flicked the lights on, As he reached the cellar floor, he could see between the first row of shelves, what looked like a smouldering bundle of rags.

"How does anything catch fire down here?" He thought, as he walked closer to the rags.

As he got within a few feet, he gagged as the drifting smoke hit the back of his throat. It was a putrid, sweet smell mixed with the unmistakable acrid odour of cordite. Sam covered his mouth and nose with his left hand, and with the other, picked up a discarded umbrella, and prodded the rags, which groaned. He stepped back, walked around the rags and prodded the other side. It groaned again.

"Back upstairs for help." Sam's better half was making a rare appearance.

"You've been remarkably quiet."

"No reason to speak until now. Just get out of here will you."

"Need to know what this is I'm afraid."

"Bollocks to you then. I'm off. Good luck."

Sam focused his attention back on the rags, and took a few steps back as the smouldering pile began to take on the outline of a body kneeling in prayer. He couldn't take his eyes away from the trembling penitent, as it began to push itself up from the kneeling position until it was stood, bent over with its hands resting on its knees. The body was still only an impression of a man, which second by second, was becoming more defined. With a terrible moan, it pushed itself upright, and stretched its back. It turned away from Sam leaving its back facing him. It shook its head and rubbed its neck. It was translucent like Adam,

432

but appeared to be more gelatinous. A sound like whale song echoed around the cellar. It coughed, seeming to clear its throat. "Jesus!" It spat out.

Sam frowned. The voice sounded remarkably familiar.

"What the fuck is going on?" It carried on.

"Oh shit no!" Sam thought in panic. *"How?"*

"Please let this be High Wood." It begged.

"My God it is."

It turned around, its hands masking its face.

"Lid … Lidsay?" Sam stuttered.

It dropped its hands to its side.

"Well if it isn't the vicar screwer." Ivor leered at Sam. "And how are you and your tart?"

HUNDRED-TWO

Arthur and Agnes were sat on a bench in the gardens.

"I've been in touch with a colleague at Craiglockhart." Arthur said. "He's been pioneering a new treatment for shell shock, and I think we could try it with James. He's going to be with us for some time yet, so my thoughts are that we should focus back on his shell shock." He cut off a piece of apple and popped it into his mouth, dabbing the juice from the corners. "Do you agree Agnes?"

"I worry constantly about him. He's buried things so deeply and I'm terrified that one day they'll surface again and destroy him." She took a slice of apple from Arthur. "I'm sure that despite his hand and knee he'll find some way of getting back to France. They're so desperate for men, they'll take just about anyone. And even if he's of no use to them as a surgeon, he could still carry a pistol and whistle." She sighed deeply. "Who were you speaking to at, where was it?"

"Craiglockhart. It's a military hospital near Edinburgh devoted to the treatment of shell shock. Dr William Rivers, is the leading doctor there. Their main claim to fame is the decorated war hero and poet Siegfried Sassoon was one of their patients. The lieutenant who condemned the War?"

Agnes nodded.

"William's belief, which matches mine, is that these damaged soldiers are repressing the terrifying experiences they had, and in order to get better, they need to confront them. I've never talked about them with James. Have you, Agnes?"

She shook her head.

"So I propose we start today."

Agnes frowned at him. "Today?"

"We don't know how much time we have, so we need to start now. You are the closest to him, so I suggest you begin, and we can then discuss your thoughts and plan his treatment."

Agnes shook her head. "We just talk about what happened to him in France?"

"Yes. Do you know everything that happened to him in France?"

She looked down at the ground and shook her head.

"So this will be a good starting point?"

"Mmmm?"

"If you ever want James completely back, then we must try this. William has had great success, and I trust his work and judgement."

"OK. Let's try. How do I, start?"

"Just chat, and draw France and the War into the conversation."

"What do I do if he reacts badly?"

Arthur, thought for a few seconds. "Bring him here to this bench. I can see you from my office, and if things don't go well, I'll be with you in a matter of seconds."

Agnes accepted this and stood up. "Strike while the iron's hot. It's almost time for lunch, so a few sandwiches."

Arthur smiled. "Excellent idea. I'll go to my office and watch you from there." He stood up and walked back to the hospital with Agnes.

Gloria was doing her rounds when three soldiers were brought in on stretchers, and laid on trolleys. She walked quickly across and met Major Watson who was examining one of them.

"Ah Gloria, excellent. Let's take a look at these men."

She stood close to the major, ready to help, and looked down at the first soldier, a private, who was lying on his right side. Major Watson pulled back the sheet exposing his injuries. Gloria took a sharp breath. She'd seen many terrible things since her return to France, but she could see the damage to this private was beyond any possibility of repair. A still glowing piece of jagged shrapnel, was sticking out at least six inches from his abdomen and was protruding another six inches from his back. Major Watson gently laid the sheets back on him and whispered to Agnes. "Morphia. Make sure that he's give *enough*."

She nodded and followed him to the second.

As Major Watson examined the sergeant, he shook his head and quickly laid the sheet back over him. "Morphia." Was all he said to Gloria.

Gloria was making some brief notes as Major Watson began to examine the third soldier.

"Can't do anything with this arm," Major Watson said.

Her heart stopped and she dropped her notes.

Major Watson turned, shocked by her expression. "Gloria? Gloria, what is it?"

She pointed at the soldier and tried to speak. "It's ... he's ..." the words were lost in tears.

Major Watson waved to another nurse to come across to him. "Gloria, go and sit down."

"I ... I ... can't ... I need ... need to be ... with h him," she said between raking sobs.

"Nurse Houldcroft can manage. We'll be OK."

"But he's ... he's ..."

"Who Gloria. Who is he?"

"R ... Roger. He ... he's ... Lieutenant Roger Lidsay."

"You know him?"

She nodded.

Major Watson waved Nurse Jones away.

"If you stay, you'll need to be in control." He said.

She nodded. "I understand. I'll be professional."

"Good." He turned back to Roger. "Let's see what we can do with what's left of this arm of yours."

Roger thankfully was heavily sedated.

Major Watson examined the ragged burnt stump of Roger's left arm, and frowned. "We need to get him to surgery. Gloria can you organise things for me."

She nodded and ran off to arrange theatre time. "Please God. Please God. Don't let him die. So many already have." She reached the theatre and quickly explained what the Major required.

"Give us half an hour." The orderly replied.

Gloria nodded, smiled and ran back to Major Watson. "Half an hour."

"Excellent. You stay with him and dress those deep cuts on his face. They'll need stitches, but for now make them as clean as you can. I've some others to take a look at before I start on, him?"

Gloria nodded.

"I'll meet you at the theatre." He walked briskly in the direction of the recovery ward.

Gloria found a dressing trolley and pulled it up alongside Roger's bed. "You're in good hands now, my darling." She tenderly washed his wounds of dried blood and caked mud. Her mind started its inexplicable game of doing its best to find the worst possible outcomes and make her focus on them.

"A man with one arm? Is that what you really want?"

Gloria struggled to ignore her thoughts.

"How can he hold you? It won't be like before."

She tried to think only of what she was doing.

"Although there's nothing to worry about, as gangrene will probably set in and kill him."

"Stop! Please stop!" She called out.

"You OK, miss?" A passing orderly asked.

"Sorry. Yes I'm OK. Just got a dreadful headache, and I can't get rid of it."

"Can I get you some aspirin?"

"Thank you no. I've been eating them all day."

He smiled sympathetically. "This place is enough to give a saint a headache. Hope that it goes soon."

Gloria massaged the side of her head and nodded. "Me too." She returned to dressing Roger's wounds.

HUNDRED-THREE

Elizabeth joined the others in the kitchen, catching up on what had happened. "So they've agreed to work with us."

"Yes," Klaus replied. "Captain Forster will decide what order they come to you in."

"Elizabeth, you go. They've agreed they will move on, so you need to be there when they need you." Klaus continued. "Karsten, you go with Elizabeth, and keep a close eye on things and help her in anyway you can."

She looked unsure, but gestured to Karsten to follow her. They walked into the hall, up the stairs together, climbed the stairs to the gallery, the air crackling with static, making strands of Elizabeth's hair fly up. They stood together looking at the rows of photographs, wondering where and how they'd start. The answer was quick in coming. In the aisle furthest away from them a blue glow illuminated the space.

"I think we start there." Elizabeth said pointing to the light.

Karsten smiled. "Follow the light."

As they walked into the aisle, they could see a private standing to attention, looking over his shoulder at his photograph. As they reached him, Elizabeth spoke gently to him. "You will need to let me hear you. Just think to yourself that it's OK for me to hear what you say."

The soldier nodded, and after a few seconds said very clearly. "Private 'enry Allingham, ma'am."

"Pleasure to meet you Private Allingham." Elizabeth replied. "Please don't stand to attention."

"Sorry, miss?"

"Stand easy." Karsten whispered in her ear.

"I'm sorry, Private. Stand easy."

"Fank you, ma'am. Beg pardon, ma'am, but why do my photo 'ave no face?"

"We're here to put that face back on you and your photo, Henry. Today we will put everything back where it should be." It was still very disconcerting for Elizabeth to be talking to a man with no face.

"Bit nerv'us, ma'am. Never a problem with the Hun, but this is all … well … it's just a bit … well bloody odd, ma'am. Excuse me, ma'am. What do we do now?"

Elizabeth put on her very best caring vicar face. "Just put your hands close to mine. That's all you need to do, and you'll be away from this and back where you belong with your family and loved ones." She smiled. "Those who've already passed over are waiting for you on the other side."

"Like angels, ma'am?"

"Just so, Henry. Like angels." She walked close to him and held out her hands. "Just bring yours close to mine and you'll be home in the blink of an eye."

His hands stayed by his side.

"It's OK, Henry. There's nothing to be afraid of. I promise you. I'm a priest. I do not, cannot, and will not lie to you. You have my sacred word."

Despite having no face, Elizabeth could sense the emotions the soldier was feeling.

"I'm ready now, ma'am. I'm coming home, my darlings." He said softly.

With tears in her eyes, Elizabeth moved her hands closer to Henry's until they were just above them. She looked up into his *face* and slowly nodded. "You're ready?"

"Ready and willing, ma'am. It'll be good to see my Martha. It's been a while you know."

Elizabeth slowly moved her hands down until they were merged with Henry's. The reaction was instantaneous and dramatic.

His translucence became more opaque, as he began to regain form and solidity. His head tilted back, arms lifted into a crucifix and Elizabeth felt that if she could see the expression on his face, it would be an image of perfect rapture.

She matched his position with some difficulty, despite pressure between their hands like the similar poles of a magnet, trying to force their hands apart. She focused on his *face*. It was the closest she'd felt to God in all her years in the ministry.

The outline of Henry started to become fuzzy and ill defined, and as she watched, what once had been the shape and form of a man, transformed into a ball of the purest white light. Her hands were now free, but she didn't need to lift them to shield her eyes. The light despite being a brilliant white, was somehow soft and welcoming.

Karsten was stood close behind her, mesmerised like a child finding Father Christmas laying out his presents on Christmas morning.

The ball of light moved close to Elizabeth, and seemed to soften its brightness. Elizabeth lifted her hand to touch the orb, but it flew like a bullet to the ceiling, burst like a child's soap bubble and vanished.

They looked at each other and without thinking hugged each other tightly.

"That was, how do you say in English, Unglaublichau?"

Elizabeth laughed. "I have no idea what you just said, but I understand from your expression. Your face tells me everything."

"But it … it was … so … so …"

"I know, and we still have so many more to help." She staggered slightly and held herself up against the panel which wobbled. "I need to sit down. This drains me emotionally." She looked at the photograph of Private Henry

Allingham, who was stood smartly at attention and grinning back at her. "But that," she pointed to Henry's photo, "that makes it all worth it. But how I'm going to manage however many more there are is questionable. Someone else may have to see if they have the ability." She looked back and smiled knowingly at Karsten.

Sam stood with his back against the cellar wall, staring in disbelief at the floating, glistening, translucent form of his nemesis. "How are you here?"

Ivor shook his head. "Not a Scooby, but what I do know is that somehow, I hold you totally responsible. How the hell I'm talking to you, and," he looked down at his feet hovering a few inches above the floor and laughed out loud, "how I'm doing this." He leaned back, cackled like one of the witches from Macbeth and flew around the rows of shelving, finishing a few inches from Sam's face. "Good that. Bloody miracle really."

"What is it you want, Sergeant?"

"Sergeant no longer. Lidsay no longer. Living no longer. But still malicious and desperately wanting you and that bitch of yours to fall, and fall a very long way." He floated back a few feet and looked at the stairs. "Where is the lovely vicar? I think I'll settle up with her first." He leered at Sam and did another circuit of the shelves. "Whooo! What did that wrestler used to say?" He closed his eyes as if in deep thought. "Ah yes. What a rush! You didn't answer my question, Sam, and even we ex-policemen like answers to questions. WHERE IS SHE?" This time there was venom in the words as they were screamed into Sam's face.

Sam's expression didn't change, although he felt a real need to change his underwear. "She's not here."

"What's that I smell." Ivor sniffed the air. "Is it Chanel? No. Is it Gucci? Not that either. What could it be?" He span around on the spot. "IT'S BULLSHIT!" He screamed at Sam. "Not horse shit or dog shit? No it's the deep unmistakable stench of someone lying their ass off." He floated close to Sam's face again. "ISN'T IT!" He screamed again. "I may be dead, you twat, but I'm not that gullible."

Sam gagged as Ivor's putrid breath hit him in the back of the throat.

"Need some mouthwash, do I Sam?" He cackled. "Where the fuck is she?" The words echoed around the cellar.

Klaus froze at the top of the steps. "What in God's name is down there with Sam?"

HUNDRED-FOUR

Agnes and James sat together, sandwiches and a flask of tea between them.

"We've never really talked about France." Agnes started tentatively. "Have we."

James shook his head as he threw the crusts from his sandwich to some fractious sparrows.

"I haven't spoken about the time we lost each other and I finished up in that trench." Agnes said. "Hell of a shock at the time, but looking back now, it turned out OK in the end. My knight on a white charger found me." She leaned across and kissed him on the cheek. "What happened while we were apart?" Agnes tried again to push the conversation in the direction she wanted it to go.

"Nothing much really." James said as he watched the sparrows squabble over the crusts. "Quarrelsome little sods."

"The sparrows?"

James nodded. "Almost as bad as the French."

"What did happen at the clearing station?" She pushed a little harder.

"Just the usual casualties. Shattered limbs, bodies and I suppose minds."

"Anyone in particular you remember?"

"Not really."

"No-one?"

James sat back on the bench and drank his tea.

"James, was there no-one who was special?"

He bent his neck back and stared at the sky. "Just one." He said almost silently. "Just the one."

"Who was it?"

"Don't remember a name."

"You must do."

"Seldon."

Agnes's expression froze. It was a name she'd buried deep in the furthest reaches of her mind.

"Seldon?" She tried to say as calmly as she could. "He was that soldier who died … when … the one who died … The soldier who died terribly when I was nursing him. The one who drowned in his own blood. The one who's blood is still soaked into my memories."

"I can't forget your uniform. I thought that, that it was your blood."

"Mine?"

James looked into her eyes. "I thought I'd lost you." He looked away. "I didn't have any concerns for the poor suffering soul dying on the bed." He looked back at Agnes, his eyes moist. "I'm a doctor. Patients are my life, and yet I had no thoughts about helping Seldon. Have I become so hardened to the horrors of this War, that I no longer care?"

Agnes said nothing but simply took hold of his hands and gently squeezed them.

"Wasn't just him. There were others. Others for whom morphia was the only solution to their agonies. It became so easy just to add a little extra to the injection. They drifted away to a peaceful death and I, well I, I had one less problem to worry about. I saw them as problems Agnes. My God what have I become? My skills are in saving, not killing. How did I get to this? This war, this damn war."

"You had no other choices James. Their injuries couldn't be repaired. Surely better to die in peace, and not like poor Seldon?"

James was staring at his injured hand. "I'm not going back."

Agnes desperately tried not to smile. "You must. You're needed. You're the best they have."

"Maybe the best at putting soldiers to sleep. That's what vets do isn't it? Put animals to sleep. That's what I've become. Who needs doctors. Vets would do a much better job than us. They've had so much more practice. I'm just a highly qualified slaughterman in an abattoir for men."

Agnes was sorely tempted to wave to Arthur to join her, but she was concerned that James would be less communicative with him present. "Why not work here with Arthur. There will be no chance of you having to put anyone to sleep here." *"Don't push too early"*. She thought.

"Still not convinced about this, this condition. So easy for them to fake it. Some will do anything to get out of the trenches. Anything."

"Move away from this." She thought. "It was a miracle you found me in that trench."

James expression dramatically changed.

"I've hit a nerve." She thought. *"And a fairly major one."*

"Miracle wasn't it that you were in that trench at the same time as me."

"Can't be in trenches. God forsaken places. Inventions of the Devil." He was throwing the remainder of his sandwiches to the grateful mass of chattering sparrows a few feet away. "Can't stay here, sir."

Agnes frowned at him. "Stay where, James?"

"The Huns have started a counter-attack." He'd started ringing his hands. "Can't stay here."

"Huns? There are no Huns here, James." She waved over her shoulder towards Arthur. She needed his help.

"Can't stay here."

"Stay where, my love?"

"Can't stay here. Can't stay here. Can't stay here." James repeated it over and over again.

Arthur came running from his office and stood staring at James. "How long has he been like this?"

Agnes sat silently staring at James.

"Agnes!"

She jumped up from the seat. "Mmmm, sorry?"

"How long has James been like this?"

"Just a few minutes. Probably seconds."

"What triggered this? Think Agnes, it's important."

"We talked about Seldon and then I mentioned the trenches, and then this started."

"Seldon?"

"A soldier who died horribly. James said that all he does is use morphia to put soldiers to sleep. He thinks that he's no better than a vet or a slaughterman. But it was only when I mentioned the trenches that this started."

"Seldon or the trenches must be at the root of his problem." Arthur sat on the bench on the other side of James. "Let me speak to him." He said.

Agnes nodded and sat back, terrified of what she'd done to James.

"James, James, it's Arthur. Where is it that we can't stay? Can none of us stay there?"

"Can't stay here. Too dangerous."

"Dangerous? That's a good reason not to stay. Where is it so dangerous? You wouldn't want Agnes to go there, would you, James?"

James stopped repeating, and turned to look at Arthur. "That trench. Keep away from that trench. Keep away from all trenches. They don't protect, they kill."

"Why is that James?"

"They only came to help me. That's all they did. Tried to help me."

"Where were you?"

"My fault."

"What was James?"

"My fault." His head dropped into his hands.

Arthur kept silent.

James started rocking back and forth.

Agnes panicked.

"My fault." He sat up his eyes welled up with tears. "I shouldn't have been there. My fault."

Arthur felt it was time to open the flood gates. "What happened, James?"

"Shelling. The shelling started. Then the counter-attack started. It wasn't safe to stay there. The shells landed in the trench. They were there and then they were gone."

"Who, James?"

"The soldiers. There were, three, no there were four of them. Came to help me. Can't stay here. They were blown to pieces. Bloody pieces of flesh, bone and brain. They'd been there, standing close me. They were boys. Only boys. Lives still to live, and then they were … they were all over me. They wrapped me in a blanket of bloody body parts that seconds before were those boys. They couldn't save me when they were alive, but they did their duty when they were …" He finally collapsed trembling and sobbing onto the floor.

Arthur shouted to a couple of orderlies, who found a wheelchair and between them they gently bundled James into it. Twenty minutes later, he was back in his quarters, heavily sedated and asleep.

Agnes stood over his bed, deeply worried about what they'd done to him. "We pushed him too far."

"We won't know that until he wakes." Arthur replied. "It's recommended that you make the patient relive the experience which has brought on the condition. I think that's what we achieved. Were you aware of this incident in the trench?"

Agnes shook her head, finding words difficult.

"We'll keep a close watch on him until he wakes, and then reassess the situation." He touched Agnes on the arm. "Do you want to stay first? Two hours on and two hours off?"

Agnes nodded.

"OK, I'll be back in two hours. If you need anyone or anything, just shout." He turned and walked towards the door. "He'll be fine, Agnes." he said as he closed the door behind him.

HUNDRED-FIVE

Sam desperately tried to show no fear, but this, whatever it was that Lidsay had become, terrified him. Not just for what it was, but that it was threatening Elizabeth.

"She's not here."

"Oh, of course not. How could I ever have doubted you, Sam." Ivor floated a few feet away from him. "Thing is," He sniffed the air like a rabid bloodhound, "I can smell her sanctimonious stench." He turned and floated back, a few inches from Sam's face. "Now how do you explain that?"

"She's lived here for weeks. Of course her scent's in the air." Sam said unconvincingly.

"Yes, of course. You've been living in sin together. The knob-head and the vicar. Good title for a film that." His eyes rolled back in his head, leaving only the whites visible. "Now if you don't tell me where the bitch is, then … well there are things I'm pretty sure I can do, and I do hope they'll be unpleasant." His eyes rolled back. "One more time. WHERE, IS, SHE!" He screamed into Sam's face.

"She, as Sam said, is not here." Klaus was half way down the cellar steps. "What are you?"

"Who am I, is more to the point, and Sam can explain that."

"He *was* Ivor Lidsay, a not very good sergeant at the local police station, and he made our life a misery. He was convinced I'd murdered Jane. Man was a moron. God only knows how he got like this."

"A little direct, but fairly accurate." Ivor hissed. "Now if you will excuse me, I have things to do." He floated towards the steps.

Sam stood in his way, but Ivor simply passed through him.

"Really, Sam." Ivor chuckled menacingly. He passed easily through Klaus and headed upstairs.

"We need to get to the gallery before he does." Sam said as he ran past Klaus.

Elizabeth had been lying on her bed for about half an hour, and felt sufficiently recovered to help another soldier. She pulled on a pair of jeans which were hanging over a chair, slipped on a battered pair of trainers, took a quick look in the mirror, didn't like what she saw, opened the door and made her way to the gallery. Karsten who'd been sitting on the landing in one of the small leather chairs, but was nowhere to be seen.

"Probably back in the gallery" She thought.

But when she got to the gallery, he wasn't there.

"Cup of coffee, or getting rid of a cup of coffee." She thought smiling. *"OK boys who's next."*

She walked down the nearest aisle, scanning the photographs.

"You, or maybe you?"

The sound of someone moving in the gallery, brought Elizabeth back from her choosing.

"Karsten." She called.

There was no reply.

"Karsten, is that you?"

Still no answer.

"Sam, Klaus, is it one of you?"

"Not exactly."

She didn't recognise the voice, but assumed it was Karsten playing the fool. "OK, Karsten, scary voice, but I've got a lot to do, so stop messing around."

"Plenty to do. Yes, plenty to do."

Elizabeth looked down towards the door to the gallery, but there was no-one in sight. "Hide and seek now is it?"

"ELIZABETH!" The urgent shout came from below. "ELIZABETH!"

"Sam? Sam is that you?" She called back.

"Yes. I'll be there now. Come down from there."

"Now, Sam? But there are so many souls still to save." She replied.

"COME ... DOWN ... NOW!"

Sam never shouted and it frightened her. "Sam your scaring me."

"Good! Now bloody come down! Elizabeth, PLEASE!"

There was no answer. Sam's blood ran icy cold.

"Over here, Elizabeth."

Elizabeth turned.

"He's messing around with you. I'm over here. Come on, as you say there is much to do."

Elizabeth frowned. "Karsten? Your voice ... it's ... odd."

"Sore throat."

Elizabeth took one look over her shoulder. *"I don't like things like that, Sam Morbeck. I'll have my turn."* She walked to the furthest aisle, where she could see what looked like a dull blue light.

Sam reached the stairs to the gallery and ran up them two at a time, but as he neared the door it slammed shut. He threw all his weight at it, but it wouldn't budge.

"Sam." Karsten and Klaus were stood close behind him.

He looked back at them, despair in his eyes. "Karsten! You're supposed to be with her!"

"I needed to pee, Sam, and Elizabeth was lying down taking a rest. I didn't know anything would happen." He looked terrified and embarrassed.

As Elizabeth turned into the furthest aisle, her mind froze. Floating a few inches above the floor, was Sergeant Ivor Lidsay.

"Hello, vicar. So nice to see you again." He hissed.

"SAM!!" Elizabeth screamed.

At the top of the stairs Sam heard her scream. *"Lidsay!"* His mind shouted. "IF YOU HARM HER I'LL …" He screamed at the door.

"Difficult to know what he could do isn't it?" Ivor sneered. "You do believe in Heaven don't you, vicar?"

Elizabeth couldn't utter a word.

"Cat got your tongue? Never mind, you won't need it soon. But before that, where did you bury her?"

Elizabeth forced out a single word. "Lidsay?

"Bravo. Yes. Sergeant Ivor Lidsay, erstwhile member of the local constabulary, married to a bitch of a woman, disliked by just about everyone, lost my job, pissed off and certain that you and your *friend*," he spat out the word, "murdered his wife and disposed of the body in this house."

"You're dead." Elizabeth croaked. "Aren't you?"

"I am the living," he chuckled "the living proof of the after life." He held out his arms mimicking the crucified Christ. "And you will soon be able to experience it with me."

"You're … you're, what are you?"

"Fucked if I know. But it's the best I've felt in years. I can highly recommend it. Don't understand why everyone's so afraid of dying. I'd have done it years ago if I'd known it was like this. Bloody marvellous."

"Elizabeth!" Sam's muted shout could just be heard.

"Ah, the cavalry's still here. Shame it's too late. Custer and all that."

Elizabeth backed away, ran to the far end of the gallery and tried to force open one of the windows. She turned, as Lidsay was menacingly floating towards her.

"No point in putting off the inevitable." As he got closer, she could smell his fetid breath. "Only, before the main event, please tell me where you buried her. If not that, then just admit you killed her, or tell me where the treasure is. Not too much to ask. Is it?"

Elizabeth could hear Sam hammering on the gallery door, but she was pinned up against the wall of the gallery, with Lidsay within feet of her face.

"Run through him. Just run through him. He's got no substance. He's like the others." She thought, her mind in survival mode.

Elizabeth swallowed hard and ran at him. She seemed to penetrate about half way through, but was thrown back like a child's spoon bouncing of a jelly.

"That's not going to work. I'm not like the others."

Her face gave away her panic.

"I know about the others. Poor saps who've been stuck here since World War One! Bunch of bloody dead beats. Why would you just sit here for a century and do nothing. It's a miracle we ever won that war. Morons in charge and pricks like this lot fighting for King and Country. God help us. Did everyone a favour, when they were killed."

A low murmuring behind Ivor made him stop and turn his head around. "Anyway, let's get down to it, shall we?" He came closer than ever to Elizabeth. "Don't know if this is going to hurt, but I do hope so."

Elizabeth's eyes weren't fixed on Lidsay, but on the changing light over his shoulder. A red mist was flowing over and under the panel of photographs closest to her.

Ivor smirked, but saw something reflected in Elizabeth's eyes which shook him. He span around and saw the red mist now rushing over the panel like the violent muddy rapids of the Colorado river, and discovered that even in death, fear wasn't very far away. The mist calmed and settled into a layer about a foot deep on the gallery floor. Ivor watched in fascination and growing concern, as shapes, at first without form began to billow up from the mist. Along the length of the aisle, at least twenty shapes grew and inexorably began to take on substance and form. The mist pulsed and eddied in whirlpools, and the shapes became more defined and clearer. Twenty transparent faceless privates in full battle dress stood with bayonets fixed waiting for orders.

"Soldiers!" Ivor thought. *"Fucking soldiers! You are having a laugh."*

"PLATOON, ATTENTION!" The barked command came from a shape of an officer at the front of the soldiers. He blew loudly on a whistle and gave his order. "ENGAGE ENEMY!"

Ivor panicked, his usual bravado lost in terror. "Now just a fucking minute there lads. Only a joke. No bloody sense of humour? Just talking with the ..." His words were lost as the platoon of Tommies drove their phantom bayonets into Lidsay's jelly like body. He emitted a scream which drove spikes of ice into Sam's heart.

"ELIZABETH!"

Elizabeth watched as they enveloped Lidsay. It was like watching white blood cells engulf a bacteria. She looked in fascination as Lidsay screamed and appeared to simply dissolve under their attack. His screams faded into silence, until after about a minute, there was nothing visible of him left. She heard the door of the gallery crash open as Sam finally forced it with a crowbar. The platoon formed up in ranks, saluted her, and like misty breath on a cold winter's morning, disappeared into the air.

Sam ran around the corner of the aisle, closely followed by Karsten, and picked her up in his arms. "What happened? Where's Lidsay? It was Lidsay, wasn't it? How are you? Did he hurt you?"

"Put me down, Sam. I'm fine. I was rescued by Tommy Atkins and friends." Elizabeth, despite everything, managed a smile. "They understand, Sam. They protected me. They know what they need to do, and the part I play in it."

Sam frowned.

"I'll tell you all about it later after I've had a very long stiff drink." She smiled at Karsten and kissed him on the cheek. "You missed quite a show."

HUNDRED-SIX

A barely audible alarm bell rang deep in Gloria's subconscious, then quickly fell silent, *almost* unheard. Nurse Gloria's will, had been significantly stronger than Gloria 2014, who she'd buried deep in the farthest corners of her mind. Very little now remained of Gloria 2014, but what did remain heard the alarm, which began to stir her from her coma.

"You OK, Gloria?" She was stood close to Roger's bed. What remained of his amputated arm, supported across his chest by a sling. Everything which could be done for him had been, and he was waiting for transport back to Blighty. For him the war was over, as it was for Gloria, who was accompanying him back to the Prince of Wales Hospital for Limbless Sailors and Soldiers, Cardiff, where she'd accepted a posting as a ward sister. It was a relatively small unit with sixty six beds for men from Wales, Monmouthshire, Herefordshire and Shropshire.

"Mmmm?"

"You seem distracted."

"No, it's just something niggling at the back of my mind. I keep thinking that I've forgotten to do something." She ran her fingers through the sides of her hair. "Do you know what I mean?"

Roger nodded. "I do it all the time." He patted the bed for her to sit down. "All packed?"

"All done. Surprising how little you have when you start packing it away."

"You're sure it's not me?"

"Mmmm?"

"It's not me that's bothering you? You know, marrying a one-armed man. Not a lot of good at dancing at the wedding, or clapping the best man's speech."

Gloria leaned forward and kissed him. "Shhh. No, but there'll be no-one better at arm wrestling, or waving goodbye, or …" She laughed. "I love *you*, not how many arms you've got. If that was a reason not to love someone, then there are going to be thousands of men who won't be loved when they get back home."

Roger forced a smile. He still hadn't properly come to terms with the loss of the lower half of his left arm, and being left handed, he was having to relearn skills which he'd last learnt in primary school. Writing, eating, washing, shaving, turning the pages of a book, golf, swimming, gardening … the list seemed endless.

She smiled at him. "Between the two of us we have three hands and that's going to be more than enough for us to do the things we need to." She winked at him. "And wouldn't you rather be sat here with me with," she nodded at his left arm, "and that little problem, or rotting in No Man's Land with all your limbs intact, but being eaten by rats?" She raised her eyebrows at him. "Mmmm?"

"Point taken and understood."

"Ready for you, sir." A corporal was standing in the doorway of the ward. "Transport's here for you and sister. I'll be outside when you're ready. Any bags I can help with?"

"Thank you, Corporal. Mine are there." He pointed to a case and a canvas bag at the foot of the bed. "Sister Perron's I believe are in her quarters." Gloria nodded. "They have tags on them."

"No rush, sir. Plenty of time to get you to the boat."

The journey from France was pleasant and they spent most of the time on deck, the English Channel as calm as a mill pond. They stayed overnight in Brighton and the next day, got to London in plenty of time for their train from Paddington to Cardiff.

As Gloria got closer to Wales the niggle at the back of her head grew stronger and stronger, until by the time they arrived in Cardiff, it had become a full-blown migraine.

A car collected them from the station, and took them directly to the Prince of Wales hospital. Gloria accompanied Roger to his ward and was then shown to her quarters by the matron.

"Headache bad?" She asked her.

"Pretty bad. It's at the lie down in dark room stage." She replied.

"I'll send an orderly up with some aspirins for you." Matron Pritchard said. "How is our hero? It's the first VC we've had at the Prince of Wales"

"Not too bad." Gloria replied. "He's still getting used to it. You know, still can only see all the things he can't do." She paused and looked intently at the matron. "He doesn't like talking about the medal. He lost a lot of friends and men in the action he won the VC."

Matron Evans nodded. "Understood. Nothing will be said about it, my dear." She smiled and put her hand on Gloria's shoulder. "He's here to rehabilitate, recuperate and get accustomed to his new arm. He's experiencing the most common thing we see, but once we have his prosthetic arm fitted, he'll begin to focus on the things he'll be able to do. We'll have problems as he get's used to the arm. It can be an uncomfortable process, but with your support I'm sure he'll get through it. Being here will also help, when he meets our other patients."

Gloria frowned, the headache getting progressively worse.

"You lie down. I'll draw the curtains and get some aspirin sent up to you. Take tomorrow off, and get to know the people and the place. I'll catch up with you at lunch." She patted the bed. "Rest. That's an order." She smiled and left the room.

Roger was settled into his ward and was sat on his bed in his best hospital issue pyjamas, reading *The Times*. He'd spread the newspaper flat on the bed, turning pages with his right hand. It was intriguing to read reports of events that he'd *lived* through.

"New?" The soldier in the next bed asked.

"Yes. Got in from France today. How long have you been here?"

"About three months I think. Name's George, George Patch." He leaned across and offered his right hand.

"Roger Lidsay." He shook hands with George and looked down at his left arm and smiled. "Shrapnel. You?"

George threw back the sheets. "Machine-gun cut me off at the knees. I'd only advanced a few yards and … I was lucky. My mates, all five of them, were killed. Couldn't have known much about it. They all dropped like stones. God, what a mess a machine-gun makes of a man's body." He pulled the sheets back up.

Roger swallowed hard. His loss paling in comparison with George's. "How are you …"

"Coping?" George said.

Roger smiled and blushed. "Sorry."

"Rule of the house. Never say sorry, or you'd be hoarse by lunch."

"Sorry, sorry about …" Roger chuckled. "No more of that word. Understood."

"I get by. Life's not easy. The worst thing is losing your dignity."

Roger raised his eyebrows.

"Lifting me on and off the loo."

Roger nodded in understanding. "Hard."

"Mmmm. Not any more." George laughed wickedly. "Bullet went through that as well. Still there, but scarred and limp."

"How do you keep going?" Roger asked.

"If I said it was easy, I'd be lying. The wife, Dora can't cope with it, but the kids are fine. Dora hasn't been to see me in three weeks. Still it's hard for her to get here from Swansea." He pointed to his artificial legs draped over the end of the bed. "They're my biggest problem. Stumps won't harden up. They keep bleeding whenever I put them on."

Roger looked down at his arm. He felt that he shouldn't be in this place with these men who'd suffered in the truest sense of the word. The one emotion he hadn't experienced was guilt. But this man, this man was …

"Do you know where the nurses sleep?" Roger asked.

"Didn't take you long."

"No. No. My … my lady … my …"

"Friend?"

Roger smiled and nodded.

"Out of the ward, turn left, up the stairs, turn right, and then you're on your own. The nurses's names are on cards by the doors, but watch out for matron. If *she* sees you then your arm will seem like a scratch." He winked. "But I'd leave it until you see her in the morning."

"Why?"

"Matron is very protective of her charges. An orderly always sits on the door to their wing, and you won't get in. Many have tried, at least those with legs have, but no-one's made it in the three months I've been here. I'd get a good night's sleep and see her tomorrow. None of us are going anywhere fast."

Roger smiled. "A good night's sleep sounds like a good idea. Don't want to upset matron." He lay back on the bed, and after tossing and turning for half an hour, he finally fell into a deep and restful sleep.

Gloria took the aspirins, but the headache didn't ease. In fact it got worse, and seemed to be concentrated at the back of her head. It was only her strength of will which was suppressing Gloria 2014. Neither Gloria was aware of the other, and as with Ivor, Gloria 2014 had faded almost to nothing, and it was only her proximity to Cardiff and home, which had stimulated her. She had no true consciousness, and all that remained of her was neural energy. Neural energy which Gloria had been feeding on, but as Gloria 2014, grew in strength, *she* began to feed off Gloria, which was causing the headaches. Gloria finally managed to get to sleep in the early hours of the morning, and the remainder of the night was spent in bizarre tortured dreams of thugs chasing her demanding money, policemen breaking down the door of her room and throwing her out of the window, a limbless Roger screaming for help, a haunted house where a mad woman chased her from room to room, and a long corridor with a door which opened into what looked like deep space. A noise behind her made her turn, and running and screaming at her like a banshee was her other self. Gloria stood with her back to the door, her hand gripped on the brass knob, and as the banshee was almost on her, she pulled at the door, for an instant it jammed, but then with another fierce tug, it flew open, pinning Gloria to the wall. The banshee, Gloria 2014, flew out of the door into the vacuum of deep space. To the other side.

Gloria woke at six in a bath of cold sweat, feeling strangely refreshed. Her headache gone.

Roger was woken at around six by an orderly. "Bathroom's free, sir, when you're ready. Able to manage on your own?"

He sat up in the bed, pushed back the blankets with his right hand and swung his feet onto the floor. "Thank you. Yes I'll be fine on my own. What do we do about breakfast?"

"Those like yourself, sir, who are mobile, eat with the staff. It's downstairs near the main entrance. I'll show you the way."

"Can you show me the bathroom first?"

"Of course, sir. Follow me."

Roger was eating toast, which a nurse had buttered for him. He was still uncomfortable accepting help with day to day things, but was gracious in his thanks. Tea hadn't been such an issue, and he looked up and grinned as Gloria appeared at the door. He waved to her to join him, and she collected some breakfast and walked over.

"Good morning." He said. "You look refreshed. Bright eyed and bushy tailed."

"I slept like a log. Peculiar dreams, but they didn't seem to disturb me." She cut the top off her boiled egg and dipped some toast in the soft yellow yolk. "How's your ward?"

"Best place I could be."

"That sounds promising."

"When you see and talk to the soldiers here who've lost so much more than I have, it puts things into perspective. George in the bed next to me, lost both his legs at Arras. *Both* legs, and there's me with this." He lifted his arm up and smiled. "It's nothing."

Gloria leaned across the table and squeezed his hand. "I prayed that this place would help, but this, this is more than I could have hoped for. I was worried about you. Desperately worried."

"I'm fine. Get my new arm and then let's see what the future holds for us."

"Us?" She smiled.

"Ah yes. I'd forgotten to mention that we were getting married."

Gloria slowly shook her head and frowned.

Roger's eyebrows almost hit his hairline.

She tried but couldn't stop herself from laughing. "Was that a proposal, Lieutenant Lidsay."

"You!" He laughed with her. "Yes, my darling, that was a practice proposal. But this is the real thing." He dropped to one knee. "Gloria will you spend the rest of this life and the next with me?"

Her expression was her answer. Words weren't needed.

HUNDRED-SEVEN

James woke from his sedated sleep and sat up in the bed. It was dark and he couldn't see very much in the room. He got up, hobbled and fumbled along the bed, until he reached the wall, and finally found the switch and flicked on the lights.

Agnes jumped out of her chair as the lights woke her from a deep and pleasant dream. "What … I … Mmmm … James! You're …"

"Awake." He smiled at her.

For the first time in months Agnes was looking at her man. Her James. The expression on his face had markedly changed, the tension in his cheeks gone, his eyes had regained their brightness, his grey pallor had been replaced by warm skin tones, his lips weren't cracked and dry, the deep frown lines were gone with the down turned corners of his mouth, but most importantly he looked like the man she'd fallen so deeply in love with in what seemed like another lifetime. "How do you feel?" She asked nervously.

"Like me." He laughed out loud.

She held his face in her hands and gently kissed him on the lips. He pulled her to him and they kissed passionately. A knock on the door, prevented it from going any further, and they laughed at each other.

"OK if I come in?" Arthur said through a crack between the door and its frame. "I saw a light on." As he walked into the room he beamed. "James! You're … well … you're …"

"Yes I'm definitely …"

James peeled himself away from Agnes, limped to Arthur and shook him so firmly by the hand, that Arthur had to prise his fingers away as they were cutting off the blood supply. James laughed in embarrassment. "Sorry about that."

"James … you look … look like …"

"Like I used to?" James replied. "What did you do to me? Never mind about *my* miracle cure."

"In time, my friend. In time. But for now …"

"Never seen you lost for words like this before, Arthur."

"Never had a patient like you before, James."

They embraced and patted each other on the back.

"I'll leave you two together, but I'd strongly recommend that you get some …" Arthur said.

"You read my mind, Arthur." James said with a wicked smile.

"You'll have plenty of time to … well … anyway …. We'll meet at breakfast and then decide what's next." He turned to leave. "Agnes, I would suggest that …"

"So would I, Arthur." She kissed him on the cheek. "I'm going back to my quarters."

James pretended to look shocked and cry, but then laughed out loud. "Where would I be without you two?"

"If you'd had your way, James, we'd be back in France." Agnes regretted the words as she said them.

The old expression started to return, but only for a few seconds. "I still want to see how I can support the war effort. But if that means working here and not at the front, well, so be it."

Agnes linked arms with Arthur. "I'll see you at breakfast. There'll be plenty of time for us to … catch up."

"Time which we're not going to waste." James replied.

"I'll send in an orderly to help you get ready. See you at breakfast." Agnes said as she closed the door to his quarters.

James laid back in the bed and pulled the sheets up to his chin.

"Agnes Wilmart, you and I are going to live every moment as if it were our last." He thought. *"None of us know how much more time we have left to walk this earth. France showed me that the time of so many can be cut short in the blink of an eye."* A knock at the door, told him that the orderly had arrived. *"I will live every extra day I have for them. Fill every day with living."*

James was late for breakfast, and Agnes was getting nervous and fidgety. "Where is he? I should go and see that he's OK."

"He'll be here." Arthur said, finishing his fried egg. "Eat your toast."

"He's … he's gone back, hasn't he? Last night was just, just a …" Agnes's nervousness was now close to panic. She was standing up to leave as James entered the canteen. He was washed, clean shaven, his hair combed, dressed in an immaculate uniform and smiling.

"Looking for me, old girl?" He said as he pulled up a chair, laid his stick on the floor and sat down. "You leaving us, Agnes? I'm starving. What's good Arthur?"

Agnes stared at him, felt like scolding him, but smiled and sat down again at the table. "You did that deliberately didn't you."

"What?"

"Got here late. That's what."

"Takes time to be presentable in the morning. Must set a good example." James thanked the orderly as he poured him a cup of coffee. "Wouldn't you agree, Masters?"

"Absolutely, sir. Shows discipline. You look very well turned out, sir. If you don't mind me saying." He poured some extra milk into James coffee. "Nice to see you back, sir." He said quietly.

James smiled up at him. "You don't know how good it feels. Thank you, Masters."

Over the coming weeks and months, James and Arthur developed a remarkable working relationship, but James's nerve damaged hand didn't improve. Brigade headquarters were finally convinced by Arthur that his skills as a doctor would best serve the war effort at Seale Hayne, with, of course, the invaluable nursing expertise of Sister Wilmart. BHQ paid them a number of visits, and eventually were convinced that the work at Seale Hayne was supporting the war effort. What they saw was fresh cannon fodder for the front, and not as James and Arthur did repaired minds ready to live a full life, and not to finish their days as discarded rotting washing hanging on German barbed wire.

They worked together until 1921, when James was offered a post as a consultant psychiatrist in Cardiff. The offer was far too good to turn down, and with the support and blessing of Arthur, he left with Agnes and mixed emotions for a new life in Wales.

His memory of the cocoon of human gore which saved his life in the trenches, never left him. It was always there, but controlled and locked away in the deepest corners of his mind, but still there, biding its time. As the years past they faded to almost nothing but dusty sepia pictures of a time that was best forgotten, when men had lost their humanity. Of a time forgotten, but not of comrades, whose memory would live on.

Marriage to Agnes and a blissful family life, strengthened his defences against the memories, and the arrival of their daughter Madeleine buried them so deeply that they seemed to be lost forever. But like dormant parasites they bided their time.

In 1944, Madeleine married Phillip Roberts, moved to Jersey and ten years later had a daughter Elizabeth, who became the final piece of James perfect life.

In May 1962 Agnes was diagnosed with an inoperable brain tumour, and three months later died. All the skills James had as a doctor could do nothing for her, and his desperation at his failure to help her and the loss of his life-long love stirred the parasites into life. At first they only entered his dreams, finding their way and corrupting them into nightmares he couldn't wake and escape from. Insomnia developed as his body desperately tried to stay awake and escape from the night terrors, but the parasites multiplied and entered his every waking moment, until his mind's only defence was to seal itself off from the world and lose itself in a time and place which had once brought him happiness.

He spent his remaining days, marching up and down the streets and roads, and sadly became the eccentric old man who lived on his own. People would walk to the other side of the street to avoid him and children would make fun and throw things at him. But all the time his personal cocoon protected him from anything which didn't fit into his reality. A reality in which he was again a skilled surgeon, where men had found their humanity and didn't slaughter each other, where his life had structure and purpose, where he was still held in respect, where his beloved Agnes and Madeleine still walked with him in the late evening sun and where the lost souls he'd seen march off to their deaths had at last found peace. In 1970 he died peacefully at home in his sleep at the age of seventy seven, dreaming of Agnes.

HUNDRED-EIGHT

Klaus and Karsten decided to spend the night in a local hotel, but were back at High Wood by nine. They walked around to the back of the house and came in by the kitchen door. Sam and Elizabeth were sitting at the kitchen table drinking tea. Captain Forster was standing close to the sink and obviously talking to Sam and Elizabeth. Jane, Rebecca and Adam were nowhere to be seen.

Sam looked across as they came in. " Guten Morgen Meine freund?."

Klaus smiled and clapped. "Sehr gute, Sam."

"I've been practising."

"Any Belgian, Sam?" Karsten asked jokingly.

"Bonjour mes amis. Is that OK."

'Très bonne Sam.' Karsten joined Klaus in his applause. "We'll make you a European yet."

"Les hommes sont prêts." Captain Forster said.

"Excellent, mon Capitaine." Klaus said. "You speak excellent French."

"Difficult not to when you've spent three years there." Captain Forster replied.

Elizabeth spoke to the captain "The men are ready?"

"Yes, ma'am. Let me know when you want to start and I'll organise things."

Elizabeth looked at her watch. "It's nine fifteen now, so I'd suggest we start at ten. That will give me time to freshen up and get ready."

Captain Forster looked at his watch and nodded. "I have the same time. First man will be with you at ten. When will you want the next?"

She smiled. "I'll need a little time to get my breath back, so lets say ten forty five, eleven thirty, twelve fifteen and one o' clock. I'll need a break for lunch, so we'll start again at two, and then two forty five," she looked across at Captain Forster who was frowning, "or would fourteen and fourteen forty five be better for you?"

Captain Forster nodded his head. "Thank you, ma'am, yes that would be better for myself and the men."

"OK, so fourteen hundred, fourteen forty five, fifteen thirty, sixteen fifteen and seventeen hundred, and that will be enough for today."

Sam looked concerned. "Ten in a day? Is that too many?"

"I'll have to suck it and see." Elizabeth replied. "If it is, then we'll just reschedule the men."

"How many men are in High Wood, Captain?" Klaus asked.

456

Captain Forster shook his head. "I don't know precisely, but it's a lot more than you can see." He closed his eyes trying to estimate their number. "Probably in excess of three hundred?"

"Dreihundert!" Klaus exclaimed. "Dreihundert?"

Captain Forster nodded. "I'd say that was a reasonable estimate."

"So viele. Dies dauert länger als ich dachte." Klaus said shaking his head.

"Yes." Karsten said. "A lot longer than we thought."

Sam was totting things up in his head. "That's going to be, three months at least, or probably four." He looked at Elizabeth. "You'll need some breaks."

"This is new to all of us, Sam, so we'll play this by ear and tweak things as we go along." She turned to Captain Forster. "That will be OK with yourself?"

"Plans should always be flexible, ma'am."

"Good. So let's get started." She walked out of the kitchen and gestured for Sam to follow. "Can you get the Bose and the iPod. Music will be helpful. It will relax me, and I've seen how much they like it, so it should make things easier for them." She headed up the stairs. "I'll see you in the gallery."

Jane, Rebecca and Adam appeared in the lounge from the map room as Sam was unplugging the Bose and the iPod. "We've been looking at the map and we can see places which seem to draw our attention. They seem to glow, and they may be where you need to look for the missing." Jane watched what Sam was doing. "Moving out already?"

"We're starting at ten o'clock."

"Starting?" Jane said.

"Starting to help them pass over."

"Can we help?" Adam asked.

"Not in the gallery, but reassuring the men would be good." Sam replied. "You'll really be able to help when I have to go to France to find the missing. What you've found in the map room, sounds like it could be a great help in locating them."

"We'll keep an eye on them for you." Jane said.

"Thanks. I'd better get up to the gallery. We can talk more, later today." Sam picked up the Bose and iPod, and made his way to the stairs.

When he reached the landing, an orderly queue of ten men were standing at ease, outside the door to the gallery. Sam smiled, but without faces he had no idea what they were feeling.

"Ah, great. Plug it in over there please." Elizabeth pointed to a plug half way along the wall. "Can I have the iPod?"

He walked across to her, kissed her on the cheek and handed her the iPod. "You're OK?"

She smiled. "Never better. Ask me again, though, at one, sorry, thirteen hundred hours. Can you get the names of the men waiting on the landing, I want to keep a record of who we help. "

"I'll pop down to the ,map room and get a notepad and pen," Sam said. "Anything else you need?"

She smiled. "I'll let you know at one o' clock."

Sam picked up the note pad, called to Jane to come with him and returned to the landing, where the men were still stood at ease. He walked to the front of the queue. "Won't be too long now." He said, realising he probably sounded like a dentist's receptionist. "Jane can you ask them their names for me."

She smiled and turned to the first soldier "We need to take your names."

"Bill Rogers 1/7th Sherwood Foresters."

Jane made her way down the line.

"Jack Easton 77th Field Ambulance Royal Army Medical Corps."

"Ernie Hodges 10th Lancashire Fusiliers."

"Fred Stevens 20th Middlesex Regiment."

"Harry Louth 15th Hampshire Regiment."

"George Patch 7th Duke of Cornwall Light Infantry."

"Dick Hawkins 11th Royal Fusiliers."

"Richard Barron 2nd London Field Ambulance Royal Army Medical Corps."

"Fred Dewing 34th Division Royal Engineers Signal Corps."

"Tom Francis 11th Border Regiment."

For some reason Sam saluted them, thanked Jane and climbed the stairs back into the Gallery.

The sound of Bob Dylan greeted him.

'Yes and how many times must the cannon balls fly
Before they're forever banned?
The answer my friend is blowin' in the wind
the answer is blowin' in the wind.'

"Elizabeth," Sam called out.

"Over here, Sam, in the last aisle."

He walked to the aisle where she was staring intently at the photographs. "How did we ever do this? Because some royal cousins didn't get on? Why, Sam? How many died?"

"Altogether?" Sam said.

Elizabeth nodded.

"In all the armies twenty million were wounded and ten million killed. I've been reading a lot about the War recently. Fill the Millennium Stadium and kill everyone, and then refill it about a hundred and twenty five times and kill all of them as well." He shook his head. "And then refill it again about another seventy five times to kill the civilians, and it sort of puts it into perspective."

They both sighed and stared at the photos.

"Didn't learn though did we? Started it all again twenty one years later." Elizabeth said.

"They only managed to kill around twenty two million soldiers that time, but they excelled themselves with civilians." He shook his head again. "Estimates vary, but it's somewhere between thirty eight to fifty million!"

'Yes, and how many deaths will it take till he knows
That too many people have died?
The answer my friend is blowin' in the wind
The answer is blowin' in the wind.'

The song ended, Dylan's lyrics encapsulating their thoughts and emotions.

"Still blowin' in the wind." Elizabeth quietly said to Sam. "Still blowin' in the wind."

Sam looked at his watch. "Almost ten!"

"OK. Who's first?"

"Bill Rogers 1/7th Sherwood Foresters."

Elizabeth smiled and nodded. "Let's get started."

Sam kissed her on the cheek. "Stop at any time you feel, well you'll know if you feel …"

"I'll be fine, Sam. Let's send Bill home shall we?"

They all met again at one o' clock in the kitchen. Elizabeth looked drained but glowing with satisfaction.

"It's going well?" Klaus asked.

She smiled. It said more than any words ever could.

"Well, we need to get to the airport. We changed our flight and its scheduled departure is in about three hours and we need to get there and check in." Klaus said. "We're always at the end of the phone, email, Face Time, text or whatever you chose, and you must come over again when you've, *helped* all these men."

"Couldn't have done any of this without you." Sam shook Klaus and Karsten's hands. "We will be over to see you. There are still quite a few things I need to ask. With their help," he smiled at Jane, Rebecca and Adam, "I think we'll be, well sort of fine." He took a deep breath as his emotions began to get the better of him. "It's been an interesting few months. Isaac … I will always miss him." He swallowed hard. "But I know that he's always there if I need him."

A loud knock at the front door made them all jump.

"We ordered a taxi." Karsten said. "Elizabeth and you, have got enough to do."

They all walked to the front door where the cases were waiting. Rebecca, Adam and Jane stayed in the kitchen, and Sam helped carry the cases to the taxi.

Elizabeth hugged and kissed Klaus and Karsten. "I'll miss you." She whispered in Klaus's ear. "Come back soon to see us. Take care of yourself, and let Guillaume know that he's in our thoughts. I know how much Isaac meant to him. He can ring me any time, if he wants to talk to someone."

They climbed into the taxi, clipped on their seat belts and lowered the windows. "Take care. This is still new to all of us, so be careful," Klaus said, and blew a kiss to Elizabeth.

"Que ton Dieu soit avec vous aussi." Karsten smiled and nodded to them.

The taxi pulled away, Sam waved and Elizabeth blew kisses to the two friends as they disappeared around the bend of the avenue.

Sam and Elizabeth looked at each other feeling suddenly very alone.

Elizabeth wiped away a tear and took Sam's hand. "OK! Who's next?"